"Well, you're nc
something fo

"What am I not goi

Margo Allende opened the door of the Situation Room—it was empty, unlike Pacino had expected. Even though the meeting with the president was postponed, the Situation Room was almost always partially occupied, but not tonight. "You want coffee? I'll fetch you one from the wardroom while you read the message."

"Yeah, that would be great. Black-and-bitter, please." Pacino found the seat he'd taken the last time there was a Situation Room meeting, on the right side of the president's end seat, three seats down, the other two seats between him and Carlucci taken by the Secretary of War and the Secretary of the Navy. Pacino pulled his pad computer out and put it on the table next to a notebook and his pen, then opened the software, submitted to the retinal scan and read the message Allende had told him about.

At the line reading, '*Panther* change-of-command ceremony successful,' he smiled to himself. That was excellent news, and a great way to summarize the op. But then paragraph three caught his eye.

3. (S) PANTHER CREW CONSISTS OF:
OIC LT. D. DANKLEFF, USN
AOIC LT. A. PACINO, USN

Pacino's mouth dropped open—*holy shit,* he thought. Seagraves had actually assigned Anthony to the boarding party. How the hell could that make any sense at all? After all the kid had been through on *Piranha,* they were sending him out an airlock in scuba gear? On one of the most dangerous missions since the search-and-destroy mission for the renegade nuclear-powered drone sub? Pacino's jaw tightened. When *Vermont* got back from this mission, he'd have a strong word with Commander Seagraves. If *Vermont* got back from this mission, he thought.

Copyright © 2021 by Michael DiMercurio
ISBN 978-1-63789-918-2
All rights reserved. No part of this book may be used or reproduced in any manner whatsoever without written permission except in the case of brief quotations embodied in critical articles and reviews
For information address Crossroad Press at 141 Brayden Dr., Hertford, NC 27944
A Gordian Knot Books Production -Gordian Knot is an imprint of Crossroad Press.
www.crossroadpress.com

First Edition

DARK TRANSIT

MICHAEL DIMERCURIO

Dedicated to the United States Submarine Force
Deep, Silent, Fast, Deadly

"The great lie at the heart of all states is that other people are not the same as us. It is the excuse for violence, the rationalization that makes it possible to wield a weapon in the first place: it's okay to kill them, they would do the same to us, they're different than us. It's the foundation of every atrocity small or large throughout history. The lie that the others are different. And once that lie is used to justify violence, it can't be relinquished. The ends become the means, and violence must be called down not just for the reason of the lie, but in defense of the lie."

"Violence and the Lie"
by Steven Lloyd Wilson
burningviolin.com, January 2013

"So let us not be blind to our differences, but let us also direct attention to our common interests and the means by which those differences can be resolved. And if we cannot end now our differences, at least we can help make the world safe for diversity. For in the final analysis, our most basic common link is that we all inhabit this small planet. We all breathe the same air. We all cherish our children's futures. And we are all mortal."

President John F. Kennedy
Address at the American University in Washington D. C., June 10, 1963

"Anyone who clings to the historically untrue—and thoroughly immoral—doctrine that 'violence never solves anything' I would advise to conjure up the ghosts of Napoleon

Bonaparte and of the Duke of Wellington and let them debate it. The ghost of Hitler could referee, and the jury might well be the Dodo, the Great Auk, and the Passenger Pigeon. Violence, naked force, has settled more issues in history than has any other factor, and the contrary opinion is wishful thinking at its worst. Breeds that forget this basic truth have always paid for it with their lives and freedoms."

Robert Heinlein

"The spectrum of conflict today is neither linear nor predictable. We must account for the possibility of conflict leading to conditions which could very rapidly drive an adversary to consider nuclear use as their least bad option."

US Strategic Command (@US_Stratcom) April 20, 2021

"The recent tragic loss of the Argentine submarine *San Juan*, the fire raging amongst moored Russian Kilo-class submarines at Vladivostok (a drill, Moscow claims), and the fortunately nonfatal but highly expensive flooding of the Indian nuclear powered submarine *Arihant* highlight that despite being arguably the most fearsome weapon system on the planet, submarines remain dangerous to operate even when not engaged in a war. Even brief breakdowns in crew discipline or mechanical reliability can rapidly turn the stealthy underwater marauders into watery coffins."

"No More Air:
How An Entire Chinese Submarine Crew
Died a Tragic Death in 2003"
by Sebastien Roblin
The National Interest, November 2019

"Unlike other warships a submarine has no peacetime role. She cannot 'show the flag' or be used to entertain foreign dignitaries. She is unsuitable for the pomp and ceremony for which war vessels of all nations are in such great demand and she is hardly the ideal vehicle for carrying a Head of State on official visits. She has no facilities or surplus space available to enable her to provide aid when natural disasters such as earthquakes, flood and volcanic eruptions occur in remote areas; and she can only offer limited assistance in a rescue situation. The submarine, unlike her surface sisters, is solely a vessel of war. Thus, by definition, her Commanding Officer is, in Winston Churchill's stirring phrase, 'a Captain of War.'

Edwyn Gray
"Captains of War: They Fought Beneath the Sea"

"The shipbuilders of Electric Boat are proud to deliver *Vermont* to our Navy, an extraordinarily capable ship. I am pleased to report that the *Vermont* has received some of the highest quality ratings in the history of the Virginia program. We wish *Vermont* and her crew a long and distinguished career in defense of our nation."

Kevin Graney, President, General Dynamics Electric Boat,
April, 2020

This black hull with all its weapons
is my home. It belongs to me.
And to all of her officers and crew
May they be strong and forever free.
Let us live to protect her stealth
And look with pride upon her sonar dome.
They say home is where the heart is
This black hull is my home.
This black hull is my home.

USS *Vermont* official song
(corrupted from the State of Vermont's official state song)

"It never happened—we were never there."
Battle cry of the USS *Vermont*

"In the name of the United States, I christen thee '*Vermont*.' May God bless her and all who sail in her."

Gloria Valdez, ship sponsor, October 20, 2018,
General Dynamics Electric Boat Division, Groton, Connecticut

PROLOGUE

The power and heat had died thirty minutes ago. The space rapidly cooled to the freezing temperature of the ocean floor. Inside, under ineffective thermal blankets, four figures shivered, their breathing marked by vapor clouds, clouds invisible in the coal mine darkness.

The youngest, a first class midshipman in the U.S. Navy, stopped shivering as he began to lose consciousness, barely aware of the blurred border between wakefulness and a coma. In the carbon dioxide-infused compartment, he had experienced a clawing drowsiness dragging him into sleep, and he had fought it as long as he could, too cold and frightened of dying to be able to think of anything but the next breath, but soon he slipped further into the grogginess and sleep came for him.

As he lay there, his heartbeat slowed and his breathing became shallower, and it would not be long before there would be breathing no more. And not long after, suddenly he was alert and awake, standing—no, more correctly, *floating*—ten feet away from his body, watching himself and the other three people he'd tried to rescue complete their last moments of life.

Perhaps the oddest thing about existing apart from his body was that it didn't feel strange at all. He felt a calmness and a deep focused awareness unlike any reality he could ever remember. It couldn't be described except to say that everything he'd ever experienced, wondered about, thought about, it all now made sense. There was a feeling that all was right with the universe, that everything that had happened and would happen was meant to happen. He could feel himself somehow fitting into a place where he was supposed to be.

He looked through the darkness, sensing the equipment inside of the deep submergence vehicle that he had climbed into as the floodwaters rose to the hatch coaming. His body lay beside the other three bodies. He floated closer, looking at the other three, seeing their heartbeats and the functions of their lungs, watching their brain activity slow. His own body seemed to struggle for life, a slight twitch kicking at the blanket, but then it went still again.

He widened his awareness and moved outside the hull of the deep submergence vehicle into the free-flood space between the deep submergence vehicle and the hull of the stricken submarine *Piranha,* which lay at a list on the rocky bottom almost two miles beneath the surface. He faded farther back away from the sunken submarine and saw the frantic robotic arms of a submersible diamond plasma arc cutting the two-inch thick high-yield steel of the hull, melting it away as if it were butter. The lettering on the side the submersible read *BERKSHIRE—HMS EXPLORER II.* His spirit moved inside the submersible and saw the sweating operator of the robot arm. He could read the man's thoughts easily—near panic and empathy for the trapped submariners inside of the *Piranha*. He wanted to tell the man it was too late, but not to worry, that there was nothing to fear about dying.

A moment later a patch of steel was lifted away from the hull, the flickering lights of the submersible revealing the curving hull of the deep submergence vehicle nestled inside the submarine. The submersible worked frantically releasing the vehicle, then began an emergency ascent to the surface. He went with it, floating outside the DSV as it rose out of the black depths of the cold Atlantic. The sea became lighter as they approached the surface, eventually the form of the undersides of the waves visible, shimmering and silvery. The DSV and the submersible broke the surface and broached. He could see the overcast and the heavy rain, the DSV and the rescue submersible bouncing in the waves in the winds of the storm. Strong crane arms reached out over the water, cables and robot grappling arms pulling the DSV up to the deck, the submersible after it.

Back inside the deep submergence vehicle he could see that all four people prone on the deck were in cardiac fibrillation, their body functions beginning to shut down. Rescue techs in air-fed facemasks rushed in and pulled out the bodies, gurneys waiting for them, the medics rushing them into the ship.

The gurney with his body arrived in an operating theater, where it became surrounded by doctors, nurses, corpsman and equipment. He watched a monitor showing one last feeble pair of heartbeats, then a flatline. The corpsman paddled the midshipman's chest, shocking him to try to restart his heart, but it didn't respond after seven attempts. The lead physician shared resigned glances with the corpsman holding the electrical paddles and shook his head. A nurse snapped off the monitor, its humming alarm going quiet.

The doctor picked up a clipboard, scribbling into it the time of death.

"What's his name?" he asked. The nurse found the top of the patient's coveralls that they'd unzipped to shock his heart. Above his left pocket, block letters of his nametag spelled MIDN. A. PACINO. The dead body had belonged to Midshipman First Class Anthony Pacino.

At the moment of the first paddle shock, on the other side of the operating theater, a black dot appeared and grew wider, opening like the petals of a flower, until it formed an opening resembling the end of the Horn of Plenty, except this funnel-like opening was black and perhaps thirty feet wide, and where it was wider than the height of the overhead, the reality of the structure of the operating room faded away, the black object more real than what almost seemed like a projection of the room around him.

The black funnel led into a long tunnel, which he could tell because the undulating walls of the tunnel seemed to be made of dark thunderclouds that lit up occasionally with lightning, the flashing giving the gloom inside the tunnel shape and form. The funnel pulsed as if trying to get his attention, but he turned away from it and floated down the hall as the corpsman who had tried to revive Pacino told Pacino's step-mother, Colleen, that the attempt to save his life had failed. That Midshipman Pacino was dead. Colleen swept her raven-black hair off her shoulder, wiped tears from her face, and asked to see Pacino's body. She was led down to the passageway outside the operating room where they had wheeled Pacino, a white sheet placed over him while someone had been sent for a body bag.

Colleen reached for the sheet covering the body's face, but before her fingers reached the linen of the sheet, the black funnel pulsed again, and this time the spirit belonging to the body who had been named Anthony Pacino was pulled into the tunnel made of thunderclouds.

He floated into the dimness of the tunnel and felt himself move away from the opening, gliding into the depths of the tunnel. He watched as the light from its opening got farther way with each moment until the rescue ship's reality completely faded from view and the only thing that existed was the tunnel, its storm cloud walls lighting up eerily every few seconds. For the longest time, he felt like he was absolutely stationary but the tunnel was moving around him, pulling him in deeper. He continued floating for what seemed hours, seemingly covering miles. The tunnel extended infinitely in each direction. Finally, after a long time, the tunnel stopped moving around him and he floated at a stationary point, and it came to him that he was waiting for something.

Then he heard the sounds. Voices. No, not sounds and not voices, but *thoughts* that communicated. They were indistinct and the words or ideas couldn't be made out, just that a conversation was happening on the other side of the tunnel wall where he floated. He remembered nights as a young child, lying in the back seat of his father's sedan at night after an evening of his parents' socializing, when he'd lie sleepily on the seat on the way home and he could hear his parents talking or arguing, their words blurry but their meaning clear from the tone of voice each used.

Here in the tunnel, he could hear one dominating voice, louder than the others and deeper. There were what seemed half a dozen others talking with the deep-voiced one, their voices softer and more feminine. The father figure, if he could be called that, was insisting on something, but the feminine beings were arguing together against his intentions. The words became clearer until he could understand the point of the argument going on, some of it lost on him, but he gathered that the females wanted to admit him to the other end of this tunnel, to what they called "the world," which seemed strange to him, since he had just left the world—or perhaps that was just *his* world and the one on the other end was a different one. Then it came clear to him that the destination was to these beings the *real* world, which would make the one he'd just departed what? A virtual world?

The females insisted that the life that had been chosen for Anthony Pacino was too hard for him, that the suffering of it would crush him. The father figure roared his response, which seemed to be that Pacino *had* to go on, that the plan—they said it as if it were capitalized, *The Plan*—needed Pacino and what Pacino would do in his future.

The argument seemed stalemated until the father figure made a picture appear on the wall of the tunnel, with images that Pacino could see, and he imagined that the arguing entities on the other side of the tunnel wall could see it too. It was more than a two-dimensional projection. He could see it in full three dimensions, but there was more—he could sense the thoughts and emotions of the person in the projection. It was an image of Pacino in scuba gear holding on to the hatch of the submarine *Piranha*. He was locking out of the ship and about to ascend to the surface only thirty feet overhead to rendezvous with a boat that would take him to shore, because he had been ordered evacuated from *Piranha* because the submarine was sailing into a combat zone and had search-and-destroy orders for the hacked and compromised robot drone sub that was searching for her. *Now watch*, the father figure commanded. *You watch this.*

From the darkness of the ocean an object could be seen traveling absurdly fast until it impacted the submarine's hull forward of Pacino and a tremendous explosion shook the ship, and as the blast was rocking Pacino, another speeding object sailed in and exploded a hundred feet aft of Pacino. He gripped the side of the hatch desperately as the shock waves rolled through him, and he could hear the thoughts of his past self, thinking it was a miracle that the explosions hadn't killed him. They had, however, blown off his scuba mask and pulled the regulator out of his mouth.

He watched his past self look upward at the waves overhead and he could hear his thoughts that he could just push up and away from the torpedoed submarine and swim to safety. But then the figure hanging on to the hatch looked back down into the hatchway. The youth seemed to freeze for a long instant, then he looked at the surface again and shook his head. He purposefully pulled himself back into the submarine's escape chamber and pulled the hatch shut after him.

The male spirit stopped the movie, or whatever this image was. *Did you see that? Did you see what he did? He didn't try to save himself. He deliberately swam back into a sinking submarine to try to help his friends! Or to die with them! He knew what he was doing the entire time! Do you seriously think The Plan continues without this soul living his full lifetime? Do you?*

The female entities were quiet for some time, and then one softly said the word, *agreed*, and suddenly he was moving again in the tunnel, the projection screen fading behind him, his motion back in the direction of where he'd started, his velocity increasing until the tunnel walls sped by him dizzyingly, until he could see the circle of white light that opened into the rescue ship's passageway, and he came to a stop floating a few feet behind Colleen as she reached for the sheet covering his dead body's face. As her hand moved to the sheet, he suddenly was pulled into his body so fast that the shock of it made him tremble and he opened his earthly eyes to find himself staring directly into Colleen Pacino's light brown eyes. He blinked and coughed weakly.

"Medic!" Colleen screamed. *"Doctor! Midshipman Pacino is alive!"*

THREE YEARS LATER

BOOK 1:

“THE MONDAY”

1

Friday, May 6

Lieutenant junior grade Anthony Pacino cut the engine of the old Corvette, the self-doubt and fear infecting him despite the colors of the ribbon of the Navy Cross shining over his left breast pocket.

He looked down at the ribbon for a moment. It sat there, next to the national service ribbon and below his airborne wings, the ribbon a simple blue field with a small stripe of white in the center. He'd shown up at his last command without wearing the ribbon, still feeling unworthy of the medal, the full citation itself so classified that his service jacket would only say the bare bones of the reason for the medal: "Awarded for classified action in the service of the U.S. Submarine Force during a mission in which Midshipman First Class A. M. Pacino—at great risk to his own life and without regard for his personal safety—performed a heroic sacrifice that saved the lives of three crewmembers." Pacino had insisted once to his father that an award like that should be given for more than just saving a few people.

But when he'd reported for Submarine School without wearing the ribbon, he'd gotten the reprimand of his life from visiting Vice Admiral Rob Catardi, the former captain of *Piranha* and one of the three whom Pacino had saved, who had nominated Pacino for the award and told him quietly and intensely that not wearing his Navy Cross dishonored the day Pacino had done what he did. What he'd had to do. So Pacino had worn the ribbon on his uniform ever since, not so much for himself or Navy regulations, but for Rob Catardi.

It occurred to Pacino then that his storied father had earned the medal himself twice, both times with citations too classified to tell anyone about and both times from incidents in which his submarines sank with most of their crews lost. Perhaps, Pacino thought, that was the thread that bound him and his father together—not their mutual suffering or their struggles in the submarine force, but that something in their karma seemed to demand that they survive catastrophes while the people around them died, with the twisted result that they would be honored by a Navy that couldn't see the reality of their losses and only rewarded courage rather than victory.

Not that it mattered. Today was Friday, the sixth of May. His orders required him to report to the Naval Security Group U.S. Submarine Force—"NavSecGru SubFor"—at 1300 and get a security indoctrination, and when that was complete, report aboard the submarine USS *Vermont* at or around 1500. That was odd, he thought, in a Navy where seemingly everything important started well before dawn and new orders required reporting aboard on a Monday. He found the nondescript building marked only with the number "112" and handed his identification to a guard stationed behind heavy glass with only a slot for the ID card. He scanned his fingerprints and put his eyes up to the retinal scanner. The guard handed back his military ID and the entrance door clicked open. Pacino pushed through it, the steel door heavier than it looked.

A scowling first class petty officer waited for him. He wore the NWU Navy working uniform with its odd-looking multicolor digital camouflage print pattern and multiple pockets with combat boots and a cloth cover, the uniform new since Pacino had graduated from the academy. The petty officer didn't salute but just escorted Pacino to a cramped, sparsely furnished cinderblock-walled room with only a metal table, metal chairs and a camera in the corner watching him, the dingy space looking like something from a Detroit police station's interrogation room. The sailor left and shut the door, leaving Pacino to wait. He stared at the wall and for the first time all day, allowed himself to think about *her.* About Carrie

Alameda. Today, like so many days, he was still sleepwalking in shock, almost a year after that night in Boston.

Lieutenant Commander and Engineer Carolyn Alameda had been his mentor on his long first class midshipman cruise on the *Seawolf*-class submarine USS *Piranha,* at first a hostile and harsh taskmaster, but softening later as he demonstrated capability in his diving officer qualifications and the studies of the submarine. They'd had to share a stateroom, and soon they both became aware of their mutual attraction, which they had both tried to keep locked down, but it had been a compelling force of nature. He would never forget the first time she had let her guard down enough to give him a smoldering look, igniting a desire in him he'd never experienced. Getting orders to evacuate the *Piranha* had been both a disappointment and a relief to Pacino—disappointment because he wanted to be with the submarine when she sailed into harm's way, into genuine combat, but a relief that leaving Alameda behind would avoid them both getting disciplined by "Big Navy" for fraternization, a Naval Academy conduct offense for him but a full-blown court martial for her.

Carolyn Alameda had been unconscious and half-drowned when he had found her after his foolish re-entry into the doomed hull. The miracle of their rescue at the hands of the Royal Navy at first seemed like the universe smiling down upon both of them. Despite the prohibition of U.S. Navy Regulations, Pacino had secretly started to see her on weekends at grad school in Boston, when she would come up from DC, avoiding having him visit her in the town where seemingly everyone was military, where their relationship would raise eyebrows.

For a long moment in Pacino's life, everything seemed so perfect. Carrie Alameda's career was going into high gear and Pacino was celebrating completing his master's thesis, only waiting for his advisor's nod before graduating and going on to the Navy's nuclear training program.

And then this brief ray of sunshine turned into black darkness. Carrie had been visiting him at the humble walk-up apartment he shared with two other grad students on Newbury Street in Back Bay Boston. They'd finished dinner, enjoying having the apartment to themselves with Pacino's roommates out of town for the long Memorial Day weekend. Pacino had carried off the dishes and poured a Merlot for Carrie and three fingers of Balvenie scotch for himself and joined her on the sofa.

"Anthony," she'd said, looking into his eyes, "I never asked you this. I didn't want to upset you. But somehow now seems the right time."

He looked at her, raising an eyebrow.

She went on. "When we were in the deep submergence vehicle and being rescued, you were clinically dead for a while. While you were, you know, *out of it,* did you see anything?"

Pacino nodded solemnly. "The more time that goes by," he said haltingly, "the dimmer the memory gets and the more unreal it seems. By now, I only remember a few fragments, and what I do remember seems more like a fever dream than an experience."

"What did you see," she asked, her hand moving up to caress his face. "What happened?"

"I was watching myself from a distance for the whole rescue. I saw the DSV's emergency ascent. I saw the inside of the rescue submersible. I could feel the Royal Navy commander's thoughts and emotions. I saw the DSV surface. I saw the guys coming in the hatch to take us out. I saw the operating room. They were trying to resuscitate me, without any luck. Then a big black tunnel appeared, sucked me into it. I lost track of time, but I felt like I was inside for a few hours. Something happened while I was in there, and as much as I try, I can't remember what it was, and it seems important, but it's like trying to grab a cloud. And then I guess the tunnel sort of spit me back out into the rescue ship. From behind, I saw Colleen leaning over to look at my body and in an instant, I was back in my body again. I opened my eyes and I'm staring right at Colleen, blinking away the visions, trying to understand what the hell had happened."

Carrie's lovely smile shone on him for just a moment, then faded. Her face froze, then went blank, and her eyes rolled up into her head. She slumped over and fell to the floor, the wine glass breaking, the red wine spilling in a pool around her unmoving body.

Pacino rushed to kneel over her, trying to find her pulse, which was weak but present. He frantically pulled her into a fireman's carry, grabbed his wallet, phone and keys and raced down four flights of stairs with her on his shoulder, hardly noticing how he was panting from the exertion. He unlocked his car and poured her into the passenger seat, slapped the seatbelt on her and roared off toward Mass General Back Bay, the emergency room entrance he had driven past a hundred times. He dialed 911 as he drove, barking at the operator to have a team standing by at the ER. He rounded a corner at a red light, the old Corvette's tires slipping on the streets wetted by an evening drizzle. Finally, he skidded to a halt at the emergency entrance, set the parking brake and left the car running while he ran to the passenger side, pulled her out and carried her into the ER, where the crash team waited with a gurney. He was following when an administrator pulled him away to move his car. He opened his mouth to argue but realized he was blocking an ambulance. He ran to the car, threw it into gear, found what passed for parking in the absurdly crowded lot, then dashed back into the emergency room entrance.

He was forced to wait in misery and shock for what seemed hours, the nurses and administrators refusing to let him back to where Carolyn Alameda lay unconscious in surgery. When the sweat-soaked surgeon walked out, Pacino could see by his expression the news. "I'm sorry, Mr. Pacino, she had a brain aneurism and it was catastrophic. We couldn't save her. There's no telling whether the trauma from that submarine incident had caused this or if it were completely unrelated. It could have been waiting to happen for five years, or it could have started developing five weeks ago."

It seemed so unreal. One moment, the most solid, real, dear person in his universe was speaking warmly to him, and the next she was gone, as if she'd never existed.

He couldn't remember the day of the wake and the funeral the same way he remembered most things. Unlike the mental video of a normal memory, Carrie's funeral was just a flash of a hundred intense images—

Her open coffin with her in her uniform with her rows

of medals and her gold submarine dolphins, her cap tucked under her arm. Her face resting, as if she were sleeping, that constellation of beautiful freckles sprinkled around her nose, one of the first things Pacino had noticed about her.

A large framed photograph propped up on an easel behind her showing her in dress whites, smiling and standing next to then-Commander Robert Catardi with the gigantic hull of the USS *Piranha* behind her. Other framed photos of Alameda as a youngster, running track in high school, graduating as a midshipman from Annapolis, all of them showing her brilliant smile, her straight white teeth and singular beauty of her soul shining out in all of them.

The enormous crowd of officers present in the church, both senior and junior, and the enlisted men and women of her former submarine *Toledo*. Her brothers, one a Marine lieutenant, the other an Air Force colonel. Her grief-stricken father, struggling on a walker with an oxygen bottle attached to it, the Tygon tubing extending from the bottle over his ears to his nose.

The size of the cathedral where the service was conducted, candles lit everywhere. Pacino's father sitting next to him, the old man's suit seeming somehow odd when Pacino had always seen him in his officer's uniform. His mother on the other side of him, holding his hand. Missing, for some reason, was his father's wife Colleen, who had not been herself since the *Explorer II* rescue.

The graveside service was held in a dreary cold June rain. The time came to leave in his father's black town car. His mind drifted during the ride to his father's house in Annapolis. He heard the clink of a highball glass as it hit the copper surface of the bar in front of the Annapolis house's stone fireplace, then the sound of the scotch pouring into the glass. From miles away, he sensed the smoky taste of the whisky as it cascaded down his throat. Then more and more until finally his father half-carried him to the guest bedroom.

He woke up the next morning, not knowing where he was. His father stood in the kitchen, tall and gaunt, pouring him a steaming cup of hot black coffee. His father stole a glance at him to see if he were okay, and the answer coming that he most assuredly was not.

The phone call came in from the detailer putting him into a later nuclear power school class and instructing him to take two months off, somehow knowing how hard this had hit him despite the secrecy of the affair, perhaps Pacino's father having intervened. The days passed, one blurring into the next, Pacino running on the cobblestone streets of the bayside village before sunrise, numbly sitting on the eastern deck staring out at the sailboats on the Chesapeake in the afternoon, quietly drinking scotch with his father in the evening and watching the sun set from the western deck.

Sometimes, when Pacino remembered their last conversation, he wondered at the timing of it. Did Carrie instinctively know she had only minutes left? Did she see the opening of that tunnel behind him as he spoke to her?

His last night at the Annapolis house, he packed his seabag and got ready to leave. It was time to return to his life. He'd reported to Navy Nuclear Power School and buried himself inside the studies and the twelve-hour days. After half a year of that, six months of nuclear prototype, where he studied, qualified on and operated a live submarine nuclear reactor plant. Then three months of submarine school, where he realized that his time on *Piranha* had taught him most of what they were trying to teach, with the exception of the tactics of how to sneak up on an enemy submerged contact and kill it before it realized it was being stalked. He took a week of leave and spent it at his father's house, then loaded his scratched and dented ancient Corvette with the modern engine and rolled it south to his newly leased apartment in Virginia Beach, commutable to Norfolk Naval Station, where his orders instructed him to report aboard his new permanent duty station, the new Block IV Virginia-class submarine *Vermont.*

This morning, a sun-drenched day in May, he donned his starched tropical white uniform with the shoulderboards of a junior grade lieutenant and the damned Navy Cross—but notably and sadly missing gold submarine dolphins that he had yet to earn and which could take over a year to be granted. And not having those dolphins while onboard a submarine would make him a second-class citizen, as berated and dismissed as he had been when he'd reported aboard *Piranha* as a lowly midshipman a million years ago. And now he'd experience the same strangeness of starting a new life chapter on *Vermont*. He took a deep breath and consciously brought himself back to the moment. With an effort, he tried to fold up and put away all thoughts of Carrie Alameda, to compartmentalize his feelings, and to some extent over the last month he'd been able to do that, but doing so seemed to drain his energy and leave him with a heavy depressed feeling. He remembered when his father's wife Eileen had suddenly died in an interstate accident, the old man had been the same way, almost in a walking dead, power-saver mode. It had taken a war that the old man was losing to knock him out of that funk.

The door to the interview room clicked, then opened, revealing a short, corpulent man in his sixties. He shuffled in, wearing over-stuffed pants and vest from a suit, the vest open, an out-of-fashion tie at half mast, the tie bearing a dime-sized stain on it, the man smelling of stale cigarette smoke. Pacino stood to shake his hand, but the gruff man waved him to a seat. He rubbed his hand over his bald scalp and opened a briefcase to withdraw a folder full of papers and a tablet computer.

"I'm Barsky, head of submarine security at SubFor. This meeting is to indoctrinate you into a program. The program's name itself is top secret. So first, sign here." The first paper slid across the desk. Pacino scanned it. The paper itself was marked as *Top Secret—Fractal Chaos,* whatever that meant. It was legalese but amounted to one long threat of life imprisonment or execution if even a minor breach of security could be tied to him. In the event of a major security breach, he'd be treated as an enemy combatant, stripped of his citizenship and Constitutional rights and either tossed into a black program cell or summarily executed. Pacino looked up at Barsky and lifted an eyebrow. "Sign it," the harsh man said, "or your submarine career ends right now." Pacino shrugged and signed the nondisclosure agreement in quadruplicate. "That just entitles you to be read into the program, which is named—and the name is special compartmented information, SCI, top secret codeword material—*Fractal Chaos*—and that codeword is three levels above the classification top secret. You're aware that SCI material includes the nation's most closely guarded secrets? Some of them so secret that only a few people know about them?"

Pacino nodded gravely, and the next hour was simply more of the same. He signed more forms, each more graphically threatening than the last, a few of the final agreements not committed to physical paper, but only on Barsky's tablet computer. The last forms required him to submit knowingly and willingly to any kind of electronic surveillance on himself at any time and to surrender his Fourth Amendment rights, agreeing to any kind of physical search of himself, his home or his possessions at any time. Pacino signed it, beginning to understand why his father had been so closed-mouthed about the operations of his submarines.

Finally, Barsky stood and waved him to the door. A different petty officer, as dour as the first one, waited and escorted him down the corridors to the entrance door, which slammed behind him. He climbed back in the Corvette and drove it to the officer parking lot for Pier 22, home of Squadron Eight and Submarine Development Group Twelve. This late in the day, the open parking spaces were a long way from the pier. He walked to the pier security building that displayed a large emblem of an angry shark pushing a billiards eight-ball, the logo of Squadron Eight, a separate emblem for SubDevGru 12, an image of King Neptune, his chest armor bearing the numeral 12. Pacino produced his identification, rescanned his fingerprints and submitted to the retinal scan. He put the contents of his pockets in a dog bowl that was scanned by the equipment. He walked through the millimeter wave body scanner, then collected his personal items. The guard pointed to his phone. "Your ship will be collecting that from you when you get to it, so any calls, texts or emails, you should send out now."

"I'm good," Pacino said, taking the phone and walking out into the early May sunshine to the long and wide concrete runway of the pier. He could see the ship in the distance. The pier was empty except for her. Perhaps an operational tempo surge or exercises were going on, but *Vermont* was the only submarine at the pier, her sister ships from the squadron at sea. He paused a few shiplengths away to look at her. As usual with nuclear attack submarines, there wasn't much to see. Just a simple cigar-shaped black cylinder with a vertical conning tower—the sail—presiding over the bow, a number of masts pointing to the sky emerging out of the sail. The sloping hull aft angled into the brackish water of the slip, the rudder sticking straight up farther aft. Doubled up heavy lines bound the sub to the pier, coiling from the bollards on the concrete jetty to the cleats on the top of the ship's hull. The hull itself was covered in a black, spongy, rubbery coating to avoid bouncing back sonar pings. A gangway, the brow, extended from the pier to the hull, and a banner was tied to the brow's structure, reading USS *VERMONT,* SSN-792.

The ship's seal was affixed to the banner. It showed an attack sub on the surface, a fragment of a Betsy Ross American flag, an image fragment of a square-rigged sailing vessel on the left, and on the right, the 1907 Connecticut-class battleship USS *Vermont,* BB-20, in the background, then below the sub image, gold and silver submarine dolphins, the seal's written motto reading, *"Vermont—Freedom & Unity."*

Pacino paused, remembering what little he knew about her, the information passed on by his father at one of their cocktail hours. *Vermont* was what the Navy called a "project boat." By that, it meant that her missions were "special projects" or operations so secret that they couldn't be spoken of aloud. She didn't report like the other boats to the squadron commander or even to the normal command structure of the force, but directly to the National Security Council and to POTUS, the President of the United States.

He walked up to the topside watch sentry, a second-class petty officer in crackerjack dress blues with gleaming silver dolphins and a splash of ribbons above his pocket, the name badge reading WATSON. His emblem showed the symbol of a ship's propeller, so he was one of the mechanical personnel onboard. Petty Officer Watson came to attention and saluted, and Pacino rigidly returned the salute.

Before he could announce himself, Watson said in a deep

South accent, squinting, "You're Lieutenant Pacino, reportin' aboard, right?"

Pacino nodded. "How'd you know?"

Watson smirked. "Ain't ever' day the son of the Chief of Naval Operations himself walks aboard your ship, and a nub non-qual airbreathin' puke at that."

Pacino smiled despite the friendly insult. "Dad's long retired," he said. "And I'm just another non-qual junior officer."

Watson seemed to appreciate Pacino's humility. He half-smiled. "I'll need to see your orders, Mr. Pacino, and your identification."

Pacino took his phone from his back pocket and pulled up his digital orders, the terse text only directing him to report to the NavSecGru and then *Vermont*, SSN-792. Watson looked it over and compared it to what was displayed on his pad computer. Pacino handed over his identification. Watson put the identification card into a scanner while he held up a portable retinal scanner. After a few seconds, he seemed satisfied at the readout.

"I'll need your phone," Watson said. Pacino handed it over. Watson opened a washing machine-sized cabinet and put the phone into a drawer inside. "Faraday cage," he said. "No signals going out or coming in. You can pick it up when you leave the ship for the day. The yeoman will have a pad computer waiting for you onboard—but remember, it never leaves the ship."

Watson pulled a VHF radio from his belt. "Duty Officer, Topside." The radio hissed with static. It took a moment for the duty officer to answer. While he waited, Pacino looked up at *Vermont*'s sail and saw the other topside watchstander, whose combat-helmeted head protruded from a cubbyhole on top of the tall fin, the man's high-powered rifle visible. A sniper, Pacino thought. Defense from an invasion, assuming a commando force could penetrate the pier security. Odds were, though, he thought, any commandos would come from the sea, not the shore. Out in the slip between the piers on the starboard side, a heavily armed Coast Guard small boat patrolled slowly, a second one on the other side of the jetty toward the cruiser piers.

Watson's radio finally clicked with the deep voice of an authoritative young man. "Duty Officer."

"Sir, Mr. Pacino is here."

"Roger, copy, on my way."

A stocky officer in working khakis appeared from the canvas tent over the aft hatch, making Pacino feel out of uniform since he himself wore tropical whites, his shirt and pants white, his hat—his cover—white, and even his belt and shoes white. Tropical whites were the more formal summer uniform, for reporting aboard. The officer approaching had the double silver bars of a full lieutenant on his collars, gold submarine dolphins above his pocket, a key on an elaborate chain around his neck, his name badge reading, DANKLEFF. He was half a head shorter than Pacino, dark-complected, with pockmarked skin showing a distinct five o-clock shadow and wore thick-lensed glasses with thick black rims. Pacino came to attention and saluted, and the duty officer waved a sloppy salute back. He reached out and shook Pacino's hand, smiling with what seemed genuine joy to meet him.

"I'm Dieter Dankleff," he said. "I'll be your sea daddy for the next few weeks."

"Anthony Pacino," Pacino said. "Glad to meet you."

"'Patch,' right?" Dankleff asked.

Pacino nodded. "Patch," his father's nickname, had seemed to stick to him as well.

"Put this on your belt," Dankleff ordered, handing Pacino a small black plastic cylinder the size of a cigarette lighter. "Thermoluminescent dosimeter, to be worn at all times on your belt to record your cumulative radiation dose. Even if you're aboard in civilian clothes, the dosimeter goes on your belt." Pacino strapped the dosimeter to his belt. "Now, come with me. The captain and exec are waiting for you below."

Dankleff walked across the gangway, turning to salute the American flag flying aft. Pacino did the same, then stepped off the gangway onto the spongy hull of the submarine, the foam coating glued to the high tensile steel for sound quieting and minimization of returned sonar pings. Aft of the sail, the conning tower, there were two hatches. The forward one had a scaffold-and-canvas "dog house" over it with the emblem of the Navy SEALs—sea/air/land commandos—and was surrounded by a locked chain. Farther aft, a larger dog house had the emblem of the ship on it. Dankleff walked to the aft doghouse, opened the curtain and stepped inside. Pacino followed him into the relative gloom. Inside the doghouse was a huge hatch, twice the size of the hatchway on the *Piranha.* As if Dankleff knew what he was thinking, he said, "Plug trunk. Bigger hatch to load bigger things without making hull cuts, like widescreen flat panels. Usually, our access is through the lockout hatch forward, but the SEALs have that tied up, what with getting all their shit loaded in."

"Down ladder," Dankleff called, then lowered himself into the trunk. Pacino followed, the bright light of the outside world vanishing, traded for the florescent lighting inside the 15-foot-wide cylinder. Inside, it resembled the escape trunk he'd used to leave the *Piranha. And to come back inside it,* he thought. Dankleff waved him through a large vertical hatch that opened into the aft part of forward compartment upper level. Pacino noticed the smell was exactly the same as *Piranha* or his father's boats—an oily mix of cooking grease, amine atmospheric control chemicals, and ozone from the electrical equipment. It made his head spin for just a moment, the scent bringing back both the *Piranha* and Carrie Alameda so strongly it was if she stood right next to him.

Just like onboard the forward spaces of the *Piranha,* bulkheads forming the tight passageway were covered with a wood trim laminated coating in the few places where there were no panels, junction boxes, cable runs, piping or valves. Unlike the *Piranha,* on top of the deck of the passageways were twelve-inch diameter tin cans of food, jammed tight and overlaid with sheets of half-inch plywood, making the overhead a foot closer. Pacino had to slouch down to get through the passageway. He followed as Dankleff continued into a narrow passageway forward and ducked down a stairway to the middle level of the forward compartment. Pacino followed him, stepping off into the crew's mess, which was oddly deserted. The deck was visible here—no plywood or tin cans. Tables and benches were gathered, café style, with a long food service line. Behind it the packed galley was likewise empty. Dankleff walked forward into the forward passageway, where the cans-and-plywood resumed, past a second set of steep stairs, where there was a door marked "XOSR," for the executive officer's stateroom.

"Listen, Patch, the XO is Lieutenant Commander Quinnivan, on exchange from the Royal Navy's fast attack sub force. Good guy, but tougher than grandma's leftover steak. In command is Commander Seagraves, who makes Quinnivan seem warm and fuzzy by comparison. So good luck in there," he said, "and welcome aboard. I just hope you're braced for a wild ride."

Before Pacino could ask what he meant, Dankleff reached up and knocked on the executive officer's door.

2

Friday, May 6

The executive officer's stateroom was the biggest aboard the *Vermont* except for the captain's, with a double rack against the far bulkhead, one wall with closets and cubbyholes, the other with two fold-down desks, a small pull-out sink in the corner.

Executive Officer Lieutenant Commander Jeremiah Seamus Quinnivan, Royal Navy, wasn't English, but rather an Irishman from County Cork, having enlisted in the Royal Navy in his youth as a choice, since it was either that or being tossed into jail. It hadn't taken long for the service to realize he had talent and after getting an engineering degree, he'd eventually found his way into a series of assignments on *Astute*-class fast attack submarines and from there to the U.S. Navy / Royal Navy joint exchange program. Quinnivan wore dark blue pants and shirt, with an emblem of his rank in the center of his chest, the emblem a dark blue background with three horizontal gold stripes, the middle stripe narrower than the others, the top stripe making a loop-the-loop in the center. On his fold-down desk was a black beret with a gold crown surrounded by laurel leaves as the center emblem. Over Quinnivan's pocket were embroidered gold submarine dolphins, their design starkly different than the American version, but still recognizable. On one shoulder was sewn a patch with the flag of the United Kingdom. On the other was an embroidered patch with the *Vermont* logo.

Quinnivan was short and slight, his close-cropped hair

salt-and-pepper, the gray invading his Van Dyke beard and mustache, both of which lent him a somewhat sinister look when he frowned, but when he smiled, his spirit seemed barely contained by his body as his eyes crinkled at the corners, revealing teeth that had been capped—some thought from a fight when he was young that had knocked them all out.

Quinnivan leaned back in his swivel chair and looked up at the captain, who stood in the doorway to their shared bathroom, the CO / XO head. Captain Timothy Talisker Seagraves was tall for submarine duty, his head threatening to bang into numerous valves tucked into the overhead, and solid as well. He had slightly longer-than-regulation black hair that swooped over his head with streaks of gray over his ears—gray arriving early for the 39-year-old—with heavy black eyebrows, dark brown eyes, a straight nose, stark cheekbones, thin lips and a square jaw, with a dimple centered in his chin. Quinnivan once joked with Seagraves that the captain looked like he could be a senator, a judge, a news anchor or a daytime soap opera star. Quinnivan considered that he and Seagraves must have looked an odd couple, with his humble looks and Seagraves' physical near perfection. Seagraves stood with an attitude of unquestioned confidence and authority as he leaned casually against the door jamb. On the collars of his working khakis, he wore silver oak leaves. Over his left pocket he wore gleaming gold submariner's dolphins, and below them, a gold capital ship command pin.

Quinnivan picked up his pad computer, which was displaying the classified service jacket of the newly reporting officer, Anthony Pacino. "Skipper, ya had a chance to look at this wee laddie's personnel file?" Quinnivan's Irish brogue was comically thick unless he was briefing senior officers, when his accent would calm down somewhat.

"I looked it over," Seagraves said in a commanding baritone voice with just a hint of a Southern accent, Atlanta or Savannah, perhaps. "I got a call from Admiral Catardi, who recommended Pacino in glowing terms. You know we had to cash in favors to get NavPersCom to assign Pacino to us, right? Are there issues or concerns, XO?" Seagraves never called Quinnivan

"Jeremiah" or "Seamus," as he'd prefer to be addressed, only using his official title of the executive officer, "XO," but not from stuffy formality but the feeling that he might lapse into calling the Irishman by the crew's nickname of "Bullfrog," from some forgotten rock 'n roll lyric about his first name.

Quinnivan stroked his short black-and-gray beard, his gesture when he was carefully choosing his next words.

"Ya know, Skipper, this kid Pacino, back home we'd call him a 'chancer.' He's got a propensity to take risks, yeah? Smart lad, good grades at the Academy and his graduate school, but almost got kicked out of Annapolis for conduct offenses. Going over the wall at three in the mornin', ya know, yeah? and then getting caught drinking in Baltimore as an underclassman. Then the kid parks his fookin' hotrod Corvette in the parking space of the Commandant of Midshipmen. That was almost the last straw, since the commandant was late for a meeting with the admiral. Sure, Pacino's brave, yeah? but reckless. I'm not sure how well I'll sleep with him standing officer-of-the-deck watch on the conn."

"You didn't read the classified citation from Rob Catardi on the *Piranha* incident, did you?"

Quinnivan shook his head. "It isn't in the file, Skipper. Just the unclassified note of the award for, well, obviously, bravery."

Seagraves pulled Quinnivan's heavy weather gear off the room's second chair, tossed it onto the upper rack, spun the chair backwards and plopped down into it, resting his forearms on the chair back.

"XO, lend an ear and let me tell you the top-secret tale that Admiral Catardi told me about the *Piranha* rescue."

As the captain spoke, Quinnivan's face changed from doubt to disbelief and then to pure awe.

A knock came at the door. The DCA, the Damage Control Assistant, Lieutenant Dieter Dankleff, cracked the door open. "Excuse me, XO, Captain, I have Lieutenant junior grade Pacino here to report aboard."

"Send him in," Quinnivan said, smiling. "And Duty Officer, rig ship for class alpha air gap."

"Rig ship for class alpha air gap, aye sir." Dankleff withdrew and Pacino stiffened his posture into rigid attention, his white officer's cover tucked under his arm. Pacino shook the captain's hand, then the exec's, looking directly into each man's eyes.

"Pacino, reporting aboard as ordered, Captain, XO." The lieutenant's voice wasn't as deep as Seagraves, more of a low-pitched tenor, but a smooth tenor, with no discernable regional accent. The lad had confidence in his voice, but also a sort of weariness, Quinnivan thought.

Quinnivan, with a practiced eye coming from years of commanding officers and enlisted men, took in Pacino with a long glance. The lad was slender and tall, his uniform pressed, starched and spotless. He carried his cover, his hat, under his arm, cradled into his ribs. He wore several ribbons, most of them the usual awards for officers with his experience, but the lone ribbon on the top row, center, was the Navy Cross, which Quinnivan had never seen before. Above the ribbons were paratrooper wings. Quinnivan wondered how the hell a junior grade lieutenant had had paratrooper training.

This kid Pacino had odd looks to him, Quinnivan thought. He seemed rugged and tough overall, yet his individual features were refined—his lips had a full, puffy look to them and his almond-shaped eyes were large and emerald green with long lashes. His nose was straight, his cheekbones sculpted, his hair looking a little longer than it should, a shade of chestnut that reflected the overhead lights. Quinnivan thought it must be a hell-ride going to a nightclub with this kid—he had to be popular with the womenfolk, but he also had this look about him that showed he had no idea about his good looks, in contrast to Seagraves, Quinnivan thought, who knew he had a striking appearance and used it whenever he could.

There was something more here, though, Quinnivan thought. There was something about the young man standing in the room entrance. He seemed engulfed in a dense cloud of something. If Quinnivan were pressed, he would have described Pacino's aura as one of exhaustion. He seemed as if he were carrying a thousand-pound backpack. He'd have to get to the bottom of that, and soon, he thought.

Seagraves spoke first after glancing quickly at Pacino's ribbons. "Welcome aboard, Lieutenant. What have you heard about the *Vermont*?"

"Actually, nothing, sir. There's not much in the open sources about her."

"That's good," Seagraves said, seriously. "We're a *project* boat. The things we do—well, let's just say *we never did them* and leave it at that. There are a few unforgiveable sins in the submarine force and particularly on this boat, Mr. Pacino, and one of them is talking about our operations. To anyone. That includes family. Decorated war hero fathers. Girlfriends, wives, mistresses—"

Quinnivan interrupted. "*Especially* those fookin' mistresses. And hookers too, yeah?"

Seagraves smiled, smirking at the XO: "Yes, XO, hookers too. Drinking buddies. Mothers. Family dog. Even submariners from other boats. Especially submariners from other boats. Even former bosses like Admiral Catardi. *Anyone*."

Pacino looked at Seagraves, the point being made that he couldn't talk to his father about anything that would happen aboard.

"Understood, sir."

"Pacino, what's the mission statement of the USS *Vermont*?"

Pacino frowned. "I don't know it, sir." Was Quinnivan talking about what was written on the *Vermont* logo on the banner strapped to the gangway, 'Freedom and Unity'?

"It never happened," Quinnivan began, looking at Seagraves.

Captain Seagraves finished with the companion statement: *"We were never there."*

"Memorize that, young Pacino," Quinnivan said.

Just then the ship-wide announcing 1MC circuit clicked. Pacino froze, knowing that in the submarine force, that *click* meant *shut up and listen.*

"Rig ship," the overhead speakers rasped with Dankleff's voice, *"for class alpha air gap."*

Seagraves looked at Quinnivan. "Well, I'll leave you to your work, XO. I'm going to shove off." He nodded seriously at Pacino. "Good to have you aboard, Mr. Pacino. Oh, XO, cigars tonight?" Quinnivan nodded and smiled at that, and Seagraves ducked into the door to the shared head and from there into his stateroom.

Quinnivan waved Pacino to the empty seat. "Shut the door and relax, willya, laddie, while I tell you about the top-secret lore of the USS *Vermont*."

Pacino shut the door and sank into the hard steel chair at the far bulkhead of the XO's stateroom, keeping his posture rigid. Quinnivan reached over to this walkie-talkie and pulled the battery out of it and tossed it and the battery onto his bed, which was crowded with papers and books. Quinnivan's desk phone buzzed. He picked up the handset. "XO. You're rigged for class-A airgap? Okay, Duty Officer, good, good." Quinnivan hung up and looked at Pacino.

"Well, okay, then, Mr. Pacino, I'm not going to tell you about all our operations in the last two years. That would take too long. But just to give you an idea what you're signing onto here, I thought I'd give you the top-secret *Fractal Chaos* briefing on our last operation, which is typical of what we do at sea. Now, there's a documentary video of this last operation, yeah? But it's too long and boring to watch. So, I grabbed a few screenshots of the optronics mast videos for you."

Quinnivan operated the software of his pad computer for a moment, authenticated himself with a retinal scan, then displayed a photograph of what looked like an aerial photo of a huge super-yacht. A second photo showed the same luxury yacht from the water level with crosshairs superimposed on it—a periscope photo.

"You've heard of Elias Sotheby, world famous billionaire industrialist, made his fortune in computer software and electric vehicles, went on to become a global philanthropist and activist, all into financing the medical health of the third world and saving the earth from dying of climate change, yeah?"

Pacino nodded. "It was all over the news. He disappeared off the face of the earth, what, a month ago? Two?"

Quinnivan shot a look at Pacino. "Yeah, forty-one days ago he disappeared, because we on the *Vermont* disappeared him." Quinnivan clicked to a high-definition photo showing Sotheby held up by two men in black wetsuits. The background was black, as if the photo were shot at night. A bullet hole showed clearly in Sotheby's left temple, with a gaping exit wound on the right side of his skull big enough to put a baseball in, but unmistakably Elias Sotheby. Quinnivan glanced over at Pacino, whose mouth hung open in disbelief.

"Why?" Pacino asked.

Quinnivan shrugged. "No idea, lad. We don't have the need to know. We involve ourselves more in the 'how' than the 'why.' Valid, authenticated orders came in from the president, and we went to work."

The 1MC clicked again, and Quinnivan paused. "Vermont, *departing!*" Another click.

"Captain's left the ship," Quinnivan noted, then continued. "And in this case, the 'how' involved finding this yacht, stalking her, popping up to periscope depth and locking out some very rough blokes, your Navy calls them SEALs, who got aboard the yacht in the middle of the night."

Quinnivan picked up his desk phone, dialed a number. "Yeah, George, XO here. Send up a pot of coffee, service for two, willya?" He hung up and continued. "You ever met any of those SEALs?"

Pacino nodded. "I went to airborne school at Fort Benning between plebe and youngster year and met half a dozen of them. Pretty closed-off group of guys, never talked to anyone outside their unit. Capable people, did phenomenally well at the physical stuff, you know, the six mile runs in combat boots, twenty chin-ups, fifty push-ups. I can tell you, I wouldn't want to meet any one of them in a dark alley."

Quinnivan laughed as a knock sounded on his door. He quickly flipped his pad computer on its face and called, "come in." A mess cook entered with a tray with a coffee carafe and two cups with milk and sugar service on the side. "Thanks, George," Quinnivan said as the messman took his leave. Quinnivan poured for them both, dumping milk and three sugars in his and looking up at Pacino while waving the milk container. Pacino shook his head, taking his coffee black.

"Damn," Quinnivan said, sipping loudly, "American coffee.

I never thought I'd like it until I'd stood about three command duty watches with no sleep in between, and Mr. Dankleff introduced me to the stuff. My eyes were opened. I had no idea how I'd survived before coffee. And just like a hotdog is better at a ballpark, yeah? Coffee is fantastic on a submarine, at sea and at depth. Just magical." He sipped the coffee. "Where were we?"

"SEALs," Pacino prompted.

"Right. So the SEALs sneak aboard, find Sotheby in his stateroom, immobilize him with zip ties, find and pack up all the computer hard drives, cell phones, pad computers and documents for transport, scour the yacht for anyone aboard, but he was alone, these computer techies relying on their AI to drive their yachts, plus Sotheby was a notorious loner. They set the yacht on fire, bring Sotheby back to the boat, we observe through the periscope until the yacht founders and then sinks, and meanwhile we interrogate Sotheby in the wardroom—well, the SEALs interrogate him. We didn't have the need to know. But I imagine most of the questions went to the passwords for his electronics, account numbers of offshore accounts, what he was really up to, who was controlling him and whom he was controlling. You know, the usual."

Pacino put down his cup. "And afterward, they just shot him? In the wardroom?"

Quinnivan laughed. "No, son, that would have made a mess. We broach the sail, just enough that they can get Sotheby's body out of the ship. SEALs do the deed, take the kill photo, weigh him down and toss him over. The sounding read nineteen hundred fathoms under the keel—well over eleven thousand feet. I guarantee no one will hear from Mr. Sotheby again, unless they get a double of him made up with plastic surgery to be a 'new' Elias Sotheby, a puppet to say what they want him to say and do what they want him to do."

Pacino looked at his cup sadly. The brew had gone cold.

Quinnivan nodded in understanding as if he knew what was going through the junior officer's mind. "Yeah, young Mr. Pacino, this is what being on a project boat means. Doin' secret but nasty stuff like this, yeah?"

Pacino opened his mouth to say something, then thought

better of it. Quinnivan shut down the pad computer, put it into his safe, then turned to look at Pacino.

"So, young lad, this ship is a three-hundred-and-seventy-seven-foot-long blunt instrument of presidential policy. We are assassins. We put the killer in hunter-killer. We do as we're told, and what we're told is sometimes very ugly. But I suppose the bright side is, by doing so we can change world politics, perhaps even the course of history." Quinnivan wasn't smiling now, Pacino noted. Quinnivan picked up his phone and dialed it. "Duty Officer, secure the rig for class alpha air gap and come pick up Mr. Pacino."

Click, from the 1MC system. *"The class alpha air gap is secured. Rig ship communications for in-port." Click.*

Quinnivan absently found his VHF walkie-talkie, put the battery in it and turned it back on. "I'll see you later at the party at my house, lad, yeah? The DCA—Mr. Dankleff—will give you the address and time."

The wardroom, a combination of conference room and mess table for the officers, was empty.

"Where is everyone?" Pacino asked Dankleff. Since Pacino had been with Dankleff, the man hadn't stopped smiling. In fact, he seemed to be having such a good time that Pacino was tempted to ask him what drugs he was on.

Dankleff smiled even wider. "Pre-lubricating for the ship's party at the XO's house. Hail-and-farewell ceremony. You're one guest of honor, the hail part. The farewell is for the officer you're replacing, Duke 'Man-Mountain Squirt Gun' Vevera, who's leaving the ship early due to medical issues. Let me show you to the three-man stateroom where you're assigned. It's half of a sixpack in the upper level. In a way you're lucky. It's the only junior officer stateroom not shared with a department head."

Dankleff led the way down the narrow passageway, turned at the steep athwartships stairway to the upper level, emerging into a passageway with more plywood laid on top of the twelve-inch diameter cans, the wood-and-can loading stretching all through the ship's upper level deck surfaces.

"I see we're loaded out for deployment," Pacino said,

hunching over to walk down the passageway.

"Oh, yeah, part of being on alert status," Dankleff said. "Can't have a sudden emergent mission fucked up by the boat running out of food. Anyway, bunking in with the engineer, navigator or weapons boss is no holiday, let me tell you. But this three-man bunkroom is half the size, so when there's an emergency and all three of you have to vault out of bed and get dressed in fifteen seconds in a space half the size of Mommy's powder room back home, it's a total cluster-fuck. Normally, as your sea-daddy, I'd give you a full tour of the boat, but the party is coming up in a couple hours, so I'll do it Monday." Dankleff handed Pacino a card with handwriting on it. "Here's the Irishman's address. Party starts at nineteen hundred sharp. Do *not* be fashionably late. XO takes roll and latecomers, well, they suffer. XO *explicitly* told me to tell you to have your ass there at nineteen hundred. On the fuckin' dot. You know what they say, Patch—*'If you're early, you're on time; if you're on time, you're late; if you're late, you're off the team.'* So I'll see you there."

Dankleff clapped Pacino on his shoulderboard, turned and headed back to the ladderway to the middle level. Pacino rubbed his eyes a moment, his head still spinning from some of the things Quinnivan had told him. He had thought *Piranha*'s combat mission was eye-opening. But *Vermont* had done things Pacino could barely believe.

Pacino put on his cover and walked on the plywood and cans, hunched over, to the ladderway to the plug hatch. It was almost 1630. He'd need to hurry to make it across town to his apartment and change before going to the XO's. He climbed out of the hull and looked down at the vessel, knowing that in the last month, she and her crew had assassinated Elias Sotheby. Farther down the pier, he turned to glance back at *Vermont*, which lay quietly at her mooring, acting innocent, but hiding deep and violent secrets.

3

Friday, May 6

Jeremiah Seamus Quinnivan's Virginia Beach house looked like ten thousand others in the suburbs of Norfolk, Virginia. When Pacino cut the engine on the old Corvette, it was 1850, ten minutes before the appointed time. He'd be damned if he'd be late for the first thing he was ordered to do, especially when cautioned by Dankleff to be spot on-time.

For the last two hours, his mind had been so filled with what Quinnivan had told him about the attack on Elias Sotheby's yacht that he realized for those hours he hadn't thought about Carrie Alameda. And with that thought, the grief came crashing back to him, as hard as it had been before, but now made worse by the guilt of forgetting her. For just the slightest moment he could swear he could feel her presence in the car sitting next to him. Hoping he could somehow connect to her, he spoke aloud to the passenger seat.

"Carrie. I miss you. I miss you terribly. I think about you all the time. I hope you're okay, wherever you are." His voice trembled and then broke on the last phrase.

He waited, wondering if he'd sense something. A scent of her, or the feeling of a caress on his face. There was nothing physical, but maybe the slightest feeling of something peaceful came into his mind, almost a soothing feeling. For some moments he shut his eyes and tried to explore the sensation to see if it were real, but then his watch beeped that it was two minutes to the hour of 1900.

He took a deep breath and told himself he was back on duty and to swallow his overwrought emotions. He dried his eyes and got out of the car, which he'd parked across the street from the house, and suddenly noticed how odd it was that a ship's party this big didn't result in a street packed with parked cars. Maybe all the officers had taken car services over, he thought, which would have been a good idea if the amount of drinking he predicted actually happened.

Feeling uncertain and nervous, but trying to make his face seem composed and cool, he rang the doorbell. He hoped he had dressed properly for the occasion. Quinnivan had said it would be a casual thing, saying even shorts, T-shirts and flip-flops would be allowable. Pacino had dressed in jeans, the kind with no holes or rips in them, a dark blue button-down Oxford shirt and his brown, scuffed harness boots. Though it was May, the weather hadn't awakened to spring yet and it was on the cool side, so Pacino had debated tossing on a leather jacket, but decided it would be silly just for the walk from the car to the front door.

The door opened and Pacino found himself looking slightly up at a stunning, slender tall brunette woman, perhaps thirty-five, with beautiful, bright sky-blue eyes, pouty lips and the features of a model or a newscaster, dressed in tall dark heels, a tight charcoal pencil dress that looked like cashmere, a diamond pendant around her throat, revealing a curvaceous figure that could stop traffic. Pacino chided himself, thinking staring at the XO's wife's chest would certainly violate protocol. And judging by her outfit, he was right to think he'd underdressed. Perhaps he should have worn a suit and tie. When she spoke, it was with a cultured London accent. "Hello, young man, come in, please, welcome, welcome, I'm Shawna, Seamus' wife, come along."

For a moment, Pacino was lost. Who the hell was Seamus, pronounced *"shame-us,"* he wondered. "Seamus?" he asked, hesitantly, as he stepped into the foyer that opened into the living room, a room tidy with what seemed fifty candles burning softly. Mellow jazz music emanated from the room's sound system.

"Seamus Quinnivan," she said. "You did meet him on the

ship today, right? And you're Patch Pacino, correct? Newly reporting aboard that wretched stinking vessel *Vermont*?" She crinkled her beautiful nose as she mentioned the name of the submarine. He nodded at her. She found a door in the kitchen, opened it and clicked a button on what looked like a wall-mounted intercom. "Seamus," she called into the squawk box, "our first guest is here, Mr. Pacino."

He could hear the XO's jolly brogue shout up from the room below. "Pacino, get your ass down here to engineroom lower level!"

He looked at Shawna Quinnivan. She smiled warmly and said in her silky English voice, "Normally I'd offer you a drink at the bar here, but Seamus is all equipped down in his man-cave."

Pacino swallowed. "If I can ask, ma'am—"

"Shawna," she corrected him, touching his shoulder.

"Shawna." He swallowed. "Where is everyone?"

She smiled. "Ship's parties never start on time and this one isn't set to kick into gear until eight pm. We won't have a quorum until nine at the earliest. Some won't even arrive until midnight. You military types, always hustling and bustling and being on-time or early for things. When you relax, you don't want to be timing things by a *clock*."

"Oh," he said. "I thought the DCA, Dieter Dankleff, said it would begin at nineteen hundred sharp. Seven pm."

"*Dieter*? Oh, you mean '*U-Boat* Dankleff.' Yes, darling, that was just for you, dear," she said, smiling brightly.

"*Pacino*!" Quinnivan bellowed from below. "Getcher arse *down* here!"

Pacino gave Shawna a grateful expression and went below to the lower level.

Quinnivan stood behind the bar fussing with the bottles and glasses. When he stepped around it, Pacino could see he wore old jeans with holes and rips, an open flannel plaid-patterned lumberjack shirt, a T-shirt with a faded image of a bottle of Jameson's Irish Whisky and old scuffed and torn steel-toed boots. Pacino thought how out of a place a suit and tie would seem now. Quinnivan hurried over and shook Pacino's hand warmly. "Welcome to engineroom lower level," he said with pride, expansively waving at the room. "Come on, we have some twenty-five-year-old single-malt rare-cask whisky waitin' for us. The two thousand dollar a bottle kind. I've been saving it for a special occasion. I held off on having the first drink until you could get here. You're fookin' *late*, by the way. If you're early, you're on-time. If you're on-time, you're late. And if you're late, you're off the team, yeah?"

Pacino found himself pulled over to the bar, where seemingly every alcoholic concoction known to mankind crowded the bar's surface. Quinnivan produced two crystal rocks glasses and poured two fingers of the Macallan 25 scotch for each of them, handed one to Pacino, then raised his own glass and clinked it into Pacino's. Pacino took a pull of the scotch, and it was smooth, smoky and mellow. Quinnivan downed his in one go and poured more for himself.

"Ah, a good scotch tastes like the dirt from the grave of an honest Scotsman," he said. "But good fookin' luck findin' tha'." He shook his head. "So, young man, what do ya think of the engineroom here?"

Pacino hadn't even noticed the room, his vision tunneled to the Irishman and his firehose stream of words so heavily accented that he had to concentrate hard to translate it all into English. The room was large, in an L-shape, one part of it devoted to two pool tables lit by dim and mellow Tiffany hanging lamps. The walls were a thick mahogany paneling in places, interrupted by areas where old bricks formed the walls. The ceiling was a grid of heavy mahogany beams with an ancient tin pattern painted an off-white in between the beams. The copper-sheathed bar presided over the corner of the room, and the area toward the stairs featured a large brown leather couch and four overstuffed leather club chairs arranged around a heavy antique mahogany coffee table. The couch faced a fireplace big enough to roast a pig in whole and it was burning a few logs, giving the room a pleasant wood smoke aroma. The wall where the stairs entered the room had one of the new gigantic flat panels mounted on it, a Samsung "Wall," a television so big that it needed a special truck to bring it to the house. Despite the stark modernity of the flat panel, the effect of Quinnivan's decorating was that it almost seemed like an old-fashioned English gentleman's club.

"It's amazing," Pacino said.

"Shawna recreated her father's old English study and retreat, but I canceled the plans for the desk and work tables over there and decided on pool tables instead, yeah? The fook do I need an office for? It's not like I can bring any of the ship's work home, what with it all being classified, you know what I'm sayin'?"

"You, um, wanted me here early, sir?" Pacino asked, wondering if prompting Quinnivan might be a misstep.

Quinnivan guided Pacino to one of the club chairs. "Indeed I did, lad, and my apologies for flim-flammin' ye to get ya here early."

Pacino sank into the leather chair and put his glass down on a marble coaster on the table in front of him. Quinnivan stepped back to the bar, retrieved the Macallan bottle, refilled their glasses and put the bottle on the table, sat down and leaned forward in his chair, as if he were a coiled spring.

Away from the formality of the submarine's XO's stateroom, Pacino looked again at Quinnivan. As imposing a personality as the Irishman was, he was not tall, perhaps lacking six feet by four inches, and wiry, all of maybe 150 pounds. He was going bald, his hairline climbing up the crown of his skull, but the effect balanced by his closely-cropped black and gray-streaked beard that gave him a sinister look unless he were smiling. Quinnivan had narrow green eyes that often lit up in amusement, crinkling the crow's feet at his temples. Pacino hadn't seen him in any moods other than expansively cheerful or soberly somber—such as when he was telling Pacino about *Vermont*'s last operation, but Pacino imagined the Irishman's expression could be frightening when he was angry.

"Listen, lad, the submarine functions as a 'SCIF,' a special compartmented information facility. When it's rigged for an air gap, no radio waves or internet signals can leave the sub's hull, avoiding a spy eavesdropping on our afternoon's conversation, yeah? Nor can sound waves from in-hull be detected. We're completely isolated from the physical universe. That was one reason the boat was a ghost town, yeah? Nobody can work very effectively when we unplug. That and this party. Anyway, places like this house are most assuredly *not* a SCIF. Anything you say here, you may as well have published in the Satellite News Network news files. So bear that in mind, yeah? Nothing, and I mean absolutely nothing, about what we do at sea or are getting ready for justifies talking about business when we're outside the hull or the tender ship or at command HQ. And absolutely never email, text or talk on the phone about it. And that goes especially for what I told you today."

"Understood, sir. I'm used to that. My father never talked about his boats. The only time I got any indication what it was like for him was when I visited his ships when he was in port."

"Well, okay then," Quinnivan said, relaxing slightly and leaning back in his seat. "Anyway, I wanted to let you in on something before this party starts. It's a hail-and-farewell, so the crowd will be greeting and meeting you, but we're also bidding farewell to communications officer Duke Vevera. Duke had a recent physical due to some abdominal pain, and turns out the fooker's got stage four pancreatic cancer that's spread almost everywhere. Probably has only a month or two left. If Monday happens the way I think it will, we'll probably never see him again, and his funeral will happen when we're a thousand feet under."

"Holy shit," Pacino gasped. "That's terrible."

"Aye, it is, but the youngster's sensitive about it. He doesn't like folks talking about his illness or making it seem like he's a goner. So we've all agreed to act like it's no big deal, yeah? We're all just going to pretend like the diagnosis never happened. Just play along, right? It'll be okay."

"Aye aye, sir, will do."

"Another thing, there, Patch. You're going to hear people talk about 'Monday' and that 'Monday' is coming. Let me let you in on that concept. Back in the old days, bomber crews used to hang out when they were on duty, playin' cards and makin' jokes, takin' naps, in a building a few feet from their airplanes, yeah? so that if the balloon went up, they could sprint to the cockpit and roar off. They called it 'being on alert.' Well, starting Monday at zero eight hundred, *Vermont* is on alert status. When we're on alert, the lines are singled up, the reactor is critical and self-sustaining, steaming the engineroom, shorepower is disconnected and a manned crane awaits to remove the gangway. The battlecontrol system, weapons control and sonar are up and online. We're fully loaded out for a forty-day run, with canned goods loaded on every deck surface forward with plywood on top, like you saw today. We're rotating and radiating on the radar. We're basically two minutes from tossing over our lines and getting our nuclear-powered asses out into the channel, yeah? There's no cell phone communications with the wife or girlfriend. There's no pizza delivery. We're essentially at sea but with the hatches open. We get the word to go, we man the maneuvering watch and we fookin' *go*."

Pacino looked at Quinnivan. "So, how often have you had to leave port when you were previously on alert status?"

"Never. We don't get into the duty rotation for alert status often, but the boats that do rarely leave. They're just on stand-by just in case, yeah? *Vermont* being a project boat, we're usually off doing our own thing with a special operation and don't have to be on the alert status duty roster. But not this time. You noticed we're the only boat at the piers."

"Yes, sir."

"Well, this alert status starting Monday seems different. It wouldn't surprise me if we're ordered out before sunset. So be ready to disappear Monday. Have someone looking after your car, your mail, your apartment, your bill payments. Make sure you don't have any plans that will disappoint someone. Sister's birthday, cousin's baby shower, whatever. Cancel everything."

"Aye aye, sir."

A knock sounded from the entrance to the room. Captain Seagraves, dressed in chinos, brown shoes and a sweater appeared. "Gentlemen," he greeted them in his deep baritone.

"Skipper," Quinnivan called, grinning, bolting to his feet. "What're ye drinkin' tonight, boss? The usual? That rotgut corn-squeezin' moonshine from Kentucky?" He headed to the bar to make the commander a drink.

Pacino stood and shook Seagraves' hand. "Evening, sir," he said. Seagraves seemed distracted, looking around the room.

"You started early, I see," he said to Quinnivan as the exec handed him a glass with two fingers of bourbon. Seagraves sank into a club chair opposite Pacino. "Did you give Mr. Pacino the rundown on the scoundrels, misfits and pirates who form the officer cadre of our good ship?"

Quinnivan joined them, pouring another scotch for Pacino and himself. "Cheers, lads," he said, toasting the captain. "I was just getting to that, Skipper. Our menagerie of zoo animals we generously call 'officers.'"

But before Quinnivan could hold court, a call came from the intercom, Shawna's English accented voice, saying, "Seamus, Elvis is here with his Ferrari. He wants to park it in the garage."

"Come on, lads, let's go see Elvis's crazy-ass sports car," Quinnivan called. He looked at Pacino. "Elvis is our engineer," he explained as they climbed the stairs. "Academy grad like you. Bloke's a little wobbly after his redheaded sexpot girlfriend left him, yeah? Anyway, he's an amateur investor from some seed money from his deceased da', and put together enough of a fortune to play with antique sports cars, but despite being the nuclear chief engineer and owning a barn full of rolling stock, the fooker can barely turn a wrench himself."

Through a doorway from the kitchen, the pristine garage waited as the fire engine red 1985 Ferrari Testarossa slowly rolled into the garage, its V-12 roaring and purring as the driver brought it in and parked it. The room crashed into silence as the driver cut the engine. The door opened and a blonde-haired, crew-cut, blue-eyed, tall skinny man unfolded himself up to his full height.

"Elvis!" Quinnivan yelled at the engineer. The engineer immediately screamed back at the XO—*"Bullfrog!"*

The exec pulled the engineer into a bear hug and smiled at him. "Lad, you're much too fookin' sober. Come on down to the lower level engineroom and grab a drink, yeah?" Quinnivan looked over at Pacino. "Eng, this young one here, Mr. Anthony Pacino, is newly reportin' aboard. He's the replacement for Mr. Vevera. And Patch, this here is Mario 'Elvis' Lewinsky, chief fookin' engineer." He'd pronounced the name *Mary-oh.* Quinnivan put his hand to his mouth as if he were disclosing a deep secret to Pacino. "Elvis is Lieutenant Commander

Lewinsky's middle name, and he hates it, which is why we call him that." Pacino nodded, remembering from *Piranha* that one thing about the submarine force was that anything that annoyed a sub sailor would be relentlessly thrown in that sailor's face, as part of the force's mysterious traditions.

The engineer shook Pacino's hand while showing his teeth to the laughing executive officer. "Dammit, Bullfrog, you know damned well it's *Mar-rhymes-with-far-ee-oh*. Pacino, glad to have you aboard, non-qual," he said, in a deep authoritative but friendly voice, smiling. A reminder to Pacino that he remained a second-class citizen until he could get qualified in submarines and earn his dolphins.

"Thank you, sir," Pacino said.

"Don't ever call me sir," the engineer said. "Even if I'm chewing your ass. I'm *Elvis* or *Feng*."

"I thought you hated your middle name," Pacino said, thinking the 'Feng' moniker seemed to embrace that he wasn't just the engineer, he was the *fucking* engineer.

The engineer rolled his eyes. "Listen, non-qual, one thing you'll quickly learn aboard a submarine is that anything that bothers you will be picked up by the crew and thrown at you a hundred times over. Why? To make sure you can don't break under pressure. Scared of spiders? For fuck's sake, don't tell anyone, or there will be a hundred spiders in your rack. So the whole 'Elvis' thing? Whatever, I no longer give a shit."

"Anyway," Pacino said, "Beautiful car."

"Testarossa," the engineer said. "Italian for 'redhead.' With all that goes with the spirit of a beautiful, sexy redhead." He sounded sad as he said that, Pacino noticed, imagining that the engineer must be missing his redheaded ex-girlfriend. Idly, Pacino wondered what had happened to the two of them. Probably the unpredictable and long absences from the schedule of the submarine.

Pacino asked to see its engine. The V-12 sparkled in the overhead lights of the garage.

Quinnivan grabbed Elvis' shoulder. "Ya know, lad, Mr. Pacino here has a classic '69 Corvette, yeah? and he changed out its engine and tranny himself with a first decade LS V-8. You should check it out." It almost seemed to Pacino like the XO was trying to cheer the engineer up.

Lewinsky looked at Pacino, blinking. "Seriously?" Pacino waved him over to the Corvette across the street. He walked to the front and hit the latch and raised the hood. Lewinsky stared at the big and modern LS engine crammed into the tiny engine compartment for several long moments before he whistled. "Wow. You swapped this out yourself? Computer control and all? And a manual six speed? *And* a supercharger?"

Pacino nodded.

"Jesus, this thing must have five hundred horsepower."

"Six hundred and forty, but who's counting," Pacino smiled.

"It'd be interesting to see which car is faster on the track, yours or mine. But listen. I could use a good mechanic," Lewinsky said. "Not on this, but I have a restoration project I could use help with. We'll talk about it after Monday."

There it was again, Pacino thought, the reference to 'Monday' as if it were a scheduled event rather than just waiting at the pier for orders that may or may not come.

Lewinsky straightened up when he saw the gray limo bus round the corner and roll to a stop in front of Quinnivan's house. A dozen or more people with duffel bags climbed out and headed into Quinnivan's house through the garage.

"Let's go meet the guys," Elvis said.

4

Friday, May 6

Pacino followed the engineer into the house and down the stairs, where in just the few minutes since the limo bus arrived, the previously whisper quiet lower-level room was crowded with people, making noise and shouting at each other. He found his rocks glass on the coffee table and turned toward the bar. U-Boat Dankleff walked up, smiling as usual. He was wearing black jeans and a black hoodie and his usual black-framed glasses.

"Wow, I hear Bullfrog gave you some of the two-grand-a-bottle scotch. You're *definitely* a VIP, he's been saving that for months."

Pacino grimaced. "I don't think a non-qual can *be* a VIP," he said. "I have a question for you, U-Boat."

"Sure. Shoot."

"How did you get the name 'U-Boat'? Because you're the damage control assistant and own the diesel generator?"

"Nope," Dankleff said, smiling mysteriously. "I'm the great-grandson of *Oberleutnant Zur See* Walter Dankleff, the captain of the German U-Boat *U-767,* which went down in the English Channel on June 18, 1944, but not before he took down a buttload of Allied shipping."

"Whoa, talk about a pedigree."

"Not really. We could have a long debate about how much talent is hereditary. You're in good shape if it is, what with your admiral father and sub captain grandfather."

"U-Boat, let's hope it is hereditary."

"So," U-Boat said, "have you met the navigator? 'Dominatrix Navigatrix'?" Pacino shook his head. Dankleff waved over a tall, slender woman wearing tight jeans and tall boots with a red sweater. Her dirty blonde hair was long, obviously attended to before the party, sweeping gracefully below her shoulders, some of it curled. She walked up and smiled with a mouthful of white, even teeth. She was compellingly beautiful, Pacino thought, reminding himself that she was a senior officer.

"So you're the new nub," she asked, extending her hand. "I'm Rachel Romanov, ship's navigator and TAO."

"TAO?" Pacino asked.

"Tactical action officer. In days gone by the position would be called the operations officer, or the ops boss, the person who's in charge of setting up the ship's mission, but now the term tactical action officer is used. I suppose it sounds more specific. So reporting to me in the operations department, I have the navigation electronics technicians, the radiomen and the crypto-spies. And the communications officer, Mr. Eisenhart, reports to me. I run the department, but tactical action operational planning is also my thing. That and, as navigator, obviously, knowing where the fuck we are."

It sounded strange to Pacino's ears to hear an elegant, attractive woman like her curse. Suddenly she yelled over his head. "Bruno! Get Mr. Pacino another Macallan! And another Merlot for me!" Then back to him, she said, "Sorry to scream like a fishwife, but it's so loud in here. Bruno's my husband. *Get over here,* Bruno, goddammit!"

A man a half-head taller than Romanov carefully ducked through the crowd to join them. His round head was shaved, giving him a tough look, but the skin at his eyes wrinkled into laugh lines as he handed Pacino the whisky. "Must be a hundred dollars' worth of scotch in that glass," he said in a deep commanding voice with an odd accent, almost German or east European.

"Bruno, this is Patch Pacino, our new non-qual. Mr. Pacino, meet Commander Bruno Romanov, in command of the missile cruiser *Javelin,*" Rachel explained. "We were assigned to a destroyer together a million years ago, back before I left the Navy."

Pacino shook Bruno's hand, nodded and said, "Good to meet you, sir." Then to Rachel, "You left? You were a skimmer?" Surface navy sailors were called, somewhat dismissively, "skimmers," although Pacino dropped the second half of the epithet, avoiding saying "skimmer puke" in deference to Bruno.

"I had a dream of being a contented housewife and having children, but it turns out that medically, it's just not meant to be. I got bored and applied for reinstatement. Submarine force recruited me. Turns out I have mad skills at navigation and tactics."

"It's true," Bruno said, just before Quinnivan heaved to, placing his arms around Bruno and Rachel.

"Ah, just the two I'm lookin' for," Quinnivan said. "Bruno, Rachel, I see you've met Lieutenant junior grade Anthony "Patch" Pacino, the replacement for Squirt Gun Vevera. Pacino here qualified dive and pilot on the ill-fated *Piranha,* ya know, just before the disaster, but he seems all healed up now, yeah?"

Healed up except for missing Carrie Alameda, Pacino thought.

"Anyway, Patch," Quinnivan said, grinning, "be careful around the navigator for two very good reasons. The first is how mean she is."

"Bullfrog!" Rachel said, exasperated. "I am *not* mean!" Apparently this exchange had been going on for some time, as it seemed a running joke between the two of them.

"You've heard of 'velvet glove, iron fist,' yeah?" Quinnivan addressed Pacino directly, grinning. "Well, the navigator here is 'silk glove, *titanium* fist.' We've taken to calling her 'Silky' for short."

Rachel rolled her eyes and whispered into Bruno's ear, who took her wine glass and headed back to the bar to get her a refill.

"The other reason?" Pacino asked.

Quinnivan put his hand up to make it look like he was disclosing something confidential, but his stage whisper was loud enough to be heard all the way at the bar. "She's been known to get just a wee bit slutty when we're in liberty ports, yeah? You'll want to watch yourself, or Silky might try to throw a fook into ya."

Rachel tilted her head back and laughed loudly, coughing and choking. "I am not *slutty* in foreign ports!" she squealed, laughing, but even more exasperated. Quinnivan laughed uproariously, enjoying the look on the navigator's face.

She caught her breath and looked at Pacino. "It was a case of mistaken identity," she explained, just as Bruno showed up with her refilled wine glass. "Bruno and I were in this cozy bar in La Spezia when he unaccountably disappeared downstairs—"

"I told you I had to hit the head—"

"And he was gone so long I think I'd had two rounds waiting for him—"

"Let's just say there was a loud argument in the men's room—"

"And so his bar stool is unoccupied for so long and then he shows back up—"

"You mean some stranger shows up," Bruno added.

"He looked just like you," Rachel said.

"He had long hair," Bruno reminded her.

"You did too, back then, and anyway, I was feeling romantic and started kissing him—"

Bruno leaned in to interject to Pacino. "I had to peel her off the poor man."

"Poor man? He seemed to enjoy it," she laughed.

"I ended up having to buy him a few rounds just to get him to agree to leave her alone after that."

"So you see, Mr. Pacino, it was not a case of being slutty in-port."

Quinnivan laughed. "You didn't tell him about the *other* incident, though, did ye?"

"Oh my God, Bullfrog, shut the fuck up!"

Quinnivan, Bruno and Rachel laughed together at what must be another inside joke. Eventually Quinnivan and Bruno went back to the bar. Rachel took a last sip of her second wine.

"Anyway, it's good to have you aboard. You go by 'Anthony'?"

"Patch," Pacino said. "My inevitable nickname."

She nodded. "Anyway, Patch, Monday's coming, so get

in early, pack a bag for a month—that means *both* pair of underwear—and be ready to go."

"You think we'll leave?"

She shook her head. "Not here. We'll talk more Monday." She saw someone in the crowd and a sour expression came to her face. "See you later, non-qual," she said, and walked to the bar. Pacino did his best not to watch her walk away, but he couldn't help but admire her perfect body. He looked up to see Dankleff, who was joined by a slightly older man. "Patch, I suppose it's time for you to meet your new boss, Sprocket Spichovich." He pronounced it *Spick-ah-vick.*

A dark-haired, youthful and underweight man shook Pacino's hand. He had a mop of too-long hair over his eyebrows, a round open face, a dark mustache and large ears. He was better dressed than most in the room, with a starched button-down white shirt, dark wool trousers and a brown herring-bone sport jacket with patches on the elbows. "You're Pacino," he said in a smooth tenor voice with a slight New England accent, not quite Boston, not quite Maine. "I'm Al Spichovich. Weapons officer."

"Sprocket," U-Boat Dankleff said. "Not drinking tonight?"

Spichovich made an unhappy face. "Duty after midnight when I relieve Doctor No." Spichovich looked at Pacino. "On the nights of a ship's party, we split the duty officer duties so everyone can enjoy, except the early half attendee has to remain sober. Which kind of flies in the face of the whole mission of a ship's party."

"You mean you want to let the others get drunk, then lure them into a poker game and walk off with all their earthly possessions?" Dankleff looked at Pacino. "This guy's a card shark. Do not ever get talked into playing a couple of hands with him."

Pacino noticed the weapons officer looking over at Romanov with an angry expression.

"Something wrong?" Pacino asked. Spichovich seemed to snap out of it.

"No, everything's fine," he said, and wandered absently off.

"Anyway," Dankleff said, "Lieutenant Commander Spichovich—Sprocket—is the weapons officer. So the torpedomen and missile techs report to him, and firecontrol, sonar and the IT guys. And of course, the torpedo division officer, Doctor No. You're relieving Easy Eisenhart as sonar officer so he can take over communications from Man Mountain Vevera. Have you met Easy Eisy?"

Pacino shook his head. *"Easy!"* Dankleff yelled toward the pool table area. A younger man walked up who could be Spichovich's younger brother, just as gaunt, with the same haircut and rounded face, but with a sharper nose and normal-sized ears. He wore jeans and an ancient Grateful Dead T-shirt.

"You rang?" he asked Dankleff.

Dankleff pointed to Pacino and said, "Meet Anthony Pacino. He's taking over your sonar slot while you take over comms from Vevera."

Eisenhart shook Pacino's hand, his face breaking into a friendly smile. "Don Eisenhart. Don't get any ideas about my nickname. Someone said I give checkouts too easily and sign people's qual cards without harsh examinations. Totally not true. I'm the toughest officer on the boat to get a qual signature from. Bear that in mind."

"Right," Dankleff said, rolling his eyes for the half-dozenth time that night. "Your easy ways with a pen hovering over a nub's qual card earned you the name 'Easy.'" He looked at Pacino. "A while back he was awarded a water-cooled pen by the XO and his little feelings have been hurt ever since."

"None of that's true," Eisenhart said to Pacino, his expression a frown that was trying to conceal a grin. "I was 'Easy Eisy' back at the Academy. Probably because I never sweated anything. Exams, PT tests, midshipman cruises, whatever. It's all easy when you're 'Easy Eisy.'"

"He just *now* made that up," U-Boat said, smiling brightly.

"Goddammit, U-Boat," Eisenhart growled.

"You were the class ahead of me, right?" Pacino asked Eisenhart.

"Yeah, and Feng was one of my firsties," Eisenhart added, referring to first class midshipmen, who acted as drill instructors for the incoming class of fourth class midshipmen, or plebes. Eisenhart drained his beer mug and added, "so he's been flaming on me for more than half a decade now. You, the Feng, I and the captain are the only Academy grads here now that Squirt Gun is leaving. Everyone else, including Silky, is an ROTC puke. Those morons barely know how to wear their uniforms."

Easy Eisy looked over at the stairwell entrance door and shouted out, "Lobabes!"

A tall blonde man appeared with a fresh bottle of scotch, this one a sixteen-year-old Balvenie. "Dump that Guinness piss water, Easy, and get a whisky glass." Without a greeting and without asking, the newcomer uncorked the bottle and poured the scotch into Pacino's glass. "You look a little dry there, non-qual," he said, smiling. "I'm Lomax. Kyle Lomax. Mechanical officer. Main Propulsion Assistant, MPA, to the fucking engineer."

He shook Pacino's hand, then poured two fingers for himself and downed the scotch like it was water. Lomax was tall, muscular, with a full head of blonde hair, blue eyes and a full mustache. He looked like someone from a recruiting poster, but recruiting for the 1939 German Wehrmacht.

"Good to meet you," Pacino said. "I'm Anthony Pacino."

"Boozy!" Lomax shouted over Pacino's head. "Get over here and meet our new nub!"

A slender medium-height young man with black hair, dark eyes and a smile joined them. "What?" he said to Lomax. "I didn't even know we were due for a new non-qual." He looked Indian or Middle Eastern, but his accent was from New York. Brooklyn, perhaps.

Lomax pointed to Pacino. "We were due. Meet the new non-qual," Lomax explained. "Boozy, meet Pacino. Pacino, this is Boozy. Boozy, what is it you do on this ship, exactly, other than catch loads of bunky?"

Pacino extended his hand and the shorter officer shook it. "I'm Muhammad Varney," he said to Pacino, ignoring Lomax's implied insult. "Crew calls me 'Boozy Moozy' or just 'Boozy' for short. And as Lobabes Lomax here well knows, I'm the electrical officer. Everything from four hundred Hertz to DC. I power your lights, your coffee-maker, your glorified stereo you call a Q-fucking-ten-vee-four, your AN/BYG-1 battlecontrol system and your thirty megawatt propulsion pump-jet. And your oxygen generator. And if Elvis' S9G reactor shits the bed, my batteries keep your asses alive until you can start U-Boat's diesel. So you want power? You want electricity? You want to breathe? Just give me a call."

Pacino couldn't help his curiosity. "Why Boozy?" he asked.

Varney smiled. "Because I drink despite being a Muslim," he said. "In moderation, of course. But these infidels act like I'm an alcoholic."

"Boozy!" Silky Romanov shouted from the bar. "Have a whisky!" She wandered back with two glasses of scotch and handed one to Varney.

Varney smirked. "Listen," he said to Pacino. "You need an electrical check-out? Don't go to Easy Eisenhart. He doesn't know shit about the electrical systems." Easy sputtered beer in Varney's direction, but the electrical officer sidestepped. "I'm your man. Knock on my stateroom door and I'll get you squared away." He looked at the drunk navigator. "And you, Silky, leave us menfolk alone to run the world—go play with Bruno, will you?"

"I'm gonna find better company," the navigator said, taking no offense and going off to talk to Seagraves.

Lomax suddenly punched Varney in the shoulder. "He may not look the part," Lomax said to Pacino, "but Boozy here played first string football for MIT."

"Running back," Varney said. "But playing first string for MIT wouldn't even get you past screening practice at UCLA."

"True," Lomax said. "And Navy's 150-pound squad could beat your asses."

"We beat Harvard my senior year," Varney said. "And Yale."

"But not NJIT."

"*Nobody* beats those thugs from New Jersey," Boozy said, shaking his head.

Pacino looked at the other officers. "So Boozy, you went to MIT, and Lobabes, you're from UCLA?" It felt odd to call people he'd met seconds before by their nicknames.

U-Boat Dankleff joined the circle, grabbing the neck of the

Balvenie bottle in Lomax's hands and pouring for himself. "Lobabes was a cheerleader," he confided loudly to Pacino. "For the UCLA football team. A fucking *cheerleader.* Can you picture Lobabes in a little skirt with pom-poms?"

"And those cute little white sneakers," Rachel shouted from across the room.

Again, Lomax controlled his facial expression, trying to act like he thought it was funny. "Don't knock it, U-Boat. You have any *idea* how many gorgeous female cheerleaders are yours for the taking if you're a male cheerleader?"

Suddenly the XO was in their crowd. "Zero!" he said, laughing. "They're too busy scoping out the football players. I hear Lobabes had a dry four years there!"

"Keep it up, Bullfrog," Lomax said, gritting his teeth.

"But at least his schooling was easy at UCLA, studying," Quinnivan cleared his throat and said the next words in a sarcastic imitation of a sophisticated English elite, *"English literature.* I'm still trying to figure out how you got into the American Navy's nuclear program," he said to Lomax. "Or how you got qualified in submarines so fast."

"Easy Eisy graped off his signatures," Rachel said, shouting again from the bar.

"I did not!" Eisenhart said, his face flushing. He looked up. "Pork Chop," he called out.

A youth who was medium height, thin, as dark as Varney joined them, and said in a Southern accent that seemed from Atlanta, "Gentlemen. Silky. Howdy do."

"Mr. Ganghadharan, sir," Quinnivan said, grinning, "allow me to introduce to you Lieutenant Junior Grade Anthony Pacino, soon to be our sonar officer, reported aboard today. He was pilot-qualed on the *Piranha.* Patch, this here's Anik Ganghadharan—just try pronouncing that when you're drunk, yeah? His name's a virtual sobriety test. Which is why we just call him *Gangbanger.* He's our supply officer. Or 'suppo.' Or Pork Chop. But I roll with Gangbanger. Fitting, if you ask me. The man has the lying soul of a criminal with the heart of a thief," Quinnivan slapped the supply officer's shoulder. "Gangbanger here has been known to pull raids to steal parts from heavily guarded Navy warehouses by dark of night to get us underway. Fooker is by the very definition of the word, a goddamned felon. Check out his stateroom cubbyholes—you'll find his balaclava hood, a black bag and a gun."

"All part of my profession," the supply officer said calmly. He looked at Pacino. "So, Pacino. I'm a proud graduate of Penn State. What about you? You one of those stuck-up Naval Academy *morons* like the Feng? Or Easy?"

"Or the captain?" Seagraves suddenly interjected, having surreptitiously joined their group from behind Gangadharan. The supply officer visibly shrank a few inches, gulping.

"Sorry, Captain, I didn't see you there," Gangadharan stuttered.

Seagraves laughed. "Perfectly fine to have an opinion, Supply Officer. Just be prepared to back it up with facts."

"Sir, yes, sir," the supply officer said, obviously intimidated by the captain. Seagraves laughed again, stole the Balvenie bottle from Lomax and poured Gangadharan and himself two fingers of the scotch. "Since Mr. Pacino here drank all the twenty-five-year-old Macallan, we'll have to make do with sixteen year old Balvenie."

Lomax grinned. "Aren't you a bourbon man, Skipper?"

Seagraves shook his head in mock sadness. "A certain Irishman and Royal Navy officer we all know and love ran out. And believe me, gentlemen and ladies, he *will* be reading about that in his next fitness report."

Pacino noticed that despite the light mood and the joking around, the officers had a definite fear of their commanding officer. For a moment he wondered if his father's officers had feared him, thinking about Rob Catardi fondly remembering Pacino's father teaching him everything he knew about being a combat submariner. The captain remained for another minute of conversation, then vanished to the bar to find Quinnivan.

"So, Pacino," Gangadharan said, as if trying to restart the dialog from before the captain's appearance, "Naval Academy?

Pacino nodded.

"How is it you're a junior grade lieutenant instead of an ensign?"

"I spent a year at grad school in Boston."

"Boston University? Tufts? Northeastern? For fuck's sake, not *Harvard*?"

"No," Pacino said, "MIT."

Varney started laughing. "You went to *The Institute*?" he asked incredulously.

Pacino looked him in the eye and spelled out seriously, "I H T F P."

"The fuck does that mean?" Lomax asked.

Boozy Varney choked on his whisky. "It's the motto of 'The Institute," or the Massachusetts Institute of Technology, as it is officially called. The motto stands for, 'I hate the fucking place.' What was your major?"

"Mechanical engineering, heat transfer. I know. Really exciting, right?"

"Don't tell the engineer that," Lomax said. "He'll have you taking my job and I'd just as soon keep it." Lomax, as the main propulsion assistant to the engineer, the MPA, was head of the nuclear mechanics.

"So, my new friend and the ship's newest non-qual nub," Varney said seriously. "How long you gonna take to get qualified as submerged OOD? We need another warm body on the officer-of-the-deck watchsection."

Just then the noise of the crowd in the room went quiet as a young man showed up at the entrance to the room, holding a black motorcycle helmet in his hand. He was of medium height but was solid, bulky, perhaps outweighing Eisenhart by fifty pounds. He had a motorcycle leather jacket on, with leather pants and black engineer's boots. He was blonde with a ruddy face, his eyes hidden behind wrap-around dark sunglasses. He came to attention and pulled the glasses off with a flourish. He raised his fist in the air and shouted suddenly, *"It never happened!"*

The room burst out the response, twenty throats shouting in unison, *"We were never there!"*

"USS *Vermont!*" the newcomer responded, then dropped his fist.

"Squirt Gun," Quinnivan shouted. "Get over here, ye fat dead man!"

Quinnivan pulled the young man into a bear hug and behind his back counted down from three with his fingers, and as he got to zero, the crowd roared in unison, *"Aren't you dead yet?"*

Lieutenant Duke 'Man-Mountain Squirt Gun' Vevera made a face at the room. "Fuck you all," he said. "It's a tiny golf-ball sized tumor. A few months of chemo and I'll be back. For fuck's sake." He walked into the room, put down his helmet and pulled off his leather jacket. Pacino stared at Quinnivan, remembering him say that Vevera was terminal and that he was sensitive about his medical condition and not to mention it. And then the officers all joked about it to his face.

Pacino found the night starting to become blurry from all the whisky he'd been putting down. And he remembered everyone showing up in a limo bus with luggage—were they all staying overnight? And then Quinnivan quieted down the room and sat Vevera down in a folding chair in front of the fireplace facing the officers while Quinnivan orchestrated the gift-giving.

"Usually, farewell gifts are given one at a time," the XO announced, "but on this solemn occasion, it's incumbent upon us all to give them simultaneously." Again, Quinnivan counted down from three, and at "one," the officers all reached into brown paper sacks and withdrew squirt guns, in various shades and sizes, some looking like black pistols, others huge colorful pump-action blasters with tanks of water, and all of them were aimed squarely at Vevera. By the time the action was over, he was soaked.

He wiped the water out of his eyes and said, "I suppose there's a reason why you had me sit on the tile by the fireplace instead of on the carpeting."

Pacino leaned over to Dankleff. "Why squirt guns?" he asked quietly.

Dankleff answered, "Vevera's nickname, Squirt Gun? See, he had a girlfriend. Nice lady. But one night in the wardroom, while eating midnight rations—mid-rats—he unwisely confessed to the XO that she was a 'squirter.' Ever since then, he was Squirt Gun Vevera. Although Man-Mountain still stayed stuck, I suppose."

Commander Timothy Seagraves joined Lieutenant Commander Jeremiah Quinnivan on the back deck leading out from the kitchen overlooking the wide backyard, the grass green in the light of the spotlights.

"Well, XO, what do you think of our new non-qual?"

Quinnivan pulled a leather container from his pocket and pulled the lid off, revealing two cigars. He offered one to the captain and took one himself, then clipped Seagraves' cigar tip and his own with a large cutter. He produced a torch lighter with the emblem of the *Vermont* on it and lit Seagraves' cigar, then puffed his own in a mellow cloud of smoke.

"Well, sir, he's an awful quiet lad. Not a swashbucklin' pirate like us."

Seagraves snorted. "I wouldn't call myself a swashbuckling pirate. *You*, definitely. Me, not so much."

"That's because your nuclear navy overlords grind into ye so much reactor safety, you've lost your tactical warrior footing. Lucky for you, Skipper, ya have *me* aboard."

Seagraves laughed. "That I am, XO." He puffed the stogie for a moment. "How did the young man react to your classified briefing?"

"The expected, yeah? Disbelief at first. Nothing in the news about it, yeah? Once he saw it was real, well, he was not thrilled. But he didn't show disgust either. Didn't shy away."

"So he's not bloodthirsty and he's not morally opposed to submarine warfare. That's about as balanced a reaction as you could hope to get."

Quinnivan thought about it for a moment, then leaned on the deck rail and turned to face the captain. "I suppose, as you Americans would say, he was raised right, yeah?"

Seagraves nodded somberly. "So, do you think Vevera is coming back like he says?"

Quinnivan looked at the captain and shook his head. "Not a chance," he said somberly. "That lad's standin' on a trap door." He checked his antique Rolex. "I guess we should return to our party before the boys get into any more trouble, yeah?"

Seagraves checked his phone. "It's nearly midnight. I'm going to leave you guys to it."

"You have a car service?"

"Already on its way," the captain said. "Good night, XO."

"Night, sir. See you Monday."

Pacino opened his eyes to bright morning sunlight. He was in a guest bedroom, tucked into the bedclothes, still wearing his jeans and shirt. The walls were a pastel blue shade, and for a moment he thought he was in Carrie Alameda's condo in Alexandria. He thrashed in the covers, vaulting out of the bed to try to find her, and then his headache punched him like a giant fist. As he stood there stupidly, he realized this wasn't Carrie's house and that she was long dead. And with that thought he seemed to deflate, and he collapsed to the floor in a heap. Then he asked himself, if he weren't at Carrie's, where the hell was he?

When he opened his eyes, he saw that his boots were placed by a high-boy and the contents of his pockets were on the nightstand. He sat up to check his phone, his head pounding. *Quinnivan's,* he thought. He'd had too much to drink. It was almost nine in the morning. Someone had carried him into bed. He tried to think. The last thing he could remember was Duke Vevera getting blasted by water cannons.

Pacino put on his boots, got his phone and wallet and went into the hallway to go down the stairs. In the kitchen, Shawna cooked breakfast, now wearing jeans and a simple top with sneakers, her long hair in a ponytail.

"Well, good morning, Patch," she said. "I see you survived your first ship's party."

"Am I the only one still here from the party?" Pacino's voice was a croak.

She laughed. "Oh no, that party went on to six in the morning. I think you were out before one o'clock AM. Everyone's crashed down below, but you seemed to have passed out first, so the boys carried you upstairs and continued on. Coffee?"

"Yes, please," he said. "And water." His head still pounded. A big man walked into the kitchen and plopped down next to

Pacino. He had a completely bald head except for short tufts of white hair over his ears, a full face, blue eyes and wire-rimmed glasses with small lenses. He had to outweigh Pacino by fifty or sixty pounds, probably from submarine cuisine. He wore jeans, a plaid shirt and cowboy boots.

Pacino went to stand to greet the stranger, but the man waved him back down. "Sit, please, sir. I'm Joe Quartane, chief of the boat. COB for short."

Pacino shook his hand. "I'm Pacino. Newly reported. Taking over as sonar officer."

Quartane nodded. "Morning, ma'am," he said to Shawna. She handed him and Pacino steaming cups of coffee. "Ensign?" the COB asked Pacino.

"Lieutenant junior grade."

"That's odd."

"Had a year of grad school before nuclear power school."

Quartane nodded. "Graduate school. Art history? Ancient cultures? Gender studies?"

"Mechanical engineering," Pacino said, smiling. "Thermodynamics and heat transfer."

"That your hotrod out front?"

"Not the Ferrari, if that's what you mean. The Corvette."

"Feng still running that hot red Ferrari, eh?"

Pacino looked at him. "So, your rating—mechanic?"

"Yep," Quartane replied. "A-gang."

Auxiliary gang was a group of tough-guy non-nuclear mechanics who tended to ships' systems and had a crazy *esprit de corps* despite what the other divisions said to deride them, that they were mere plumbers.

"Senior chief?" Pacino guessed.

"Master chief," Quartane replied.

"Whoa," Pacino said. He'd only met one in his life, and he was now at the bottom of the eastern Atlantic.

From the entrance behind Quartane, Duke Vevera walked in, wearing only boxer shorts and a black T-shirt with a snarling skull and gothic script spelling *It Never Happened. We Were Never There. USS Vermont.* He plopped down opposite Pacino, next to the chief of the boat.

Shawna brought him coffee and smiled at him. "Man Mountain, dear, aren't you a bit underdressed?"

"Two things," Vevera smiled. "The Quinnivan residence rules prohibit wearing leather pants at the breakfast table. And also, I can't seem to find them. After I rested my eyes, some scumbag seems to have run off with them."

Pacino tried not to smile or laugh. Vevera seemed genuinely hurt by the prank. As Shawna put down plates of eggs, sausages and bacon, Mario Lewinsky came in, white as a ghost, smelled the food and waved it off, disappearing for the bathroom.

"Tough night," Pacino said, waving his thumb to where the engineer went.

"*You* seemed to have had fun," Vevera said, smirking. "I don't think I've ever seen anyone dance with the Dominatrix Navigatrix quite the way *you* did."

"Oh hell," Pacino groaned.

"Don't worry about it, kid, I doubt she'll even remember. But every cell phone in the house will, so, perhaps you'd better stand by for the blackmail photos later. Oh, and if I were you, I'd watch out for the wrath of Bruno. Damned good thing you'll be working for the weapons officer and not the navigator."

Pacino finished his food. "I should go," he said. Suddenly all he wanted was a shower and a nap. He said good-bye to Vevera and Quartane, thanked Shawna, who kissed him on the cheek. He walked out to his Corvette. At least, he thought, he had the keys. Vevera was missing everything that he'd had on him, phone, keys, wallet. Motorcycle helmet. A large black Indian Chieftain classic motorcycle was parked in front of Pacino's car—it must be Vevera's, he thought, which would explain all the leather. Perhaps the leather was also meant for shielding against the deluge of squirt gun water that he may have anticipated. Odd that Vevera still rode the motorcycle, as allegedly seriously sick as he was.

Pacino rolled to his apartment and dragged himself inside.

5

Sunday, May 8

After crashing all day Saturday, horribly hungover, Pacino woke early on Sunday. He'd intended to unpack his apartment, but when he looked around at how stark and dark and dingy it was, he decided to save doing all that for later. It made more sense to go the base and spend Sunday night on the boat. That way, he'd be ready for whatever Monday threw at him.

He opened several boxes and found toiletries, clothes, and uniforms and packed them into a duffel bag, grabbed his electronics and packed his backpack. After showering and changing into working khakis, he clicked his phone's app for a car service and waited the eight minutes it took for the driver to arrive.

The driver dropped him at pier security. As before, they took the contents of his pockets for scanning and put him into the millimeter wave scanner. He rolled his baggage onto a conveyor leading to a large machine, presumably X-raying the bags. The security petty officer opened Pacino's duffel, rifled through the contents, did the same to the backpack, then zipped them back up, nodding at Pacino and buzzing open the heavy bulletproof glass door.

Pacino hurried down the pier to the *Vermont*. To the right, the looming gigantic hull of the tender ship *Olympus* took up half the length of the pier, the support vessel a cruise ship painted gray, but with the bowling alleys and shops replaced with weapons storage bays and machine shops, with offices for the squadron staff and the commodore in command.

It was a little after eleven in the morning when he arrived at the brow to the ship. A different petty officer awaited him. He returned the man's salute, the youth a third class petty officer in a formal white crackerjack uniform, his rating emblem showing an arrow and a headset. A sonarman.

"Petty Officer Sanders," Pacino said, reading the man's nametag. "I'm Pacino, taking over sonar from Mr. Eisenhart."

"I know, sir," Sanders said. "Welcome aboard. Your identification?"

Pacino handed his military ID to Sanders, who scanned it into a device by the phone Faraday cage. It beeped green lights and Sanders handed it back. Pacino handed over his phone, then headed over the gangway to the aft hatch. He stopped, faced the flag, saluted it, then turned to the "doghouse" over the plug hatch, shouted "down ladder!" and dropped his duffel to the deck below. He looked around him at the sunny May Sunday morning, took a deep breath of real air, then climbed down the ladder into the chamber. As always, the overpowering smell of the submarine invaded his senses, as if to command him to leave the surface world behind and concentrate on the submerged universe. Pacino grabbed his duffel and backpack and muscled it all through the hatch, then followed the passageway around forward on the port side to the three-man bunkroom.

The ship was quiet, the only sound the bass hum of the air handlers blowing air in the diffusers in the overhead of the passageway and the bunkroom. Pacino looked around. Inside the door of the three-man room, the deck was two feet wide and four feet long, with three cubbyholes on the forward bulkhead, three racks opposite the door from the passageway. The wall to the right of the door had hooks with hanging uniforms. The upper and middle bunk were strewn with books and folders and clothes. He'd barely unpacked his duffel into the lowest cubbyhole and the space under the bottom bunk when a knock came at the doorjamb. Pacino straightened up and turned to see a tall thin white-haired man with wire-rimmed glasses in working khakis, his anchor-and-star collar emblems showing him to be a senior chief petty officer, his name tag reading "R. NYGARD, TMSC(SS)." The chief torpedoman, Pacino thought. Above his pocket were pewter-colored submarine dolphins.

"You're Pacino?" the chief asked in an unfriendly, no-nonsense tenor.

"Yes, Senior Chief," Pacino said. Nygard didn't extend his hand, so Pacino didn't offer to shake hands. "Duty Officer wants to see you in the wardroom," Nygard said.

"Who's the Duty Officer?" Pacino asked to Nygard's back as he was withdrawing down the passageway.

"Doctor No," Nygard called over his shoulder. Pacino hadn't met a person named "No," or was it "Noe"?

Pacino took the aft ladder to the lower level, through the crew's mess to the wardroom, where spread out on the table were three tablet computers, multiple printouts, binders and a slight, short officer, like Pacino, a junior grade lieutenant, obviously of Chinese descent. He had a round, full, almost chubby face, wearing a half-smirk as if he'd break into a grin in a second. His expression was open and friendly. He glanced up at Pacino over his half-frame reading glasses, stood up and reached across the table to shake Pacino's hand.

"I'm Lieutenant No, first name Li," he said. "Torpedo Officer. I work for Sprocket like you do." His accent reminded Pacino of a midshipman in his company at the Academy who'd been from Chicago.

"I didn't see you at the ship's party," Pacino said.

"I was there, got there half past midnight. On party nights, we split the duty. Weapons Officer had the duty after midnight, which was why he wasn't drinking. By the time I got there, you'd already shlunked."

"'*Shlunked*'?" Pacino asked, wondering if that were some Mandarin or Cantonese word.

"Shlunk. Irish slang for someone who disappears from a party without saying good-night, whether by sneaking out or passing out. I take it, your case was the latter. Be careful, the XO will give you that as a nickname. *Shlunk Pacino.* Too bad you don't remember, though. I hear you had a wonderful time dirty dancing with the Dominatrix Navigatrix."

Pacino rubbed the hair on the back of his head, not knowing what to say. He'd better toughen up his alcohol tolerance, he thought. Hard liquor on the deck with his dad hadn't prepared him for this fiasco.

"Anyway, I wish I'd known earlier you were coming in today. I'd have had more time for you." No stood up, removed a key around his neck and handed it to Pacino. "As of right now, you're the duty officer under-instruction. First task? Get the reactor started."

Pacino looked at No, nodded, and reached for a phone. He looked up the code for maneuvering and punched in the three buttons and heard the phone buzz. "Engineering Duty Officer," Dankleff's voice called.

"It's Pacino," he replied. "I'm duty officer under instruction."

"Ah, Mr. Pacino," Dankleff said, sounding pleased. "Just the man I want to speak to. I need permission to start the reactor. You'll need to call the engineer. Tell him we have no class alpha discrepancies. Tell him we did the estimated critical position and it's in the expected range. Tell him we're on shorepower running in natural circulation on both loops. And tell him we're manned aft for reactor startup."

Pacino grabbed a pen and a blank pad of legal paper belonging to Li No and scribbled notes.

He took the landline phone and dialed the engineer's cell phone.

"Lewinsky," the engineer's deep voice barked.

"Engineer, this is Pacino, Duty Officer Under Instruction."

"Go ahead," Lewinsky said, his voice clipped and almost angry.

"Engineer, the reactor is natural circulation on both loops, ship is on shorepower," Pacino said formally. "Estimated critical position is calculated and is within spec. Watches are manned aft for the startup. The out-of-commission log shows no class alpha discrepancies. Request permission to start the reactor, sir."

"Don't call me 'sir,'" Lewinsky said. "You have my permission to start the reactor and my recommendation to the captain is we start the reactor now. Get back to me after you call the skipper."

"Understood, Engineer," Pacino said, unconsciously standing at attention. Lewinsky hung up. He looked at Li No. "Engineer concurs."

No shrugged. "Call the captain."

Pacino dialed the commanding officer's cell phone number. Immediately Seagraves' baritone came over the phone line. There was noise in the background, as if he were in a restaurant. Pacino identified himself and that he was the under-instruction duty officer, then repeated the status to the captain and added that the engineer recommended reactor startup now.

Seagraves said, seriously, "Duty Officer Under Instruction, you have permission to start the reactor."

Pacino acknowledged and the captain hung up on him. Pacino was already seeing some of what he'd seen on *Piranha,* the casual first-name-basis joking around among the officers off duty, the iron-hard formality on duty.

"Mr. No," Pacino said, "We have permission to start the reactor."

No nodded. "Call the Feng back and tell him the skipper okayed the reactor startup."

Pacino got up to grab the land line, called Lewinsky and made the report to him.

"Call aft," Li No ordered.

Pacino buzzed maneuvering again and relayed the order to Dankleff. He sat down at the table. Li No looked up.

"Paratrooper pin?" No pointed to Pacino's chest, where his silver airborne wings were pinned above his pocket, the eagle's wings surrounding a parachute canopy.

Pacino nodded. "I went to jump school at Fort Benning before third class year, spent a month training with the Army, some SEALs and a bunch of zoomie cadets." *Zoomies* were Air Force Academy cadets, in the dismissive lexicon of Annapolis midshipmen. "Did PT in full combat gear. Thirteen-mile group runs. Twenty-mile forced marches. Jumped out of half a dozen jets. Managed to avoid breaking my legs." That was the year before the *Princess Dragon* terrorist attack that almost killed his father and took him out of his chief of naval operations position, Pacino thought glumly. How easy and simple life had been before the *Princess Dragon* and *Piranha* disasters.

Li No nodded. "Nice. Oh, where is it?" He moved the piles on the table, finding a slender box with a pad computer inside. "Eisenhart said to give you this," No said. He motioned Pacino to sign for it on No's tablet. "It's got the secret, top secret and codeword-classified data file apps, plus information on all ship's systems. It has everything in there you need to know to qualify in submarines. Put in your military identification number and answer the security questions. The software will guide you in from there. If you lose it, you may as well kiss your career goodbye, so my recommendation to you is, don't lose it. It's got a sensor in it that knows if it's leaving the ship's hull. If you were to bring it topside, it would self-destruct. Lomax was standing duty a year or so ago and liked to tuck his computer inside his belt in back. Fucker forgot it was there, climbed out the plug hatch, computer destructed and literally set his pants on fire and burned his ass. You can imagine the jokes he faced after that."

"Got it," Pacino said. He opened up the tablet and started entering security information, and finally it opened up to a page full of app icons. He found the classified news files and opened them up, scanning through the headlines, none of which in any way resembled the open-source news articles. He decided to enter a search for Elias Sotheby.

A warning notification flashed up, stating he wasn't approved to read the information at his clearance level. He'd have to petition to Eisenhart to get the right clearance, he thought. He canceled the search and looked up at No.

"Can I ask you a serious question?"

Li No answered absently, his concentration remaining on his work. "Ask away."

"Before I do, can you rig the ship for an airgap?"

No looked up and stared at Pacino for a moment. He picked up his VHF radio. "Duty Chief, Duty Officer," he called.

The wardroom door opened and Nygard stepped in. "You rang?" he said.

"Rig ship for a class alpha air gap," No ordered, putting his radio down.

"Sir, we're all in the middle of pre-underway checks and a thousand other things, not the least of which is emails to and from squadron."

"We'll rig communications back to in-port in five minutes."

Nygard sighed wearily. "Aye aye, sir, rig ship for class alpha air gap." He set down his radio and pulled the battery out of it. Li No did the same. Nygard left and No grabbed a microphone with a black coiled wire out of a cubbyhole by the captain's seat. His accent rang throughout the ship, *"Rig ship for class alpha air gap."* He waited a few minutes, and then Nygard came back in.

"Ship's rigged for class alpha air gap by me, checked by Petty Officer Miller."

"Very well," No said. Nygard stepped out. No got up and locked both doors of the wardroom.

"What do you want to know?"

"XO said that *Vermont* sank the yacht belonging to Elias Sotheby. That our SEALs killed Sotheby. Is all that true?"

Li No blinked, then frowned. "Yeah. So what?"

Pacino blinked. "So during peacetime, you just sank a yacht and killed its owner?"

No acted as if he didn't care. "Yeah. What of it?"

Pacino stared at No. "You just killed him in cold blood?"

No slapped shut his tablet cover, tossed it roughly aside and looked up at Pacino, frowning. "That's what we *do*. We're a *project* boat. Didn't XO clue you in to that?"

"He did," Pacino said. "It's just kind of hard to believe."

No shrugged. "There had to be a good reason for it. We don't do things randomly, we just follow our very specific orders. We just aren't privy to the entire context of the op. The story of why we did that is compartmented six ways at least. There are all of maybe five people on earth who know the complete story."

"That's amazing," Pacino said.

"Hell," Li No said. "That's *nothing*. Wait till you see what we do next."

"What is next?" Pacino asked.

"Nothing. Forget I said that. Any other questions?" When Pacino shook his head, No reached for the phone and dialed three numbers. "Yeah, send the Duty Chief to the wardroom."

Nygard reappeared. Li No looked up at him. "Secure the rig for class alpha air gap and rig ship for in-port communications."

Nygard repeated back the order. No announced on the 1MC, *"Secure the rig for class alpha air gap, rig ship for in-port comms."* He and Nygard resuscitated their VHF radios and Nygard left.

The 1MC clicked again. Dankleff's voice. *"The reactor,"* he announced dramatically, *"is critical."*

"About time," No said. "Oh, by the way, Pacino, you're on the maneuvering watch's watch bill as junior officer of the deck. If and when we get ordered out, you're driving us out of port."

"Okay," Pacino said. He'd done that on *Piranha* without incident. If he could drive a submarine as a midshipman, he thought, he sure as hell could as an officer.

No pointed to Pacino's computer. "Get in there and study the charts and the tides. Memorize it so you know this port inside and out."

Nygard put his head in. "Duty Officer and Duty Officer U-I, the ship's communications are rigged for in-port by me and checked by Petty Officer Miller, and the SEALs have arrived topside. They want one of you up there."

"Get topside and get the SEALs signed in." No ordered. "I'll meet you in lower level aft of the torpedo room. Starboard side, there's commando berthing. And just some advice from me to you. Don't try to mess around with them. Those guys are scary."

Pacino climbed the ladder of the plug trunk to the topside doghouse and emerged through the tent flap to the outside world, noticing that the morning's clouds had cleared and bright sunshine illuminated the pier. He took a deep breath, the air smelling odd after being inside the submarine. He saluted the ensign flag aft and Petty Officer Miller, the topside watch, and stepped over the gangway to the pier.

On the pier was a flat black two-ton truck with staked sides loaded with equipment containers. In front of it stood a tough-looking black man, maybe forty years old, wearing scuffed black boots with skulls on them, ragged black jeans, a Harley T-shirt showing a burning skull and a leather vest with biker outlaw patches on it. Under his biker vest was the butt of a large caliber handgun peeking out from a shoulder holster. On his other side, a fourteen-inch K-Bar combat knife was secured in a black leather sheath. He had a thin face, prominent cheekbones, hollow cheeks, a few days of beard growth over pockmarked skin and a scar on his forehead disappearing into his hairline. He was about Pacino's height but outweighed him by forty pounds at least, most of it muscle. He looked at Pacino, his hard face easing into an intent, kind look. Pacino's eyes narrowed, thinking a facial expression of kindness was out of character to the SEAL's costume, or uniform, or whatever they called this grubby outlaw look.

"I'm Pacino, duty officer under instruction," Pacino said, looking at the biker. The biker stepped close and held out his hand, his crushing grip dry and sandpapery rough, a slight smile coming to the big man's lips.

"Commander Fishman," he said in a deep, sonorous baritone. "Eb Fishman. I'm in charge of SEAL Task Group Eight Zero, the crew detailed to your boat."

Fishman produced his pad computer from an internal vest pocket on his right side, opposite the holster's side. "Our orders."

Pacino read the official message, from the commander of the special warfare command to SEAL TEAM TASK GROUP EIGHT ZERO with a copy to SSN-792 USS VERMONT. Pacino was no expert, but it seemed in order, and the group was expected aboard. Pacino gestured to Petty Officer Miller, the second class machinist's mate from Auxiliary Gang who was standing topside watch duty.

"Let's get you signed in."

As with Pacino on Friday, Miller took Fishman's identification and biometrics, which had been sent over from SubCom prior to the arrival of the commandos. Miller nodded at Pacino as Fishman's identification checked.

A tall man dressed in black jeans, a long black ranch coat, and pointy-toed black cowboy boots emerged from behind the truck, dusting off his hands from unloading the equipment crates. He wore a large pistol, a chrome-plated semi-automatic, holstered on one hip, the end of the holster strapped around his thigh above his knee. He looked corn-fed, solid, perhaps an inch taller than Pacino and Fishman, and much younger, perhaps in his mid-twenties. He had trimmed black hair and a salt-and-pepper beard, round and friendly green eyes, pronounced facial features and a face that seemed to relax into a smile. His smile deepened into a grin as he approached Pacino and offered his hand.

"I'm Lieutenant junior grade Elias Aquatong," he said in a southern Midwest accent, perhaps Kentucky or Tennessee. "My friends call me 'Autoloader.' The other SEALs on this team call me 'Grip,' the assholes. You drop *one lousy crate* of grenades and boom, your damned call-sign changes to 'Grip.'" He leaned over and pointed to Fishman, confidentially stating in a stage whisper, "you can call Fishman 'Tiny Tim.' His first name is Ebenezer, but the handle 'Scrooge' didn't fit him. He's way too sweet and nice to be a Scrooge."

Fishman tipped his head without smiling, the banter obviously having become banal to him. He withdrew a Camel unfiltered from his inside vest pocket and produced a scratched-up lighter with the emblem of the USS *Barracuda*. He lit it and blew the smoke in a perfect ring that rolled toward the submarine. The entire time, he cupped his hand around the lit end, as if shielding it from someone watching. He looked at Aquatong with an amused expression, almost like a grizzled uncle at an apprentice nephew. "You know, Grip, I did you a *huge* favor. Because, you know, 'Aquatong,'" he paused, "is a stupid and distracting name." Aquatong just laughed and shook his head.

Pacino looked up as an unmarked black SUV drove up behind the cargo truck. Two men climbed out, one medium height and thin, looking Japanese, wearing a black windbreaker, red baseball cap, black T-shirt and black jeans. None of the clothing had any markings or for that matter, wrinkles, looking like the pants, shirt, jacket and hat just came off a rack at a department store. The other man was a lanky black man of medium height, wearing blue jeans and a starched white button-down shirt under a sport jacket. The Japanese SEAL looked thirty, though he could be older. The thin black SEAL was definitely older, but his exact age was indistinct.

Aquatong pointed to the older man. "That's Senior Chief Tucker-Santos. He's a commando *and* a corpsman. Call him 'Scooter.' So named because he dumped an expensive bike on an easy ride."

Tucker-Santos came over and shook Pacino's hand, snarling at Aquatong. "It was a hard ride up a New Hampshire mountain through four inches of blowing snow, actually," he said. "And it was an emergency." He looked at Pacino. "Story for another day, Lieutenant. Glad to be riding your fine submarine." As the senior chief leaned over, Pacino could see his holstered pistol beneath his sport jacket. The piece was huge, at least a forty-five. He gestured at the Japanese man. "This is Petty Officer First Class Hoshi Oneida. Just call him 'Swan Creek.'"

"Not 'Swan Creek,'" the slender first class petty officer said in a gentle voice, approaching Pacino and shaking his hand. "Just 'Swan.'" He smiled. "Good to be aboard again with you fine gentlemen of the Silent Service. This should be a good op."

There it was again, Pacino thought. First the XO's vague thought that the ship would depart Monday, then Li No's hints, and now the SEAL operator calling this an 'op,' short for *operation*—Navy slang for a secret mission.

Pacino shepherded the men to the lower level aft of the torpedo room where the SEALs' berthing room was located. Li No was there with Senior Chief Nygard. Both men met the four commandos and showed them their bunks. Nygard went to help with their equipment load, some of which would go into the lockout trunk, some into the lower-level torpedo room. Pacino and No returned to the wardroom. Pacino brewed a pot of coffee. When it was done, the two SEAL officers came in and plopped down into chairs next to Pacino, facing Li No. Pacino offered coffee and both accepted cups.

"Hot water for me, Mr. Pacino," No said. Pacino heated a cup and set it in front of Li No, who pulled a teabag from his briefcase. The two commando officers both poured seemingly toxic levels of sugar into their coffees, then sipped from their cups.

"Submarine coffee is the best," Fishman said. Aquatong nodded. "I don't know if you know this, Mr. Pacino," Fishman said. "The Navy has its own coffee plantations in Columbia. Rumor has it we had to make a covenant with the cartels to be able to operate down there."

It seemed surreal, sitting in the wardroom and drinking coffee with the commando officers in their odd civilian clothes. Fishman still wore his biker vest and shoulder-holstered weapon. Aquatong had lost the long coat, revealing a cowboy-style black shirt with snaps instead of buttons. He still wore the belt with the pistol holstered to his thigh.

"Have you been aboard *Vermont* before?" Pacino asked the SEALs.

"We just rode, what, Grip, only a month ago?" Fishman asked Aquatong.

"Yeah, Tiny Tim, about then."

"That one was wild," Fishman said.

Pacino was tempted to ask if that run had been the superyacht operation, but decided to keep his mouth shut. His mind went to the thought of an upcoming operation, but knew it would require re-rigging the submarine's communications for an air gap, and it was possible even the commandos didn't know, or if they did, they might not tell him. After all, he didn't have the need-to-know. The phone near the captain's chair buzzed. Li No motioned Pacino to pick it up.

"Duty Officer U-I," he said.

"Engineering Officer of the Watch here," Lieutenant Dieter "U-Boat" Dankleff said formally. He'd stopped being 'engineering duty officer' and started being 'engineering officer of the watch' when the reactor was started. "Reactor is self-sustaining and shorepower breaker is open. Request to divorce from shorepower and remove the shorepower cables."

"I'll call you back," Pacino said, replacing the handset. He looked at Lieutenant No. "The EOOW," he said, pronouncing it *ee-ow*, "wants to remove shorepower cables."

"So, Mr. Pacino, whose permission do you need to do that?"

Pacino considered. "I think it was part of the captain's permission to start the reactor."

"You sure, or are you guessing?"

Pacino looked at Li No. He *wasn't* sure, but this was a

submarine. Indecision was penalized harshly here. Better to miscalculate and beg forgiveness than to seem uncertain.

"I'm sure."

No nodded and waved a hand in the air. "Well, then, divorce from shorepower."

Pacino dialed maneuvering. Dankleff picked up.

"Engineering Officer of the Watch, divorce from shorepower," Pacino ordered Dankleff.

Dankleff's voice was jovial. "Divorce from shorepower, EOOW aye."

Pacino sat back down and took a pull from his coffee. While he'd been up at the phone, the SEALs had pulled out their weapons and put them on the table in front of Li No, who for the first time showed an interest in something other than his WritePad tablet. Fishman looked over at No.

"Mark nineteen Desert Eagle," he said. "Fifty cal. The *actual* most powerful handgun in the world. And it actually *will* blow your head clean off."

"That sissy piece of shit only holds seven rounds and weighs a ton," Aquatong sneered. "Now *this* is a real man's weapon. Sig Sauer chrome-plated model 1911 shooting a magazine of twenty-one rounds of forty-five caliber freedom nuggets. Stars on the grip, the number 1776 engraved on the barrel."

"Grip actually wanted a pink one with a Powerpuff girl riding a unicorn on one side and Hello Kitty on the other, but the stars and the 1776 inscription were all he could get."

"Shit, Tiny Tim, all I have to do to win a gunfight with you is wait till you've got off seven rounds, then unload three times that number into you."

The SEALs took back their weapons and put them back into their holsters.

Grip Aquatong looked over at Lieutenant No. "U-Boat Dankleff still around?"

Li pointed his thumb aft, still staring at his tablet computer. "He's back aft, starting the reactor."

"He still getting divorced from Eurobitch?"

Li No nodded. "They couldn't work it out."

Pacino lifted an eyebrow. "U-Boat's getting divorced?"

"It's been coming for years," No said. "Eurobitch was introduced that way to the crew when U-Boat reported aboard as a non-qual nub two years ago. That tells you something right there. Now U-Boat's the Bull L-T and she's worse than ever."

"Bull L-T?"

"Bull lieutenant," No explained. "Senior man amongst the junior officers aboard."

"So, what's U-Boat doing about a place to live?" Pacino asked. If he'd known U-Boat were becoming single, he might have been able to get an apartment with him and saved on rent.

"Probably move onboard the boat," No said. "It's been done."

"Damned shame," Pacino said.

"Hello, gentlemen," Navigator Rachel Romanov said from the forward wardroom door.

"Navigator," Li No said, looking up. "What are *you* doing here?"

Romanov walked past the SEALs and Pacino to the pod coffee maker. "Bruno got underway Saturday. Nothing to do at home but drink vodka and take care of the cats, so I got a cat-sitter and came in. No sense being hungover and late for Monday. Especially not for *this* Monday." She looked at the SEALs. "You," she said to Fishman. "Commander Fishman, commanding officer, right? Tiny Tim?"

Fishman stood and offered his hand and the navigator shook it. "You remembered. You're Romanov? Silky Romanov?"

"That's me. And you? I remember you but I forgot your name."

Aquatong stood and offered his hand. "Grip Aquatong, executive officer of our little task group."

"Rachel Romanov, navigator of this humble boat." She got her coffee and took her normal chair, the one forward of the executive officer's, tipping it back on its back two legs, her face becoming serious. "So what's going on with U-Boat?" Romanov asked the table.

Li No shrugged. "Trouble with Eurobitch. He's moving out."

"It's a shame," she said. "But then a lot of folks saw that one coming."

"Divorce ain't for wimps," Aquatong said. "I'm going through one myself."

"Yeah," Fishman added. "He has to sell his loud-ass Harley for money to pay the ex her half of the—quote—marital estate—unquote."

"Don't remind me," Aquatong said, his perpetual smile fading away.

"What kind of Harley?" Romanov asked, sipping her hot brew, her chair back on all four legs.

Aquatong pulled out his tablet computer and showed the navigator the photos of the bike. "2014 Heritage Softail Classic, leather bags, windshield, double pipes, tuned for high torque, loudest motorcycle in a three-state area. If Elvis Presley ever rode a motorcycle, this would be the bike he'd ride."

"Oh yeah?" she said, taking Aquatong's handheld so she could see the photos close up.

"Oh yeah," Fishman confirmed. "Remember that bike rally last summer?"

"That was awesome," Aquatong said, his smile returning.

"So there we are at this bike rally," Fishman said, leaning far back in his chair and settling into telling the story while Romanov scanned intensely through the photos. "We're all there. I'm on my Dyna Wide Glide. Scooter's there with his Fat Bob. And Swan Creek is there with that rice burner of his, what is that thing—"

"Suzuki Hayabusa," Aquatong said.

"Right. Hayabusa. A horrible thing painted baby blue, looks like a teenaged girl's dream of a motorcycle. Second fastest production motorcycle in the world, as Swan Creek keeps telling us."

"Not that he got to prove it," Aquatong added. "He got pulled over for going a hundred and thirteen in a fifty-five. He was trying to see if he could get to the advertised 195 mile per hour advertised top speed."

"I had to bail him out that time," Fishman said. "Anyway, so we're there waiting for the bikes to get lined up and finally we're ready. In fact, that guy from your boat was there too, what's his name?"

"Vevera," Aquatong said. "You introduced me to him, Tiny Tim. *Vermont*'s communications guy. Squirt Gun Vevera."

"Yeah, that fat fucker," Fishman continued. "He's on that shiny, fancy Indian bike. Chieftain or something. Only a yuppie like you, Grip, would own a sissy bike like that."

"Hey. Them's fightin' words, Tiny Tim."

"Anyway, finally the rally leader gives the signal to start engines. So about a thousand motorcycle engines all start at once. Swan's bike's two hundred horsepower engine just does this little whispering sizzle, sounds like a sewing machine. Can't even hear it even if it's pin-drop quiet. Anyway, all those bikes cranking at once? You'd think that would be the loudest sound you'd ever hear, right? Oh no. Grip here, he waits about six seconds and only *then* hits the starter on that Heritage of his, and suddenly the eardrums of a hundred people shattered as *his* engine cranked up."

"It was epic," Aquatong said, grinning. "Suddenly three hundred people spin their heads around to stare at me."

"Yeah, but you didn't even get a single biker girl's phone number out of it, you pathetic loser."

"Hey, fuck off, at least I'm single now, not like a certain boss of mine who has to ask permission to go to a strip club."

"So this bike," Romanov said seriously. "How many miles and how much you want for it?"

"Whoa," Fishman said, "hold on there, little lady. *You* couldn't handle a bike like this."

"I used to own a Fat Bob back in the day," Romanov said. "I burned so much rubber on that bike I had to replace tires every season."

"Wait, you're a, you're a...*biker chick?*" The commandos stared at Romanov. Li No didn't even glance up.

Romanov shrugged. "I used to be. Back when I was a surface ship Navy officer."

"Man," Fishman said, getting up to get a refill. "A skimmer, a bubblehead, *and* a biker chick. You got any sisters at home, kid?"

Romanov laughed. "You'd hate my sister. She has four kids and gained a hundred pounds."

"Hey, Tiny Tim," Aquatong said, "you're getting in the way of negotiations, here. Navigator, she's got eight thousand on the clock. A mere ten grand gets you the keys to this fine scooter."

Romanov handed back Aquatong's tablet. "Nine grand and you've got a deal."

"Nine thousand five hundred."

She looked at him, frowned, and said, "Nine-five and you buy me a helmet and leather jacket. *And* boots."

"Nine-five, helmet, jacket, and you buy your own fuckin' boots."

"Deal," she said, bursting into a smile as she shook his hand. "Is it on base, officer parking?"

"That it is, Madam Navigatrix."

"Let's go see it," she said, getting up and leaving the wardroom with Aquatong.

Pacino decided to go aft and visit the engineering spaces and say hello to U-Boat Dankleff.

6

Monday, May 9

Pacino had been in the wardroom since 0600, staking out a seat near the supply officer's end of the table, with his back to the bulkhead, drinking coffee, reading the classified intelligence digest and reviewing ship's information, starting with the layout.

So far his caution about being early for things had paid off. The room began to fill with frowning officers who seemed sleepy or grumpy. The merriness of Saturday night had inevitably yielded to the tense edginess of Monday morning. The chair to the right hand of the captain's end seat, the aft end of the wardroom, would be reserved for the XO, Pacino knew, the chair to the left, the engineer. Next to the XO's seat would be the navigator's, and next to the engineer, the weapons officer. At the far end, opposite the captain, was the supply officer's seat. The other chairs were up for grabs for the junior officers. Generally, if they did things on *Vermont* the way they did on *Piranha,* the engineers' officers—the main propulsion assistant, damage control assistant, and electrical officer—would sit on the XO's side so they could face the engineer. The engineer's side would then fill up with the torpedo officer, the sonar officer, and the communications officer. That left two open seats, one on each side, then the supply officer's seat at the end.

The coffee maker was doing triple duty, with the pod coffee maker gurgling loudly and the espresso machine making angry steaming noises. Navigator Silky Romanov flipped her long hair into a ponytail while she waited for coffee, then grabbed her cup and sat down next to the XO's seat. Romanov opened her tablet computer and paged through it. Damage Control Assistant U-Boat Dankleff and Main Propulsion Assistant Lobabes Lomax entered the room, grabbed coffee and took their seats to the navigator's right, their attention also taken up with their tablet computers. There was no sign of Boozy Varney, the electrical officer. Pacino guessed he had relieved U-Boat aft to run the nuclear plant since U-Boat was seated next to Silky. Engineer Elvis Feng Lewinsky came in then and made himself a double espresso, his booming baritone voice addressing U-Boat.

"So DCA, your report?"

U-Boat straightened his posture in his chair and answered formally. "Engineer, estimated critical position coincided with the calculation to within one half of one percent. Plant is in a normal full-power lineup running natural circulation in both loops, propulsion is on the main motor, motor tested ahead and astern, test sat. All tanks are full or higher than nine zero percent with the exception of San One and San Two, which are at ten percent. Out-of-commission log has ten discrepancies, all minor. Engineering is ready for alert status."

Elvis nodded. "Very well."

The supply officer arrived, made his coffee from the pod machine, a hideous smelly witch's brew of hazelnut and vanilla, then plopped down near Pacino as Li No came in, sitting one seat over from the weapons officer's seat. Eisenhart, the outgoing sonar officer and incoming communications officer, came in from the captain's end door and squeezed past the engineer, the weapons officer's seat and Li No's seat and settled to Pacino's right. He leaned over to say something to Pacino.

"You catching up with the intel digest?" he asked.

"I'm locked out of half of it," Pacino said quietly. "Clearance level isn't high enough, according to the software."

"Okay, I'll fix that after officers' call," Eisenhart said. "If the XO asks, though, tell him you're running hot, straight, and normal."

"Got it."

When Quinnivan entered the room holding a coffee cup,

everyone in the room seemed to stiffen up, sitting at attention in their chairs. The executive officer frowned and took his seat, annoyance in his voice when he said, "Where's the weapons officer?"

As if on cue, Spichovich came into the room on the supply officer's side door and made his way aft to the seat by the engineer. "Good morning, XO. Morning, everyone," he said gravely. Quinnivan seemed satisfied, looking around the room as he took a mental roll call of the officers present.

Quinnivan looked at his old watch. "Let's start, people. Officers' call. We are on alert status in exactly fifty-nine minutes and thirty seconds. Readiness for alert—Engineer?"

"Engineering's ready," Elvis said, his face serious. "Ship is divorced from shorepower with propulsion on the main motor. Ready to answer all bells."

"Good work, Eng. Weapons?"

"Weapons department is ready," Sprocket said. "Battlecontrol is online and nominal, self-checks complete."

"Very good, Weps. Navigation and operations?"

"Operations department is ready," Romanov reported. "Charts are updated and uploaded to the tactical apps. All lines are singled up. The crane is ready and manned and prepared to remove the gangway. Ship is rotating and radiating. The harbormaster's pilot is in the mess decks, standing by. Both tugs are in the slip with engines at idle, on stand-by. Radios to the tugs tested, tested sat."

"Very well, Nav. Supply?"

"Supply department is ready," Gangbanger said, quietly. "Load-out complete for forty days, spares inventory complete and sat, no major items on the out-of-commission log and no major discrepancies."

"Whatever happened to the fookin' washin' machine?" the XO asked, his tone aggressive. On Friday, the day Pacino reported aboard, the ship's washing machine had burst into flames. Pacino had heard it from Gangbanger at the party and the long story of what he had to do to get it fixed. The part couldn't be borrowed—"cannibalized"—from other ships of the same class, since they were all at sea.

"Sir, we just needed the rotary switch for a replacement, but there were none in the fleet, so we ordered and found an entirely new washing machine, ripped the rotary switch out of it, brought it to A-gang and abandoned the rest of the new unit on the pier."

"Gangbanger's brute force method comes through again. Well, okay then," the executive officer said. He looked up at the gathered officers. "We won't be going over admin today, people, but take any time while we're on alert to catch up on your deliverables. Also, the captain and I will be walking the spaces to inspect stowage for sea, so get with your divisions and take a strain to ensure seaworthiness, and for God's sake, clean the hell up. Everything better be goddamned sparkling and shiny. Eng, you have anything?"

"No, sir," Elvis said.

"Nav?"

"Yes, sir," Romanov said, her pretty face clenching into a hard frown. "The watch officers on the way out—Mr. Lomax and Mr. Pacino—need to study the tides and charts, and be aware of the tide situation as the day goes on. If the alert turns into an order to get underway, take a few minutes to review the tides for that time of day before you get to the bridge. Once the maneuvering watch is stationed, you won't have time to look at the tides and chart, so make sure you're doing it now and throughout the day. Clear?"

Pacino and Lomax nodded. "Yes, Nav," Lomax said obediently.

"Weps?"

"Nothing for me," Spichovich replied.

Quinnivan slapped the table. "Very well. Officers' call is complete and sat. Let's go make some money." Without another word he grabbed his cup and his tablet and vanished through the captain's end door.

Pacino showed Easy Eisy the warning notification that flashed when he put in his search for 'Sotheby superyacht.' If Eisenhart were disturbed at Pacino's search, he didn't show it. He went into his own tablet and adjusted settings for what seemed like fifteen minutes while Pacino studied the charts of Norfolk, Hampton Roads and Virginia Beach, checking the nominal depths of the channel, the outbound traffic separation scheme east of Virginia Beach, the buoy numbering, then the tides, starting with the tide situation as of 0800. Finally Eisenhart said, "Try it now."

Pacino entered the intel files and searched for information on Elias Sotheby's disappearance. A long article came up, marked TOP SECRET–*FRACTAL CHAOS*, with video clips available and photographs. The photos XO had shown him were embedded in the article. Suddenly, finally, it seemed all too real.

Pacino checked the brass bulkhead chronometer. Just as the minute hand clicked to the twelve of the hour of 0800, the overhead speakers of the 1MC announcing circuit clicked with XO Quinnivan's voice.

"Communications emergency, communications emergency. Navigator, Communicator and Radio Chief, report to radio."

"And here we go," Lomax said, standing.

"What's happening?" Pacino asked.

"Suit up and look at the chart and the tides one final time," Lomax said. "This communication emergency will be a message to us to go, the go-code. We're outta here."

The 1MC clicked again, then Quinnivan's voice came over. *"Station…the maneuvering watch!"*

Pacino made his way through the mad crowd of crewmen hurrying to their maneuvering watchstations, up the ladder to the upper level and across to the narrow passageway to his half-a-six-pack berthing room. He ditched his working khaki uniform and put it on one of the hooks on the wall, grabbed his digital camo working uniform from the lower locker along with his binoculars, jumped into the uniform, put the binoculars around his neck and grabbed a USS VERMONT baseball hat with the ship's name embroidered above gold dolphins and below, the embroidery spelling SSN-792. The uniforms they'd given him already had his name embroidered over the pocket, with an American flag patch on the left shoulder and the *Vermont* emblem patch on the right. All that was missing were gold submarine dolphins, he noted with dismay.

Pacino debated whether to take his jacket with him, then decided that despite it being May, the winds topside from their passage would make it cold. He pulled it on, thinking if it were too hot topside, he could toss it somewhere in the bridge cockpit. He grabbed his handheld computer and clicked again to the chart and the tides, seeing that high tide would be in ninety minutes. He clicked to a real-time satellite image of Port Norfolk and noted the traffic, which was light for a Monday morning. He put the handheld in a pocket in his jacket, the pocket sized for the tablet, then opened the door and hurried into the passageway.

He stepped down to control to check in with the officer of the deck, Lieutenant Lomax, and the navigator, Lieutenant Commander Romanov. Pacino looked around the room, which seemed large when unoccupied with the ship shut down in port, but which was now cramped and bursting with people, all shoulder-to-shoulder, every console seat filled, the crew all donning wireless headsets with boom microphones. Lomax stood behind the ship control station, checking the status displays for tank levels and the main ballast tank vent indicator lights. He seemed far away, absorbed while he handed Pacino a full body harness and a lanyard. Pacino stepped into the harness. He looked over at the navigation console, the large electronic table displaying the harbor chart.

The navigator stood at the electronic chart table, holding her hand to her earphone as if straining to hear someone. She looked up at Pacino as if she sensed his glance and nodded once at him, deeply serious. Lieutenant Commander Lewinsky, the engineer, stood at the command console, standing contact coordinator watch, his job to monitor the radar display and periscope to keep an eye on shipping traffic and report the contacts to the bridge. Lewinsky's best engineering officer of the watch, Lieutenant junior grade Li No, would be aft running the engineering watchsection in maneuvering. The ship control pilot for the run would be the DCA, Lieutenant Dankleff, with the chief of the boat—the COB—Master Chief Quartane, as copilot.

The exec, Lieutenant Commander Quinnivan, stood next to the navigator at the chart table, frowning at the track laid down by one of Romanov's navigation electronics technicians. As Lomax had told him before the watch, the XO would be supervising all the action from control, being wary for any mistake by a watchstander. When it came time to leave, the captain, Commander Seagraves, would be on the bridge with them, standing on top of the sail surrounded by the temporary handrails that made up the "flying bridge."

The navigator's almost hostile voice was grating as she nagged him one final time, her voice projecting at him though she kept her eyes on her chart. "Mr. Pacino, you checked the chart and the tides?"

"Yes, ma'am."

Lomax spoke quietly to the engineer at the conn command console, with its large ultra-high-definition periscope display, the periscope view trained aft to look into the channel. When they finished, Lomax had a few words with Quinnivan, the two officers looking over at Pacino for an instant. Pacino felt his stomach quiver with nerves as the harbormaster's civilian pilot walked into the room. An old, grizzled sailor well into his sixties clamped his harness on, spoke quietly to the navigator, then vanished out of control.

Executive Officer Quinnivan motioned Pacino over.

"Yes, sir," Pacino said, standing at attention.

"Listen, young Pacino, *Vermont* is a combat submarine. You fookin' drive it like you stole it, understand? The navigator and captain will step in if you're standing into danger. But the biggest mistake a conning officer can make is being tentative. You be aggressive up there. Remember, Patch, when that last line comes off? The USS *Vermont* is at war."

"Yes, sir."

"And listen up for anything the captain has to say to you, laddie. I read about your underway on the *Piranha*. You can do this." Quinnivan clapped Pacino on the shoulder and drilled his gaze into Pacino's eyes, as if searching for weakness. Pacino swallowed hard.

"Aye aye, sir. Understood."

"Good luck, lad," Quinnivan said, his eyes crinkling as he smiled.

"Mr. Pacino, let's go," Lomax interrupted seriously.

Pacino looked around control one last time. There was none of the levity of the ship's party from Friday night, nor even the calm professionalism of officer's call an hour before. The atmosphere was as tense as anything Pacino had witnessed, even more than those frightening "comearounds" to the upperclassmen during Plebe Summer at the academy.

His heart beginning to hammer in his chest, Pacino followed Lomax to the upper level and the ladder under the bridge access tunnel. "Officer of the Deck to the bridge," Lomax shouted up the tunnel, then vanished up the ladder. Pacino waited for him to get all the way up, then shouted, "Junior Officer of the Deck to the bridge!" He checked that his lanyard was tucked in, then took the ladder rungs until the submarine's upper level disappeared and he was in the darkness of the vertical tunnel, only a few hooded lights illuminating the empty cylinder of steel. Above him, he could see the circle of bright light shining down from the outside world, and a momentary flash of memory tugged at him as he remembered something dimly from the *Piranha* sinking, but he put it aside and climbed close to the upper hatch.

"Junior Officer of the Deck, permission to come up?"

"Permission granted, come on up," Lomax called, and Pacino climbed up through the upper hatch and stood aside as Lomax put down the grating allowing them to stand on top of the opening to the tunnel. Pacino looked around him. He stood in a crow's nest of steel, the coaming of the bridge coming to chest level. Pacino slipped past Lomax and went to the port side and leaned over, looking down on the linehandlers on the pier and on the topside deck, all of them looking up at him expectantly. Ahead of him, a large Plexiglass windshield was bolted to the sail, and below it was the bridge communication box, with a microphone on a coiled spring, a large speaker and two rotary switches to select communication circuits and adjust volume. Lomax handed Pacino the microphone.

"Test your comms with all stations," he ordered.

Pacino looked at the box and checked that it was selected to "7MC," the maneuvering and ship control circuit.

"Pilot, Bridge, comm check," he said into the mike, hoping his voice didn't tremble.

"Bridge, Pilot," Dankleff's voice boomed out of the speaker. "Comm check sat."

"Bridge, aye," Pacino said. "Navigator, Bridge, comm check."

"Bridge, Navigator, aye," Romanov's harsh voice called back. "Check sat."

Lomax laughed. "Goddamn, that woman's voice penetrates to the marrow of your bones. I feel sorry for Bruno." Pacino smirked.

"Bridge aye, Contact Coordinator, Bridge, comm check."

"Bridge, Contact, check sat," Lewinsky's deep booming voice reported.

"Maneuvering, Bridge," Pacino called, "comm check."

"Bridge, Maneuvering," No replied in his harsh Chicago accent, "communications check satisfactory."

Pacino looked at Lomax. "Officer of the Deck," he reported formally, "communication circuits tested, tested sat."

Lomax nodded. "Very well, JOOD."

Behind Pacino's left shoulder, the radar rotated, atop its tall mast, the radar array rotating once every two seconds. To Pacino's right rear was a small commercial DynaCorp radar unit mounted on a temporary mast tied into the flying bridge handrails. As Pacino had learned on *Piranha,* sometimes the boat would sneak out of port using only the commercial unit so a waiting spy ship wouldn't see their unique military spec's radar signal, but today, apparently, it was acceptable to be identifiable as a Navy submarine. Pacino checked over the port side again, where the lines holding them to the pier were singled-up, linehandlers impatiently standing by. Forward, through the windshield, Pacino could see the nose of the ship sloping downward into the brackish water of the slip. To starboard, on his side, the two tugs could be seen, idling in the channel. At the end of the slip he could see the pier's security building with its tall guard tower, almost looking like a mid-size airport's control tower. Pacino frowned, wondering why they'd moored with the bow pointed landward. This would be so easy if they were parked nose-out, but then, bow-in like this had been how *Piranha* had been moored when he drove her out, back what seemed a hundred years ago.

Pacino pulled out his handheld and mounted it on a support to the left of the bridge box. Lomax's was already mounted on the right, his display showing the chart. Likewise, Pacino brought up the chart, showing their position flashing on the pier leading into the Elizabeth River's Norfolk Harbor Reach.

"So, JOOD," Lomax said, his voice dead serious, "listen up. The captain and XO heard about your 'back full, ahead flank' underway when you drove out your midshipman cruise submarine. So the CO wants to see how you'd do that now. You think you can do it again?"

"Yes, OOD," Pacino said, turning around to see the waters astern of them. He could see the rudder pointing straight aft and the open water of the river far astern. He could feel his heart beating harder and faster than before. Being pulled out by two tugboats would have been so easy. But a back-full, ahead-flank underway? That risked the ship, not to mention his reputation.

"Don't fuck it up like Man Mountain Vevera did," Lomax said.

"Why? What happened?"

Lomax laughed, breaking the tension of the morning. "Fucker put on a weak back one-third bell instead of back full. The river current overcame his rudder. Instead of the propulsor pulling the stern south in the river so the bow would point north—the way out of Norfolk—the current pushed the stern *north,* so that the ship was exactly backwards. Normally the captain would have taken the conn and gotten it all figured out, or at the very least, given Vevera rudder orders so *he* could recover and get the bow pointed north. But the captain was gagged. It was this oddball exercise simulating a nuclear first strike, with SubCom staff onboard simulating that half the crew were injured or dead, with no comms to command HQ, and one of the simulated injured was the captain. We had to get underway with a random officer, so they picked Vevera since he happened to be the one in the wardroom slamming down sausages when the staff rats walked in.

"So Man Mountain Squirt Gun Vevera, what does he do?

Does he bring the ship to all stop and use the thruster to rotate the hull 180 degrees to face north? *No.* That fucker decided to just keep going backwards. He shifted the rudder so the stern kept coming around from north to east to south again. Eventually he was pointing north in the river, after having executed a full *two-seventy-degree turn* going *backwards.* In a goddamned river channel. Goddamn, he got lucky, it was high tide and there were no sandbars, but any other time he would have hit something or run aground. The crew was screaming and howling in hilarity, and the goddamned navigator almost passed out. And the entire time? I think the captain had turned purple in the face, the ComSub staff guy was furiously taking notes, and Vevera? He was as cool as if he had no problem with it at all. As the bow came around to the north, he ordered the ship from back one third to ahead two thirds, then looked up at the staff rat and said, and I quote, 'I planned that very carefully.' I'm telling you, it was fucking *legend!*"

Lomax paused, his face going from exhilarated hilarity of the memory to a sad, hopeless expression. "Fucking Squirt Gun Vevera," he said. "Now that fucker's gonna die."

"We don't know that," Pacino said. "Maybe he'll beat this thing."

"No chance. My uncle's an oncologist. I forced Squirt Gun to get a second opinion from Uncle Joe. Joe can't tell me what his professional opinion is due to doctor-patient confidentiality, but Joe's face spoke for him. For Vevera, it's just a matter of time, and not much time at that." Lomax hoisted his binoculars to his face and scanned the channel. "Let's get our heads into the operation, Mr. Pacino. Just don't do what Vevera did. When you back into the channel, do it with a back full bell with right full rudder, and train the outboard to zero nine zero, start it, and don't stop it until we're pointed fucking north, you got that?"

Pacino nodded. "I've got it. Don't worry. I did it before. The current was faster in the Thames River than here."

Just then a voice came up from below. "Captain to the bridge!"

Pacino replied, "Come up, sir." He bent and pulled up the

grating so the commanding officer could climb up into the cockpit.

"Hello, Mr. Pacino," Seagraves said in his deep baritone, emerging fully into the bridge cockpit. "Mr. Lomax." Seagraves kept going, climbing up to the top of the sail behind them, to the handrail-enclosed flying bridge, latching his safety lanyard to one of the flying bridge's horizontal rails.

"Morning, Captain," Lomax and Pacino replied, almost in perfect unison.

"Mr. Lomax," Seagraves called, "did you brief your JOOD on the procedure to get underway?"

"Sir, yes, sir," Lomax said, facing the captain.

"Very well." Seagraves checked his watch. "Brief the navigator on your intentions, Mr. Pacino."

"Aye aye, sir," Pacino said. He picked up the bridge box microphone, still selected to the 7MC ship-control circuit. "Navigator, Bridge," he called.

"Bridge, Navigator," Romanov's voice crackled.

"Navigator, Bridge, intentions are to back into the channel without tugs or pilot and proceed to Thimble Shoal Channel unassisted."

There was a pause. Obviously Romanov was not comfortable with the announcement, but she knew Pacino was on the bridge with the captain and that the departure method, however unconventional, was approved.

"Bridge…" There was a long second as Romanov showed her displeasure. "Navigator, aye."

The captain looked down at Pacino. "Mr. Pacino, let's go."

Pacino noticed that the harbormaster's civilian pilot was not on the sail, but walking across the gangway to the pier. Pacino pulled up his bullhorn. "On the pier, pier crew remove the gangway!"

The diesel engine of the pier cherry-picker roared as its boom hoisted the gangway off the hull and put it back down on the pier.

Pacino checked his chart and tides one last time. The damned current from the south was pushing the hull against the pier to the north. He'd need to push off the pier with the thruster, the "outboard," which was mounted on a pedestal far aft and withdrawn into the hull. A hydraulic mechanism could push it down out of the hull by five feet to be in the clear water away from the hull.

He pulled the microphone to his mouth. "Pilot, Bridge, lower the outboard and train the outboard to zero nine zero."

Dankleff's voice boomed out of the bridge box. "Lower the outboard aye, and the outboard is rigged out. Train the outboard to zero nine zero, aye, and the outboard is trained to zero nine zero."

"Pilot, Bridge, aye."

"Shift your pumps, JOOD," Lomax ordered.

"Right," Pacino said. "Maneuvering, Bridge, shift main coolant pumps to fast speed."

"Bridge, Maneuvering," Li No said, "Shift main coolant pumps to fast speed, aye." There was a short pause. "Bridge, Maneuvering, main coolant pumps are running in fast speed. Ready to answer all bells."

"Maneuvering, Bridge aye," Pacino acknowledged. He peered down onto the pier and hull and lifted the bullhorn. "On deck," he ordered, "Take in lines six, four, five, three and two!"

The deck crew chief acknowledged and the pier crew hurriedly took the lines off the pier bollards and tossed them to the crew on the submarine's deck. Finally the deck chief, the auxiliary division chief, Dysart, yelled up in a gravelly voice, "two, three, four, five and six are in, sir!"

Only line one at the bow held them to the pier. That and the goddamned current, Pacino thought.

As he gave his next order, he felt his armpits melt into sweat. He could feel the beads of sweat on his forehead. His blood was pumping so hard it made a rushing noise in his head. "Pilot, Bridge, start the outboard!" he ordered.

"Start the outboard, Bridge, Pilot aye, and the outboard is started."

"Pilot, Bridge, right full rudder."

"Bridge, Pilot, right full rudder, aye, and my rudder is right full."

"Very well, Pilot," Pacino called. He looked aft, making

sure the rudder was put over to the right, or left as he peered backwards toward the river. Pacino glanced at Lomax. "OOD, be ready to sound the ship's whistle." Lomax nodded seriously.

"On the flying bridge," Pacino called up to the captain and the lookout standing next to him, "Be prepared to shift colors."

The lookout of the watch acknowledged, his hands on the flag's lanyard.

Pacino's heart felt like it would beat clear out of his chest any minute. What if this went wrong like it did with Vevera? Would he himself have Vevera's cool panache? He seriously doubted it. Pacino bit his lip, his nerves jangling. This was it, he thought. The eyes of the entire crew were on him, the new nub non-qual officer, seeing if he could pull this off. He shut his eyes for just a half second, reminding himself that his father had done this every time he'd gone to sea, and that he himself had done this once before, as a mere midshipman.

"Pilot, Bridge," he called on the 7 MC microphone, "all back full."

"Bridge, Pilot, back full, Pilot aye, and Maneuvering answers, all back full!"

Pacino looked aft at the foam bubbling up astern of the rudder. He picked up his bullhorn.

"On deck! Hold line one!"

Pacino looked at the pier, seeing how it was moving away from the stern. The bow was still tied tight to the bollards on the pier. Pacino watched as the force of the outboard thruster battled the current, the outboard trying to pull the stern up-river, the current trying to push it back against the pier. The wake was boiling up around the rudder.

It was time to go.

"On deck," Pacino shouted into his bullhorn, "take in line one!"

The moment the line was pulled off the bollard and tossed over to the deck, the USS *Vermont* was officially underway.

"Shift colors!" Pacino shouted aft. "Sound one long blast on the ship's whistle," he ordered Lomax. Lomax reached under the cockpit lip forward and found the handle to the air horn and pulled it toward him. An earsplitting baritone shriek

roared across the water of the bay, lasting what seemed two dozen heartbeats. Pacino spun to look to the stern, to make sure there was no traffic in the channel and to see if the stern would break south as he intended. On the flying bridge, the lookout hoisted the American flag and the Jolly Roger flag of SubCom, the black field with the white skull-and-crossbones.

"OOD," Pacino said to Lomax, "Three short blasts on the ship's whistle."

Lomax pulled on the freakishly loud air horn and the blasting roar came again for a long second, quieted, then again and finally a third time. All this deafening noise, Pacino thought, made it so no one could hear his orders. But it was a safety signal to anyone sailing behind them in the channel to let them know they were backing into the river.

The submarine started moving slowly, an inch at first, then gradually accelerating, first at a leisurely stroll, then walking speed, then jogging speed, the ship's smooth motion making it seem like it was stationary and it was the pier that was moving backwards. Soon the pier was fading backward at what seemed twenty miles an hour. The end of the pier came even with the sail. Pacino looked aft, and the rudder, propulsor and outboard thruster were losing their struggle with the current. Despite the back full revolutions and the outboard's thrust, the current was pushing the stern northward, the stern now headed almost due west. Vevera's nightmare was happening to Pacino.

"Kick it up to back emergency," Captain Seagraves commanded sternly, his jaw clenching.

"Aye, Captain. Pilot, Bridge, all back emergency!" Pacino yelled into his 7MC mike, only after giving the order realizing he'd shouted, his hand shaking. He leaned far over the aft part of the bridge coaming, praying that the stern broke south. He could feel a sudden violent trembling of the deck under his feet, the ride no longer smooth, the power of the propulsor at maximum revolutions in reverse boiling up foam so furiously it frothed higher than the rudder.

"Come on, rudder, you motherless whore," Pacino muttered, or at least he thought he'd said it under his breath, but the captain

himself nodded and said, "Exactly, Mr. Pacino, that rudder is *definitely* a motherless whore."

And just then, the stern broke south, the force of the propulsor at one hundred percent reactor power, the outboard thruster, and the full rudder angle only now overcoming the current of the Elizabeth River, the stern going south, the bow rotating to come north. Pacino let the ship turn for just a few seconds, then hoisted his 7MC mike.

"Pilot, Bridge, all stop, rudder amidships, train the outboard to zero-zero-zero and retract the outboard!"

"Bridge, Pilot, rudder amidships, aye, all stop, aye, and Maneuvering answers, all stop. The outboard is trained to triple zero, rigging in the outboard ... and the outboard is rigged in!"

"Very well, Pilot. All ahead flank!"

"All ahead flank, aye, and Maneuvering answers, all ahead flank!"

For an agonizing ten seconds, the hull's backward motion continued, but then slowed until the ship froze in the channel, the steel of it shaking with the power of the reactor as forty thousand shaft horsepower went from full reverse to full ahead, and finally the ship started to move forward, picking up speed, the bullet nose starting to burrow into the water and forming a small bow wave.

"Ease it back down, Mr. Pacino," Captain Seagraves advised, "or your bow wave will drown the deck crew."

"Aye, Captain," Pacino said, clicking the 7MC mike. "Pilot, Bridge, all ahead two thirds, steady as she goes."

"Bridge, Pilot, all ahead two thirds, steady as she goes, steering course north, and Maneuvering answers, all ahead two thirds."

"Bridge, Navigator," Romanov's voice intoned, smoother this time, less harsh. "Hold the ship ten yards west of track, recommend course zero-zero-two to regain track."

"Pilot, Bridge," Pacino said, "Steer course zero-zero-two."

"Bridge, Pilot, steering zero-zero-two."

"Mr. Pacino," the captain called down. "That was an adequate job. But don't get cocky. Watch yourself in the channel."

"Yes, sir," Pacino said, realizing he'd soaked through his

uniform with nervous sweat. The first thing he'd do when he got off watch was take a long hot hotel shower. He looked down at the deck. The deck crew was furiously stowing the heavy lines into the line lockers and rotating the deck cleats into the hull. Soon the hull was clean and rigged for sea. Aft, he could see the deck crew descending into the plug hatch, then the hatch coming shut.

"Bridge, Pilot," Dankleff called, "Deck is rigged for dive, last man down, plug hatch rigged for dive."

"Pilot, Bridge, aye," Pacino acknowledged. "All ahead standard," he ordered.

"Bridge, Pilot, all ahead standard, aye, and Maneuvering answers, all ahead standard."

Finally Pacino felt like he could breathe again. He traded places with Lomax, moving to the starboard side of the cockpit. To the right, the Norfolk Naval Base surface fleet piers appeared and moved aft. First the destroyer piers, then the cruiser piers, then the gigantic piers for the aircraft carriers, where the colossal USS *Gerald R. Ford* was moored. The sheer size of the aircraft carrier was staggering, the deck towering over *Vermont*'s sail.

"Bridge, Navigator," Romanov's voice blasted from the 7MC speaker. "Distance to turn one hundred yards. New course will be zero-three-four."

"Navigator, Bridge, aye," Pacino called, checking his chart display. At the end of the naval base, the channel turned northeast and headed toward the Interstate-64 bridge-tunnel.

"Bridge, Navigator, mark the turn to course zero-three-four."

"Pilot, Bridge," Pacino called into his mike, "Right fifteen degrees rudder, steady course zero-three-four."

Dankleff acknowledged. Pacino glanced aft to see that he'd turned the rudder correctly, then picked up his binoculars and scanned down the channel. There was no traffic. The sun from the east was intense. Pacino took out his sunglasses and put them on.

"Let's increase speed to full, Mr. Pacino," Seagraves called.

"Aye, Captain. Pilot, Bridge, all ahead full."

"Bridge, Pilot, all ahead full aye, and Maneuvering answers, all ahead full."

As the ship accelerated, below, forward, on deck, the bow wave climbed up the hull and broke on either side of the sail, the spray kicked up into the cockpit. The thrumming of the propulsor could be felt below, the wake boiling up to a furious frothy white behind them. The wind of their passage became loud, and the flags aft flapped in the wind of it. The sound of the radar spinning once every two seconds, combined with the wind and the blasting noise of the bow wave, seemed hypnotic. Pacino realized there was a certain magic in the sights and sounds of the ship getting underway. He had a half-second thought about his father, but put it away and concentrated on the channel navigation as the interstate's tunnel came closer.

He looked to starboard at the bridge and its ramp into the tunnel, the trucks and cars vanishing below the water to proceed beneath them. Soon they were past the tunnel and the buoys of Thimble Shoal Channel beckoned, seeming to stretch into the distance to the left and right, like a runway formed in the harbor. Navigator Romanov guided them through two turns until the ship was lined up into the long channel pointing toward the Chesapeake Bay Bridge Tunnel. At the exit of that tunnel, they'd be almost clear of the harbor.

"JOOD," Seagraves said, his voice loud to overcome the wind of their motion, "Increase speed to flank."

"Aye sir," Pacino said. "Pilot, Bridge, all ahead flank."

"Bridge, Pilot, all ahead flank, aye, and Maneuvering answers, all ahead flank."

The deck beneath Pacino's boots began to tremble harder until finally the hull was shaking violently. The flags aft flapped even harder, the noise from them competing with the blast of the hurricane wind and the earsplitting roar of the bow wave, which had now flowed over the forward half of the hull, the only part of the deck not underwater far aft, the sea spray becoming constant, wetting Pacino's sunglasses and making them opaque. He took them off and pocketed them.

"Bridge, Navigator, JOOD 1JV." The navigator wanted to speak to him privately on the 1JV phone. Pacino hoisted the phone to his ears, plugging the other ear against the noise.

"Junior Officer of the Deck."

"JOOD, Navigator," Romanov said. "Speed limit in the channel is fifteen knots. You're going twenty-one."

Pacino glanced up at the captain. "Navigator," he said slowly, "We're in a hurry."

"Navigator, aye," she snapped and hung up.

In what seemed no time, the Bay Bridge Tunnel was behind them and the submarine was in open water. Romanov had them turn south after Fort Story, paralleling the Virginia Beach coast, until the resort hotels had faded astern, then turned them due east into the traffic separation scheme. Twenty minutes later, they were officially out of Norfolk Harbor and into the Atlantic Ocean.

"Secure the maneuvering watch," Quinnivan's voice boomed on the 1MC shipwide announcing circuit. "Station underway watch section one."

Captain Seagraves climbed down from the flying bridge. "Disassemble the flying bridge, gentlemen," he said, addressing both Pacino and Lomax. "I'll be in my stateroom." With that, he vanished into the vertical tunnel to the upper level.

"Control, Bridge," Pacino called, "Captain has left the bridge."

Pacino took a deep breath, looked aft at the fading beachfront of Virginia Beach, and scanned the horizon with his binoculars. The ocean was empty except for them. The sun rose higher in the sky as the radar rotated, the flags flapped, the wind blew and the bow wave roared, and for a long moment, Anthony Pacino realized something—that here, in this moment, he was actually happy. The sea had seemed to have infected him. All the heavy weight of losing Carrie Alameda and the *Piranha* seemed much lighter now. He smiled as he scanned the horizon again.

7

Monday, May 9

Pacino found a seat at the wardroom table, the same one he'd used at officers' call, for the mid-day meal. It was starting to feel like an assigned seat. Watch relief had gone down at noon, but the "turnover" from Pacino and Lomax to Lieutenant Eisenhart had taken a quarter hour, so that by the time they were relieved, it was almost 1220 hours, almost an hour after the meal started for the oncoming watch section.

Pacino had walked into the wardroom and found the captain finished with his plate, as were the engineer and XO, all of them lingering with coffee after the meal. On behalf of himself and Lomax, as off-going junior officer of the deck, it fell to him to give the watch relief briefing to the captain. Pacino had taken a deep breath and said, "Captain, off-going JOOD, sir, Mr. Lomax and I have been properly relieved by Lieutenant Eisenhart of the deck and the conn, sir, steaming on the surface as before, course zero-nine-five, all ahead flank. Last fix on our watch was noon by GPS satellite and concurs with SINS inertial nav to within ten yards. Sounding is three zero fathoms and correlates to charted depth. Time to the Point Delta dive point at the hundred fathom curve is seven hours. Electric plant is in a normal full-power lineup, main coolant pumps one, two, five and six running in fast speed. Forecast calls for us hitting a squall line in the next hour. From what we could tell, sir, it looks like we're going to be in for it—it's going to be wet and rough out there."

Captain Seagraves had nodded up at Pacino. "Very well, Mr. Pacino. I just wanted to say, you and Mr. Lomax did a somewhat adequate job today."

Lomax smiled in pleasure. Apparently, doling out weak praise was a running joke for the captain. "Why, thank you, sir," Lomax said, taking his seat.

The captain, XO and engineer finished and left the room. There was no sign of the weapons officer or navigator, and after a moment the room was empty but for Li No, Lomax and Pacino.

Soon Pacino's plate was taken up by sliders—hamburgers so greasy they virtually sailed down one's throat—and fries. As he washed it down with a searingly sugary bright red colored "bug juice," he considered how good this would have tasted with a beer. But no doubt, he'd have to watch his intake, because inhaling chow like this four times a day would make anyone pack on pounds.

After the meal, Pacino grabbed coffee in a USS *Vermont* mug and opened his handheld and scanned the news files. As the ship steamed through the rising sea state, the room and deck started to sway and roll in the waves, his coffee threatening to spill out of his cup. He concentrated on his display screen. There were multiple alerts sent to him by the XO, the navigator and the weapons officer, things that were required reading. They were odd, seemingly unconnected articles.

The first was an article about China's Peoples' Liberation Army Navy, or "PLAN," which was commissioning their fifth gigantic supercarrier. A second, an editorial about how nations hostile to America were planning to send their naval forces to conduct operations in the Western Hemisphere—Iran and North Korea and China, all seeking blue water naval status by sailing in Atlantic waters, a traditional lake of the western powers of the USA, the UK and the European Union. That one gave Pacino pause—imagine a Chinese carrier battle group in the damned Atlantic, steaming off Norfolk.

There was a third secret-classified article about the Iranian and North Korean submarine programs, with the North Koreans concentrating on putting a sub-launched ballistic missile into a quiet diesel-electric submarine while the Iranians had aspirations to put a nuclear reactor into a retrofitted old Kilo Russian-built diesel-electric attack sub.

A fourth article about the Taiwanese building submarines intent on deterring China from invading them. A fifth about experimental new tactics of nuclear attack submarines *versus* diesel boats, since operating on batteries alone, diesel boats could be between three and nine decibels quieter on broadband sonar than a nuclear boat. It boiled down to some complicated acoustic physics of narrowband tuning to seek out low frequency bell tones—tonals—put out by large electrical motors. And a sixth about the new amphibious Chinese PLAN helicopter carriers.

The seventh was about drug smuggling by the Medellin cartel, and how they were building and using narco-subs to ferry cocaine from Medellin, Colombia, their submarines becoming progressively more sophisticated, and that their competitors, the Barranquilla cartel, had secretly succeeded in putting in service a much larger submarine, rumors persisting that the operational Barranquilla narco-sub was a replica of an old World War I American design, sailing out of Santa Marta, Colombia, but no one in the open sources or the top secret intelligence community had yet seen it. It was elusive. It was a ghost.

The eighth article covered what was known about the capabilities of China's new antisubmarine warfare maritime patrol aircraft and the heavy antisubmarine weapons they carried, including a hypersonic nuclear-tipped weapon that dropped a hundred kiloton bomb in a depth charge.

The ninth and final article was classified top secret, higher than the others, and laid out the schematic plans of the Russian Status-6 Poseidon / Kanyon nuclear powered, hundred megaton torpedo, meant to loiter off the coastal cities of an enemy—the EU or America—or even lay dormant on the bottom for months, and when triggered, detonate a cobalt-laced dirty bomb powerful enough to kill tens of millions and make an area inside of fifty miles uninhabitable for three hundred years. And the last paragraph was the most chilling, that to date, there was no effective countermeasure to this nuclear-powered death machine.

To judge by the selected articles, the future looked far less than peaceful for a submarine like *Vermont*.

After Pacino finished the required reading, he turned to studying for his qualifications for his dolphins, concentrating first on the diving officer / pilot section. The trim system, the drain system, the high-pressure air system, the steering and diving hydraulics and what to do when each system failed. He shut his eyes for a moment and remembered his qualification watch held for him by Alameda and Catardi on *Piranha,* when he'd stood diving officer of the watch and had every casualty known to man thrown at him, and when he'd managed to pull through it, every man in the control room exchanged twenty-dollar bills, most betting against Pacino's ability to prevail, but both Alameda and Catardi betting he would succeed and beat the scenario.

He'd been put on the watchbill for the next week as copilot at the ship control station, he saw from a notice on his handheld. He'd be standing watch beside Chief Dysart, the auxiliarymen chief—A-Gang—who would be manning the pilot station. Dysart had to be the most intimidating presence Pacino had run into in the submarine force, taciturn and wearing a perpetually angry face. The officer of the deck on their watch section would be the navigator, Lieutenant Commander Romanov, and Pacino didn't relish that idea, not after whatever foolishness had happened at the ship's party. The sonarman of the watch would be his soon-to-be-chief, Chief Albanese, a wiry redhead who had so much energy he had to be freebasing coffee grounds. Torpedo Officer Li No, the engineering officer of the watch for that watch section, had hinted Pacino would stand copilot watch for a few days, then rotate into the pilot seat, and after a qualification checkout, would start standing submerged officer of the deck under instruction. That, he looked forward to, that and eventually getting his dolphins when he qualified, perhaps eight, nine or ten months in the future, assuming Captain Seagraves waived the one-year requirement. But he couldn't pick a better qual boat than *Vermont,* he thought. The coming months promised to be busy with operations, where qualification in submarines went fast. The minute they made port, quals would effectively stop, whether in a liberty port where everyone would be partying or at home port, where the crew would be frantically working to repair the ship and get it ready for the next op.

Hours seemed to pass in a moment, Pacino thought, because already the mess cooks were setting up for evening meal. Pacino looked up from his handheld, coming out of the trance of studying and thinking about qualifications. The deck was rocking hard and trembling violently from the power of the propulsor as the ship rocketed through the waves at flank speed. The motion of the boat that made some people seasick only made Pacino drowsy. At one point the deck was doing slow corkscrew motions, both rolling and pitching in what must be waves a third the length of the ship and as tall as the sail. It felt like being rocked to sleep, he thought. Just then, Lomax walked in wearing foul weather gear, holding a safety rail at the wardroom credenza to keep his footing. "We've got the evening watch for the dive, Mr. Pacino. It's raining hard topside and the sea state keeps climbing, so you might want to think about whether you want to skip dinner."

"I'm okay," Pacino said. Lomax called in the mess cook, who set down plates for the two officers earlier than the normal start for the oncoming watch section. "Cold cuts," Lomax said, packing turkey, ham, cheese and onions into a bun dripping with mustard. "Sea state is too high to cook." Pacino joined him, making a sandwich and wolfing it down with chips. After what could only be five minutes, Lomax stood and gestured to Pacino. "Go get appropriately dressed and meet me in control. And leave your handheld in your safe. They may be water resistant, but it's insane out there."

Pacino got into a full-body rain slicker and pulled a safety harness over it, clamping the blue *Vermont* ball cap onto his head. He debated leaving his binoculars in his cubby, since it was raining so hard, he'd probably see nothing through them, but decided to hang them around his neck anyway. He traded out his at-sea sneakers for combat boots and headed down to the middle level.

In the control room, Lomax held on to a hand-hold bar at the command console, looking at the periscope display, where

Lieutenant Varney had the contact coordinator watch, his headset covering one ear, with a boom microphone extending down his jawline. As contact coordinator, Varney was responsible for tracking surface contacts, using the periscope, the radar set and data from sonar, analyzing their relative motion and making sure there was no risk of collision.

"Anything out there?" Lomax asked.

The unmistakable sound of someone vomiting came from forward, the ship control station. Pacino looked over as the copilot finished puking into a black plastic bag and wiped his face.

"You okay, Copilot?" Lomax asked. "You need to be relieved?"

Torpedoman Senior Chief Nygard, the copilot at the right-side console in the cocoon of flat panel displays, joysticks and interface variable function keys shook his head. "I'm fine, sir," he said, just before hurling up again. Lomax gave Pacino an amused look. "So, Contact Coordinator, contacts?" Lomax prompted Varney.

Varney shook his head. "Sea state is too high to see much and we've got wind-driven rain falling horizontally. We're not going to get much with optronics on visible light spectrum. We've been running infrared for the last hour. Nothing but a few brave seagulls." Varney checked the bulkhead chronometer, then his watch. "Sunset's in five minutes, but it looks more like midnight out there. Nothing on sonar to report, but with these waves, everything is drowned out or attenuated. Radar's as clean as it could get with these waves. So, as best we can tell, we seem to be alone out here. Looks like everyone else had the good sense to stay home."

"Keep a sharp eye out anyway," Lomax advised. "We *are* on or close to a major shipping lane. Merchant traffic is out there somewhere. I don't want to look up and see the bow of an incoming supertanker fifty yards dead ahead of me."

"Absolutely," Varney said, his voice iron hard.

"Sounding?" Lomax asked.

"Only five eight fathoms," Varney said, turning around to point at the chart. "The continental shelf goes all the way out to here," he said, pointing to Point Delta, "then the ocean depth falls off a steep cliff. Sixty fathoms here on this side of Delta, almost eight hundred here on the other side."

Lomax turned to the navigation console, staring down at the chart. Their location, "own-ship's position," was marked with a slowly pulsing bright red dot, their path from Norfolk—their "track"—marked with a thin but bright red line. Their intended course extended with a dotted blue line from own-ship's position ahead in the sea to a second point, this one a bright "X" drawn in blue, marked "Point Delta." Point Delta was the dive point, where their intended course intersected the hundred fathom curve, where it would be safe to dive the boat. The run out almost due east to the continental shelf was an eleven-hour transit. It must be nice, Pacino thought, to be assigned out of Pearl Harbor, where you could submerge half a mile from the pier. He looked forward to being submerged, because being under meant no rain and no waves—and hot food.

"Mark the distance to the dive point, Mr. Pacino," Lomax ordered. Pacino manipulated a cursor to own-ship's position, then extended a line to Point Delta.

"Twenty-eight point five nautical miles," Pacino reported. At their present speed on the surface of 19 knots, losing a few knots from laboring through these waves, they'd be there in a little over ninety minutes. Of course, just five minutes in this weather would leave them as soaked as if they had fallen overboard.

"Pilot, Copilot," Lomax announced to the two chief petty officers at the wrap-around console displays of the ship control station, "Mr. Lomax and Mr. Pacino to the bridge to relieve the officer of the deck."

"Aye, sir, wait one," Chief Goreliki, the pilot, replied. She spoke into her boom microphone to the bridge. The navigator's piercing soprano voice came in reply, "Send them up."

Lomax led the way to the upper level to the bridge access trunk step-off pad, which had a grating under it to catch any water coming in from above, but even so, that section of the passageway was flooded with the rainwater and spray from the bridge. "Watch your footing," Lomax said. He looked up into the dimly lit vertical tunnel, only two hooded red lamps illuminating the ladder extending upward. "Lieutenant Lomax to the bridge!" he called.

"Come up!" Lieutenant Commander Romanov shouted down.

"Up ladder!" He climbed up. Pacino waited for him to get to the top, knowing that in a sea state like this, if Lomax fell on top of Pacino, there'd be two injured officers rather than just one.

"Pacino to the bridge," Pacino called, imitating Lomax.

"Come on up!" Navigator Romanov ordered.

Pacino climbed the ladder, the rungs wet and salty from the spray above. He reached the bridge grating, which Lomax held open for him, and climbed up. Immediately he was hit with the showering spray from the boat hitting a tall wave, the water like a cold firehose stream. This would be a long hour, he thought, as he fastened his safety harness' lanyard onto the safety rail.

He faced Romanov, the off-going officer of the deck. "I'm ready to relieve you, ma'am," he shouted over the roaring noise of the bow wave and the rain. It was startling how dark it was when it should have been a bright May twilight. He couldn't help glancing to starboard as the boat rolled right, a towering wave seemingly far over his head, illuminated by the green starboard running light. One thing he hated, Pacino thought, was looking *up* at water. The boat rolled slowly, sickeningly back to port, the huge swells now over his head on that side, these colored red from the port running light.

"I'm ready to be relieved," the soaked-to-the-skin navigator yelled. "We're on course zero-nine-five, steaming at flank even in this sea state. Captain is anxious to get to the hundred fathom curve and get under this weather. Dive point is approximately twenty-three miles ahead. In an hour, I'll be back in the control room to take the watch while you two rig the bridge for dive. Once you come on down, I'll keep the watch long enough for you guys to shower and change, then relieve me again when you're ready."

"Got it," Pacino shouted over the gale.

"There's no surface contacts but you and the lookout back there, Petty Officer Williams, keep your eyes out. If someone is there, we won't see him until he's right on us." She leaned in to put her face close to Pacino's, the rainwater running off the brim of her ball cap and into his face. "You got it, Mr. Pacino?"

He stood straighter, as much as he could, given the bucking of the deck. "I have it, ma'am. I relieve you, ma'am."

Romanov nodded. "I stand relieved." Lomax held up the grating and the tall, slender navigator disappeared down the access trunk.

Pacino looked out at the miserable seascape, amazed at the anger of nature. It would definitely be good to get submerged and under this, he thought.

The 7MC speaker clicked, then rasped Romanov's voice. "Bridge, Navigator, I'm ready to relieve the JOOD of the deck and the conn."

"Navigator, Bridge, pick up the 1JV," Pacino said into the microphone as a spray of saltwater smashed into his face. The bridge cockpit's windshield was useless in this.

"Navigator," Romanov said into the phone.

"I'm ready to be relieved," Pacino shouted. "Ship is on course zero-nine-five, all ahead flank, no contacts, steaming toward Delta."

"I relieve you, sir," Romanov said crisply.

"I stand relieved," Pacino replied, hanging up the phone.

"Let's hurry," Lomax said, reaching for the clamps holding the bridge communication box to the steel of the cockpit.

Petty Officer Watson, the A-ganger who Pacino had first met topside, arrived at the bridge grating over the access trunk. Over the next fifteen minutes, Lomax and Pacino disassembled the bridge cockpit equipment and passed it down to Watson, who lowered it down to a second man in the access trunk. There must have been a hundred pounds of stuff up here, Pacino thought, as he took a wrench to the bolts holding the windshield in place, passing the tool, the bolts and the windshield down to Watson.

Lomax scanned the cockpit with his flashlight, finding a stray coffee cup, but otherwise it was clear. He looked at Pacino. "Take a last breath of real air, Mr. Pacino."

Pacino complied, knowing this to be a tradition in the

submarine force. He lowered himself into the bridge access trunk, looking upward as Lomax pushed shut the panels that would streamline the sail, making the bridge cockpit disappear. Finally his boots appeared in the upper opening. Pacino lowered himself out of the way. Lomax shut the upper hatch and rotated the dogs so it clamped itself locked shut.

"Check the hatch rigged for dive," he ordered Pacino, who climbed even with Lomax and checked the hatch.

"Shut and locked," Pacino said, lowering himself all the way back into the submarine. Lomax emerged down the ladder and pulled the lower hatch shut and spun the wheel to dog it shut.

"Check it," Lomax said. Lomax reached for the drain valve from the access trunk and shut it. "Check that, too."

"Hatched checked locked. Drain valve checked shut."

"Follow me," Lomax said. They hurried down the ladder and into the control room.

"Officer of the Deck," Pacino said to Romanov, "Sail and bridge access trunk rigged for dive by Mr. Lomax, checked by Mr. Pacino."

"Very well, gentlemen," Romanov said. "You have exactly eight minutes to shower, change and get back here."

Nothing could feel as good as the hot freshwater of the shower as Pacino rinsed off the seawater. He dried, ran to his stateroom and climbed into his blue at-sea coveralls, rigged with the American flag and *Vermont* patch. He hurried to the control room, arriving a few seconds before Lomax.

He and Lomax reassumed the watch, and Romanov went back to her chart table. Pacino checked the chart. They were almost on top of the Point Delta dive point.

"Well, Mr. Pacino?" the captain's voice sounded behind Pacino. "Your report?"

"Yessir, ship's ready to dive. Rig for dive made by Chief Dysart and checked by Lieutenant Junior Grade Ganghadharan with the exception of the bridge and bridge access trunk and bridge upper and lower hatch, which was rigged for dive by Mr. Lomax and checked by me—"

"JOOD, Navigator," Romanov interrupted. "Mark the dive point!"

"Sounding!" Pacino called to the navigation electronics technician of the watch.

"One five four fathoms, sir!" the petty officer called from aft.

"Captain," Pacino continued. "Ship is at the dive point, sounding is one hundred fifty-four fathoms. Request permission to dive, sir."

Seagraves nodded. "Junior Officer of the Deck, submerge the ship."

"Submerge the ship, JOOD, aye, sir," Pacino repeated back formally. "Pilot, submerge the ship to one five zero feet!"

"Submerge the ship to one five zero feet, Pilot aye," Chief Goreliki repeated. "Ordering all ahead two thirds," she reported, "and Maneuvering answers all ahead two thirds." Over the 1MC shipwide announcing circuit, her voice boomed throughout the ship.

"Dive, dive!"

She reached into the overhead and hit an alarm lever, and a loud screeching *"OOOOOO-GAAAAAAAH"* blasted out of the speakers. She spoke on the 1MC again.

"Dive, dive!"

"Copilot, open forward main ballast tank vents," she ordered. The copilot, the torpedoman chief, Nygard, repeated the order and selected the "open" selector and the confirmation button on his touch screen for the forward ballast tank vents.

Pacino stood behind the command console, his eyes on the periscope screen. He trained the view to the bow, the venting coming out of the forward ballast tank vents barely perceptible above the rolling swells.

"Venting forward," he called.

"Going to ten degree down bubble," the pilot announced. The deck, with all its rocking and rolling, started to tilt forward.

"Copilot, open aft main ballast tank vents," Goreliki ordered, and Nygard operated the touch screen buttons.

"Aft MBT vents open," he called.

Pacino trained the periscope view to dead astern. In the waves and wind, he could see vertical spray coming out of the aft vents.

"Venting aft," he said.

The deck plunged into a steeper tilt. Pacino was still holding on to the command console's safety hand-hold bar.

"Six five feet," Goreliki called.

The waves and spray had grown closer to the view.

"Sail's under," Pacino said.

"Seven zero feet, seven two."

"Scope's awash," Pacino said. "Scope's awash."

"Seven five feet."

"Scope's under," Pacino said, reaching for the selector on the console that would lower the periscope.

BOOK 2:

MODERN PIRATES
WEAR AT-SEA COVERALLS

8

Wednesday, May 11

In the flank sprint to the Caribbean, there had only been one excursion to periscope depth, at the Tropic of Cancer southeast of Nassau, Bahamas, to collapse the "fix error circle" of the ship's inertial navigation system, what Romanov called an "overgrown fucking gyro." Once Romanov knew exactly where they were, she could be confident in her navigation past the island approach to the entrance to the Windward Passage between the eastern tip of Cuba and the northwestern point of Haiti. The ship slowed down to standard speed, 15 knots, to navigate from the windward islands through the Cuba-Haiti shipping lanes and past Jamaica at "Point Whiskey," where the ship sped back up to flank speed and headed south.

From Pacino's glances at the navigation chart console before his copilot watches, and a few days later, pilot watches, they had diverged from a course toward the Panama Canal, so they were headed elsewhere. Obviously, they wouldn't go through the canal and they wouldn't be waiting to ambush someone exiting the canal, so what possible mission was this? Pacino asked at least once a watch, but still Romanov would divulge nothing about their destination. She'd stand next to Pacino and make sure there was one navigation point and only one entered beyond their immediate sailing point.

"Nav," Pacino said, glancing at his watch before assuming the pilot console seat, "where are we going? What are we doing? What's the mission?"

It had almost become their inside joke. He'd ask and Silky Romanov would give him a mysterious, teasing smile, her eyes bright, and say in a false Southern accent, "ain't sayin.'" But today she looked at him seriously and said, "after evening meal, Mr. Pacino, at nineteen hundred, there will be an op brief for the officers and SEALs. And I promise, all your eager non-qual questions shall be answered in full."

Pacino had nodded and taken a briefing from the off-going pilot of the watch, Chief Cruz, the jocular and friendly storekeeper chief.

The watch dragged on, the ship ramming through the Caribbean Sea at flank speed at five hundred feet below the waves, with nothing happening. After watch relief, Pacino went to the wardroom and studied for his qualifications, but couldn't concentrate, so he opened up the assigned NewsFiles his boss, the weapons officer, had assigned him to read, both open-source and classified, although none were higher than secret level. Pacino searched for context. There had to be a reason Spichovich would send these, but like the first batch from the XO, these seemed unrelated and random. Another update on the Russian Republic's Status-6 Poseidon / Kanyon nuclear powered, nuclear-tipped autonomous torpedo. An update on North Korea's nuclear ambitions and desire to build the sixth modification of their SLBM submarine-launched ballistic missile and test it from a modified diesel-electric submarine. Great, Pacino thought, the hostile North Korean regime arguably run by a madwoman builds a nuclear-powered ballistic missile sub, a "boomer," with unlimited range and duration. She'd be tempted to shower down doom on the U.S. west coast.

A second Iranian update about them attempting to design a nuclear reactor for a submarine, with apparent failure on that score up to the present, but there were ominous signs that the Russians were equipping an old Iranian Kilo-class diesel-electric submarine with a radical, new design of a liquid metal reactor, using the Iranians to test it. Apparently, according to the intel, it was too dangerous for the Russians to test in their vast boondocks, and they had gotten the Iranians to agree to take it to the Indian Ocean for a test run. If it worked, it would be the

Iranians to own, but odds were, the unit would explode with the yield of half of Hiroshima's energy release. But the Iranians didn't seem to care, so intense were their desires to enter the nuclear submarine club.

With all *that* going on in the world, Pacino thought, why would a "project boat" like *Vermont* be ordered on this oddball flank run toward the South American coastline? With a task force of SEAL commandos on board?

Eventually the table was set for dinner, which would be Chinese food with sesame chicken or spicy beef, brown rice, eggrolls and the supply officer's favorite, fortune cookies with custom-made fortunes he had written especially for the crew. Gangbanger's strange sense of humor was evident in some of the outrageous fortunes. Chinese night was tremendously popular with the crew, but Pacino would have been happier with a steak and potatoes. The officers at dinner were subdued and quiet, none of the usual banter going on, all of them waiting impatiently for the op brief.

Finally, after the cutlery was removed and the table cleared, the officers produced their handhelds on the table's leather-covered surface. The captain, XO and navigator got up and followed the captain forward through the door by the supply officer. Engineer Elvis Lewinsky passed a large carafe of coffee to Weapons Officer Sprocket Spichovich, who filled up and passed it to Torpedo Officer Li No, who shook his head, his cup already filled with his eclectic tea brew, the pot then passing to Communicator Easy Eisenhart, who freshened his half-full cup and passed the pot to Pacino. Pacino filled his cup and handed the pot to the SEAL XO, Grip Aquatong. Aquatong was already drinking from a large energy drink can and passed the pot to Supply Officer Gangbanger Ganghadharan, who set it on the center of the table.

The middle level of the forward compartment started at frame 87, the bulkhead between the massive reactor compartment amidships and the forward compartment's crew's mess, which was the largest open space aboard, spanning the width of the boat, with café seating style tables that could seat a group of forty, more if they crowded three to a bench seat. The messroom ended forward with a door to storage on the port side, a steep centerline staircase—called a "ladder"—going up to the upper level, and the galley on the starboard side with its long cafeteria-style tray-slider for food service to the crew. Opposite the galley along the centerline passageway was the wardroom, a combined officer's messroom, conference room and office, where the officers and SEALs officers were waiting for the operation brief.

Forward of the wardroom, there was a small room for the chief yeoman's office, adjoining the executive officer's stateroom, with a pass-through opening that the XO could open so he could talk to the yeoman—his administrative aide—without getting up and leaving his stateroom. Farther forward was the head between the XO's stateroom and the roomier captain's cabin. To starboard along the central passageway was officers' country, the three main staterooms of the department heads and the junior officers who reported to them, with their own narrow passageway leading to their staterooms and the two-hole unisex toilet and shower. Forward of officers' country and the captain's sea cabin was the control room. The layout considered that a sudden call to battlestations could empty all the officers into control in seconds without them having to dash up or down the steep staircases.

The captain held court in his stateroom with the XO seated at the aft seat of the pull-out table and navigator on the outboard seat by the door, the captain's high-backed leather command chair rolled up to the table at the forward end so he could see them both at the same time.

"So, Nav," Seagraves said, looking down at his coffee cup, then refilling it from a carafe on the table. "What are you going to tell Spichovich when he asks about the written op order? You know you don't have much of a poker face."

Romanov frowned, a slight color coming to her cheeks. "I'll tell him the truth. He's not cleared for it."

"How's that make any sense?" Quinnivan snorted. "He's cleared high enough to execute the order. How can he not be cleared to read it? You do know his other nickname, right? '4-Wall'? Fooker doesn't just roll around on his little girly bicycle.

He plays handball at an almost semi-pro level. He earned the name from beating people using all four walls—and the ceiling and floor too. I'm thinking he won't buy your bullshit."

"I'll tell him it's a multi-mission operation order and he's only got the need to know for the first mission."

Seagraves nodded at Quinnivan. "Sounds credible, XO. Still, there *is* no written op order. And we only have this one mission assigned."

"But there *is* an op order, Captain," Romanov said quickly. "It's just not aboard this ship. Or with any of us. For reasons I gather have to do with the very slight chance of us getting caught being naughty and a hostile power going through our paper and electronic business."

Seagraves nodded approvingly again at Quinnivan, obviously liking what he was hearing.

"And we were briefed by ComSubCom himself."

Vice Admiral Catardi had personally brought them into his SCIF adjoining his headquarters office inside the Commander Submarine Command complex, their briefing held with him and the CIA's Deputy Director of Operations himself and three of his direct reports.

"So, just like there's no written contract for a wedding or a marriage, it's a verbal thing witnessed by, well, witnesses."

"She makes another good point, XO," Seagraves said, but Quinnivan still shook his head.

"I don't know, Captain, I'm not sure I've ever sailed into anything remotely like this without orders. The last mission, we had a detailed op order. And the one before that."

"We *have* orders. You heard the admiral."

Seagraves nodded and downed the rest of his coffee and stood. "Well, Nav, it's showtime. Let's do this," he said. He led the way aft down the passageway, the exec following.

The officers stood when the captain entered. He waved them to seats and he and the XO sat down. Navigator Romanov hurried into the room and grabbed a remote control from the table, standing at the large flat panel screen over the supply officer's head. She clicked the remote and a large screen became filled with a chart of the Caribbean Sea.

Quinnivan spoke up. "Navigator, everyone in here cleared for this briefing?"

"Yes, XO," she said.

"Go ahead, Nav," Seagraves said, leaning back in his chair.

Romanov's pointer hovered over a spot in the sea labeled *Colombian Basin*. "Good afternoon, officers," she began. "We're here," she said, operating the screen, a red dot flashing at their position, "One hundred and seventy nautical miles north of our arrival at our destination, Point X-Ray, which we should reach early in the mid-watch, zero one hundred local time, Thursday the twelfth." The dot labeled "X" was north-northeast of a small city on the Colombian coast labeled Santa Marta. "Once at X-Ray, we'll be commencing a slow speed bow-tie barrier search pattern here, from Point X-Ray due west to Point Yankee, here." Yankee was north-northwest of Santa Marta. "The width of the bow tie pattern is twenty nautical miles. When the ship reaches Yankee, we'll turn back east and proceed at bare steerageway back to Point X-Ray."

"And what are we searching for, exactly?" Spichovich asked, his chair turned so he was directly facing the navigator, his arms crossed, a frown wrinkling his forehead. Pacino glanced at his boss, the weapons officer, whose voice had taken on an unfamiliar edge. In Pacino's short dealings with his boss, Lieutenant Commander Spichovich had been a complete gentleman, a friendly and sensitive superior, asking Pacino what he could do to speed along Pacino's qualifications, sitting with Pacino, Eisenhart and the sonar chief, Albanese, as they "turned over" command of the sonar division from Eisenhart to Pacino, the turnover completing last night as Eisenhart, Pacino and Spichovich had visited the captain and XO in the captain's stateroom to report the turnover. As of last night, Pacino was officially the sonar officer and Eisenhart was officially the communications officer, or "communicator."

Romanov turned from the screen to address the room. "Gentlemen, welcome to *Operation Bigfoot*. That's what we're searching for. 'Bigfoot' because like the monster of myth, everyone has heard about it, but no one has ever actually seen it. Until now." She clicked the remote and the next slide came up. The wardroom's officers immediately began talking and pointing.

"Quiet down, everyone. The photograph you're looking at is from 1916. This is the submarine *L-4*, a diesel-electric submarine designed by our good friends at Electric Boat, about 90 years before they were acquired by DynaCorp, and built by their shipyard in Quincy, Massachusetts." Romanov clicked the remote, the next slide showing the L-class submarine in profile and in plan, the drawing showing the interior compartments. Below the schematic diagram, a blur of statistics were displayed.

"Let's review some things about this submarine—a miraculous ocean-going American submarine—built well over a century ago. 457 tons surfaced, 557 tons submerged. 167 feet length overall. Seventeen-and-a-half feet in beam. Two NELSECO diesels, 1300 horsepower total. Two Electro Dynamic main motors, 800 horsepower total. Two bays of 60-cell batteries. Speed, 14 knots surfaced, ten-and-a-half submerged. Range, 4300 nautical miles surfaced at seven knots, 150 nautical miles submerged at five knots, which, officers, is a submerged endurance of thirty hours. From a boat designed in the year of our Lord nineteen fourteen."

Spichovich spoke again, his voice dripping with sarcasm. "So, Nav, we're going back in time to fight Diesel Boat Eddie in his 1914 L-class diesel submarine? A World War I diesel sub named," he coughed sarcastically, "'*Bigfoot*'?"

"Not exactly," Romanov said, her cheeks reddening slightly. "This is a narcotics smuggling submarine. The narco-subs have progressed tremendously, but they've mostly just been speed boats with the topside flattened out. Ten years ago, the Medellin cartel built a small diesel-electric submarine with a snorkel mast and a diesel that could smuggle ten tons of cocaine, but it had trouble in the open seas, balance trouble, and it had problems trying to submerge, even more trying to surface. It sank a few times, each time killing the four-man crew. They kept resurrecting it, but eventually it sank in deep water, killing the crew, and three hundred million dollars' worth of product was lost. Designing a submarine is not for the inexperienced. We think the Colombian Barranquilla cartel tried their hand and started off with a blank sheet of paper and started designing a special purpose submarine, but like their competitors, their prototypes were ridiculously underpowered, or heavy, or unbalanced. Or they simply sank. The cartel finally realized that reinventing the wheel made no sense. So they took a look at past designs, designs they could get their hands on from open sources. Their shipbuilders found the detailed plans for the *L-4* and visited the actual submarine, rusting away in a Massachusetts coast museum. They had just enough unclassified data from dusty old Navy archives and DynaCorp file rooms to be able to build a new one.

"For secrecy, they assembled it in the hold of a cargo freighter lying-to in Port Saint Marta. They've fitted it out with modern Edison battery Giga-Packs, with battery power density four times what the 1914 versions had, with half the weight and less than half the volume, and modern diesel engines, with twice the fuel efficiency, so they could maintain the same range with half the volume of fuel. Which makes for even more space available for cocaine. With a ten-ton load of coke, the most anyone's been able to smuggle in a narco-sub, you make upwards of three hundred million dollars. This ship can transport over fifty tons, perhaps even sixty. That's over one point six *billion* dollars. And no depth control or instability problems with this boat—it was a success over a hundred years ago, and they have the detailed specs. They just copied it. We've been looking for it ever since our good friends in the intelligence services got wind of it. But no one has ever even gotten close to this thing. We think this ship has made at least half a dozen successful smuggling runs already, and with that load of coke, the cartel will corner the market."

"Wait, we're doing *drug interdiction*," Spichovich asked, incredulously. "You sent us down here at flank speed to, what, intercept and sink a fucking *narco*-sub?"

"No," Romanov said dryly. "We were sent down here at flank speed to *steal* it."

The wardroom burst into loud crosstalk. Pacino looked over at Tiny Tim Fishman and Grip Aquatong, who were smiling in pleasure. Grip reached out and fist-bumped Fishman.

"Quiet, people," Quinnivan said from the aft end of the room.

"This makes no sense," Spichovich said, acid in his voice, "why would they replicate a World War I sub where there are a thousand more advanced subs they could copy? A late-flight World War II German U-boat, for one."

"The L-class is perfect for them," Romanov said, staying calm, only her slight blush a sign that Spichovich's harassing questions were bothering her. "The World War II subs could be twice this size or even triple the size. Too cumbersome, too difficult to hide, too long to build and too expensive. This one could well be called 'Goldilocks' instead of 'Bigfoot.' It's not too big, not too small, but just right. Small enough to be assembled in the hold of the cargo mother ship, which was modified to have under-hull opening doors and a crane mechanism to lower the sub into the water unnoticed. So for now, gentlemen, this is the state of the art narcotics smuggling submarine. It has a test depth of 200 feet, deep enough to avoid any Coast Guard activity. And you guys will enjoy this. The boat has fully functional torpedo tubes—not to attack with weapons, but to offload the drugs. They have neutrally buoyant torpedo shaped cargo containers holding the coke, and when they get to the Florida coast, they rendezvous with the coastal boats and shoot the cargo out the tubes, which the receiving boats catch in nets. The L-class stays submerged the entire time, then sneaks back to Santa Marta, Colombia, for another load. We think that her maiden voyage paid for the submarine's construction ten times over. Multiple trips? That, gentlemen, is a *business plan*. Questions?"

"So," Quinnivan said, "tell us more about stealing this sub. How do we do it? I'm assuming this is the reason the SEALs are embarked."

Seagraves broke in. "Let's ask our newest non-qual junior officer, who will be the approach officer for this op so that he can fulfill the requirements of his qual card. Mr. Pacino, knowing what you know now, and seeing that we have our SEAL friends here, how do we hijack a diesel-electric sub?"

Pacino shook his head, feeling warmth come to his cheeks.

"I'd have to say, force it to the surface. Sneak up under it, blow ballast, bang into her undersides and bring her up to the surface. Then the SEALs open a hatch, toss down a nerve gas grenade and make off with the sub."

Fishman laughed and smiled. "That's actually not half bad, Captain. Not very subtle, but not bad."

The other officers were rolling their eyes, shaking their heads or making dismissive noises.

"No, Mr. Pacino," Seagraves said. "Do you want to try again?"

Pacino shrugged. "I've got nothing, Cap'n."

"What about you, Weapons Officer?" Seagraves looked over at Spichovich. "You have a better plan?"

Spichovich nodded. "Gentlemen and Navigator, back during the Cold War, one of our attack submarines was trailing a Soviet Akula nuclear attack sub that had arrived on a top-secret patrol in the western Atlantic, right off our shores, coming to see if he could himself shadow a missile sub leaving Kings Bay or one of our attack subs leaving Norfolk or Groton. The incident is still highly classified, but the basics are that our boat managed to get too close to the Russian at an odd angle and got his towed array sonar completely wrapped around the Russian's screw. With his screw fouled, the Rooskie came to a stop, then surfaced to see what happened. There he is, on a super-secret hush-hush covert mission off American shores, and he surfaces in broad daylight, and a dozen members of his crew—probably a bunch of smelly A-Gangers," he said, shooting a smirk at Dankleff, the head of the auxiliary mechanics, "come out of the hatch and stare dumbly aft trying to see what happened. Eventually divers got equipped and went over the side."

The towed array was a thick cable a shiplength long towed by a steel wire rope that could be a mile long, intended to process high frequency narrowband sonar signals, the cable length intended to get the array far away from the noise generated by the sub streaming the array. The cable of it wrapping around a ship's screw would completely immobilize it, as would the thick diameter array itself.

"Without propulsion," Spichovich continued, "a submarine would have to have *perfect* trim and a *fantastic* hovering system to avoid sinking or popping to the surface. There *is* no standard operating procedure for a fouled screw, just common sense to use the engines at maximum revs to try to break whatever is fouling the screw, and if that doesn't work, come to the surface and send over divers to get rid of the fisherman's net or whatever it was that got wrapped around the screw."

"Nicely done, Weps," Seagraves said. "So, Mr. Pacino, what do you think now?"

"Sir," Pacino began, "I'd come up beside the L-class when she's steaming submerged, lock out the commandos, and get them to wrap a net of some type around the L-class' screw."

"Hopefully without getting *ourselves* wrapped around the screw," Fishman said.

Pacino continued. "That's going to be tough at five knots, though."

Aquatong put his hands behind his head and grinned. "That's what we do for a living, Patch. That's why we get the big bucks."

"So then what?" Seagraves asked Romanov.

"Well," Romanov said. "The sub surfaces. A hatch pops open and one or more crewmen come out. The SEALs use non-lethal weapons to take out the crewmen and take over the submarine, or in the worst case, use lethal force. We augment them with a crew of two of our qualified officers so they can operate the boat and steam it to Andros Island, Bahamas, at the Navy/DynaCorp AUTEC test range, where the CIA will be waiting to study the boat."

Pacino raised his hand self-consciously, wondering if he'd be ridiculed for acting like he was a second-grader trying to get the teacher's attention.

Romanov smiled warmly at him. "Yes, you in the back, Mr. Pacino, you have a question?"

"Yes, ma'am," Pacino said. "This target is diesel-electric. We'll hear him when he's on his diesels—assuming he can snorkel—but when he's submerged on his batteries, he's going to disappear into the ocean background noise."

"Spoken like the sonar officer he is," Spichovich said harshly, his annoyance again directed at the navigator. Pacino glanced at the weapons officer. Obviously, there was some beef between the two department heads.

"He'll come out of port in the belly of this freighter," Romanov said, clicking to the next slide, showing a photograph of a fairly large container ship, the slide after that showing the ship in a schematic drawing in profile view. The hold below the waterline had a submarine stowed in it, dotted lines marking underwater panels of the ship's hull that could be removed to allow the submarine to submerge under the freighter. "This design partially replicates the CIA-commissioned Howard Hughes' ship *Glomar Explorer,* which was built in the 1970s to recover a Soviet submarine off the seafloor and pull its hull into the hold of the ship, but in this case, the submarine is assembled and constructed *inside* the freighter, and when it is ready to launch, leaves the freighter's hold and disappears for the Florida coast. When this happens, there will be a thousand transients as divers open up the under-hold panels to allow the sub to leave—"

"Divers?" Spichovich asked. "Divers in this crystal-clear Caribbean seawater? Do you understand that if we're close enough, they'll see us visually? What happens to this mission then?"

Romanov inclined her head, her jaw clamped. "We'll stay a clear distance from the freighter when he's preparing to launch the L-class, for that exact reason. Once the L-class clears the freighter and makes his way north, we believe he will be submerged and snorkeling to charge his batteries. Once the operation has progressed to the point that the L-class is under the control of the SEALs, we'll lock out the two officers who will take the boat back to AUTEC. Narco-sub submerges and heads north. We submerge and clear datum. The entire incident? It never happened. We were never there. Any other questions?"

Spichovich waved his hand. "Can we see the op order?" The navigator opened her mouth to speak, but before she could, Spichovich put his palm out and said, "You know what—I don't even want to know. But tell me this—why wouldn't the L-class leave the freighter's hull with a full battery charge, then just steam silently away?"

"Intelligence on the L-class says it can get shorepower when its mother ship is tied up at the pier but not once the freighter puts to sea. It's a short sail to the hundred-fathom curve, but still, unrigging the bracing inside the hold takes time, there could be problems or issues getting the hold doors open, and that entire time, the sub is on internal power on her batteries, and she isn't rigged to snorkel inside the hold. That would be like warming up your car in the garage with the garage door closed. I know," she said, as Spichovich raised his hand, "that would be easy to fix with a ventilation system or an exhaust plenum to get the diesel exhaust out of the hold, or a shorepower connection inside the freighter, but things are not yet that sophisticated. There's obviously plenty of money to make ship alterations, but maybe the profits from the previous trips are paying for production expansions. Plus, if it works—if it ain't broke—don't fix it."

The engineer spoke up then. "What about the crew of the *Bigfoot*? What do we do with them?"

"Commander Fishman?" Romanov asked.

The SEAL commander shrugged. "Hostages create trouble. There's the risk of them escaping their restraints and thwarting the mission and killing us or sinking the boat. And hostages consume manhours. Someone has to keep an eye on them, allow them to use the bathroom, give them food, water. You need one person on our team for every three hostages to be safe. That's a 24-hour thing, so three men standing one eight-hour watch a day or two four-hour watches a day. We don't have six extra people for this mission. So we either kill them or leave them."

"Leave them?" Lewinsky asked.

"Put them in a raft with some rations and water and leave them to be rescued. Or apprehended and arrested."

"Any other questions?"

Every officer in the room had a question, it seemed, until they reached the limits of what was known about the L-class. Seagraves stood, thanked the navigator, and he and the XO left the room. Romanov gathered up her tablet and shot a glare at

Spichovich, shook her ponytail off her shoulder and stormed out of the room. Pacino looked at Spichovich, who shrugged as if there were no explanation for his issues with the navigator.

"My advice, Mr. Pacino? We'll be on a barrier search. This could go on for days. When we eventually detect this guy, we could be at battlestations rigged for ultra-quiet for hours, even days, with no sleep and the only food a plate of peanut butter sandwiches with coffee cups of bug juice to wash it down. So, while we search and wait, I suggest you get as much sleep as you can."

Pacino nodded and left, taking the steep stairs to the upper level and around two passageway corners to his stateroom. He hung up his coveralls and climbed into the bunk and tried to sleep, but his mind wouldn't stop spinning about the operation and his part in it. Approach officer. Every eye in the control room would be on him, from the captain on down.

After an hour of anxiety, he finally sank into sleep and a dream about carrying a hunter's rifle into thick woods, searching for something that never appeared.

9

Thursday, May 12

Pacino had drifted into a deep sleep, coming out of it abruptly as the messenger of the watch violently pulled his bunk curtain aside, stuck his head in, shook Pacino's shoulder and whispered intensely, "Man battlestations!"

"What time is it?" Pacino asked groggily.

"Zero five hundred, sir. Come on, out of the bunk."

Pacino got hastily out of the bunk and found his coveralls and sneakers, yawning, the grogginess making him wish he hadn't taken Spichovich's advice and stayed awake. He'd kill for a steaming cup of coffee, he thought, taking the ladder down to the middle level and making his way to the crowded control room. He felt his nerves vibrating the way they had just before he'd driven the ship out. But that had just been shiphandling. This was a real operation. A combat operation, even if the opponent were unarmed. Or armed with only shotguns, rifles and pistols, not missiles or torpedoes.

He walked into the control room and walked up to the midwatch officer of the deck, Lieutenant Varney, at the command console. The messenger of the watch, the same petty officer who'd awakened Pacino, arrived with a large tray of coffee cups. Pacino took one gratefully, the brew hot enough to burn his tongue. For the next five minutes, Varney walked Pacino through the initial contact with Master Two, the cargo ship. The main target, the L-class submarine, would be designated "Master One" when it emerged out of the belly of the cargo ship. The cargo ship was making loud transients, and it was considered likely this was the beginning of the operation to launch the narco-submarine, but the cargo ship was still steaming slowly northward out of Port Santa Marta and hadn't slowed yet, and they all believed it would need to stop to be able to launch the submarine.

Romanov asked a few quiet questions. She would be battlestations officer of the deck while Pacino would be the junior officer of the deck *and* the "approach officer." During battlestations, the XO would take up a roving position behind the battlecontrol and weapon control consoles, his job to get the magical, mystical holy grail of information called "the solution," which was the distance to their main target and his heading and speed. If one knew the solution, one could easily put a salvo of torpedoes right on top of where he'd be in the near future—assuming the target didn't suddenly change course or speed—a very bad event known as a "zig." The XO's position was called the "firecontrol coordinator" or simply "coordinator."

The "approach officer" was usually the captain, who rode herd over the firecontrol coordinator, the weapons officer and the officer of the deck. That holy trinity always spoke up just before a weapon launch, the coordinator responsible for the solution, the weapons officer for the health and settings of the weapons to be employed and the officer of the deck for the behavior of the ship in the moments prior to launch. For Pacino to be acting as approach officer seemed insane, but this was how this was done in the force, he knew. Thrust the maximum amount of responsibility and demands on the non-qual and harden him to be qualified and "heavy," the submariner's term for knowledgeable. He consoled himself that the captain would be right behind him, as would the navigator, in the event he made a critical mistake.

Pacino nodded at Varney. "I relieve you, sir," he said.

Varney faced Captain Seagraves. "Captain, I've been properly relieved of the officer of the deck watch by Lieutenant Commander Romanov and Lieutenant junior grade Pacino."

"Very well," Seagraves said quietly.

Varney hurried to the starboard side attack center console nearest Quinnivan, "pos one," where the officer most adept at tracking contacts sat and, dancing with the computer and the sonar data, originated his best guess at the solution to the target. Lieutenant Lomax at pos two would compete with Varney, coming up with his own suggestion of the solution. Lieutenant Eisenhart joined them at pos three, his console usually selected to the geographic plot, which showed the contrasting solutions of pos one and pos two so the captain and XO could see which made more sense. Absent an active sonar pulse, using passive listen-only sonar required some intuitive guessing about what the contact was doing, but emitting active sonar gave away their position and intent, and was not stealthy. It contradicted *Vermont*'s battle cry of *It never happened, we were never there.*

Pacino took up his position at the command console, its large flat panel screen tuned to the navigation chart display, since the periscope was retracted and switched off. He reached down with two fingers and blew up the scale of their position shown in blue, north of Santa Marta, with the exiting freighter's position blinking in blood red.

"Your headset, Approach Officer," Romanov said from over his shoulder. He gave her a look of gratitude and strapped on the headset, only one ear covered to monitor the phone circuits, the other open to the sounds of the room around him. "Better darken the room so we can see the displays."

"Pilot," Pacino called to Lieutenant Dankleff at the ship control console, "rig control for black!"

The lights went out in the control room, the room lit only by the sonar display consoles on the port side, the firecontrol and weapon control consoles to starboard, the command and navigation console displays and the large screen periscope monitors forward port and starboard.

The navigation electronics technician suddenly piped up from the aft port corner of control. "Approach Officer, mark sunrise!"

"Very well, Nav ET," Pacino said. With the seascape brightening, it meant a greater chance any divers helping the cargo ship launch the narco-sub might see them.

"Approach Officer," Romanov said, "make sure battlestations are fully manned."

"Coordinator," Pacino barked at the XO. "Are we manned?"

Quinnivan spun to face him, coming to attention as if Pacino were the captain himself, and said formally, "Approach Officer, battlestations are manned."

"Very well, Coordinator," Pacino said, trying to force his voice to be deep, loud and commanding, hopefully not wavering from his intense nervousness, a hint of absurdity occurring to him that his boss' boss was treating him like a superior officer.

"Ready for your speech?" Romanov asked. He nodded, trying to remember all the tactics drilled into him by the navigator, hoping he looked cooler than he felt. He cleared his throat self-consciously.

"Attention in the firecontrol party," Pacino announced to the crowd in the room and the phone circuits, "my intention is to parallel the slow course of the freighter, designated Master Two, who is on course north, speed four knots, range, one thousand yards, maintaining our present depth at one two zero feet. We will hold station with Master Two as he slows, stops and prepares to open his hold and lower and release the target diesel submarine, Master One. We are at risk at that moment of being seen by divers in this clear water from any floodlights inside the cargo ship and the early morning sunlight, if the divers exit the freighter's hold, so we'll hang back, more deeply submerged so we won't be counterdetected, but hovering close to Master Two, with both scopes raised. I will be controlling number one scope while the Coordinator and pos one will control the number two scope. Number one will display on the forward starboard display, number two on the forward port.

"Once the noise of the hold doors opening fades, we will come shallow and trail Master One until he's clear of the freighter. We don't want the freighter to see the *Bigfoot* surfacing and having trouble, or else it would heave-to and render aid. We'll need to commence the operation to force the sub to the surface as soon as the freighter is over the horizon.

"Before Master One secures snorkeling on his diesels and goes deep, we'll match his speed and take station slightly ahead of him at periscope depth so we can fine-tune our position. Being ahead of him gives the SEALs the advantage of the current moving them toward the *Bigfoot* hull. At my call the SEAL force will lock out with their propulsor units and drive to the hull of Master One. We will continue steaming beside the target but fading slightly astern of him in case there's a failure and one or more SEALs need to return to own-ship. The SEALs will deploy the net to stop Master One's screw. Expectations are that Master One will go dead in the water and surface. SEALs will conduct tactical steps to overcome the crew and take command of Master One on the surface. We will enter phase two of the op at that time. Are there any questions?"

"I have a question," the weapons officer, Spichovich said, from his position at the weapons control console, the aft end of the consoles of the AN/BYG-1 battlecontrol system. "What if Master One doesn't use his diesels? What if we're wrong about him needing to charge batteries and he leaves the freighter on batteries and his main motor and goes quieter than a hole in the ocean?"

Pacino looked at Romanov. As the brand-new sonar officer, Pacino had spoken briefly to Chief Albanese, who was not optimistic he could track a diesel sub on batteries. *All the exercises we did with NATO diesel boats,* he'd explained, *maybe one time in three we could track them, but most of the time they vanish like ghosts. A diesel boat on batteries? All you have are transient noises and maybe a slight thrum from his main propulsion motor. Otherwise, those bastards are invisible.*

Romanov spoke up. "He'll be going slow enough on batteries that we can keep up with him with periscopes raised," she said. "If sonar has trouble tracking him, we'll be able to see his snorkel mast. Odds are he will be below five knots, perhaps only going three to conserve battery power. His max submerged speed is just over seven knots and we can sail with a periscope deployed up to ten knots before it risks getting snapped off in the slipstream. Anyone else?"

The control room was pin-drop silent.

"Be watching for The Glitch," Romanov said quietly in his free ear. She'd explained that *The Glitch* was that first thing that went wrong on an operation, something that would take it off the battle plan. And once off-plan, they would all be improvising.

The most likely glitch was that the *Bigfoot* wouldn't snorkel on his diesels but would slip away from the launching freighter quietly on batteries, and in the worst case, vanished into the noise of the ocean and got away from them. Which would lead to mission failure.

"Coordinator, Sonar," Albanese's voice came over the headset. "Master Two zig, turn count going down. Master Two is stopping."

"Very well," Pacino said. "Pilot, all stop and prepare to hover."

"All stop, Pilot aye," Dankleff replied, "and Maneuvering answers, all stop, preparing to hover, sir."

"Pilot, mark speed one knot."

"Mark speed one knot, Pilot, aye, speed two knots." A second later, Dankleff announced, "Speed one knot, sir."

"Pilot," Pacino ordered, "engage the hovering system and hover at present depth."

"Hover at present depth, Pilot, aye, and commencing hovering, depth one two zero feet, sir."

This was it, Pacino thought. He looked down at his right hand. It was trembling. Pacino gripped the command console safety handrail, hoping no one noticed.

In the lockout trunk, Lieutenant junior grade Grip Aquatong tightened the strap of his full-face helmet and adjusted the tactical camera on top of the helmet. His integrated helmet included the air from his rebreather and communications interface, with a small heads-up display on the upper portion of his visor screen. He looked over at similarly clad Commander Tiny Tim Fishman, who nodded and gave him a thumbs-up sign.

To the port side, Senior Chief Scooter Tucker-Santos was readying the four Mark 17 Mod 2 propulsion units, small devices resembling a scuba tank but that had a powerful battery, a shrouded propulsor and motorcycle handlebars protruding aft of the propulsor. On the starboard side, Petty Officer First Class Swan Oneida was breaking out their weapons, multiple Mark 6 Mod 1 electrical shock directional weapons, each one able to fire enough current and voltage at a person to kill him if dialed up high enough, the unit functioning something like a civilian Taser, but far more powerful with a much longer range, but which also worked underwater.

Oneida had assembled four M4A1 carbines, fully automatic 5.56 mm rifles, each encased in a waterproof casing that with one click on one of several quick-release buttons would disconnect the casing and drop it to the deck. Oneida passed out the Mark 6 tactical directional shock units and the encapsulated M4A1s while Tucker-Santos equipped each man with a Mark 17 propulsion unit.

"Nothing to do now but wait for the word to flood down and open the upper hatch," Fishman said to the men. "Go over your assignments to yourselves. What's the rule, Grip?"

Aquatong answered up, belting out, "Fucking up is *not* an option, boss!"

"That's right, gentlemen."

This was always the worst part of any mission, Fishman thought, the interminable wait for the action to start. There was no doubt, if one hoped to succeed in the military, he'd be well advised to get good at the art of waiting.

Perfect, Pacino thought, as he looked at the display of the optronics of periscope number one. The high-definition image was a blurry blue of the Caribbean Sea, but visible at a high angle overhead was the underside of the freighter.

"Coordinator, Sonar," Chief Albanese said, "loud transients from Master Two."

The freighter would be opening his hull doors any minute.

"You're too close," Romanov coached quietly. "Take us down."

"Pilot, make your depth two hundred feet."

"Two hundred feet, Pilot, aye, and descending to two hundred feet, sir."

The image in the screen lost focus but was still visible in the sea, the light having faded some with the depth.

"Two hundred feet, sir," Dankleff announced.

"Very well, Pilot."

"Coordinator, Sonar, very loud transients from Master Two."

He was either opening his hold doors or getting ready to, Pacino thought. Pacino strained to look at the periscope image.

"Coordinator, Sonar, transients continue."

They all waited for what seemed an eternity, until Albanese announced, "Master Two has gone quiet."

"Listen for a turn count," Quinnivan ordered Albanese.

Seagraves shot a look at Romanov and gestured with his thumb—unmistakably ordering, *get us up.*

"Let's get closer," Romanov said. "To hell with the freighter's divers, we *can't* lose this target."

"Pilot, make your depth one hundred feet," Pacino called. Dankleff acknowledged, but for Pacino, the only thing that existed in the world was the image on his periscope display screen. He zoomed the view closer until he could see it in the blue haze of the ocean. Discernable in the distance was the underside of a ship with cargo bay doors dropped open, bright lights from floodlights inside the hull shining on a large metal claw device coming slowly deeper in the water, the claw holding a shape. The claw exactly resembled the claw named "Clementine" used in *Glomar Explorer*'s Project Azorian / Project Jennifer to pull that sunken Soviet "Golf" submarine, *K-129*, off the sea bottom decades before. This, Pacino thought, had to be the disadvantage of declassifying military secrets. God alone knew how bad actors would use information developed by the military and intelligence community. The black blur in the claw had to be the L-class narco-sub. *Bigfoot*. In the flesh.

"Coordinator, Sonar, slight transients again. Mechanical in nature. Scraping noises."

"Listen up for a main motor startup," Quinnivan advised over Albanese's shoulder.

Pacino waited, hearing his heart beating thunderously in his chest, his pulse throbbing in his neck.

"Transients stop and we've got something, something rotating very slowly, believe it's a turn count," Albanese announced, one hand over his right ear as if that would help him hear better. "Oh, out-fucking-*standing*," Albanese said, half to himself, his voice sounding oddly happy.

"What is it?" Seagraves demanded.

"I've got a turn count," Albanese said, "bearing to Master One at zero-four-zero, making three zero RPM and he's got a sound problem, Captain, a bearing rub or a ding on his screw, we're hearing it every revolution." Albanese spun around from his triple-screened master sonar console. "We'll be able to track him when he's on his batteries with this, sir."

Quinnivan, Seagraves and Romanov crowded the command console, surrounding Pacino and the periscope display.

"He won't be able to fix that underway," Quinnivan said, one hand over his boom mike, a crooked grin on his face.

"It's like a lottery win, Skipper," Romanov said, smiling. For an instant Pacino stared at her, her usually frowning, dour face erupting into a shining beauty when she smiled.

"Let's get ready to trail him," Seagraves commanded.

"Coordinator, Sonar, Master One is making transients."

"What is it, Sonar," Quinnivan barked, turning from the command console.

"Could be, wait … wait, yes, we have a diesel engine startup at zero-four-one, bearing to Master One."

"Take it up to PD, Approach Officer," Seagraves said, leaning close to the periscope display.

"Periscope depth, aye, Captain. Pilot, vertical rise to six eight feet!"

"Better make it six four," Romanov said. "We're not sweating periscope exposure. We don't even know if Master One has a periscope himself—yet. And the freighter isn't a threat any longer. It's not like he's going to radio his coast guard people to report his illicit drug boat's being followed."

"Pilot, make your depth six four feet!"

"Six four, Pilot, aye, depth eight zero. Seven five. Seven zero."

The periscope display showed the undersides of the waves approaching. This view seemed bizarre to Pacino. The underside of the water surface was an oddly shimmering silver, like looking through the reverse side of a mirror. A wrinkly mirror. Some waves admitted slight glimpses of blue sky and white clouds above. At the pilot's call of seventy feet, a wave trough approached and for just a split second the periscope view became foamy and blurry.

"Scope's breaking," Pacino called.

"Seven zero feet, sir, coming up."

"You're *sluggish*, Pilot, get us up," Pacino said, more out of instinct or perhaps unconscious imitation of the officers on *Piranha* than his own intention.

"Six nine feet, sir."

The periscope view went through two cycles of foam splashing over the view, then cleared, the view blurry from the unit being wet, but it dried rapidly and the view became crystal clear.

"Scope's clear," Pacino said.

"Six seven, six six, six five feet, sir, and six four feet."

"Very well, Pilot."

"Pos One, do a surface safety sweep," Quinnivan ordered Lieutenant Varney at the pos one master console of the BYG-1 battlecontrol system. The periscope view of unit two rotated quickly on the display mounted in the port forward corner of the room, the intention to identify any close contacts missed by sonar that posed a danger of collision. The blur of motion showed only the freighter, Master Two. After the sweep, the view zeroed in on the freighter. On its rusty stern, the Panamanian flag flew over block white letters spelling *MV SARGASSO CAUSEWAY.*

"Approach Officer, we have a name for Master Two," Quinnivan said. "The motor vessel *Sargasso Causeway* bears one-six-five, range, three divisions in low power, angle-on-the-bow port sixty."

"Get a laser range," Romanov ordered Pacino. "Odds are the freighter won't know what it is even if he sees it."

"Coordinator, get a laser range on Master Two," Pacino said to Quinnivan, who acknowledged quickly and repeated it to Varney on pos one.

"Range twelve thousand five hundred yards," Lieutenant Varney, the pos one operator, reported. The freighter was six nautical miles away. At this range, the *Vermont*'s periscopes would be as good as invisible.

"Coordinator, Sonar, Transients, Master Two," Albanese

said. "He may be rigging in the hull doors."

Pacino looked up at the number one scope's display. Interesting, he thought. *Sargasso Causeway.* It was as if the owners of the freighter were consciously or unconsciously revealing their intention to smuggle. He returned his concentration to his periscope display, trained to the bearing of the target, Master One, the L-class, the *Bigfoot.* For a moment he wondered what the owners called *it.* A number? The name of a wife or sweetheart?

There, he thought, a slight wake boiling up from a pole extending vertically several feet over the wave crests—no, two poles. He must have a periscope in addition to his snorkel mast.

"I have Master One on visual," Pacino said. "Showing extensions of two masts." He zoomed as far in as the unit could magnify. In 96x, the view bounced slightly despite gyro-stabilization and post image computer processing, and it was blurry, but still, that higher mast unmistakably resembled the old-fashioned attack periscopes of the diesel submarines of fifty years before. The other mast had a wider cylinder on top of it, which must have been the head valve for the snorkel, which should shut if the mast suffered a wave rolling on top of it, preventing the induction piping to the diesel suction from pulling in water and damaging the diesel—and flooding the submarine. No doubt, this submarine was as sophisticated as Navigator Romanov had promised. Pacino watched his display. He could see smoke boiling out of the ocean slightly behind the *Bigfoot*'s masts. Exhaust fumes. Evidently, they didn't use low-smoke diesel fuel.

Pacino took the magnification down to 8x to see if he could still detect the masts, and he could make them out, the rooster tail of the motion and smoke trail making it easier.

"Coordinator, Sonar, turn count, Master One, four zero RPM on one four-bladed screw. He's headed out of town."

"Get in trail," Romanov ordered.

"Pilot, all ahead one third, turns for three knots, steer course three five zero."

"All ahead one third, turns for three, steer three five zero, Pilot aye, and Maneuvering answers, one third, turns for three knots."

For the next ten minutes Pacino concentrated on falling in behind the L-class target, close enough he could make out the periscope and snorkel mast at 8x magnification but far enough away that Master One probably wouldn't see his own periscopes. Pacino wondered what *Bigfoot* would do if he did see the scopes. Probably secure snorkeling and go deep on batteries and try to evade—at least that's what Pacino would do if it were his call. He added RPM a few turns at a time to close in the range, then dropped revolutions off as he seemed too close, all the while coached by Romanov. For those ten minutes, Pacino felt a triumph, that this mission was going well. Soon the freighter would be distant and over the horizon behind them and the mission of the SEALs could begin. And then the bad news came in.

"Coordinator, Sonar, loud transients have stopped from Master Two, but I now have a turn count on Master Two and he's making one two zero RPM on two three-bladed screws. Master Two is speeding up and turning, bearing one-six-eight. Coordinator, Master Two is getting louder. I believe Master Two is steaming toward us."

Quinnivan grabbed Varney's shoulder. "Pos One, turn the scope to Master Two to the south!"

There in the port forward control room overhead, the number two periscope view showed Master Two, the *Sargasso Causeway,* with a large bow wave forming. "Observation, Master Two, number one scope, bearing mark," Quinnivan said, leaning over Varney's Pos One console. "Range, mark, four divisions in high power, angle on the bow port five. Take a laser range."

"Now two four zero RPM," Albanese reported.

The freighter was approaching at full throttle.

"Bearing one six five," Varney reported from Pos One. "Range thirteen thousand two hundred yards."

Quinnivan looked over at Pacino, Seagraves and Romanov. "He's either seen us and is coming to investigate, or perhaps worse, he's going to steam beside the submarine and escort it out of the area, maybe all the way to Miami. Which would put a damper on our plans with our good friends, the SEALs. If they tried to force Master One to surface in sight of the freighter, the freighter would render aid. And for all we know, start a shootout with the SEALs."

"The freighter has never done this on prior voyages," Romanov said dejectedly. "He's always turned around and gone back to port, leaving the narco-sub alone. Why is this different?"

There it was, Pacino thought. *The Glitch.* Maybe the freighter had seen Vermont's twin periscopes and grown alarmed, and was either coming to investigate or their procedures had changed, and now the revised base plan had them escorting the narco-sub.

Without conscious thought, Pacino looked at the senior officers and said breathlessly, "Let's toss a Tomahawk Mod EMP Kakivak cruise missile at the freighter. That'll shut him down dead in the water without hurting the submarine."

A Mod EMP Kakivak was a "NNEMP," a non-nuclear electromagnetic pulse weapon that would fry the electronics and major electrical components of anyone or anything in its blast radius. Pacino had encountered its detailed specifications in the course of this qualification studies. *Vermont* was loaded out with two of them, despite no one expecting to use them.

For a long moment, Lieutenant Commander Romanov stared at Pacino, then found her voice. "Are you *insane*? You can't just launch a *warshot* cruise missile at a civilian freighter!"

Pacino took in the room. Every eye was on him. Quinnivan looked like he'd just been slapped, his face turning red. Varney, the pos one battlecontrol console operator, looked at Lomax on pos two, then at Eisenhart on pos three. Ganghadharan, at the navigation console, shared a look with both of them. Pacino thought for a moment he heard Lomax murmur to Eisenhart, *Jesus, check out the big brass balls of non-qual Pacino.*

It was Weapons Officer Spichovich at the weapon control console, the WCC pos one, who broke the moment of silence.

"Captain," he said, addressing Seagraves, who had put his hand to his chin and stared at the deck, deep in thought, "I have Mod EMP Kakivaks in the number two VPT in tubes eleven and twelve. Recommend spinning up both, sir."

Quinnivan turned from the periscope display at Varney's pos one. "Master Two is making way, fast, maybe twelve to fifteen knots, and his angle-on-the-bow is narrowing. We're on the same bearing from him as Master One, and he's coming straight toward the both of us. If he aims to escort the *Bigfoot* out of the area, he's sighting in her periscope and snorkel mast. Which means he might also be seeing ours. Recommend dipping scopes."

Romanov hissed at Pacino. *"Down scopes!"*

Pacino hit the hydraulic control levers to lower both periscopes. "Scopes one and two coming down," he said to the room.

Seagraves glanced at Romanov and Quinnivan. "Mr. Pacino has a point," he said, his baritone voice quiet and confident. "An EMP *would* shut down the freighter. And he's not going to complain about it to the authorities. And we buy time. None of his radios will work to call for a tow. He's near enough to shipping lanes he'd eventually be spotted and rescued. Worst thing that can happen is we fry the electronics of an innocent passer-by. Sonar, report all contacts."

"Captain, the only contacts held by sonar," Albanese said crisply, "Are Master Two, bearing one-six-zero, distant, and Master One, bearing three five zero, close range."

"Captain," Romanov said, her voice uncertain, "that EMP could knock out the *Bigfoot*. And us."

"After we launch, we'll take her deep," Seagraves said. "If it paralyzes Master One, we'll deal with that at the time."

Pacino spoke up. "We could place the detonation a few thousand yards on the other side of Master Two, opening the range to us and Master One, but still close enough to the freighter to shut him down."

Seagraves spoke to Pacino. "No. At an airburst height of four hundred feet, the damage radius is two thousand yards, more or less, Mr. Pacino. I don't want to risk launching an EMP, having it go off but being ineffective. When we launch, that warhead is going off directly over his bridge. Straight down his throat. And we'll be well outside the damage zone. And so will Master One." Seagraves winked at Romanov. "I can't bring myself to call him *Bigfoot*, Officer of the Deck." He looked back at Pacino. "Approach Officer, drive off west, five knots. You have permission to open the number two VPT door and launch one EMP Kakivak at Master Two, the *Sargasso Causeway,* with the aim point directly overhead at a detonation altitude of four hundred feet. Immediately after launch, take her deeper in the layer, two hundred feet."

Pacino acknowledged the captain, then turned toward the command console, the display selected to the same output as the navigation chart plot aft of him, showing the God's eye view of the sea around him. He looked hard at it, memorizing the image.

"Pilot," he ordered Dankleff, "Left fifteen degrees rudder, steady course west, all ahead one third, maintain depth six four feet. Weapons Officer, open the number two VPT outer door and make the Mod EMP Kakivak in vertical launch tube twelve ready in all respects for a tactical launch at Master Two, aim point directly overhead Master Two, detonation altitude four hundred feet."

The flurry of acknowledgements floated in the air of the control room in slow motion. Time seemed to slow down until he realized Quinnivan, Romanov, Seagraves and Spichovich were all staring expectantly at him.

"Firing point procedures," Pacino said, hoping the litany of commands he'd memorized were correct. "Tube twelve, Mod EMP Kakivak, Master Two."

"Ship ready," Romanov reported formally to him.

"Weapon ready!" Spichovich barked.

"Solution ready," Quinnivan said, a look of uncertainty wrinkling his forehead.

"Shoot on generated solution," Pacino ordered.

"Set," Varney said from pos one, sending his final data on the target to Spichovich's panel, the electronic instructions traveling at the speed of light down to the torpedo room's master weapons consoles and from there to the aft Virginia Payload Tube's interface, then to the missile loaded in vertical launch tube twelve.

"*Stand*-by," Spichovich said, pulling his panel's master trigger lever up to the "stand-by" position.

"Shoot!" Pacino ordered.

"Fire!" Spichovich announced, pushing his trigger down to the "fire" position.

Tube 12, the twelfth tube in the aft-most Virginia Payload Tube module forward of the sail, detonated a steam charge under the cruise missile and blew it out of the tube toward the sky, its rocket motor firing as it cleared the sea, the rocket lifting it up to almost half a mile, a slight smoke trail extending backward to the launch point.

"Pilot, all ahead full, make your depth two hundred feet, steep angle!" Pacino ordered.

"All ahead full, Pilot, aye, make my depth two hundred feet, steep angle, and Maneuvering answers, all ahead full, fifteen-degree down angle on the ship," Dankleff spat.

In a matter of seconds Dankleff pulled the ship out of the dive. "Two hundred feet, sir!"

"All ahead two thirds," Pacino said from the navigation console. He had to get them back toward the target submarine. "Right fifteen degrees rudder, steady course three-one-zero. Sonar, mark the bearing to Master Two."

"Master Two bears one-five-eight."

"Sonar, how is Master Two's signal?" Seagraves asked.

"SNR to Master Two is fading but still hold him on broadband on the Q-ten wide aperture bow array and spherical array," Albanese reported.

"Narrowband?"

Albanese shook his head. "Narrowband's only showing random noise, Captain."

"Acoustic daylight?"

"Noise as well, sir."

High above and behind them, the Kakivak missile's rocket motor ran out of fuel. Twenty-four explosive bolts fired and detached the booster stage and it tumbled toward the sea. The missile's jet engine, spooled up by the air ramming into its drop-down intake during the rocket boost phase, lit off, the thrust increasing as the missile arched over and dived toward the sea, now five miles from the target, or thirty seconds at the missile's just-under-supersonic speed. The missile sailed closer to the hull of the target, the huge ship growing large in the seeker window flashing as the Kakivak executed a pop-up maneuver, its winglets rotating to guide the jet powered weapon skyward again. A hundred yards short of the aim point, directly overhead of the freighter, the missile dived back down and sped downward vertically toward the ship. The fuel valves shut and the engine shut down. Another two dozen explosive bolts fired and ejected the warhead payload. The winglets of the now-empty missile body guided it away from the target and the warhead, and four hundred yards south, a self-destruction charge blew it to fragments that fell to the ocean below.

Aboard the warhead, an explosive charge blew a stabilizing streamer out of the top, followed by a small parachute. At an altitude of four hundred feet, the warhead's trigger detonated and the NNEMP unit's high explosive charge flashed into incandescent life, the force of it blowing an iron core through the tunnel of a high voltage electrified armature, the sudden and immediate speed of the core relative to the armature generating an intense and focused electromagnetic pulse traveling at the speed of light. There was little to see or hear but a gray puff of smoke and the thump of the explosion, but the electromagnetic pulse traveled straight down, focused on the target until it fried every electronic circuit aboard the freighter *Sargasso Causeway*. The force of the trigger charge acted as its own self-destruct mechanism, the remains of the EMP unit littering the sea around the freighter.

The freighter's navigation lights winked out. She slowed in the water, half a dozen crewmen emerging from her bridge structure to the bridge wing to find out what happened.

"Detonation bearing one-five-one," Albanese called.

"That would be the EMP," Romanov commented, seemingly to herself.

"Turn count, Master Two?"

Albanese listened intently, one finger raised in the air, then said, "Target zig, Master Two. Turn count Master Two is decreasing. I no longer hold diesel engines from her bearing on broadband. Master Two is slowing down."

A quick cheer erupted in the room. Seagraves frowned. "Quiet in control!" he barked.

"*We got her,* Captain," Romanov said, smiling that beautiful smile and clapping Pacino on the shoulder. "Thanks to our young non-qual here."

Seagraves gave Pacino a brief look of approval, just the slightest crinkling of his eyes and a nod. "A somewhat adequate job, Mr. Pacino." Then, as before, the warning: "Don't get cocky, though. Now close up on Master One and prepare to commence the operation."

In the blur of the minutes that followed, Pacino ordered the ship turned to the bearing of the *Bigfoot* and sped up to twenty knots for the few minutes it would take to close the distance to the target. After the five minutes he'd calculated it would take to get within half a mile of Master One, he ordered *Vermont* slowed to nine knots and raised both periscopes uncaring of the twin rooster-tail wakes rising from behind their periscopes.

In his periscope view, the snorkel mast and periscope of Master One steadily grew. At Romanov's direction, he hit the target's snorkel mast with a laser rangefinder burst and reported the range now closed to five hundred yards. The target hadn't sped up, gone deep or changed his behavior. They were still undetected.

"Pilot," Pacino ordered, "Left one degree rudder, rudder amidships, steady as she goes."

"Steady as she goes, course three-five-eight, sir."

Pacino watched the periscope display, keeping the unit trained to the scope and snorkel of Master One, the crosshairs of the display showing the bearing changing as *Vermont* drew up even with the *Bigfoot* and surged ahead.

"Pilot, steer course north, all stop, mark speed five knots," Pacino called. Dankleff acknowledged and the ship slowed, now just ahead of and on the port side of the L-class narco-sub.

"Speed five, sir," Dankleff said. "Steady course north."

"All ahead one third, turns for five knots," Pacino ordered, all his concentration focused on the snorkel and scope of the target, now just abreast of *Vermont*'s propulsor shroud aft.

"It's time, Patch," Romanov reminded him. "Let's go."

"Captain," Pacino stood erect as he addressed Commander

Seagraves, who stood to the port side of the command console. "Request to open the lockout trunk hatch."

Seagraves nodded. "Permission granted to open the lockout trunk hatch."

"Lockout Trunk, Control," Pacino said, keying his boom microphone into the 7MC ship-control circuit. "Flood the lockout trunk and open the upper hatch."

The repeat-back rasped over Pacino's headset, Grip Aquatong making the report. *"Flood down the trunk and open the upper hatch, Lockout Trunk, aye."*

"Officer of the Deck," Dankleff called a moment later, "Lockout trunk upper hatch indicates open."

"Very well," Pacino said. "Captain, request to lock out SEALs."

Seagraves nodded. "Approach Officer, lock out the SEALs."

"Lockout trunk, Control," Pacino said over the 7MC. "Lock out and commence the operation." Fishman in the lockout trunk's dry station acknowledged.

It was all in the hands of the SEALs now.

10

"Approach Officer, lockout trunk hatch indicates shut," Dankleff reported from the ship control console.

"Very well, Pilot," Pacino acknowledged.

"Take us slowly deeper to one hundred feet," Seagraves ordered. "Underhull maneuver, but maintain station relative to Master One. When you clear seventy feet, raise both scopes."

"One hundred, scopes at seventy, maintain station, aye, sir," Pacino said, then barked to Dankleff, "Pilot, make your depth one hundred feet, shallow angle, report depths."

"One hundred feet, aye, and passing six five feet, down two degree bubble, sir."

"V'well, Pilot."

"Seven zero feet, sir."

"Raising scopes," Pacino said to Quinnivan. He pulled up both yellow-and-black striped hydraulic control levers for the number one and two periscope. The chart view on his command console blacked out, then displayed the view out the periscope, which was automatically trained toward the bow when he'd retracted it before. He pushed the "train" lever on the periscope controller, a unit that startlingly resembled a computer game console controller, to the right to change the bearing to the target, beside them on the starboard side and slightly behind.

"Eight zero feet, sir."

The waves were getting farther away up above. Pacino trained the view downward from the waves to try to see the hull of the target submarine. Blurry in the blue haze, he could barely make out a black shape. It was bigger than he expected.

He could see the bow and the conning tower, but the sub extended into the haze farther aft.

"Nine zero feet, sir."

"Very well." Pacino could see other shapes. The commandos who'd locked out and left the *Vermont* were visible, two of them forward of *Bigfoot*'s conning tower, no sign of the other two.

"One hundred feet, sir."

"Approach officer, energize the sail's under-ice lights," Seagraves ordered, staring at the display for the number one scope.

"Pilot, turn on the sail's under-ice lights," Pacino called.

"Sail's under-ice lights coming on," Dankleff said. "Under-ice lamps are lit, sir."

"Very well."

The view out the periscope sharpened slightly as the sail's lights came on, the units designed to allow approach to the underside of the polar ice if they were in the arctic maneuvering under a pressure ridge or preparing to vertical surface.

"Let's fade back, Approach Officer," Seagraves ordered. "See if we can get a better look at the screw-fouling effort, and be positioned if one of the SEALs falls off the target's hull."

"Pilot, drop two turns," Pacino ordered.

"Drop two turns, aye, and Maneuvering answers, dropping two turns, present RPM two eight turns."

"Very well."

The target slowly rolled past them, now crystal clear in the periscope view in low power. Pacino could make out the detail of the conning tower, saw the two SEALs forward, then the black hull passed slowly by until Pacino could see two SEALs near the aft rudder, with a package—no, two packages—that slowly started expanding. Unfurling. Almost like an underwater parachute, a blooming surface, silk or canvas or some modern polymer with nano-fibers, expanded, flapped slowly in the water flow, then spiraled downward aft of the rudder, the motion of the target submarine and the vortex of the screw pulling the packages downward and inward, until the strange objects were no longer visible. No doubt, they were wrapped hard around the *Bigfoot*'s screw.

"Master One's screw is fouled," Pacino said to Seagraves.

"Get ready to slow and stop," Romanov said. "You may need momentary reverse turns, but stay close to him."

"Coordinator, Sonar," Albanese said, his voice unmistakably happy, "Master One turn count dropping, and Master One's screw is stopped, turn count zero."

"Pilot, all stop, prepare to hover," Pacino ordered.

"All stop, prepare to hover, Pilot, aye, and Maneuvering answers, all stop."

Quinnivan turned and grinned over at Pacino, Romanov and Seagraves. "We got the fooker," he said quietly.

The target was slowing too fast. *Vermont* was starting to pass him, still too fast.

"Pilot, all back one third." Pacino took a breath. "Mark speed one knot."

"All back one third, Maneuvering answers, mark speed one knot."

Pacino waited tensely as the target came back toward them. Being submerged with a backing bell ordered was not a comfortable situation, he knew.

"Speed, one knot," Dankleff called.

"Pilot, all stop. Commence hovering at present depth."

"All stop, aye, sir, Maneuvering answers all stop, commencing hovering, depth one hundred feet."

"Coordinator, Sonar, transients from Master One. Sounds like blowing noises. Believe he's surfacing."

"Take us up to PD," Seagraves ordered Pacino, "and adjust position to be abreast of Master One."

"Pilot, make your depth six four feet," Pacino called.

"Rising to six four feet, Pilot aye, depth nine zero. Eight five."

"Belay reports," Pacino said, staring at the periscope display. The view was getting too distant.

"Pilot, all ahead one third, turns for two."

"Ahead one third, turns for two knots, aye, and Maneuvering answers, all ahead one third, turns for two. Depth seven five."

Pacino waited until the hull of the target was drawing nearer. If he called it right, he could slow *Vermont* to coast to a halt right beside the *Bigfoot*. "All stop," he said, guessing this would be enough thrust to get them beside the target. "Hover at present depth."

The periscope view grew foamy and blurry as the optics penetrated the waves, then slowly cleared, the bright blue sky above, the deep blue of the ocean below, the waves rolling by slowly, the crests perhaps a foot or a foot-and-a-half tall.

"Six five feet. Six four. Hovering at six four feet, sir," Dankleff reported.

Pacino trained the scope slightly aft. The target submarine, its hull a dark, glossy black, had stopped, its conning tower moving slightly as the ship rolled in the slight swells. He could make out two figures, hugging tight to the conning tower. The tower was smooth, with no handholds or ladder rungs or openings. The SEALs had wrapped cable around the conning tower to use to be able to hold on to the submarine. Pacino could see two of their thruster units hanging suspended from the cable, and one small equipment bag. The SEALs waited, crouched down low.

Pacino trained his view upward to the top of the conning tower, wondering if the sub's access hatch was at the top. The snorkel mast and periscope were still extended. Pacino zoomed in to look at the target's periscope mast. As he'd expected, the sloping glass of the optic opening was pointed right at him.

"He can see us," Pacino said to Seagraves and Romanov. "There's nothing happening."

For two long minutes, the control room crew froze, all of them except the pilot and copilot staring at the periscope displays, waiting for a hatch to open on the sub's deck or conning tower, waiting for a crewman or multiple crewmen to emerge to troubleshoot the fouled screw, but nothing happened.

"That's odd," Quinnivan said.

"Glitch number two," Romanov said, staring at the command console's display.

"We have a contingency for this?" Pacino asked Romanov.

She shrugged. "SEALs do. They'll try to break in. Either an external hatch-opening mechanism or a salvage connection. If that doesn't look possible, we'll have to pass over a diamond-plasma cutting rig so they can torch their way in."

Seagraves frowned. "I have a bad feeling about this," he said. "They may have a plan in case of being caught or detained."

Romanov shot the captain a look. "Like the North Korean sub a few years ago," she said slowly.

"Exactly. Approach Officer, surface the ship."

"Surface, aye, sir. Pilot, vertical surface!"

"Vertical surface, Pilot, aye." A blasting alarm boomed through control, the *OOOO-GAAAH* of the diving alarm. The 1MC shipwide announcing circuit blasted out Dankleff's voice. "Surface! Surface! Surface!" The diving alarm sounded again, but by that time Dankleff had blown forward and aft main ballast and the periscope view rose higher. Pacino looked downward as their own hull emerged from the waves.

"Prepare to place the low-pressure blower on all main ballast tanks," Dankleff's voice crackled again on the 1MC. "Approach Officer, raising the snorkel mast."

"Very well, Pilot."

Another 1MC announcement, Dankleff saying, "Placing the low-pressure blower on all main ballast tanks!"

A dim roaring sound vibrated the deck from below and aft. The LP blower was a positive displacement unit, much like the supercharger on Pacino's hotrod, moving air into the ballast tanks. Slowly the hull came fully out of the water.

"Securing the LP blow," Dankleff said, and the blower's noise quieted and stopped.

On the hull of the target, the SEALs continued to wait in their crouch, hugging the conning tower. Pacino glanced at the chronometer. It had been a full twelve minutes since he'd surfaced, and still no sign of anyone emerging topside.

"Sonar," Seagraves called to Albanese. "Any transients from Master One?"

Albanese turned from his console, his hand pressing his right headphone to his ear, as if that would help him detect transients better. He shook his head. "Master One is dead quiet, Skipper."

Suddenly a speaker crackled in the overhead above the command console. *"Victor Three Papa, this is Sierra Four Alpha, over."* Fishman's voice.

Romanov grabbed a microphone from an overhead cradle, the coiled cord of it extending into a small red unit the size of a shoebox, the VHF Nestor secure voice circuit. She glanced at Seagraves. "Request to answer, Captain?"

Seagraves put out his hand and Romanov handed him the mike.

"Sierra Four Alpha, Victor Three Papa, go ahead." Seagraves voice echoed back in a strange bubbly burbling tone as his voice was encrypted for transmission.

"Stand by to recover the team."

The SEALs wanted to come back in, Pacino thought. Something must be very wrong.

"Prepare to return, Victor Three Papa, out," Seagraves said, handing the mike back to Romanov. "XO, get to the lockout trunk and find out what the hell is going on," Seagraves ordered. Quinnivan handed his headset to Varney and half-ran out the room.

Romanov nudged Pacino. "Get the upper lockout trunk door open, now."

"Captain, request to open the lockout trunk hatch?"

"Open the lockout trunk hatch," Seagraves said, his face a scowl.

"Pilot, open the lockout trunk hatch and drain the lockout trunk."

Dankleff acknowledged.

Below, on the deck, one of the SEALs had climbed up on the hull, then a second. They'd taken off their gear but for weapons and left the equipment on the target's deck. Soon all four had vanished down the hatch and the hatch started shutting behind them.

"Lockout trunk hatch indicates shut," Dankleff said.

It seemed to take another ten minutes before Fishman and Aquatong came into the control room, Quinnivan behind them, the commandos holding white towels around their necks, their wetsuits glistening wet, dripping slightly.

Fishman addressed Seagraves. "We think there may be a self-destruct protocol going on. There could be a big bang coming from that thing." Fishman crossed his arms over his chest and stared at the deck. Lieutenant junior grade Elias Aquatong stood beside Fishman, running his fingers through his soaked hair.

Pacino kept his eyes on the periscope display, wondering if the target submarine would scuttle itself, or worse, explode with a self-destruct charge. It came to him that they might be too close to his hull.

"What do you want to do?" Seagraves asked Fishman.

"We're going to break in, Captain, but before we do, you'd better get *Vermont* to a safe distance. And submerge it. At this point, anything is possible."

Fifteen minutes later, the SEALs had locked out again and climbed up on the deck of the *Bigfoot* with several tool bags. Pacino watched them on the periscope display of the command console, having submerged *Vermont* and driven her out a thousand yards, now hovering half a mile from the narco-sub, his view trained on the conning tower of the target. Two of the commandos were on the foredeck and two were atop the conning tower, attaching the equipment bags to lines tossed down by the crew up high, who lifted them up and stowed them in the conning tower's cockpit.

The Nestor satellite secure voice radio circuit crackled with static and blooped with the distorted, decrypted voice of Fishman. "Victor Three Papa, odd situation up here. There's no hatch opening mechanism on the upper hatch and no ISO salvage connection, just smooth steel. As I stepped close to it to try it with a crowbar, the hatch came open by itself. The hatch is fully open now."

Captain Seagraves took the red microphone from the overhead. "Sierra Four Alpha, were there lights on inside the submarine when the hatch opened?"

What was he getting at, Pacino wondered.

"It's bright out here, so it would look dark even if it were lit by floodlights in there, but I'm fairly sure it was dark and some lights flashed on when the hatch came fully open."

"This day just keeps getting better and better," Romanov muttered.

"Curiouser and curiouser," Pacino replied, still staring at his display.

"You can say that again," Romanov said to him.

"You mentioned a North Korean submarine to the captain," Pacino said. Romanov looked at him blankly. "Well. What did you mean?"

"I forget the specifics," she said. "It was a while ago. A North Korean submarine got snarled in a trawler net inside the territorial waters of South Korea and the sub surfaced. The fishermen alerted the South Korean Navy. A South Korean destroyer grabbed the sub and started towing it to a South Korean naval base, but it sank on the way. So the South Koreans salvage it, and inside? Entire crew was dead, some with a bullet in the forehead, a few with throats slit. There were four cases of suspected suicide, the senior officers in command. The rest of the crew were executed by the senior guys. The conclusion being, none of the officers wanted it known they were captured submerged by their blood enemies, and you know, death before dishonor. They were also probably terrified of what an interrogation would be like. In any case, suicide made more tactical sense to them than surrender."

"You think that could be happening here?"

Romanov shrugged. "Maybe, but it's hard to imagine smugglers turning to murder and suicide when caught. Every other narco-sub detained, they took the crews for questioning. At first, they had to let them go, because there were no laws on the books prohibiting sailing a submarine full of coke on the no-man's land of the high seas. So a year later, there were brand new international laws making smuggling coke in the open ocean a felony, and the crews apprehended after that, well, they won't be seeing the outside of a high security prison for a long time. They were all hired guns, though, making ten or twenty grand to move the product. A pittance, really, considering the street value of the cargo. And the risks of the trip."

"Victor, this is Sierra," the Nestor radio speaker blared with Fishman's voice. "My XO and I are going inside the hull. I'm leaving a relay unit on top of the conning tower to relay my helmet cam to your displays. Testing it now."

"Select the tactical freq for your console display," Romanov said.

"I don't know how to do that," Pacino admitted. Romanov moved him over with her hip and showed him how to manipulate the software to change the display readout to receive and display the SEAL commander's helmet camera. For just a tenth of a second he became aware of the feeling of the touch of the attractive older woman, and he had to blink back his hardwired male response.

The display winked out, then showed the view of Fishman's head-mounted tactical camera as he looked down at the open hatch. "Am I patched into the Nestor circuit?" he asked someone out of the camera view, his voice coming out of the Nestor speaker in the overhead.

"You're coming through five by five," Seagraves said into the red mike.

"Grip and I are going in now. I'll go first."

The view out the helmet camera showed Fishman's view as he looked down in the maw of the hatchway. He stepped down to the first ladder rung inside, climbed down several rungs, then his hands reached out for the ladder. The rungs of the ladder moved by the view until Fishman's boots landed on the deck, some twenty feet down from the conning tower cockpit.

He did a slow turn through a full circle to show the inside of the boat.

There was almost nothing there.

He looked up at the ladder and ordered Aquatong to wait on the conning tower. "I'm inside the sub," he said, "and there's only room for one person in here. I'm standing in a rectangular space barely a meter square and two-and-a-half meters high. The forward wall is a server rack, nothing but computers. In the forward starboard corner there is a video display that seems to be showing the view out of a camera mounted on the forward server rack. To starboard there's a bulkhead completely taken up with cables and piping. Aft is another server rack. And the port side is like the starboard side, all cables, wires, junction boxes and piping, with a few valves. That's it."

Seagraves grabbed his microphone, ready to say something or ask a question, when Fishman's voice came back, louder this time.

"Oh, *that's* not good," he said. The video screen mounted in the forward starboard corner suddenly came to life, its display showing Fishman's face, then rewinding slowly to view his face when the camera had seen him best. The screen froze with his face in the video, but with straight lines superimposed on his face, tracing the shape of his face, measuring his cheekbones, nose and eye spacing. "That's facial recognition for sure," he said as he vaulted back to the ladder and took the rungs as fast as he could.

"Fuck, hatch is coming shut!" The camera view showed the world spinning as Fishman threw himself out of the upper hatchway onto the deck of the cockpit. He turned his head and the video view showed the hatch almost half shut. Pacino watched as the hatch slowly and smoothly shut all the way.

"Evacuate!" Fishman ordered. "Victor, stay where you are. We're getting out of here. Sierra, out."

The helmet cam view winked out. Pacino tried to return the display to the periscope, managing to get it to work on the second try. The SEALs were tossing down equipment bags and rappelling down the conning tower to the sub's deck. One of the SEALs on the foredeck had inflated a Zodiac rubber boat and outfitted it with a small motor. Within seconds, the equipment and SEALs were embarked and the boat was plowing through the small waves toward *Vermont*. Pacino kept his view trained to the submarine, noticing in 8x magnification he could see the sub's periscope optical opening pointed straight at him. Was it possible the submarine had defensive weapons?

"Broach the sail, Mr. Pacino," Seagraves ordered. "We'll bring them in through the bridge hatch. XO, go up and meet them." Quinnivan left the room in a haste.

"Aye, Captain. Pilot, make your depth five zero feet."

"Five zero feet, Pilot aye. Depth six zero, five five, five zero feet, sir."

"Very well." The SEAL boat reached their sail, then became too close to see in the periscope view.

"Approach Officer, bridge trunk upper hatch indicates open."

"Very well, Pilot," Pacino said, his periscope view locked

onto the narco-sub, which was floating motionless.

"Approach Officer, Sonar," Albanese called. "I have transients from Master One. Sounds like thumping noises."

Pacino watched the submarine. Was it getting lower in the water?

"Scuttling charges," Romanov said. To Pacino, she whispered, "Get a sounding."

"Nav-ET," Pacino called, "Mark sounding."

"Approach Officer," a young voice said from the aft port corner of control, "Sounding one thousand seventy fathoms."

"Six thousand feet plus," Romanov said, her tablet out as she noted the exact latitude and longitude of the target submarine. "A bit too deep to salvage without military equipment."

On Pacino's console display, the decks of the sub vanished beneath the waves, only the conning tower still visible, until soon that too vanished.

"Approach Officer, upper bridge access hatch indicates shut."

Seagraves tapped his gold Annapolis ring on the command console, impatient for word from the SEAL commander. As if on cue, Fishman stepped into the room, wrapped in towels. He looked over at Seagraves.

"Well?"

"You saw what I saw, Captain. Sub was run by some kind of artificial intelligence. With over a billion dollars in cargo, the AI was reluctant to self-destruct until it looked at my face and realized I wasn't on its list of friendly faces. Then it decided to sink. I'm just lucky it gave me enough time to get out. I wonder if they programmed that as a safety feature in case one of their own guys didn't get his face recognized properly. So, now, that sub is on its way to Davey Jones' locker, never to be seen again."

"I wouldn't be too sure about that," Seagraves said. "I imagine we'll salvage it to see what was up with its artificial intelligence setup. And to destroy those drugs, of course."

Fishman shrugged. "In any case, Captain, the mission's over. I'm going to take a shower."

"You and your XO please join us in the wardroom once you're squared away," Seagraves said.

"Roger," Fishman said, spinning on his wet heel and heading for his quarters.

Seagraves turned to Pacino. "Mr. Pacino, secure battlestations and station the normal watch section. Take us to patrol depth, course north, ten knots while you wait for the navigator to lay in a course for Andros Island, Bahamas. Once you're relieved, convene a patrol report party."

"Aye, Captain," Pacino said. He picked up the 1MC microphone and clicked it, his voice blasting through the ship. *"Secure battlestations, station underway watch section two."* He projected his voice toward the ship control station. "Pilot, make your depth five four six feet, all ahead two thirds, turns for ten knots, steer course north."

Pacino looked at Romanov, who was leaning over the chart display and plotting a turning point on the approach to the Windward Passage. "What's a patrol report party?" Pacino asked Romanov.

"We get the control room watchstanders together and get our story straight for the quick reaction situation report and then the top-secret patrol report to the National Security Council and ComSubCom. You're the junior officer, so lucky you, you get to write the report for all of us to critique."

Pacino smiled at her. "I am lucky," he said. "Who else gets to be approach officer on a tactical mission at the tender age of twenty-three?"

Romanov winked at him and clapped his shoulder. "You did well, non-qual. But like the captain said, don't get cocky."

Romanov grabbed the 1MC microphone. *"Convene the patrol report party in the wardroom,"* she said.

What a difference a week made, Pacino thought. A week ago he was a bundle of anxiety and had zero confidence. Today, he was a veteran, swashbuckling pirate. Quite a week, indeed.

11

Saturday, May 14

Lieutenant Commander Romanov was surfaced officer of the deck with Pacino as junior officer of the deck on the short surface run to the AUTEC complex on Andros Island, Bahamas. The sea was a sparkling deep blue, so transparent that the hull of the submarine could be seen below her massive bow wave as she steamed at flank northeast toward the AUTEC piers. A pair of dolphins suddenly burst out of the flow of the sea and arced gracefully over and dived beneath the bow, then jumped out again, the pair playing in the bow wave. For almost two solid minutes, the dolphins swam and jumped joyfully beside them, sometimes on the starboard side, sometimes to port, sometimes one on each side. Romanov looked at Pacino.

"Dolphins are always good luck, non-qual," she said, her voice loud to overcome the gale force wind of their passage.

Pacino lifted his binoculars and scanned the horizon, but they were alone in the sea. The speed of the ship on the surface made the howling wind feel like a hurricane, but it was warm despite the salty sea spray. The sun shone on them brightly, glinting off the waves. Pacino could feel the skin of his face starting to burn despite the sunscreen he'd applied when they'd surfaced. He looked over at Romanov. Her long chestnut hair, gleaming in the sunshine, was pulled back in a smooth ponytail, the ponytail going through the back of her *Vermont* ballcap, her eyes obscured by her dark Ray•Ban sunglasses, her tall, slender form revealed by the working khaki uniform. Pacino scolded himself for being aware of her as a woman and not as his superior officer. Sometimes he wished he could just disconnect his central nervous system, or the part of it that reacted to the opposite sex. Dammit, he thought, this was work. He wondered how long this mission would last.

"So Navigator," he asked Romanov, "What happens when we get to AUTEC?"

Romanov shrugged. "The captain will disembark and go talk to whomever he talks to after an op like this. Probably an ultra-secure videolink to some mid-level staffer at the National Security Council."

"Cool," Pacino said, taking another scan of the sea with his binoculars. The howling wind, the bow wave's sound and fury, the furious flapping of the flags aft, the sun, the sea, the sky and the ruler straight horizon, all of them seemed to warm his cold soul. He could steam on the surface like this all day, he thought.

The admiral-in-command of the combined U.S. Navy submarine force, Vice Admiral Robert Catardi, emerged from the relative gloom of the Navy Gulfstream SS-12 supersonic eight-passenger jet into the bright sunshine of the strip on Andros Island, Bahamas. His aide, Lieutenant Commander Wanda Styxx, carried his overnight bag and briefcase as well as her own luggage. A waiting staff car had its trunk open. A female lieutenant saluted him and he returned the salute and climbed into the back of the car with Styxx. As the car rolled off the airfield, Catardi took a look around at the volcanic rocks of the island. Andros wasn't like Nassau—there was no natural beauty here. This place could have been used as a training ground for moon landings, he thought. The unbroken stretches of volcanic rock extended to the horizon in every direction, which accounted for the large island being completely deserted.

Deserted, that is, except for the DynaCorp / Navy AUTEC installation on the east end, the nearest point to TOTO. AUTEC stood for Atlantic Undersea Testing and Evaluation Center, and TOTO was "Tongue of the Ocean," a vast deep hole in the sea surrounded by shallow shoals, keeping the area a place unable to be spied on by an underwater adversary, since the only entrance to it was a channel that any submarine would have to surface to transit. TOTO was a bathtub used by the Navy as a submarine testing ground, big enough for submarine vs. submarine exercises and exercise weapon shots. The tub was fully instrumented with 3D sonar, where the submarine doing training could see a projection of their battle after the action ended, in a large theater with a giant projection screen.

But this visit had nothing to do with testing or evaluation, Catardi thought. He turned his tablet machine back on and went over the situation report from the *Vermont*. He studied it for the tenth time, then reread the text of the patrol report. He'd review the video files again when they reached the guest office at AUTEC. He switched to the summary of the decision theory geek, Gustuvson, and his computer simulations of the attack on the *Bigfoot*.

The car arrived at the AUTEC complex and Catardi and Styxx got out of the car to get scanned into the security post. Long legged and slender Styxx got out on her side, all hundred and five pounds of her, the brunette younger woman thin and lithe, a veritable ballet dancer, making the two of them an odd couple. Catardi was of medium height, solid, perhaps twenty pounds shy of "stocky," but still an imposing presence. His formerly coal black hair now had pronounced streaks of gray in it, one streak extending from the center of his forehead all the way back to the nape of his neck, looking ridiculously like a skunk stripe, he thought. Every morning in the mirror, he contemplated dying his hair, and every morning he decided against it. Catardi had a rugged, chiseled face with dark circles under his eyes, not from lack of rest but inherited from his Sicilian father. He could have been credibly cast in a cigarette ad or a movie about a Wyoming sheriff—although his thick south Boston accent would make the latter impossible—but in fact he had once been dragged in to get a screen test for a pharmaceutical ad by his then-girlfriend, Monica Eddlestein, the local Channel Eleven news anchor. He'd failed the screen test, he thought ruefully, which he believed had contributed to the eventual breakup.

Since Monica, there had been no one. He had a bitter, standard Navy-issue ex-wife, or as she described herself, a widow of his extended sea time, and a daughter heading into middle school in another year. Those were the women in his life, for now, he thought. There were females he could attract, he knew, including his dark beauty of an aide, one Wanda "River" Styxx, despite some of his fire-and-brimstone ass-chewings directed her way, but life was full and busy with his trying to run the combined Atlantic and Pacific fleet submarine forces.

Life must have been simpler back when there had been one admiral-in-command of the Atlantic and a second in command of the Pacific fleet, but in the reorganization of the military ten years ago, the forces had been combined into one post. He had purview over both fleets and administratively reported to his boss, Commander-in-Chief U.S. Naval Forces Atlantic/Pacific, or CINCUSNAVLANTPAC, Admiral Greyson Rand, who was a brilliant but demanding boss, always just as close to an explosive lava-filled rant as Catardi himself was. And God knew, talk about difficult bosses—the National Security Council's leader, former Illinois senator and current National Security Advisor Dana Brady-Hawlings, who couldn't be meaner if she'd had twelve snarling snakes growing out of her damned head, was whom he reported to for the *Fractal Chaos* projects. Projects executed by his project boat, the USS *Vermont*.

After being cleared by security, the car dropped them at the AUTEC administration building. Styxx gave the driver orders to take their bags to the bachelor officers' quarters, the BOQ, then followed the admiral into the admin building, where a petty officer escorted them to a large guest office. Styxx got them coffee from an adjoining galley while Catardi settled down at the desk to go over the sitrep, patrol report and decision theory results again. He sipped the boiling hot coffee and turned to the situation report first.

1600Z12MAY22
IMMEDIATE
FM USS VERMONT SSN-792
TO NATSECADV / NSC; COMSUBCOM
CC COMSUBRON 8; COMSPECWAR NORVA
SUBJ SITREP // OPERATION BIGFOOT

TOP SECRET FRACTAL CHAOS // TOP SECRET FRACTAL CHAOS // TOP SECRET FRACTAL CHAOS

//BT//

1. (S) USS VERMONT ARRIVED ON-STATION SANTA MARTA HOLD POINT XRAY 0320Z12MAY22 AND ESTABLISHED BARRIER SEARCH.

2. (S) USS VERMONT INTERCEPTED OUTBOUND FREIGHTER "SARGASSO CAUSEWAY" CARRYING TARGETED NARCO-SUB 1000Z12MAY22. FREIGHTER OPENED HULL DOORS AND LOWERED TARGET SUBMARINE INTO CARIBBEAN SEA.

3. (S) USS VERMONT ESTABLISHED COVERT AND UNDETECTED TRAIL OF TARGET SUBMARINE. TARGET SUBMARINE STEAMED NORTH SUBMERGED WITH A RAISED SNORKEL MAST AND PERISCOPE. TARGET SUBMARINE WAS SNORKELING ON HER DIESELS AND PRESUMED TO BE CHARGING BATTERIES BEFORE SHIFTING TO SILENT RUNNING ON BATTERIES.

4. (S) SITUATION BECAME COMPLICATED WHEN FREIGHTER RECONFIGURED HULL DOORS AND COMMENCED STEAMING TOWARD TARGET SUBMARINE AND USS VERMONT. INTENT UNKNOWN BUT BELIEVED THAT FREIGHTER WAS GOING TO ESCORT TARGET SUBMARINE PART WAY OR ALL THE WAY TO TARGET SUBMARINE'S DESTINATION. THIS WOULD CAUSE MISSION FAILURE BECAUSE WHEN TARGET SUBMARINE SURFACED, IT WAS EXPECTED THAT FREIGHTER WOULD RENDER AID AND INTERRUPT MISSION.

5. (TS) USS VERMONT LAUNCHED MOD EMP KAKIVAK AT FREIGHTER. EMP DETONATION SHUT FREIGHTER DOWN. SHE LIES DEAD-IN-THE-WATER OFF SANTA MARTA.

6. (S) USS VERMONT TRAILED TARGET SUBMARINE, MATCHED SPEED, DEPLOYED SEAL TEAM TASK GROUP 80. SEALs INCAPACITATED TARGET SUBMARINE WITH NET OVER TARGET SUBMARINE'S SCREW. TARGET SUBMARINE SURFACED. SEAL FORCE AWAITED PERSONNEL COMING TOPSIDE TO TROUBLESHOOT PROBLEM. A HALF HOUR LATER, NO ONE HAD COME OUT OF THE HULL.

7. (TS) SEAL TASK GROUP 80 COMMANDER ENTERED HULL

AND DISCOVERED THE TARGET SUBMARINE WAS AN ENTIRELY COMPUTER-CONTROLLED VESSEL. THERE WERE NO ACCOMMODATIONS FOR PERSONNEL. THE ARTIFICIAL INTELLIGENCE ABOARD TARGET SUBMARINE EXAMINED SEAL COMMANDER'S FACE AND PRESUMABLY CONCLUDED IT DID NOT MATCH ANY FACES IN ITS DATABASE. TARGET SUBMARINE IMMEDIATELY IGNITED SCUTTLING CHARGES. SEAL TASK GROUP 80 PROMPTLY WITHDREW AND WERE SUCCESSFULLY RECOVERED ABOARD USS VERMONT.

8. (S) TARGET SUBMARINE SANK IN CARIBBEAN SEA OVER 1,000 FATHOMS DEEP, EXACT POSITION TO BE RELAYED IN OFFICAL PATROL REPORT.

9. (S) MISSION CONSIDERED CONCLUDED. USS VERMONT EN ROUTE WINDWARD PASSAGE AND REQUESTS FURTHER ORDERS.

10. (U) CDR. T. SEAGRAVES SENDS.
//BT//

"Jesus," Catardi muttered. A goddamned ultra-secret warshot Kakivak EMP missile, tossed at a civilian freighter by a covert submarine, which after that was no longer covert and could have left American fingerprints on the botched operation. What if it had been a dud? Then the bad guys would have a copy of their most secret weapon system. Catardi manipulated the tablet to take him to the *Vermont*'s patrol report. It was a fleshed-out version of the situation report, but with charts and images of the chart output and the periscope display. There was a video, a long one.

Catardi linked his tablet to the wide-screen television on the side of the office away from the windows, shut the blinds, and played the video, finding one of the leather club chairs facing the television, deep in concentration as he watched the control room video. When Lieutenant junior grade Pacino suggested launching the Kakivak missile, Catardi froze the frame, thinking about his history with the young man. There was no doubt, that kid was even more crazily ballsy than his old man. Catardi watched the faces of Seagraves, Quinnivan and Romanov as they reacted to the non-qual junior officer's suggestion. They'd weighed the risks, he thought, and had done what they thought was right. He would have to convince the National Security Advisor of that, he thought. He pressed "play" and watched the video stream from the SEAL commander's tactical helmet cam.

After the video ended, Catardi went back to his desk and opened his tablet again to the scenarios described by his artificial intelligence decision theory experts. After an hour, Styxx reminded him it was time to meet the officers of the *Vermont.*

When they arrived at the pier and stationed the in-port duty section, a message came in marked "personal for commanding officer." Romanov was summoned to the captain's stateroom, where Executive Officer Quinnivan was already seated at the captain's small table.

"Have a seat, Nav, and read this message."

She read aloud the terse message displayed on Seagraves' tablet. "USS *Vermont* CO, XO, TAO/NAV ordered to report to AUTEC's special compartmented information facility 13 May at 1300 for a debrief with ComSubCom Vice Admiral R. Catardi." She looked up at Seagraves, the tension evident in the lines of his face. She glanced at Quinnivan, who had looked back with a dour expression of disappointment, perhaps even sadness.

"Catardi's never had us do a debrief before," she said uncertainly.

"We've never had mission failure before," Quinnivan said, shaking his head slowly.

The words hung heavily in the air. Romanov realized the term *mission failure* had never been connected with the previously unblemished record of the USS *Vermont.*

"I know what this is," Seagraves said. "It's a 'comearound.'"

Quinnivan raised an eyebrow. "Pray tell, Captain, what's a *comearound*?"

"Listen up, you poor uninitiated personnel. Plebe year at the Naval Academy," Seagraves began. He crossed his arms and leaned back in his command chair and continued, "*plebes* being the newly reporting freshmen, found themselves in a harsh prisoner-of-war environment characterized by being forced to memorize huge amounts of information—famous naval sayings, every coach of every Navy sport, the scores of each bowl game played by the Navy football team in all of recorded history, the quarter-by-quarter story of the last three Army-Navy football games, the hometown and birthday of every man-Jack in the company, every officer in the tactical and academic departments, on and on, with more added every miserable day—and reciting said data without hesitation when demanded by the ruthless *firsties*—first classmen, the seniors acting as drill instructors—at a meeting of the twelve man platoon in the passageway of *The Hall*—the corridor of the dorm—while standing braced up—a rigid posture of attention with your chin pulled so hard into your neck that you make at least a dozen wrinkles, while keeping your head up, eyes locked in front of you, staring into the far distance, while the firstie would scream at you from an inch in front of your nose at the slightest mistake or hesitation. It was called a *comearound*.

"Perhaps the most unpleasant half hour you'll ever spend in your life, and it happened four or five times a day. And it was a verb as well. *'Come around,'* Mr. Seagraves, a pissed-off firstie would bark, which meant your meeting with the firstie would be one-on-one, for that extra *special* attention. Now, keep that up for over two months including weekend days, and there you have your introduction to the hallowed traditions of the United States Naval Academy."

"Jaysus," Quinnivan said. "Sounds like an abusive little boarding school for wayward boys."

"Explains why you 'boat school' guys are such hard-asses," Romanov said. "No offense, Captain."

"None taken," Seagraves said, almost smiling, but the smile turning back to his dark expression from before. If this meeting were a comearound, it meant the boss was displeased with their mission result. Or as Quinnivan had put it, *mission failure.*

Commander Seagraves, Lieutenant Commander Quinnivan and Lieutenant Commander Romanov were escorted by a scowling petty officer in blue-gray digital camouflage NWUs, the shapeless Navy working uniform, to a SCIF secure conference room on the ground floor. They entered the conference room's airlock's outer heavy wooden door, then a steel door, then finally a heavy composite door with sound-isolation padding on the inside. The petty officer shut the door behind him. The silence in the room after the door closed seemed eerie.

Romanov took in the room. On a solid oak conference table, there was a pitcher of water with glasses and coasters and a coffee service set up in the center. Seagraves waved Quinnivan and Romanov to seats on either side of the seat he chose at the center of the table, the XO on his right, the navigator on his left. He passed out coffee mugs and filled Romanov's cup, then raised an eyebrow at Quinnivan.

"I'll definitely have coffee, Captain." He poured cream and dumped sugar into the brew and stirred it up.

Romanov glanced nervously at the door. Several minutes after the appointed hour of 1300, the door of the conference room came open and Vice Admiral Robert Catardi rushed in, dressed in sharp tropical whites, with his aide, a slender worried-looking female lieutenant commander with a nameplate reading STYXX, following behind him.

"Attention on deck," Seagraves commanded, and the *Vermont*'s officers bolted to their feet and came to attention, Romanov thinking about Seagraves' definition of a comearound.

"Stand easy," Catardi said, frowning as he reached out and shook Seagraves' hand, then Quinnivan's and Romanov's. His grip was strong but momentary, without warmth. The admiral was in a foul mood, Romanov realized. He walked around the table and pulled out a seat opposite Seagraves and tossed his hat on the table. Putting a hat on a table was strictly prohibited by Navy protocol with the one exception—if an officer or sailor had been to the North Pole, it was *obligatory* to put his hat on the table. Few but submariners could boast of visiting the pole. He waved Styxx to a seat on his right and took his tablet computer when she handed it to him. He paged through a few displays, then looked up at Seagraves.

"Let's get right to it," Catardi said grimly. "What the hell did you think you were doing, tossing a warshot Kakivak at a civilian merchant ship?"

Seagraves seemed ready for the harsh question. "The cargo ship buttoned up his hold and then ran up to full speed at a vector directly aimed at the narco-sub, and our own periscopes were in his same line-of-sight. He was either going to position himself to escort the submarine part way or all the way to his destination or he was investigating why another submarine's periscopes were following his narco-sub. Either way, the cargo's ship's unanticipated interference spelled the *certainty* of mission failure."

Catardi frowned, leaning back in his seat and looking into Seagraves eyes, then over at Quinnivan and finally at Romanov.

"Yesterday, while you were on your flank run on the way here, I called in the AI decision theory geeks. I had them program two different and competing artificial intelligence systems. One of them was given all the data from your sitrep and patrol report. The other only knew what you did when you began the mission. Then we ran scenarios with various levels of *bias* of the *Vermont* programmed into the simulation. For our purposes today, the term 'bias' means aggressiveness."

Romanov stared at Catardi, thinking that if his simulations showed a viable way of mission success, this would *not* go well for the three of them. She went back to the moment that Pacino recommended the Kakivak launch and wondered what else they could have done.

"Scenario one. Low level of bias programmed. Twenty percent aggressiveness. Artificial *Vermont* dipped periscopes, drove off the line-of-sight to the cargo ship, steamed east and monitored the position of the cargo ship to see if it were escorting the narco-sub or trying to intercept *Vermont.* With a probability in the high ninety percent level, the cargo ship fell in alongside the narco-sub to escort it out of the Caribbean Sea. The alternative to go after *Vermont* was low probability after *Vermont* dipped her periscopes. After the scope dip, *Vermont* was undetectable from the cargo ship. From that point, there was a fifty percent probability that *Vermont* lost contact with the narco-sub and could only trail the cargo ship. Mission failure.

Then a fifty percent probability that *Vermont* tracked the narco-sub but couldn't stop and board it because of the company of the cargo ship escort. Either way? Mission failure with the worst possible outcome—the narco-sub completed its mission and delivered its cargo."

Catardi paused to pour himself coffee, dumping in three artificial sweeteners handed him by Styxx. The room was pin-drop silent, waiting for Catardi to continue.

"Scenario two. A higher level of bias of the *Vermont*, at about forty percent aggression. Cargo ship starts up and heads for the narco-sub. *Vermont* dips scopes, drives off east, verifies that the cargo ship is headed for the narco-sub and not *Vermont* herself, then commences trailing the cargo ship and the narco-sub, following them all the way to the Windward Passage, *Paso de los Vientos*, between Cuba and Haiti's northwest tip. At the entrance to the Atlantic, the Sargasso Sea, *Vermont* waited to see whether the cargo ship would turn back to Colombia or continue the escort operation all the way up Cuba's northeast coastline to Miami.

Catardi downed his coffee and Styxx refilled his cup and put the sweetener in. Romanov studied Styxx's face, wondering if there were anything going on between the admiral and his aide. Styxx seemed clingy, but the admiral was cold as steel.

"We divided the scenario at that point. Scenario two alpha—the cargo ship continued escort operations northward and all *Vermont* could do at this level of bias was radio ahead to the U.S. Coast Guard, which boarded the cargo ship but lost the narco-sub. Mission failure again, with failure to interdict the cargo. Or steal the target sub. Scenario two bravo—the cargo ship turned back and *Vermont* deployed the SEALs. At a high percentage, the commandos captured the narco-sub, broke in, and the sub sank, but in *much* shallower water. Mission failure, but a situation far worse than your actual reality, with the narco-sub lost in shallow water, which means she could be salvaged by the bad guys and the drugs recovered."

Catardi finished this coffee and swiveled in his chair to put the cup back on the credenza behind him. Romanov looked for a sign from him. So far, the low level of aggression of the simulated *Vermont* had resulted in worse situations than the actual mission result. But Catardi's mood still seemed dark. Maybe one of the simulations triumphed.

"Scenario three. Bias dialed up to eighty percent, the AI's estimate of the equivalent of its evaluation of your real-life aggression level."

Seagraves' face revealed his tell, just the hint of his lips drawing back, as if he were about to smirk, Romanov thought. That the computers evaluated their aggression level at eighty percent seemed to please him. His face returned to his normal attentive poker face.

"Cargo ship follows the narco-sub into the Atlantic, staying close to Cuban shores. *Vermont* says 'fuck it' and deploys the SEALs anyway. Narco-sub surfaces. SEALs board the sub. Sailors on board the cargo ship open fire on the SEALs with automatic weapons. Two of the commandos are killed. The other two took cover behind the conning tower and returned fire. Cargo ship sailors fired two RPGs at the SEALs."

Rocket-propelled grenades, Romanov thought, which she knew were in the weapons inventory of the cartel.

"Then five more. Conning tower blown apart, remaining two SEALs dead. Cargo ship heaves to and takes the narco-sub in tow, back to Columbia. The mission result—the loss of four Navy SEALs and the cartel's recovery of the drugs and the sub, able to try again later. Mission failure, but again, much worse than your actual mission's outcome.

"So, scenario four. Bias dialed up to a full one hundred percent. At the point the cargo ship starts driving in to establish its escort operation, *Vermont* fires a salvo of four Mod nine ADCAP torpedoes at the cargo ship. Cargo ship *spectacularly* explodes and sinks, killing some four dozen cartel sailors, so none of them could be captured and interrogated. SEALs board the narco-sub and it sinks, but this time two SEALs were trapped aboard when it went down. Loss of two commandos, the cargo ship's exploding on the front pages of the news files, loss of the narco-sub and cargo, but in deep water. So a similar mission result with respect to the target sub and the drugs, but with fifty souls lost, including two of our own, and a reputational problem if the cargo ship's exploding and sinking is linked to the U.S. Navy. It would be a scandal."

"So, Admiral, we seem to have found the sweet spot," Seagraves said, that tell happening again, Romanov thought. The captain was secretly pleased.

The first glimpse of light seemed come into Catardi's mood. He pursed his lips, then smiled just slightly, just for a fragment of a moment.

"That's what I'm going to tell the National Security Advisor, Dana Brady-Hawlings." Catardi said her name contemptuously as if cursing and spitting. "And now this whole Kakivak fiasco becomes *my* goddamned idea." Catardi took his tablet from the table, made a few corrections to a document, clicked the screen and looked up at Seagraves. "Check it, Commander."

Seagraves looked over at Romanov's tablet while Quinnivan clicked into his own machine. It was an order, an operation order, an op-order. Dated from five days ago, May 8, the time stamp just before midnight. It ordered *Vermont* to make haste to Santa Marta and take charge of the narco-sub, and if there were the *slightest* interference from the cargo ship, to immobilize it with a Kakivak EMP cruise missile. Seagraves looked up at Catardi.

"Thank you, sir."

Romanov breathed a deep sigh of relief. They were off the hook after all. That bitch of a mission may have failed, but none of the AI could do any better. And now Admiral Catardi had given his imprimatur to their tactics with a backdated order to do exactly what they'd improvised.

"Which brings me to the real purpose of this meeting," Catardi said, while Styxx lowered a screen at the far end of the narrow room. She clicked her tablet to pair it to the projector, and a view of the earth from overhead Andros Island and the Atlantic Ocean appeared, the deep blue of the sea and emerald green of the land masses making the view seem inviting.

"Just a side comment before we go on," Catardi said. "Did you note that the difference between eighty percent aggression and a hundred percent aggression is pure undistilled stupidity?"

Romanov nodded. She'd been thinking the same thing.

"Anyway, here we are, Andros Island, Bahamas. I'm ordering you to take a great circle route to the southern tip of Africa, the Cape of Good Hope and Cape Agulhas and up northward into the Indian Ocean."

An animated bright dotted line appeared, drawing a curve on the globe from Andros Island and extending south toward the south Atlantic and around South Africa and turning north-northeast up the eastern African coastline toward Saudi Arabia.

"You'll enter the Gulf of Oman, here, off Cape al-Hadd, Oman and head toward the Strait of Hormuz and loiter off the Iranian Navy base at Bandar Abbas, which has access to the Persian Gulf to the west and the Gulf of Oman and the Arabian Sea to the east. And yes, Madame Navigator," Catardi said to Romanov, "it would, in fact, be much faster to route you through Gibraltar, the Med, the Suez Canal and around the Saudi peninsula, but surfacing *Vermont* to transit the Suez Canal in front of a thousand spies would only happen if we *wanted* the bad guys to know we were coming. For *this* mission, stealth is important. Vital, in fact. Your run to South Africa and up the Indian Ocean will be a *dark transit* done at flank speed, with only one excursion to periscope depth per day for a navigation fix. By 'dark transit,' I mean *no* communications in or out. Complete radio silence until the mission is complete. That means no emails, in or out. After you leave the pier here, the next thing I expect to hear from you is your situation report. Your sitrep reporting *complete* mission success."

Catardi looked at Romanov again. "This means you'll be going over seven thousand nautical miles full-out at flank speed, with only daily excursions to periscope depth to grab a NavSat fix. However, once you round the cape and enter the Indian Ocean, no more periscope depth excursions. You'll be navigating solely using bottom contour and gravity contour the whole way to keep SINS behaving. Bottom contour nav loses accuracy at high speed without you slowing down to explore an area to cross reference the bottom contours, but we're going to have to live with your fix error circle growing to the size of Connecticut until you approach the Saudi peninsula. Then you'll downshift main coolant pumps, go to natural circulation, rig for ultra-quiet and sneak into the Gulf of Oman at no more than eight knots, only popping the scope up long enough for a navigation fix."

Catardi expanded the map, zooming into an area drawn around Bandar Abbas Naval Base.

"You're authorized entry within the territorial sea of the Republic of Iran as directed by the president. There will be no written directive to penetrate nor will there be a written op-order for this mission. Your radio suite and crypto equipment will be rigged for programmed self-destruct if the unlock codes aren't input every hour."

"What *is* the mission, Admiral?" Seagraves asked, looking at the blown-up chart of the Strait of Hormuz.

Catardi clicked the next slide, showing a submarine inside a huge assembly building, with massive steel bridge cranes overhead, scaffolding surrounding the vessel, which was placed on top of blocks on the factory floor. The submarine looked weathered. It had seen sea duty.

Romanov looked at the photograph closely. "Is that a Kilo-class?" she said.

"Indeed it is," Catardi said. "Iran has three older Russian-built Kilo-class diesel-electric attack submarines. Enough of a threat to sink shipping in the gulf. But the Iranians and their nuclear ambitions have progressed to the point of initiating 'Project Panther.'"

Catardi clicked to the next slide. In this photograph, the Kilo diesel submarine had been torched into a forward portion and an after half. The halves had been moved apart by thirty feet.

"Guess what's going in there?"

"A missile compartment for ballistic missiles?" Romanov asked. "Nuclear-tipped ballistic missiles?"

"Nope," Catardi said, turning to the next slide. In this photo, a cylindrical can had appeared between the submarine's halves. In the photo's center, the inside of the new module could be seen with bright work lights shining on the interior's equipment.

"That's a—that's a *reactor*," Quinnivan breathed.

"Exactly," Catardi said. "The Russians are lending Iran an experimental lead-bismuth liquid metal cooled nuclear fast reactor, the UBK-500 model, the grandson of the reactors that powered the storied Lira Project 705 class, the submarine class we and NATO called 'Alfa.' This unit puts out eighty megawatts thermal from a reactor vessel smaller than your water heater at home. The remainder of the module is the steam generator, ship's service steam turbine and propulsion steam turbine. The propulsion turbine's output goes to the Kilo-class' main motor, which can now run on electricity generated by the nuke in addition to the diesel propulsion generator or the batteries."

Catardi clicked to the next slide, a profile drawing of the Kilo with the new fast reactor and generator module plugged in. It made the Kilo longer, but the Kilo was a stubby submarine in its original configuration. With the reactor module installed, the submarine looked like it had been meant to have a nuclear reactor.

"The reactor is of key interest to us. The Russians seem to have vaulted ahead in technology with this unit. As you may know, liquid metal reactors have one big problem. At a temperature below 123 degrees Celsius, the metal coolant freezes. It 'rocks up' and can't be melted again without damaging the nuclear fuel modules and making the thing hellishly radioactive, and ruining it permanently. The Russians added something to the mix that makes the coolant stay in liquid form at ambient temperature. That's ambient temperature in freezing Murmansk, people. And whatever it is that the Russians added to the coolant, it doesn't become radioactive at a level any higher than the lead-bismuth itself."

Romanov spoke up. "If this unit is new and secret, why are they giving it to the Iranians to test? Why wouldn't they test it on one of their own prototype submarines after trying it out in a controlled lab setting?"

"Question of the hour, Madame Navigator. We only have theories. There's no intelligence about this reactor being tested on land or sea. There are those who think that this thing being a fast reactor—that is, critical on fast neutrons—could go supercritical and become uncontrollable. A reactor runaway on this unit could even go prompt critical and experience a rapid disassembly."

"Prompt critical rapid disassembly," Romanov said slowly.

"*Explosion,* you mean," Quinnivan said. "You mean just blowing itself apart and scattering radioactivity all over God's green earth? Or a *nuclear* explosion?"

Catardi shrugged. "Odds are, just the dirty, radioactive blowing-apart scenario, but there is the possibility it could have a small nuclear yield in the five to ten kiloton level. About half of a Hiroshima bomb."

Quinnivan whistled.

"So," Seagraves said, that slight smirk appearing on his face. "Let me guess."

Catardi began to smile. "Don't steal my thunder, Commander. That's right, officers of the project submarine USS *Vermont,* the United States Navy wants you to steal this submarine. You'll be keeping the SEALs you had embarked for the narco-sub operation for this op. And you'll take the *Panther* the same way you took the narco-sub."

"So that whole narco-sub mission, that was just a dry run for *this?*" Romanov asked.

"Goddamn, you're smart," Catardi said, his brilliant smile finally appearing. "You got any sisters at home?"

Romanov blushed. At least Catardi's sarcasm hadn't been too biting.

"The only difference is you'll be breaking into a submarine that's definitely manned, not computer controlled. Which means, to sail it out of the gulf and the thirteen thousand miles back here, you'll need to man the *Panther* with some of your officers and sail home short-handed. Commander Seagraves, I leave it to you to decide how to man the stolen *Panther* to sneak it submerged out of the Gulf of Oman and sail it back to AUTEC on the same route you took to get there. Once here at Andros, we'll bring in a crew and run it through the Tongue of the Ocean test range, then it'll go to a facility we're hastily putting together here for us to rip it apart. Normally, we'd take it to a naval shipyard to peek at this unit's guts, but given the dangers of this particular nuclear reactor, we're going to analyze it right here on uninhabited Andros Island. If it does blow up like a nuke, it'll only damage the DynaCorp complex. And officers, as before, there will be no written op-order. This is the operation order, our discussion in this room."

Seagraves took a glass from the center of the table and filled it with an inch of water. He looked at it. "You know Admiral, hearing all this, I could really use something stronger than water in this glass."

"You read my thoughts exactly," Catardi said, standing, smiling at the *Vermont*'s officers. "I want you to convene your wardroom at the AUTEC officers' club at eighteen hundred. Drinks and dinner are on me tonight. Bring the SEAL officers with you. And I want to see young Pacino again before I fly back."

"Absolutely, Admiral, and thank you."

Catardi stood and reached for his hat. "I'm going to grab a room at the Q," Catardi said, referring the bachelor officers' quarters, BOQ, or just, 'the Q.' "Uniform for the O-club tonight is ultra-casual. As for me, I'll be in jeans and a Grateful Dead T-shirt."

Ten minutes later on the walk back to the pier, Romanov looked at Seagraves. "Do you think there will be any more information coming our way about this *Panther* submarine?"

Seagraves shook his head. "For now, we sail with only the tactical files we have, but it wouldn't surprise me if our systems get an update when we reach the Gulf of Oman."

Romanov nodded and grimaced. For fuck's sake, she thought. Stealing an improvised drug sub was one thing. Stealing an Iranian nuclear submarine, now that was quite another.

12

Andros Island, Bahamas
Saturday, May 14

The knock came to Robert Catardi's BOQ room door as he was changing out of the Grateful Dead T-shirt into the Harley shirt displaying a skeleton in flames zooming in a crazy speed demon's motorcycle, the bike trailing flames as well. Somehow it just seemed more appropriate to his mood, he thought.

He pulled on the shirt and opened the door. It was Wanda Styxx, done up in tight jeans and full combat makeup, with tall black boots and a tight red top that dipped low into her décolletage, but she needn't have bothered. Catardi knew his aide liked him, but that was not to be. Navy Regulations aside, she wasn't his type. Styxx had that athletic dancer's body, Catardi thought. He liked voluptuous women with lots of curves. The kind of woman who, when she entered a room, conversation stopped. Like his ex-wife. Damned shame they'd broken up, he thought. Before she had turned into a rage-filled bitter lunatic, she'd been perfect for him.

"Admiral," Styxx said breathlessly, shaking her long hair off one shoulder. "You've got to see this." She held out her tablet, opened to a Satellite News Network article and pointed to it with a manicured fingernail.

**NATIONAL SECURITY ADVISOR BRADY-HAWLINGS DISMISSED—
UNDER FBI INVESTIGATION FOR CORRUPTION**

SNN—The White House released a statement late Friday that National Security Advisor and former Illinois Senator Dana Brady-Hawlings had been asked to leave the staff, just an hour after FBI Director Rita Molotov announced Brady-Hawlings was under investigation for corruption charges related to her dealings with failed oil company EndoNat.

"Wow," Catardi said, handing her the tablet after scanning the text of the article, but Styxx forced it back into his hands.

"You've got to read the last paragraph, Admiral."

He paged the article down to the last sentence.

Brady-Hawlings' replacement is rumored to be the former Chief of Naval Operations, Admiral Michael A. Pacino, a longtime friend of the president and the architect of the defeat of the Chinese PLA Navy in the War of the East China Sea.

"Holy shit," Catardi breathed. It was too good to be true, he thought. Pacino had been Catardi's first submarine captain, a million years ago aboard Pacino's first command, the USS *Devilfish*, the Piranha-class ship, not the SSNX submarine of fifteen years later. Catardi had been a young non-qual, reporting aboard Pacino's *Devilfish* just after the change-of-command ceremony. Two years of serving with then-Commander Pacino, Catardi had grown from being a shy, uncertain non-qual newcomer to a swashbuckling, cocky, dolphin-wearing senior lieutenant. Catardi had rotated off for a three-month temporary assignment to study for his chief nuclear engineer's exam, and as chance had it, that was just before the secret orders came in that resulted in *Devilfish* sinking under the polar ice cap, with the loss of all souls aboard except for Pacino himself. He'd never seen the senior officer again, and other than serving under his command of the Unified Submarine Command years ago, and later when Pacino was CNO, Catardi hadn't thought about him until his son, Midshipman First Class Anthony Pacino, reported aboard Catardi's submarine command, the USS *Piranha*, for his midshipman cruise.

This would certainly change things. Instead of the ass-chewing he'd expected from Brady-Hawlings over the Kakivak attack, he could explain it to an understanding fellow submariner. He wondered if young Anthony Pacino had heard the news.

Catardi handed back the tablet to Styxx. "Come on. We'll be late for the *Vermont* officers and SEALs."

Andros Island, Bahamas
Saturday, May 14

Lieutenant junior grade Anthony Pacino stood up from the wardroom table when the outside line's phone rang. He shot a look at Lieutenant Li No, who was the duty officer, who nodded toward the phone, as if to say, *you* answer it, non-qual.

Pacino picked up the handset. "USS *Vermont* wardroom, this is a non-secure line, duty officer under-instruction Pacino speaking, may I help you, sir or ma'am?" It was a mouthful to bark out instead of simply saying "hello," but it was required.

"Hello Anthony," his father's baritone voice crackled on the connection, his tone warm.

"Dad! How *are* you? *Where* are you? How did you know you could reach me here?"

His father's laugh came over the phone. "I got asked to take a job in D.C.," he said. "Turns out I now have the clearance and the need-to-know to be briefed on what you're up to, so I thought I'd reach out and tell you I'm thinking about you."

"I miss you, Dad. I wish we *could* talk about, you know, stuff." There were so many things Pacino wanted to tell his father about. The narco-sub operation, his suggestion to lob an EMP weapon at the cargo ship, the crew of the *Vermont,* but no matter what his father's new clearance was, all that was off the table.

"Listen, I have it on good authority you'll be going out to dinner with my old buddy Robbie Catardi tonight. Make sure to tell him I send my warmest regards."

"I would, Dad, but, well, I'm kind of inport duty officer under-instruction. No liberty at the O-club for me."

The older Pacino laughed again. "I doubt that, Son. But

anyway, I'd better bounce, the boss is standing in my doorway."

"It was good to talk to you, Dad," Pacino said.

"You too, Son. Good luck and good hunting."

The line clicked off. Pacino hung up the phone. *Good hunting*—a submariner's term for "get out there, find 'em and sink 'em." What the hell did his father know about the next mission?

Li No looked over. "Must be nice to have a high-powered father. That's a hell of a connection."

"Not really," Pacino said. "Dad's been retired for years."

"I don't think so," Lieutenant No said, sliding his pad computer across the wardroom table to Pacino. Pacino leaned over and read the article about Brady-Hawlings, eventually getting to the sentence that ended the article.

USNewsFiles—Friday May 13—President Carlucci tapped the former chief of naval operations and the fighting admiral of the War of the East China Sea, Admiral Michael Pacino, for the position of his National Security Advisor. Pacino had no comment for the press, but his spokesman promised a statement before the end of the weekend.

"You know what that means, right?" Li No said. "Your boss is Captain Seagraves. Seagraves' boss is Admiral Catardi. And Catardi's boss is none other than Admiral Pacino, daddy dearest. A complete circle. Talk about nepotism."

Pacino shook his head. Somehow his world was coming together again after the horror-filled years after the *Piranha* sinking. At the moment the captain had accepted his recommendation to launch the Kakivak missile, Pacino finally felt like himself again, not the walking ghost of a month ago.

The supply officer's side door to the wardroom opened. Executive Officer Lieutenant Commander Jeremiah Quinnivan leaned in. He was dressed as he had been for the ship's party, an old T-shirt over jeans, falling-apart boots, with a lumberjack open shirt worn over the ensemble.

"Pacino! Let's go, dammit. You're late and you're fookin' out of uniform!"

"I'm sorry sir, I'm duty officer under-instruction."

"No you're not. Now get your fookin' ass into casual clothes and join us on the pier. You've got two minutes and thirty seconds."

"Yessir," Pacino said, rushing to the ladder to the upper level. He changed and climbed out the plug hatch and emerged into the brilliant Caribbean sunlight of the late afternoon.

Washington, DC, USA
White House Situation Room
Saturday, May 14

President Vito "Paul" Carlucci opened the door to the crowded room, flashed his dazzling smile at the personnel who all rose to their feet at attention. Carlucci was slender, well over six feet tall, in his late fifties, with a distinguished look owing to the gray streaks of hair that swooped over his ears. Normally never seen out of an expensive suit, on this Saturday, he was dressed in golf clothes—chinos, a short-sleeved Polo shirt, multicolored patterned socks and sneakers. The rest of the room's inhabitants looked like they'd dressed for Monday morning. Generals and admirals in dress uniforms, cabinet secretaries in suits, their aides sitting along the wall likewise formally dressed.

"Let's make this fast, people," Carlucci said, seating himself in his leather swivel chair at the end of the polished table and opening a briefing book.

"Mr. President," Secretary of War Bret Coppin Hogshead began formally, "the Vice President is remote in Austin, Texas and is present by secure videolink. Also present by video is CIA Director Allende, who is at Mossad headquarters in Tel Aviv, Israel. Presenting today will be CIA's Director of Operations, Angel Menendez. Co-presenting will be General Zvi Amit of the U.S. Cyber Command, under the Department of War. Also present today are the chief officers of the Joint Cyber Warfare Task Force, a joint development group of the War Department's NSA and CIA's international cyberwarfare team. The briefing book in front of you has a hardcopy of Angel's presentation."

Carlucci yawned into his fist. Famously bored by technology

and especially computers, he had wanted to delegate these meetings to his VP, Karen Chushi, but after the Stuxnet flap, all cyberattacks had to be personally approved by the president himself. Like authorizing a nuclear strike, it required presidential authority.

"Fine. Let's start," Carlucci said. "But give me the Cliffs Notes' version."

"Yes, sir," Menendez said. Solid and shorter than medium height, Menendez sported a goatee and spoke with a slight Cuban accent. His great grandfather had fought in the Cuban Bay of Pigs conflict, and he came from four generations of CIA officers. "The name of the operation and the name of the worm itself—"

"Worm?" Carlucci asked.

"Sorry, Mr. President," Menendez said. "By 'worm' we mean an algorithm. A computer program. A virus. A piece of software code that gets inserted into an adversary's computer systems with the intent of causing various forms of damage, like the Stuxnet virus did to Iran's Natanz nuclear facility some time ago."

"Right," Carlucci said. "Please ignore my ignorance and proceed."

"The name of the operation and the name of the worm—the algorithm—are the same, and that name is *Harmaakarhu*, which in Finnish means 'grizzly bear.'"

"Wait, why Finnish?"

"Well, sir, of all the languages' translations of the word 'grizzly bear,' the Finnish version is the coolest."

Carlucci laughed.

"Actually, sir, it was a random word generator run by CIA, but I like my version better," Menendez smiled.

"Go on then, Mr. Menendez."

"Yes, sir. Anyway, the effect of the worm will be to invade Iranian Navy computer systems and cause them to stop communicating with each other. Most of them will just brick—go black, sir, and stop functioning. The worm is intended to paralyze Iranian logistics networks and operational control assets of the Iranian Air Force, Naval Air Force and Iranian

Navy's surface action forces. Pretty much everything in the Iranian Navy with the exception of their submarines."

Carlucci frowned. "Why not their submarines?"

"Sir, that ties into a separate operation that we will be briefing you on next week."

Carlucci waved. "No problem. So, why are we doing this, exactly?"

"Well, sir, technically, it's not *we* who are doing it. The Mossad will be executing the cyberattack. We'll hand the worm code over to Mossad after you sign off with your permission, and then they will get it inserted into a normal system software patching and update version, so it will be accepted into the Iranian networks and then go to sleep for five days, then it will become active."

"Okay, understood, but that's tactics, Mr. Menendez. What is the grand strategy here?"

"Functionally, Mr. President, we're fundamentally attacking Russian systems from a vector they trust—the Iranians. We infect the Iranian systems, and within days, the multiple interfaces between Iranian systems and Russian systems put the worm deep into the Russian networks. All their analysts will see is a threat vector from Iran. Sir, they will chase their tails for three weeks over this, minimum. At the point you deem appropriate, you can order the kill code. Boom, worm dies. All Iranian and Russian systems return to nominal. And the attack on Russian systems, well, it flanges into your directive regarding an operation we can't talk about here, at this time." Because, Menendez thought, the Israelis weren't read into the Fractal Chaos program.

"Okay. I understand the front end. I understand the objective. Now tell me about the downside. First, can we or Israel be blamed for this attack?"

"Sir, we can't promise the answer is negative, but we have done everything technically possible to scrub the code of any agency fingerprints. We've actually hired amateur coders—hackers, if you will, Mr. President—to give the line-by-line code the look and feel of it being originated by civilians, not state actors. We've run it through the AI that guards our own networks to see if it could detect it. It was not able to detect it. So confidence is high, sir."

"Mr. Menendez, if our guardian AI missed detecting this virus, isn't that cause for concern? If you and your band of scruffy hackers can defeat it, what's to stop some angry Venezuelans from penetrating *our* systems?"

"We have a briefing for you on that on Wednesday, sir."

"Oh my God, this never ends, does it?" Carlucci remarked in frustration.

"Sorry sir," Menendez said in sympathy.

"And what, Mr. Menendez, are the unintended consequences of us releasing this bug? Sorry, this *worm*?"

"Nothing that can be foreseen, sir, but let me reassure you that everything that can be anticipated that could blow back on us has been considered."

"This will affect Iran and Russia only? No chance of it breaking out of those two cages and getting into Germany's defense systems? I don't need Iron Ida Schwarzzen to be pissing in my ear that all her naval systems are down." Ida Schwarzzen was the renown prime minister of the new German government, a scrapper who had no affection for America or Americans.

"Not a chance, sir. It will definitely stay in its lane."

"Well, okay then," Carlucci said, sounding almost sleepy. "You have permission to proceed." Menendez handed Carlucci a leather folder with a document inside it. Carlucci scanned it and signed it with a fountain pen enclosed in the folder. He stood up. "Well, have a good weekend, all." With another politician's smile flashed at the crowd, he disappeared out of the room, the crowd of military officers and cabinet officials leaving after him.

Angel Menendez looked up at the video screen and saw his boss, Margo Allende, turn to talk to a man partially off-screen. For a moment, he leaned in to point at something on Allende's tablet computer, and when he did, Menendez recognized the famous billionaire and software mogul, Elias Sotheby, one of the architects of the *Harmaakarhu* worm. Allende smiled at him and nodded, and he left. She turned back to the screen. Menendez gave a crooked smile to Allende. "Well, Madam Director, get that worm going and get back here. You know what they say about when the cat's away."

Allende smiled. "I have it on good authority that you love when your boss is out of town."

"Total lies," Menendez laughed. "Whoever says that is totally lying."

"See you soon, Angel."

With that, Allende clicked off.

Andros Island, Bahamas
Saturday, May 14

Pacino blinked in the bright sunshine of the pier, his eyes used to the relative dimness of the submarine's interior. The air smelled funny, then he realized it was because it was fresh sea air that didn't stink of atmospheric control amines, diesel fumes, ozone and cooking grease. He half ran over to the waiting white bus with the DynaCorp logo painted on the side. He stepped in the bus door and took the two steps up to the aisle between the seats, and immediately the *Vermont*'s officers started jeering at him.

"Look at *this* guy," Quinnivan teased. "Khakis and a damned Polo shirt. And fancy little topsiders."

Pacino surveyed the crowd, who all seemed to sport cargo shorts, flip-flops and T-shirts as if they were headed to the beach rather than dinner with the admiral in command of the submarine force.

"Well, Bullfrog, he *is* sort of royalty," Romanov said, smiling that beautiful smile of hers at Pacino, her eyes sparkling. "He has to dress the part." Pacino looked at Romanov, who looked stunning, wearing shorts that revealed her long, tanned legs, with a tight, revealing tube top and sandals that had three-inch heels. Her hair shone, cascading in loose curls down to her shoulders. Her eyes were made up, the eyeliner making her eyes even more gorgeous. Lip gloss graced her full lips. For a moment he stared at her, unable to deny an animal attraction to the woman, and when she noticed, she winked at him and said, "sit down, you non-qual air-breathing puke."

Pacino blushed, hoping no one noticed him ogling the navigator, and plopped into a seat for the short ride to the officers' club. The club was a humble, rusted Quonset hut with a neon domestic beer sign in the front window. Inside there were what seemed dozens of cheap tables and chairs, with the bar and grill in the back of the long narrow structure. The club was deserted except for them, Pacino imagining that the DynaCorp personnel had flown back to the mainland for the weekend. At the back, near the bar, half a dozen tables had been pushed together. Standing at the end of the table was Vice Admiral Catardi with his attractive aide. Catardi wore jeans, sandals and a motorcycle T-shirt. His aide wore tight jeans, boots and silk blouse, made up with warpaint and looking like she'd be going to an upscale nightclub later in the evening. Catardi broke into a warm grin when he saw the *Vermont*'s officers walking in. Pacino walked over and waited for the admiral to greet the captain, XO, navigator, engineer and weapons officer, then shook Catardi's hand.

"Patch Pacino, how are you doing with this scurvy crowd of rough pirates, son?" he asked, pumping Pacino's hand, his other hand clapping his shoulder.

"Good, sir, fine. Best officers in the fleet." Pacino smiled back. "Oh, I heard from my father—he called the wardroom, sir, and said to give you his warmest regards."

Catardi smiled even wider. "That man taught me everything I know about being a combat submariner. And now we have the privilege of teaching you."

Catardi found Seagraves and asked him where the SEALs were.

"They decided on a ten mile run before coming out drinking," Seagraves said, a slight smirk on his lips.

"Speaking of which, Wanda! Get that bartender over here! Let's get some beers and whisky out."

A few moments later, when they were all holding a drink, Pacino sipping from a frosted mug with a beer that tasted fantastic, Catardi called the group to silence.

"Before we go too much further, officers, I have two promotions to make." He looked at Styxx. "This is the best part of the job. Can I have Lieutenant Commander Quinnivan step up? Front and center, Executive Officer."

Styxx produced an envelope. Catardi took out the insignia

badge and held it up for the crowd to see, the three gold stripes with one of them making a loop.

"Jeremiah Seamus Quinnivan," Catardi said officiously, "you are hereby promoted to the rank of commander, Royal Navy, by order of the Admiralty on this date, thirteen May." Catardi accepted a safety pin from Styxx and pinned the badge to the center of Quinnivan's T-shirt.

Pacino clapped with the rest of the crowd, noticing that Quinnivan was choked up. The tough-as-nails senior officer was actually tearing up.

"Thank you, Admiral," Quinnivan said, his voice trembling. "I honestly never thought I'd see this day." He looked up and smirked at the crowd. "It's not April Fool's Day, is it?"

Catardi shook his hand as Lomax took a picture, then a second picture with Seagraves shaking his hand.

"Now, I'd like our young non-qual to step up," Catardi said. "Mr. Pacino, get up here."

What was all this, Pacino wondered, taking the half dozen steps to join the admiral, the XO and captain at the head of the table. Styxx handed Catardi another open envelope.

"Mr. Pacino," Catardi said, "you are hereby promoted to the rank of lieutenant, United States Navy, by order of U.S. Naval Personnel Command on this date, the thirteenth of May."

The officers clapped enthusiastically. Pacino stared at Catardi with his mouth half open. Full lieutenant. Senior lieutenant. The same rank as all the other veteran junior officers in the wardroom. He hadn't expected to be a full lieutenant for another year. He wondered if Seagraves and Catardi had made this happen inside the bureaucracy of the Navy.

Catardi withdrew the new insignia, double silver bars, from the envelope and pinned one on Pacino's left collar, the other on his right. Pacino supposed if he'd worn a T-shirt, Catardi would simply have pinned it to the fabric near his throat.

Catardi pumped his hand while Lomax took another photograph, then one shaking Seagraves hand, the captain grinning for the camera. Pacino realized until now he'd never seen the captain smile, which was odd, because Seagraves had teeth so perfect he could have been in a toothpaste ad.

"And now, as is tradition when in port," Catardi said, "with a promotion like this, you'll have to drink your bars." He looked at Quinnivan. "Your weird Royal Navy insignia, being cloth and all, won't go well inside a glass of whisky, but you're drinking anyway."

Quinnivan laughed, mumbling he'd be fine dunking the commander's insignia.

Styxx handed Pacino a tall tumbler half full of brown liquid in it.

"That's the best scotch available in Andros," Catardi said. "It's some cheap off brand, but we can reasonably expect it'll work as well as the good stuff. So go ahead. Wanda, put Mr. Pacino's new bars in the glass."

Styxx unfastened the new insignia from Pacino's collars and dropped them into the scotch. Pacino realized everyone in the group was staring at him, the SEALs included, who had just shown up.

"You're still a non-qual puke," Romanov said to him, her smile shining on him, her long-fingered hand on his shoulder, her touch warm. "But now a full *lieutenant* non-qual puke," she added. "Next, we're going to get some fucking *dolphins* on that uniform of yours. Now drink up and don't stop till you've got your silver bars in your mouth."

Andros Island, Bahamas
Sunday, May 15

Pacino woke before daylight, unsure of where he was. He opened one eye in the dim light of a clock-radio on a nightstand, and realized that there was an arm on top of his chest. He touched the hand. It was warm, soft and small. He traced his way up the arm, slowly turning in the bed to face where the arm met the torso. It was a slender naked woman with brown hair, her skin warm against the skin of his chest. He stealthily moved her hair away from her face to reveal who she was.

Wanda Styxx.

Wanda "River" Styxx.

Lieutenant fucking *Commander* Wanda "River" Styxx.

Oh my God, he thought. Seriously? He drank his lieutenant's bars and woke to this?

Styxx stirred and opened her eyes, smiling slowly at Pacino.

"Good morning, Tiger," she said, a look of happy satisfaction on her face.

Pacino's mind raced, trying to remember the evening before. He remembered Styxx pulling him to the dance floor. Then fragments of a conversation.

Oh, for fuck's sake, this wasn't happening. Pacino vaulted out of Styxx's bed and lunged for his khaki pants and Polo shirt, searching the room for his wallet and the lieutenant's bars. Styxx looked up at him.

"Leaving so soon?" she pouted.

"I have to go, I'm starting the reactor and then driving us out today." God, his head hurt. Note to self, he thought. No more slamming down cheap scotch the night before an underway. "I can't find my silver bars. Where are they?"

"Probably on top of my clothes," Styxx said sleepily.

Pacino found the collar devices, leaned over Styxx, kissed her briefly on the lips and half ran out of the room, down the hall, down the stairs, luckily finding the island's van idling in front of the hall.

"Can you take me to the pier?"

"Absolutely, sir," the Jamaican driver smiled. "Your captain had me posted here waiting for you."

Dammit, Pacino thought. The captain himself knew about this indiscretion.

At the pier, Pacino rushed out, crossed the gangway, hurriedly saluted the American flag, dived down the plug trunk, hustled to his room and dumped the casual clothes on his rack, then climbed into his khaki uniform, pinning the new lieutenant's bars onto his uniform shirt, then rushing to the wardroom to grab coffee before officers' call, after which he'd assume the watch in maneuvering to start the reactor.

It was five in the morning, but there must have been eight officers there already, all of them in uniform and all of them sober as judges. The moment he entered the room, all of them broke out in howls of laughter. Pacino looked at Spichovich, who looked like he would burst at the seams from laughing. Li No spurted tea on his tablet computer. And Gangbanger, the supply officer, stood up, pointed and guffawed. Quinnivan looked like he was going to suffer a hernia, bent over and laughing so hard he started coughing.

"What? What is it?"

A scowling Rachel Romanov pulled him roughly down the narrow passageway of officers' country to the unisex head and shoved him against the sink so he could see himself in the mirror.

Pacino's face had lipstick smeared all around his lips, from his chin all the way to the bottom of his nose, and twice as wide as his mouth. He looked like he was wearing the makeup of a clown.

"Admiral's aide, huh?" Romanov said in blistering hostility. "Get the stink of that *skank* off you and join us in the wardroom for zero five thirty officers' call. What the hell were you thinking? Fucking gross."

Pacino washed his face, watching in the mirror as Romanov stormed angrily down the passageway. What was *her* problem? Could this be—no, not jealousy. Certainly, he and Romanov had the beginnings of a connection, but it was a professional friendship, right? And she was a married woman, right? A *happily* married woman. Right?

Once the lipstick was scrubbed off, Pacino walked back to the wardroom, thinking he could sneak into his seat without further ado, but Quinnivan pointed his finger at Pacino and said, "your new callsign, Lieutenant, is 'Lipstick.' Officers, I present to you Lieutenant Lipstick Pacino!"

Pacino frowned, not pleased at their roaring laughter at his expense. Dieter Dankleff clapped him on the shoulder. "Don't worry about them, they're just jealous *you* were the one to get that Styxx chick. She shot down a half dozen of us before she pulled you onto the dance floor. You're a regular ladies' man, Lipstick."

"Oh fuck you, U-Boat," Pacino said. It was all he could think of as a comeback.

BOOK 3:

POLLIWOGS, SHELLBACKS, PANTHERS

13

North Atlantic Ocean, near the equator
Thursday, May 19: Wog Eve

Lieutenant Anthony Pacino walked into the wardroom shortly after 0800 and made straight for the coffee machine. He'd missed breakfast so he could find an open treadmill and weight machine in the torpedo room, the breakfast period one of few slack times for the equipment. After a fast shower, he needed caffeine before beginning the grind of a new day of submarine qualification studies and checkouts.

A *checkout* was a submarine ritual, in which a non-qual studied and memorized a particular system, digging into the tech manuals and SOP procedures, interviewed the men who operated the system and physically touched the major components of it. That could even mean crawling into the oily bilge under the deckplates of aft compartment lower level to touch the drain pump, the massive unit the size of a compact car, able to keep the ship alive during flooding by forcing floodwater overboard through the huge drain piping system. When the non-qual felt he was ready, he would go to a qualified officer and undergo a verbal exam on the system. It usually entailed going over the basics, moving on to making the non-qual draw the piping system or block functional diagram or even the circuit diagram.

Non-quals rarely passed a checkout on the first try. The questions escalated in difficulty and esoteric nature until the non-qual became clueless, and at that point, from one to four "lookups" were handed down from the dolphin-wearer to the non-qual. Tradition had it that reporting with the answers to lookups required bringing the qualified person his favorite drink or snack, spitting out the lookup answers, then getting his "qual card" signed. There were hundreds of checkouts required for an officer to acquire dolphins, and the process could take over a year, depending on the operational tempo of the boat. The most difficult requirement was for the non-qual officer to make two approaches as approach officer, but Pacino had the first one signed off. One to go, and only a few dozen more checkouts, and all that was left was the minimum six-month requirement. By early November, the gods of the seas willing, Pacino should be wearing gold dolphins.

He tossed his pad computer to the table, took his habitual seat and looked over at his boss, Weapons Officer Al Sprocket Spichovich, who was reading his tablet across from the engineer, Lieutenant Commander Elvis Lewinsky. The wardroom was pin-drop silent, and the three of them were the only ones in the room.

"Morning, Patch," Spichovich said, hoisting a coffee cup and draining the thick black liquid. Lately, Spichovich was the only officer in the wardroom other than the captain who stilled called Pacino *Patch*. His new nickname, *Lipstick*, seemed to have stuck much harder. And unlike the other officers, Pacino was rarely referred to by his job title, like *DCA* Dankleff or *MPA* Lomax or *Communicator* Eisenhart. It didn't sound right to address a person, even if the person were the sonar officer, as *Sonar*. "Are you looking for another weapons checkout? You know, my sleaziest checkouts are when you play poker with me and the other junior officers while you submit to my interrogation. A zero eight hundred checkout, absent cards, poker chips and cigars? I don't think even the Feng here could pass that."

Engineer Lewinsky grinned at Spichovich over his coffee. "Bullshit, Weps," he said. "I know more about *your* shit than you know about *my* shit."

Spichovich laughed and made a dismissive motion with his hand. "All *your* shit does is push us through the water. *My* shit finds the bad guys, then puts warheads on foreheads, the very purpose of us being here. The fucking *mission*."

"Yeah, your warheads would still be at the pier if not for me and my boys. Plus, we make the hot water for your shower and laundry and the potable water for your coffee. Where would you be without coffee?"

"Fine," Spichovich conceded, smirking. "Maybe so, maybe so." He looked at Pacino. "So, Patch? A checkout?"

Pacino considered the question, glancing at his cup. The coffee in the cup made ripples and waves when Pacino set the cup on the table from the vibration of the deck with the submarine speeding southeast at flank speed in its headlong rush, its *dark transit,* toward the southern tip of Africa.

"I don't think so, Weps. Last time I played poker with you, well, I went back to my bunky with my wallet empty."

Spichovich was a card shark, and loved playing *Vermont* Hold 'Em, which was just Texas Hold 'Em with aces as low cards instead of high. So far, Pacino had had five easy checkouts during five poker games with no lookups from Spichovich—one on the Mod 9 ADCAP torpedo, another on the conventional Tomahawk land attack and ship attack cruise missile, the third on the new Mod 80 Tomahawk SACM-N, which stood for ship attack cruise missile, twenty kiloton nuclear warhead-equipped, a fourth on the Kakivak Mod EMP and a fifth on the Tomahawk SubRoc antisubmarine cruise missile with a nuclear depth charge, also with a twenty kiloton nuke. Each time Pacino had lost over a hundred dollars in chips, and Spichovich was the bank for the chips, demanding or making payment to cash in or out.

Cash-poor on this run, Pacino had decided to attempt a checkout with Spichovich when they weren't playing poker, a checkout on the horrendously complex AN/BYG-1 combat control system, and Spichovich had tortured Pacino for over two hours, making Pacino draw a dozen block diagrams of the interconnected systems and subsystems, and leaving him with eleven challenging lookups. Any sane non-qual would only get checkouts from the weapons boss while playing poker with him, where the questions were easy and the lookups few, but the potential for financial loss was tremendous. By Pacino's calculations, he could be three thousand dollars in the hole getting qualified that way.

"No, Weps, no poker for me and no checkouts, not on Wog Eve. Just advice. From you and the engineer. You know, while I've got you both in the same room."

Lewinsky smiled, leaning back in his chair. "You know, Lipstick, I'm an expert on two things—sports cars and women. I'll bet you want advice on one of the two."

"Yeah, Feng," Spichovich laughed. "You don't know which end of a wrench to hold for that Italian rig of yours, what's its name again, *Ferrari Testarossa*—doesn't that mean *redhead* in Italian? Oh, wait, wasn't Redhead that last girlfriend of yours, that sexpot with the big chest, you know the one, the nymphomaniac? Wasn't she, you know, a redhead? And left you for what, an attorney? So yeah, the two things you're an expert on? Lord have mercy that you're better at running a nuclear reactor than you are at the two things you're a supposed expert on."

Pacino looked at Lewinsky, who was laughing so hard he was choking back tears. Insults between friends on a submarine were routine, but the weapons officer's striking for Lewinsky's deep cuts—in another environment—would have caused fists to fly. But on a submarine? That was called "Thursday." Pacino waited for the engineer, no, the *fucking* engineer, to make his comeback.

"Oh, look at me being lectured by a guy who hasn't kissed a girl in, what, five years?"

"Hey," Spichovich said without a moment to think about it, "I had a *spectacular* girlfriend before this damned boat got between us, and I'd remind you that's only two years ago, not five, and she was blonde and beautiful and virtuous, unlike your Ms. Redhead, and my mother liked her and my sister told me to marry her, and she was herself an attorney, so no need to leave me to find one."

"Hell, Weps, if you'd married Legally Blonde Attorney Girl when your sister told you to, you'd be divorced by now."

"Tell me about it," Spichovich said, returning to being serious. He looked back at Pacino. "So, Patch, advice from the two heaviest department heads on board the project boat USS *Vermont*, on Wog Eve, no less. Must be some kind of luck thing. Hey, Feng, is it a full moon too?"

Wog Eve, Pacino thought. At zero one forty hours on the upcoming mid-watch, the *Vermont* would cross the equator and pass from the North Atlantic to the South Atlantic. The crossing ceremony would begin at midnight in the crew's mess, and would feature half a dozen hazing rituals of the uninitiated *Polliwogs*—those who'd never crossed—by the *Trusty Shellbacks*—the crewmen who'd crossed the equator before. Even in the modern Navy, the hazing would include absurd rituals, some passed down from antiquity, others made up by "King Neptune," the senior Trusted Shellback of the crew, which in this case was Executive Officer Quinnivan. Even Captain Seagraves was a Polliwog and would have to undergo the hazing during the crossing.

"So, advice?" Spichovich said, prompting Pacino while pushing his overgrown black bangs out of his eyes. The weapons boss was well known for refusing to cut his hair or shave his beard during the duration of any operation, preferring a Virginia Beach salon where rumor had it he had a huge crush on the woman who owned the joint. Unrequited love, Pacino thought, was an awful thing.

"Yessir," Pacino said. "It's a delicate situation."

Spichovich looked at Pacino with rapt interest, then shot a glance at Lewinsky. "Pray tell, oh non-qual Sonar Officer. What's up?"

Pacino took a deep breath. "It's the navigator. Ever since AUTEC, Romanov's been hostile. Total silent treatment. How can I learn anything as junior officer of the deck under her if she won't talk to me? She won't even look me in the eye. And why the hell is she doing that? Because of my night with Catardi's aide? What's going on? What should I do?"

Spichovich took a long pull of his coffee and tried to refill his cup, but the carafe was empty. He stood and walked around the captain's end of the table to brew a fresh pot, looking at the coffee pot as it brewed, then looked into Pacino's eyes.

"It's a mild form of PTSD," he said. "You remember her

husband Bruno? You met him at the party."

"Yeah, he was great. Hilarious, friendly. Good guy."

"Not that good. He's apparently a ladies' man and may have stepped out on young Silky Romanov a few times when he was on deployment and his missile cruiser would pull into port. Broke her heart a few times over, I understand. So, when she sees you getting lucky a few hours after we tossed over our lines, well, I think it just put her mind right back to where it was when she found out about Bruno cheating on her. She's just giving you what she would have given Bruno. The smoldering silent treatment. I wouldn't take it personally."

Pacino stared at Spichovich for a moment, speechless, then looked at Lewinsky, who nodded solemnly. "Keep it to yourself, Lipstick," the engineer cautioned. "The navigator's been known to flame on people who bring up her burden of pain."

"Meanwhile I'll talk to the XO about getting you on my watchsection," Spichovich said. "I'll school you, but good, in the ways of driving a combat submarine."

"Wow. Thanks, Weps, Eng. Glad I came to you guys. If you'll excuse me, I'm going to see Chief Albanese. I have a sonar lookup." Pacino picked up his pad computer from the table, put his cup away in the small pantry sink and walked forward to the supply officer's end of the table and out into the passageway, walking as if a weight had been lifted from his back.

Lewinsky looked at Spichovich after the younger officer had shut the door behind him. "That was complete horseshit, Sprocket. But goddamn, you sure sold it. And he bought it."

"Thanks to you, Elvis. We make a good team. I lie, you swear to it. I'd hate for the lad to learn the truth. Goddamned Romanov and her open marriage with Bruno."

A realization dawned on Lewinsky suddenly. "Hey, didn't your thing with the blonde attorney end suddenly after you reported aboard? And didn't you get along great with Romanov until about six months in? And now you guys hate each other. *You*, Sprocket? And Dominatrix Navigatrix?"

"Let's make it our secret, Elvis. I admit it," Spichovich said. "I was one of her many victims. I just didn't want her claiming another one. I need my sonar officer functional, not broken-hearted after being another toy of the nymphomaniac navigator."

Lewinsky let out a low whistle. "I saw you whisper something to Wanda Styxx at the AUTEC party. Wasn't long after that she dragged Lipstick onto the dance floor. So that was you?"

Spichovich nodded. "She and I go way back. She owed me a favor."

"You're just full of surprises, aren't you, Weapons Officer?"

"Maybe I am, Chief Engineer."

"You'd better hope Lipstick doesn't guess the truth," Lewinsky said, looking at the wardroom door.

"When I talk to the XO when he wakes up in an hour," Spichovich said. "I'll tell him I need Pacino on my watch section to supervise his quals and watchstanding. He'll take Patch off her afternoon watch and put the boy on my evening watch."

"You think he'll figure out the real reason?"

"Eng, the XO misses nothing. I assure you, he already knows."

North Atlantic Ocean, near the equator
Friday, May 20: Wog Day

"Polliwog Lipstick, King Neptune commands you to rise to your feet and stand here next to the Polliwog captain of this fine ship!" Quinnivan's Irish brogue was comically thick and dripping with obscene pleasure.

Lieutenant Anthony Pacino was kneeling on the vibrating, trembling deck of the crews' mess, the ship shaking from the power of the propulsor pushing against the thrust bearing deep inside the aft compartment, propelling the submarine through the deep sea at thirty-two knots, the speed she made at one hundred percent reactor power at all-ahead flank, full-out. The deck was cold on his bare knees. The tables had been unbolted and stowed, creating a large open space in the ship. Pacino's wrists were taped together in front of him with five turns of duct tape. He wore a blindfold and his underwear and nothing else. He was smeared with a mushy mix of jello, pasta sauce, soggy spaghetti and the remains of a fish dinner. Louisiana hot sauce ran down his soaked hair into his eyes. In his mouth was a sock that had been soaked in an awful tasting liquid they'd named "Kickapoo Joy Juice." He was trying hard not to retch.

Pacino did as instructed, the trip from the deck to standing complicated by his tied hands and blindfold, but he was shoved next to Captain Seagraves, who was in the same situation, minus the dirty sock. Next Quinnivan called Navigator Romanov to her feet and she was shoved next to Pacino, the barest impression reaching him that Rachel Romanov stood next to him in nothing but bra and panties, her warm, soft skin a hairsbreadth from his own. U-Boat Dankleff, Easy Eisenhart and Gangbanger Ganghadharan were summoned to their feet and shoved roughly next to the navigator. King Neptune then called upon the Polliwog chiefs to rise to their feet. Chief Fire Controlman Kim, Senior Chief Mechanic Krevin, Radioman Chief Goreliki and Chief Sonarman Albanese were all pushed into the group of officers. Then the first class petty officers, the second class and finally the third class, until all sixty-some Polliwogs stood in front of the King.

"Attention to orders, you scurvy, lower-than-whaleshit Polliwogs!" Quinnivan read from a long text of arcane nautical prose, something handed down centuries ago from the traditions of square-rigged sailing ships, finishing just before the 1MC shipwide announcing system clicked and the deep booming voice of the chief engineer, Elvis Lewinsky, blasted from the mess deck loudspeaker.

"Attention all hands, this is the Officer of the Deck. In ten seconds, the good ship *Vermont* will cross the equator at longitude west twenty-four degrees, fifteen minutes and twelve seconds. All you Polliwog scum, prepare to become Trusted Shellbacks. Three seconds, two, one, *equator crossing!* Welcome to the South Atlantic, Shellbacks. That is all."

"Polliwogs," Quinnivan shouted. "Remove your blindfolds!"

Pacino did as ordered, blushing as he looked at the other underwear-clad officers, chiefs and petty officers. He couldn't help noticing Romanov kept her eyes straight ahead, not looking at Pacino. "King Neptune" Quinnivan was costumed in a flowing green cape, purple coveralls, tall rubber Wellington boots and a large gold crown, holding a long scepter with a three-pointed trident at the end.

"Any of you with socks in your mouths, remove the socks and stomp them into the deck!"

Feeling like an idiot, Pacino complied, smashing his bare foot onto the damp sock.

"Now, all of you, give me the USS *Vermont* battle cry!"

"It never happened!" they all shouted in unison, Pacino screaming with the rest. *"We were never there!"*

"What? I can't hear you," Quinnivan said, cupping his hand to his ear. Three more times he made the crowd repeat the battle cry until finally he looked at them with deep satisfaction. "By the power vested in me by the Universe, the United States Navy and Her Majesty's Royal Navy, I hereby pronounce you, all of you, Trusted Shellbacks. Congratulations, Shellbacks!"

The veteran Shellback members of the crew clapped and cheered, laughing at them.

"Now get the fook out of here and clean your ragged asses up," Quinnivan barked.

Pacino waited for Navigator Romanov to finish in the head, then a few minutes more for the more senior junior officers to shower, then jumped in and shampooed the hot sauce out of his hair.

"This is nothing," Eisenhart said, toweling his hair. "Wait till we cross the Arctic Circle. Now *there*'s a crossing ceremony."

"I can wait," Pacino said.

"Pacino!" Commander Quinnivan bellowed, leaning into the supply officer's door to the wardroom. "My stateroom! Now!"

U-Boat Dankleff and Lobabes Lomax glanced up at Pacino from the remains of their breakfast dishes. Pacino had skipped working out this morning. The "Grand Convening of the Polliwog Scum" had started at midnight UTC—Zulu time—and had gone on until the crossing at 0140. After all that, Pacino hadn't seen his bunk until two in the morning and had barely slept but for a short, disturbed dream that the navigator was glaring at him.

"Great way to start the day," U-Boat smirked, grabbing the coffee carafe.

"Could be worse," Lomax said. "DCA, what are the nine most frightening words in the English language?"

Dankleff laughed. *"'The captain wants to see you in his stateroom.'"*

"Exactly."

Pacino grabbed his tablet, pushed his chair in and stepped forward to the supply officer's door, then down the narrow passageway until he reached the XO's stateroom door. He knocked twice.

"Come in!" Quinnivan shouted.

Pacino entered and shut the door quickly but quietly behind him and stood at attention. "Yes, sir," he said, staring at the bulkhead straight ahead, reminded of a Naval Academy comearound.

"Relax, Patch, and take a seat. Tea? Coffee?"

What was this all about, Pacino wondered as he sat in the chair next to the XO. Being summoned to the senior officer's stateroom had made his stomach melt in anxiety, and now Quinnivan offered coffee? Pacino considered saying no to the offer, but thought it would make the atmosphere colder.

"A black-and-bitter would be great, sir, thank you."

Quinnivan smiled and dialed the galley and asked them to have the messenger of the watch send up coffee. Almost within seconds, a knock came at the door and the messenger—obviously anticipating the executive officer's habits—brought in a carafe and two cups. Quinnivan frowned at the messenger. "What took ya so long, lad?"

The messenger hastily withdrew, and Quinnivan poured for himself and Pacino. Pacino waited for the exec to say something and reveal why he'd ordered the meeting, but the XO just took a deep pull of the brew and looked at the cup.

"You know why this cup—this simple conveyance of a hot beverage—has two blue lines on it drawn parallel to the rim?" The Pyrex white cup was inelegant, a simple cup adorned only with two blue lines.

"I guess I've never thought about it, XO," Pacino said, trying not to stare at the senior officer to figure out what was going on.

"Well, then, pay attention. The top line is the fill line for inport—or submerged. The lower-level line is the fill point for high seas, when we're rocking and rolling. Makes sense, yeah?" Quinnivan smiled warmly at Pacino.

"I suppose so, sir." The executive officer's charm was taking this somewhere, Pacino thought.

"So, lad, do you know why I called you here?" Quinnivan stared seriously into Pacino's eyes.

What had Weapons Officer Spichovich said the first night out of AUTEC on this run, when Pacino tried and failed at the last few hands of poker with him, Dankleff and Lomax? *Patch, you have no poker face. You couldn't bluff your way out of a wet paper bag. You'd better work on that, boy. Someday you'll be in command and on the business end of a bad guy's torpedo, and the entire crew will be looking at your expression to see if they'll live or die. If your face shows fear and resignation, all is lost, the battlestations crew will go limp, or worse. If your jaw tightens and you glower with a determination to fight the ship against the odds and win? Well, hell, maybe you will. And if not, you'll go down with a crew to whom you gave courage in their final moments. Not so bad a way to die, eh?*

But lying to the XO, whether through words, omission or his facial expression, that seemed more than wrong. Pacino took a deep breath.

"Well, XO, I suppose this has something to do with Weps asking to take me off Nav's watchsection and put me on his."

"Bingo, yeah? And pray tell, young non-qual, why would he do that?"

Pacino considered telling the XO that it was about having more face time with his boss, to keep Spichovich up to date on the goings-on of the sonar division, and to get qualification checkouts during prime time, when Pacino could actually sit at the sonar stack or the firecontrol console, and in truth that was part of the answer. But the real answer was that Navigator Romanov was freezing him out and it was straining his nerves.

"Well, sir, I came to him and the engineer for advice."

"About?"

"I'm not getting along very well with the navigator, sir."

Quinnivan unexpectedly laughed, his head tilting back in mirth. He picked up the phone and dialed a number, then said into the phone, "Weps? I win. That'll be a hundred bucks, as soon as Mr. Pacino shoves off." He replaced the phone and looked at Pacino. "Sorry for the interruption. I had a bet with the weapons officer about your answer. He insisted you've been working on your poker face and your bluffing skills."

Pacino could feel the color rise to his cheeks. Quinnivan opened a bound diary and made a notation in it, then shut it and looked seriously at Pacino. "Mr. Pacino, report for duty with Mr. Spichovich on this evening's eighteen-to-twenty-four watchsection. He may have you on copilot watch for a while to get a sense of your knowledge level, then pilot watch, then he may put you on the sonar stack, and finally junior officer of the deck. I expect that before we get to Point Echo for the run northeast, you'll have all your weapons department qualification signatures and you'll be operating smooth as the junior officer of the deck."

"Yes, sir," Pacino said, wondering if he should stand.

"That's all, lad. If you would, send the weapons officer to my stateroom."

Pacino grabbed his tablet computer and vaulted to his feet, opened the door and almost ran into Spichovich, who smiled at him and clapped him on the shoulder before shutting the XO's door behind him. Pacino walked back aft to the wardroom, wondering it there would be blowback from the navigator for his complaining about her. Not that his relationship with her could get any worse, he thought.

Lieutenant Commander Spichovich shut the XO's stateroom door behind him and took a seat in the chair just vacated by Pacino.

"Well, XO?"

Quinnivan just smiled his crooked smile and pointed to his open palm. "Well, my Irish ass. I need one-hundred-dollar bills, fresh from the ass crack of a Fort Lauderdale stripper, in my hands, right fookin' now."

Spichovich withdrew a huge wad of cash from his coveralls

and snapped off five crisp, newly-minted twenties and handed them to Quinnivan. "I should probably get a receipt," he said. "You'll forget tomorrow I paid up today."

Quinnivan put the money in his safe, smiling to himself.

"So XO, your secret evil plan to put a wedge between Silky and Patch-slash-Lipstick all went to plan," Spichovich said, smiling.

"I have to admit, I had my doubts Wanda Styxx would just go ahead and do as you asked, when the ask was that big. What did it cost you?"

"A favor to be named later, XO."

"So—expensive."

"Yeah, exactly."

"Well, we're back on an even keel now. Good order and discipline, Weapons Officer. Good order and discipline."

Spichovich grinned. "And what about the Nav?"

"Ah," Quinnivan said, waving his hand in the air. "She'll get over it. Just like with you." Quinnivan drilled his eyes into Spichovich's. "Except that with you, *she* moved on, but *you're* the one who's still hostile. If you'd just lighten up on her, just a little, it'll all be cool."

Spichovich stared sadly at the deck. "Yeah. I guess I'd better work on that, XO."

"You do that, Weps."

"Good order and discipline, right, XO?"

"Yes, Weps, my thoughts exactly." Quinnivan was smiling again. Spichovich stood.

"You need to see anyone else, boss?"

"Nah, I think I'll grab a little bunky before the evening watch. Those fookers on the eighteen-to-twenty-four watch are morons." The 1800-2400 watch belonged to Spichovich.

"Fuck you, Bullfrog."

"And your mother too, Sprocket," Quinnivan said, grinning.

"Have a good nap, sir."

14

South Atlantic Ocean
Point "Delta"
Tuesday, May 24

At 1220 Zulu time, the *Vermont* reached Point "Delta," the bottom of the great circle route from the Bahamas to South Africa, and the turning point to due east toward the Indian Ocean. In another seventeen hours, the ship would reach Point "Echo," marking the start of the northeastern run up the coast of Africa toward Saudi Arabia and the Gulf of Oman. The ship was due at Point "G," the entrance to the gulf, five days after that, on the afternoon watch of Monday, May 30.

Reaching Point "Delta" also marked a change in the ship's routine. Up to now, the submarine's flank run south had been uneventful, steaming full-out during the day, rising one time per 24-hour period sometime during the mid-watch to periscope depth, the PD period busy with obtaining a navigation fix to correct the inertial navigation unit, executing trash disposal and steam generator blowdowns, and receiving a passive intelligence update from the CommStar, which would automatically update all their intelligence news files and archives. Then back down below the thermal layer and speeding up to get back to "chasing PIM," in which "PIM" was their point of intended motion, or "where the brass wants our ass," as the navigator would say. The officers worked quietly on division business, worrying over equipment that might break down or had already fallen out of repair, writing endless personnel evaluations, generating the hundreds of status reports on the health of the submarine for the maintenance facilities and the squadron engineer. The SEALs onboard had been passing the time in poker games in their berthing room on the lower level adjacent to the torpedo room or working out. The chiefs stood their watches, worked on their division chores during the day, crashed in their space, the "goat locker," a sort of combination conference room, movie screening area, berthing area and head, segregated from the rest of the crew. The enlisted sailors stood their watches, occasionally rousted for "field day" to clean up the ship or participating in the many "school of the boat" sessions to learn the ship's systems and procedures in the course of their own qualifications, attempting to earn silver dolphins just as Pacino was striving to earn gold ones.

Now that they were getting closer to their destination, the senior officers had decided to conduct the operation brief, the brief going down last night, Monday evening after dinner. The department heads and junior officers were, to a man, still reeling from the disclosures made at the brief.

An Iranian diesel boat, cut in half and a liquid metal-cooled nuclear reactor shoehorned in, a fast reactor that could become unstable and blow itself apart in a superheated radioactive cloud or worse, detonate in a small nuclear explosion, if the word "small" could ever be applied to a fission bomb explosion. A reactor so potentially dangerous that the Russian designers wouldn't even test it in their vast wilderness or their backyard Arctic Ocean, but had convinced the Iranians to take it to sea and test it for them, dangling in front of the Iranians having a nuclear-powered attack submarine. There was no information on whether Russian technicians would be aboard the Kilo, a boat they'd renamed *Panther* to coincide with the name of the liquid metal reactor's design program, "Project Panther." They would sneak the *Panther* out of its base at Bandar Abbas eastward through the Gulf of Oman, presumably submerged on batteries or snorkeling on its diesel southward en route the deep Indian Ocean, "the IO," a thousand miles away from land, where intelligence estimates asserted it would then go to initial criticality on the fast reactor.

And sometime during *Panther*'s run south through the Arabian Sea on the way to the Indian Ocean, *Vermont* would sneak up on her and steal her, the same way they'd briefly hijacked the *Bigfoot* narco-sub. A group of six officers and chiefs would be chosen to lock out of the *Vermont* after the SEALs had secured the Kilo and rounded up the crew, to run the stolen submarine from the Arabian Sea back the way they'd come, down south into the Indian Ocean, around South Africa and into the South Atlantic, then speed all the way northeast to AUTEC in the Bahamas.

There was tremendous debate in the wardroom about who would be chosen to operate the hijacked submarine. All but Lieutenant Li No wanted to be chosen to conn the *Panther* back to AUTEC, Pacino first among them. It seemed low probability, he was told, because he didn't even have his dolphins yet, so why would the captain trust a non-qual to operate a stolen foreign submarine and bring it to the Bahamas?

At midrats, the meal served from 2330 to 0130, usually consisting of something simple but gut-busting, like beanie-weenies over rice, or chili with crackers, the engineer looked over at Spichovich and said, "You know, Weps, only the *least* useful officers to *Vermont* will be chosen to go, so the bosses might decide to pick *you* to go on the *Panther*. I mean, really, what do you do for a living anyway? Wait for us to shoot one of your missiles? Take inventory of torpedoes daily to make sure no one shoplifted one?"

"No way, Feng," Spichovich said without looking up from his tablet computer. "Your theory is just your way of coping with the fact that *you'll* be left behind on *Vermont* because, let's face it, tactically, you *suck*. I mean, that's why, at battlestations, you're just the engineering officer of the watch, splitting atoms and making the screw go roundy-roundy while we adults find the bad guys and put them on the bottom. So no heroics or medals for you. Just keep playing with your reactor. Oh, and as to usefulness, all you and your boys do is stare at gauge needles that don't move for the entire watch."

"Yeah, until something breaks, and then you'll be damned glad I'm useful enough to restore propulsion and get you air to breathe."

"When it was your incompetence that got it broken in the first place?"

The engineer stood and cocked his fist, but he was grinning.

"Knock it off, you two bastards," XO Quinnivan said, suppressing a smile.

"So XO, who's going on the *Panther*?" Dankleff asked, shoveling a spoonful of rancid-looking chili into his mouth.

"My fookin lips are sealed," Quinnivan said, pushing his plate away and standing.

"Can't you at least say what the selection criteria are?"

"I suppose I can say this. It comes down to our opinions of you scurvy junior officers, with maybe some metrics thrown in.

"Metrics, XO?" Dankleff stopped chewing.

"The war game simulation results. Once the Nav gets the simulations staged and ready, we're going to see how the officers do individually and as a team. Once we see how it goes, we'll know which round peg to put in which square hole."

"So, basically you're just going to draw straws?" Lewinsky grinned.

"Exactly," Quinnivan said, leaving the wardroom by the forward supply officer's door.

Reaching Point "Delta" began the simulation phase of the transit. As Lieutenant Commander Rachel Romanov had said during the op brief, "Our mission failure with the narco-sub began with a failure of imagination. No one thought that the cargo ship would escort the *Bigfoot* out of the Caribbean Sea, and we didn't have a contingency plan for that. Which forced us to improvise. And no one imagined *Bigfoot* would be conned by artificial intelligence. So, on *this* mission, long before we get to the op-area, we're going to war game this operation. We'll split into multiple teams, three blue and three red. Each blue team will play *Vermont* and give the simulation app their actions and reactions. The red teams will steal the Kilo, the *Panther,* and upload their actions and reactions to the app. A third group will be the God group, consisting of the captain, XO and me. The God group are observers from high over the earth watching as things happen, with perfect knowledge of what the tactical situation is. The God group will introduce scenarios and glitches to the simulation to see what the red and blue teams will do. The God group will also play the part of any interception force—Iranian or Russian—and upload their actions and reactions to the app. We're going to churn the assignments and make you switch from red to blue and back, with the roster changed each time, so we can evaluate which team make-up is the most effective. Gentlemen, we will be doing this for five solid days, after which the captain, XO and I will be reviewing the results. From what we see, we'll reevaluate the op plan and form contingency plans."

Pacino had volunteered to be on a red team, but Romanov put him on a blue team with Supply Officer Ganghadharan and Electrical Officer Varney. The opposing red team for the first round of simulations included Li "Doctor" No, U-Boat Dankleff and Lobabes Lomax. The first simulation went down promptly at 0800 and concluded just before noon. The second started at 1300 and continued for several hours. Pacino reported for his 1800 to 2400 watch with Spichovich, standing pilot watch for six hours. When the watch was over, he was exhausted, and slept a dreamless sleep until his alarm woke him to go aft and work out.

Southern Indian Ocean
Saturday, May 28

Navigator and Tactical Action Officer Rachel Romanov shut the captain's stateroom door behind her and took her seat at the captain's table next to Quinnivan.

"What do you think, Nav?" the XO asked.

Romanov sighed.

"You're going to think I'm crazy for recommending this," she started hesitantly. "But of all the officers, Lieutenant Pacino had the highest success rate in the simulations. He's also the most original and takes the highest risks."

"I told you he was a 'chancer,' Skipper," Quinnivan said.

"Yeah," Seagraves said, his chin in his hand, his gesture when he was deep in thought or wrestling with a difficult decision. "It was Pacino who lobbed that nuclear weapon into the sea between the Kilo and the attacking Russian submarine force farther south in the Indian Ocean."

"It made a handy blue-out across half the horizon from the Russian submarines," Romanov said. "Those zillion bubbles in the sea that blocked the Russian passive and active sonar allowed the *Panther* to clear datum, and it also got *Vermont* off Scot-free."

"Leave it to that Lipstick to reach for a nuke straight out of the chute," Quinnivan said.

"Pacino's blue team won against the scenario at a much higher percentage than the other blues. When we switched him into a red team, he didn't lose the *Panther* one time. Meanwhile, the other red teams got boarded or torpedoed by various interception forces," Romanov said.

"Or their reactors blew up when *you* were on God group watch," Quinnivan said, his eyes crinkling into a smile as looked at Romanov.

"Are you saying I put my thumb on the scale to favor Pacino?" Romanov said, a sharpness in her tone, her eyes narrowed at the XO.

Quinnivan put his palms out as if in surrender. "No, no, no, I'm not saying that," he said, trying to calm the navigator down.

"So," Seagraves said, "you're recommending we put Pacino onboard the *Panther* even though he isn't even qualified on an American sub."

"More than that, Captain," Romanov said. "I'm recommending he be put in as OIC." OIC meant officer in charge.

"*Captain* Pacino," Quinnivan mused. "I like the sound of that."

"Who would go with him, then, Nav? Pacino's the most inexperienced of the officers aboard. It would be awkward to put Dankleff or Varney or Lomax onboard with him if Pacino's in command."

"More than awkward, Skipper," Quinnivan said. "It would violate your U.S. Navy Regulations."

"I'm thinking we send in Supply Officer Gangbanger

with him. Ganghadharan is a junior grade lieutenant. Pacino outranks him."

"Who else, then?" Seagraves asked.

"We send in Chief Radioman Goreliki—she's a wizard at anything that communicates and she can modify the Iranian radio gear to accept our crypto and transceivers. We send in Chief Fire Controlman Kim—she can figure out the *Panther*'s firecontrol system if anyone can. And then Chief Sonarman Albanese, to decode the *Panther*'s sonar system. Then we send in the crypto tech we picked up in AUTEC, Indian guy, what's his name, Saurabh, who's fluent in Farsi, because we'll need translations to operate their systems."

"You've thought this through, haven't you, Nav?" Seagraves said.

"It's my best recommendation, Captain, XO," Romanov said, looking first at Seagraves, then Quinnivan.

"Let us think about it, Nav," Seagraves said. "Sending those chiefs onto the *Panther* takes our first-string operators away."

"You'll need them more on the Kilo than here. If the mission goes to plan, this is relatively uneventful for *Vermont*. The action will all be for the *Panther*."

"I hear you, Nav. It's late. Why don't you get some rest?"

"By your leave, sir," Romanov said, standing.

"Goodnight, Nav," Seagraves said.

When the door shut behind her, Seagraves looked at Quinnivan, who pulled a leather cigar carrier from his pocket, a cutter and a lighter. Seagraves opened his desk and withdrew a crystal ash tray and placed it on the table between them. Soon both officers were puffing smoke into the overhead.

"Nothing like watching cigar smoke rise to help you think, eh, Captain?"

"You know what I'm thinking, XO? It's just interesting that Romanov puts Pacino into the stolen *Panther* at the same time she's furious with him. Makes you wonder what's going on in her subconscious."

"Jaysus, Skipper," Quinnivan said, cigar smoke emerging from his nostrils. "Are you saying she's trying to get him killed?"

"You know what the simulations said in the aggregate, right,

XO? This mission has a nineteen percent chance of success. *Nineteen*. Sixty-one percent chance the *Panther* is lost at sea, from an opposing force or from its own hellish reactor exploding."

"What's the other twenty percent?"

"That we'll never know what happened. *Panther* simply vanishes. Either the Russians or the Iranians grab it or torpedo it. Or it sinks out of sensor range of the *Vermont* or an opposition force."

"Nineteen percent chance of success," Quinnivan said. "Do you think the Nav knows that little statistic?"

"How could she not, XO?"

"Still. There *is* something to be said about that young lad Pacino. He may be a chancer, but he has something I've never seen before. It's like, hell, I'll sound foolish saying this out loud to you, Skipper, but it's like that kid carries destiny itself with him. That thing on the *Piranha,* what do you think the chances were of surviving *that?"*

"About zero point zero," Seagraves said.

"Exactly," Quinnivan said, taking a puff and blowing a smoke ring. "That kid has a special kind of luck, Captain. He brings it with him. With him on the *Vermont,* we can't fail and we can't die. If we put him on the *Panther,* well, he just won't be on the *Vermont*. And I'm not afraid to admit, that scares me."

Seagraves thought for a moment, tapping a long ash off the Churchill cigar into his ash tray.

"XO, if your metaphysical argument is correct, that this kid quote, *carries destiny with him,* unquote, we'd be derelict in our duty to *not* put him on the *Panther* mission."

"You make a damned good point, Skipper. But now, let's look at this from Admiral Catardi's point of view. You just put his boss' son on a mission that has a nineteen percent chance of success. And not just any boss' son. The son that personally risked his life to rescue Catardi himself from certain death in the *Piranha* sinking. How career enhancing will it be to send Catardi a situation report stating that *Panther* sank with all hands, including one Lieutenant Anthony Pacino?"

Seagraves tamped his cigar out in the ash tray. "XO, knowing what we know? Catardi would do the same thing. And if we have to give an officer special treatment, what good is he to us? And don't forget, Pacino volunteered for this mission in the strongest possible terms. And a final point? It was Catardi who sent us on this damned mission in the first place. So we're all in this together. So it's settled. Pacino goes."

Quinnivan seemed satisfied with Seagraves' answer. "So, are you going to make him OIC?"

"XO, I just can't put a non-qual officer in command of the *Panther.* Maybe I could be convinced to make him assistant officer in charge, the AOIC, but that brings up the question, who should be OIC? Who does Pacino work best with? If Pacino is second-in-command, who can complement his tactical instincts?"

"Maybe we ask Pacino himself."

"Not a bad plan, XO. You might even call it...adequate."

Quinnivan smiled and put out his cigar.

Gulf of Oman
Point "Golf"
Monday, May 30

"Pilot, all stop," Lieutenant Commander Rachel Romanov ordered.

"All stop, Pilot aye, and Maneuvering answers, all stop," Lieutenant junior grade Ganghadharan reported.

"Mark speed four knots," Romanov said.

Almost immediately, the deck stopped its mad shaking and trembling, the sudden smoothness of the ride seeming strange after being constantly at flank speed for fifteen days.

"Mark four knots, aye."

The USS *Vermont* glided slowly to a halt at Point "Golf" at the entrance to the Gulf of Oman.

"Officer of the Deck, speed four knots," Gangbanger reported.

"Very well, all ahead one third, turns for four."

The pilot acknowledged. Romanov pulled the 7MC microphone from the crowded overhead. "Maneuvering, Conn, downshift and de-energize main coolant pumps and engage natural circulation."

The 7MC speaker overhead rasped with Li No's voice. "Downshift and de-energize reactor coolant pumps and rig for natural circulation, Conn, Maneuvering aye." A pause. "Conn, Maneuvering, the reactor is in nat-circ."

"Maneuvering, Conn, aye," Romanov said into the mike. "Pilot, left fifteen degrees rudder, steady course three-one-five." She picked the phone at the command console and buzzed the captain.

"Captain," Seagraves' baritone came over the phone.

"We're at Point 'Golf,' sir, turning northwest into the Gulf of Oman. You wanted to make a 1MC announcement."

"Be right there."

Seagraves appeared in the control room seconds later. "Captain's in control," Romanov announced. She handed Seagraves the 1MC microphone. It clicked just before the captain's voice boomed through the spaces.

"Attention all hands, this is the captain. We've completed the flank run to the entrance of the Gulf of Oman and we're slowing and turning to the northwest for the slow approach to the Strait of Hormuz. We will be setting up a chokepoint barrier search at Point 'Hotel' at the exit of the strait in order to detect and trail our target, a modified Iranian Kilo diesel-electric submarine called the *Panther.* As always, I will rely on the discretion of every member of this crew to keep our secrets. After all, what is the battle cry of the USS *Vermont?*"

Throughout the ship, the shouting of *It never happened—we were never there!* rang out.

"That's right, crew. This, all of this, never happened, and we were never here. We will be rigging the ship for ultra-quiet. The galley will accordingly be shut down—sorry about that—but we will have an abundance of cold cut sandwiches and peanut butter and jelly with cheese and crackers. Wash that down with bug juice, and you've got yourself a battlestations feast. Immediately, upon detection of the *Panther,* we will station battlestations and fall in trail. This may be a long mission, crew, so between now and reaching Point 'Hotel,' I urge you all to get whatever sleep you can. There may not be much of that after acquisition. If any of you have questions about the mission, get them to your division chiefs and division officers and, to the extent we're able to, we'll put your mind at ease. Let's all have a safe and successful mission. That is all." The 1MC clicked off and Seagraves returned the microphone to its cradle.

"Pilot, rig ship for ultra-quiet," Romanov ordered.

"Ultra-quiet, Pilot, aye." The 1MC announcing circuit clicked and rasped with the last announcement until ultra-quiet would be secured. *"Rig ship...for ultra-quiet."*

"I'll be in my stateroom with the XO," Seagraves said to Romanov. "Send Mr. Pacino to see us, please."

"Right away, sir," Romanov said.

Pacino walked down the passageway, lit with red lights as a reminder that the ship was rigged for ultra-quiet, then knocked carefully on the door of the captain's stateroom, bearing in mind what Lomax had said before, that the nine most frightening words in the English language were, *The captain wants to see you in his stateroom.*

"Come in," Seagraves called through the door.

Pacino opened it and came to attention. The overhead lights were off, the room lit by three sepia-shaded lamps, making it seem like it was evening, even though it was just after 1500 in the afternoon.

"Have a seat at the table, Mr. Pacino," Seagraves said, waving to the seat at the door side of the small café style table and seats.

"Yessir." Pacino put his tablet computer on the table.

"So, lad," Quinnivan said. "Any idea why we've called you here?"

"I suppose it's about my volunteering to be on the crew of the *Panther* when we hijack it and take it to AUTEC."

"'Hijack' is such a nasty word," Quinnivan smirked. "It sounds so unfriendly, like you're putting a gun to someone's head."

Seagraves smiled. "The XO makes a good point. We're just going to *borrow* the *Panther* for a while."

"A long while, and then we're going to take her apart all the way down to her fookin nuts and bolts," Quinnivan added.

"But you're correct, laddie, we wanted to talk to you about this mission."

Pacino waited, but neither man said anything. Seagraves was manipulating a document on this pad computer and Quinnivan was just looking at him. Finally, Pacino broke the silence.

"So, do I get to board the *Panther?*"

"Mr. Pacino," Seagraves said grimly. "You are aware, aren't you, that according to our war game simulations, this mission has one chance in five of success. Eighty percent chance says we face mission failure. Which is a nice way to say that the *Panther* goes down."

Pacino made a dismissive face and waved his hand. "What do those simulations know, Captain? That's all bull dreamed up by theorists who live their lives in cubicles. Look at the real situation. If we can board this Kilo with an element of surprise, we'll vanish into the noise of the ocean. We'll have Onur Saurabh with us, the crypto tech Farsi translator, so we can figure out their systems. And I've been thinking, sir, we could find one of the Kilo's officers who's willing to cooperate with us and give us some help."

Seagraves looked at Quinnivan, then nodded. "Mr. Pacino," he said slowly, "the XO and I have decided to place you aboard the *Panther* as assistant officer in charge. You'll be second-in-command."

Pacino wasn't prepared for that. He figured the best he would be able to do would be to be the junior officer of those selected. "May I ask, sir, who you're putting in command? Who will be OIC?"

Seagraves and Quinnivan glanced at each other.

"Laddie, who would *you* nominate?" Quinnivan asked.

"No question, Lieutenant Dankleff. He's great with diesel engines and generators, he's a great leader and he's a tactical innovator. And he's good under pressure."

"He's also pretty much your best friend aboard," Seagraves observed. "And your sea daddy when you first reported."

"That'll help the mission, Captain, not detract from it. Who else is on the *Panther* crew?" Pacino asked.

"Lieutenant Varney will come along as your operations officer and third-in-command. He's an electrical expert and knows reactor controls. You'll be accompanied by Chief Goreliki on radio, Chief Albanese on sonar and Chief Kim on artificial intelligence battlecontrol systems. And the cryptotech translator. And, of course, the SEALs."

"But as to who is OIC, that's still under discussion," Seagraves said. "Mr. Pacino, send up the navigator, will you?"

"Aye, sir. By your leave, sir."

"Granted, Mr. Pacino."

When the door shut behind him, Quinnivan looked at Seagraves. "Interesting. We'd zeroed in on Lomax as OIC, but Pacino went immediately to Dankleff."

"Let's see what Romanov thinks about that combination. But at least we have Pacino's role figured out."

A knock came at the door. Rachel Romanov came in and sat down at the captain's table.

Fifteen minutes later, aft in the wardroom, Pacino was reading news files on his pad computer when U-Boat Dankleff walked into the room—or more precisely, *danced* into the room. He grinned, offered his fist to Pacino and said, "Guess who just got named officer in charge of the *Panther*?"

Pacino grinned back and bumped U-Boat's fist. "Captain U-Boat," Pacino said.

"And I hear you're my XO."

"Yes, sir, Captain, *sir*," Pacino said, mockingly stiffening at attention in his chair.

He could already tell it would be a good mission.

The crew's mess was cordoned off at the forward and aft ends. With the galley shut down and dark, the only food was served out of a refrigerated cart placed outside the room. A petty officer was stationed at the forward door to make sure anyone wanting to enter was cleared for the goings-on inside. The aft hatch to the engineering spaces was shut and dogged, a second petty officer seated near the door to escort personnel through if they entered from aft.

Lieutenant Commander Ebenezer Fishman and Lieutenant

Commander Rachel Romanov stood at the forward bulkhead at a large dual-purpose whiteboard, which could be paired to a tablet computer or used the old-fashioned way, with dry-erase markers.

"Okay, people, listen up," Romanov said sternly. "Glitch matrix review. The following glitch possibilities have been identified for this mission. Commander Fishman will present the glitch and I'll call one person to state the contingency plan corresponding to defeat the glitch. If that person blows it, I will call on someone else until we arrive at a satisfactory answer. You people got that?"

"Yes, ma'am," several of them said in unison.

"Fine. Commander, if you'll start with the easy ones?"

"My pleasure, Navigator, but shouldn't we reveal the perfect scenario first?"

"Good point. Mr. OIC, Mr. Dankleff, recite for us, please, the textbook mission plan."

U-Boat Dankleff stood. "Yes, ma'am. Okay, pay attention, pirates. Here's the nominal mission profile. The *Panther*—which, until we take her over, is "Master One"—out-chops the Strait of Hormuz right into our barrier search trap. We follow it in complete stealth southeast out of the Gulf of Oman and continue in trail until Master One slows and rises to periscope depth for whatever reason, the most likely reason to snorkel and charge her batteries. It's possible she sends a situation report back to her base saying all is well. The SEAL force is ready in the lockout chamber. Own ship is positioned to match the speed of Master One, but slightly forward on her port bow, at her ten o'clock, and we're deeper so we can use the scopes to see what's going on, without our scopes penetrating the surface and alerting Master One.

"SEALs lock out and foul the screw of Master One. Master One surfaces and a hatch comes open and a crewman or several pop out to say 'what the fucking fuck happened to our screw?' and they are overcome by the SEALs, preferably by non-lethal means but lethal if need be. SEALs invade the ship and take out the crew, again, Plan A being the use of non-lethal shock, but Plan B being lethal means. In a perfect world, no bullets will hit equipment. The *Panther* crew is locked out and placed on or near a provisioned raft with an emergency locator beacon that will fail to work for 48 hours, and only then go off automatically to call for rescue. By that time, we'll be long gone.

"At this point, the boarding party locks out of *Vermont* and locks in to the *Panther* and the submarine is ours. The base plan is to drive off the track of a great circle route around Africa to the southeast, parallel to the west coast of India, then due south to the a point midway between South Africa and Antarctica, then westward into the Atlantic—the idea being that this course keeps us off shipping lanes and isn't a predictable route from the point of the successful hijacking. We continue westward, again, off the great circle route to the Bahamas, only turning when we can go north-northwest, finally turning due west slightly north of the Tropic of Cancer to head in to the Bahamas and AUTEC.

"All this time, we are submerged deep on batteries by day, at a moderate speed that allows battery endurance until dark, which we'll need to figure out once we're aboard. Our intelligence on the watt-hours of the Kilo's battery is all over the map. During the night, a few hours before dawn, we go to periscope depth, make sure we're alone in the sea, and snorkel to charge the batteries. By the time the sun rises, we're deep again, running silent until the next excursion to PD.

"How was that, Nav?" Dankleff sat back down.

"You forgot that *Vermont* will be in trail of you to make sure no one sneaks up you to try to take you out, whether Iranian or Russian, and to keep track of you," Romanov said, frowning, her eyes briefly locking on Pacino's, her frown growing more angry. "It would be nice to be able to know what's going on with you guys, in case anyone in authority asks."

"Right, Nav," Dankleff said, unruffled by the navigator's frostiness.

"So, can we go to glitch number one, Commander?" Romanov said, addressing Fishman.

"Glitch numero uno, people. Master One comes barreling out of the Gulf of Oman submerged, deep, at high speed, on her batteries," Fishman said.

"Mr. Dankleff?" Romanov pointed at U-Boat.

"*Vermont* chases Master One, keeping in trail, SEAL force ready to suit up so that when Master One does eventually go to PD, we can take her. Easy day."

"Okay, next, Commander Fishman."

"Glitch two starts out as glitch one. Master One blasts out of the Gulf of Oman deep and fast. We chase her and remain in trail. But somewhere during Master One's underway, she starts her reactor and is independent of the surface. Master One continues hauling ass to wherever she's going, without going up to periscope depth."

"Let's hear from the AOIC, Mr. Pacino, for this one," Romanov said, looking at Pacino.

Pacino stood up and addressed the room. "Same as glitch number one, Nav. *Vermont* chases Master One. He may be independent of the surface, but he can't stay submerged forever. His navigation will eventually go to shit and he'll need a navigation fix. The Kilo's atmospheric control equipment is okay, but any malfunction means he'd need to ventilate. At some point, his mission ends and he has to bring the boat back to base. He'll want to come to periscope depth to refine his navigation fix before entering restricted waters, like the Gulf of Oman. Chances are high we could get him before he in-chops the gulf."

"What if he remains submerged deep well into the Gulf of Oman, only popping up before the Strait of Hormuz?"

"Mission failure," Pacino said, looking Romanov in the eye. "But that scenario would never happen. Hell, even with *our* inertial nav, the Goddess of the Fix Error Circle eventually has her way with you. Any sub doing what you described would run aground or hit an underwater seamount if it tried to do that for the thousands of miles we're talking about traveling."

"You can only hope, Mr. Pacino," Romanov said coldly. "Commander, glitch three?"

"Master One comes to periscope depth when the SEALs foul its screw, and like the narco-sub, it turns out it's operated by an AI computer system."

"Ops Officer, Mr. Varney, go," Romanov said.

"Let's say the SEALs can get in," Varney began, rising to his feet. "They'll have to react to whatever the AI system is doing. If the ship is stable with the invasion force onboard, they'll have time to bring aboard the boarding party, and Chief Kim will disable the AI and shift to manual control. Then the mission continues as before. If the AI looks like it is taking hostile action, such as a ship self-destruct, Commander Fishman pulls the pin on the Mark 14 NNEMP pod and the electromagnetic pulse takes out any electronics not directly shielded from the blast."

"Won't that destroy the nuclear reactor electronics?" Romanov asked.

"We think the heavy steel bulkhead between the forward compartment and the new reactor compartment would prevent reactor electronics from being affected. There's a large shield tank with a lead lining between the compartments, for shielding from neutron and gamma radiation from the reactor, but it will work the opposite direction, shielding the reactor electronics from the EMP."

"What about ship control systems?"

"If the EMP makes ship control impossible, we may have bigger problems," Varney admitted.

"Let's say you start to sink. What do you do?"

"Look for a ballast tank blow system or the levers to an emergency ballast tank blow system. This Kilo isn't designed ground-up to be run by AI, so any AI in command is superimposed on top of the original manually controlled systems. Somewhere in the control room is the ability to blow ballast. We'd use it to surface. *Vermont* would have to call for a surface task force to tow the Kilo out of there."

"And what if you're going down?" Romanov persisted.

"We evacuate the Kilo, lock out of it, attach a sonar locator beacon to the upper hatch so we can find her on the bottom, climb on to a raft and await rescue from the *Vermont*. And *Vermont* will chart the position of the sinking with precision so we can come back and salvage or explore the wreck at a later date."

"So, not exactly a good day at sea, eh, Mr. Varney?"

"No, ma'am."

"Okay, Commander, glitch four."

"At the point the SEALs enter the hull, the crew of the *Panther* resist heavily with small arms fire, maybe automatic rifle fire. Maybe they start to act to initiate a manual self-destruct or scuttle the sub."

"Chief Goreliki, what happens then?" Romanov said, addressing the radio chief.

Radioman Chief Bernadette "Gory" Goreliki stood up. She was petite, barely five feet tall, with sleek, straight black hair, dark skin and a Cuban accent. It was a shipwide mystery why she had a Polish surname, but she would only smile and change the subject when asked.

"The first SEAL in pulls the pin on an H2S grenade—and hopefully his scuba rig has a good airtight seal."

"So, hydrogen sulfide gas, Chief. What will it do to the *Panther* crew?"

"At a thousand parts per million, Nav, it will cause immediate death. One grenade in a room will give us about ten times that. Two or three are the base plan. We can be confident it would kill anyone in the control room and give the SEALs time to search the other compartments, but even in lower concentrations elsewhere in the ship, the H2S will immobilize other crewmen from the ventilation system spreading the gas. The gas is flammable and corrosive, so at the earliest opportunity, we'll want to ventilate the submarine."

"Chief, why lethal H2S?" Romanov asked. "Why not use non-lethal halothane and fentanyl, like the Russians did to retake that theater from Chechen terrorists back in the day? That drops people in their boots but doesn't kill them."

"That combination is effective but unpredictable," Goreliki said. "To this day, we're still not exactly sure what the chemical combination or formula was for the gas the Russians used. And while some survived, it did kill others. Meanwhile, H2S is a no-nonsense, more certain response to a counterattack by ship's force. It's lethal, but that's life in the big city."

"It could also hurt our people, though, right?" Romanov said.

"Our procedure is that no one takes off their scuba rig until we've tested the atmosphere in the *Panther*."

"Very well, Chief, thank you. Commander?"

"Glitch five. We take the *Panther* successfully, but we miss a hidden member of the Iranian crew or the Russian test technicians, and when we least expect it, the person either sabotages the ship or comes out with weapons to kill us."

"This one's for you, Chief Albanese," Romanov said, pointing to the sonar chief.

Albanese stood, his voice nervous, obviously uncomfortable speaking to an audience. "Prevention is the key to this one, Nav. We do a thorough search of the ship visually and with infrared sensors. We tested these in the torpedo room bilges and the aft compartment lower level. If a warm body is hiding, we'll find him. We're vulnerable to attack from a hidden crewman until we conduct the search, so by procedure, we'll all be armed with weapons drawn until we can verify we're clear. Kind of like when cops kick down a door, unsure of whether there are hidden bad guys."

"Nicely done, Chief," Romanov said, smiling at the sonarman. "Commander, glitch six?"

"This is my favorite," Fishman said. "On the way out of the Gulf of Oman and continuing into the Arabian Sea and perhaps even into the Indian Ocean, Master One is escorted by and guarded by an Iranian gunship or gunships, perhaps even a frigate or destroyer."

"Chief Kim, this one's for you," Romanov said, smiling at the chief.

Firecontrol Chief Nancy "K-Squared" Kim rose to her feet. Like Albanese, she wasn't used to public speaking. A daughter of a South Korean immigrant and business mogul, Kim was technically brilliant and confident of that fact, never stumped by the myriad problems presented by *Vermont*'s AN/BYG-1 combat control system, but then, she'd been in on the birth of the unit in the DynaCorp AI labs that brought the complex system to fruition.

"Well, let me see," she said in a thick Korean accent, speaking just a notch too loud, which Pacino had always found somewhat odd. "I think Mr. Pacino solved that riddle once before, Commander. We launch a Kakivak cruise missile at the surface force and the EMP blast knocks them dead. Then we proceed to take the *Panther* as before."

"Do our rules of engagement allow us to do that?" Romanov asked.

"Yes ma'am. The ROE allows non-lethal weapon employment."

"What if the escorting surface force is Russian? And what if there are several of them? A task force?"

"It doesn't matter whose flag the ships fly. We launch an NNEMP Kakivak at them and they'll all shut down."

"Well done, Chief. Next, Commander?"

"Glitch seven, people. *Panther* will need refueling four, five or six times en route AUTEC. What if she gets attacked on the surface while refueling or re-provisioning?"

"Back to Mr. Varney," Romanov said.

"We've all got these laminated cards with latitude and longitude of your disguised refueling ships. It's preferred that we re-provision on the surface, but if the area's considered hot, there's a procedure for refueling us while we're submerged and hovering. It sounds like a recipe for an oil spill to me, or seawater contamination of the oil bunkers, but whatever."

"What if you lose the cards or run out of fuel far from one of these refueling ships?"

"We lock out a diver with the sat-phone in a waterproof pouch. Speed dial one gets us a dispatcher. The phone provides our location automatically, fueling ship comes to us. But if we have to loiter in one place waiting for a refuel, it could be hazardous to our health. And use of the phone could get us detected if surveillance direction-finder equipment is listening."

"Not much we can do about that, Mr. Varney," Romanov said sternly. "Next, Commander."

"The escort force is a Russian attack submarine. Let's say, for the sake of argument, it's a Russian Akula III class."

"Let's go back to the OIC. Mr. Dankleff, what then?"

"We've talked about this among ourselves," Dankleff said, standing. "Let's assume the Akula can trail the Kilo-class but can't counterdetect *Vermont*. In that case, we're looking at mission failure, because presumably if the *Panther* surfaced, the

Akula would heave-to and render aid, and if at that point it *did* discover *Vermont*, *Vermont* might end up shooting at us trying to defend the *Panther*. And if the Akula can somehow detect us, it could shoot at us preemptively. Of course, we'd shoot back, but we'd have a messy international incident on our hands, and it's predictable that it could get worse. Of course, any shoot-out between two opposing submarines, well, it could go either way. Naturally, we're confident we could prevail over an Akula, but what if a Yasen-class decides to show up? We might be evenly matched, or God help us, outmatched. Any hesitation on our part to shoot him could prove fatal, and our present rules of engagement prevent us from shooting first. If we have to wait to fire on a submarine escort, not only are we talking about mission failure, we could be risking the *Vermont*'s survival. And in addition to attacking us, the Akula or the Yasen might decide to sink the *Panther* just to protect Russian secrets. This glitch—to use technical terms—is a total clusterfuck."

"Thank you for that color commentary, Mr. Dankleff. So what do you recommend?"

"I know this is a dark transit, but we need to transmit a request to revise our ROE."

"You'd change our rules of engagement to what, DCA?"

"We need authorization to employ weapons against an opposing submarine escort force."

Romanov stared at Dankleff, finally dropping her eyes for a moment, then looked at Fishman. "Let's skip to the final glitch, Commander."

"Okay, glitch nine. The *Panther* is armed with torpedoes and decides to shoot at us while we're trying to hijack him."

"Mr. AOIC?" Romanov asked, looking at Pacino.

Pacino stood. "Let's assume we have at least three tube-loaded ADCAP Mod 9s in CMT mode." CMT mean countermeasure anti-torpedo mode. "I'd launch a salvo of them at the likely inbound bearings to the *Panther*'s torpedoes, clear datum deep at flank, and at the right point, slow and hover to eliminate any doppler sonar returns."

"You know, CMT mode is expected to be a dismal failure in a real encounter, right?" Romanov snarled.

"I know."

"So, twice your scenarios face mission failure, right, Mr. Pacino?"

"There's still something we could do," Pacino said. "I could detonate a SubRoc depth charge in the path of incoming torpedoes. That would do the trick, and probably prevent the *Panther* from firing again."

"Mr. Pacino, the rules of engagement prohibit first use of weapons against a Russian submarine counterforce, and they *absolutely* prohibit your use of *nukes*."

Pacino could feel the anger rising in him, knowing his face was flushing.

"But you have to admit, it *would* work, Nav."

"I think we've run through quite enough," Captain Seagraves' hard baritone voice said from the forward entrance to the room. Pacino looked over, wondering how long he'd been listening. "I want to see the boarding party in the wardroom along with you, Navigator."

Romanov swallowed hard. She shot an angry look at Pacino, then gathered her pad computer and walked past him toward the wardroom.

15

Gulf of Oman
Monday, May 30

Pacino found his usual seat in the wardroom. Captain Seagraves took his seat at the aft end of the table, XO Quinnivan to his right, Navigator Romanov to his left. Opposite Pacino was U-Boat Dankleff and Boozy Varney, then Chiefs Albanese and Kim next to Varney, with Chief Goreliki seated to Pacino's left on his side of the table. Dankleff passed around a carafe of coffee and Pacino filled up and passed it to Chief Goreliki.

"So, Nav, I notice we have problems with our rules of engagement," Seagraves began, opening the meeting.

"Captain, any escorting forces with teeth cause mission failure," Romanov said evenly. "We need to know how badly the bosses want the *Panther*. Enough to let us turn some ADCAP torpedoes loose on an escorting Russian attack sub or pop a nuke in the ocean to confuse things? We need authorization to use lethal force pre-emptively at the discretion of *Vermont*'s commanding officer. We need to send a message requesting revised rules of engagement."

"We're in a radio-silenced dark transit," Quinnivan said to Romanov. "Do I really have to remind you?"

"We could pop a SLOT coded for a delayed transmission," Pacino offered. "Wait twenty-four hours, come up to PD in the gulf and raise the HDR and see what the brass say." A SLOT was a submarine-launched one-way transmitter buoy, the unit the size of a baseball bat and fired while submerged from one of two signal ejectors, each a miniature torpedo tube pointed skyward. The SLOT would be loaded with an encrypted coded preformatted message, and when it broached the surface, it would transmit in a brief burst communication to the CommStar communications satellite constellation in low earth orbit, then self-destruct and sink. The reply would take some time, presumably requiring permission from the president himself, but when it arrived it would come back down from the satellite to their HDR high data rate radio antenna, which was more sensitive and faster than the receiver on the periscope.

Seagraves considered for a moment. "You have a problem with that XO, Navigator?"

Quinnivan and Romanov glanced at each other. Romanov found her voice. "It violates the op-order, sir," she said, "but I think we could be forgiven for coloring outside the lines this one time."

"I say we do it, Captain," Quinnivan said, his hand making a fist on the table.

"Navigator, bring the coded draft of the message to my stateroom and have the communicator standing by with a SLOT buoy. Then notify the OOD."

"Yes, sir," Romanov said, standing, shooting a piercing glare at Pacino for a moment before she left, the captain and XO following behind her, the chief petty officers rising and clearing out, their clan famous for not liking being in the wardroom any longer than they had to be.

Dankleff stared into the distance. Pacino snapped his fingers in front of U-Boat's eyes.

"Hey, OIC, where are you?"

Dankleff blinked and returned to the present. "This mission just started to feel real," he said. "It's not just a war game simulation or a scenario anymore. And I'm just wondering what the chances are of the Russians *not* guarding their nuclear reactor test platform. I feel like, fuck, Patch, I feel like I can *hear* Russian subs out there."

"Can you hear the sounds of their hulls imploding as they go down from our ADCAP torpedoes?"

"Whoa, there, Mister Aggressive. Just because Dominatrix Navigatrix isn't your sweetheart anymore doesn't mean you should go all *firing-point-procedures* on our Russian friends."

"Hey," Pacino said, smirking. "I'm a pirate *and* a warrior."

Washington, D.C., USA
The White House
Monday, May 30

National Security Advisor Michael Pacino put President Carlucci's torch lighter to the tip of the Cuban Cohiba and puffed it to life, peering through the smoke at the president as he passed the lighter back, the torch lighter showing the worn emblem of VFA-41 with its ace of trumps emblem, the logo of the F-18 squadron that had once been attached to the aircraft carrier USS *Ronald Reagan*.

"Two fingers?" Carlucci asked, a crystal carafe of Balvenie 30 scotch poised over Pacino's empty crystal rocks glass.

"Perfect," Pacino said.

Vito Nunzio Carlucci, who went by the first name "Paul" in an effort to defuse a name that the local Ohio media had once characterized as sounding like it belonged to a New Jersey mob enforcer, was a tall, slender, distinguished fifty-year old with a full head of gray hair that swept over his ears, his features seeming more aristocratically British than Italian. He had once been in the Navy as a young junior officer, leaving the fleet to run for mayor of his native city of Cleveland. The lore of his Navy career had boosted him in the lion's den of Ohio politics since Carlucci had flown one of the fighter jets off the aircraft carrier USS *Ronald Reagan* in the Bo Hai Bay rescue mission of the captured submarine *Tampa* and the *Seawolf*, which was how he and Pacino eventually met, when Pacino paid him a visit to thank him for saving his *Seawolf* from the relentless depth charging of the Red Chinese surface action force. Carlucci's F-18's missiles had blown apart three Chinese destroyers and sank a fast frigate, allowing the *Seawolf* to survive and live to fight another day. By the day of their meeting, Carlucci was running for the American Party's U.S senate seat from Ohio, and the two men became fast friends.

Carlucci avoided the Oval Office, much preferring the remodeled presidential study a few doors down, the room done in dark mahogany paneling with a large tigerwood desk and overstuffed leather chairs facing a ridiculously huge fireplace, where Carlucci kept a fire going even in sweltering Washington summers, the new air conditioning unit able to keep the room feeling freezing despite the logs crackling in the hearth. The windowless room was outfitted as a SCIF, a special compartmented information facility, with air-gapped electronics, no wifi, no ethernet connections, and best of all—according to Carlucci—no phone. A fan of Cuban cigars and scotch, Carlucci particularly enjoyed brainstorming with Pacino, since they could fill the room with smoke and get creative under the mild influence of Scotland's finest.

Former Admiral Michael Pacino had turned sixty last fall, but was still as gaunt as he'd been as a midshipman. Well over six feet tall, Pacino's stark cheekbones and penetrating emerald-green eyes shone under a canopy of snow-white hair, the legend that his once coal-black hair had gone to white after the Arctic Ocean mission's sinking of the first USS *Devilfish*. Other than the wrinkles at the corners of his eyes and the weathered skin of his face, Pacino looked like a youngish fifty-year old, as if he could be in a commercial for one of those Florida retirement golf-course neighborhoods.

"You know, Patch, the media scolded me for appointing you." Carlucci put down his glass and made a sweeping motion with his arms and hands, as if framing a large headline. "'Carlucci appoints warmonger admiral as top advisor in nod to military-industrial complex.' Can you believe that?"

"Well, sir, the War of the East China Sea *was* somewhat bloody," Pacino admitted. "Are you sure you still want me on the payroll?"

"Hell, yes, Patch. Those wonks can suck wind. You're the one I want doing my thinking. Seriously, this office, this position? There's way too much going on to think clearly, cohesively, about the one thing that truly matters—national security. No doubt about it, you're the man."

"Glad to help, sir," Pacino said, peering through a cloud of smoke at the president.

"So, Patch, this just came in. The duty officer rushed in here right before you arrived. Gave me this."

Carlucci handed over a clipboard with a simple printout on it. Pacino scanned it, then read it slowly from the beginning, then read it a second time. The USS *Vermont* had broken radio silence to request a change in the rules of engagement to capture the Iranian nuclear submarine test platform, the enhanced ROE to include approval to attack and sink foreign submarines, surface ships and employ nuclear weapons—presumably in an effort to confuse the opposition force, but also with the possibility that they'd be used on the opposition forces themselves. Finally Pacino looked up at President Carlucci.

"So, Mr. President, how vital is capturing and keeping this Iranian submarine? Is it worth slaughtering Russians over? Is it worth the public relations disaster of tossing a nuclear weapon in anger?"

"Assuming you know what I know, what do you think the answer to that question is?"

"Shouldn't we be convening the joint chiefs at the Pentagon, and the Secretary of War, SecNav, SecAirForce and SecArmy?"

"You'd think that would be logical, Patch," Carlucci said, pouring himself another two fingers. "But none of them are cleared for *Top Secret Fractal Chaos.* They have this annoying tendency to leak juicy things to the SNN NewsFiles. So, for the moment, it's just you, me, Admiral Catardi and two top officials at CIA."

"You didn't answer the question, sir."

"What question?"

"How important is it to grab this nuclear-powered Iranian sub? The context of this mission suggests that if Russian or Iranian forces oppose the *Vermont* crew, that *Vermont* should clear datum, get out of there undetected and let the Kilo test platform go. It's a test of a revolutionary new reactor and the placing of a nuclear-powered sub in the hands of the Iranians—neither of which are good news for us, but not something to risk a shooting war with the Russians over."

Carlucci considered for a long moment, then looked up a Pacino. "You remember, just now, I said to assume you know everything I know? Well, no surprise, you don't. There's another program I'm reading you into now. It's classified Release-12. A program run by the Director Combined Intelligence, Margo Allende, and Admiral Rand, the CINC of the Atlantic and Pacific fleets. Its codename is *Operation Blue Hardhat*." Carlucci opened his desk and withdrew a folder, broke the top-secret seal and handed it to Pacino. Pacino scanned it, then stood to put pen to the twelve places he had to sign to acknowledge the secrecy of the program. He handed the folder back and sat back down, raising an eyebrow at Carlucci.

"*Blue Hardhat* is a human intelligence operation," Carlucci began, "infiltrating Russian shipyards with our own engineers, technicians and scientists. There's an encyclopedia of information that's come out of it, but it boils down to one disappointing fact. The Russian submarine program has leapfrogged over our own. Their improved 'Yasen-M' class, built on the old Severodvinsk submarine platform, is suspected to have an acoustic advantage over our Virginia class. They're now believed to be quieter and stealthier, at least by the *Blue Hardhat* guys."

Pacino frowned. "That's not good."

"Vostov is starting to brag about his weapons systems. He talks about Russian resurgence as a superpower. He's rattling his saber louder and louder every time we talk."

"Is he bluffing?"

"I have no idea. But something comes to mind, a chat I had with Vostov a year ago, and God help me, I hope this isn't part of his thinking now."

"What do you mean, Mr. President?"

"Let's assume for a moment that at that time, Dmitri Vostov and I had a close and trusting friendship in spite of all the craziness of our military-industrial complexes and our differing views of the roles of our nations in the world. I told Vostov there was a huge gap in both of our knowledge of the other—that is, who had the most capable attack submarine. With programs that both our nations are investing tens of billions into? So I was thinking, shouldn't we know, not guess, whose submarines are superior? I told Dmitri that I had this crazy idea that we should each send one submarine into an open sea and let them take each other on. One submarine only. And no surface ships and no antisubmarine warfare aircraft. Just submarine vs. submarine. And each one would have unlimited weapons release. Who would win? Of course, Vostov laughed and said his Yasen-M would put my Virginia-class on the bottom without breaking a sweat. As for me, I told him I remained confident and convinced that our submarine would prevail. Don't you feel the same way, Patch?"

Pacino considered for a long time. "Sir, beyond the ships' acoustic advantage or disadvantage, it comes down to the crews of both ships, the rules of engagement and the scenario. Hell, it could come down to which crew is more rested and who had the better breakfast. But on a good day, yes, I think a Virginia could put down a sole Yasen-M. But against two or three? That's a different story. And no realistic scenario in the open seas would result in a hot battle happening between two lone attack submarines. There would always be a surface warship force involved, destroyers with antisubmarine helicopters. And MPA marine patrol aircraft dropping sonobuoys all over the place and using the magnetic anomaly detectors and hydrogen stream detectors. The slightest sniff of an unfriendly submarine and that submarine would be on the bottom, perhaps even hundreds of miles from the other submarine. So, it would never, ever come down to our sub vs. their sub." Pacino's words about 'open seas' were significant, he thought, because a million years ago, his USS *Devilfish* was sent into just that situation, one American submarine taking on a Russian, but that had been under the polar icecap where no aircraft could detect a submarine and no surface ships could intrude.

Carlucci nodded. "Anyway, enough about that fantasy of one submarine going up against the other. Back to the present. This mission came up, and now it's clear we need to take that Iranian submarine. And now there's the worry that it may be escorted by a Yasen-M sub. And Patch, despite the possibility of an escort Russian force, we *have* to grab that Iranian. There's no question about it. And as to rules of engagement, we were going to wait until *Vermont* arrived in-theater, and then send them a directive authorizing any and all force to be used at the discretion of the USS *Vermont* commanding officer against any opposition force. That the mission is of the highest importance to the national security of the United States. That this is a must-win situation. That *anything* standing between *Vermont* and mission success should be, well, blown to bits."

Pacino looked at his cigar, which had gone cold. He put it in Carlucci's ash tray.

"I know what you're thinking, Patch. Your boy is on the *Vermont*. And here I am sending his sub on this mission."

Pacino consciously tried to harden his expression. "My son will be fine, Mr. President." Could Carlucci detect that Pacino's voice had quivered, just slightly, from the emotions rushing through him?

"He's quite a kid, isn't he, Patch? That story from the *Piranha* sinking, just amazing."

"He is, sir. Listen, Mr. President, I looked into the crew of the *Vermont*. They're our best officers, chiefs and enlisted, driving our newest Virginia-class, which is loaded with every weapon that would ever be needed. A Yasen-M trying anything—with our new rules of engagement—might be defeated, sir, assuming the action happens fast. But if this develops over an extended period of time, the Russians could send in destroyers and frigates with helicopters and blanket the sea with sonobuoys dropped by antisubmarine aircraft, all of which are loaded with torpedoes. A concerted and coordinated Russian antisubmarine effort from submarines, surface ships and aircraft would simply doom our Virginia-class. And the mission would fail."

"I see your point, Patch. Let's hope it won't come to that. With luck, we'll get in, get out and sneak out of there, and no one gets hurt, and the Yasen-M's never even hear us. Don't worry, Patch. The *Vermont* and your boy will be fine."

But as Pacino drove back to the Annapolis house, long after dark, all he could do was worry. Anthony, Pacino's flesh and blood, was at sea on a project submarine with orders to arm its weapons and use any and all force against Russian opposition, on a mission that was dangerous on a good day.

There was no doubt. If Anthony's mother ever heard about this, National Security Advisor Michael Pacino was a dead man.

Gulf of Oman
40 hours from Point "Hotel,"
central point of Hormuz Strait barrier search
USS Vermont
Wednesday, June 1

"Depth two hundred feet, ma'am," Pilot Ganghadharan reported to Officer of the Deck Romanov.

The phone at the conn's command console buzzed. "Officer of the Deck," Romanov said.

"Radio," Chief Goreliki's voice came over the circuit. "Flash message in the buffer, marked 'personal for commanding officer.' Also, there's an immediate priority intelligence file update."

"Send the message to the captain's stateroom," Romanov said.

She clicked into her pad computer to look at the intelligence file update. There was a recent set of aerial photographs taken by a Predator drone, looking down on the Iranian Navy's Bandar Abbas base, the photos showing a submarine steaming out of the interior basins of the base and past the breakwater to the Strait of Hormuz. She zoomed far in, and it was definitely a Kilo-class, a stretched hull Kilo-class. No doubt, that was the *Panther.*

Dammit, she thought, *Vermont* wouldn't be at the Point "Hotel" barrier search point near Bandar Abbas until Thursday after midnight. They should have been at the barrier search outside the straight when the Kilo was towed out of the base and into the deep waters of the gulf. The previous intelligence had the test run starting with the Kilo leaving port next Monday, June 6. This was almost a week early. Now they would have to intercept the Kilo on his run eastward out of the gulf, toward the Arabian Sea and beyond to the Indian Ocean. And if he submerged and went silent on his batteries, there was risk he'd get by them, with the result a mission failure. *Another* mission failure, she thought.

The conn phone buzzed again. "Officer of the Deck."

"Captain," Seagraves' baritone came over the circuit. "I'm sending the flash message to your pad computer. Get the engineer to relieve you on the conn and come to the wardroom. Emergent op brief."

"Yessir," Romanov said. She hung up the phone and turned to see Lieutenant Commander Lewinsky standing behind her. "What took you so long, Feng?" she said, smirking. She gave him a brief on the tactical picture.

"I've got it. I relieve you, ma'am," the engineer said.

"I stand relieved," Romanov replied. "Pilot, Nav-ET, Lieutenant Commander Lewinsky has the deck and the conn." She was already out of the room as they acknowledged her. She hurried aft in the passageway to the wardroom while scanning the incoming flash message. As she reached the middle of the message, she stopped and read the remainder. "Holy shit," she gasped.

The wardroom was crowded. Seagraves and Quinnivan were already seated. She made her way to her seat, since she wouldn't be presenting.

"Okay, quiet, everybody," Quinnivan said, frowning at his computer. He projected his tablet's display onto the large flatpanel screen, showing the text of the incoming message.

"As all of you can see," Seagraves began, "we have a change to the rules of engagement. We are not only authorized but *ordered* to use all quote, *necessary force,* unquote, to accomplish this mission, including the tactical use of nuclear weapons, all at the complete discretion of the commanding officer."

There was a shocked silence in the room for a moment. Romanov spoke up. "Captain, if that's the case, we need to get back to the simulation war games. At the time we did them, we considered Russian or Iranian opposition forces to be unlikely or something that would cancel the operation. Any simulated battles we did with those forces were somewhat whimsical." *And ended with mission failure or worse, the sinking of the Kilo or* Vermont *herself,* Romanov thought. "With this ROE change, we need to practice in earnest against attacks and counterattacks from a Russian attack boat or an Iranian destroyer."

Seagraves checked his watch. "You have less than forty hours before we reach barrier search Point Hotel," he said. "I suggest you all get busy. XO, my stateroom, if you please."

Quinnivan shut the door and sank into his usual seat at the captain's table.

"What do you think, XO?" Seagraves' arms were crossed across his chest.

"I think there's more to this mission than stealing an Iranian modified Kilo submarine. Maybe there's something on that sub that the brass aren't telling us."

"I don't think so. This order," Seagraves slapped the display of his pad computer, "almost makes it seem like the NSC and the president *want* us to pick a fight with an opposition force. And sink it. As if this is some type of demonstration of capability. Or a message to Tehran or Moscow. Or both."

Quinnivan thought a moment. "That's one thing if it's a submarine we're up against. Sinking a sub doesn't leave much of an immediate forensic trace. Submarines are lost at sea every year. Too many bad things can happen deep underwater, yeah? But a surface ASW force? Sinking an antisubmarine warfare destroyer is going to make for a juicy headline. Satellite News Network will be blasting that all over the globe within minutes. Every swingin' dick out there owns a satellite-synched cell phone with video capability now. There's a good chance a destroyer sailor could film the whole thing, or even live-stream it, while it's attacked from an apparently empty ocean. Worse if we use a Tomahawk cruise missile. A flame trail would lead right down to the launch point. And to us."

"That last doesn't worry me," Seagraves said. "If I have to attack by daylight, I'll use the delay function on the cruise missile capsule. It'll just float there until the timer goes off, then launch, and by then we'll be a mile away. What does worry me is if a Russian Akula III or, God help us, a Yasen-M-class attack sub shows up. No one's very certain back in the hallowed halls of Submarine Force HQ whether, on an even playing field, we could take them down."

"Bah," Quinnivan said dismissively. "The fookin *Severodvinsk* was dreamed up in the late 1980s. They laid the keel in, what, 1993? Then it rusted till they found the money to complete it in the teens. Sub didn't get operational till 2013. And I'd remind you, for the last ten years, it's been at the bottom of the Atlantic, in a million pieces, put there by an American torpedo. The Yasen-class are an old, obsolete, hunk of junk design, Skipper. We'd take a Yasen to the bottom before it even had a *sniff* of us on its sonar."

"*Severodvinsk* was a Yasen class," Seagraves said, paging his computer to an intelligence file. "The only one. The Yasens after that are 'Yasen-M,' for modernized. An understatement. Everything is new. You can hardly compare the Yasen-M to the old rustbucket *Severodvinsk*. The Yasen-M should probably have been given a new class name, but the Russians were doing something funny with their budget office, wanted to make it seem like they were just cost-effectively building the next unit of the model, but the M-class is *new* from the propulsor to the sonar dome. All new electronics, with a high level of automation. From a tonnage standpoint, the M is twice our size, almost fourteen thousand tons to our eight thousand. Her reactor is a two-hundred-megawatt monster to our mere ninety. Her crew is all of sixty officers and enlisted, less than half our hundred and thirty, a sure indicator of automation and the incorporation of AI systems. The M can do thirty-five knots to our thirty-two, and in silent mode with natural circulation, it'll do twenty-eight to our twenty-five. XO, our test depth is twelve hundred feet. Yasen-M can take it down to over two thousand, and do I need to remind you, that depth is knocking on the door of the crush depth of the Mod 9 ADCAP torpedo? If we ever got into a hot war with the Russians, hell, they'd just take her to test depth plus a little more and wait till our torpedoes implode, then shoot us out of the water. We're still guessing how many weapons she carries, but I'd lay you odds she's got the jump on us in sheer number of torpedoes. And don't get me started on the hellish weapons she has. And acoustically? Should I remind *you* that we've never yet been able to trail a Yasen-M submarine? Our Virginias have lurked outside the Zapadnaya Litsa Northern Fleet submarine base for the M-class and fell in trail for all of half a mile before the target would vanish. For all we know, they can hear us before we can hear them. Our so-called acoustic advantage may have flipped in favor of the M-class. Let's just admit it, XO, we wouldn't want to run into a Yasen-M-class in a dark alley."

Quinnivan whistled as he paged his own tablet through the intelligence. "Maybe we'll get lucky," he said after a moment. "Maybe there won't *be* an opposition force. Maybe the *Panther* will go out alone to do his reactor test. It's dangerous, so going out there alone without an escort is a damned good probability."

"Yeah," Seagraves said. "I'm sure you're right."

Gulf of Aden, Yemen
Port Aden Container Facility,
K-573 *Novosibirsk*
Wednesday, June 1

Captain First Rank Yuri Orlov stood on the pier looking at the seemingly combat-ready Yasen-M-class attack submarine K-573 *Novosibirsk* of the proud Russian Federation Pacific fleet.

"Another one, Captain?" his first officer, Captain Second Rank Ivan Vlasenko asked. When Orlov nodded, Vlasenko shook out another cigarette, the highly coveted American brand, Camel, almost impossible to get on the Russian Pacific coast. They tasted so much smoother than the Russian brands, Orlov thought, which tasted like toilet paper and left an aftertaste like cleaning chemicals.

"Where did you get these?" Orlov puffed the cigarette to life, inhaling the smoke deeply, then looking at the glowing tip of the cigarette. There was no doubt about it, a man could think with a cigarette between his fingers.

"My wife's sister travels for business. Somehow she got them through customs. I suspect she has a thing going on with a customs agent."

"If your wife's sister is anywhere as good-looking as your wife, I'd say that is totally possible."

"You know, Captain, having a gorgeous wife is a blessing *and* a curse. Long sea voyages? With all those hound dogs at the base? It keeps a loving husband up at night."

"Try being divorced, Ivan. I guarantee you, it is a scenario much worse than having a beautiful, sexy wife whose faithfulness you have to worry about."

"Damned shame, Captain," Vlasenko said, blowing out smoke from his nostrils.

"Definitely, Mr. First. Anyway, we should turn our attention to the mission."

Vlasenko glanced for a moment at *Novosibirsk*'s commanding officer. Yuri Orlov was tall for submarine duty, with dirty-blonde hair, blue eyes, a sculpted face, though his face was pockmarked from his adolescent acne, but the roughness of his facial skin made him look tough. He was thin, almost too thin, Vlasenko thought. Perhaps that was the fault of the *Novosibirsk*'s mess cooks. As for his own appearance, Vlasenko didn't have that problem. His wife was a self-proclaimed master chef, and had fattened him up much more than he had been when they had said their vows, yet another reason Vlasenko worried about his wife finding another suitor more to her liking than chubby Vlasenko.

"Agreed, Captain. If the gods are with us, we should be putting to sea tomorrow."

Five days ago, a reactor casualty had forced an end to their maximum speed run to the Gulf of Oman, originating from the Pacific Submarine Fleet's Rybachiy Nuclear Submarine Base in Kamchatka. The reactor controls had alarmed and the unit had tripped, and it had taken the ship out of the deep to periscope depth, barely making way while snorkeling on the emergency diesel. The engineer, Captain Third Rank Kiril "Chernobyl" Chernobrovin had taken an hour to thread through the distributed control system's history module to diagnose the problem, and when he did, the problem was serious—a dropped control rod from a burned out control rod drive motor. Dropping a rod while critical meant the neighboring fuel modules would pick up the load and it was possible they could reach melting temperature, and melted fuel meant a bad day at sea—radiation levels within the hull rising to near fatal for the crew, and to complicate the miserable situation, a failed rod drive was not repairable at sea. No one carried a spare for that, and to Orlov's knowledge, no one had ever dropped a rod in real life. It had always been a dreamt-up drill run for training, but here it was, cursing this mission.

The dropped control rod in the reactor that happened the day they arrived in the Arabian Sea had forced *Novosibirsk* to turn sharply west to pull into the port of Aden, Yemen, to await repair crews to arrive from Vladivostok with the exotic parts and tools needed to repair a control rod drive. And every minute it had taken that crew to arrive and fix the reactor was another minute that *that asshole* Boris Novikov had to get *his* submarine in-theater. Orlov frowned. "Mr. First, if that asshole Novikov beats us to the Gulf of Oman, I'm going to be seriously annoyed."

"Your history with Novikov is the stuff of legend, Captain."

Orlov nodded somberly. "That scum. I'd torpedo him myself if I could get away with it. But that aside, Mr. First, where do we stand with the repair?"

"Let me call Chernobyl, Captain." Vlasenko pulled a VHF radio from his belt. "Topside Duty Officer, First Officer."

The radio clicked as the topside watchstander, who stood aft of the graceful conning tower, waved and held his radio to his lips. "Topside, sir."

"Get the engineer up here. Tell him we want an up-to-the-minute report."

"Right away, sir," the duty officer said, the radio clicking back to silence.

"You know, Captain, this will be our last night ashore for five, maybe six weeks. T.K. Sukolov reported he found a bar called 'The Tent' in the Sheraton hotel. We could get a cab, maybe grab some dinner, put away some vodka. You know, for good luck."

"Fat chance of that, Ivan. You're standing on the soil of a country that has outlawed alcohol."

"The Western restaurants allow you to bring in two bottles per party as long as you drink behind closed doors."

"Really?"

"Sukolov was very hungover this morning, Captain. And

very happy. Seems he met a flight crew and they invited him and Dobryvnik to their private dining room. So vodka *and* a little female company."

"Sukolov's a dog," Orlov said, suppressing a smile. The young communications officer, Captain Lieutenant Mikhail "T.K." Sukolov, was perpetually looking for excitement ashore, and not the sort that an upstanding citizen would seek. "But let me ask you, Mr. First, do we even *have* any vodka onboard?"

"Officially, sir? *Nyet.*"

"And unofficially?"

"Unofficially, Trusov could fill a bathtub."

The weapons officer, Captain Lieutenant Irina Trusov, was a teetotaler. Everything about that woman was prudish, cold, severe and wrapped up entirely too tight, in Orlov's opinion, but he wouldn't say that aloud to Vlasenko. Trusov was Vlasenko's protégé, his creation, recruiting her personally from a distant branch of his family. They were third cousins, if Orlov remembered right.

"Good plan, having a non-drinker guard the vodka. But tell me, will she give it up if you ask?"

"I'll probably have to resort to stealing it like Sukolov did."

Orlov made a hissing sound. "Sukolov probably tried to sweet talk her first."

"I have it on good authority he hit a brick wall with Iron Irina Trusov."

"Grab the navigator to come with us, and Irina as well—she can make sure we don't get into too much trouble. I'm assuming the engineer will have to stay with the technicians to supervise the repair."

Vlasenko snickered. "And as punishment that it's *his* equipment that interrupted our mission."

Captain Third Rank Chernobrovin stepped quickly down the gangway from the boat to the pier, snapped to attention and saluted Orlov and Vlasenko.

"Engineer, reporting as ordered, sir."

Orlov casually waved a salute back as he took in Chernobrovin, who wore sweat- and grease-stained blue coveralls with horizontal high-visibility reflective stripes across the top and bottoms of his sleeves. The youth looked underfed and hungry, with a perpetual five o'clock shadow on his face even if he had just shaved, his usual at-sea beard gnarly and atrocious, but he was newly married, and apparently the wife didn't approve of facial hair. That in itself seemed odd, since a woman who liked baby-faced men would never ordinarily connect with a swarthy lad like Chernobrovin, but who could predict feminine attraction? And there was one perpetual constant in the universe, Orlov thought, the undeniable female urge to change her man from what he *was* to what she *wanted* him to be.

"So what's the status, Mr. Chief Engineer?"

"Sir, the new control rod drive is installed and is mechanically complete. We're loop checking it now. It's responding. But we need to test it at operating temperature and pressure, and the only way to do that is to start the reactor and warm it up. The shipyard will ask to start it up and heat it up, then perform a normal shutdown, then restart it, then trip it manually to make sure it responds to a manual trip, then restart it again and send it a trip signal from the reactor control panel to make sure it responds to a programmed trip. Since there are five programmed trips, we'll have to do that test five times. Only then will they clear us for sea."

Orlov looked at Vlasenko, frowning. "How long is all *that* going to take?"

Chernobrovin checked his watch. "About twenty hours from now, Captain, if you give me permission to test the reactor and start up and shut down as the testing dictates."

Orlov looked at the sky, then at Vlasenko. "We could test it while we maneuver out on the diesel. Assuming the weather cooperated."

"Shipyard techs want to document a thousand data points from the testing, Captain. And if the unit fails to respond to a trip signal, it's not safe. And it could even run away from us in a control rod withdrawal accident if the power connections got their polarity reversed or if a connection shorts out. And they want us tied up to the pier in case they have to call for more replacement parts."

"Twenty hours, then," Orlov said, shaking his head in frustration. Goddamned Sevmash Shipyard. They'd humped the pooch yet *again*. "You have permission to start up and shut down the reactor as necessary to accomplish the tests. When you're done, remain steaming and critical. We're heading out to sea the moment the ink on the closeout paperwork dries."

"Yes, sir." Chernobrovin saluted and turned and walked back down the gangway. Orlov watched him, then looked at the hull of the *Novosibirsk.* The ship was black and sleek, her hull covered with anechoic foam tiling to absorb sonar pings and to suppress noise from the inside. She was 130 meters long and 13 meters wide at her beam. Her graceful conning tower was tall and long, rising at a slight angle at the forward edge, continuing straight aft, then sloping down gently to the after deck. The vertical rudder aft rose almost as high as the conning tower, the cigar-shaped hull continuing as a simple cylinder forward to where the bullet nose vanished into the brackish water of Port Aden. She was, in a word, beautiful. Not like the drab, boring, functional cylinders of the American submarines. Their naval architects had no souls. Give him a Russian ship designer any day, Orlov thought, but it would be nice if they could manufacture their gorgeous designs with some goddamned workmanship. And throw in some reliability. Maybe Russia could get the Germans or Swiss to build submarines for them some day in the far future. Or even the Italians.

An hour later, as the sun was beginning to set, Orlov, Vlasenko, Sukolov, Trusov and the navigator, Captain Third Rank Misha Dobryvnik, were led to red leather seats at a cherrywood table in a room paneled in the dark mahogany. The waiter brought out glasses and a large bottle of Coca Cola with a bucket of ice, handed them menus and left.

"Madam Weapons Officer, would you do the honors?" Orlov asked Trusov.

Captain Lieutenant Irina Trusov smiled with straight white teeth at the captain, tossing a lock of white-blonde hair out of her blue eyes with a shake of her head, her expression worried at the prospect of getting caught committing a crime in a foreign country.

"Happy to, sir." She pulled a large bottle of vodka from a dufflebag and filled up four rocks glasses. "Ice, sir?"

"Only amateurs put ice in vodka," Orlov said, winking at Dobryvnik as the navigator dropped three ice cubes into his drink.

"Only cretins drink it straight," Dobryvnik said, smiling at Orlov.

"A toast," Vlasenko said. "To a successful mission for us—"

"—and a failed one for that asshole Novikov and his stinking boat, the *Voronezh,*" Orlov finished. They all held up their glasses, Trusov having put ice and cola in her glass, then drank the contents. Trusov, without being prompted, immediately refilled their glasses.

"Captain," Dobryvnik said, "tell us the story of you and 'that asshole' Novikov. I'm the only one who hasn't heard it."

Dobryvnik was a big man with black hair, dark skin, narrow eyes, a flattened wide nose and a round face. In a wardroom composed of mostly blue-eyed Slavic blondes, he stood out. As a junior officer on the Akula III-class submarine K-419 *Kuzbass,* he had excelled at under-ice navigation, earning his navigation billet on the *Novosibirsk*. He was the newest officer to report aboard, but Orlov already had a good feeling about the younger officer. He was sharp-witted, sarcastic and funny. The crew had a taken a liking to him from the first day.

Orlov shook his head sadly. "The others only know the first half of the story. The second half is much worse."

"Pray tell, Captain," Vlasenko said, passing around the bottle for the third round, "what could *possibly* be worse than you two loading a torpedo onto the *Severodvinsk* and having its engine start, blast out of the torpedo tube and zip across the harbor and blow up a tugboat?"

"What?" Dobryvnik almost spilled his drink.

The waiter came in then to take their orders. Orlov and Vlasenko put in their orders, the others hurrying to scan the menu, their minds previously far from thinking about their dinner orders. When the waiter had collected their menus and shut the room's door behind him, Orlov continued.

"Totally not my fault," Orlov said, smirking, the worn

expression he used when telling the story an inside joke between him and Vlasenko. "The board of inquiry blamed it all on that asshole Novikov, since he was on the loading platform and had direct control of the weapon, but some of his stink rubbed off on me, since I was on the wharf supervising."

"Did it really blow up and sink the tug?" Dobryvnik stared at Orlov, his eyes wide.

"Not with the full force of the warhead." Orlov put out his glass for a refill. Vlasenko poured for the captain and himself. "Only maybe ten percent of the high explosive went off, but the impact and that small detonation put a hole in the tugboat big enough that it took on water, and fast. We got lucky. It was right under a six-hundred-ton rail-mounted crane, and a quick-thinking crew and operator put the hook to a cable wrapped around the tugboat's deck cleats and lifted it up so it wouldn't sink and held it long enough that they could rig a drain pump and pontoons and patch the hole. But it occupied the crane for a week, and that delayed some important depot-level maintenance."

"It's a better story when you have the tug blow up and sink, though, Captain," Vlasenko laughed.

"A few more vodkas in, and that tugboat in the story gets blown to holy hell," Orlov smiled. "That asshole Novikov got knocked down a rank and I got one of those letters in my service jacket, the kind that's not entertaining reading."

"So what's the second half of the story, Captain?" Dobryvnik asked.

"Let's just say that that asshole Novikov was as furious at me as I was at him."

"Why, what did you do to *him*?"

"He thinks I could have argued he was blameless before the board of inquiry, that the weapon was defective. Stupid idea, they recovered what was left of the torpedo and they would have seen we were both lying. I told the board Novikov took the safety bolts off to make the weapon easier to load. It was a common practice, but frowned on, and I personally told Novikov that would be unacceptable, but I didn't check personally that the bolts were installed. Weapon got cockeyed in the tube and the arming circuit went off, had an internal short, started the engine, and the force of the screw on the metal of the tube walked it outward from the hull despite Novikov and his midshipman trying to stop it. Finally, they had to run out of the way and the torpedo started its journey. He blames me for his reduction in rank."

"Didn't hurt his career any, not that I saw, Captain," Vlasenko said. "He may be only a captain second rank, but he's in command of the Yasen-M boat *Voronezh*."

"You know why, right? That asshole Novikov is the adopted son of Admiral Gennady Zhigunov, and Zhigunov is married to the daughter of the Minister of Defense. So. Connections."

"You said there was more?" Vlasenko prompted.

"That asshole Novikov is pretty much the reason I'm divorced."

Irina Trusov stared at him. "Really, sir?"

Orlov poured another vodka. "After the board of inquiry, he apparently decided to strike for me where it hurt. While I was on an under-ice run in the Arctic Ocean, that asshole Novikov was busy chatting up and seducing my wife."

The room went silent, almost as if someone had let all the air out of the room. Orlov looked up from his glass and shook his head. "Yeah, and the story doesn't have a happy ending, not for either of us."

"What do you mean, Captain?" Trusov put her hand briefly on Orlov's sleeve, a gesture of empathy.

"She left me for him," Orlov said. "And that asshole Novikov was stupid enough to fall for her, just like I did. And would you believe it? She did the same thing to him that she did to me, not even a full year later. His next Barents Sea exercise, she ended up in the bed of the captain of the *Kazan*."

"Mother of God," Vlasenko said. "That woman certainly has a thing for submarine commanders."

Orlov pulled out his phone and selected a photo of his former wife and passed it to Vlasenko, who handed it to Sukolov—who whistled—who handed it to Dobryvnik, then to Trusov.

"She could be a movie star," Trusov said, impressed.

The woman in the photo was a platinum bombshell blonde

with deep blue eyes, puffy red lips, a small upturned nose; she was slender but with an enormous chest and mile-long legs. She looked like she stepped right off one of those graphics that graced the noses of the bombers of the Great Patriotic War.

"She stopped traffic everywhere she went. It was stupid of me to marry her. Stupider still for that asshole Novikov to fall in love with her."

"Damn," Vlasenko said. "Now I feel sorry for *both* of you."

"I didn't mean to turn the evening into a downer," Orlov said, standing. "I'll close out the tab. You guys finish without me. I'll find a cab back to the boat."

On the cab ride back to the port facility, Orlov leaned his head against the window, berating himself for spilling his sad life story to his officers. For the thousandth time, he cursed the day he met Natalia.

And for the ten thousandth time, he cursed that asshole Novikov. Orlov wondered where that asshole Novikov was at that moment. Probably speeding at full ahead, reactor circulating pumps at fast speed, leaving the Arabian Sea and entering the Gulf of Oman, making his 8300 nautical mile passage from the Northern Fleet Kola base at Zapadnaya Litsa through the Suez Canal look like a breeze compared to Orlov's 8100 mile run from Rybachiy in the Kamchatka peninsula. The thought of that asshole Novikov entering the Gulf of Oman ahead of them made Orlov sick. As the cab arrived at the pier, Captain First Rank Yuri Orlov, Navy of the Russian Republic and captain of the frontline nuclear fast attack submarine *Novosibirsk,* opened the door and vomited what seemed like gallons.

16

Mediterranean Entrance to the Suez Canal
Port Said Southbound Convoy Waiting Area Anchorage
K-579 *Voronezh*
Thursday, June 2

Captain Second Rank Boris Novikov climbed the four steps from the conning tower interior to the bridge of the Yasen-M-class submarine *Voronezh*. The ship was anchored in the southbound convoy waiting area a few miles north of Port Said, the northern mouth of the Suez Canal. The route plan had *Voronezh* passing surfaced through the canal over a week ago, but all traffic had been suddenly held up for reasons unknown. Instead of 97 ships a day going through, half of them southbound, those vessels had all piled up, filling the southbound convoy waiting area until the new arrivals were forced to steam in slow circles, burning their fuel and annoying their crews.

Novikov lifted the satellite phone from his belt and stared at it for a moment, knowing it was prohibited for personal use, but unable to help himself. He dialed the number, *her* number, a number he'd had memorized since the day she'd given it to him, what seemed half a lifetime ago.

The voice that came over the connection was beautiful, Novikov thought, sweet and soprano, her tongue caressing the consonants, her throat wrapping around the vowels, more musical than an opera singer, but unfortunately, the voice was a recording.

"You have reached Natalia Orlov, and I am so very sorry I am unable to connect with you live, but if you'll leave me your message, I promise I will call you back at my very earliest opportunity, and until then, may God and all his angels be with you."

He'd gotten that stupid recording for the last eight days, ever since the Suez Canal shut down. That recording constantly promising she'd call back, a false promise for certain. And she'd kept that foul name *Orlov,* as if to toss it in his face. Novikov knew she hadn't gone back to that pud-thumper Orlov. And he doubted she was still seeing Alexeyev, the captain of the *Kazan.* And if not, where was she? What was she doing? She'd made noises about leaving Murmansk and going back to Moscow, but even so, her phone should have worked.

Novikov decided to leave yet another message. "Natalia, it's me, Boris. If this number is unfamiliar, that's because it's a secure satellite phone. I'm halfway through a voyage and delayed, so I thought I would call you and tell you again how I feel about you. Natalia, I can't sleep, I can't eat, I miss you so much—"

The first officer just *had* to pick that very moment to intrude on his space in the upper conning tower.

Novikov clicked off the connection, hoping Captain Second Rank Anastasia Isakova hadn't heard much of his message. It was unmistakably not an official call, and his whispering romance into a goddamned Navy satphone would not sit well with the crew. Or with the bosses. With an effort to control his expression, he turned to face the first officer.

"Madam First," he said.

Isakova stepped up to the upper conning tower platform, binoculars hanging from a strap around her neck. The slender brunette was wearing her blue at-sea coveralls with the high-vis stripes, the belt of the one-piece garment tied snugly around her small waist, making her breasts seem bigger. Her hips were narrow, her legs thin, leaving her seeming top-heavy. Her hair was cut ultra-short, giving her a pixie look. Some men liked that, Novikov thought, but she seemed less feminine than he liked. Not like the nightclub singer body of Natalia. Dammit, he thought, could he have one thought to himself without Natalia invading his mind?

"Captain. I came up to talk to you and take a look around. Do you mind?"

"Be my guest. What did you want to talk about?"

"It's strange, sir," she said. I've been scouring the news from all sources. Egyptian, Israeli, Russian, English, American, French."

"We all know your amazing talents in languages, Madam First. What did you find out?"

"Exactly nothing, Captain. This situation could go on. The 2021 blockage was a week, but the canal was closed for *seven years* when the Egyptians and Israelis had a scrape sixty years ago. I suppose the mission could wait a week, but there's no telling how long this could take. It's shrouded in secrecy. Something is up. I thought maybe you could call the admiral and ask if he knows anything."

"I send daily status reports to Northern Fleet HQ. The admiral knows we're stuck here."

Anastasia Isakova put her binoculars up to her eyes, but stole a long glance at the captain. Boris Novikov was tall and lanky, with a mop of black hair and dark eyes, a straight nose over strong cheekbones, with a narrow, tough-looking face and a sculpted chin. His teeth, when he smiled, were straight, perhaps unnaturally white—could that be from the vanity of a dental treatment? He reminded her of how the movies depicted Moscow mafia solders or bosses—mean and criminal, with a dark energy seeking release, a large pistol inevitably holstered under a sharkskin sport jacket. That his girlfriend or wife or whatever she was to him, Natalia, had left him seemed incredibly stupid. Isakova had been denying her feelings for the captain for the last year, and had finally started thinking about asking for reassignment.

What had Novikov said at the wardroom table a few months ago? "That pud-thumper Orlov used to always say, 'put a reasonably attractive female in a room with a reasonable looking male and make them work together for a year, and they're either going to fuck each other or murder each other.'"

And the engineer, Yevgeny Montorov, who had zero tact, had smiled and said, "sometimes both, eh, Captain?" as if he were unaware that saying that would bring Novikov face-to-face with his life crisis, Natalia moving on. And the navigator, Leonid "Luke" Lukashenko, had tried to break the tension by adding, "hopefully in that order, because the reverse would be, well, socially unacceptable." Novikov had smiled at Lukashenko gratefully for just a split second.

"Maybe a secure video conference is in order," Isakova said. "Tell him you're thinking of leaving the Med and going around Africa. With the canal closed, it's the only way to get in-theater."

"Draft a message for me to see before you send it, requesting a video link for this afternoon. Maybe we'll either find something out or get a blessing to go around the horn. Just sitting here cooling our heels won't do."

Morningside, Maryland, USA
Joint Base Andrews
Thursday June 2

Michael Pacino leaned over and opened the passenger-side door while he pushed the button to open the rear hatch.

Vice Admiral Robert Catardi, clad in jeans, harness boots and a golf shirt with a black sport jacket over it, half jogged up, a briefcase in one hand and an overnight bag in the other. He tossed his bags in the back and the hatch began to close slowly by itself. He stood back a moment, staring at the car. "What. The fuck. Is this?"

"Good to see you too, Rob," Pacino grinned, holding out his hand. Catardi ducked to fold himself into the sleek black sports car and shook the National Security Advisor's hand.

"You too, sir," Catardi said.

"No 'sirs' around me, Robby, just 'Patch'. How long has it been?"

Pacino took the shift lever to first gear and the engine roared as he swung away from the Andrews Military Aviation arrival and departure lounge, the engine screaming as Pacino shifted to second, the car already going insanely fast before he hit third.

"It's been since the days of the old *Devilfish*," Catardi said, reluctant to mention the name of the submarine Pacino had commanded that had so disastrously gone down under the ice, but he hadn't been in the same room with the older man since then. "And we used to call your son 'Patch.'"

Pacino looked over as he drove down the winding backroad, taking the scenic route out of Washington.

"I talked to him after you tipped me that he'd be at the—well, where you said he'd be. He sounded like his old self, before the whole, well, you know."

Before the *Piranha* sinking, Catardi thought sadly. Their history with sunken submarines was not something either wanted to think about. Catardi decided to change the subject. Plenty of time to talk about the mission of the USS *Vermont* once they reached Camp David and got into a secure SCIF conference room.

Catardi glanced at Pacino for a moment, seeing what time had done to the man since they'd last met. Back then, Pacino had had a head full of thick hair black as a coal mine, shallow cheeks below strong cheekbones, a straight nose and emerald-green eyes, and stood at a height that should have been too tall for submarine duty. Today, he was still as gaunt and thin as he'd been then and he still had all of his hair, but the hair had all turned pure white. It made for an odd look, since his eyebrows were still black. His eyes were still that weird color of green, but duller somehow. The smile lines at the corners of his eyes had gotten deeper, and he looked tanned. Like Catardi, he was wearing jeans, a golf shirt and a sport coat.

Catardi decided to break the silence and ask about Pacino's sports car.

"What *is* this car?" At the moment he asked, they were taking a turn at what had to be over half a G, the car's engine roaring, then purring, the screaming again as Pacino raked it smoothly through the manual transmission's gears.

"Aston Martin DB11 AMR. V-12 engine with six hundred and thirty horsepower. She'll do two oh eight on a flat course, zero to sixty in three point seven."

"Jesus, Patch. How fast have you driven her?"

"One of my pilot friends took me to an abandoned airfield with an eight-thousand-foot runway. I got to about two hundred and two miles per before I decided I was either going to melt the brakes or go off the end of the runway."

"This thing must cost a fortune. A lot more than my damned house if I'm guessing right."

Pacino shrugged. "I sold the sailboat. After that scrape with the drone sub, the sea holds no relaxation for me. I got a good price, from one of my Annapolis neighbors who'd been lusting over it for years. So then I saw this car at a distressed estate sale. Owner found himself in the kind of trouble that needed a million-dollar legal defense, so instead of taking six months to auction it off to some Saudi prince and the hassle of shipping it overseas, he let it go for pennies on the pound. So, really, I paid less than you would for one of those fancy mid-engined Corvettes."

The truth of it was, Pacino thought, that he'd desperately needed something to cheer him up after Colleen moved out, over a year into her giving him the silent treatment, furious at Pacino that Anthony had chosen to go submarines for his service selection. Seeing him clinically dead and then return had changed her, he thought, and not for the better. He glanced at his left ring finger. This morning he'd decided to take it off and put it in the polished wood box he kept his Rolex in at night. The tan-line on the finger seemed a rebuke.

"Even *that* price is eye-popping. I hope you're enjoying it."

"You know what, Rob? It's okay."

Catardi laughed. "Okay, right. Are you getting any time to drive it?"

"Not after Scorch hired me. I guess you can say I'm his consiglieri on military affairs."

"Scorch?"

"President Carlucci's handle back when he was pushing a fighter jet off an aircraft carrier for a living. Apparently his afterburners caused some minor damage to a car parked too close to an Air Force Base taxiway."

"Minor damage?"

"Well, the way Carlucci tells it, the car went up in flames

and the gas tank exploded and he didn't even know it, he was all the way down the runway and going vertical by that time. Turns out the car belonged to the Air Force base commander. Not very career-enhancing for poor Lieutenant Commander Vito Carlucci."

"I can imagine."

"He stuck out his tour, then punched out shortly after the Bohai Bay conflict, decided to try politics."

"'Scorch'—he's probably the *last* guy I could see having a name like that."

"I know what you mean," Pacino said. "He's pretty cautious for an ex-fighter jockey."

"Cautious? More like weak. You're aware the political cartoons all depict him holding a purse, right?"

"That's why he brought *me* in. But from what I've seen so far, he's pretty tough behind the scenes. Far tougher than I would have ever thought."

"Press flamed on him pretty hard for appointing *you*, Patch, you warmonger."

Pacino smiled, his eyes on the road as he downshifted to third for a tight curve, then down again to second, the engine squealing as he throttled up out of the curve.

"You sink one little Chinese fleet and they call you a warmonger. So unfair."

Catardi grinned. "So, Camp David. What's it like?"

"It's nice. Forested, secluded, rustic. It's quiet there. The cabins are a bit basic and haven't been updated or remodeled since Gerald Ford hung out here, but I guess that's part of its charm. I'm told Carlucci doesn't use it like other presidents did. It's an absolute no-media zone, a total comms lockdown. No photographers, videographers, news reporters, nobody. No presidential family members. Cabinet and top-level staff only. And as few of those as possible, and none of their lackeys are invited. That's why I had to tell you to leave your aide behind, what's her name? River something."

"Wanda. Wanda Styxx. Apparently she's your son's type. They danced one dance at the AUTEC O-Club and then disappeared together."

Pacino stared over at Catardi for a split second. "Wow, really?"

"Didn't see her again until late the next morning, just before your son's boat shoved off." Catardi decided to be discreet and not mention that Wanda Styxx was in an uncharacteristically excellent mood for the morning after an O-Club drink-fest.

"I guess he's starting to get over Carrie," Pacino said. Catardi lifted an eyebrow.

"Your former engineer, Robby, Carolyn Alameda."

Catardi whistled, shaking his head. "I couldn't make her funeral in time. Admiral Rand had me at a comearound at Pac Fleet HQ in Pearl Harbor. She died so suddenly. But you said Patch Junior was quote, *getting over her,* unquote. They were—?"

"Yeah, they were seeing each other. I thought I'd have to talk him out of getting married, it was that serious."

"Holy shit. I never knew."

"Going through what you guys suffered, I guess they stayed in touch after that. And you know the story. Tale as old as time. Boy meets girl. Girl calls boy a non-qual. Boy falls for girl. Boy rescues girl from certain death. Girl falls for boy."

Catardi felt a moment of guilt that he'd tried to bury the *Piranha* incident in his mind and hadn't kept in contact with Alameda, Schultz or the younger Pacino, probably unconsciously thinking that seeing them would bring him right back to that horrible deep submergence vehicle where he'd almost died.

"You were telling me about Carlucci and Camp David," Catardi prompted.

"Yeah," Pacino said. "Carlucci doesn't like the usual presidential accommodations at Aspen Lodge with all its facilities for meetings and communications. He holes up in the super-humble Birch Cabin. He's got us bunking in the old Holly Lodge, which was the presidential house before they built Aspen Lodge. It has enough gigantic bedrooms to host half a dozen heads of state at a time. The Secretary of State and the Director of Combined Intelligence will be there with us along with the VP. When Carlucci calls, we walk over to Birch's back deck if the weather's nice, or indoors in the small den with the fireplace going if it's raining or snowing or just cold. And that fire's always going."

"Sounds cozy. I guess. But the outside deck at the Birch Cabin can't be secure enough for what I think we'll be talking about. I suppose I can't really ask why I got called here."

Pacino shook his head. "This car's a lot of things, Robby, but it ain't a SCIF. But the den at Birch Cabin is."

An hour later, they parked and took their bags to the security building to check in and get their belongings scanned. After clearing security, a golf cart waited for them, a young, pretty staff aide ready to drive them over the narrow road to Holly Lodge.

"It's pretty humble for presidential digs," Catardi said, following Pacino into the house.

"Hey," Pacino said, "we're camping, remember?"

Mediterranean entrance to the Suez Canal
Port Said southbound convoy waiting area anchorage
K-579 *Voronezh*
Thursday June 2

The officers' wardroom doors were both shut, with leather covers affixed to their small circular windows and warning signs posted outside reading *SECURE VIDEO CONFERENCE IN PROGRESS.*

Captain First Rank Boris Novikov sat in a chair in the middle of the long edge of the table on the inboard side. To his left sat the navigator and chief of tactical operations, Captain Third Rank Leonid Lukashenko. To his right sat First Officer Anastasia Isakova. On the other side of the room, against the outboard bulkhead, a large flatscreen display showed the surface of a table, an ornate green tablecloth on it with elaborate gold stitching, the wall behind the table a dark wood paneling with a framed oil painting of a Project 671 Shchuka-class submarine on the surface, plowing through a high sea state.

As the officers of the *Voronezh* waited, they each took out their tablet phones and scanned the news again, as they had for the last week, but there was still nothing but a single sentence about the Suez Canal closing.

Finally a large older man appeared in the screen, taking his seat and putting his officer's cap on the table surface. Someone off-screen handed him an ash tray and a silver cigarette case. The officer opened the case and took out a cigarette, accepted a lighter from the person off-screen, lit up and let out a cloud of smoke. He was in late fifties or early sixties, with all his hair, albeit mostly gray, with a face that was probably once handsome but had given up to the infirmities of age. His face was stern as he got settled and lifted a remote to turn on his screen.

"Good afternoon, Admiral," Novikov said. "This is First Officer Isakova and Navigator Lukashenko, sir. Officers, allow me to present Admiral Zhigunov, commander of the Northern Fleet Submarine Force."

The mean expression on Zhigunov's face melted into a warm smile. "Hello Boris Alexandrovich. And hello also to your officers. I hope you are all well, yes? My chief of staff said you had an urgent matter. What is it that is so urgent that you can't put it in a radio dispatch?"

The truth was that Novikov wanted to see the expression on his adopted father's face when the matter of the closed canal came up. Novikov outlined the situation.

"I'd heard," Zhigunov said, letting smoke out of his nostrils and taking another puff.

"It's just that we're stuck here and there's no contingency plan for this. If this goes on too much longer, I would lag behind where I would have been if I'd immediately backed out of the Med and gone around Africa. It's fifteen thousand kilometers farther. We could have done that in fourteen days at a speed-of-advance of twenty-five knots, sir. And maybe we still should."

"I've spent a week talking with the secretary general of the *Rossiyskoy Federatsii*, the SVR."

The SVR, the federal state security agency, was the successor to the KGB, Novikov thought, but from what he heard, things were no different at the secret spy shop since the hammer-and-sickle flag was struck in favor of the colors of the Russian Republic.

"Yes, Admiral?" Would Novikov have to drag the information out of the teeth of Gennady Zhigunov?

"I hate to tell you this, Boris, but let's attribute this to secrecy and 'the left hand doesn't know what the right hand is doing' department, because while we, the right hand, were putting you into the Gulf of Oman via the Suez Canal, the left hand, the SVR, were busy with a client organization, the Algerian FLN, who they've been financing for years. Turns out the FLN had plans to detonate a very large bomb in the Suez Canal at the Al Salam bridge. Large for a bomb but small for an atomic bomb, I suppose you could say. A suitcase nuclear demolition explosive, as my source said. The secretary general knew nothing of your mission until I told him. The unintended consequences, he told me, were unknown. After we talked, the SVR gave an anonymous tip to an Israeli Mossad agent and that's why they shut down the canal, so they could find this bomb and the freedom fighters responsible for placing it. So *his* operation is ending, to allow *our* operation to continue."

Novikov stared at the screen. "So, Admiral, what does that mean for us? Should we continue waiting or head west to Gibraltar?"

"I told the SVR secretary general to set up an ambush for the FLN with a second friendly tip to their counterparts at Mossad. Because once Mossad interrogates the people captured, they'll find the demolition charge, defuse it and reopen the canal."

"That could take weeks."

Admiral Gennady Zhigunov looked at his expensive, antique watch given him by Novikov several years before. "No, Boris, they captured the bombers this morning, and an hour ago found the suitcase nuclear weapon. They should be reopening the canal any—"

Just then the forward wardroom door came half open and the head and shoulders of the communications officer appeared. Captain Lieutenant Maksimilian Kovalyov whispered intensely, *"Apologies, Captain, but the canal just reopened!"* As swiftly as he'd appeared, the radio officer vanished, the door shutting behind him.

Zhigunov smiled, apparently hearing the off-screen voice.

"You see? All is taken care of, Boris Alexandrovich. I expect the southbound convoys will start very soon."

"Thank you, sir," Novikov said, feeling relief.

"I have another matter for you, Boris."

"Yes, Admiral?"

Zhigunov held up a clear plastic-wrapped package. Visible inside were the gold uniform epaulets of a captain first rank.

"I hope your ship's store has these uniform devices, Boris. You're officially promoted to the rank of captain first rank as of this morning. Message to follow from Northern Fleet Personnel Command. Congratulations, Boris Alexandrovich."

Novikov smiled. "I ordered the collar insignia and epaulets before we sailed, Admiral. I just had a feeling."

Zhigunov smiled. "Good luck on your mission, son." Zhigunov ended the video link and the screen went dark.

Novikov stood up. "What *is* this damned mission anyway?" he said half to himself. Isakova looked at him, startled. Lukashenko, the navigator and operations officer, froze as he reached for his tablet phone.

"Why, to get to the Gulf of Oman as fast as possible," Isakova said.

"Yes, but *why*? What are we *doing* there?"

"I assume they'll tell us when we arrive on-station," she said. Novikov looked at her.

"You're right. I guess I'm just frustrated by this wait. Navigator, have the engineer see me in my stateroom. Madam First, prepare to get underway. I want us to weigh anchor the second they call on our convoy."

In his stateroom, as he waited for the engineer, Novikov lifted up his tablet phone as it beeped, then read the message traffic. *Great,* he thought. The canal authority, Port Said Operations, was prioritizing for the southbound convoys the ships that hadn't been able to anchor and had had to steam in circles waiting for the canal to reopen, so those ships low on fuel could dock at the refueling facility at Bitter Lake. The second priority would be anchored ships with livestock or perishable goods. The wait for their convoy to get clearance to sail would not come for at least one, maybe two more days. Dammit, he thought, this was insane. It was almost at the point that if he'd turned back immediately when the canal had shut down, he'd have arrived on-station sooner than he would with this new wrinkle.

The engineer came in after knocking. Captain Second Rank Yevgeny Montorov was sweating and dirty. He was shorter than average, but muscularly built, with bulging biceps under his blue at-sea coveralls, the weight-lifting perhaps an attempt to compensate for his lack of height, whether conscious or unconscious. His hair had been going prematurely bald, so he always cut it so close to his head it was a mere shadow. He was a brilliant and a dedicated engineer, having a master's degree in mechanical engineering and bachelor's in electrical and a third degree in instrumentation and controls. Unmarried, he always seemed on the prowl for a wife, but so far, he'd been rejected by what seemed all of the available women in the greater Murmansk metro area. Perhaps the females sensed he was too hungry, Novikov thought, or they all detected some character flaw in the youngster in that odd second sight all women seemed to have.

"Looking after the diesel, I see, yes, Yevgeny?" Novikov almost never used an officer or enlisted person's first name, but Montorov was an exception, reminding Novikov of himself when he was that age, full of energy and wild-eyed patriotism and unfortunately more than a little recklessness. Novikov had made it his personal mission to mentor the youth and save him from the heartache that Novikov himself had suffered. He couldn't just say, "follow torpedo loading procedures to the letter and avoid overly sexual large-breasted women," but he *could* pay attention to the officer's life and offer sage advice when called for. Perhaps intervening. Perhaps even interfering, when necessary.

"Yes, Captain. The emergency diesel will be very happy to go back to sleep once we start the reactor. I assume you called me here to give me permission to start the reactor."

"Originally I did, Yevgeny, but it looks like this wait will continue."

"Really? How long, Captain?"

"Another day, maybe two. They're forming up convoys of fifty ships and only two southbound convoys will go per day. According to the latest from Port Said Operations, we're in convoy four. So that's a day-and-a-half minimum. I'll have you start the reactor tomorrow, Yevgeny. Until then, make that diesel happy."

"Yes, sir, understood."

"What's the status of the battery?"

"Fully charged, Captain, on a trickle discharge as of an hour ago."

"Very well. That'll be all, Yevgeny. Oh, and try to get some sleep before we roll out."

"Sleep will be no trouble at all, Captain," Montorov grinned. He shut the door behind him.

For some reason, when he left, Novikov was left with a sense of loneliness. For once, that loneliness wasn't for Natalia. He picked up the phone handset and dialed the first officer's stateroom.

"First Officer," Anastasia Isakova's crisp voice said.

"Madam First, when convenient, can you come to my stateroom?"

"Right away, Captain."

Novikov put the phone down, thinking about that pud-thumper Orlov's statement about men and women working together. Consider the source, he counseled himself. Orlov was an idiot. Still, Isakova was looking more attractive lately.

Gulf of Aden, Yemen
Port Aden Container Facility
K-573 *Novosibirsk*
Thursday June 2

Captain Yuri Orlov zipped up his at-sea coveralls, laced up his boots and left his sea cabin to go to the wardroom. First Officer Ivan Vlasenko was there, as were Navigator Misha Dobryvnik and Weapons Officer Irina Trusov.

He took his seat at the end of the room that abutted the galley and nodded at the other officers. There was tea service on the table. He poured a cup and dropped in two sugarcubes.

"Status, Mr. First?"

Vlasenko said from the seat to Orlov's right, "Chernobyl's still starting the reactor. The repair techs are still here. They want to do a reliability check."

"Now what, for God's sake?" Orlov asked glancing at the overhead.

"They want to run it against the load bank at various power levels and let it settle out. Then they'll increase power. Eventually the engineer will request to run fast speed pumps and they'll take it up to a hundred percent for an hour."

Orlov sighed. "You know, Ivan, there comes a time in every repair work-order when it's time to shoot the repair technicians."

Vlasenko laughed and Iron Irina Trusov smiled. Orlov thought for a moment—could he remember her ever smiling? He hadn't noticed, but when the woman smiled, she was really quite beautiful. That head of white-blonde hair, pouting red lips, big blue eyes. But, he thought, for him to be noticing Irina Ice Queen Trusov, his mind must be giving him a notification that he needed to search for female companionship. Maybe it was time, after Hurricane Natalia had done her damage and he'd healed for almost two years. For a moment he was distracted and didn't hear Vlasenko's question.

"What was that, Ivan?"

"Sir, I *could* go back aft and tell them to stop the test and get the hell off our ship. We do have a mission to perform."

"Yeah, a mission no one's bothered to tell us about other than to get our boat to the Gulf of Oman."

"It's supposedly urgent, Captain."

"Go back aft and tell those idiots, whatever amount of time they're spending at each power level, to cut it in half."

"Yes, *sir*," Vlasenko said, leaving and shutting the door behind him.

"I'd better check the charts and current, Captain," Misha Dobryvnik said, standing and putting his cup away in the bin. Orlov waved, taking a pull from his tea. He figured Irina Trusov would leave the wardroom as well. It would give him time to review the news files and see what was going on in the

Gulf of Oman. Perhaps there was some context to this oddball mission.

But Trusov remained behind, refilling her cup, blowing on the hot tea and looking over the rim at Orlov, smiling at him with her eyes.

"Did you see the dispatch on the hack, Captain?" she asked.

"No," he said, embarrassed that there was something he'd missed. "Was it addressed to us?"

"No, Captain, just a general update message. But it's serious. The Northern and Pacific Fleet's air and surface warfare systems all got some kind of worm that shuts down their computers. They can't fly and the surface ships can't even start their engines. It's severe."

"When did this happen? Do we know where it came from?" Orlov should have known about something this major. It might be a reason why their operational orders were delayed getting to them.

Trusov shook her head in disgust. "Who *could* it be, Captain. The damned Americans, of course."

"Did the update say it was a state actor that originated this worm, like Stuxnet?"

"Yes, Captain."

"It might not have been the Americans. The Chinese are making things difficult now. After they pulled out of the joint space mission, things have been pretty chilly with them."

Trusov pursed her lips. "It's the Americans, Captain. It's *always* the Americans. You know my uncle went down on the *Kursk*, right?"

"Vlasenko told me," Orlov said, hearing his own voice become gentler. "I'm sorry."

"You know the intelligence agencies think the Americans sank her."

"If they did," Orlov said, "it was the perfect crime. There's no evidence. It's a conspiracy theory, Irina." Suddenly it felt strange to address her as 'Weapons Officer' or 'Miss Trusov.'

"Maybe so, sir, but it does fit a lot of facts about the Americans."

"Do you ever wonder sometimes," Orlov asked, "about the

American submarine force? Their sailors, their officers, their ships?"

Captain Lieutenant Irina Trusov looked over the rim of her cup at Orlov again. "Only in passing, I suppose, the way I think about the Americans in general."

"And how's that, Irina?"

"They're *villains*, Captain. They remain the *glavny protivnik*, the main adversary. They never go a year without starting a war, sometimes two, or continuing a war that never should have happened. Korea, Vietnam, Laos, Cambodia, Iraq, Bosnia, Somalia, Libya, Afghanistan. Every day their bombs rip apart the bodies of women and children, destroying schools, bridges, bus terminals, causing starvation, disease and death everywhere they go. They pretend to be proponents of peace while their intelligence agencies assassinate anyone who is in their political way. Captain, Mother Russia is the only force that stands between the Americans and total world domination."

Orlov looked at her indulgently. "I know about one point four billion Chinamen who would disagree with that last point."

"It's the hypocrisy, Captain," Trusov continued, ignoring his comment. "The Americans pretend to be a moral force for good, yet the sheer extent of racism in their culture is baked in. They eliminated slavery, but the descendants of their slaves live in ghettos. Meanwhile, their ultra-elites light cigars with hundred dollar bills while their media and entertainment industries crank out the vilest, most immoral and shocking content. It's enough to make a red-blooded Russian girl sick. I'm friends with the first officer of the *Voronezh*, Anastasia Isakova. She was a mentor to me, recruited me into the force, back when she was in the Pacific Fleet. She told me her father lived in Star City and worked at the Baikonur Cosmodrome. He told her a hundred stories of how the Americans won the space race by cheating."

"Cheating? In the space race?"

"Sabotage. They blew up more than a dozen of our rockets, one of the explosions killing the first chief designer. They even shot down our cosmonauts. The Americans are a wretched culture of killing and death and evil, Captain. The world would be a better place if they just stopped existing between breakfast and lunch."

Orlov smiled. "Remind me to keep my nuclear release codes locked up tight, Madam Weapons Officer. Still," he said, looking into the distance. "Consider if you will one of their submarines—"

A knock came at the door and Engineer Kiril Chernobrovin stuck his head in. "Captain, we are in the final hour of testing. We should be ready to answer all bells in fifty-five minutes, sir."

"Very well, Engineer." Orlov checked his watch. It was 0530 hours local time. The tea was helping clear his head, but losing a night's sleep wasn't as easy as it had been when he'd been in his twenties. He picked up his phone and dialed the central command post.

"Watch Officer," the navigator's voice said.

"Navigator, the repair work will be complete in less than an hour. Are you ready?"

"We'll set maneuvering stations watch in thirty minutes, sir, then get underway as soon as the repair crew walks to the pier."

"Very well," Orlov said, putting up the phone. Finally, this ridiculous wait was coming to an end.

Trusov refilled his cup and spooned two teaspoons of sugar in it for him. "You were saying about the American submarines, sir?" she prompted.

"Yes, Madam Weapons Officer. Consider for a moment, if you will, one of their new Virginia-class submarines. Half our tonnage, twice our crew. That points to less automation. Manual control. Sailors back in the engineroom sweating through long propulsion plant watches. Other sailors in their central command post manually driving the ship. And their weapon control is probably primitive compared to ours. There's no centralized AI system, no second captain, just a bunch of wobbly, off-the-shelf computers. I think of their crew, bottled up in their submarine, fighting against the sea just like us, scanning their sonar screens, straining to hear one of our subs, going days without daylight, without relaxation, without even a single shot of vodka, with bad canned food, and, well, I feel sorry for them. In a way, they are just like *us*. We would have more in common with the crew of an American nuclear submarine than with any collection of people off the street of Murmansk. Or Moscow, for that matter. I think, often, perhaps too often, that if we went out drinking together, just we and our American submarine counterparts, we might reach a deep understanding. Perhaps, we could even be friends." Orlov paused, reluctant to look at Trusov, who certainly wouldn't understand, and who probably thought he'd suddenly gone soft.

"I wonder," he continued. "If our souls could move through the ocean, through the waves, through the air and past the clouds, in the direction of the closest Virginia-class submarine to us that's steaming at sea, and just fly unseen into their central command post, what would we see? What are the sailors of that Virginia-class submarine doing *right now*?"

17

Gulf of Oman
41 Nautical miles north-northeast of As Sib, Oman
USS *Vermont*
Friday, June 3, 0110 UTC

The control room mid-watch was quiet, the lights set to red in accordance with the rig for ultra-quiet, to remind watchstanders of the need to maintain absolute sound silence. In the old days, when periscopes of submarines featured actual optics, control rooms were lit with red lights to keep the eyes of the officer of the deck night-adapted, so at periscope depth he'd be able to see in the dark. Conning officers in decades past had worn red goggles or even a pirate's eye patch over their periscope eye, to maintain that night vision capability. Today, with the periscopes constructed of non-hull-penetrating optronics, able to see in normal optical frequencies and also infrared, with laser range-finders, their output piped to high definition flatscreen displays, there was no longer a need for lighting the control room with red lights, and yet the tradition lived on. Somehow, red lights—the human perceiving red as an indicator of danger, from the sight of blood—kept the crew mindful of how close to real danger they all were.

Officer of the Deck Lieutenant Mohammed "Boozy" Varney paced the deck in the crowded space aft of the command console, the display selected to the athwartships beam of the sonar narrowband display of the TB-33 thin line towed array sonar, which showed exactly nothing but multifrequency noise, the array searching for a tonal frequency from man-made rotating machinery, hoping to catch the thrum of the electrical generators or the main motor of the modified-Kilo submarine *Panther*. But so far, it was all noise.

Varney paged his display software to show the output of the BQQ-10 large aperture bow array, which was scanning for broadband noise, and was full of contacts. All 37 of them—merchant ships all, steaming through the gulf with their three or four-bladed screws, tankers laden with oil coming outbound, or tankers empty and riding high, lumbering inbound to get loaded. He squinted his eyes shut and touched his stomach. He checked the bulkhead chronometer—0110 hours Zulu time, or 5:10 am local time. It was barely over an hour into the midwatch, and already his guts were churning.

"Goddamn chili for mid-rats," he said to no one.

"Someone feeling Chubby Cruz's famous hot and spicy Tex-Mex chili?" Radioman Chief Bernadette Goreliki said, snickering, from the pilot station. "Just don't be polluting the control room air, sir. That's an atmospheric contaminant for sure." Chief Antonio "Chubby" Cruz, a bony and gaunt Californian with blonde hair and sparse facial hair that only dimly aspired to be a beard, worked for the supply officer and was the boss of the SK division, which kept the boat stocked with spare parts and food, and as such, he ran the messcooks. Cruz was the one who approved the menus, taking only input from the captain and executive officer, and he delighted in serving gut-busting and spicy mid-rats food.

"Shut up, Gory," Varney said, smiling. "And mind your panel, Pilot."

"Yeah," Torpedoman Senior Chief Roderick "Blackie" Nygard said, piling on, from his station as copilot. "Mind your panel, Pilot."

"Mind my panel, aye, Officer of the Deck, sir. And Copilot, go fuck yourself."

Nygard smiled. "Go fuck myself, Copilot, aye."

Varney paged the software on the command console to display the amidships wide aperture hull array's acoustic daylight output, thinking that there was a remote chance a submerged contact would appear out of the distant noises of the biologics—the fish—that so filled the gulf with noise, that and the damned crowded shipping lanes. He stepped to the port side forward sonar stack position, a console with three large flat panel displays. In the seat was the sonar division's leading petty officer and the midwatch's sonarman-of-the-watch, Sonarman First Class Jay "Snowman" Mercer, who was a youthful, short and slender sonar tech who, like Chief Albanese, had been aboard the SSNX that was lost in the revenge attack on the hacked and hijacked drone submarine. They said it was the horror of that operation that had turned his beard stark white and filled his head with gray, but in truth he'd been going gray since he turned twenty. He kept the beard trimmed to a goatee, and looked almost academic with half-frame reading glasses perched on the end of his nose.

"Got anything?" Varney said, leaning over the sonar stack.

Mercer picked up a grease pencil and, on a small white plastic area of the lower console, wrote a hash mark. The hash marks added up to 11. He looked up at Varney and said in a south central Tennessee accent, "That's the eleventh time this watch you've asked that. And we're all of an hour in. You're going to beat yesterday's record."

"Fuck," Varney muttered, wandering back to the chart table, calculating the time on this leg until they'd reach the southwestern point of the bow-tie-shaped barrier search pattern, Point Lima, which was hours away at the slow crawl they were doing, four knots, to absolutely minimize own-ship's noise, the minimum speed that would keep the towed array from dropping toward the sea floor.

"Actually," Mercer said over his shoulder.

Varney skidded to a halt at Mercer's console chair a second later. "What?"

"I was just going to say that *this* is interesting." Mercer's grease pencil circled a graph that was the data from the athwartships towed array beam. There was a slender peak forming at 50.2 Hertz.

"Yeah, big deal, fifty cycles," Varney said dismissively. "Half the ships out here are running fifty Hertz electrics."

"And if the *Panther* is on batteries, that's all we're going to hear from him. That and maybe a LOFAR detect on his low freq main motor."

"You got a low freq hit?" Varney asked, leaning far over Mercer's console.

"No."

"Fuck," Varney said, turning away again to go back to the command console.

"But I *do* have an acoustic daylight detect on something submerged on the same bearing the athwartships beam is looking."

Varney bounced back again. He leaned in to stare at the top console's display. To the uninitiated, it would be like staring at the white noise of a broken television, but Varney had qualified under the tutelage of Sonarman Chief Tom "Whale" Albanese, *Vermont*'s revered top sonar operator, reportedly the best in the Atlantic Fleet, and The Whale had taught Varney the mysteries of the acoustic daylight array. It was mostly noise, but a repeating series of black vertical bars kept recurring off to the side. Mercer rolled his cursor ball over to the there-one-second-gone-the-next black spots, the bearing 310. Then he selected the time-frequency graph in the middle display and rolled his cursor to the bearing spread of the beam, which was from bearings 300 to 325. Then he rolled his cursor to bearing 310 on the broadband waterfall display, which showed a slight trace at 312, which was not unusual, because that was the direction to the shipping lanes.

"You're sure the acoustic daylight array's not picking up a surface ship?"

"It's screening out everything above the thermal layer. I'm only looking deep with it. If the *Panther* is sailing the way I think he is, he's at keel depth one hundred meters, and the thermal layer is at fifty."

"So Petty Officer Mercer, you're saying—"

Mercer straightened up in his seat and turned to face Varney. "I'm calling it, sir. We've snapped him up." In a louder voice, he announced formally to the entire room, "Officer of the Deck, new sonar contact, designate Sierra Fifty-Seven, bearing three one zero, held on narrowband, broadband and acoustic daylight imaging, possible submerged warship."

"Hot diggity fuckin' *dawg*, and about time," Varney said, lunging for the phone at the command console. "Good job, Petty Officer Mercer. Don't fucking lose him. Designate Sierra Five Seven as Master One." Varney dialed the XO's stateroom.

"Command Duty Officer," Quinnivan's voice came over the circuit. During the midnight watch, Quinnivan relieved Captain Seagraves of most of his command responsibilities so the captain could get some uninterrupted sleep. While stationed, the command duty officer had the same authority as the captain.

"Officer of the Deck, sir," Varney said breathlessly, his heart pounding. "We fucking got him! I'm calling silent battlestations, sir."

"I'll wake the captain," Quinnivan said, a jolly tone in his voice.

Gulf of Aden, Yemen
Port Aden Container Facility
K-573 *Novosibirsk*
Friday, June 3, 0115 UTC, 5:15 am local time

The gathered officers waited silently in the wardroom, counting off the last minutes before stationing the watch to get underway.

"Still no word of what the mission is, Captain?" the navigator and operations officer, Misha Dobryvnik, asked.

Orlov shook his head. "Nothing, just the original orders to make all haste to the terminus point at the entrance to the Gulf of Oman. Safe to assume that once we report that we're on-station, we'll get a new op-order."

The aft wardroom door opened and a sweaty Chernobrovin came in. "Repair crew signed off the work package, Captain," he said, pouring a cup of water for himself from the credenza. "The electric plant has all ship's loads and we're divorced from shorepower, removing cables now. Propulsion turbines are warm and loaded by the load bank, and the main motor is ready."

"Very good, Mr. Engineer," Orlov said, standing. "Mr. First, set the maneuvering stations watch." It would be damned good to get back to sea, he thought.

The announcing circuit clicked and Vlasenko's hard-as-steel voice came over. "Attention all hands. Set the maneuvering stations watch for getting underway."

Orlov returned to his stateroom and grabbed his binoculars and his VHF radio. In the central command post, people rushed to their stations and donned headsets. He walked to the forward door of the room, to the ladder and tunnel leading vertically to the conning tower interior. He waited for one of the lookouts to get all the way up, then took the ladder upward, the dim fluorescent lights of the ship giving way to the bright sunshine of the morning. He took the four steps up to the conning station on top of the conning tower, the area featuring two leather seats for the conning officer and assistant conning officer, the seats positioned behind an open space where the officers could stand behind the windscreen. As he stepped into the conning station, the communications officer, Captain Lieutenant Mikhail TK Sukolov was connecting and testing the conning tower's communication box, a device the size of a toaster oven that bolted to a post aft of the windscreen and was connected electrically by a large cable with multiple connectors. He stood, saluted and smiled at Orlov.

"Conning station communications tested, Captain. All is in order."

"Very well, Mr. Communicator," Orlov said formally, returning the salute. Sukolov had been inport duty officer last night, so evidently no hangover for him this morning.

"Excuse me sir," he said, and passed by Orlov on his way to the control room. He passed Vlasenko and saluted the first officer as he was on his way up from the tower interior to the conning station.

"Lines are singled up, Captain. Pier crew is ready to lift the gangway."

"Lose the gangway, Mr. First. Did you decide to drive us out yourself?"

"Yes, Captain. I can use the sea air and maybe a little sunshine."

Orlov nodded, smiling at Vlasenko. "We could all use some sea air and sunshine. Probably our last for a long time."

The pier crane rumbled as it pulled off the gangway. Vlasenko stood on the port side of the conning station, leaning over the coaming to look down at the pier. He reached for a megaphone and projected his voice down to the linehandlers below. "Pier crew, stand ready to toss over all lines!"

He looked over at Orlov. "Permission to take in lines and get underway, sir?"

"By all means, Mr. First, take in all lines and get underway." It was high time they got the hell out of here.

Ten minutes later, the Pacific Fleet's submarine K-573 *Novosibirsk* plowed through the small waves at maximum surfaced speed, headed northeast for water deep enough to dive.

Gulf of Oman
USS *Vermont*
Friday, June 3, 0117 UTC, 5:17 am local time

The command console of the USS *Vermont* was crowded as Captain Seagraves leaned over the periscope display from the inboard side. Lieutenant Anthony Pacino stood aft of the display and held the controller to the scope in his hands. To his left he could feel the fabric of the navigator's coveralls against the bare skin of his forearm, having rolled up his sleeves in the warm control room. To Navigator Romanov's right, the executive officer—the battlestations firecontrol coordinator—stood, alternating his gaze between the large flatscreen periscope display repeaters on the forward bulkhead, one showing Pacino's, the other showing Lieutenant Varney's Pos One's scope, and the firecontrol "dot stack," representing the best solution to the target, Master One. The *Panther.* This close to the target, the data source had been shifted from narrowband to broadband, and the dot stack had become sloppy, the phenomenon called "near-field effect." With a half shiplength between the two submarines, there was wide range of bearings to the target. The approach had been shifted to visual, first on periscope infrared, and now to normal optics.

"Add turns," Romanov said to Pacino, who was acting as approach officer under the watchful eye of Captain Seagraves.

"Pilot, add two turns," Pacino commanded.

Lieutenant Dankleff, at the ship control console, acknowledged. "Add two turns, Pilot aye, and Maneuvering answers, now making five six turns and seven point zero knots."

"Very well, Pilot."

The target was ahead of them and slightly shallower, at a depth of 328 feet. He was cruising at seven knots, steady at this depth since they'd acquired him. It seemed an odd depth at first, but it was well below the thermal layer and correlated to the target's depth gauges reading exactly one hundred meters. The speed of seven knots would seem to optimize his range on his batteries.

It was only a matter of time before he came to periscope depth and the operation to take him over could begin.

The voice of the navigation electronics tech came from aft and port. "Approach Officer, Navigator, mark sunrise."

Mediterranean entrance to the Suez Canal
Port Said southbound convoy waiting area anchorage
K-579 *Voronezh*
Friday, June 3, 0130 UTC, 5:30 am local time

Captain First Rank Boris Novikov poured tea into the first officer's cup. Isakova declined the offer of cream and sugar. They were seated at the table of his stateroom, trying to kill time before Port Said Operations called their convoy to form up and proceed south into the Suez Canal.

Kovalyov stuck his head in. "Captain, our convoy commences forming up in one hour."

"Very well, Communicator." Novikov checked his watch. It was 0530 hours local time. He picked up his phone and dialed the central command post.

"Watch Officer," the navigator's voice said.

"Navigator, the convoy will start forming in an hour. Are you ready?"

"We'll set maneuvering stations watch in twenty minutes,

sir, then weigh anchor and position ourselves in preparation."

"Very well," Novikov said, putting up the phone. Finally, this ridiculous wait was coming to an end.

Catoctin Mountain Park, Maryland, USA
Camp David
Birch Cabin SCIF
Friday, June 3, 0145 UTC; Thursday, June 2, 8:45 pm EDT

National Security Advisor Michael Pacino gratefully accepted the steaming coffee from Vice Admiral Robert Catardi. They were the first to arrive at Birch Cabin's special compartmented information facility, a SCIF that had preserved the rustic look and feel of the cabin's former den, complete with wood-burning fireplace, the out-of-date tables and upholstered couches and chairs that looked like they came straight out of Great Aunt Maude's front parlor from the year of our Lord 1943.

"Did you get in a nap?" Pacino asked Catardi. The call to assemble in Birch Cabin's SCIF had come at 2030 after Pacino had been unable to fall asleep for a nap, knowing that once they got Carlucci's call, they might be up for two days straight. He'd finally slipped into an uneasy rest, the images of a nightmare vaporizing with the jangling of the 1950s bedside table phone, but the residue of unease had lingered behind.

"You kidding? You get the word to fly to Joint Base Andrews for a comearound with the President of the United States, cool your heels over hamburgers and sausages on the Holly Lodge back deck grill with the muckety-mucks, sip a little Kentucky whiskey, but you know that any moment you'll be standing tall, braced up, in front of the president? For maybe days at a time without being able to go to bed? Who sleeps with *that* going on?"

Pacino smiled and nodded his chin toward the newcomer coming through the door, Jehoshaphat Taylor. "I bet *he* did." Taylor was a vice admiral in the Navy's Special Warfare Command, or SpecWar, as they liked to say. He was built like a refrigerator, weighing in at something like 270 pounds, all of it bone and muscle. He was swarthy, with black hair, bushy eyebrows and an overgrown beard extending to the collar button of his starched black Harley-Davidson button-down shirt, worn under a leather jacket and above black jeans and black steel-toed boots. He had a look of half-mad violence about him, as if one wrong word and he'd break someone in half. But he saw Pacino and broke into a grin that lit up his caveman face.

"Patch Pacino. Admiral. Sir," Taylor said, coming up to Pacino and pumping his hand in a hairy paw that dwarfed Pacino's. "It's great to meet you in the flesh. The stories about you—my mentors were on the *Seawolf* with you in the Bo Hai Bay. The stuff of legend, sir."

Pacino smiled. "No 'sirs' around me, Admiral. It's just 'Patch' now."

Taylor continued pumping Pacino's hand. "It'll always be 'sir' to me, sir."

Pacino laughed. "Have you met Rob Catardi, boss of the submarine force?"

Taylor smiled at Catardi. "You mean the boss of the bus drivers who take my commandos into action?"

"Bus drivers?" Catardi said, almost getting irritated.

"I'm just kidding, Rob," Taylor offered. "Jehoshaphat Taylor. You can just call me 'Jumpin Joe.' God knows, I've answered to worse."

"Coffee, Joe?" Pacino asked Taylor.

"I'd rather it were something stronger, it being after happy hour and all," Taylor said, "but I'll settle for a blonde-and-sweet."

The fourth arrival into the SCIF was Admiral Grayson Rand, the commander of the Atlantic and Pacific Fleets. He walked up and shook their hands, smiling. "Gentlemen," he said, "and I use the term *very* loosely." Rand stood barely five foot six, wiry and energetic, his hair going bald but trimmed to a crew cut, making his appearance seem tough. He had a Bayonne, north Jersey accent that accentuated his projected toughness. Dressed in a herringbone sport coat over jeans and brown Bruno Magli loafers, he looked ready to accept an umbrella-decorated cocktail at a megayacht's party. "So what, pray tell, is going on here?"

"I imagine the president will tell us when he's good and ready," Pacino said, refilling his coffee cup.

The door opened again and a chunky man of average height came in, appearing in his forties. He wore a black fedora cap, a Hawaiian shirt and chinos. He seemed dark, with a black goatee and mustache, wide eyes so dark brown they seemed black. He was nowhere near as imposing as Taylor, but certainly formidable. He walked to the coffee pot without a word and poured a cup for himself, acting as if the gathered admirals weren't even there. Theatrically, he took a deep pull on the coffee, then comically seemed to wake up and realize there were other human beings nearby. He smiled and offered his hand to Pacino.

"Angel Menendez, CIA deputy director of operations." His accent seemed familiar to Pacino. Cuban, perhaps.

"I'm Patch Pacino, the new national security advisor," Pacino said, then introduced the other admirals. Menendez shook their hands while sucking down his first cup of coffee.

"Anyone know what this mysterious meeting is about?" Menendez asked. Obviously, he was not used to being in the dark.

The door opened and a confident attractive woman in her late forties walked in carrying a laptop computer.

"Uh, oh," Menendez said in a stage whisper. "Stand by for action. The dragon lady is here."

The woman walked up to the coffee area, smiling slightly at the gathering, and poured herself a cup, tilting the sugar container into it.

"Some coffee with that sugar, boss?" Menendez asked, smiling.

The woman greeted them all with a smile that lit up her face. She needed no introduction. Her Senate confirmation hearings had been plastered over all the news files. Margo Allende, former CIA deputy director of operations and master of clandestine services, had been accused by the senators of the National Party of torturing enemy combatants. She had been confirmed by a one-vote margin after answering that she would never allow such an action under her leadership of the Combined Intelligence Agency.

"Good to meet you, Ms. Allende," Pacino said, shaking her

hand. He was surprised. He'd expected her to look older, but the woman was youthful, perhaps in her mid-forties, tall, slender, her straight auburn hair pulled back into a bun, revealing her perfect jawline and long throat. She had a small upturned nose, strong cheekbones, and behind her thick-rimmed glasses she had wide, deep blue eyes, with long auburn lashes under thin arcing eyebrows. She held his gaze, her eyes smiling at him along with her mouth.

"Please. Call me Margo. 'Ms. Allende' is my mother. God help us all if *she* shows up to this meeting." Allende's south-of-Atlanta accent was thick as warm honey. Pacino noticed she was still holding his hand in hers, her hand soft and warm.

Pacino introduced her to the admirals and the six of them got to their third cups of coffee, until Director Allende looked at her watch. "Not sure what's holding up the silver spoons," she said, "but why don't we get comfortable in the seating area while we wait?"

"Silver spoons?" Pacino asked.

Allende bit her lip, as if weighing her words. "The VP, Secretary of State and Secretary of War, all go way back together. They tend to disapprove of Carlucci's, well, let's just say *sensitive initiatives* that he tries to get accomplished. So I'll be nice and just say that when it comes to clandestine activities and projects, those three all need *lots* of convincing." She took a club chair by the side of the fireplace facing the door.

When the door opened, the vice president strolled in with three cabinet members, and like the admirals and spymasters before them, found their way to the coffee machine. Pacino stood, as did the others. As the three newcomer men shook the hands of the others, Vice President Karen Chushi came up to Pacino. She stood a head shorter than he did, slim in a tight dress that complimented her figure. She stood too close to Pacino, close enough he could sense an alluring perfume, and she looked up at him with wide light green eyes. He felt her soft hand reach for his.

"Admiral Michael Pacino," she said in a nasal and irritating south Texas-accented voice, even as she spoke in, what to her, must have been a tone of intimacy. "I've waited a long time to meet you. I'm Karen Chushi."

"Madam Vice President," Pacino said respectfully. Her nickname of "The Voice" seemed apt, Pacino thought.

"Maybe we would have met sooner if the president had read me into your little 'Fractal Chaos' security program." Her tone took on a resentfulness.

The Secretary of State arrived, his great bulk seeming to dwarf the petite vice president. He held out his hand to Pacino. "Seymour Klugendorf, State Department," he said in a sonorous voice, smiling in what seemed genuine pleasure. Pacino tried to keep a neutral facial expression, but the man's tremendous size was freakish. Where, Pacino wondered, did he buy pants that big? The secretary had to be well over four hundred pounds. Before Pacino could say a word, the Secretary of War and the Secretary of the Navy strolled up, sipping from their mugs with the presidential seal.

A tall, slender, man with a marathon runner's physique, in his late forties, bespectacled with steel-framed glasses, nodded at Pacino. The Secretary of War, Bret Coppin Hogshead, was one of those cool, logical figures, known to get through hostile wartime press conferences with calm, low-voiced sound bites that made him a favorite of the Washington think tank crowd, but unpopular with the rank and file of the military. He looked more like an actuary or an accountant than a major member of the president's cabinet. Hogshead came from old money, his ancestors arriving on the *Mayflower* four hundred years ago.

Beside Hogshead stood Secretary of the Navy Jeremy Shingles. He and Pacino had become acquainted in the aftermath of the drone submarine incident, where Pacino found himself having to brief Shingles, then an undersecretary of cyberwarfare in the War Department, about the drone incident and the loss of the *Piranha*. Shingles was a former civilian test pilot, and later Space Shuttle astronaut, who had taken over the helm of his father's corporation, McDermott Aerospace, a major defense contractor, second only to DynaCorp. Once, over drinks, Shingles had told the tale of his childhood being raised by Caspar Shingles, the "barnstorming billionaire" who had founded McDermott Aerospace with former Air Force General

Billy McDermott. Two years into the company's history, the elder Shingles had fired McDermott, but decided to keep the name of the company despite McDermott's lawsuits and claims on the company's profits. Decades later, McDermott Aerospace supplied the military with most of their fighter jets. A political cartoon had once derisively depicted the front of the Pentagon with a sign reading "Property of McDermott Aerospace." President Carlucci had known Shingles from years before, and Shingles was one of Carlucci's few allies in the contentious politics of the administration's cabinet.

People thought, Shingles once explained, that the president's cabinet functioned like the direct reports of a corporate chief executive officer, but it most certainly did not. Cabinet level appointments had to be confirmed by the U.S. Senate, which meant that in the partisan political realm, each cabinet member had to somehow appeal to both sides of the aisle. They also had to have connections to the Washington, D.C. power networks, and be scandal-free. In the swamp of D.C., having a clean record was not something that came easily. After having five of his proposed cabinet members rejected by the Senate on a partisan vote, Carlucci threw up his hands and appointed people who could be Senate approved, and the eventual result was a cabinet that was anything but a rubber stamp.

It was one of the reasons, Carlucci had explained to Pacino, that he hadn't read the three cabinet members and the vice president into the "Fractal Chaos" program. Pacino knew it wasn't that their offices tended to leak secrets, though there was more than a little truth in that, but that Carlucci knew that these particular members of his administration would have opposed their operation to steal the Iranian modified Kilo submarine, and Carlucci was in no mood to be scolded by his own cabinet or have his orders questioned. But since the operation was about to happen, he had decided to read them into the program and invite them here, perhaps so that if it failed, they too would be accountable for the mission. It had seemed a dangerous decision to Pacino, but Carlucci had proceeded anyway.

Finally the interior door to the room opened, three Secret Service agents appeared, two moving toward the outside entrance, the other staying at the interior door, and in walked President Vito "Paul" Carlucci, dressed in a track suit and sneakers. He smiled and walked through the room, greeting everyone personally. When he came to Pacino, he leaned in and whispered, "Careful with these cutthroats, Patch." He went on to greet Catardi before Pacino could respond.

"Okay, everyone," Carlucci said above the noise of the conversations. "If I could have your attention, let's get seated and discuss a few things."

The large room's chairs and couches were arranged in a long oval, but all offered a view of a wall-sized flat panel display. Carlucci took a seat to the right of the display, Karen Chushi to his left in a club chair, then Klugendorf, who occupied a small sofa, barely fitting into it. A sofa had been claimed by Hogshead and Shingles, then another chair occupied by Jehoshaphat Taylor, then a couch with Pacino, Allende and Menendez. A second couch seated Rob Catardi and Grayson Rand.

"I've asked you here to brief you on an operation that is about to commence, and to watch the progress of it in real time if you'd like, although we may have some time to wait before the real action happens. You're all cleared for 'Fractal Chaos' now, and I don't have to remind you of how secret this all is. Admiral Catardi, could you present your portion of the operation for us? I took the liberty of having some slides made up in anticipation of what you'd be talking about. You haven't seen the presentation, but you can ad-lib based on what the slide shows."

Catardi stood and the display screen came to life. The first slide that Carlucci selected was a standard security statement of the extreme level of classification of the slide deck. Then a photograph of earth from high earth orbit zoomed slowly down over the Indian Ocean and the Arabian Sea until the screen was filled with the Gulf of Oman, the Strait of Hormuz, with the northward-pointing triangle of Dubai on the south side of the strait and the Iranian Navy's Bandar Abbas base on the north side.

"Well," Catardi began, "What you're seeing is the Bandar Abbas base of the Iranian Navy."

Carlucci's view zoomed far in to show the protected basins

of the base, the larger warships on one side, the smaller patrol boats on the other, drydocks and building ways on the northeast side, with a floating drydock shown, an oblong black shape in it. The view then zoomed closer so the floating drydock occupied the entire screen.

"This is an Iranian Kilo-class diesel-electric submarine, built by the Russians for export sale."

Carlucci's slide changed to show a profile view of the Kilo-class submarine, the outside skin of the submarine graphically melting away to show a drawing of the interior.

"The Kilo has been considered one of Russia's greatest submarine construction achievements. It's quiet, fast, capable, reliable, has extended battery endurance and can carry 22 torpedoes or Kalibr cruise missiles."

The drawing in the slide suddenly split into two pieces, a forward section with the torpedo compartment and the second compartment with the control room beneath the conning tower, and the aft section that contained the diesel ship's service generator and the larger diesel propulsion generator, the latter electrically connected to the large main motor that drove the shaft and the single propeller. The gap of empty space between the compartments flashed red for a moment.

"We think the Iranians, with Russian help, have split the Kilo hull as shown here, with the combat spaces forward and the propulsion plant aft. They intend to fill that space with a new module."

A cylinder appeared between the hull sections. A darker red piece of equipment appeared in the front section of the cylinder.

"This is a new Russian-designed liquid-metal cooled nuclear reactor, fueled by bomb-grade plutonium. It's what physicists call a 'fast reactor,' in that it needs no 'moderator' to slow down the neutrons produced from the fission of the heavy elements of plutonium, and those neutrons go directly on to create the next generation of fissions. The heat produced by the fissions goes to heat a liquid metal piping system, which then heats water in the steam generators—the boilers—to make steam."

Two new vertical cylinders appeared near the reactor, with piping connecting them. "What you see next to the reactor are steam generators—boilers—where the hot liquid metal heats water that then boils."

The animation then showed piping emerging from the steam generators and running aft to a large piece of equipment, bigger by far than the reactor itself. "This is the steam propulsion turbine and generator that will now put power—nuclear power—to the ship's main motor for propulsion. A second, smaller steam turbine, will supply electricity to the ship's service generator. So now, the main motor can either be driven by the diesel propulsion generator or the new steam turbine generator or the batteries, and the ship's electricity can either come from the batteries, the diesel generators or the new ship's service steam turbine generator."

In the animation, all three hull sections rejoined themselves together, and the skin reappeared, turning the profile view into a longer, more slender submarine.

"The Iranians have renamed this submarine *Panther,* which was also the name of the entire program. Integrated together, the modified Kilo is now a nuclear submarine."

The view changed again to show the Bandar Abbas base, the view zooming back out to show the Gulf of Oman. A red dotted line extended from Bandar Abbas southeast into the gulf. "The submarine will be tested far south of here, either in the southern Arabian Sea or in the Indian Ocean." The view zoomed farther out, until the Saudi Peninsula shrank in size and the Indian Ocean was screen center between the east coast of Africa and the west coast of India. The dotted line ended in an "X" slightly north of the equator.

The slide returned to showing the new module to be inserted into the Kilo submarine. Carlucci spoke up for the first time.

"Rob, tell the crowd here why this nuclear fast reactor is of such interest to us."

"Yes, Mr. President." Catardi turned from the display toward the cabinet members and the VP. "This reactor is revolutionary, a giant leap forward in technology. In fact, we don't understand how it can function without, well, exploding. If the Russians have managed to make this work, reliably and safely, it revolutionizes everything. This reactor is smaller than a refrigerator in the average home, yet produces enough power to pull a mile-long train at eighty miles per over the Rocky Mountains. The applications are endless. They could use it in space for their moon base. They could power up the Arctic remote areas. And their future submarines will be world-beaters. Compared to their current pressurized water reactors, this has five times the power with an sixth of the weight and a third of the volume. We want to know what makes this reactor tick."

VP Karen "The Voice" Chushi looked at Margo Allende and frowned. "So, couldn't Margo's spies just, I don't know, bring us the plans? We could study them and figure out what's going on."

"Not so easy," the CIA director said. "But we already did it." Menendez nodded, as if there were a story there he was remembering.

"The plans gave us more questions than answers," Catardi said.

"Wait a minute," Klugendorf said, holding his fat hand up like a child in school. Pacino looked at him, thinking that academic circles were where the Secretary of State had spent his career, eventually making his way to becoming dean of faculty at the Harvard Kennedy School. "If this is a Russian creation and it's to be tested, why aren't the Russians testing it? Siberia somewhere, or Novaya Zemlya where they dropped that hundred megaton monster hydrogen bomb? Why would they entrust it to the Iranians?"

"Mr. Secretary," Catardi said, "From studying the plans, this reactor could be unstable. It could blow itself apart in a dirty radioactive cloud. Or it could go so 'prompt critical' that it could blow up in a nuclear explosion—not a big one, maybe ten to twenty kilotons, but that's on the order of the bombs dropped on Japan. Big enough to vaporize the submarine and all the technicians testing it. But it's more than that. It's national prestige. The Russians don't want a nuclear failure or to be accused of intentionally making another Chernobyl. They're hiding in the skirts of the Iranians, who are all too happy to test the reactor for them. If it's a success, Iran gets itself a nuclear-powered attack submarine. Imagine the mischief they could get into with that. If it fails, well, it was just another hare-brained Iranian nuclear project."

"Okay, then," Klugendorf said, apparently satisfied.

Pacino glanced at Shingles and Hogshead, who were both studiously and calmly looking at the screen. VP Chushi was frowning, a dark expression on her face. Perhaps she sensed where this was leading.

Carlucci changed the slide again. A green line appeared, extending northeastward along the east coast of Africa to the Arabian Sea and into the Gulf of Oman.

"This is the track of *our* asset," Catardi said, "the Block IV Virginia-class project submarine USS *Vermont*."

The screen changed to show a picture of a Virginia-class submarine on the surface, the bow wave breaking at her sail as she plowed through the waves, an American flag flapping on a pole on the conning tower.

The screen changed again to a view of the Gulf of Oman, where the green line moved toward the Strait of Hormuz and touched the red line that showed the outbound *Panther*'s movement.

"This is where the operation will start," Catardi said.

"What *is* the operation?" Chushi asked, a tone of suspicion in her voice.

Catardi paused for a moment, glanced at the president, then looked at the vice president. "We intend to steal the *Panther*."

Through the sudden din of the loud response of the cabinet members to Catardi's statement, Pacino could hear the shrill voice of Karen Chushi saying, "Are you fucking *kidding* me?"

18

Catoctin Mountain Park, Maryland, USA
Camp David Presidential Retreat
Birch Cabin SCIF
Friday, June 3, 0210 UTC; Thursday, June 2, 9:10 pm EDT

"Quiet, please, everyone," President Carlucci said. The side of the room toward the exterior door with the VP and cabinet members had broken into loud chaos a moment before. The other side, by the fireplace, with Pacino, the CIA officers and the admirals, had remained quiet, all of them still in their seats. "Let me switch on a short video of how this will work."

A video clip rolled on the large flatscreen, the operation of the USS *Vermont* in its attempt to steal the narco-sub in the Caribbean Sea. Pacino had never seen it before, and was startled to see his own son acting as the approach officer, guided and coached by a stunningly beautiful female lieutenant commander. He watched as the control room battlestations crew made the decision to launch the EMP cruise missile, and stole a glance at Chushi, Klugendorf and Hogshead, who were all frowning. They all watched attentively as the SEALs locked out and got to the deck of the submerged target submarine, immobilized it, then tried to take it over. The clip ended with the SEAL commander hurriedly evacuating the sub at the conning tower hatch and the periscope view of the narco-sub as it scuttled itself and sank.

Carlucci nodded at Vice Admiral Catardi. "Thank you, Admiral. I wonder if Admiral Taylor could say a few words about why this upcoming operation will succeed when the narco-sub operation didn't."

Jehoshaphat Taylor stood. "Thank you, Mister President. The only real difference between the operation to hijack the *Panther* and the narco-sub is that the *Panther* will be operated by a human crew."

"You're sure?" the VP asked.

"We had almost no intel on the cartel operating the narco-sub," Margo Allende said in her smooth Georgia accent. "Our intelligence money is better spent watching the Iranians, North Koreans, Russians and Chinese. And we've done our due diligence on this *Panther.* The crew will be human, I promise you."

"So what happens after you get this sub to come to the surface? Are you going to kill the crew?" Klugendorf asked.

"That's not the plan," Taylor answered. "We prefer non-lethal tools. Shotgun shells and bullets, according to Admiral Catardi here, are considered bad for submarine equipment. We'll leave the crew in a life raft, give them rations and a distress beacon."

"Okay then," Klugendorf said, satisfied.

Odds were, Pacino thought, non-lethal means wouldn't be enough, but maybe Taylor's men would prevail without shooting. Catardi's concern was legitimate. A bullet in the ship control console could ruin the whole plan. Pacino noted that Taylor left out the fact that the emergency beacon would be designed to be inert for 48 hours, and only *then* broadcast the distress signal, allowing the hijacked *Panther* to clear datum and exit the area.

"After that," Catardi said, standing as Taylor sat back down, "a small crew from the *Vermont* will cross over to man the *Panther.* They'll drive it to our Bahamas Atlantic Undersea Test and Evaluation Center, AUTEC. Sort of the Navy's version of Area 51, if you will." The display screen zoomed out from the Indian Ocean, the globe turned and the view zoomed back in to the Bahamas to an overhead shot of the DynaCorp / Navy test facility at the barren Bahaman island labeled Andros Island. "We'll take the reactor apart here and study it."

"Are you planning on testing this reactor when the *Panther* is at sea? On the way to this test facility?" Bret Hogshead asked.

"Not on the run from the Indian Ocean, Mr. Secretary," Catardi said, addressing the Secretary of War. "We'll keep the reactor shut down and inert and use the batteries and snorkel on the diesel to get the ship back to AUTEC, so it will be a long, slow—but safe—voyage. After we examine it, we will get a test crew and take it out into the deep central Atlantic and test it there. I'm sure we'll have the same worries as the Russians. We don't want this thing exploding in the Bahamas. That would impact the tourist industry for a season or two. We're still trying to figure out how to select the test crew, since the risk is so high."

"So that brings us to the present moment," Carlucci said, standing. "Thank you again, Admiral," he nodded to Carlucci. The screen darkened, then lit up with a view of the eastern Gulf of Oman. "This is a live view from a Predator drone looking down on the approximate area of where this operation will commence. But we're not exactly certain of when or exactly where the operation will happen, so this drone will be orbiting at a high altitude and looking for signs of a surfacing submarine. You're free to take a break or go back to your cabin and grab a nap. We'll call your room when we detect action, or you can stay here and wait for this to happen in real time."

"Mr. President," Karen Chushi said, standing and smoothing out her dress, "I and Secretary Klugendorf, Secretary Hogshead and Secretary Shingles would like a private word with you." She turned to the admirals, Pacino and the CIA officers. "Could we have the room, please?"

Pacino left and walked slowly back toward Holly Lodge. Rob Catardi fell in step beside him. Once they got there, Pacino motioned Catardi into Holly Lodge's special compartmented information facility, a more conventional conference room that resembled a rustic version of the White House Situation Room. "We didn't even get to the issue of a hostile opposition force," Pacino said, turning on the screen and selecting the Predator drone view, which still just showed empty, unremarkable ocean. "Wait till Chushi gets word that Carlucci already gave *Vermont* permission to release weapons as deemed necessary to succeed."

"And nuclear weapons at that," Catardi said.

"She and Klugendorf are going to melt down over that."

"Yeah, definitely."

"Rob, something I meant to ask in the briefing. What's the range of the *Panther*? Won't she need to refuel? And won't she run out of food?"

Catardi nodded, reaching for the pod coffeemaker. He raised an eyebrow at Pacino, who nodded. Catardi brought two cups to the table and both men sat facing the video screen. "*Panther's* range is limited on diesel fuel, advertised at six thousand nautical miles, but we think it may be as low as four thousand. The trip is around fifteen thousand miles, depending on how far *Panther* will deviate from the great circle route. So she'll need to stop four or five times before she reaches AUTEC and take on fuel. We'll re-provision her then."

"When she surfaces to load diesel, she'll be vulnerable, Rob. That could be when an opposition submarine could torpedo her and destroy her. And to track the *Panther*, all the Russians will need to do is keep track of every Navy oiler in the hemisphere."

"Your buddy Margo and company came up with a work-around. Tramp steamers, rust-bucket tankers, lying-to on shorelines, anchored out, biding their time. The latitude and longitude of all these rusting derelicts given to the *Panther* boarding party ahead of time. Each one of them can refuel the *Panther*, and if we absolutely, positively have to, it can be done while the *Panther* hovers submerged."

"What about food? How would you load food while submerged?"

"Those rusting hulks that refuel *Panther*? They'll be dumping trash overboard, but it won't be trash. It'll be food. Submerged *Panther* divers snatch it up and lock it in. Boom, extended range. Patch, I assure you, we've thought of everything."

"What about this nuclear weapon release issue? What happens when the VP and the silver spoons find out about that?"

"Maybe Carlucci keeps them in the dark about it. Maybe he thinks it's just a deep contingency plan. What do *you* think, Patch? Do you think it's a low probability contingency?"

Pacino stopped, thinking about what Carlucci had said to him in confidence about the Virginia-class and the Yasen-M, and Carlucci's intentions to demonstrate to the Russian president that American submarines remained superior to Russian subs. And Carlucci was essentially cheating by giving *Vermont* advanced permission to fire warshots at any Russian submarines trespassing into the operation. Even allowing her to hammer the Russians with nuclear depth charges. Pacino stood up from the table and walked to the display screen, touched the screen absently, then slipped his hands into his pockets and turned to look at Catardi. "Rob, if *we* were the Russians, do you think there's a chance in hell we'd let the Iranians test our reactor without a submarine escort out there?"

Perhaps unconsciously imitating Pacino, Catardi stood up to look closer at the screen and put his hands into his pockets. "No way."

"So the only question is, do they send a front-line boat or a clunker out there?"

Catardi considered. "Clunker. Definitely. An Akula II maybe. Or a Sierra-class. Maybe even an improved Kilo-class. Something they're not afraid to sacrifice in case the *Panther* reactor blows up and takes the escort boat with it."

"Yeah, you're probably right."

"I know your worry, but no way in hell Moscow would risk sending a Yasen-M-class out there."

"I hope not. From the intel I've read, I don't know that we could beat one, even with the new Virginia-class."

"We still have the edge," Catardi said. "Weapon release rules of engagement. Russians would probably have to ask fleet HQ for permission to shoot at us, whereas *we* have warshots loaded in all tubes, powered up and ready to fire. And a note from home giving Mommy's permission."

"Let's just hope it doesn't come to that," Pacino said, a dark worried expression crossing his face. "But we haven't mentioned the elephant in the room, Rob."

"What's that, Patch?"

"Aircraft. Think about it. Four or five of our P-8 antisubmarine jets could find the *Panther* between breakfast and lunch. Find her and take her out with torpedoes carried aboard. The Russian version? The older Il-38 or the newer Il-114 are more than capable maritime patrol aircraft. They might not snap up *Vermont*, but they could easily nail down *Panther*. And it's easy to mobilize half a dozen of them, even from the Pacific Fleet HQ or the Northern Fleet's airfields. It's a long flight, but *Panther* will be doing an exfiltration for six, seven or eight *weeks*, Rob."

"Don't forget, Patch, *Vermont* is equipped with Mod Charlie SLAAM-80 missiles. One of those would ruin an Il-114's entire day." SLAAM stood for submarine launched anti-air missile, and had gotten submarines out of several scrapes since its introduction.

"You can run out of missiles, be out of range, or late to detect an aircraft, Rob. It's small comfort."

Margo Allende walked in then, her eyes drifting toward the screen and back to Pacino, then nodding at him and Catardi. "Hello, boys," she said, a half-smile on her face. She reached behind her head and removed a pin holding her hair in a bun, and her flowing hair fell down on her shoulders, long and straight and sleek. She shook her head to arrange her hair and looked seriously at Pacino.

"You're worried about your boy?"

Pacino nodded glumly. "If the Russians blanket the Arabian Sea and the Indian Ocean with antisubmarine aircraft, they could find *Panther* and *Vermont* and torpedo them, or relay the information to any in-theater attack submarines. Or to Iranian destroyers and frigates. Weapon release permission aside, there are a hundred scenarios where this just isn't survivable. For either boat."

"You don't have to worry about any Iranian or Russian surface ships or antisubmarine aircraft," Allende said, staring into Pacino's eyes. "If you're up against an opposition force, I guarantee it will *only* be from submarines."

"Why do you say that?" Catardi asked. "How do you know that?"

"Ain't sayin'," Allende smiled mysteriously. "You're not read into the program. Well, I'll leave you boys alone. Come on out to the bar if you want a drink."

Pacino nodded, then looked at Catardi.

"I wonder what she's got up her sleeve to keep airplanes and destroyers out of the mix," Pacino said, his mood suddenly lighter.

Catardi shook his head. "No telling. But if that's true, mission success just became much more probable." He was quiet for a moment, then looked at Pacino. "You know, this whole nuclear release thing must be just a deep contingency plan, Patch."

"Yeah. You're probably right."

"Your son looked good in that video clip," Catardi offered.

"I hope like hell this goes as planned," Pacino said, frowning. "You don't think my boy will be on that crew that takes over the *Panther*, do you?"

"Hell, no, Patch," Catardi said. "He's good tactically, but he's still a non-qual. No way Seagraves puts him on the *Panther* crew."

Gulf of Oman
65 Nautical miles northeast of Muscat, Oman
USS *Vermont*
Friday, June 3, 0245 UTC, 6:45 am local time

Lieutenant Anthony Pacino, clad in a form-fitting wetsuit, stood at the forward hatch of the SEAL lockout chamber, his scuba bottles, regulator, mask, fins and weight belt placed in a neat pile by a passageway corner by the canisters of things they'd take aboard the stolen Kilo sub, including SatNav receivers, radio equipment, clothes and food, and the large container that would inflate into the raft they'd pour the Iranian crew into.

The AI division under Chief Nancy "K-Squared" Kim had set up two large flatscreens on the bulkhead opposite the lockout chamber hatch. One was patched into the number one periscope of the command console, the second a view of the control room taken from aft overhead in the room and looking down on the attack center consoles, the firecontrol coordinator and the command console. Sound was piped in, the conversations in the control room audible from the screen.

Chief Kim looked up at Pacino from her seated position on

the deck. "Might as well get comfortable, Mr. Patch. It might be a long time before we need to prep."

Pacino sank down to the deck at a spot where he could see the control room monitor. "Can you turn that up?" he said to Kim. She increased the volume. He shut his eyes and listened to the hum of conversation. The *Panther* was still deep, 328 feet, going at a battery-endurance speed of seven knots. The control room crew was on a trip-wire alert, waiting for the target to make a move that would indicate he was coming above the thermal layer up to periscope depth. Perhaps a maneuver like turning in a 180 degree turn to hear shipping behind him in his "baffles," the area directly astern where his sonar in the bow couldn't hear, the baffle-clear an attempt to avoid colliding with surface shipping.

Coming to periscope depth was always hazardous for any submarine, with some of the loaded supertankers drawing up to 120 feet to the bottoms of their hulls. A sub coming out of the cold thermal layer into the warmer water stirred by the sun would be in an entirely new sonar environment—sounds up there would reflect off the interface between warm and cold and not penetrate deep. Almost the ocean version of a mirage in the desert. The only way to come to PD safely was to come up slowly and maneuver the ship to hear all sounds from all points of the compass, and only then allow the top of the conning tower to rise above 120 feet.

So there would be plenty of signs that *Panther* was on his way up, Pacino thought, and told himself to relax. Last night had been sleepless. Watchstanders were rotated in and out to sleep for a few hours, then returning to their battlestations watch, the captain and XO deciding who was fading out and directing team members in and out, almost like a professional coach pulling a player off the field and sending in a fresh replacement. Seagraves had taken over the approach officer duty four hours ago and directed Pacino to his bunk, but all Pacino could do was stare into the dark. A combat operation like this, he thought—anything and everything could go wrong.

He thought about the simulations they'd run before snapping up the *Panther*. This tranche of simulations began by assuming the boarding party had successfully taken over the Kilo submarine, but then the Kilo and the *Vermont* ran into opposition forces—Iranian destroyers, Russian destroyers, Russian Kilo-class submarines, even Russian nuclear submarines. Even two Russian nuclear submarines operating together. Seagraves had kept the Russian nuclear submarine attackers at older submarine classes to see how they fared, and against the older Akula II-class and older vessels, they'd prevailed, sometimes easily, sometimes with a bit of a struggle. But in all of them, *Vermont* heard the bad guys long before said bad guys heard *Vermont,* and assuming the Russian opposition force was there to stop the *Vermont*'s mission and recover the Kilo, *Vermont* had immediately fired upon and destroyed the older attack submarines. In those simulation runs, the main issue was positioning *Vermont* out ahead of the *Panther,* so there would be little chance of a *Vermont*-launched torpedo homing in on the *Panther* instead of the Russian attacker. And that was a challenge because *Panther* couldn't hear *Vermont,* even if she were right alongside. It had been up to *Vermont* to maintain battlespace awareness and keep herself ahead of *Panther.* That, of course, made the pair vulnerable to torpedo attack from the rear. *Panther* wouldn't hear it and the incoming torpedo would sink *Panther* before *Vermont* could even react. A torpedo dropped from astern from an MPA, a maritime patrol aircraft? Mission failure. Every time.

Eventually, after enough simulations had been run that both *Vermont* and *Panther* crews were reaching the same results over and over, Captain Seagraves upped the ante and tossed in a modern Russian Yasen-M-class attack submarine, approaching from the south.

Those simulations had all ended in disasters. The Yasen-M submarine, commanded by Romanov in the simulations, every single time, heard *Vermont* before *Vermont* heard the Yasen-M, and it had come down to what the Russian's rules of engagement were. If the Russians had permission to attack on detection, both *Vermont* and *Panther* went down. Mission failure. And all the good guys died. If the Russians had to go to periscope depth to ask for permission to shoot warshots from fleet HQ or Moscow,

Vermont had enough time to detect the Yasen-M, mostly from the transient sounds the Russian boat made as it ascended to periscope depth, or increasing noise from "clearing baffles," exposing all sides of himself to *Vermont*'s sonar arrays, with one angle being the "bingo angle-on-the-bow" where his emitted noise was louder than other angles. But even in those scenarios, it was *not* an automatic victory for *Vermont*.

When both *Vermont* and the Yasen-M were aware of each other and shooting, the scenario would degrade into what was called a "PCO waltz"—so called since prospective commanding officer school featured prospective captains acting as approach officers in submarine vs. submarine exercises, and whenever two attack subs could hear each other and were shooting at each other, the world dissolved into a crazy, mixed-up melee where anything could happen, the fog of war intruded and no one knew what was happening. Likely as not, an attacking submarine could go down from his own torpedo fired into the cloud of confusion. The massive uncertainty of a PCO waltz was to be avoided at all costs, Seagraves had cautioned. "If you're in a PCO waltz, withdraw and clear datum, and try to sneak up on the bastard again when he least expects it."

Something about that last advice had rubbed Pacino the wrong way. Retreating in the face of the enemy? That wasn't the American way, or what he imagined the American way to be. Romanov had chided him harshly for being naïve. "Sticking around for certain death isn't dagger-in-the-teeth courage, non-qual. It's dagger-in-the-teeth *stupidity*. Above all, in submarine operations, stupidity is punished harshly, either by the sea itself or the enemy. So if you're fighting an attack submarine that knows you're there and is shooting at you, get the hell out. Clear datum, come back later and sneak up on him." Pacino had put his head down and yes-ma'amed her, but he doubted he could ever do that. Perhaps, he thought, that was his fatal flaw. Perhaps that was a terrible thing in a harsh future, lying in wait to kill him.

He tried to banish all negative thoughts like that from his mind. The SEAL commander, Fishman, kept saying freakish things like *we create our own reality* and *the universe you live in is built and furnished by you and only you—you live what you create.* That was a little too New Age for Pacino's taste. At his core, he thought, he was a pragmatist, and all too often, pragmatists were mistaken for pessimists. Reality was what it was, he thought. Reality was as solid as a cold brick wall.

In the lockout chamber of the attack submarine USS *Vermont,* Lieutenant junior grade Elias "Grip" Aquatong reclined against the bulkhead, clad in a wetsuit, weight belt, scuba tanks, fins, his mask strapped on but up high on his head. His thighs were heavily laden with the non-lethal Mark 6 modified Taser, and the M4A1 carbine with attached grenade launcher, with his Sig Sauer 1911 .45 ACP pistol in a watertight container. His shins were strapped with two long K-Bar knives and the one his sister had bought him, a slender ten inch stiletto knife that would stop a man the size of a grizzly bear in his tracks. His weight belt was crowded with watertight containers of .45 ammo, grenades and the 5.56 mm ammo for the carbine. *Guns are great,* Commander Fishman had preached, *but they're useless without ammo. And in combat, ammo goes fast, and the battle goes to the party who brings more bullets to the fight.* Aquatong put his hand on his belt and felt for that ammo, trying to reassure himself.

Commander Ebenezer "Tiny Tim" Fishman came up to him. "How you doin', Grip?" he asked quietly, looking into Aquatong's eyes.

Aquatong smiled. "I'm good this time, Skipper," he said. "Not like last time. No need for your 'simulation theory' speech." Fishman didn't smile. "I'll tell you what, though. I think the AOIC, Pacino, could benefit from it."

Fishman thought for a moment, stroking his chin. "I'll be back in ten," he said.

On the passageway deck outside the lockout chamber, the entire *Panther* boarding party, with the exception of Lieutenant Anthony Pacino, slept. Chief Bernadette "Gory" Goreliki snored quietly next to Pacino. Pacino looked up to see the SEAL commander, Fishman, leaning over him.

"How you doin', AOIC?" he asked.

Pacino squinted up at him, at first intending to give him the story Pacino was trying to make himself believe, that he was perfectly calm and unafraid, but that was so far from the truth that there was no way he could pull off that lie. Despite Spichovich's warning about needing to learn to have a poker face and learn how to bluff credibly, Pacino thought this was a bad time to practice telling a bald-faced lie just to see if he could get away with it. What a world, he thought, where his homework assignment from his boss was to learn how to lie.

"The *truth*, Commander? I'm nervous as fuck." His voice had trembled, just slightly. Pacino picked up his canteen and tried to unscrew the top, but his hands were shaking too hard. Fishman reached for the canteen.

"Totally understandable," Fishman said, his voice low, gentle and reassuring as he unscrewed the canteen cap and handed it to Pacino, who took a drink, some of it spilling out of his mouth and running down the front of his black wetsuit. Fishman dropped to one knee and looked left and right at the sleeping *Panther* invasion crew, who all remained asleep. "I want to share something with you that might make this easier for you. Maybe it will lighten the load you're carrying."

Pacino looked at Fishman. "Anything you could do to make this easier for me, Commander, by all means, proceed."

"Have you ever heard of the simulation theory?" Fishman asked.

"Sure," Pacino said. "Ever since Elias Sotheby made it mainstream. *We're all living in a video game. This is all a simulation. A computer-generated quasi-reality. None of this is real. The one true god is a software engineer, watching what happens in this simulation.* Of course I've heard of it. And it's all bullshit."

"But is it? Consider this," Fishman said. "I believe the one thing in the universe that matters is a *decision*. Have you heard of the branch of analysis called 'decision theory'?"

Pacino made a dismissive gesture. "I haven't, but it sounds like a business school buzzword like 'paradigm shift' or 'the new normal.'"

"Far from it, Mr. Pacino. Let me ask you a personal question.

What was your last major decision? Your last life-changing decision?"

Pacino bared his teeth in what he thought was a tough expression. "To go back into the airlock of the *Piranha* after it got torpedoed. But that felt more like instinct than a conscious decision."

"Exactly the point I'm about to make," Fishman said. "Do you ever wonder what would have happened if you'd pushed yourself to the surface and saved your own life and just let the submarine sink without you?"

"Sure," Pacino said. "A thousand times."

"That," Fishman said, "is exactly what I'm talking about. *Alternate endings.*"

"Alternate endings? I'm not sure what you mean."

"Imagine, if you will, you're a person who has lived a nice, safe life that ends when you're ninety-five years old. Call that the 'Base Life.' And after you die, you go to the afterlife, and in that afterlife, you wonder about what *would* have happened if you had made different major decisions. Example, that bully on the school bus in third grade? What would your life be like if you'd punched him so hard he hit the deck, and all your classmates witnessed you being a badass and gave you a standing ovation?"

"Okay," Pacino said uncertainly. "I guess I'm following you."

"So, Mr. Pacino, imagine reality—for your life or any life—being a tree. Every time you make a major decision, you create two new branches of that tree. One branch is the decision you made and the reality you live as a result. The other decision leads to a different branch and its reality is completely different. If you look at this, with all the major decisions you make in life, that tree has thousands of branches. Yes?"

"I'm with you so far, Commander." Pacino wondered where this was all going.

"So what you're living right now, this is an *alternate reality*, played out to demonstrate to your soul, which is right now residing in the afterlife, what your life would have been like if you'd made a different decision. So, basically, the reality actually happened for your base life. But this?" Fishman gestured to the passageway and the sleeping *Panther* invasion force. "All of this? This is a digital simulation. A computer simulation. A video game. All constructed to demonstrate to your base life's soul what *would* have happened if you made a different decision than what your base life had actually decided."

"Whoa," Pacino said. "So, this, none of this, is real?"

"It's totally real," Fishman said. "For us, in *this* version of reality, this is *completely* real. But for every reality we sense, there are ten thousand other realities going on at the same time, each one of those created out of a different decision."

"So you're saying that in my 'base life,' I took the safe way out. I swam to the surface and let *Piranha* go down without me."

"No. I think that in that long and safe base life, you didn't even go to the Naval Academy—too much risk of eventually having to do something dangerous. You probably went to Purdue and studied mechanical engineering and lived your working life out in a cubicle, with a nice safe wife waiting for you in a nice safe home. And this? All this? This is you wondering what life *could* have been like if only you'd taken more risk."

"And so there are a thousand variations. There's lives where I did swim to the surface, right?"

"There's lives where on that midshipman cruise, you decided to go on a nice, safe aircraft carrier, not down to the scary depths of the submarine force."

"So what's the point of all this?" Pacino asked.

"The point is, in the afterlife, after watching all the thousands of lives that resulted from different decisions, your soul will eventually have no regrets. Your soul will see every decision's result, every outcome. And in that review of every life that emerges from a decision, your soul will learn and evolve and find peace. You'll become a more powerful you. And then, who knows, maybe you decide to do it again, and you come back. A new you, without the conscious memories of your past lives, but the unique individuality of your soul is always with you."

"You know, Commander, that sounds completely whacko," Pacino said, but finding himself smiling.

Fishman smiled back. "I presented that theory in my doctorate board in philosophy at Old Dominion U."

"And?"

"They failed me, sent me back to do another thesis, but by that time I was done with philosophy. But at least I learned that the world isn't ready for the real truth."

"Sorry to hear, Commander. Maybe it is a bit odd, but something to think about, I suppose. At least it's making me feel better about going out that hatch."

Fishman clapped Pacino on the shoulder. "Good man. So when we invade this target submarine, remember, it's just a video game."

Pacino smiled. "I will, Commander."

Against the aft bulkhead of the lockout trunk, Senior Chief Ronald "Scooter" Tucker-Santos strapped on his Mark 6 non-lethal attack weapon, his Mark 17 propulsion unit and a waterproof, portable emergency medical kit, then looked over at Petty Officer First Class Hoshi "Swan Creek" Oneida.

"Skipper giving that newbie officer that speech about 'this is all a video game'?" Tucker-Santos asked.

Oneida looked at Tucker-Santos. "Yup. Works every time. Something about someone making you doubt the reality of walking into combat makes it bearable. 'It's only a movie.' It helped me in Tokyo, Doctor Scooter."

"Yeah? Do you still believe in Fishman's theory?"

"I wonder." Oneida said. "The Skipper *is* crazy. But something happened and I've been meaning to ask Skip about it. If every decision creates a unique branch and a new reality, do those branches ever touch each other? And if they touch, is it possible that you'd be moving along one branch and suddenly find yourself in another?"

"Something happened? What?"

"Back in Japan, my cousin was very close to our grandmother, and in her last days, he sat with her by her hospital bed, only leaving her side for bio-breaks and the occasional shower, having food brought up from the cafeteria for him to eat in her room."

"Okay, Swan," Tucker-Santos said.

"So my grandmother died on a Tuesday in May. My cousin left the hospital and went home, completely overwhelmed with grief. He can't sleep, but finally naps at maybe five in the morning, Wednesday morning, mind you, and at eleven the hospital is calling him. It's grandmother's favorite nurse on the line, asking when he'll be at the hospital, because his grandmother was awake and asking for him. The day after she died, she's there, asking for him."

"What?"

"Yeah. So he goes to the hospital, gets there at noon Wednesday, and grandmother is sitting up and having a few bites of lunch. She lasted ten more days before she died again."

Tucker-Santos looked over at Hoshi Oneida.

"Yeah," Oneida said. "Two complete parallel realities."

"Did your cousin ask Grannie if she remembered dying?"

"He told her the whole story. She told him he was crazy. She told him he dreamed it all from exhaustion that Tuesday. But my cousin? He still had the pamphlet the favorite nurse gave him when grandmother died, labeled, 'When Your Loved One Passes Away' with a hand-written recommendation of which undertaker to call. And that pamphlet? Favorite Nurse Girl had no memory of giving it to him or of writing anything on it."

The two SEALs were silent for some time. Grip Aquatong, having heard the exchange, came over and leaned on the aft bulkhead by Scooter and Swan. "You know what I wonder?" he asked the others.

"What's that, Grip?"

"In a video game, does taking a bullet still hurt?"

"If we fuck up," Oneida said, deciding to check his ammo one more time, "we'll find out."

Pacino realized he was truly exhausted, thinking about Fishman's alternate endings theory. He shut his eyes and concentrated on making his muscles relax in his toes, then his feet, then his shins, then his thighs, working his way up to his neck, until he was completely relaxed. He imagined himself in a dark movie theater, where he was alone in a row a few from the front in the center, and the screen was blank, with a word dimly appearing on the screen, the word spelling *SLEEP.*

Five minutes later, Lieutenant Anthony M. Pacino, U.S. Navy, lay in a deep sleep on the deck of the submarine USS *Vermont,* headed into a combat mission.

BOOK 4:

CHANGE OF COMMAND

19

Gulf of Oman, entrance to the Arabian Sea
70 Nautical miles north-northeast of Sur, Oman
USS *Vermont*
Friday June 3, 1012 UTC, 2:12 pm local time

USS *Vermont* AN/BYG-1 History Module // Ship's Deck Log—
Date: 3 June.
Time: 1012Z.

Status: USS *Vermont* in trail of target submarine *Panther*. Target has been steaming deep and submerged since trail operation began. Awaiting target's next excursion to periscope depth.

Update: *Panther*'s noise signature indicates target is preparing to come to periscope depth.

"This is finally it, gentlemen," Commander Fishman said. "What's not an option?"

"Fucking up," Lieutenant junior grade Aquatong replied, pulling his mask down over his face.

"Control, Lockout Trunk, request permission to flood down the trunk," Fishman said into the 7MC communication box nestled in the overhead of the trunk, in a protected space separated from the rest of the trunk by a vertical wall. When the trunk flooded, this space would maintain an air bubble and stay dry.

"Lockout Trunk, Control, flood the trunk," the pilot said over the comm box's speaker, the COB, Master Chief Quartane, at the pilot station, having taken the battlestations watch over from Dankleff, since Dankleff was on the *Panther* boarding party.

"Flood the trunk, Lockout Trunk, aye." Fishman looked at Tucker-Santos. "Doctor Scooter, check shut the side hatch."

"Side hatch shut and locked, Skipper," Tucker-Santos reported.

"Check shut the trunk drain valve."

"Aye, Skip, and trunk drain valve is shut."

"Let's get some ocean in here, people," Fishman said, pulling down a lever that opened a hydraulically controlled ball valve that flooded the space. In just a few seconds' time, the warm gulf water came into the trunk, the water level rising fast, over two feet per second. As the water rose, the air in the space compressed, coming close to the pressure of the water outside the skin of the ship at periscope depth. The pressure gauge read 18 psi. Fishman's ears popped as the air pressure rose. The air above the water began to form a thick, impenetrable fog. The four SEAL commandos were gathered close together in the air bubble space, waiting for the trunk to flood all the way. Other than the air bubble space, in another minute, the trunk was fully flooded with seawater.

"Control, Lockout Trunk, trunk is flooded. Request to open the outer door."

"Lockout Trunk, Control, open the outer door."

"Open the outer door, aye, and outer door coming open."

Fishman moved a second hydraulic lever, and the upper lockout trunk hatch came open. The lockout trunk was now open to the ocean above. He pulled his mask down over his face and gestured to the others with his thumb. *Let's go.*

Fishman ducked down from the air bubble into the trunk's water, then looked up at the circle of light from the world above. He pulled himself up by the ladder rungs until he and his scuba bottles rose through the open hatchway.

The water of the gulf was warm and startlingly clear, almost as clear as the waters of the Mediterranean, he thought.

Aft of the ship, slightly above them, he could see the entire hull of the *Panther* as it moved at periscope depth, using its diesels to charge its batteries. The target submarine looked long and slender and graceful, he thought.

He pulled himself farther out of the hatchway, holding on to the hatch operating mechanism, and watched as the other three SEALs emerged. Once they were all out of the hull, he motioned to the target submarine, letting go of the hatch.

The current formed by the movement of the ship floated him backwards to the target submarine, requiring only slight thrust of the Mark 17 propulsion unit to lift him up the proper depth to the target's deck. Fishman swam to the target's conning tower, noticing the side of the conning tower had a large graphic of a prowling, snarling panther. He smirked, admiring it in spite of himself. As they'd practiced a dozen times, he unpacked a cable from a small container, unfurling it along both sides of the conning tower, the flow of the current pulling each end of the cable aft. Scooter Tucker-Santos held the cable at the forward end of the conning tower while Fishman floated aft along the *Panther*'s port side. At the trailing edge of the conning tower, he found the other half of the cable on the starboard side and fastened the two lengths of cable together with a special grip mechanism, then cinched the grip forward to the trailing edge of the conning tower. That left two cables trailing aft toward the screw. Fishman hand-over-handed himself aft with Scooter right behind him, Scooter latching on to Fishman with a safety cable, attaching them both to the conning tower cable.

Fishman was dimly aware of the massive black shape of the *Vermont* slowing down and fading back astern of the *Panther*, there in case one of the SEALs fell off the *Panther* hull. As the Kilo submarine's hull angled downward toward its rudder, horizontal stabilizers, and screw, Fishman followed the cable aft, concentrating hard not to lose the package. The package was a special carbon fiber net that he would deploy and wrap around the *Panther*'s screw, fouling it so hard that no amount of horsepower or torque of the screw's driveshaft would overcome the net.

He pulled the package out of its container and let go of the container and let the current carry it away. He found the carbon dioxide pressurized canister attached to the net, designed to blow the net up into a cloud, and pulled its pin. The net, a mere brick-sized solid, immediately blew up into a large fuzzy mass in front of him. Fishman guided it down toward the screw and watched as the screw's flow vortex sucked the net into it. After several revolutions, the net was fully wrapped around the screw, and two seconds later, the screw stopped. The submarine was coasting to a stop. Any moment, Fishman thought, the sub would surface to see what had happened to their screw. He looked over at Scooter and gestured forward. The two commandos hand-over-handed themselves forward against the rapidly dying current of the submarine's motion, the work getting easier by the second as the target sub slowed.

Up forward, Grip Aquatong and Swan Oneida were waiting by the forward hatch. Behind him, Scooter Tucker-Santos was grabbing the handholds to pull himself up to the top of the conning tower in case that was the hatch that opened first. As the ship glided to a halt in the warm gulf water, the commandos unsheathed their non-lethal weapons, waiting.

But something was wrong. The *Panther* wasn't surfacing. Fishman looked at his diver's watch. The screw had been immobilized for at least four minutes, maybe longer. He looked up at the surface, then at the conning tower, with the periscope extended and penetrating the surface, a second mast behind it, which must be the snorkel mast, bringing fresh air into the submarine for the diesel generator to breathe to charge the battery bank. Finally the current generated by the ship's motion completely died. They were stationary in the sea.

He looked over at Grip and Swan, who were gesturing with "what the fuck" signs. He shrugged. Who knew what was going on inside the control room of the goddamned *Panther.*

In the central command post of the Iranian Navy's submarine *Panther,* commanding officer Commander Resa Ahmadi looked over at his second-in-command, Lieutenant Commander Hossein Kharrazi. The two men had an uneasy relationship, since Kharrazi was older and more experienced, having come up through the Iranian Navy's enlisted ranks, and obviously thought that command of the *Panther* should have gone to him, not the inexperienced, Harvard-educated upstart who had family connections in both the Revolutionary Guards and the General Staff of the Armed Forces. How many times had Kharrazi muttered under his breath things like, "It's not what you know, it's who you know."

"What in the name of Allah is going on?" Ahmadi said from the periscope.

"Let me look," Kharrazi said. Ahmadi stepped back from the number two periscope and Kharrazi grabbed the grips and put his eye to the periscope optics. On the surface, there was nothing obviously wrong. But the ship had unceremoniously come to a stop in the ocean. Yet there were no fishing trawlers in the surroundings that could account for the screw becoming fouled.

"We can't surface," Kharrazi said, his voice muffled by the periscope. "Our orders prohibit surfacing, no matter what."

"I know," Ahmadi said. "But we can hover and send out divers to see what's wrong with the screw."

"Excellent idea, Captain," Kharrazi said. Ahmadi could never tell when the man was being sarcastic or genuine when he said things like that. "I'll see to it."

"Who are you sending to the escape trunk?"

"The engineer and chief of the boat are both diver qualified. I'll send them out."

"Very well," Ahmadi said, taking the periscope from Kharrazi. "Boatswain," Ahmadi called, "Commence hovering at present depth."

"Hover at present depth, Boatswain aye," the watchstander at the starboard command console acknowledged.

"What's happening?" the heavily accented voice of Alexie Abakumov asked. Abakumov was the lead test engineer for the upcoming test of the UBK-500 fast reactor, which lay silently sleeping in the reactor compartment far aft. And as usual, Abakumov had been drinking, his stash of vodka taking up more room than the rest of his personal belongings. Ahmadi disapproved, but the Russian was a VIP rider and was owed a certain professional deference.

"We're troubleshooting a problem," Ahmadi said, trying to make his voice sound calm and controlled.

"What problem?"

Ahmadi pushed the periscope away from his face and glared at the Russian reactor physics engineer. "There's a problem with the screw. We are sending divers out to investigate."

Ten minutes later, Lieutenant Commander Ahmad Kazemi, the chief engineer, and Chief Petty Officer Mehdi Bakeri gathered at the forward escape trunk's lower hatch in the torpedo room, both clad in wetsuits, weight belts, scuba tanks, regulators and masks, their fins in their hands ready for the climb up the ladder. First Officer Hossein Kharrazi could barely tell them apart. They both looked like frightening phantoms.

Kharrazi picked up the microphone to the inter-ship communications circuit. "Central Command, First Compartment, request permission to enter the forward escape trunk, flood the trunk and open the outer hatch for diver operations."

The word came through the circuit from the captain's voice. "Enter the forward escape trunk, flood the trunk and open the outer hatch for diver ops."

When the upper hatch came open, chief engineer Lieutenant Commander Ahmad Kazemi pulled himself through the hatchway into the clear blue warm water of the Gulf of Oman and immediately felt himself stung by what seemed a huge wasp, but it wasn't a wasp, it was another diver. His body went completely limp and he could barely breathe. He felt himself floating. A second diver grabbed his inert body and lashed it to a cable at the conning tower leading edge. Kazemi, though he could no longer move, could definitely still feel emotions, and the emotion of the moment was stark panic and fear for his life. He should have been thrashing in the water or fighting these other divers, but nothing worked but his lungs. He felt a moment of gratitude that whatever they'd hit him with hadn't paralyzed his diaphragm and his chest muscles, at least not yet, but that and his eye muscles were the only parts of him that were still functional.

Kazemi watched as the second *Panther* diver, Chief Bakeri, emerged from the hatch, and whatever these alien divers had stung him with, they used on Bakeri, who went immediately limp. They moved him back to the conning tower and secured him to it.

One of the divers came over to him and lashed his wrists together behind his back with cable ties, then his ankles, then did the same to Chief Bakeri. Kazemi watched as the divers unlatched him and Bakeri from the conning tower and pulled them to the forward escape trunk hatch. He and Bakeri were maneuvered into the airlock. The divers shut the upper hatch. If only there were a way to alert central command, he thought, but whatever they'd injected him with seemed to be getting stronger rather than weaker, and within another minute, Kazemi found himself fighting to stay awake, and it was a losing battle. He shut his eyes and the world faded away.

The four SEALs crowded into the forward escape trunk of the Iranian Navy's submarine *Panther* along with the two paralyzed divers. It was unknown how long it would take the SEALs to secure the Kilo submarine, and if it took too long, the Iranian divers would drown. Fishman had no problem with the *Panther* crew meeting their ends, but only if it were necessary. Letting a diver drown when his air bottles ran out was not a death Fishman would wish on anyone. He wondered if this were one of those major decisions that would bifurcate his reality and send him down the branch of the universe where he let the divers live, and what that *other* universe would be like.

Consciously trying to be more present in the moment, Fishman reached up, pulled the upper hatch down and shut it, spinning the hatch wheel that dogged the hatch shut. He searched for a drain valve and a vent valve, found two valves nestled side-by-side in the overhead, and made the assumption that they were the drain and vent valves. He opened the valve in the smaller pipe first, probably the vent valve, then the one in the larger pipe, which had to be the drain valve, and immediately the water level in the chamber fell down from over their heads to their chests, then lower to their knees, until all the water drained from the trunk. Fishman leaned down to the wheel of the lower hatch and spun it, watching as the hatch dogs came off the seating surface. He pulled the hatch open and found himself face to face with someone looking up at him expectantly. The person at the bottom of the ladder apparently thought he was one of the ship's divers, not a commando invading the ship. The man said something in Farsi.

In response, Fishman hit him with a blast from the Mark 6, and the Iranian went down hard, collapsing to the deck. Fishman reached for cable ties and tied the man's hands behind his back, then tied his ankles together. He looked up as a second Iranian sailor approached, and hit him with a shot from the Mark 6. The other SEALs handed down the Iranian divers, took the regulators out of their mouths, and piled them by the other two paralyzed members of the *Panther* crew while Fishman tightened the zip ties on the interior Iranians' wrists and ankles.

A communication circuit in the crowded overhead rasped with an Iranian voice, undoubtedly inquiring about what was happening. Aquatong pulled the Iranian divers and the two men who'd been at the bottom of the trunk ladder farther into the torpedo room, checking their zip ties, then reached up and shut the lower escape trunk hatch, nodding seriously at Fishman.

The band of commandos made their way aft to the control room, their weapons leveled for the next Iranians they'd encounter.

Dankleff shook Pacino awake.

"Wake up, wake up, wake up! Let's go, AOIC. Time to get to work."

Pacino yawned, not sure how long he'd dozed. His entire body ached from lying against the hard deck and bulkhead of the lockout trunk. Pacino stood and strapped on his gear, preparing to lock out of the trunk once the *Panther* surfaced. The trunk was still flooded with the outer door open, in case one or all of the SEALs needed to return. When *Panther* surfaced, the plan was shut the upper hatch, drain down the trunk, then the *Vermont* crew would enter the trunk and lock out for the short swim to the surface, where the SEALs would help them climb onto the hull of the *Panther*. The hardest part of the operation would be moving all the cargo they needed—the raft that would house the survivors of the crew, the radio and navigation equipment, canisters of clothes and food. The only thing they were relying on the *Panther* for was oxygen and water. And, he supposed, watertight integrity.

For the tenth time today Pacino wondered about whether the *Panther* were loaded with weapons, and if so, what were they? And would Chief Kim be able to figure out the firecontrol systems to allow Pacino and Dankleff to shoot at submerged targets, assuming Chief Albanese could find them on what had to be a primitive sonar system?

"So far, glitch-free," Grip Aquatong said to Tiny Tim Fishman.

"Don't jinx it, Grip," Fishman ordered. They stood in the cramped control room of the modified Kilo-class submarine *Panther*. There were two older men in the room with three younger ones. The older men had to be the officers, the younger ones enlisted watchstanders or perhaps junior officers, all of them immobilized. "Figure out a way to surface this tub."

Aquatong looked at the ship control area, which had a steering wheel and two control joysticks. "Damn if I know how this works."

"Maybe on that panel behind you on the starboard side."

Grip turned and leaned over the horizontal portion of what looked like a control panel. "It's all in Farsi. I can't figure any of this shit out."

"They said to look for big levers, with big operators on them, like the *Vermont*'s emergency ballast tank blow levers."

Grip shook his head in frustration. "Nothing."

"Dammit."

Scooter and Swan showed up, their Mark 6s ready to fire.

"Status?"

"All ship's company immobilized. We used half the zip ties we brought. Smaller crew than we imagined," Scooter reported.

"You check all the nooks and crannies? All the possible hidey-holes?"

"We went over it all once. We'll need a second and third tour once we get the *Vermont* crew in here."

"And don't forget that translator, what's his name?"

The short and slight kid with buck teeth and thick glasses, Cryptotechnician First Class Saurabh Onur, had a thick Indian accent, and hadn't really been adopted by the *Vermont* sailors, at least, not yet. He was fluent in Russian and Farsi, and he was an expert at encryption and decryption technology. He'd definitely be useful here, but Fishman worried that there was only one of him. There should have been a second CT in case something happened to Onur, he thought.

"Grip, go get the OIC and AOIC in here and bring that CT guy with you. Pacino and Dankleff can figure out the operation of this sub once the CT guy translates all this gibberish. Meanwhile, Swan and Scooter, make another sweep of the sub for anyone we haven't found and immobilized."

The three commandos left Fishman alone in the submarine's control room. He leaned over the older officers, if that's what they were, wondering if he should put them on the raft with the other crewmen or keep them as hostages to help run this submarine. Obviously, this was harder than they'd imagined.

Dammit, he thought. Another major decision. Another two realities coming his way. But which one led to mission success?

"What the hell?" Dankleff said to Pacino. "Upper hatch is coming shut. But the *Panther* is still submerged."

"Must be glitch number one," Pacino said. "*Panther* crew must not have wanted to surface—probably in her op-order to remain submerged no matter what. The SEALs must not have been able to figure out how to surface her."

"Shit. Trunk is draining down." Dankleff picked up the 1JV phone. "Control, the lockout trunk upper hatch is shut and trunk is draining down. One or more SEALs is coming back in."

Finally the forward side-door of the lockout trunk opened and Grip Aquatong pulled off his mask.

"You're next on-stage," he said. "Let's go."

"Why isn't *Panther* on the surface?"

"Goddamned if we could figure out how to surface her. We

didn't want to just try stuff. Not sure we can trust any of the Iranian crew. We need that cryptotech, Onur."

"Petty Officer Onur, get in here," Dankleff barked.

The cryptotech climbed into the lockout trunk, looking like a fourteen-year-old boy. The kid was tiny, Pacino thought, surprised the SEALs hadn't given him a call sign like 'Heavy' or 'Fatty' or 'Massive.'

"What do they call you?" Pacino asked the petite cytotechnician.

"Saurabh, sir. My first name."

"From now on," Dankleff said, "you answer to 'Crypto Geek,' or just 'Geek.'"

Onur stared at the OIC as if he'd spoken another language.

"Come on, Geek, get your mask on."

"First trip, I'll take OIC and AOIC and the Geek," Aquatong said.

"I'll inform control," Pacino said, reaching for a phone on the bulkhead of the crowded passageway. At first he picked up the 1JV official circuit, but realized half the tactical team would be listening in. He put the phone back, found the inter-station phone and dialed the conn. Officer of the Deck Rachel Romanov answered, her voice seeming perplexed that she'd been called on the unofficial phone circuit. For a moment, Pacino felt something dark blow through his soul.

"OOD, Lockout Trunk," Pacino said. "SEALs couldn't figure out how to surface *Panther*. So OIC, AOIC, cryptotech and Aquatong are going to lock out and get over to *Panther* and try to surface it."

"Very well," Romanov's cold voice replied.

"And Nav," Pacino said, hesitating.

"Yes?"

Pacino could hear her breathing.

"I just wanted to say," he said, "I'm sorry for what I did. I hope someday you'll forgive me. I treasured our friendship. I was hoping we could be friends again. I wanted to tell you now because, well, I feel like I may be running out of time. My life may be out of days. So. You know. I just wanted to leave you with that."

There was silence for a moment. Dankleff was waving at him from the hatch, as if to say, *let's go.* Finally Romanov answered him.

"Don't think that way, non-qual," she said softly, almost gently. "You are going to *win* this thing. We *will* prevail. We will *all* survive this. Because, goddammit, you owe me a fucking drink when we get to AUTEC."

"I could throw in a steak and some more drinks to go with it, Nav," he smiled into the phone.

"Good plan. Good luck out there, non-qual. Anthony."

She hung up the phone. He stared at the handset for a moment, then looked up. Dankleff was staring at him.

"Okay," Pacino said. "Control has the word. Let's go."

Pacino, Onur and Dankleff climbed into the side hatch. Pacino dogged the hatch, shut the drain valve and vent valve and hit the hydraulic lever to open the trunk-flood hull and backup valves.

"Control, Lockout Trunk, flooding down." Dankleff said over the 7MC communication circuit.

"Trunk, Control, aye," the box rasped.

The water began to rise in the lockout trunk, and for a moment Pacino felt a visceral panic grip his chest and it became hard to breathe. He consciously tried to take a breath, screaming at himself that this was *not* the *Piranha.* But the water had risen above his chest and as it approached his chin, he found himself hyperventilating, and as the panic blew into his mind, the edges of his vision began to darken.

Aquatong slapped his mask, hard. "Lipstick. Lipstick! Patch! *Patch!* You with us?"

Pacino violently shook his head, trying to clear his mind.

"Shut the flood valve!" Aquatong yelled.

The noise of the flooding stopped. The water was up to Pacino's shoulders. Aquatong took off Pacino's mask and regulator, pulling his own mask to his forehead and dropping his regulator.

"You okay, Patch? You gonna make it?"

Pacino saw Dankleff and Onur staring at him. He inhaled. "Just some, you know, anxiety from what I went through on

Piranha," he choked out. "I'll be okay," he said, more to himself than the others. "I'll be okay." He took a deep breath, put his mask back on and put his regulator into his mouth, clamping his teeth down on the rubber.

Through the mask he saw Dankleff looking at him, knowing that since Dankleff was in command, he was making a decision—whether to leave Pacino behind or soldier on.

"I'm *okay,* U-Boat," Pacino said around his regulator.

"Come into the air space with me," Dankleff ordered, pulling Pacino with him into the space that remained dry while the rest of the trunk flooded, where the valve operating mechanisms and comms box were housed.

"Let's get going," Aquatong said.

Dankleff hit the flood valve handle again the sound of water flowing in restarted. Outside the air space, through a round porthole, Pacino could see the water level started rising again until it had risen all the way to the upper hatch. Dankleff shut the flood hull and backup valves, then looked at Pacino, his mask on the top of his head.

"You don't have to do this, Patch."

Pacino lifted his mask and dropped his regulator. "It was a momentary thing, boss. I swear I'm okay." He drilled his eyes into Dankleff's, hoping he sounded believable.

Dankleff exhaled and put in his regulator and nodded. Pacino pulled his mask down and clamped his teeth into the regulator and took a few breaths. Dankleff turned to hit the hydraulic lever for the upper hatch, then pulled Pacino under the water's surface with him, the two of them emerging into the flooded lockout trunk.

Inside the trunk, Aquatong was already out the upper hatch, pulling Petty Officer Onur after him, then Dankleff, finally Pacino. As Pacino emerged into the clear water, he could see the entire hull of the black *Vermont* extending into the distance. He noticed a faint trace of green algae at the waterline, showing how the boat rested in the water when surfaced. Farther back and above them, the hull of the Kilo submarine was also visible, the sub stationary nearer the surface.

Aquatong had strapped a safety lanyard to Pacino's belt,

the lanyard attached to Dankleff and the crypto tech. Aquatong maneuvered his Mark 17 propulsion unit and started off for the *Panther* hull. Pacino stared at the hull of the *Vermont,* thinking, *there, right there, that's where the first torpedo hit the* Piranha. He clamped his eyes shut and shook his head, forcing himself to be in the present. He saw Dankleff looking at him, giving him a "thumbs-up" sign, but it wasn't a statement, it was a question. *Are you okay?* Pacino nodded and shot a thumbs-up back at him, and by that time Aquatong had maneuvered them over the forward hatch of the *Panther.*

The *Panther* was bigger than in Pacino's imagination, but then, he thought, reality always is, and that thought made him think about Fishman's ideas about the nature of reality. Could this, all this, really be just a simulation? "It's only a movie," he thought to himself as his fins went down into the hatch of *Panther*'s forward escape trunk.

20

Gulf of Oman, entrance to the Arabian Sea
70 Nautical miles north-northeast of Sur, Oman
B-902 *Panther*
Friday June 3; 1101 UTC, 3:01 pm local time

Grip Aquatong pulled the upper hatch of the *Panther*'s escape trunk shut and spun the hatch-wheel to dog the hatch, then opened the vent and drain valves. The water in the tight space drained, and as the level sank below Pacino's chest, he dropped his regulator, put his mask on the top of his head and pulled off his flippers. Dankleff was staring at him. Pacino grinned.

"I'm okay, Skipper," he said.

"Better to be dry, eh, AOIC?"

Pacino nodded. Aquatong opened the lower hatch, the last drops of water falling down to the space below. He climbed into the hull, then Onur, Dankleff, then Pacino. Pacino emerged into a space crowded with weapon racks and torpedoes, lit by weak overhead fluorescent lamps. Valves and piping and panels choked the walls of the space, interspersed with a thousand runs of cable. At least one question he had was answered—they *did* have torpedoes, but what kind?

"Jesus, look at this," Dankleff said, looking around. "It's like 1950 in here."

"Come on," Aquatong said, "Hurry up."

The four of them took off their diving equipment and put them into four separate piles—who knew if they'd have to use them again, so no sense mixing them up into a chaotic stack.

"Follow me," Aquatong said, and walked quickly aft, where a circular hatch was set into the thick steel of the watertight bulkhead. They emerged into a narrow passageway, the walls of it done in a light birch paneling. The passageway extended far aft, but Aquatong only went thirty feet down it before arriving at an alcove where a steep stairway extended up in one direction and down in the other. Aquatong vaulted up a steep staircase to an upper level. Pacino followed Dankleff and pulled himself up by the stair's stainless steel railing into a narrow area, boxed in in three directions, each wall of it filled with junction boxes, cables and piping, with an open space amidships of the stairway, the opposite area filled with what looked thousands of valves in piping, most with large, red, circular handles, a few of the larger ones high up in the overhead with bar-type handles, these valve handles engraved with large letters in Farsi.

Pacino stared at the valve manifold wall. "You weren't kidding about it being 1950 in here. Maybe 1940. Look—there's got to be a million valves in that rats' nest of piping—it's 'The Million Valve Manifold.'"

"More like a World War I sub with *that* jumble of valves. No way we're going to figure out how to operate this with just a translator."

"With any luck, the Iranians are still alive," Pacino said.

Aquatong kept going forward through a narrow space past the Million Valve Manifold into what had to be the control room, but it was barely twenty feet square. Unlike the U.S. Navy's submarines with their drab gray paint, the predominant color of the room was a bright corn-on-the-cob yellow. Jammed into the center of the brightly lit room were two periscopes, the forward one slender and retracted, the smooth stainless steel of its pole extending downward into its well. The aft periscope was larger, possibly the navigation unit, and it was extended, the grips still horizontal, the eyepiece glowing with light from the surface.

To the port side of the scopes was a command seat shoehorned in by a bulkhead of more valves, junction boxes and cabling. Forward of the command seat was a panel in the port forward corner, with what looked like a radar repeater or sonar repeater, or maybe both, the console jammed with a hundred switches and annunciator lights. To the right, at about the centerline, was a console built to be stood behind, with a display at eye height, possibly an upward-looking sonar, reminding Pacino of an underice sonar, but what use would that be to a non-nuclear submarine? To starboard of that, in the forward starboard corner, was a small ship control console, with a horseshoe-shaped panel, a steering yoke in the center, joysticks on either side of it, one seat centered behind the yoke, the second jammed against the starboard bulkhead.

Immediately aft were three consoles built to be stations where watchstanders sat facing outboard to starboard, with fairly expansive table-like horizontal sections with keyboards and function keys set into them, communication circuit microphones, vertical sections jammed with rotary switches, gauges, more annunciator lights, toggle switches and buttons. Aft of the three sit-down consoles was the Million Valve Manifold bulkhead. Pacino looked around in wonder. He could fit this entire tiny control room into his father's kitchen, he thought.

"Figure out how to surface this bitch before it sinks," Aquatong urged.

"Geek, get over here, Petty Officer Onur," Dankleff commanded.

"You hear that?" Pacino asked Dankleff.

"What?"

"Diesel engine," Pacino said. "We're snorkeling, and apparently hovering while we snorkel."

"Well, we ain't goin' *anywhere* till the SEALs free up the screw. So let's hope whatever hovering system they've got keeps us level here. We sink a few feet and the induction mast goes under, if they don't have a head valve or the head valve controller fails, that diesel engine could suck all the air out of the boat and kill us, like in that Chinese diesel-electric sub a few years ago. God knows if they have a vacuum switch interlock."

"Or even if they have one, does it work?"

"Geek, can you read this panel?" Dankleff said, focusing the crypto tech on the middle console. "This 'pos two,' if you can call it that, seems to be a combined ballast control panel and electric plant control panel. We need the BCP part of it. Onur, there should be a switch or lever somewhere that says 'main ballast tank blow,' or two of them, with one of them for the forward group and the other for the aft group."

Petty Officer Onur looked at the panel and shook his head. "OIC, it's all abbreviations and knobology. There's nothing a landlubber can figure out from this. I know technical terms in Farsi, but these abbreviations are all what you guys call 'inside baseball.'"

"I was afraid of this," Dankleff said. He looked around. "Nothing resembling emergency blow levers. Fucking designers built all the functions into this BCP slash EPCP."

"Look for a SOP manual," Pacino said.

"Yeah, Geek, look for a book, an instruction manual, procedure manual, something labeled 'Standard Operating Procedures.'"

Petty Officer Onur pulled out an orange one-inch-thick plastic binder. "Says 'Operating Procedures.'"

"Try to find something that says 'surfacing.' Or 'emergency surfacing.'"

Petty Officer Onur studied the manual, frowning.

"This is taking too long," Pacino said. "We need one of the Iranian crew."

"The officers are all in the wardroom, or at least we thought they were officers," Aquatong said. "But they're all kind of tied up at the moment."

"Not funny," Pacino said. "Take me to them. U-Boat, you and Onur keep trying to figure out how to surface this bitch."

"Hey, who's in command here?" Dankleff said, but he was smiling.

Down the birch-paneled passageway, a side door opened into the wardroom. Pacino took it in at a glance. Fairly large for a wardroom, almost as big as *Vermont*'s, which was an odd contrast to the cramped design of the tiny control room. There were bookshelves along two walls, a seating area at the far end, and the long ends of the table each had four seats, with a larger one at the door end—for the captain—and a normal chair at the other end, with a door that opened into the galley, a pass-through in the wall for bringing in food.

There were teacups and plates on the table and a tea service that had gone cold, a serving tray of pastries and small sandwiches in the table's center. Seated at the end seating area were three tied-up Iranian officers. The end chair and the six seats at the table were taken up with more immobilized Iranians. All of them were zip-tied to their chairs and had duct tape over their mouths. Pacino pulled Onur over.

"Which one is the captain?"

Onur read the name badges over the left breast pocket of their at-sea coveralls.

"There's just names, sir, not rank or station."

"For God's sake, Geek, *ask them*."

One of the Iranians started moving violently in the seat he was cable-tied to. Pacino walked up to him. He was maybe forty years old, with a well-groomed haircut, a full handlebar mustache, clean-shaven otherwise, slender, medium height. He looked a little too young for central casting to send in as the commanding officer, though. Pacino carefully pulled the duct tape off the man's mouth.

He took a gasping breath. "*I'm* the captain," he said in perfect, almost British, English, the stress of the moment making his voice a half-octave higher than Pacino imagined it normally was. "Commander Resa Ahmadi, commanding officer of *Panther*. And who in the name of Allah are *you*?"

"Anthony Pacino, Lieutenant, United States Navy," Pacino said, his face close to the Iranian's, looking into his eyes to try to read if the Iranian were truly the captain, and if he'd try to sabotage the mission, perhaps even sink them all intentionally. "Why do you speak English so well?"

"I went to high school in London. For college and grad school, I went to Harvard in America," he said. "Double major—quantum physics and international relations."

"Funny combination of studies for a submarine officer," Pacino said, weighing the Iranian's words, and noticing that the officer next to him, an older, thickly bearded and heavier man, was glaring at Ahmadi as if he wanted to kill him. "If you went to Harvard," Pacino asked, "tell me this—there's a restaurant just east of the Harvard Book Store, across the street from Lamont Library. What is it?"

Without hesitation, Ahmadi answered. "It's the Grafton Street Pub and Grill when I was there, but there was talk about closing it down."

"Really?" Pacino asked. It had been a favorite haunt of his and Carolyn Alameda's when he'd been a grad student in Boston. "So what does it look like inside?"

"Lots of brick, old wood floor, dark wood tables, dim lighting. Atmosphere. And a rowdy crowd, Mr. Pacino." Ahmadi looked up at him imploringly.

Pacino unholstered the Glock .45 ACP from its waterproof container at his belt that he'd been issued for this mission. He had no intention of using it, because God alone knew what a stray bullet would do to a submarine designed like this one, but it did a good job of intimidation. He pointed it at Ahmadi's right eyeball.

"Okay, I believe you, Captain Ahmadi. Now, I need to *trust* you. I need you to come with me to the control room and surface the boat."

"Control room? You mean the central command post?"

"Yeah, the goddamned central command post. You think you can do that without me having to put a hole in you big enough to toss an apple through?"

"Lieutenant, I don't want to die any more than you do."

"Geek, take my knife and cut Ahmadi's zip ties."

Petty Officer Onur took Pacino's K-Bar knife from his shin sheath and cut the cable ties holding Ahmadi to the chair.

Just then the deck tilted downward and the air pressure in the room sank. Pacino's ears popped with a *BANG*, and a second later the sound of the diesel engine cut off, the ensuing quiet boding ill, because if the snorkel mast had gone under, with the deck tilting and the diesel shutting down, it meant one thing.

They were sinking.

Sonarman First Class Mercer put his hand to his ear and raised the other hand to signal attention.

"Approach Officer, Sonar, Master One's diesel has shut down."

"Very well, Sonar," Seagraves said calmly. "Officer of the Deck, what do you think that means?"

"Captain, I was hoping it meant the SEALs and Dankleff and Pacino were preparing to surface, but look!" Romanov gestured to the periscope display. The *Panther* was taking on a down angle, the angle increasing, and drifting vertically downward. "Dammit, sir, she's sinking!"

"Mark the depth here, NavET," Seagraves called to the navigation technician.

"One thousand six hundred seventy fathoms, Captain. Ten thousand feet."

Seagraves shot a look at Romanov, and Quinnivan stepped over from the firecontrol's attack center. "What's crush depth for a Kilo, OOD?" Quinnivan asked.

"We think it's three-fifty meters, sir. Eleven hundred fifty feet. Give or take."

"Vertical dive the ship and keep up with it, OOD," Seagraves ordered, "so we can check its depth."

"Aye sir. Pilot, insert negative depth rate, ten feet per second. Shifting scope to IR," she said, shifting the periscope optics to infrared.

"Negative depth rate ten, Pilot, aye, and negative rate increasing, three, five, seven, nine and ten feet per second, OOD, depth three one zero feet."

"Very well, Pilot, call out depth every fifty feet."

Romanov concentrated on the periscope display. The *Panther* was deeper than *Vermont*. And from its bowplanes and horizontal stabilizers, it had started to glide forward, the range opening.

"Pilot, secure hovering, all ahead one third, turns for three knots. Take the bubble to a twenty degree down angle."

The deck in the room dramatically tilted downward. Everyone standing had grabbed a hand-hold, including

Romanov. She stared at the IR periscope display. The *Panther* kept sinking deeper, its down-angle steeper.

"Pilot, take the bubble to thirty degrees."

"Down angle to three zero degrees, Pilot, aye. Present depth five five zero feet."

"Dammit, Captain, *Panther*'s angle is steep, she's going down at thirty degrees now, maybe more."

Seagraves shot a look at Quinnivan. This mission might be over five minutes from now.

Ending in mission failure.

Ending in the death of their subordinates and friends, Lieutenants Dankleff and Pacino. And the SEAL commandos.

Seagraves clamped his jaw shut, fighting hard to keep the emotions from showing on his face.

"Depth seven hundred."

"Master One's angle's increased to thirty-five, maybe forty degrees."

"Depth seven five zero. Depth eight hundred feet. Eight fifty. OOD, you got a depth order for me?"

"Pilot, pull out at twelve hundred feet."

"Nine fifty feet. One thousand feet. Eleven hundred. Eleven hundred fifty, feet, Officer of the Deck, and pulling out. Depth twelve hundred feet. Test depth, ma'am."

Romanov looked up at Seagraves. "Fuck, Captain."

"I know," he said quietly.

Pacino's last words suddenly filled Romanov's mind. *I treasured our friendship. I was hoping we could be friends again. I wanted to tell you now because, well, I feel like I may be running out of time. My life may be out of days. So. You know. I just wanted to leave you with that.*

Oh my God, she thought, and a hot tear leaked out of her right eye and ran down her cheek.

"Hurry up!" Pacino screamed. He pushed Captain Ahmadi up the steep stairs to the upper level. With the steep down angle the ship had taken on, the stairway had become more horizontal, the rungs at odds with gravity. They both slipped twice on the ascent. "You've got to blow ballast. Emergency blow!"

"We have to shut the vent valves first," Ahmadi said. "Or the air in the ballast tanks will just float away."

"Why the fuck," Pacino said, gasping for breath as he reached the top of the ladder, "would you sail around with the goddamned ballast tank vents *open?*"

"Otherwise, they rust shut and you could never submerge," Ahmadi said, as if it were obvious. Dankleff was holding onto the middle console they'd named "pos two."

"Well, dammit, shut the damned vents!" Pacino shouted, thinking the Russian designers hadn't yet gotten a grip on the metallurgy that could keep main ballast tank vents shut without rusting shut. Their design ignorance was about to get him, Dankleff and the SEALs killed.

The down angle was getting worse. Pacino shot a glance at an inclinometer, a simple bubble level device he'd seen on the port bulkhead above the command chair, and it read 30 degrees down. He scanned for depth and found a gauge that said 400. Was that meters? And what was test depth? For that matter, what was crush depth?

Ahmadi lunged to the overhead forward portion of the Million Valve Manifold and rotated a bar handle on a hydraulic valve, the handle marked with bold Farsi lettering, then rotated a second handle farther aft of the first valve. He skidded to the middle console, pos two, and looked at eight annunciators, which changed from red to green.

"Vent valves are shut," he gasped. He pulled himself back to the manifold and found two more bar handles on massive ball valves set into six-inch piping and rotated the first ninety degrees.

Immediately a blasting noise slammed Pacino's eardrums and the room filled up with condensation, a fog so thick he could barely make out Dankleff at pos two.

"That's the forward group emergency blow." Ahmadi operated the second valve handle. The noise in the room got even louder and the fog from the piping in the manifold grew even thicker. "Aft group."

"U-Boat, mark our depth. Pressure gauge is at that ship control station."

"There's one at pos two," Dankleff called. "It reads four hundred twenty-five." He looked at Ahmadi, whose face had turned white, but perhaps that was just the effect of the fog. "Is that meters?"

"Dear Allah," Ahmadi breathed. "Three hundred and fifty meters is *crush depth*."

Pacino vaulted back to the port side so he could see the inclinometer. The deck had stopped inclining madly downward. He had to put his face a foot away from it to read the bubble indication, the fog in the room from the blow system still thick. "Angle has eased to ten degrees dive," he shouted above the roar of the high-pressure air flow.

The flow noise in the room gradually died down, the fog began to clear and the angle came off. The inclinometer read five degrees rise. Ahmadi reached up and shut the handles of the two large ball valves.

"What's depth?" Pacino barked at Dankleff.

"Three hundred meters and rising!"

"Thank the Sevmash design engineers," Pacino said. "They may be stupid about ballast tank vent valves and placement of emergency blow valve actuators, but at least their hull took us to design crush depth and beyond."

"Two fifty," Dankleff said, a note of hope creeping into his voice. "Two hundred meters."

The deck angle climbed. The inclinometer read ten degrees, then fifteen, then twenty. Pacino grabbed a handhold at pos three to steady himself and looked at Ahmadi. "Thanks. I didn't want to spend eternity at the bottom of two miles of ocean."

"You and me, both," Ahmadi said.

"When this is all over, I'm buying you a stiff drink at the Grafton Street Pub and Grill, Captain," Pacino said.

"And despite my faith's prohibition of alcohol consumption, Lieutenant, I shall drink it. What is 'all this,' anyway? What are you doing here? What's your mission?"

"Isn't it obvious?" Pacino asked. "We're stealing your submarine."

"Why?"

Pacino shrugged. "The nuclear reactor, well, it interests us."

"Are you going to kill me and my crew?"

"Hell no," Pacino said, the deck suddenly leveling off and starting to rock from port to starboard in the surface waves.

"We've surfaced," Dankleff said.

The SEAL commander ran into the room and looked around. "Nice recovery, boys," Fishman said. "We're going back to *Vermont* to get our stuff."

Pacino wiped sweat from his forehead, realizing it would be nice to get out of the hot wetsuit and get a shower.

"So," Ahmadi said, "you're not killing us?"

"We brought a big-ass raft to put you guys in," Dankleff said. "You can even take your personal effects, framed pictures of your kids or wifey or whatever. We'll set you adrift with rations and an emergency beacon. You'll be home in no time."

"Except for you, Captain Ahmadi," Pacino said. "You and whatever Russian reactor technicians are aboard are coming with us. When we reach our destination, you'll be repatriated. It'll be a first-class ticket, I promise. After that drink at the Grafton."

"There's no going home for me if I come with you, Lieutenant. I'd be shot for a traitor, or imprisoned for my mission's disaster. I'll be forced to request asylum in the United States."

Pacino looked at Ahmadi. "For you to be educated in London and Boston, you must have some pretty heavy connections to, you know, the guys who run things."

"I do. I mean, I did. But after this, they'll disown me, swear they never knew me, or knew all along I'd disappoint them."

"Yeah. I get that. Damned shame."

Ahmadi looked at the deck. "There was a woman I wanted to marry. I'd be leaving her behind."

"Hey," Pacino said. "Maybe we can get her out to join you."

Ahmadi shook his head. "She's a fundamentalist and has never left Iran and only speaks Farsi. She'd drown if she were to leave."

"People change," Pacino offered lamely. What else could he say? "Why don't you help me get the Russian technicians in a room so I can talk to them? I'm going to need them, too."

"There's only one, that drunken infidel Alexie Abakumov."

"Let's go meet him."

21

Catoctin Mountain Park, Maryland, USA
Camp David Presidential Retreat
Friday June 3; 1141 UTC, 6:41 am EDT

Every time he tightened up the laces on his running shoes, Michael Pacino missed his old black lab, Jackson. The enthusiasm that puppy had would overcome any thought of skipping an early morning workout. Pacino remembered when he came back from the sinking of the SSNX after the drone sub incident, Jackson seemed suddenly older, gray hair at his muzzle, still wagging his tail, but too tired to get up from his bed for a run. Pacino had taken him in to the vet a week later when the dog could no longer eat or drink, just lying in his bed, trembling. That last night, Pacino had put his pillow and blanket on the floor next to the dog and kept him company, the lab occasionally crying in what little sleep he did get. Finally, at sunrise, Pacino had packed him up into the Lincoln SUV and driven him to the Sandbridge Pet Hospital, that last walk through the door reminding him of all the times he'd taken the dog there in the past. Unlike most dogs, Jackson had enjoyed the vet's office, making friends with the other animals and pet-owners in the waiting room, and smiling up at the nurse or the doctor. As the dog had shut his eyes for the last time, Pacino wept, and as if prepared for that, the vet had a box of tissues handy. The walk back to the truck had been a long one.

The wait for action in the SCIF had continued for hours until Pacino had decided to get some sleep, leaving Catardi to watch the display. But sleep had been impossible, what with worrying about Anthony. At 4 am, Pacino had made coffee and checked the screen, but still nothing. He figured he could squeeze in five or six miles running the circuit of trails around the facility before checking back in to see what was happening with the operation. As he shut the door of Holly Lodge behind him, Vice Admiral Catardi called out to him from a golf cart parked in front.

"Patch. I was just dialing your cell. There's signs of action. Come on."

"I'm not exactly dressed to see the President of the United States," Pacino said, self-conscious in running shorts and a black T-shirt with a leering skull and crossbones on it, gothic script reading, "U.S. Submarine Force."

"You look great. Come on."

Catardi rushed them to Birch Cabin, parked the cart and hurried inside, Pacino behind him, half jogging to catch up.

"Oh, Patch, Rob, just in time," President Carlucci said, smiling.

Gathered in front of the flatscreen were Vice President Karen Chushi and Vice Admiral Jehoshaphat Taylor. Both glanced at him, Taylor nodding respectfully, Chushi smiling slightly, then both returned their attention to the screen.

The television was in a split-screen mode, the right side an overhead view of the ocean with a timestamp and the notation, "Video age: 10 minutes 17 seconds." On the left side, the modified Kilo submarine *Panther* was stationary on the surface, a large raft being inflated on the forward deck.

"Take a look at the clip from eleven minutes ago," Carlucci said. Pacino stood in front of the display, watching the calm square of ocean.

A moment into the video, the nose of a submarine suddenly and dramatically burst forth from the water, the waves and splashing foam rising violently on either side of the hull as the black cigar shape came almost halfway out of the ocean, slowed to a stop and in what looked like slow motion, crashed back into the surface, almost disappearing underwater for a moment before resurfacing and rocking in the gentle waves.

"Now that's style," Carlucci said.

"They emergency blew to the surface," Pacino said.

"Something else you'll want to see, Patch," Carlucci said, operating the remote and spinning the history video forward as divers on the port side of the Kilo submarine surfaced and were helped aboard by the SEAL commandos. Carlucci zoomed the screen of the history video so faces could be made out.

"The magnification of this drone is incredible," Pacino said.

"Our facial recognition is online," Taylor said. As each diver climbed aboard the sub, a name and rank appeared in a text box with an arrow leading to the person. Pacino saw Lieutenant M. Varney, a dolphin-qualified officer from *Vermont*, look at the sky, then a petite woman took off her mask, and her label read Chief B. Goreliki, RMC(SS)—a radio chief—and Chief T. Albanese, a sonarman, then FTC(SS) N. Kim, a firecontrol and weapons system tech and AI specialist.

"See, Patch," Catardi said. "Your son's not in the boarding party."

"What about a translator?" Pacino asked. "And that's a pretty slender crew to be manning a submarine for a long voyage, having to stand watches around the clock."

"They've got *my* guys," Taylor said.

"Yes, they have the SEALs," Catardi said. "See, Patch? You son is safe and warm inside *Vermont*, probably sipping a black-and-bitter in the control room watching the success of this operation on the periscope display." Catardi clapped Pacino's shoulder, smiling.

The boarding party entered the ship, then two SEALs emerged from the hatch, both in full diving gear, and walked aft to the stern, diving into the water.

"Clearing the screw from their net," Catardi said.

Once the SEALs had climbed back aboard the sub, the history video shrank to a dot, the entire screen now devoted to a real-time view. The large, black, oblong raft was fully inflated, and two of the SEALs were pulling Iranians out of the hull and loading them on to the raft.

"How big is the crew?" Pacino asked.

"We think forty, maybe fifty," Catardi said.

After the SEALs loaded the last Iranian and lifted large containers into the raft—rations, water, the emergency locator beacon—they withdrew into the boat and shut the hatch after themselves.

"Any of these Iranians identified in our facial recognition database?" Pacino looked closely at the video screen.

"No," Taylor said.

"I don't see any Russians."

"You can tell a Russian from an Iranian from thirty thousand feet?" Taylor was smiling to remove any offense from his comment.

"I guess not. I just imagined a Russian reactor technician would be wearing a different color set of coveralls."

"Or a lab jacket," Taylor said.

"What's the count?"

"Thirty-five," Catardi said.

"Still seems light," Pacino said.

"Russians are big into automation, Patch," Catardi said. "They run with half the number of officers and enlisted we sail with."

"Maybe so," Pacino said, but he had his doubts. The intel files he'd seen on the original Kilo class showed minimal automation. The improved Kilo, by contrast, had a modern AI system, a "second captain," as the Russians called it, the system considered a glorified autopilot, but rumor had it that their front-line AI systems could actually operate the ship in combat, and in some case "fight the ship" better than their human counterparts. After all, AI didn't get nervous or tired. It didn't have to recover from a fight with the spouse. It didn't get hungover. It didn't hesitate or take into account the morality of sinking another ship filled with human beings. It just fought the enemy. But this hull was the older, original Kilo, built from the technology of World War II German U-boats. The Russians had operated a sub the West called the Foxtrot well into the 1970s, and the Foxtrot was just a Nazi Type XXI U-boat. No automation, just valves jammed everywhere with rudimentary sonar and firecontrol. Pacino imagined that's why the Russians put their effort into smart torpedoes, which could be fired by even a dumb U-boat, since they were truly fire-and-forget weapons that didn't need much programming by the launching ship other than the bearing to the target.

Suddenly a large geyser of water and foam sprayed out of the bow of the submarine, then a similar gusher of foam from the rear.

"Ballast tank vents opening," Pacino said to himself.

The submarine began to settle into the water, and as the foredeck sank low enough that it became awash with the surrounding waves, the raft floated free, the submarine sinking under it. Soon only the conning tower was visible, and then it too got lower in the water until only its top surface was visible, waves breaking over it, until it too sank into the ocean, only the periscope visible extending from the conning tower, and eventually that too vanished, and there was only the raft and the Iranians—and maybe Russians.

A vertical dive, Pacino thought. Submerging vertically took skill. Ideally, it took automation to keep the boat level. Vertical diving an ancient Kilo like this? With a boarding party unfamiliar with the boat? They had to have help from the original Kilo's crew, Pacino thought. Maybe the captain or some cooperative junior officers or chiefs. Someone who knew what he was doing.

That was both good and bad, Pacino considered. Good because someone from the original Iranian crew could help them operate the stolen submarine, avoiding the thousands of disasters that could befall an uneducated crew from the hazards of the ruthless ocean itself. But bad because having original crewmembers risked retaliation. Sabotage. The *Panther,* now that she was submerged, could simply vanish into the deep from a crewmember intent on her destruction from within. And if the SEALs were busy standing watches around the clock to drive the ship, they wouldn't be paying enough attention to whomever Lieutenant Varney had recruited to help them.

In any case, there was nothing to do now but wait for status reports from the USS *Vermont,* which was ordered to communicate with coded, preformatted SLOT buoys.

"Did *Vermont* send a status report?" Pacino asked Catardi.

"She popped a SLOT a few minutes after you got here. A simple 'code one' with a latitude and longitude. Means success in hijacking the *Panther* at that position. I doubt we'll hear much more from her unless there's trouble."

"This is going to be a long trip, right?" Pacino asked.

"Mr. President, can you show the intended track of *Panther* and *Vermont* back to AUTEC?"

Carlucci operated the screen remote, pulling up a view of earth from high above the Indian Ocean. Twin tracks, one in blue, the other red, extended from the point of capture of the *Panther* in the mouth of the Gulf of Oman, heading south-southeast, hugging the west coast of India, then proceeding due south to Antarctica and hugging its coast until the point due south of the Atlantic between Africa and South America, then north to a point west of Western Sahara and Morocco—the approximate latitude of their destination—then west to the Bahamas.

"A trip like this, at battery optimization cruising speed, six to ten knots, that could take six weeks, maybe more."

"Seventeen thousand miles," Catardi said, "With an average point-of-intended motion speed of seven knots, well, that's a hundred days. *Panther* won't arrive at AUTEC until mid-September. We've programmed in refueling operations and re-provisioning four, maybe five times, along the voyage."

That seemed a weak point of the operation, Pacino thought. Surfacing to load food and fuel would leave them vulnerable to an opposition force. Satellites would photograph them. Enemy submarines could lie in wait knowing their location at a certain time. Even if the harebrained scheme to load them up while submerged and hovering worked, there was still vulnerability if they'd been trailed there by an opposition submarine.

"Did they load on rations?"

"They loaded a lot of stuff, Patch," Catardi said. "Some of it was equipment. Radio, SatNav. Some clothes. But the rest of the load-out was food. Enough to get to the first refueling point. They'll be okay. The *Vermont* will be with her the entire way, making sure she's safe."

"Goddamned long wait for this mission to be over," Pacino said.

"Well, I guess we can enjoy the rest of the weekend here," Carlucci said. "Nothing more to see. Patch, if you and the admirals need to go, no problem. Go spend the weekend at home. I'll catch up with you Monday afternoon."

"Thank you, sir," Pacino said.

Outside Birch Cabin, at Catardi's golf cart, Catardi asked Pacino if he were headed back to Annapolis.

"You need a ride, Robby?"

"I'm a little afraid of that thing you call a car, Patch."

"I'll drive gently. Interstates, even."

"I'll call Styxx. She can get a Gulfstream for me at Andrews. It's on your way, right?"

"That it is, Robby."

Kola Peninsula, Russian Republic
Polyarny Naval Base
Northern Fleet Headquarters
Friday, June 3, 1254 UTC; 2:54 pm Moscow time

Admiral Gennady Zhigunov sat down in the sparsely furnished secure conference room at Northern Fleet Headquarters. The room was empty except for him, the metal table, four chairs, a large flatscreen and the camera mounted on top of the screen. He poured half a glass of water from a pitcher on the table, opened a notebook and switched on his pad computer while he waited for the secure link to come up with the Admiralty building in St. Petersburg. This meeting would be the kind that took half a liter of vodka to get over, he knew, because the Kindly Old Gentleman, as they sarcastically called the volatile Admiral Anatoly Stanislav behind his back, had called for the video conference with him from the Northern Fleet and his counterpart and bitter rival from the Pacific Fleet, Admiral Aleksander Andreyushkin. Stanislav was the Chief Commander of the Navy, and Zhigunov had only met him once, and the diminutive, older, gray-haired man had shouted so loud he'd rattled the windows of his office about that regrettable nuclear incident at the Polyarny base. That had to be four or five years ago, but Zhigunov had never forgotten.

Today's meeting would feature not only the explosive Stanislav but his Chief of Staff and First Deputy Commander of the Navy, Vice Admiral Pavel Zhabin, who despite being a rank below Zhigunov himself, used the rank of his boss as a weapon, having sent Zhigunov dozens of blisteringly furious emails when things hadn't gone to plan.

Zhigunov took a deep breath as the screen lit up, but the expected view of the Admiralty's ornate secure conference room didn't appear, but rather a room much like the one Zhigunov occupied, this one with the emblem of the Pacific Fleet on the wall behind the man in the room. It was Admiral Andreyushkin, the commander of the Pacific Fleet. Stanislav and Zhabin were slightly delayed. Soon the right side of the screen lit up with the Admiralty conference room, Stanislav and Zhabin seated together in the room, the screen's left half devoted to the figure of Andreyushkin.

Before he could even greet the senior admiral and his chief of staff, Stanislav began, his voice so furious it wavered.

"Are either of you aware what happened an hour ago?" he demanded. Zhigunov glanced briefly at his pad computer. He had cleared out all his messages just before walking into the room so he wouldn't be blindsided by the admiral.

"No, Admiral," Zhigunov said.

"What about you, Andreyushkin?"

"I have no information, Admiral," Andreyushkin said, his voice low.

"Well, *gentlemen,*" Stanislav spit, as the word 'gentlemen' were an epithet, "allow me to display for your edification this video clip, taken from our newest Comsomolets satellite I spent fuel to retask to monitor the Gulf of Oman, since your *submarines* were both late to get in-theater." Stanislav's pronunciation of 'submarines' dripped with contempt. He'd come up through the surface navy and had always been annoyed at submariners, Zhigunov thought.

The screen changed to an overhead view of the calm, deep waters of the Gulf of Oman. Suddenly the ocean burst into foam and spray as a Kilo-class submarine blasted out of the water after performing an emergency blow. The Kilo was elongated—the modified Iranian submarine that his command's submarine *Voronezh* had been tasked with escorting into the Indian Ocean.

Zhigunov watched in horror as the video showed four commandos emerging from the sea and invading the submarine, being helped onto the deck by multiple men in wetsuits, the bags of equipment being loaded onto the Kilo submarine, a huge raft being inflated on her foredeck, then the commandos pulling the crewmembers onto the raft, finally re-entering the hull and shutting the hatch behind them. Zhigunov had clamped his hand over his mouth as the Kilo submerged beneath the raft, until the square of ocean in the video only showed the raft and the crewmen on it. Finally the video winked out and the snarling face of Stanislav returned to the screen, the frowning first deputy commander likewise glaring at the camera with a dark expression.

"So, you first *Admiral* Andreyushkin. Your submarine *Novosibirsk* was due in the Gulf of Oman four days ago. I'm told it's still two days away, off the coast of the Saudi peninsula, south of Oman. Why is your submarine late to its position to rendezvous with and escort the *Panther*?"

Zhigunov watched as Andreyushkin swallowed hard. "Sir, the Iranians took the Kilo to sea nearly a week early. What happened?"

Normally Stanislav couldn't be taken off his relentless interrogations, but this time he sat back heavily and glared at Zhabin. "Something disastrous. The Americans successfully cyber-attacked the Iranian computer systems. The worm they uploaded caused the crashing of all systems related to their surface ships and their air force and navy aircraft. Their aircraft are grounded and their surface warships are welded to the pier. The Iranians were worried that the Kilo might be attacked by the same worm, so they thought it was safest to get it into the Indian Ocean immediately before any submarine systems became affected, so they jumped off early.

"But there's more. Somehow the worm injected into the Iranian systems found its way into ours. And now *our* naval air assets are grounded. Our surface ships are bricked. And there's no telling when we will recover, when we'll be able to fly. Gentlemen, the reason I'm so fixated on the performance of your submarines are that you are all we have. There will be no overflights by Il-114s or helicopters. There will be no destroyers or frigates or even patrol torpedo boats. We are relying completely and totally on you. So, now, tell me, Admiral Andreyushkin, what is going on with your submarine?"

Andreyushkin sighed. "The *Novosibirsk* suffered a material failure in the reactor system, Admiral, that required shutting down and flying in replacement parts and technicians to fix it before the boat could get underway again."

"A material failure? The only failure I see here is *you*, Andreyushkin, you and your miserable maintenance facilities. I wouldn't trust those lazy alcoholics with fixing my *lawnmower*. And their incompetence is *your* incompetence. You failed. You failed the Navy and you failed the motherland."

There was no doubt, Stanislav could make a grown man cry in a hundred words or less. At least his own reprimand would be demonstrably not his fault, Zhigunov thought. At least he hoped.

"And you, *Admiral* Zhigunov. Your command's submarine *Voronezh* was likewise scheduled to be at the rendezvous point at Bandar Abbas four days ago. Where in bloody hell was it? Why was it late?"

"Sir, Admiral, I routed it through the Suez Canal and the canal closed for almost a week, for what turned out to be an operation by our own—"

"I don't care *why* the canal was closed," Stanislav said, cutting him off, and pointing at him, his hand trembling, either from his anger or his age, or perhaps both. "It's just another damned excuse. You should have routed your ship around Africa and sent her on her way the week prior. The intelligence bulletins were practically shouting about trouble in the Suez. Did you listen to them? No. You let that idiot son of yours linger for another week in port and then sent him the shortcut to the Gulf of Oman by a route you should have *known* would be problematic."

There had been absolutely nothing in the intelligence bulletins about the Suez Canal, Zhigunov knew. He'd learned long ago to read them carefully enough that he could pass a comprehensive test on them from memory alone. Which meant Stanislav was blowing off steam—who in his right mind would sail eight thousand kilometers farther around a continent if he could go the direct route through a canal? Had he done that, right now he'd be getting flamed on by Stanislav for having taken the long, slow route to the rendezvous point.

Stanislav must have gotten his ears boxed by the president, Zhigunov thought, and was taking his ire out on Andreyushkin and Zhigunov.

Stanislav took a drink from his water glass, his tirade apparently leaving him with a dry mouth. He pointed at the screen again, his face furious.

"I expect both of you to make this horrible situation right. Your orders are no longer to escort the nuclear-powered Kilo submarine to the safe test area. Your new orders are to find the *Panther* and destroy it. Sink it before the Americans or whatever rabid dogs stole our submarine can take it apart and study it. Am I making myself clear? Zhigunov, what will be your orders to *Voronezh*?"

"To find the *Panther* and sink it."

Stanislav looked at the screen. "Do you think that will be easy?"

"Yes, Admiral. *Voronezh* is a front-line Yasen-M-class. The best in the world. The boat will hear the *Panther* long before the *Panther* is even aware we are shooting at it."

"Oh my God," Stanislav said to Zhabin. "Can you believe the stupidity?" He turned back to Zhigunov. "Zhigunov, where do you think those commandos came from? Deep space? The sky? You didn't see parachutes did you?"

"No, sir."

"So, where did they come from?"

"Perhaps another submarine, Admiral."

"Look at this brilliant mind at work, Zhabin," Stanislav said the first deputy, who shook his head in contempt. Zhigunov could feel his face flushing with anger.

"That's right. Another submarine. So Andreyushkin, why don't you try your luck at this? Where do you think the commandos came from?"

"An American submarine, sir."

"And do you think the Americans sent their second string, their bottom shelf submarine, to execute their savage mission violating international law, their piracy on the high seas?"

"No, Admiral," Andreyushkin said quietly. "I think they sent their best submarine."

"And what would that be?"

"A Virginia-class, sir."

"Well, we're banging on all eight cylinders today, aren't we, Andreyushkin? So, if they sent a Virginia-class, does that worry you?"

"No sir, My boat *Novosibirsk* will find it and sink it. All they need is the order, sir, to fire upon first detection."

"If you think this will be easy, Admiral Andreyushkin, you are sadly mistaken. And you too, Zhigunov. All this drivel you read about in the newspapers, about the Yasen-M-class being the best in the world—that's not for *your* eyes, it's for the eyes of the rest of the world, so they'll fear us. But now we come down to it, gentlemen. Are your two submarines, with all their weapons and sensors, equal to a fight with one Virginia-class?"

"Absolutely, sir," Zhigunov said. "Do I understand you that we have permission to release weapons upon initial detection, sir? No radioing fleet headquarters for permission?"

"Listen to me and listen damned good, Zhigunov, and you too, Andreyushkin. You are *ordered* to fire on first detection. Put the *Panther* and the Virginia-class on the bottom. And there's more."

More, Zhigunov thought. What more could there be?

"You have nuclear weapon release authority, both of you. It will be coming to you in a coded, authenticated directive issued by the office of the president within the hour."

Zhigunov stared at the screen. Nuclear weapons?

"And one more thing. None of this goes in writing to your submarine commanders. You bring them up into secure video conferences. I want you to look into their eyes and make damned sure they understand the orders. Is that clear?"

Both Zhigunov and Andreyushkin answered in the affirmative at the same time.

"That's all. I expect a call from you on a secure line, any time, day or night, the second you get word that the *Panther* and the Virginia are destroyed. You got that?"

"Yes, sir," the junior admirals both answered.

The moment the screen went blank, Northern Fleet Commander Admiral Gennady Zhigunov stood up so fast his brushed steel chair fell back to the floor and bounced on the wall. He picked up his paper notebook and threw it at the screen, hard, just as it flashed back to life and the red face of the Pacific fleet commander came up.

Embarrassed, Zhigunov righted the chair and sat back down. Admiral Andreyushkin was far from a friend, but after their reprimand from Stanislav, they were almost compatriots. Comrades, even.

"Aleksandr," Zhigunov said.

"Gennady," Andreyushkin said. "I think we should get our orders out to our boats immediately, before they get in-theater, so our recalling them to periscope depth won't endanger them. We need to tell them not only about the search-and-destroy mission, but that they are steaming into a hot combat zone, because if we have shoot-on-detection orders, surely the Americans do as well."

Four submarines out there, Zhigunov thought. Perhaps only one would sail home.

"I'm listening," Zhigunov said, looking at his watch.

"We need to coordinate together, Gennady. We can't afford to face Stanislav with a broken mission. What if one of our boats shoots the other?"

"Friendly fire," Zhigunov said. "I doubt either of us would survive that eventuality."

"Precisely. We need to direct *Novosibirsk* and *Voronezh* to work together. It's the only way."

"You have a plan?"

"Allow me to show our present situation."

Admiral Andreyushkin vanished from the screen, replaced

with an overhead view of the Arabian peninsula and the Arabian Sea. A black line extended southeast from the Bandar Abbas Iranian Naval base into the Gulf of Oman. The line, once it entered the Arabian Sea, turned due south toward the Indian Ocean.

"This is the track that the *Panther* intended to take on its way to the test area," Andreyushkin said.

A red circle bloomed over the black line at the point the black line left the Gulf of Oman and entered the Arabian Sea.

"This red circle is the point where *Panther* was taken."

Two blue flashing dots appeared, one off the east coast of Oman, perhaps 300 kilometers southwest of the red circle of the hijacking. The second blue dot was farther southwest, off the coast of Yemen, another 250 kilometers southwest of the first dot.

"The northern blue dot is *Novosibirsk*. The southern one is *Voronezh*."

Suddenly Zhigunov realized the hopelessness of the situation. The search area was huge, a triangle almost 2500 kilometers wide at its base and 900 kilometers tall. East to west, it would take one of their submarines 48 hours to traverse the area at maximum speed and 16 hours from north to south. In that time, anything could happen.

"This is a huge ocean, Aleksandr."

"Not so much, Gennady. First, what speed do you imagine the *Panther* and its escort sub to be making in their escape?"

"Well, they will keep the reactor shutdown and inert," Zhigunov said, thinking aloud. "They don't know how to start it up, and if they did, they'd accomplish our mission for us by exploding. So they would proceed at a speed that would maximize their battery endurance. Six knots, maybe seven."

"Exactly, and then they'd come up shallow to snorkel on the diesel to charge batteries, and that speed might even be slower so as to minimize a rooster-tail wake from the periscope and snorkel mast, but let us imagine that speed to be six knots as well. So from the point that *Panther* was taken, here is a time-based expansion circle."

The red circle from the hijacking point expanded slowly,

the time stamp on the map rolling hour by hour, each hour the circle barely moving, going so slowly.

"Here is the circle at time-zero plus twenty-four hours," Andreyushkin explained. "As you can see, the possible places *Panther* can be has only moved less than two hundred seventy-five kilometers from the hijacking point. At maximum speed, that's a distance we could cover in five hours. At time-zero plus forty-eight hours, the circle is another two hundred seventy-five kilometers from the hijacking point. At seventy-two hours, the circle looks like this, perhaps seven hundred kilometers wide. If we approach this without panicking, Gennady, we could search this effectively.

"I propose the northern boat, my *Novosibirsk* proceed northeast into the northern part of this expanding circle of probability while your *Voronezh* turns due east to capture the southern part. From there, *Novosibirsk* will seek the targets from the north, while *Voronezh* approaches from the south." Andreyushkin sat back in his seat, looking satisfied.

Zhigunov thought. "The area is still too big. And if our units are facing each other, there is risk that a weapon from one homes in on and blows up the other friendly unit. No, Aleksandr, your plan won't work. All we will do is sink each other, at best. Our ships must face the incoming vector of the *Panther* and her escort together. Then our weapons will leave from our torpedo tubes and go the same general direction, with no friendly submarine in the seeker cones of our torpedoes."

"You make a good point," Andreyushkin said.

"Let us look at this from another point of view," Zhigunov said. "First, are we in agreement that it was the Americans who took the *Panther*?"

Andreyushkin nodded.

"Who else?" Zhigunov asked.

"The British, perhaps. The Chinese."

"What possible motive would they have, Aleksandr?" Zhigunov asked.

"I can't see one. But what is the motive for the *Americans* to steal the *Panther*?"

"They want the reactor technology," Zhigunov said, "and

they want to keep it out of the hands of the Iranians. This ongoing conflict between the Iranians and Americans makes it obvious. It had to be the Americans."

"Very well," Andreyushkin said. "But what difference does that make?"

"It determines their destination, Aleksandr. If the Americans took this submarine, they aim to bring it back to the Atlantic, and they would avoid the Suez Canal and the Panama Canal. That means a transit through the Indian Ocean and going around Africa into the Atlantic."

"I'm with you, Gennady."

"Allow me to control the display," Zhigunov said. He zoomed the display outward until the entire globe was visible, the eastern Africa coast on the west, the Arabian peninsula on the north, India to the east. He drew a bold yellow line extending from the mouth of the Gulf of Oman along the east coast of Africa and extending west at the southern tip of Africa. "This is the great circle route from the point of their taking the *Panther*." Zhigunov drew a second line, this one green, extending due south from the Gulf of Oman into the Arabian Sea, then into the Indian Ocean, then a third line in red, from the hijacking point southeast, hugging the west coast of India. "Now, Aleksandr, if we had taken *Panther* and aimed to get it to America without being intercepted, which route would we take?"

"The shortest one," Andreyushkin said. "The great circle route along the east coast of Africa."

Zhigunov made the bold yellow line fade into a dull, weak yellow. "I don't think so, Aleksandr. You are correct that it is the shortest route, but we are hunting down a burglar, and a burglar won't take an obvious escape route. All we would have to do would be to set up in the narrows between Mozambique and Madagascar, in the Mozambique Channel, using it as a choke point, and the *Panther* would steam right through it at six knots. We'd find it and sink it easily."

"You're saying that's too obvious, and that the Americans are going to try something sneakier?"

"Of course," Zhigunov said. "They were sneaky enough to steal the submarine in the first place. And they won't just go due south, since that was the way to the test area, and they would suppose we would have support ships in that direction to monitor the reactor test. We didn't, by the way, but they don't know that, and they would want to avoid being detected by one of our destroyers or our patrol aircraft—and we should assume they don't know about the worm that has paralyzed our air assets and surface ships. That leaves the red route, extending southeast, close to the shores of India. This is perfect, it takes them far away from the great circle route to their destination and from the test route. Plus, the western coast of India is absolutely rotten with shipping. There's more sonar noise in that part of the world than anywhere other than the approaches to the Suez Canal, Panama Canal or Cape of Good Hope. And a submarine can hide in that ambient noise. That, Aleksandr, is the escape route."

Andreyushkin nodded. "I see your point, Gennady. I agree. So how should we deploy our forces?"

"This gets easy. The red route extends here. It will take us, let's see." Zhigunov manipulated his pad computer. "Thirty hours for *Novosibirsk* at maximum speed, forty for *Voronezh,* to reach this point here, approximately halfway down the Indian coastline, west of this town of Marmagao. If we start promptly, *Novosibirsk* arrives on-station June 4 at 2000 Moscow time and *Voronezh* June 5 at 0600 hours. Our submarines rendezvous there, in contact with other using underwater encrypted Bolshoi-Feniks sonar, and they will proceed northward together until *Panther* and the American escort sub drive into them. They should probably have twenty or thirty or even forty kilometers between them, but search slowly north-northwestward at best search speed of six knots after their rendezvous. At the six-knot transit speed of *Panther,* it will take her days to drive into the search sector of our sonars. With her southward speed of six knots and our northward speed of six knots, we'll intercept her about five days after the rendezvous. That would put detection on or about June 10, Friday, plus or minus a day."

"Heavens, Gennady, that's a week from now. A long time to wait to tell Stanislav the good news we've found and put down the *Panther* and the American submarine."

"Like we both know, Aleksandr, it is a gigantic ocean out there."

"We could shorten this up. Have our boats rendezvous much farther north along the Indian coastline."

"No, Aleksandr, we risk arriving at a point that the *Panther* has already passed by. We have to make sure we intercept them. We will scour the route from the coast of India all the way north to the shores of Pakistan. We'll find her, if we are smart and patient."

Andreyushkin thought for a moment. "We double our chances of detecting her if one boat goes to the northernmost point of the Pakistan-India coastline and the other begins from Point Marmagao, Gennady. They would converge on the targets. With an ocean this big, only one of our units will have the enemy in detection range at one time. The chances of going down from friendly fire are not that great."

"Are you willing to risk that, Aleksandr? Risk your men's lives, risk one of the most expensive weapons systems Russia has ever built? And risk that you'll find yourself explaining to Admiral Stanislav that you lost a submarine to American torpedoes, or worse, from your own force's torpedoes?"

Andreyushkin sighed. "I suppose you're right, Gennady. Still, it seems overly conservative. And, what if the Americans actually do decide to take the great circle route?"

"Why would they do that?"

"They might think we'd reject that as a tactic, since, as you said, it is too obvious. They'd expect us to head to the other escape route, the Indian coastline. So, by hugging the coast of Africa, they've fooled us. They get away with their operation."

Zhigunov thought for a long time. "There is no way that Americans think like that, Aleksandr. They are sneaky thieves. They are cowards. They will skulk along the Indian coastline. If we go with my proposal, yes, it will take longer. The longer the Americans go from having stolen the *Panther,* the more overconfident they will be, and the greater the chance of them making a mistake. We know the sound signature of the Kilo-class, Aleksandr. We will find them. We will sink them. We will report to Stanislav a successful mission."

Andreyushkin thought a moment, then manipulated his pad computer. "We show arrival in-theater very early. We could hedge our bet, and instead of proceeding to Point Marmagao at maximum silent speed, thirty-one knots, we could do a sprint-and-drift tactic. Twenty-five minutes at max silent speed, then ten minutes at a best sonar search speed of eight knots, then another twenty-five at thirty-one knots. That makes a speed-of-advance of, let's see, twenty-seven knots. A very slight degradation in speed over ground, but with the benefit that if the Americans get even sneakier than we think they are, we'd definitely detect them in the middle of the Arabian Sea. And if we stagger the drift time, with *Novosibirsk* drifting at the top of the hour and *Voronezh* at the bottom, we almost double our chances of picking up the trace of the *Panther* if it did diverge from the west coast of India."

Zhigunov smiled at Andreyushkin. "You know, Aleksandr, I don't care what people say about you. You're actually quite bright."

The Pacific Fleet admiral made a face at his Northern Fleet counterpart, as if they were two brothers antagonizing each other in the back of their parents' car.

"Let us call our submarines to communication depth and present these orders to them now," Andreyushkin said.

Arabian Sea
K-573 *Novosibirsk*
Friday, June 3; 1412 UTC, 4:12 pm Moscow time

Captain First Rank Yuri Orlov took his tea to the wardroom table and sat at the center of the long end, facing the video screen. Captain Second Rank Ivan Vlasenko took the seat to Orlov's right, with navigator and operations officer, Captain Third Rank Misha Dobryvnik, and Weapons Officer Captain Lieutenant Irina Trusov to his left.

The screen came up, splitting into three screens. On the left were his opposite numbers from the attack submarine *Voronezh*, Captain First Rank—apparently promoted since Orlov last saw him—Boris Novikov, his first officer, Isakova to his right and his navigator, Lukashenko, on his left. The other screens each showed a senior officer, the center screen showing Pacific Fleet Commander Admiral Aleksandr Andreyushkin, the right screen showing Northern Fleet Commander Admiral Gennady Zhigunov.

After the admirals briefed the officers of the *Novosibirsk* and *Voronezh* on the taking of the *Panther* submarine, and their orders to proceed together up the Indian coastline to intercept her and the assumed American submarine escort, Novikov objected.

"Putting two submarines together defeats the purpose of having two submarines. We need to spread out and cover more ocean."

"No, Captain Novikov," Zhigunov said calmly, "we believe the American hijackers and their escort sub will avoid a direct path back to the Atlantic, and they'll believe a southward route will run them into the Russian support ships waiting at the test site. They'll sneak away along the Indian coastline."

"Fine, sir," Novikov persisted. "Send *Novosibirsk* up the Indian coastline. Let me and my *Voronezh* prowl the center of the Arabian Sea and the Indian Ocean."

"No, Captain. The area is too big to search without reliable intelligence."

"Well, sir, then send out MPA antisubmarine aircraft and drop sonobuoys. Hell, drop so many a man could walk from India to Africa on them."

"There's a slight problem with that," Andreyushkin admitted. "There is an ongoing cyber-attack that has paralyzed all of our aircraft and surface ships. Those of the Iranians as well. There will be no MPA aircraft or destroyers to help you two. All the Navy's hopes rest on your two submarines."

There was silence for a moment while the submarine crews absorbed this horrible news.

"There's another problem with this," Novikov said. "If we're operating together, we'll have to coordinate together using the sound communication system of the MGK-600. The Bolshoi-Feniks."

The MGK-600 sonar had a spherical bow array, flank arrays and a towed array, all linked into the Mark VII Second Captain system. The unit's bow array had a submarine-to-submarine communication and identification-friend-or-foe mode, called Bolshoi-Feniks, which emitted a series of high frequency tones sent in pulses, like Morse code, but with a much faster rate, almost like broadcasting a barcode. The code was encrypted with a daily-changing code, and was able to transmit to another friendly submarine within ten kilometers. Communication at a long distance required shifting the MGK-600's spherical array's hydrophones to low frequency, but the data rate was much slower.

"It's like transmitting active sonar," Novikov continued. "We could be counterdetected by the American."

"American sonars are not that good," Andreyushkin said. "And a transmission is short with the high frequency data rate. It'll probably be mistaken for a school of shrimp, if the Americans hear it at all."

"So," Orlov said, "When we detect the target submarines, what are our rules of engagement?"

"Sink them," Andreyushkin said. "You are authorized nuclear weapon release. You will each receive an order from the president and the Minister of Defense authorizing use of nuclear weapons. Once both submarines are on the bottom, send an urgent after-action message to both fleet headquarters and the Admiralty with the results of the battle and your own ship's material condition."

"Understood, sir," Orlov said.

"Aye aye, Admiral," Novikov said.

"Well, gentlemen, you have your orders," Zhigunov said. "Good luck. Good hunting."

The screen went black. Orlov reached for the phone and buzzed the central command post.

"Watch Officer," Captain Lieutenant TK Sukolov's voice answered.

"Take us back deep and fast, course east, Watch Officer, while the navigator lays in a track for the rendezvous at Point Marmagao."

"Deep and fast, course east, Watch Officer, aye."

Orlov drank the dregs of his tea and stared into the distance.

"You worried, Captain?" Vlasenko asked.

"I don't like these orders," he said. "Our side has two attack submarines, but we may as well only have one, with these search tactics. And I don't like using the Bolshoi-Feniks to coordinate. It risks us losing stealth."

"We'll minimize its use, Captain," Vlasenko reassured Orlov.

Orlov grimaced. "And if the president and the Kremlin have authorized us to use nuclear weapons, it means the bosses are worried. I wonder, what is it that is scaring them? Do they think that American sub can sink us before we find him? Please. We're much superior. We'll hear him long before he hears us. We'll put him and the *Panther* down like the dogs they are."

"Your lips to God's ear, Captain. Let us hope so."

22

Arabian Sea
100 nautical miles south of Karachi, Pakistan
B-902 *Panther*
Monday, June 6, 2200 UTC;
Tuesday, June 7; 2:00 am local time

Lieutenant Anthony Pacino leaned against the chart table in the navigation chart room, a five-foot-by-ten-foot closet jammed in aft of the central command post. After dealing with the electronics of *Vermont*'s chart table, going back to a paper chart and a pencil seemed strange, as if he'd wandered back in time.

"So everyone agreed," Pacino said, tapping his pencil on the line on the chart, "the best route out of here is to hug the India coastline. We proceed southeast, and from there, as we depart the Arabian Sea and in-chop the Indian Ocean, turn due south to Antarctica. We stay as far away from the great circle route back to AUTEC as possible. That way we avoid any opposition force lying in wait for us, such as here, in the Mozambique Channel. Or the south shores of Africa. And off the coast of India, the shipping traffic is heavy. It'll hide us."

Lieutenant Dieter Dankleff, officer in charge, leaned far over the chart. "I still say we'll be going hundreds of miles farther than the great circle route. We'll burn fuel and go through our food. How long is the total transit time by doing this?"

"A hundred days, give or take," Pacino said. "But I have an idea that can get it done in three weeks."

"No," Lieutenant Muhammad Varney, the *Panther*'s operations officer, said. "I know what you're thinking. There's no way we're doing that."

"What?" Dankleff asked.

"Lipstick here wants to start the goddamned fast reactor, then take us up to flank speed. He thinks we can squeeze thirty knots out of this pig. That's assuming we don't melt the reactor down, break open the hull or, you know, explode."

"Explode?" Dankleff said, smirking. "Exploding would be somewhat non-optimal."

"I spent some time with Captain Ahmadi," Pacino said. "He's no fan of the Russian technician, Abakumov, but even Ahmadi thinks the Russian can start the UBK-500 safely and bring it into the power range."

"UBK-500? You know the model number of the fast reactor?"

"Ahmadi told me all about it. He was translating the Iranian version of the tech manual. First chapter of the operating instructions, anyway. 'Normal startup.'"

"Okay," Dankleff said, his voice taking on a commanding tone. "Here's what we're going to do. We're going to keep going at six knots to optimize battery endurance, snorkeling at night to charge batteries. And right after Gory Goreliki whips us up some dinner, we're going to talk more about this fast reactor."

"I'll get with Abakumov about this so he can prepare," Pacino said.

Dankleff smiled. "I'm beginning to like the idea of getting home in a couple weeks instead of three months."

Varney shook his head. "I'm beginning to *fear* the idea of hitting the ocean bottom in a day when that reactor blows."

"Don't be a pessimist, Boozy," Pacino said.

"Now, boys, be nice," Dankleff said. Pacino watched him and Varney leave the navigation space. Dankleff had a spring in his step while Varney slouched out of the room.

He hoped like hell he was right about all this.

After the pasta and meat sauce meal that Gory Goreliki served, Pacino spread out a large-area chart of the Arabian Sea on the wardroom table. Pacino had drawn their course in pencil. He took dividers and walked them down the track, scribbling in a notebook he'd found, then sat back and frowned at the chart.

After an hour, Ahmadi and Dankleff joined him. Varney was in the central command post, manning the evening watch. Standing in the far corner of the room was Grip Aquatong, strapped with a Mark 6, his Sig Sauer 1911 .45 pistol and two K-Bar combat knives, one strapped to each thigh, and a long stiletto knife strapped to his forearm, his gaze fixed on Ahmadi. Ahmadi and the Russian reactor engineer were monitored at all times by one of the SEALs.

Pacino had his head in his hands.

"What's the matter, Lipstick?" Dankleff asked.

"Something's bothering me, U-Boat," Pacino said. "The Indian coast idea seemed like a good idea when we first thought of it, but now it seems too obvious. An opposition force would be looking for us to escape either by the great circle route on the African east coast or to hug the Indian or Saudi peninsula coastline."

"Say that's true. What do you propose?"

Pacino took a pencil and marked a south-southwest track starting from their present position.

"A big zig-zag. We head this way to the equator, then turn southwest toward Madagascar, running south of the island, then actually southeastward, here, southeast to our original course that circled Antarctica. It's random enough that we can hide in the Indian Ocean. No one looking at the possible escape routes from the Arabian Sea is going to nail it."

Dankleff picked up a phone and dialed the central command post.

"Varney."

"New plan. Change course to one nine zero."

"That'll take us away from the Indian coastline."

"I know," Dankleff said. "Someone walked on Lipstick's watery grave. Just do it."

"Aye aye, OIC," Varney said and hung up.

"Happy now?"

"No," Pacino said. "Our number two problem. Fuel. Captain Ahmadi, were you loaded out full with diesel oil on departure?"

"Yes, Mr. Patch. One hundred percent. Twenty thousand gallons."

"Your range on full tanks?"

"About four thousand nautical miles. Give or take. Sprinting above battery optimization speed makes the diesel go faster."

Pacino looked up at Dankleff. "So for the sake of argument, let's say we *don't* use the reactor. We'll run out of gas about here." He pointed to the chart. "Southern tip of Madagascar. Unless we fill it up, we'll be adrift with no fuel. To add in some margin of safety, I'd get to the northeast coast of Madagascar. With our tank range, we'll need four refills to make it to AUTEC. This hairbrained plan for us to rendezvous with rustbucket tramp steamers with bunkers full of diesel is a loser, U-Boat. There's no way this scheme to refuel submerged can work, and even if it did, we are totally vulnerable for hours while that goes down. And refueling surfaced is even worse. And we do survive this, we'll have to do it four more times, U-Boat. Eventually, they'll catch us. Eventually, we're going down."

Dankleff went to the credenza and made a boiling hot cup of Arabian coffee. "I'll say one thing for you Iranians," he said to Ahmadi. "Your coffee is goddamned rocket fuel." He sat at the table by Pacino, looking at the chart. "We're not used to thinking like this," he said. "Being nuclear-powered means never having to say you're out of gas."

"But we *are* nuclear-powered, U-Boat," Pacino said.

"Your first reason to start that beast, to get home sooner, was a good one. But this reason is *much* more compelling."

"Look, the longer we're out here, the longer an opposition force has to find us. And, U-Boat, they probably have shoot-on-detection orders. If we get snapped up, we're dead men."

Dankleff nodded. "If I were the Russians, that's what I'd do."

"We need to crank up the fast reactor first. Then The Whale needs to figure out the sonar system, and K-Squared has to make the firecontrol system work. And Gory has to configure our secure VHF, UHF and EHF to talk to the CommStar. And we need to figure out the torpedoes and launching mechanisms."

"I can help with all that," Ahmadi said. "I'd just as soon not get shot down by a Russian Yasen-M-class."

Something dark blew into Pacino's soul. "Why did you mention a Yasen-M?"

A voice from the door said in Russian-accented English, "We were sending two of them."

Pacino looked up to see the Russian reactor engineer, Alexie Abakumov, standing in blue ship-issued coveralls with a white lab jacket over it, as if the lab coat made him appear more scientific. He was a big man, not fat but solid, almost six feet tall, his full head of dirty blonde hair touching the door sill. He had a straight nose, blue eyes, thin lips, and shallow cheeks that looked like he hadn't shaved in a week, maybe more. He moved into the room and took a seat opposite Pacino. Commander Fishman shadowed him into the wardroom, his Mark 6 unholstered.

The Russian pulled over a coffee cup, withdrew a flask from his jacket pocket, and half-filled the cup, then took a pull from it.

"Care to share?" Dankleff said, putting a cup beside Abakumov's. The Russian looked up at him and shrugged, then poured for Dankleff, who sipped the contents and made a sour face.

"What the hell is this?"

"The only vodka I could get, smuggled into Bandar Abbas Naval Base. I know. It's not exactly Jewel of Russia or Nemiroff, but it takes the edge off."

"I'd say you could use this stuff to degrease the engineroom if you had enough of it," Dankleff said.

"The Russians were sending two Yasen-M-class submarines?" Pacino asked.

"That was original plan. Iranians got scared. There was a cyber-worm. Invaded Iranian systems. Made all their aircraft inoperative. Made their surface ship control systems go black. Iranians worried that the worm would infect *Panther*. So they sent it to sea early. Original plan was to be escorted out by the Yasen-M subs from the moment we left Bandar Abbas."

"So they're out there, trying to find us," Pacino said.

"I thought I heard you talking about starting the UBK-500," Abakumov said.

"You're damned right we're going to start it. If we don't," Pacino said, glancing at Dankleff, "we risk running out of fuel in the middle of the ocean, and going too slow for too long, or refueling with some poorly imagined plan, risking getting detected by one of these Russian attack subs."

"Are you able to start it and put it online?" Dankleff asked the Russian.

The Russian ran his hand over his hair, down to the nape of this neck. "It will be easy." Abakumov and Fishman stood to go back aft to the reactor controls room aft of the new reactor module. Pacino stood up to go with them, then stopped at the door.

"Goreliki needs to get that radio functional. We'll have to transmit, to warn *Vermont* that two Yasen-M submarines are coming for us."

Dankleff nodded solemnly. "What about the risk of being detected from transmitting?"

"The risk of a Yasen-M surprising the *Vermont* far outweighs that. And two Yasen-Ms? Fuck, U-Boat. We're toast."

"Not if you get that fast reactor started. We could kick this tub into full thrust and get the fuck out of here."

"Now *that* thought is worth a shot of that rotgut vodka."

Arabian Sea
200 nautical miles west of Porbandar, India
USS *Vermont*
Tuesday, June 7; midwatch: 0115 UTC, 5:15 am local time

The watchbill had been completely scrambled by the loss of Varney, Dankleff and even non-qual Pacino. It also put a big hole in the 18-24 watch, where Chief Albanese had stood the watch on the number one Q-10 sonar stack. Lieutenant Commander Mario "Elvis" Lewinsky, the engineer, leaned over the command console, debating calling for the swivel command chair that could be inserted into a hole in the deck directly behind the console. He decided that would be a temptation to sleep, and stood up straighter.

Instead of the engineer's preference, to stand his daily watch aft as engineering officer of the watch from 0600 to noon—where he could keep an eye on his engineering spaces, the health of the machinery, and the alertness of the watchstanders, and even go through some of the paperwork of his engineering divisions—he found himself on the conn, standing officer of the deck watch. Worse, the watch was on the goddamned midwatch, when Quinnivan and Seagraves wanted someone senior and sharp watching over *Panther* and keeping a weather eye for any incursion of an opposing attack force.

But Lewinsky felt anything but sharp tonight. In fact, his sleep had been thrashed by this change in schedule. That and worry over the mission. Too many damned things could go wrong. He tried to avoid counting them in his mind when he did have time to lie down in his bunk, but they presented themselves for counting almost like an insomniac's sheep crowding the fence. So, for the number one malfunction, they could lose sonar contact on the *Panther.* It was loud when snorkeling—that wasn't a problem—but it only snorkeled at dark, then maintained slow speed on the batteries. And on batteries, it had a low frequency emission from the main motor and a fifty-cycle whine from the ship's service generator. And if *Panther* got out ahead of them too far, it's signal-to-noise ratio would plummet and it could easily vanish into the noise of the warm Arabian Sea, which was teeming with fish and underwater mammals, all of them calling to each other at once, filling the broadband sonar stack with static. And if they lost sonar contact with the *Panther,* they would be well on the way to mission failure, because the next submarine to pick up her trail might be Russian.

Which led the way to glitch number two—a Russian attack submarine sent to stop this messy submarine theft. Odds were, an incoming Russian SSN had strict orders to shoot the *Panther* the second it was detected, to keep that super-secret fast reactor from falling into American hands. And it was up in the air—a fifty-fifty chance—that the attacker could have orders to sink the American escort sub in retaliation for stealing the *Panther* in the first place. Or out of a defensive analysis, that the best defense is a good offense.

Glitch three? *Panther* would eventually run out of fuel, and the refueling rendezvous with a disguised merchant oiler could go wrong or an attacking force could find her on the surface when refueling. Or a storm came up while refueling, strong enough to sink her.

The list of worries and glitches went on and on.

Lewinsky knew he shouldn't worry, that worrying did nothing but erode combat effectiveness, but that was his personality. What had *been* his personality, anyway, until he'd gotten help. At Annapolis plebe year, his nickname was "Wart," shortened from "Worry Wart," because he had sweated everything. Would he fail the next physical strength test? Would the firsties scream at him at the next comearound? Would he fail plebe chemistry? Would his term paper on World War I differences from previous conflicts get an F? Would the company officer barge into his room and find it unsat and give him a class A conduct offense? And if he got a class A, would it snowball into conduct grades so severe that he'd get kicked out of the Academy? Eventually, his worries got so severe he'd had to see a counselor about it, during Christmas break, the sessions kept completely secret in case seeing a psychologist would get him kicked out of the Navy—and that formed yet another worry.

In working with the shrink, a pretty woman named Deb who was perhaps 35, he'd slowly managed to overcome his constant anxiety. Doctor Deb had offered to refer him to psychiatrist to get him anti-anxiety meds, but he'd refused. He couldn't add to the worry list that some mind-altering medication showed up in a random drug test.

It had taken years with Doc Deb, with her making him learn a technique of visualizing alternate futures, one in which his worry came to nothing, and one where it happened. Then, she taught him, if the worry came true, he would deal with it. He'd have the strength to deal with it.

The shrink's other effort came in forcing him to have interests outside the military. As with almost all men his age, his most intense interest was in women, but Lewinsky had anxiety levels too high to approach a female, and the only woman he'd seen socially at the Academy was at the plebe "tea dance," also known as "the pig push," where random chance matched up plebes with visitors of the opposite sex. The girl that had been forced on him was pretty but quiet and she'd liked him. They'd danced for a few hours before she'd had to leave. But he hadn't kissed her, worrying that doing that might endanger their connection. And he hadn't called her later either, because he worried she'd reject him.

So he decided upon an alternate hobby. Cars. There was a mechanic's facility across the Severn River where midshipmen could rent a space with a lift and borrow tools, so they could work on their cars. With a thousand dollars Lewinsky had managed to save, he'd bought an old Mustang. A 1970 Boss, with the original, now faded, radical orange paint job with black stripes. The car was somewhat sound, having spent decades in a barn, but nothing mechanical or electrical worked, and it would all have to be replaced. The entire power train had to go. He'd scrapped the 351 Cleveland V8 and saved for a big block V8 crate engine with a manual five speed performance transmission, spending his weekends putting the engine into the car and solving the thousands of problems of an engine transplant in a car that old.

He'd worked on the car for his entire time at Annapolis, his father even deciding to pay the rent on the space and pay for the new parts, apparently pleased at the results of this auto-restoration-therapy. By the time Lewinsky was a first class midshipman, a senior, he was a double major in mathematics and physics, a nominee for a Rhodes scholarship to Oxford, and the proud owner of a newly painted orange muscle car that was the envy of his entire company. And the funny thing about that car was that it made people talk to him, without him having to do anything. He'd drive it around Annapolis that summer before first class year, the exhaust roaring, the engine purring, the wheels a gleaming polished chrome, the tires wide and black and shiny, the slick orange paint job so outrageous that seemingly everyone at the Academy knew it belonged to him. People came up to him when he'd fill it with gas or when he parked, talking about their own project cars or simply admiring this blast from the past. People of every sort flocked to the car, old duffers who remembered when that was a car they'd lusted over in high school, young teenagers asking how he'd restored it and was it difficult, and then the groupie girls, the women who loved cars, and so it happened that he met Anne, who had fallen in love with the Mustang first, Lewinsky second.

And from that point on, all the worries and anxieties seemed to fade into the past. Lewinsky went on to Oxford, did more work in physics, found it almost unbearably difficult, but managed to squeak by and get a master's degree. Then on to the nuclear power training pipeline, nuclear prototype, submarine school, and his first submarine, the Norfolk-based USS *Montpelier*, SSN-765. Three years there, qualifying in submarines, then shore duty teaching physics at Annapolis for two years, then on to the *Vermont*.

All those years, he'd restored cars, selling the Mustang for a wrecked 1963 split-window Corvette, which had been in such bad shape it had to be lifted from its collapsing garage with a crane. Two years later, it looked as new as when it had rolled off the factory floor. Lewinsky had used the amazing profits from the Mustang to restore the Corvette's original parts rather than replacing everything as he had with the Mustang. Corvette enthusiasts talked about "the numbers matching" as if putting a new crate engine into a Corvette were some kind of mortal sin.

When he'd sold the Corvette, it had fetched an eye-popping six-figure amount. It left him enough to buy the Ferrari Testarossa, Italian for "redhead."

So there were cars in his life, but no women. That girl Anne at Annapolis had been kind to him, and they'd dated until he'd had to leave for Oxford, and as people told him to expect, the distance eventually strangled the relationship. She'd found someone else and had gotten married and by now was working on having her second child. As for Lewinsky, while he'd conquered much of his anxiety, he was just too shy to ask a woman out or approach someone at a bar. He began to imagine he would die alone.

He'd steamed on alone until he'd reported back to Norfolk when his instructor duty at Annapolis concluded, and it was time to take on the hardest job in the Navy, engineer of a nuclear submarine. He smiled to himself—his old worrywart self could never have done this job. He'd driven the Testarossa to a beachside café in Virginia Beach one sunny Saturday, thinking he'd have a beer and a sandwich outside on the beachfront deck, enjoy the sunshine, maybe go for a run later in the afternoon when it would get cooler. He'd just bitten into a club sandwich when a stunning redheaded woman walked up to him wearing a short skirt, tube top and running sneakers. She was slender, with curvaceous hips, tiny waist, and what had to be double-D-cup breasts that pointed outward like the front bumper of a '57 Cadillac. She was practically falling out of her shirt. Her skin was smooth and tanned, her body was toned, and she had a long graceful neck, a lovely face with pouty red lips, strong cheekbones, an upturned nose, wide brown romantic eyes with long lashes, her face framed by long, straight, shining naturally red hair that came down to her nipples, and it had so much sleek body that she could have been in a shampoo commercial.

Without a word, she pulled back the seat opposite Lewinski's and sat down, smiling at him slightly. She motioned the waitress over. "Old fashioned, neat, please," she said in a slight Southern accent, her voice silky and feminine, "and ask if they could use Angel's Envy bourbon. And then I'll have what he's having."

He stared at her, his mouth half open, then he remembered to chew his food and swallow, and it had almost gone down the wrong way.

"Um," he said. "Hello." His voice had been an adolescent squeak. He coughed, cleared his throat, and tried to make his voice deep again. And make it sound like every day of the week a gorgeous, hot model sat down at his table, uninvited. "I'm Mario. Mario Lewinsky. Who are you?"

"Hello, Mario. I'm Redhead."

He found himself smiling at her, despite the strangeness of the situation. Was she a hooker, sent by the officers of the *Vermont* to tease him and make fun of his reaction? He'd only just met them at the hail-and-farewell party at the executive officer's house, and they were definitely a rowdy crew of pranksters. It would be just like Man Mountain Squirt Gun Vevera to arrange to have a hooker approach him at a Saturday lunch.

"No, what's your *real* name?" Using 'Redhead' as her name was a stripper thing, he thought, the way all strippers seemed to be 'Amber' or 'Tiffany' or 'Crystal.'

She smiled with a row of absolutely perfect white teeth. Which meant there was no way this was legit, he thought.

"I quit using it. You'll laugh." The tiniest micro-expression of sadness crossed that gorgeous face.

He smiled back at her. "Listen, try going through life with a name like Mario Elvis Lewinsky. It can't be worse than that."

She looked down at the table for a second, then whispered something he couldn't hear. He cupped his hand to his ear. "Eh?" he said, imitating a hearing-impaired octogenarian.

"Please don't laugh. It's *Bamanda*. Like Amanda, but with a big *BAM* at the start. My father's idea of a cool name, with him going through life bragging about how he invented my name. I would have used my middle name, but he put his fingerprints on that too. I don't tell anyone what that name is. Since middle school, I just told people my name was 'Redhead,' and they started going along with it. I make sure the color stays the way it looked when I was young. These days, decades down the road, I have help from a flamboyant stylist name Jorge. So yes, it's my natural color, but yes, I dye the fuck out of it. And does the carpet match the drapes? There is no carpet. Hardwood floors, you might say."

It sounded strange to Lewinsky to hear her curse with that beautiful voice with just a trace of the South. Alabama? Georgia? Memphis? His Indiana-raised ears weren't trained enough to figure it out. What was even stranger that she had just plopped down and started talking to him as if they were friends. Or more.

"I'm sorry," he said, "but can I ask you, Redhead, why are you sitting here with me? Don't get me wrong, I'm not complaining, it's just, well, it's not every day a guy like me," he ran his hands thought his flat-top haircut and adjusted his black-framed glasses on his nose, "gets visited by a woman who looks like the real-life version of Jessica Rabbit. Shouldn't you be crooning in a dark smoke-filled nightclub somewhere, wearing six-inch heels and a silk gown with a slit up the side?"

Redhead tilted her head back and laughed, her laugh as musical as her voice. "I noticed the Ferrari," she said. "I did a photo shoot next to one once, and I thought it was hot, but I mean, you never see one, even here in snooty Virginia Beach. Then a week ago I saw yours and I saw you get out of it. So I checked you out. You're a Navy lieutenant commander. Engineer on the *Vermont*. Newly reported aboard. Extremely handsome. Extremely sexy. Extremely smart. And *extremely* shy. So—no girlfriend. Well, at least until today. As of today, you *do* have a girlfriend." She winked at him.

"First, Ms. Redhead, how did you find out all that about me?"

"Hey, Mario. A girl's got to have some mystery, doesn't she?"

"Come on."

"Okay, fine. I used to date Bruno Romanov. He was my first naval officer. I guess you could say I got hooked. I'm sort of a naval officer groupie now. I was out for drinks with Bruno and that bitch Rachel and they mentioned the Ferrari. They said it belonged to you, that you were hot and single and ripe for the taking. So. That brings you to now." She smiled brightly as if it were a done deal.

"Want to go for a ride?" Lewinsky said, smiling at her. Even if this were a trick by Vevera, Lewinsky decided to roll with it, maybe even have some fun with it. What was the harm? Then he heard his own question, and realized it sounded like a sexual proposition.

Redhead tossed back her whiskey, put down four crisp twenties on the table, using her whiskey glass as a paperweight, and took Lewinsky by the hand out to his car. He opened the passenger door and watched her as she folded those long legs to get in.

Four hours later they were naked in bed and sweating after the most amazing sex he'd ever had in his life. He had never believed in love at first sight, but Redhead was *it* for him.

It had taken two years for the relationship to fall apart, and when it did, it came apart as suddenly and strangely as it started. If Redhead had a fatal flaw, it was jealousy, and somehow she'd gotten it into her head that Lewinsky had something going on with Rachel Romanov—which he most certainly did not—but his working closely with the ship's navigator had made Redhead stew in boiling anger, particularly when *Vermont* would disappear on an op for weeks on end. Redhead finally revealed that Rachel had a crush on Lewinsky, and had put Redhead up to sleeping with him as an odd way of, as Redhead put it, "Rachel fucking you by proxy," saying, "she used me, she made me into a *sex torpedo* that she fired at *you*." Redhead was convinced that the *Vermont* navigator had sent Redhead his way in order to obtain juicy details about what sex with him was like, because Romanov lusted for him. The reality of this crazy situation was that Redhead couldn't live in a world where she thought another woman wanted her man, or one where she thought her man wanted another woman.

Redhead eventually left him, slamming the door after her. She'd taken an ice pick to the Testarossa and in white epoxy paint had written the word ASSHOLE on every surface. It had taken a twenty-thousand-dollar repair and a new paint job to fix that, but there would be no fixing Mario Lewinsky's heart. He was still deeply, profoundly in love with Redhead, and he imagined he always would be, their terrible ending notwithstanding.

It was then that his reverie was interrupted by Sonarman First Class Jay "Snowman" Mercer, the midwatch sonarman of the watch. "Officer of the Deck, we've got some strange transients coming from the *Panther*."

"Transients? Like what?" Transients could be bad news. A mechanical malfunction? Something rupturing and breaking? A fire breaking out with the crew making noise trying to battle the flames?

"I've got a pump startup. Not just any pump. A *big* pump."

"A pump? Why would a diesel-electric submarine be starting a *pump*?"

"Maybe because it's about to become a *nuclear* submarine."

"Oh, holy hell, no."

"I've got flow noise, Eng. There's definitely steam flowing in pipes, a fuck-ton of it."

"Exactly how much is the quantity 'fuck-ton,' Petty Officer Mercer?"

"A buttload, in technical terms, Eng. Now I've got a turbine starting up. No, two turbines, a small one and a big one. Definitely a big-ass turbine. Do you want that quantified also?"

"Is this for real?"

"I've got transient clicks or booms, Eng. Could be breakers shutting. The turbine noise is getting louder. Wait, what the hell?"

"What?"

"Possible zig, *Panther,* sir. She's speeding up. Jesus, she's speeding up. Can you get a TMA leg? With speed across the line-of-sight of at least fifteen knots?"

"Pilot! Left full rudder, all ahead standard! Steady course east."

"Left full rudder, steady course east, Pilot aye, and all ahead standard," Torpedoman Senior Chief Nygard said. "Maneuvering answers, all ahead standard. Present course one six zero, seventy degrees from ordered course."

"FT of the Watch, once we steady on course east, get a curve."

"Get a curve, aye."

Lewinsky was already dialing the XO's stateroom.

"Command Duty Officer."

"Sir, we have a zig on *Panther.* Looks like they lit off that fast reactor and they're speeding up like a bat outta hell, sir. I'm getting a perpendicular leg to get a fix on his speed."

"I'll be right there," Quinnivan said.

Ten minutes later, after *Vermont* had taken data on the first leg, then turned to the reciprocal course, west, and gathered data on the other perpendicular leg, the answer was in. *Panther* was doing thirty-one knots.

"Thirty-one goddamned knots, XO," Lewinsky said.

"That reactor seems to be working quite nicely," Quinnivan said. "And good news. It didn't explode."

"Yet," Lewinsky said, old worries from the past deciding to visit.

"Your optimism is noted, Eng," Quinnivan said. "I'll inform the captain."

BOOK 5:

THE WAR OF JUNE 7

23

Arabian Sea
K-579 *Voronezh*
Tuesday, June 7; 0140 UTC, 0340 Moscow time

Captain Second Rank Anastasia Isakova blinked hard, trying to become more alert. She'd had the first watch for almost four hours and was trying to make the adjustment from having had the afternoon watch.

She sat in the captain's console seat, the far-left seat of the three seats of the command console, in the central command post. In front of her was a large flat panel display that could show anything from any of the other displays, whether ship control, sonar, battlecontrol, weapons control, communications or navigation. The console could be set to rotate through all available displays if desired, or it could be turned over to the AI system, the Second Captain, and left to have the Second Captain decide what was display-worthy. The number two and three screens in front of the seats to her right were selected to Second-Captain-discretion display modes, but Isakova insisted that her own screen show only what she herself selected. In her opinion, the Second Captain was a bit of a moron, or as she was fond of saying, AI—artificial intelligence—would be better named artificial idiocy.

Isakova was standing command duty officer watch for the midnight to 0600 watch run by Captain Lieutenant Maksimilian Kovalyov, who was the communications officer. Kovalyov was seated at the middle seat of the starboard side battlecontrol attack center console, where he liked to spend most of his watch, but he rotated through the sonar-and-sensor consoles on the port side or stood at the aft port navigation display as well.

The central command post of the *Voronezh* was startlingly large. The center of the room was occupied by the three-seat command console, with three large displays, with annunciators and phones set into the console between displays. Behind the command console, directly behind Isakova, was the number two periscope, the number one periscope beside it, behind the far-right seat of the command console. Behind the periscopes, the bulkhead was crowded with navigation equipment and electrical junction boxes, communication panels and bookshelves. The far aft starboard corner had a door that opened into the aft passageway. The starboard side of the room, on the aft end, was filled with the battlecontrol's attack center, a long console with three seats in front of it, with eight large displays, arranged in two rows of four, an extended gauge panel above the top row. This console was manned only with the middle seat during normal steaming, a battlecontrol petty officer of the watch normally studying the displays, but the watch officer sometimes liked to station himself at the console so he could see all eight displays at once, rather than one at a time at the command console. With Kovalyov taking his normal seat, the displaced battlecontrol petty officer of the watch had taken the forward-most of the three seats.

Forward of battlecontrol, on the starboard side of the forward bulkhead, was a three-display console with two seats facing the displays, both seats occupied by the boatswains of the watch, controlling the ship's bowplanes, sternplanes, rudder, auxiliary ship's systems, complex ballast systems and the masts and antennae in the conning tower. To the left of the ship control console was a long slender credenza with the stand-behind under-ice sonar console, several navigation displays showing the health of the inertial navigation system and the status of navigation satellite downlinks when at periscope depth, with the upper center section occupied by two large flat panel screens, the left displaying the output of the number two periscope, the right tied into the number one scope. Farther to port, the credenza ended at the door leading forward. To the left of the door, on the forward port corner of the room, was the sonar-and-sensor console, the longest console in the central command post, with four seats placed facing the port side to attend to twelve large displays arranged in two rows of six, the horizontal section of the console jammed tight with keyboards, fixed function keys, trackballs and annunciator lights.

Aft of the sonar-and-sensor console was the navigation electronic chart table, a meter wide and two meters long, with navigation cabinets behind it on the port bulkhead, interrupted by the port aft door. Both aft doors led to a wide spot in the central passageway that led aft to the officer's berthing and several equipment spaces, one for radio, one for sonar, another for battlecontrol. Isakova would usually spend much of the watch at the navigation chart, trying to imagine where the target submarines were in the Arabian Sea, but at this moment, she had just selected the navigation chart to display on her command console display. This ocean was vast, extending from the farthest south point of India to the southern tip of the Arabian peninsula and northward all the way to Pakistan and the Gulf of Oman.

At the battlecontrol console, Kovalyov's tablet computer beeped. He looked away from the display screens to check it, then turned to Isakova.

"Madam First," he said, "messages are in from our excursion to periscope depth. There's one marked 'personal for first officer.'"

They'd spent a half hour at periscope depth, only going deep ten minutes before, the surface rotten with shipping this close to the Indian coastline, Isakova's time at the scope exhausting and sickening, the sea state high, the boat rocking hard in the heavy waves, while she took laser ranges to various surface contacts and fed them to the battlecontrol system, tracking them over time to make sure none of them got within a thousand meters, requiring two maneuvers to avoid the closest ones, Isakova finally lowering the scope and taking *Voronezh* deep as the third appeared inside the kilometer safety range.

Once they'd gone deep, she'd hoped there would be an

intelligence update—perhaps a satellite sighting of the *Panther* or the American target submarine, unwisely surfacing. Without aircraft or surface ships thanks to the worm, there would be no eye-in-the sky of an antisubmarine warfare patrol plane or a surveillance drone. They'd have to hope for other intel, such as an intercepted message with some inkling of where they were and their course and speed. Or some human intelligence, perhaps one of the Americans consorting with a well-placed prostitute working the town of the submarine's home base. But there was absolutely nothing. All that time at periscope depth, fighting the surface traffic, tossing in the damned waves, gone to waste.

"Send it to my tablet," Isakova ordered. The message was switched to her pad computer, which beeped with a notification. She opened the message and read it, and no sooner had she closed out the message than her eyes filled with water. She blinked it back as hard as she could, finding a roll of tissue paper and wiping her eyes, suddenly aware that Kovalyov was staring at her.

The message had been from her mother, with whom she had been in a running cold war for over a decade over her supposedly "unwomanly insistence on joining the Navy." But this message wasn't cold at all, it was tender and full of empathy for her, because Mother knew full well that Isakova was close to her beloved father, and the message was sent to report that Father was lying on his deathbed, finally succumbing to the lung disease from the mineral insulation he'd worked with for fifty hard years at the Baikonur Cosmodrome, and that at this point he wasn't expected to live for more than a few days. He had hidden his illness from Isakova on her last visit, but she'd suspected he wasn't himself. But now, here she was at sea, unable to rush to his bedside, and the knowledge settled into her soul that she'd seen her father alive for the last time.

She put her head in her hands, the unwelcome tears flooding into her palms. *Daddy,* she thought desperately, *please don't leave me.* She was sobbing too hard to notice Kovalyov pick up the phone at the station between battlecontrol display two and display three and dial the commanding officer's stateroom.

"Captain," a sleepy Captain First Rank Boris Novikov answered, his voice laced with anxiety. After all, why would the watch officer call him when the command duty officer—Isakova—was stationed right there with him in the central command post?

"Sir," Kovalyov whispered, "I think you need to come to central."

"On my way." Novikov clicked off.

Arabian Sea
B-902 *Panther*
Tuesday, June 7; 0140 UTC, 5:40 am local time

Lieutenant Dieter Dankleff leaned over the chart table in the navigation chart room, walking dividers down a line drawn south from where they'd started the reactor and increased speed to thirty-one knots a half hour ago. The deck shook and trembled violently from the speed of their transit.

Lieutenant Anthony Pacino walked in and handed Dankleff a cup of coffee. "Something's bothering me."

"Dammit, again? And shouldn't you be in the control room if we're going flank?"

"Central command post, you mean? I'm not the one who laid out this submarine. Who puts the navigation chart in a closet outside the central command post? How can the officer of the deck figure out where the hell he is?"

"Who's got the wheel?"

"Grip Aquatong. He's good. He's alert. Maybe a little scared."

Dankleff laughed. "What, a big tough-guy armed-to-the-teeth SEAL commando is scared?"

"I told him all the things that can go wrong on a maximum speed run. A jam dive, for instance, that takes us below crush depth before he could recover."

"That poor kid. You're going to give him nightmares."

"Better scared and alert than complacent and sleepy."

"You said something was bothering you, Lipstick."

Pacino half sat on a stool with a red leather cushion. "We have to slow back down."

"What? You're the one who wanted to get the hell out of Dodge and flank it out of here."

"It's not right," Pacino said. "It's not smart. We're probably making more noise than a freight train on loose rails. This reactor system wasn't sound-mounted. It wasn't designed for stealth, it's just a big test rig. We proved what we had to prove, that the *Panther* can haul ass if it absolutely has to. Now it's time to get quiet again."

"What happened to the Russians bragging that their Kilo-class was a quote, black hole in the ocean, unquote?"

"Yeah, a new one, the improved class. This thing is old. Hell, we were in grade school when this hull was laid down. And Kilos *are* quiet on the batteries, even this one. But blasting through the sea at thirty-one knots with a gigantic feed pump and a steam turbine bigger than a moving truck? We're probably waking people up on either coastline of the entire damned Arabian Sea. Not to mention, *Vermont*'s top speed is just a little over the same speed we're going right now. Which means all she can do is trail us with fast speed main coolant pumps, so even *she's* not stealthy. The original plan had *Vermont* out in front of us, so any weapon she'd shoot wouldn't home in on us. Now she's behind us after we left her in the dust a half hour ago, in a tail chase."

"So what do you want to do?"

"Shut down the plant and cruise deep on batteries, six knots. *Vermont* can get back out ahead of us. We can use our rudimentary sonar to search, but it won't see much, and we don't know how to use it even if it did. The Q-10 on the *Vermont* can scout the sea around us. When we get to the point the battery bank is depleted, instead of snorkeling, we restart the fast reactor, speed up to say, fifteen knots and charge the batteries. Once the batteries are back at a hundred percent, we shut down and cruise on the batteries again."

"Now we're back on the hundred-day transit. Maybe a little less. But still. And although we won't run out of diesel, we will still need a rendezvous with one of those CIA tramp steamers or else we run out of food."

"We'll figure out the food situation later."

"Got it. Understood. Shut down the reactor plant and take her to six knots, then. Hurry up."

Pacino vanished back into the central command post, and soon the buzzing, rattling, trembling deck at their maximum speed run settled back down. Somehow, Dankleff had felt safer at thirty-one knots than he did at six, even if this speed on batteries were much quieter.

"OIC?" Chief Goreliki said from the door to the navigation room.

"Yeah?" Dankleff said, sipping his broiling hot coffee. "What is it, Chief?"

"With the radio passing self-checks, I'm thinking we should take it up to periscope depth and put up an antenna. Now that we've slowed, we won't lose time by going to PD. We need to get a precise NavSat fix. And if I can grab the CommStar broadcast, anything from *Vermont* or ComSubFor will be in our messages. There might be intelligence we need to read. And if you feel like you can risk transmitting, you can tell *Vermont* about the two inbound Yasen-M submarines that Abakumov reported."

Dankleff nodded. "Go tell Pacino that. See what he thinks."

Dankleff recalculated their average speed. Sixteen hours at six knots, then eight hours at fifteen. Dammit, he thought, a speed-of-advance of only nine knots. He sighed, realizing he'd be losing his entire summer.

After twenty minutes on the batteries, Pacino came back in and plopped a notepad on the table. "Assuming we can transmit, I recommend we transmit that." Chief Goreliki stood outside the room, waiting for Dankleff's decision.

Dankleff read the draft message and nodded, adding a sentence at the end.

"Let's take her to PD. First let's try to receive the broadcast and get a NavSat fix. Then we'll go through any messages for us. Scout the intelligence updates. Then if there's nothing new, we'll transmit this."

"Periscope depth, aye, and grab the broadcast and a fix."

Dankleff shook his head at the chart again as the deck inclined upward, the slight swaying of the deck a sign of rough seas topside. There was a thump as hydraulics raised the radio antenna. He walked into the central command post, where Pacino was doing slow circles on the aft periscope.

"Any contacts?"

"Two. Distant merchant ships by the look of their lights. Want to look?"

"Sure."

"Low power, on the horizon, relative zero zero zero," Pacino said, turning over the periscope.

Dankleff put his eye to the warm rubber of the eyepiece and scanned the dark horizon, lit weakly by moonlight that came down through an overcast sky. To the right, there was a surface ship, a supertanker, showing a green, starboard running light, with white lights aft. He was distant. Dankleff found the control to magnify the view, the magnification done with the left periscope grip. He clicked it up twice, and the merchant ship became larger, jumping in the view. He went back to low power and scanned the horizon again, seeing another merchant, this one far distant, barely showing up even in maximum magnification. He returned the periscope to point forward and handed it back to Pacino. "Low power, on the horizon, relative triple zero."

Pacino took back the scope and continued slow sweeps of the horizon. Dankleff walked aft to the radio room, a small enclosure opposite the navigation room.

"Anything?" he asked Goreliki.

"Nothing for us."

"We get a fix?"

Goreliki handed Dankleff a printout. He stepped across the passageway to the navigation alcove and plotted the fix, making a dot with a small circle around it and the time of the fix, then plotted their course leading from the dot. His dead reckoning had been off by over thirty miles. He went back to the radio room.

"Can you transmit?"

"We won't really know until we get a reply," Goreliki said. "But your message is coded in and ready to send."

"Send it."

Goreliki operated her screen, a modified, hardened laptop

connected by cables to a temporary panel she'd duct-taped to the submarine's radio equipment rack in a space once occupied by Iranian equipment that now lay on the deck.

"Okay, it's transmitted, OIC."

"Great," Dankleff said, returning to the central command post.

"Message is out. Lower the antenna. Let's take her back down, Patch."

"Helm," Pacino called to Grip Aquatong as he operated the hydraulic lever to lower the radio antenna, "make your depth one five zero meters."

"One five zero meters, Helm, aye," Grip answered, pushing his control yoke forward. The deck inclined down.

"Scope's awash," Pacino said. "Lowering number two scope." He hit the hydraulic control lever to lower the periscope.

At a hundred meters, the hull popped from the pressure, a booming roar overhead in control.

"Is it just me, Lipstick, or are those sounds louder on this boat than on the *Vermont*?"

"Seems that way to me, too," Pacino said.

"Leveling out at one five zero meters," Grip called.

"Very well, Helm," Pacino said.

"You know, he's more like the diving officer than the helmsman."

"I feel strange calling him 'diving officer' if he's got the rudder and planes. And 'pilot' isn't right, not on an ancient setup like this."

"Yeah. Well. I'm going to try to catch a few hours. I'll be back at zero six."

"I've got the bubble, OIC. Get some rack," Pacino said, taking a seat at the pos two console.

Arabian Sea
USS *Vermont*
Tuesday June 7; 0155 UTC, 5:55 am local time

"Got a curve on this leg, Officer of the Deck," Fire Controlman First Class Ralston, the Fire Controlman of the watch, reported, only turning his head enough from the attack center to allow the engineer to hear his voice.

"Pilot, right fifteen degrees rudder, steady course west," Lieutenant Commander Lewinsky ordered from the command console.

"Right fifteen degrees rudder, steady course west, Pilot, aye," Senior Chief Nygard acknowledged from the ship control station.

"What are they doing?" Lewinsky wondered to himself. Forty minutes before, after the transients were detected coming from the *Panther,* she'd sped up and screeched southward, and had ended up going so fast that Lewinsky had to order fast speed main coolant pumps started and kick the reactor plant up to a hundred percent power to follow her, keeping up, but in a blind tail chase, the clanking and loud Kilo submarine a dark streak of broadband noise on the Q-10's spherical array. And then, ten minutes ago, just as suddenly as she'd sped up, *Panther* shut down her reactor and went dead quiet again, going slow on her batteries.

"Steady course west, sir," Nygard called.

"FTOW, get a leg." Lewinsky dialed his display to the same output that Ralston was looking at, a vertical dot stack of fixed interval data units sent from sonar to the battlecontrol system, each data package combining twenty seconds of passive sonar data into a smoothed out best bearing to the target. Lewinsky checked his watch for the third time in two minutes, waiting impatiently to see what the target solution came out to be. As the new sonar data came in, it skewed off to the right. He could see what Ralston was doing to the dot stack. By dialing in assumed ranges and speeds of the contact, the dot stack after two "legs" of data—one bearing rate from driving *Vermont* east, the second from driving her west—could generate only one target range, course and speed based on how the bearings to the target changed with the parallax maneuver.

"Petty Officer Mercer, what's your best guess on speed?"

The sonarman of the watch, Mercer, turned to look over at Lewinsky. "She's back on batteries, Eng. Most probable is six knots. But you'd better close on her, I'm losing SNR." If the signal-to-noise ratio sank too low, the target would vanish into the loud background noise of the sea.

"What speed are you using, FTOW?"

"Speed six, OOD," Ralston said. "This is about as good as we're going to get without a third leg, sir. *Panther*'s solution—range, six thousand one hundred yards, speed six, course one nine five."

"Pilot, left ten degrees rudder, steady course one nine five, make turns for twelve knots." Slowing down three knots was not what Lewinsky wanted, because at the fifteen knots he'd been going, he'd catch up to *Panther* faster, but twelve gave him less own-ship generated noise, which would help sonar with its struggling signal-to-noise ratio. Anything he could do to improve the sonar equation, he'd do it.

"Pilot, aye, my rudder's left ten, passing one zero zero to the left, and Maneuvering answers, all ahead two thirds, turns for twelve knots. Passing one two zero to the left."

"Belay headings, Pilot."

The dot stack on the display diverged again and became meaningless, the previous data no longer useful. Lewinsky dialed his display back to the navigation chart, zooming out to show the entire Arabian Sea, then zooming in to show ownship's position, then the position of the *Panther*. For the fourth time in ten minutes, he muttered to himself, *what is that boat doing?*

"Officer of the Deck, steady course one nine five."

"How's your signal now, Mercer?"

"Better," Mercer replied from the number one sonar stack. "No, wait, I lied. He's fading, with a high D-E." *D/E* was deflection/elevation, or the sonar's way of saying the angle to the target had changed so that the Q-10 sphere was now looking upward. "I've got transients too, sounds like hull pops."

"He's going shallow," Lewinsky said. "Maybe going to periscope depth to grab a fix, or maybe he got his radio working. Pilot, all stop, make your depth one five zero feet, report speed seven." Lewinsky picked up the phone and buzzed the XO's stateroom as the deck started tilting dramatically upward, Lewinsky grabbing the handhold bar on the command console.

A loud groaning sound came from the overhead, quiet at first, then louder, as the hull expanded from the lower pressure as they came shallow.

"Command Duty Officer," Quinnivan said on the phone.

"He's popping up to PD, XO. I've closed range from six thousand to maybe four. Request permission to proceed to periscope depth, no baffle clear."

"Take her up to PD, OOD, no baffle clear," Quinnivan said. "I'm coming to control."

"Aye sir, PD, no baffle clear." Lewinsky put the phone down. He hated the idea of going shallow above the thermal layer without looking around to see what was going on in the radically different sonar environment near the surface, where the water was stirred by the waves and wind, the tremendous thermal power of the sun heating this upper layer of a hundred or so feet of water to bathtub warmth, where back deep, it was barely above freezing temperature, and the interface between warm and cold was often stark, almost like the surface of a mirror. A submariner could think he had the whole tactical picture when deep, then when ascending through the layer, there could be a dozen ships up there, some of them close enough to risk being rammed. And a submarine hull was built to take the even pressure of the deep, not a puncture force of a supertanker hull collision. There were dozens of incident reports of submarines being run into up above the layer. Photos of destroyed sails and huge dents in hulls came to mind. Submarines had even caused surface ships to sink after a collision. The classified after-action report from the Bo Hai Bay rescue mission came to mind, when the *Seawolf*, under the command of Lipstick's dad, had run out of torpedoes and decided to use her sail to ram a Chinese destroyer. She'd cut the destroyer cleanly in half, and both halves sank. The force of the ramming had mostly sheared off *Seawolf*'s sail, but she'd bought herself a few hours' time.

But worrying about collision was a waste of time, Lewinsky thought, and yet another worry for him to consciously leave behind.

Commander Jeremiah Quinnivan appeared to Lewinsky's right at the command console. "How you doin, lad?"

Lewinsky nodded at the XO. "I'm runnin' hot, straight and normal, XO. You?"

"Most groovy," Quinnivan said, turning to peer over Ralston's shoulder at the attack center console.

"Speed seven knots, sir," Nygard called.

"Very well, Pilot, make your depth six five feet, smartly, all ahead one third, turns for six knots."

Nygard acknowledged the string of orders and the deck tilted upward again. Lewinsky changed his command console display to the output of the number two scope, which was black. He opened the panel to reveal the hydraulic control switches for the periscope and actuated the number one scope's raising hydraulics.

"Raising number one scope." The large flatscreen in the starboard forward corner of the room came on, and it and the command console display showed a blurry black that gradually got lighter.

"One hundred feet, sir," Nygard reported, the deck becoming more level. "Nine zero feet."

"Very well," Lewinsky said, his screen starting to get lighter still until he could see a shimmer from high above, the moonlight shining down from the waves. Lewinsky maneuvered the scope in a circle, making a full revolution in a few seconds.

"Eight zero feet."

"No shapes or shadows," Lewinsky called, holding his breath, and hoping there was nothing up there. No doubt, a close, fully-loaded supertanker barreling in at twelve knots could ruin the whole day. Lewinsky continued rotating the scope through full revolutions, looking upward at first, then leveling the view to see farther away, looking for the shadow formed by an incoming surface ship hull, but there was nothing. They were safe, at least so far.

"Seven five."

The undersides of the waves came into focus, the sea state above heavy. The deck had taken on a roll to port, holding there tilted for a moment, then rolling back to starboard and hanging up there, then returning to port.

"Seven zero."

"Scope's breaking." A frothy blast obscured the view, the clear focus lost as there was nothing but bubbles and foam in the viewscreen. The foaming continued. "Scope's breaking. Get us up, Pilot."

"Six nine feet."

"Scope's clear," Lewinsky called, making three fast circles in the periscope, the features of the surface above blurred by the motion. There was nothing to see but the tall waves of the sea, the horizon and the crescent moon. "No close contacts." Lewinsky slowed the periscope revolutions to make a slow search around them, the magnification set to low power. The sea was empty. He increased the magnification to 4x and started a slow surface search, taking a full thirty seconds for each twenty degrees of arc. Still no lights or shapes out there, just the waves and the moon above.

"Report bearing to the *Panther,*" he called.

"*Panther* bears one-two-seven," Ralston said.

Lewinsky trained the scope to 127 degrees and zoomed the magnification to 8x, but didn't see anything in the view. He hit the infrared, but still nothing. The periscope of *Panther,* and her radio antenna, if she were using it, were the same temperature as the sea, or colder from having been freezing in the deep.

"What's your range?"

"Thirty-five hundred, but it's rough. If you'll drive us across the line-of-sight, I can do better."

"Pilot, left fifteen degrees rudder, steady course zero five zero, all ahead two thirds, turns for nine knots."

Vermont turned toward the *Panther,* swinging around to the northeast, attempting to drive the bearing to the target right and improve the range calculation.

"Sir," the radioman of the watch said to Lewinsky, showing up from behind him on his right. "We have flash traffic aboard." Radio messages were classified by their urgency, ranging from routine, priority, immediate and flash. A flash message had to be read within seconds, as it would contain information crucial to the survival of the addressee. Lewinsky had never before seen a flash message. What in holy hell was it?

"I'll take it," Quinnivan said. "Send it to my machine."

Quinnivan scanned the message, then reread it, stroking his beard. It was a mix of good news and bad, but the bad news was very bad indeed.

01155Z10JUN22
FLASH / FLASH / FLASH / FLASH / FLASH
FM B-902 PANTHER
TO USS VERMONT SSN-792
CC NATSECADV / NSC; COMSUBCOM
SUBJ SITREP // OPERATION PANTHER
TOP SECRET FRACTAL CHAOS // TOP SECRET FRACTAL CHAOS // TOP SECRET FRACTAL CHAOS
//BT//
1. (TS) PANTHER CHANGE-OF-COMMAND CEREMONY SUCCESSFUL.
2. (TS) PANTHER TRANSITED WITHOUT INCIDENT THROUGH GULF OF OMAN AND IS STEAMING SOUTHEAST IN THE ARABIAN SEA, PRESENTLY THREE HUNDRED FIFTY (350) NAUTICAL MILES SOUTH OF KARACHI, PAKISTAN. ORIGINAL PLAN OF TRANSIT ALONG COASTLINE OF INDIA DISCARDED AS BEING DISCERNIBLE BY OPPOSITION FORCE. PANTHER CURRENTLY PURSUING RANDOM ZIG-ZAG COURSE SOUTHWARD TOWARD ANTARCTIC COAST.

3. (S) PANTHER CREW CONSISTS OF:
OIC LT. D. DANKLEFF, USN
AOIC LT. A. PACINO, USN
OPS LT. M. VARNEY, USN
AI FTC(SS) N. KIM, USN
ST STC(SS) T. ALBANESE, USN
RM RMC(SS) B. GORELIKI, USN
TF80 CDR. E FISHMAN, USN
TF80 LTJG E. AQUATONG, USN
TF80 SOSC R. TUCKER-SANTOS, USN
TF80 SO1 H. ONEIDA, USN
902 CDR. R. AHMADI, IRANIAN NAVY
RR ENGR. A. ABAKUMOV, RUSSIAN REPUBLIC

4. (TS) RUSSIAN ENGINEER ABAKUMOV REPORTED TWO (2) RUSSIAN REPUBLIC ATTACK SUBMARINES INBOUND, BOTH YASEN-M-CLASS UNITS, BOTH DELAYED EN ROUTE.

5. (TS) RECOMMEND PAST RECENT HISTORY OF SATELLITE IMAGES BE SEARCHED FOR YASEN-M SUBMARINES TRANSITING TOWARD GULF OF OMAN. ANY INTEL ON YASEN-M POSITIONS URGENTLY REQUESTED. YASEN-M UNITS SUSPECTED TO BE HOSTILE COMBATANTS AND MAY FIRE ON DETECTION OF PANTHER AND / OR USS VERMONT.

6. (TS) PANTHER COMMISSIONED AND TESTED FAST REACTOR AND ASSOCIATED PROPULSION SYSTEMS, TEST SAT, MAXIMUM SPEED RUN AT THIRTY-ONE (31) KNOTS ATTAINED FOR THIRTY (30) MINUTES. FAST REACTOR SHUT DOWN AND PANTHER STEAMING ON BATTERIES FOR STEALTH. WILL START FAST REACTOR NIGHTLY TO CHARGE BATTERIES.

7. (TS) SHIP'S FORCE ABOARD PANTHER WORKING WITH FORMER COMMANDER OF PANTHER, WHO IS COOPERATIVE, AND RUSSIAN TEST ENGINEER, ALSO COOPERATING.

8. (TS) PANTHER SHIP'S FORCE ATTEMPTING TO MAKE PANTHER FIRECONTROL AND WEAPONS SYSTEMS FUNCTIONAL FOR POTENTIAL EMPLOYMENT AS A CONTINGENCY.

9. (TS) PANTHER CREW THANKS USS VERMONT FOR THE ESCORT.

10. (S) THE FIRST ROUND FOR USS VERMONT CREW AT DESTINATION IS ON PANTHER.
(U) LT. D. DANKLEFF SENDS.
//BT//

Arabian Sea
K-579 *Voronezh*
Tuesday, June 7; 0155 UTC, 0355 Moscow time

Captain First Rank Boris Novikov took his seat at the far portside command console. He'd sent Isakova to her stateroom to try to recover from her personal issue. He felt sorry for her. A woman like her, hard as steel and cold as ice, but tell her that her father is dying and she dissolves into a six-year-old daddy's girl, he thought. But he couldn't allow her grief to interfere with the ship's mission. But God also knew, he couldn't let his sleep deprivation interfere either. He wondered if Isakova would pull herself together before the start of the next midnight watch.

He selected his display to the Second-Captain-discretion display, and the Second Captain put the screen immediately to the notifications section. There was only one notification, but it was flashing red.

0320 Moscow Time: Sonar history module irregularity

He clicked the notification. The voice of the Second Captain came up, an emotionless, sterile, uncaring female voice, that the crew delighted in, because it so visibly irritated Isakova. The navigator, that prankster Leonid "Luke" Lukashenko, could do an amazing impersonation of the Second Captain's voice, and loved to use it on Isakova if they were off the ship just to see her face get red.

"Zero three twenty Moscow time," the Second Captain said. "Sonar history module irregularity. Detected signal-to-noise ratio below the thermal layer, bearing two-nine-five. Noise signature is high sound-power-level of sustained transient noises correlating with high mass-flow-rate steam flow, with high frequencies associated with a fifty cycle large generator. There is an unknown loud steady-state noise, also flow-related, correlated with a medium probability of being a boiler feed pump. Sonar history module irregularity began at zero three twenty Moscow time."

"Is it still present?" Novikov asked.

"The irregularity lasted until zero three forty-five Moscow time. At that time, all sound-related irregularities ceased."

Novikov stood up from his seat and hurried to the chart table. "Second Captain, display own-ship's position at zero three forty-five."

The chart responded with a pulsing blue light from the track behind them, perhaps six kilometers aft.

"Generate a bearing line from that point to two-nine-five." A red line grew from their past position, extending to the northwest, pointing just south of a line entering the Gulf of Oman.

"Watch Officer, are you seeing this?" Novikov asked in irritation.

"Yes, Captain. It must have come in while we were at periscope depth."

"No, it was noticed when you were still deep." Then to himself, "goddammit."

He studied the chart. If this were the *Panther,* going almost 300 RPM meant she'd figured out how to start her reactor and had sped up to an ungodly velocity. But he shouldn't jump to a conclusion, he cautioned himself.

"Second Captain, calculate probability that this sound irregularity is a Virginia-class submarine."

"Calculating. Probability of a correlation with this sound irregularity and a Virginia-class submarine is zero point two percent."

So, that wasn't the answer. "Second Captain, calculate the probability of this detection being a Kilo-class submarine."

"Calculating. Probability of a correlation with this sound irregularity and a Kilo-class submarine is eight percent."

Novikov considered. That seemed way too low. What did that mean? Was it something else?

"Second Captain, slow the noise history down by a factor of five. That is, replay it for analysis at twenty percent speed. With the slowed-down history, is there a correlation between the sound irregularity and a Kilo-class?"

"Calculating. Probability of a correlation with this sound irregularity, slowed down to twenty percent speed, and a Kilo-class submarine is forty-six percent."

Dramatic improvement, Novikov thought. "Second Captain, are you able to analyze a signal correlation if you remove the feed pump, the steam flow noise, the steam turbine and the large electrical generator? Then account for the slowing of the fifty-cycle generator?"

"Yes. It will be somewhat degraded, but it could be analyzed."

"Second Captain, calculate the probability of a correlation of the sound irregularity with a Kilo-submarine, with the elements I mentioned subtracted out."

"Calculating. Probability of a correlation of this sound irregularity, slowed down with elements subtracted, with a Kilo-submarine is eighty-four percent, however, the confidence interval is low-to-medium at fifty-eight percent."

Eighty-four percent chance the noise was from the stolen Kilo. That was good enough for Novikov.

"Watch Officer, man battlestations," Novikov ordered. "That's him. And open up the Bolshoi-Feniks function of the MGK-600 and prepare to establish secure sonar telegraphy with K-573 *Novosibirsk*. Warm up the Fizik-2 torpedoes in tubes one through six. Then spin up the Kalibr antisubmarine cruise missiles in vertical launch silo tubes one and two. Settings to full yield, thirty kilotons."

Kovalyov stared at him, dumbfounded. Finally he found his voice. "The Kalibrs are *nuclear weapons*, Captain. We'll need the first officer's concurrence."

"Have her awakened and tell her to open my outer safe, then get the navigator to open the inner safe and instruct them to withdraw nuclear launch codes for cruise missiles one and two, and to keep the codes in two-person control at all times and bring them to the central command post."

"Yes, Captain, right away sir." He pulled a microphone to his lips. "This is the central command watch officer," Kovalyov's voice projected throughout the ship. "All hands, action stations for tactical launch. This is not a drill. I repeat, all hands, *action stations*."

24

Arabian Sea
K-579 *Voronezh*
Tuesday, June 7; 0205 UTC, 0405 Moscow Time

First Officer Captain Second Rank Anastasia Isakova rushed into the central command post, holding two sealed packages over her head, the navigator, Captain Third Rank Leonid Lukashenko following her, his hand gripped on the wrist of her arm holding up the packages. She stopped at the far portside station of the command console, where Captain Novikov waited impatiently.

The room was filling up rapidly with watchstanders, four taking seats at the portside sonar-and-sensor console, one at the under-ice console and Bolshoi-Feniks control station of the MGK-600 sonar. To Novikov's right, at the battlecontrol consoles, the communications officer, Maksimilian Kovalyov, occupied the center seat, the forward seat taken by the torpedo and missile officer, Captain Lieutenant Seva Laska, the aft seat a combined firecontrol console and weapons control console, reserved for the weapons officer, Captain Lieutenant Pyotr Alexandrov. The empty center seat of the command console was where Isakova took her battlestation, the navigator taking the far starboard side seat.

Isakova looked at Novikov through eyes made bleary by hours of crying. With her free hand, she wiped her running nose with a handkerchief, stuffing it back in her coveralls pocket.

"Sir, what's going on," she whispered urgently to Novikov,

who took the sealed packets from Isakova. He looked at them, each one a sealed set of codes that would unlock the nuclear-tipped Kalibr cruise missiles and allow them to dial in the yield settings.

"We've detected the target, the stolen Kilo submarine. Actually, *you* detected it. There was a notification from your watch, before you went to periscope depth. You should have been more alert."

Novikov looked up at Isakova, who was in sad shape. Her entire face looked swollen. Her nose was running and her eyes were so bloodshot it looked like she'd lost a back alley fight. Under normal circumstances, Novikov would have sent her to her cabin to sleep off her grief, but firing nuclear weapons required her concurrence, and he had no choice but to plug her into the tactical situation.

Navigator Leonid Lukashenko was charged with monitoring that the captain and the first officer fully agreed on nuclear weapon release, able to veto a weapon release if there were any suspicion of duress or the unfitness of one of the officers. Should one of them become incapacitated, he himself would function as one of the authorizers of weapon release, the duty of being the referee of rectitude passing to the next most senior department head, the weapons officer, Alexandrov. Novikov glanced quickly at Lukashenko, wondering if he should have Isakova relieved, but as if understanding what was happening, she seemed to snap out of her fugue state.

"The Kilo is northwest of us, range unknown, but it lit off its fast reactor and bolted southward out of the Gulf of Oman," Novikov said. "I've turned toward the target, increased speed to twenty-five knots and I'm preparing to conduct an active sonar search of the probable location of the target."

"No, sir," Isakova said, louder now, her voice settling into its usual cadence and tone. "For one thing, that Kilo is escorted by a Virginia-class. If we go pinging at the Kilo, the Virginia submarine will counterdetect us and put weapons in the water. And have you forgotten we are operating with the *Novosibirsk*? And neither you nor Captain Orlov of *Novosibirsk* is in tactical command. You both have to agree on tactics and weapons employment."

On some ships, Isakova's strident assertion of something contrary to the captain's intention could be considered borderline mutiny, but after the loss of several nuclear submarines over the years, the Admiralty had borrowed the concept of "crew resource management" from the aviation sphere, where officers had significant input and captains were strongly cautioned to listen to the advice of their officers. The Navy called it "command post resource management" and all the fleet's officers had been forced into training simulators. Novikov thought it was more harmful modern management and coddling of the sensitive feelings of the younger generation of sailors, but with Isakova he tolerated it. What made it easier was that she was so often right. He wondered if Orlov's first officer were as talented.

That pud-thumper Orlov again, Novikov thought, his blood pressure rising at the thought of having to get that idiot's agreement on weapons release and approach to the Kilo, but Isakova was right. And he'd been right not to have her relieved. With a feeling of relief, he nodded at her middle console seat.

"Fine," he said. "I'd intended to toss a Kalibr missile at the contact the minute I got a return ping. I figured the detonation would neutralize the Virginia-class escort, since he's probably following the Kilo close enough that a nuclear explosion would sink him or incapacitate him."

"A sound tactic, Captain, but we need a range first, and if we approach the probable location of the Kilo, we can reacquire him on passive sonar, and we can put a salvo of torpedoes into him. Much more surgical, and remember, Captain, a nuclear detonation will make miles and miles of ocean water impenetrable to active or passive sonar—a blue-out from all the bubbles created by the detonation. If our shot goes wide, the target—or targets—could hide from us on the other side of the massive blue-out. Did the second captain even have a bearing rate to the target? If it were going fast enough to make that noise, what, twenty knots? More? He'd have a significant bearing drift. If he were going southward, the bearing to the target must have changed from the original value of two-nine-five to something lower. Two-nine-four?"

"Second Captain," Novikov said into a microphone mounted

on a small pedestal and plugged into his console, "report the bearing rate of the sonar anomaly detected at zero three twenty. Did you detect a bearing drift over the time you had the target?"

"Captain, there was no bearing drift detected for the time of acquisition of the irregularity. It remained at two-nine-five for the duration of the detection, within the accuracy of that beam of the sonar sphere."

Novikov looked at Isakova. "Dammit, that means he was extremely distant."

"Once we establish communications with *Novosibirsk,* we need to proceed on a southwest course at high speed to intercept, even though that will cause our own emitted noise to rise and lower our ability to hear the target. He could be a hundred or even two hundred kilometers away. Or more."

Novikov cursed to himself. This mission might already be a failure. If the target never sped up again, and were two hundred kilometers away, he'd escape. And they had the devil's choice—chase him at high speed to close range with his own submarine, and Orlov's, making tremendous noise of their own while their sonars were deaf, or keep the approach at slow speed where they could hear, but the target disappeared.

"Perhaps the *Novosibirsk* has a better fix on the target," Novikov said reluctantly. That goddamned Orlov again. "But we're not in communication with him yet. Nor do we hold him on sonar. The boat is either out of position or too far away for secure sonar telegraphy."

Isakova took a deep breath. "You know the standard procedure calls for sending out a pulse to get him to respond with a return ping."

"But you just scolded me for active sonar employment. It's not stealthy. That Virginia-class might hear us pinging at each other."

"It would just be one pulse. It sounds like a biologic and it's short duration. It's not ideal, but truly, Captain, what tactical situation against a worthy opponent is ever ideal?"

"Fine." Novikov turned to the sonar-and-sensor console. "Sonar Officer," he called. Senior Lieutenant Svetomir Albescu turned from the forward-most seat of the sonar-and-sensor console. Albescu was a scrawny pimple-faced youth with wireless glasses, whom one would think wouldn't garner a second look in a bar, but every liberty port visited, he always seemed to find a beautiful woman who would drape herself across him. There was no accounting for feminine attraction, Novikov thought.

"Yes, sir," he said, blinking behind his glasses.

"Line up a secure active pulse on the MGK, wide azimuth pulse, medium frequency, short duration."

"Power level, Captain?"

Novikov looked at Isakova. "If I dial it up to maximum, perhaps we only have to do this once," he said. She nodded.

"One hundred percent, Lieutenant."

"One hundred percent, aye, Captain." Albescu lined up his panel, leaning over to consult with his *glavny starshina,* who was the technical expert on the equipment. After a moment, Albescu turned to Novikov. "Ready, sir."

"Transmit, Sonar Officer."

"Transmit, aye." Albescu hit a variable function key backlit with a red light.

A booming, roaring, groaning sound like an angry whale suddenly slammed Novikov's eardrums, the sonar sphere's transducers projecting a hundred percent sonar power into the water. The reverberations from the pulse took some seconds to die down.

Novikov's screen was selected to the sonar active display, the output looking like a conventional radar screen, but it was filled with blotchy colored stains from all the ocean noise. A small dot pulsed brightly for just a half second, then faded.

"I have a return echo, Captain," Albescu reported. "Bearing zero-four-five, range, ten point five kilometers." The screen pulsed again, three times from the same position. "We're receiving a three-ping secure pulse in response, Captain."

"Watch Officer," Novikov said to Navigator Lukashenko at the far-right console, "take us toward the *Novosibirsk,* heading zero four five, speed ten knots."

"He was farther away from the Kilo than we were," Isakova said, pursing her lips. "Most likely, he did not hear it."

"Once we establish communications with *Novosibirsk,* we can report our findings and see if he had a detect. Then we can coordinate the approach to this damned target," Novikov said, shaking his head. This operation was already getting messy. It would have been better if that pud-thumper Orlov and his incompetent submarine *Novosibirsk* had stayed behind in Petropavlovsk. Let them play in the Pacific Ocean and leave the Arabian Sea to the professionals.

Arabian Sea
K-573 *Novosibirsk*
Tuesday, June 7; 0215 UTC, 0415 Moscow time

Navigator Captain Third Rank Misha Dobryvnik yawned as he took the teacup from the tea service brought from the galley. He yawned as he spooned sugar into the cup and looked over from the far port side seat of the command console at the command duty officer, Captain Second Rank Ivan Vlasenko, who was already halfway through his tea.

"First watch starts getting wearing about this hour," he said to Vlasenko. Vlasenko nodded, not saying anything. When the first officer was tired, Dobryvnik thought, he seemingly lost all the upper functions of his brain, operating on the lizard brain alone. He could walk, breathe, blink and swallow, but otherwise he was somewhere else. Which was fine, Dobryvnik thought, since he himself was senior enough that he could run the central command post watchsection by himself during the tense search for the escaped Kilo submarine.

Dobryvnik checked his pad computer, selecting it to the calendar. It was the wee hours of Tuesday June 7. They'd been given orders to make haste to the west coast of India at mid-day Friday June 3, arriving at Point Marmagao after a maximum-speed run, arriving the morning of June 5, Sunday. Since then, they'd crawled north-northwest at walking speed, barely enough velocity to keep the towed array close to being level, searching for the stolen Kilo submarine and the rumored American escort submarine. Dobryvnik had theorized, during an operational briefing in the wardroom, that there *was* no American escort submarine, that the Kilo was operating alone.

"Where did the commandos raiding the Kilo come from, then?" Iron Irina Trusov, the weapons officer had asked.

"Madam Weapons Officer," Dobryvnik replied. "They may have been dropped by a helicopter from a distance with a swimmer delivery vehicle, the vehicle either parachuted with them or dropped there, waiting for them. They could have come in a swimmer delivery vehicle dropped by one of the hundreds of merchant ships in the gulf. There's a hundred ways to deliver commandos."

"How would *you* know?" Trusov had said coldly, tossing a lock of platinum blonde hair off her shoulder.

"My roommate is a senior lieutenant in the Spetsnaz GRU," Dobryvnik said. "He should keep his mouth shut about what he does for exercises, but his stories of insertion and extraction are epic."

That was all the opening the communications officer had needed. Captain Lieutenant Mikhail "TK" Sukolov, hearing 'insertion' and 'extraction,' had made an obscene gesture with his hands simulating copulation.

"Oh shut up, TK. Why don't you go to the radio room and lock yourself in for a couple of watches?" Dobryvnik had said, smirking. "The point is, we have no confirmation of an American submarine escort ship. There's *zero* intelligence that one was present."

His was definitely the minority opinion. The rest all believed that the only way the Kilo could have been taken was with a front-line American attack submarine. A Virginia-class.

Dobryvnik lazily selected the console to do a rotation through all screens, selecting the hold time on each screen to seven seconds. Long enough he could absorb information, not so long that he'd get bored or distracted, the screen rotation time discovered from long first watches, trying to stay plugged into the tactical situation, more often just trying to stay awake.

They said anything important always happened on the midnight watch, but Dobryvnik didn't believe it. His thoughts were interrupted by the appearance of Chernobyl Chernobrovin, the engineer, who grabbed Dobryvnik by both shoulders and shook him, as if to wake him up.

"Wake up, Watch Officer! Vigilance is our creed!" Chernobrovin said, grinning.

"Who let *you* forward of frame two-oh-seven?" Dobryvnik asked in jest.

The engineer had freshly showered and had donned fresh coveralls, the straight creases still in them from being pressed at the base's dry cleaners.

"Special occasion, Chernobyl? For some reason you're not covered in lube oil and soaked in sweat. Hot date tonight?"

The engineer smiled. He and the navigator had been junior officers on the Pacific Fleet's Project 971 Shchuka-B submarine K-157 *Vepr.* Dobryvnik had started as sonar officer, then had become the weapons officer, while Chernobrovin had maintained core engineering duties, starting as the reactor controls officer, then after a year, taking over the mechanical and auxiliary mechanical battle sections. They had requested to take department head tours on the same submarine, and getting assigned to a freshly commissioned Yasen-M submarine was like a lottery win. They'd contemplated renting an apartment and being roommates, but Chernobrovin maintained that they saw enough of each other as it was, and Dobryvnik would cramp his bachelor lifestyle. Dobryvnik had snorted at that, as if Chernobrovin had been with a woman alone in all the years he'd known him, since graduation from the Marshal Grechko School of Underwater Navigation.

"The special occasion is this, that *this* is the watch when something happens, I can feel it in my bones, my navigator friend—which, by the way, as the ship's navigator, do you have the slightest *idea* where we are?"

Dobryvnik smiled and vaulted out of his seat at command console three and stepped to the portside navigation chart table. The chart showed the upper Arabian Sea, the coastline of India forming the east side, the far distant Arabian peninsula on the west side, the top of the triangle formed by the coastline of Pakistan to the northeast and Iran to the northwest.

"We're here," Dobryvnik stabbed his finger at the pulsing blue dot off the Indian town of Veraval, perhaps 180 kilometers northwest of Mumbai, a dark blue line extending behind it, marking the history of their recent motion.

"Yeah? So where's the Northern Fleet sub, *Voronezh*?"

"Wow, you *do* pay attention to tactical briefings, don't you? I didn't think you could get your head out of the crankcase of the emergency diesel long enough."

"Hey, it takes real intelligence to comprehend both engineering *and* tactics," Chernobrovin said. "Anybody can navigate. Hell, my grandmother can navigate better than you, and she's been dead for two years."

"Fuck you, Chernobyl," Dobryvnik said, smiling.

"The hell is wrong with you guys?" Vlasenko said in irritation from command console position one. "Why don't you two get a room?"

"Oh, the first officer awakens," Chernobrovin said.

"Listen, Engineer," Vlasenko said, his blood rising.

"Mr. First! Mr. Navigator! We have a sonar pulse!" Senior Lieutenant Arisha Vasilev yelled from the port forward sonar-and-sensor console. Vasilev was the new sonar officer, arriving just before *Novosibirsk* sailed from Petropavlovsk. Dobryvnik and Chernobrovin had shared private comments about her, that with her long, gleaming black hair, perfect petite ballerina body and pretty face, she was much too hot to be a submarine officer, and would do better to be the *wife* of a submarine officer, and then they'd argued for hours about which officer she should become the wife of.

"Is it ours or foreign?" Dobryvnik yelled back.

"It's Russian, sir," Vasilev said.

Dobryvnik rushed to the sonar-and-sensor console to look over Vasilev's display. He looked back at Vlasenko. "It's *Voronezh*, Mr. First. We should respond. With a three-pulse narrow aperture high frequency active pulse, centered on the bearing to the *Voronezh*'s pulse."

"Very well, respond with a three-pulse narrow aperture high freq active," Vlasenko ordered. "And maintain your course and speed. Let *Voronezh* close the distance to us with our track staying predictable." The last time two submarines tried to rendezvous together using active sonar, they'd collided, ruining careers. He pulled the console's phone to his ear while dialing the captain's cabin.

"Captain," Captain First Rank Yuri Orlov answered. "I heard the pulse and your return pings. I'll be right there."

Washington, DC, USA
White House West Wing
Tuesday, June 7; 0240 UTC; June 6, 2240 EDT

The town car pulled to a halt at the lobby entrance to the West Wing. National Security Advisor Michael Pacino had already had his biometric identification checked at the entrance and his briefcase scanned. At the lobby door he relinquished his cell phone to a Secret Service agent and walked through a whole-body scanner, his briefcase scanned a second time. CIA Director Margo Allende was waiting for him, her sleek auburn hair pulled back into a ponytail, dressed for business, as was Pacino himself, having donned a black suit and tie for the meeting with the president.

"I got here as fast as I could." He glanced at his scratched, ancient Rolex Submariner watch. They'd wanted him here at 2230 and he was ten minutes late.

"You're fine, Patch. The president decided to postpone the meeting until morning. Joint chiefs will be here at zero six hundred for breakfast and the president will be down at seven. The VP and Admiral Catardi will join by secure video conference. But I'm glad you're here. I need to brief you on a late-breaking development."

As they took the steps to the lower level and the entrance to the Situation Room, he had the thought that he missed Camp David and its rustic informality.

"You probably haven't seen the message, I take it."

"I haven't. My pad computer said it wouldn't load until I was in the Situation Room."

"Well, you're not gonna like it," she said. "But I've got something for you that might ease the pain."

"What am I not going to like?"

Margo Allende opened the door of the Situation

Room—it was empty, unlike Pacino had expected. Even though the meeting with the president was postponed, the Situation Room was almost always partially occupied, but not tonight. "You want coffee? I'll fetch you one from the wardroom while you read the message."

"Yeah, that would be great. Black-and-bitter, please." Pacino found the seat he'd taken the last time there was a Situation Room meeting, on the right side of the president's end seat, three seats down, the other two seats between him and Carlucci taken by the Secretary of War and the Secretary of the Navy. Pacino pulled his pad computer out and put it on the table next to a notebook and his pen, then opened the software, submitted to the retinal scan and read the message Allende had told him about.

At the line reading, '*Panther* change-of-command ceremony successful,' he smiled to himself. That was excellent news, and a great way to summarize the op. But then paragraph three caught his eye.

3. (S) PANTHER CREW CONSISTS OF:
OIC LT. D. DANKLEFF, USN
AOIC LT. A. PACINO, USN

Pacino's mouth dropped open—*holy shit,* he thought. Seagraves had actually assigned Anthony to the boarding party. How the hell could that make any sense at all? After all the kid had been through on *Piranha,* they were sending him out an airlock in scuba gear? On one of the most dangerous missions since the search-and-destroy mission for the renegade nuclear-powered drone sub? Pacino's jaw tightened. When *Vermont* got back from this mission, he'd have a strong word with Commander Seagraves. If *Vermont* got back from this mission, he thought.

He'd reached the end of the message by the time Allende brought him a mug with the seal of the president on it, the hot steaming coffee's aroma the only good thing about the evening. She looked at him, sat next to him and put her hand on his forearm.

"I know you're upset about Little Patch, but he's going to be okay."

"Jesus, Margo, the most dangerous mission since we went after the drone submarine and my son's on it. He's not even qualified in submarines yet!"

"I know, but apparently his superior officers were impressed with his tactical ability. You have to imagine that with him being the son of the most storied fighting admiral since Halsey and Nimitz and fucking Horatio Nelson, some of your DNA would rub off on him and make him a tactical genius too. And I doubt anyone on that boarding party is a conscript, Patch, they're all volunteers."

Pacino smiled at that. He had to admit, he liked that expression—'fighting admiral.' "Well, then dammit, I'm going to have a strong word with my *son* when this is over." He took a pull of the coffee. "You said you had something that might make this miserable situation better?"

"Yeah, there's an update on Operation *Blue Hardhat,*" Allende said. "We have a small transmitter—more of a transponder, actually—placed on submarine periscopes. We managed to steal power for it from inside the periscope's systems without being detected. If the periscope is dry, the transmitter radios us the submarine's position. It's useless, of course, if the sub is deep, but most submarines come up for navigation purposes and to get radio traffic passively every day or two, and when the subs with this transponder come up, they tell us who they are and where they are."

"You have these on seven Yasen-M-class submarines?"

"We have them on the two Yasen-M boats that the Russian engineer said were inbound the Arabian Sea."

Pacino's face lit up. "Where?"

Allende projected her pad computer to a large display monitor opposite where they sat at the table. A projection of the Arabian Sea came up with the Saudi peninsula on the west side and the India coast on the right.

"One unit, Yasen Four, showed up in Port Aden in Oman. We believe he had maintenance trouble after traveling in from the Pacific fleet. The other unit, Yasen Six, was in the Med, at anchor waiting for the Suez Canal fiasco to get cleared up. Both units, by our analysts' reckoning, were inbound the Gulf of Oman to escort out the *Panther,* but when they were both delayed, the Iranians decided to send the *Panther* to sea early."

Pacino looked at Allende. "Did you put one of these transponders onto the periscope of the *Panther*?"

Allende looked back at him. Pacino could tell she was trying hard to control her facial expression.

"I can neither confirm nor deny, Patch. That's a different program."

Pacino considered—if there were a separate special compartmented information program on the *Panther,* maybe the CIA *did* know where it was. And what about *Vermont*? Would the Pentagon have outfitted it with a stealth-breaking transponder?

Suddenly the weight of this mission seemed to fall down on Pacino's head. Was it survivable? For the *Panther*? For Anthony? For *Vermont*? For the Russians?

Allende touched his forearm again and looked into his eyes. "It'll be okay, Patch. Your son will be fine. I promise."

Pacino nodded, hoping she would prove to be right.

25

Three days ago, the phone call had come in at three in the morning. One moment, he had been snuggled happily in bed with Natalia Orlov, the woman who had bewitched him, with whom he was desperately in love.

Even before answering the jangling phone, he stroked his finger down Natalia's long naked thigh, wondering at the amazing luck he'd had in winning her affection. Two weeks after he'd been sleeping with her, she confessed to her double sins of having been married to Captain First Rank Yuri Orlov and leaving him for Captain Second Rank Boris Novikov, and then leaving Novikov for him. He remembered that moment, when the world seemed to stand still, and she looked up at him with moisture in her big blue eyes, seemingly waiting for him to dismiss her, to reject her, but he had taken her face in his hands and kissed her, and told her that he didn't care, that all he saw when he looked at her was the love of his life. He had felt stupid saying that so early, but she had cried happy tears and thrown her arms around him, and they had only left his bed that weekend for food.

He glanced at her face in the dimness of the room, illuminated only by the lit up display of the phone, hoping the buzzing phone hadn't awakened her, but she slept on. For a moment, he regretted that she hadn't awakened, since phone calls arriving at three in morning usually meant there was a car waiting for him downstairs and an angry admiral on the other end of the connection.

"Go for Alexeyev," he said into the phone, trying to sound as if he'd been awake.

"This is Zhigunov," the deep gravelly voice of the admiral in command of the Northern Fleet said. Alexeyev sat straighter in the bed.

"Yes, Admiral," Alexeyev had said. "What is it?"

"Get your crew and report to the *Kazan*. Phone ahead and have the reactor started and prepare to get underway. I shall meet you on the pier in twenty minutes."

So had this oddball mission begun, unlike anything Alexeyev had ever seen. K-561 *Kazan*, the first Yasen-M-class submarine built, lay at her mooring on the dark moonless night, lit only by the sodium lamps of the pier, being hastily loaded out by a pier crew, trucks and pallets of food arriving and being offloaded. On the hull, two men were working beside a small handhole in the flank of the conning tower, taking off the shorepower cables. At the gangway, his first officer and department heads waited for him.

He stepped up to them and returned their salutes. It still felt strange, he thought, that the four highest ranking officers under his command were all women. Doubtless the idea of Zhigunov's deputy, Olga Vova, the first female admiral in the submarine force, a square-jawed bruiser of a woman, who must have outweighed Alexeyev by at least ten kilograms and could probably easily take him in a fight. The famous "Admiral OV" had wanted an all-female officer ship, but Admiral Zhigunov had made her settle for just the department heads and the first officer being female, under an experienced and trusted male captain.

"Madam First, what do we have?" he asked Captain Second Rank Ania Lebedev, a plain-looking woman with short chestnut hair, brown eyes and thin downturned lips, her normal expression one of constant disapproval. He was reminded of when he was a child and his mother informed him that if he made a face, it would freeze like that.

Lebedev frowned and looked at the hull of *Kazan*. "Well, Captain, the Admiral wants us in the channel before dawn. Perhaps worried about an overhead satellite observation. But we're held up by the stores load. The boat was almost completely empty of food."

The ship had been offloaded deliberately last week as a preparation for entering the drydock for a refit. Today, the boat had been scheduled to offload all weapons. Obviously that wasn't going to happen. Oddly, despite a refit period making the crew work much harder than at sea, the crew enjoyed being in port and with their families for weeks on end, rather than disappearing to sea for months, sometimes being called on for surprise mobilizations, like tonight's.

"Navigator?" Alexeyev looked at the female navigator and operations officer, Captain Third Rank Svetka Maksimov, who was as lovely as Lebedev was plain, with long shiny black hair, beautiful features, straight white teeth and deep brown eyes. Even gorgeous Natalia had gotten a little jealous at the last ship's party. There was no doubt, Natalia was still the traffic-stopping beauty of the crew's families, but Svetka Maksimov was a decade younger and had a way about her that endeared her to the crew. Alexeyev was convinced that even had Maksimov been homely, her outgoing and friendly personality would win over the crew.

"I've got the tides and current for the time period from now to dawn, Captain, but once clear of restricted waters in the Barents Sea, I have no idea where we're going. I can't lay in a track if the destination is so secret even I don't know it."

"Understood, Nav. Engineer?"

Captain Third Rank Alesya Matveev nodded at him. Matveev could have been an Amazon, the crew all thought. She was over 180 centimeters tall and solid. Her hobby was mixed martial arts, and it was said that no man aboard could win a cage fight with her. Her combative nature had made its way to her dour frowning face. Alexeyev suspected if she let her hair down and put on some makeup, she might be pretty, or at least less plain, but that wasn't Matveev's personality. Alexeyev suspected, if given the choice to transition her gender to being male, Matveev would jump at the chance.

"Captain, the reactor is in the power range and self-sustaining in natural circulation," Matveev said in a voice almost deeper than Alexeyev's, "with the propulsion turbines warm and connected to the load bank. The main motor is likewise warm. Removing shorepower cables now. There are no class one deficiencies. We are troubleshooting a problem with the redundant electrical evaporator. The air banks are full. Oxygen banks are at fifty percent, since we were bleeding them off slowly for the refit, but the bleed is stopped. We'll make oxygen and recharge once we're in open sea. The battery charge is at eighty percent. I'd feel better with a battery charge before we submerge but we may have to leave it as-is for now, sir."

"Very well, Engineer. Weapons Officer?"

"Sir," Captain Lieutenant Katerina Sobol said in a startlingly high-pitched cartoon character voice, standing straighter, "vertical launch system is loaded with thirty-two Oniks antiship cruise missiles, all conventional warheads. The torpedo room is loaded with twenty-four Futlyar Fizik-2 torpedoes, ten of them tube-loaded." Sobol was a small woman with a ballerina's body and looked way too young to be an officer, Alexeyev thought. She still had pimples on her face and tried to cover them up with makeup. She couldn't weigh a gram over 45 kilograms and barely stood over 150 centimeters. Her best friend aboard was the Amazon engineer. When the two of them went out drinking, people around them insisted on taking pictures of the giant female next to the tiny one.

"Do the Futlyar units have the latest software update for torpedo countermeasure employment?" Alexeyev frowned. Could his torpedoes stop an incoming American torpedo? When Alexeyev had nightmares, they were always of him in the central command post, helpless as the sound of an incoming torpedo sonar got louder and louder.

"Sir, yes, sir. I supervised the software load personally, a month ago, before the refit had been scheduled."

"Don't we also have two Shkvals?"

"Yes, Captain, sorry, I failed to mention the Shkvals."

"I want them tube loaded. We'll move weapons when we're submerged. Once they are in the torpedo tubes, I want them checked hourly for high temperatures."

"Yes, Captain, I'll put a weapon move plan together and present it to you once we clear restricted waters."

"Well, people, you'd better get your departments ready to put to sea," Alexeyev said, trying to make his voice sound forceful, while looking toward the end of the pier, awaiting Admiral Zhigunov, who was now ten minutes late. Just then the admiral's black limo drove up and Zhigunov got out and waved Alexeyev over. Alexeyev half ran to the end of the pier.

As he left the group of women officers, the navigator looked appreciatively at the retreating form of Captain First Rank Georgy Alexeyev. He was tall, slender, in good shape and had a thick head of amazingly shining dark black hair that swooped over his forehead to his ears, his hair just slightly longer than regulations allowed. Matveev called his hair "politician hair," the kind of looks only Kremlin elected officials sported. He had blue eyes that could freeze water when he was angry or boil a woman's blood when he smiled. He had rugged features, thin cheeks below strong cheekbones and a ruler-straight jawline, and he was one of those men who seemed to have a perpetual five o'clock shadow, and it made him look tough, masculine and strong. For the part of a front-line nuclear submarine commander, Maksimov thought, he looked like he had been cast by Moscow's movie industry.

His personality was hard to crack, though, she thought, the captain seeming somewhat remote, lost in thought, sometimes having to be prompted to concentrate on a briefing or a conversation. All too often, he seemed mentally somewhere else. The first officer, in a moment of being angry at him, once called him autistic, but that certainly wasn't the case. Of course Alexeyev had people skills—after all, look at that gorgeous beauty he was living with—but his remoteness and mentally distracted nature were a weakness, and he needed a good first officer to help him. It was a shame, Maksimov thought, that *she* couldn't be his first officer. That bitch Lebedev was one of those officers who was in the Navy just to advance her own career and become the fleet's first female commanding officer. With her, there was no thought of patriotism or spirit for the ship. Or to help her captain. As if reading her thoughts, the first officer looked at her and frowned.

"Navigator," Lebedev said coldly, "I suggest you get aboard and make sure you are ready to lay in a course once the captain has his orders."

Maksimov saluted her. "Yes, ma'am. By your leave."

"Dismissed," Lebedev said. "That goes for you too, Weapons Officer and Engineer. Let's get this mission going."

"Won't the captain be briefing us in the wardroom before we sail?" the engineer asked.

"If he does, you'll be the first to know. Come on, let's get aboard. Weapons Officer, you're driving us out. May I suggest you get yourself to the bridge and study the current and charts? And make contact with the tugs and pilot, make sure they're ready."

"Yes, ma'am," Sobol said, seeming glad to get away from the overbearing first officer, stepping quickly across the gangway to the hull.

At the end of the pier, Alexeyev walked up to Zhigunov and rigidly saluted the older man, who waved a salute back.

"What's going on, Admiral? What's the mission?"

"It's very bolloxed up, Georgy," Zhigunov said, his deep voice even more gravelly than usual. He pulled out a pack of cigarettes and offered one to Alexeyev, who nodded and accepted the admiral's lighter flame, inhaling the smoke of some foreign brand the admiral had managed to get his hands on. "We were sending *Novosibirsk* and *Voronezh* to the Gulf of Oman to provide a routine escort for the Iranian Navy's testing of our new fast reactor on the Kilo-class submarine *Panther*. But the *Medved' Grizli* worm uploaded into the Iranian computer systems—presumably by the Americans—destroyed the Iranian Navy's ability to send destroyers and frigates to sea with the *Panther* and completely grounded their air force, and so the Iranians sent *Panther* to sea early before the worm could affect submarine computer systems. And you know the rest of the story, Georgy, the *Medved' Grizli* cyberattack crossed over and infected *our* systems, and our surface fleet is still down hard, as are the naval air assets. Somehow we submariners were fortunate and the submarines' systems remained intact, but we have further firewalled them off from the rest of the Navy's systems. All the more reason to get *Kazan* submerged as soon as possible, to avoid this damned cyberattack infecting your boat."

"Yes, Admiral, I'm with you so far. But something worse happened, right, Admiral?"

Zhigunov sighed. "Yes, Georgy. Somewhere in the Gulf of Oman, the Americans managed to steal the *Panther*."

"What?"

"I know. Serious shit, Georgy. We still don't know exactly how or where it happened, but we think an American submarine brought in commandos who took the *Panther* while she was submerged at periscope depth at slow speed. So the operation orders for *Voronezh* and *Novosibirsk* changed from simply escorting *Panther* to test her reactor into a search-and-destroy mission to *sink* the *Panther.* And there must be an American submarine that is escorting her out of the Arabian Sea and into the Western Hemisphere. That's where you and *Kazan* come in. If *Voronezh* or *Novosibirsk* fail, you are the insurance policy. You'll establish a barrier search at Africa's Cape of Good Hope and lie in wait for the *Panther* and her escort submarine to exit the Indian Ocean and enter the South Atlantic. And when they do, put them both on the ocean bottom."

What had followed were three straight days of steaming at 100% reactor power, reactor recirculation pumps in fast speed, making good 35 knots speed-over-ground, from the Kola Peninsula through the GI-UK gap between Greenland, Iceland and the U.K. and into the North Atlantic, their loud transit unavoidably alerting the Americans' sonar web laid at the bottom of the sea, acting as a trip wire and notifying them of when a loud submarine left the northern waters for the Atlantic. Down past the United Kingdom, past France and now at the latitude of the northern shores of Spain. From here, their track took them around western Africa and south to the South Atlantic, to Africa's Cape of Good Hope, where *Kazan* would establish her barrier search.

If *Voronezh* and *Novosibirsk* succeeded, there was nothing for *Kazan* to do but cruise home, the whole mission a fool's errand. But if they failed, it meant the operation would become real for *Kazan*. Very real indeed, Alexeyev thought. Certainly, as a patriot, he wanted his competitor submarines to succeed. But as the captain of *Kazan*, he wouldn't mind if they failed. It could put Alexeyev and his crew into a position of glory. And really, what military commander didn't relish the idea of glory?

Arabian Sea
K-579 *Voronezh*
Monday, June 7; 0320 UTC, 0520 Moscow time

Captain First Rank Boris Novikov put his ten fingers on the keyboard of command console position one. *Voronezh* had driven up to the *Novosibirsk,* both of them deep at two hundred meters keel depth to avoid the noise of the shallow layer with all its merchant shipping this close to the Indian Coast. The MGK-600 sonar's Bolshoi-Feniks submarine-to-submarine telegraphy system was lined up, with the bow sphere preparing to transmit an active focused high-frequency series of pulses in the direction of the *Novosibirsk,* the system's pulses reminding Novikov of a barcode, each letter taking up a half second of rapid pulses. It was so high-frequency and transmitted with such low power levels that outside of five shiplengths, it was virtually undetectable, the system half a century in the making.

Novikov typed:

> **0520 Moscow Time: K579 requests K573 come to periscope depth and establish secure video link with K579.**

It took a moment for *Novosibirsk* to respond.

> **0522 Moscow Time: K573 acknowledges and agrees.**

"Watch Officer," Novikov ordered the navigator, Captain Third Rank Leonid Lukashenko, "take us to periscope depth."

"No stern clearance?"

"No stern clearance. If you maneuver, you could hit the *Novosibirsk*. Just be vigilant for shapes or shadows near the surface."

"Madam First," Lukashenko said to First Officer Anastasia Isakova, "Please darken the command post." Lukashenko was wearing red wrap-around glasses to keep his eyes night-adjusted. By local time, it was still early in the morning. The lights in the room clicked off, the room illuminated only by the wash of light from the control consoles. Lukashenko pulled off his red glasses and pocketed them. "Boatswain! Make your depth twenty-one meters, ten-degree angle maximum, engine stop, report speed seven knots."

The boatswain at the starboard forward console responded, acknowledging the orders. The deck inclined in what seemed a steep angle despite keeping it to only ten degrees, the captain grabbing his teacup.

"Seven knots, depth two hundred and fifty meters, sir."

"Engine ahead slow, turns for four knots." Lukashenko stepped to the portside number two periscope pole and reached into the overhead for a circular ring set into the overhead, the hydraulic controls for raising the periscope. He rotated it counterclockwise and the unit thumped with hydraulics. "Raising number two scope," he called to the silent room. The optics module came slowly out of the deck. Lukashenko stooped and put his eye to the cold rubber eyepiece and pulled the control grips down to their horizontal unstowed position.

"Two hundred meters, sir, angle at up ten."

"Very well." Lukashenko clicked the right grip control for rotation assist, and the scope turned slowly clockwise, the optics on low power. With the right grip he dialed the angle of view upward, but so far it was dark. He continued his slow circles.

"One fifty meters, sir."

"Very well," Lukashenko said. Above, on the surface, it would be dark, but there should be some moonlight, he thought, and just there, to the right, there was a shimmering faint beam of light penetrating down to the deep.

"Fifty meters."

They were hanging up, the boat coming up too slowly. "Boatswain, engine ahead two thirds, turns for seven knots, increase your angle to up fifteen."

"Two thirds, seven knots, up ten. Forty meters. Up twelve."

Lukashenko made several quick sweeps looking upward. With no stern clearance maneuver, they were tempting fate, especially in the crowded seaways here, but there was apparently nothing overhead.

"Thirty-five meters, thirty. Twenty-eight meters. Twenty-seven."

"Ease your angle," Lukashenko ordered, his voice muffled by the periscope optic module. The front of his coveralls were starting to soak through with sweat, the large optics module almost too warm to touch from all the electronics coursing through it. Up above, through the inky blackness of the water, the moonlight's shimmer grew stronger and the undersides of the waves came into view, looking wrinkled and silvery from below, a mirrored surface from a fever dream.

"Twenty-five."

The view approached the waves and then dissolved into foam and a million bubbles.

"Periscope is broaching."

"Twenty-four, twenty-three, twenty-two. Twenty-one meters, sir."

Finally the foam cleared and Lukashenko found himself in a different universe, here where there was the sky above, puffy clouds surrounding the first quarter moon, waves below. To the right of the ship's travel, were the running lights of a large container ship. "Periscope is dry." Lukashenko rotated the periscope through four complete circles, making sure no one other than the container ship was close, but they were alone in the sea. "No close contacts, one distant at three kilometers, container ship."

"Watch Officer," Novikov ordered the navigator, "turn your watch over to Engineer Montorov and get the communications officer to the wardroom to set up the videolink. Assemble the first officer and weapons officer in the wardroom for the link. I'll be down in a moment."

Lukashenko felt a tap on his shoulder and a voice at his ear. "Morning, Luke." It was his friend, the chief engineer, Yevgeny Montorov, who must have been called to the central command post by the captain. Lukashenko turned the periscope straight ahead.

"Low power, on the horizon," he said to Montorov.

"Do you know what's going on?" Montorov whispered,

taking the periscope.

"Videolink with the *Novosibirsk*," Lukashenko said. "Maybe they have news—a detect, maybe."

"I relieve you, sir," Montorov said.

"I stand relieved," Lukashenko replied. "In the command post," he announced loudly, "Captain Second Rank Montorov has the conn."

Lukashenko hurried to the wardroom, where Captain Lieutenant Maksimilian Kovalyov was establishing the secure link, but the screen was filled with snow. Kovalyov reached for the phone in the corner and made a call. "Central, wardroom, I need the multifrequency high-gain antenna. Periscope feed is not sufficient." A distant thump sounded in the room. Hydraulics, Lukashenko thought, raising the MFHG antenna.

The weapons officer, Captain Lieutenant Pyotr Alexandrov, stepped into the room, yawning behind his fist, putting his cup on the table and pulling out his pad computer. Then First Officer Anastasia Isakova entered, finding the tea service and pouring for herself, taking a seat on the long edge of the table opposite the screen mounted on the outboard side. Captain Novikov came in and sat in the center seat directly opposite the screen. Isakova sat to his right. Lukashenko took the seat on the captain's left, with Alexandrov seated to Isakova's right. Lukashenko took out his pad computer and flipped through several screens, waiting for it to be updated by any incoming intelligence being fed from the high gain multifrequency antenna.

The screen's snow cleared and a sharp, high-definition image appeared. On the screen were the senior officers of the *Novosibirsk*. Lukashenko had never met them before, but he knew Captain Novikov and the *Novosibirsk* commander, Orlov, had a long history together, none of it positive.

"Hello again, Captain Orlov," Novikov said, his voice controlled, almost a monotone.

"Captain Novikov," Orlov replied formally, perhaps coldly. "These are my senior officers," he continued. "First Officer Ivan Vlasenko." Vlasenko nodded at the camera. "Navigator Misha Dobryvnik. And Weapons Officer Irina Trusov."

Lukashenko stared at the weapons officer of the *Novosibirsk*.

Irina Trusov was a stunning platinum blonde, her coveralls trying but failing to conceal her expansive breasts. Lukashenko suddenly felt reminded of how long it had been since he was with a beautiful woman. Or any woman, for that matter.

"This is First Officer Anastasia Isakova," Novikov said, "and Navigator Leonid Lukashenko. And Captain Lieutenant Pyotr Alexandrov is our weapons officer. So Boris, why have you called us here? You have news?"

"Good news and bad news, Yuri," Novikov said. "At zero three twenty Moscow time, our MGK detected a very loud submerged contact at bearing two-nine-five. The signal continued for twenty-five minutes, then faded. We believe it to be the *Panther*."

"For God's sake," Orlov said, his voice loud, "that was two hours ago! What have you been doing since?"

Novikov bit his lip in frustration. "The AI system didn't alert us to it until well after the contact's noise shut down. By then, the contact was gone. There was zero bearing rate on the contact—he was far distant. We did a full spectrum sonar scan, but there was nothing. The contact, we believe, was doing thirty knots."

"Wait," Orlov said. "For *Panther* to be going that fast and that loud, he would have had to light off his fast reactor."

"Yes, we believe *Panther* was under nuclear power. The captured and analyzed signal showed steam flow transients and turbine noises. But when we slowed it down, the AI believed it to be a Kilo-class."

"Well, where is he now? What's the data package?"

By data package, Orlov meant the combination of the contact's distance, his speed and the direction of his travel—data that would allow a torpedo hit, since torpedo combat required precision. For a torpedo to inflict damage, it had to get close, and to do that, one would have to put it in the same exact spot in the sea that the enemy would be at a precise moment in the future. It was like trying to hit a flying soccer ball with a tennis ball. You couldn't just throw the ball the at the bearing of the moving soccer ball or you'd miss; you'd have to aim to put the tennis ball at a point in space where the soccer ball would be in the *future* after the tennis ball had time to travel there. And the only way to know where the soccer ball would be in that future moment was to know its data package. There had been much leaked to the media that the new Futlyar torpedoes were so smart that they didn't need a data package, and that they could be launched only knowing the target bearing, yet would still hit the target, but that was disinformation, intentionally injected into the world's open-source information sphere to frighten and deter the Americans. The cold, hard reality was, without a data package, even an advanced Futlyar torpedo would miss.

"We have no data package," Novikov said, his jaw tightening. "Only the bearing and the sound signature. And the sound pressure level."

"No bearing rate?" Orlov frowned. This made no sense. A submarine blasting through the sea, loud and clanking, at thirty knots, would move across the compass bearings as it soared by.

"Constant bearing and very, very distant. Perhaps hundreds of kilometers," Novikov confessed. "And no way to understand where he'll be in the future."

"You're wrong, Boris." Orlov bit his lip, as if he'd wanted to say more, but had stopped himself. "You have a wealth of data to calculate the future position of the *Panther*."

"No we don't," Novikov said, sadly. "It could have been hundreds of kilometers away. Who knows where it is now? All we know is it didn't come down the Indian coastline as we expected. So, we have no idea where it is now."

"Yes you *do*." Orlov shook his head as if in frustration that he had to deal with fools. "Send us all your second captain's data from the half hour before the detection to a half hour after. I want it all."

"Fine," Novikov said, grabbing the phone handset from under the table surface to call the communications officer. He said a few terse words into the phone, no doubt ordering Communications Officer Kovalyov to order the AI system's history module data packaged up for uplink to the satellite and retransmission back to the *Novosibirsk* so that Orlov's crew could further analyze it. "While we wait, you tell me why you think you can come up with a probable data package."

"Listen, Boris, I'm only going to say this once." Orlov's voice was biting, as if having to explain something simple to a hated and slow-witted ex-wife. "You know the location of *Panther* when it left its base at Bandar Abbas and the time it departed. You know its speed as it sailed east-southeast to the mouth of the Gulf of Oman. You know approximately where it was when it got hijacked. From that point, you need to get into the minds of the adversary. The Americans were stealing the Kilo submarine." At the mention of *the Americans*, the *Novosibirsk*'s pretty blonde weapons officer's face grew dark with some hidden fury. Somehow, for her, Lukashenko thought, this was personal. "They mean to escape the Arabian Sea and the Indian Ocean and sail it back to the Western Hemisphere."

Orlov looked up as the communications officer, TK Sukolov came into the room and whispered in Orlov's ear. Orlov nodded and Sukolov withdrew.

"The data stream is aboard for us to analyze now," Orlov said. "As I was saying, the Americans mean to get back to the United States. They may not follow exactly a great-circle route around Africa's Cape of Good Hope, but their approximate path will get them there. Even if they steam slightly eastward, their predominant vector is southward."

Novikov frowned. "They might be going to the Pacific, Yuri, to bring the *Panther* to their Pearl Harbor base in Hawaii. Or their base on Guam."

"No, Boris," Orlov said, shaking his head. "The only way out of the Arabian Sea for someone headed to the Pacific is southeast down the India coastline. We've already proved that incorrect. And even if they *were* headed to the Pacific and decided to avoid breaking eastward until they reached the equator in order to confuse us, their vector would *still* be predominantly southward."

Novikov pursed his lips in thought. "Fine. If they are headed to Africa's southern tip, we should steam at maximum speed to the Cape of Good Hope and catch them there when they transit from the Indian Ocean to the Atlantic."

"Forget that, Boris," Orlov said, still in a tone of lecturing a dullard pupil. "The South Atlantic between the Cape of Good

Hope and the Antarctic coast is bigger than the Arabian Sea by five hundred percent. It's just another haystack for you to cry about losing your needle in. No, we must catch these thieves now, here, *here* in the Arabian Sea." Orlov looked at his navigator, Dobryvnik. "Misha, pair your screen to the videolink and bring up the second captain's command screen."

Onboard the *Novosibirsk,* Navigator Misha Dobryvnik operated his pad computer, seeing the data that had come in from *Voronezh,* the second captain standing by for Orlov to give it commands. The flatpanel video screen split into two displays, the main one the text-entry commands for the onboard AI system, the second a small window showing the videolink and the crew of the *Novosibirsk.* Dobryvnik slid his pad computer over to Orlov. Orlov began typing.

Captain to Second Captain: Analyze data stream to calculate a probability of location, course and speed-of-advance of contact with the following assumptions:

Orlov continued typing in his assumptions, that the *Panther* had continued east-southeast after being captured for some time, then turned to escape the Arabian Sea with a bias toward sailing in the general direction of the Cape of Good Hope and the Atlantic Ocean, then inserted the high-speed run for half an hour, starting 0315 Moscow time until 0345, then slowing back down to a six-knot battery-conserving crawl. Finally he finished by typing:

Display the probability distribution of Panther's present location.

A view of the Arabian Sea flashed on the main screen, looking down from high overhead, the image from a satellite composite with cloudcover removed. The sea was a glistening deep blue, almost black, the Arabian peninsula a bright sand-color, the coast of India light green in the north and a more lush green farther south.

A red dot flashed at their present location, off India's Gulf of Khambht, a few hundred kilometers west of the city of Surat. Soon the second captain started sprinkling white spots into the Arabian Sea, each dot representing a probability calculation. As the dots filled the sea, they formed a narrow, oblong oval running north-to-south, the oval perhaps three hundred kilometers long and perhaps thirty wide. Oddly, as the probability dots littered the sea, a smallish triangle formed north of the oval, the point of it pointing southward, the overall impression of the white probability dots forming what looked like a fish sailing due south. The probability distribution was heaviest in the center of the oval, the probabilities becoming lower as the dots grew less dense toward the fuzzy edges of both shapes. The center of the oval was due west of their present position by about five hundred kilometers.

Orlov typed into the screen, a third window flashing up on the screen showing what he was typing.

Display dimensions of probability envelope and bearing a distance to its center.

The typing screen vanished and the view of the Arabian Sea took up the display again, but now there were dimensions noted in slender yellow lines. North-to-south, the probability oval was 286 kilometers long and 36 kilometers wide, not counting the fish tail. The display showed the oval's center to be at bearing 274 from their present position, at a distance of 487 kilometers. Orlov typed again.

Display the course and speed-of-advance of probability envelope.

The display at the center of the oval formed by the white dots flashed in bold red:

Course 177
Speed 6 knots

Novikov considered for a moment. A transit speed of six knots meant they were running on batteries to keep silent and conserve battery amp-hours. And instead of having to come to periscope depth and snorkel on the diesels to charge the battery bank, they could restart the fast reactor and charge the batteries with the nuclear turbine-generator. Odds were, the reactor at low power levels was quieter than the loud clanking, banging and rumbling of the diesel.

"So we should calculate an interception course from here to the southwest," Novikov said. "We'll position ourselves farther south of the probability oval, and *Panther*—and his escort, if he has one—will drive right into our trap. Then we take him down, and whatever is escorting him. We could be home in three weeks."

"You're half right, Boris," Orlov replied. "*One* of us is going southwest to lie in wait for the probability oval to drive into a barrier search, but a barrier search formed by one of us, not two. Whoever doesn't go to the southern intercept hold point will be pursuing a course to arrive at a point *north* of the probability oval, then turn south to overrun the oval from the north. Submarine one catches *Panther* from the south while submarine two attacks him from the north. A rundown, if you are a fan of American baseball."

"I don't know American baseball, Yuri, but this sounds like a circular firing squad. Any torpedo fired by the northern attack submarine at the *Panther* to the south could home in on and destroy the southern submarine. One of us could perish by friendly fire."

"That won't happen, Boris," Orlov said confidently. "And even if it does, the Futlyar torpedoes have a TCM feature."

TCM stood for torpedo countermeasure. On the video screen, Novikov made a sour face. Dobryvnik knew what he had to be thinking, that the TCM mode had never worked in submarine vs. submarine testing, never, but the bureaucrats in the weapons testing labs swore with the new software upload, it would magically gain the capability to intercept and destroying incoming American, Chinese and French torpedoes—assuming that software upload wasn't as hacked as the compromised surface and air force computer systems. And on this mission, they might well be facing an attack from *Russian* torpedoes, the older UGST units loaded onto the *Panther.* Well, Dobryvnik thought, this mission might well bring those lab-jacketed idiots the evidence they lacked. Of success or failure, although if the TCM subroutines failed, who would live to tell the tale?

"So who goes north and who goes south?" Novikov asked. Obviously the plum combat position was lying in wait to the south, waiting for the *Panther* and her escort to drive up on them. The boat to the north would be in a tail-chase. Odds are, detecting *Panther* on her stealthy transit on her batteries would be insanely difficult, and if she were escorted by a Virginia-class U.S submarine, that ship would be even more quiet—although the nuclear-powered escort would emit tonals detectable by the MGK-600's narrowband processors. In a world of loud ocean noise, detecting a diesel boat on her batteries and a stealthy nuclear attack submarine would be an impossible mission. Unless, Novikov thought, the *Panther* lit off his fast reactor, in which case he'd blast out transients and narrowband tonals—the Kilo's fast reactor module was not sound-mounted for stealth. It was just a test platform. Detection might be aided if *Panther* fired torpedoes—or God help them, the Americans fired torpedoes. Submarines might well be stealthy, but torpedoes were loud. The technicians had worked on quieting them for decades and come up with nothing. If one wanted a weapon to travel fast, one gave up on stealth. There was a 'stealth mode' for the new Futlyar torpedo, but all it had turned out to be was making the weapon crawl at fifteen knots instead of screaming in at fifty. But an ultra-slow torpedo had a higher chance of missing, giving the target too much time to randomly maneuver or counterdetect the incoming torpedo.

Still, there were ways around the impossible problem. A cruise missile dropping a depth charge from overhead was one way. A supercavitating torpedo was another—it was indeed much louder than a conventional torpedo, being an underwater rocket, but it traveled so fast that transit time was minimal, meaning that evasion time was also reduced.

There was no doubt, though, the northern position would

go to the lesser of the submarine captains.

"We should go to the south," Novikov asserted, clenching his jaw. "We made the initial detection."

Orlov made a dismissive noise and rolled his eyes. "You also failed to realize it until, what, an hour later, and then you failed to analyze it properly—that all fell on us. No, Boris, you'll go to the north and *we'll* go south. And for God's sake, don't launch torpedoes at ghosts or shadows. You make damned sure you're shooting at the *Panther* or the American and not at us. You got that?"

Not wanting to be further humiliated in front of his crew, Novikov decided to accept Orlov's insistent proposal with grace.

"Fine, Yuri, but the same goes for you. Don't you shoot northward unless you have a damned good data package on the targets. Preferably, hit them with active sonar before you shoot—or after, and wire-guide steer the weapons to the targets."

"Leave the tactics to me, Boris. After I and my crew destroy these targets, we'll allow you to claim victory with us."

Novikov frowned. Orlov was being even more of an asshole than he was face-to-face. He supposed Orlov blamed Novikov for Natalia leaving and eventually forming a relationship with Novikov, but there had been almost a year between the ending of one relationship and the beginning of another. Novikov had *not* stolen the woman, only accepted her affection much later when offered it. Was that morally wrong? Perhaps it would have been if the other man had been a friend, but Orlov had hated Novikov ever since the torpedo incident of their youth. Besides, it was moot point now, because Natalia had left Novikov and moved on. Novikov shook his head. The sooner they ended this call, the better. Then the rest of the mission he could forget about Orlov.

"So, Boris, I've calculated my intercept course, speed and waiting time for the probability oval to reach me. I've bracketed the speed of the target, using an initial assumption of a six knot transit, but I also laid in a nine knot transit in case *Panther* decides to speed up when he's underway on nuclear power. If *Panther* transits at six knots for eighteen hours on his batteries, then speeds up to eighteen knots for six hours while charging his batteries, his overall speed-of-advance is nine knots, so we accounted for that. I plan on using a speed of twenty-eight knots, enough to be swift while still remaining silent in natural circulation reactor loops. That gives me a course of three-zero-nine and a transit time of eleven hours and a waiting time-on-station of seven hours if the target is transiting at six knots, and a wait of one hour if he's going an average of nine knots with a sprint-and-drift tactic. That means contact time is somewhere between twelve hours and eighteen hours from now. Moscow time, that's somewhere between eighteen hundred and midnight tonight. By the early hours of tomorrow, Boris, we will be writing the after-action reports to the Admiralty."

Novikov nodded. Orlov continued.

"Now, Boris, you should do the same kind of calculations to place yourselves sufficiently close to the tail of the probability oval so that you cross the oval's north end at eighteen hundred hours today. You have the shorter distance to travel, so you can approach slower than twenty-eight knots. You will be more stealthy than we will be. When you get to the northern envelope of the probability oval, you should transit into it heading south at a speed of nineteen knots—this will be faster than a possible *Panther* sprint speed, and is still stealthy with natural circulation. You should have your AI calculate contact time based on that—if it is earlier than midnight, trail in stealth until then, and at midnight, open fire. That will give *Panther* time to drive into our barrier search, and we can attack in coordination. Is all that understood? Are we in agreement?"

"No, we are *not* in agreement," Novikov said, "If I have a solid detect on *Panther* at a time before you're on-station, I'm taking my shot. I'm firing at him. *You're* the one who wanted to go south for the glory position and left me with the low-probability tail-chase of the northern approach zone. It's entirely possible, Yuri, that your entry into this battle will start with *you* detecting the sound of *my* torpedoes exploding and the target sinking. So, is all *that* understood?"

Orlov pursed his lips. "Fine. Then good luck to us both."

"Wait," Novikov said. "We need an emergency distress signal."

"Use four loud, three-second low-frequency pulses from the MGK's spherical array active. It's not stealthy, but I assume such a situation of distress would dispense with stealth. If possible, launch a coded radio buoy out the countermeasure ejector."

"Agreed," Novikov replied. "And I also agree—good luck to us both. Anything else from you or your crew, Captain Orlov?"

"Nothing from our side, Captain Novikov. Good hunting."

The screen winked out. Novikov smirked at Lukashenko, relieved that the confrontational meeting with Orlov was finally over. He picked up the phone handset from its cradle bolted to the underside of the table and punched the button for central control on the handset.

"Watch Officer," Novikov said, "depart periscope depth and proceed to three hundred meters, course west, speed twenty. You'll get new sailing orders from the navigator in a few minutes."

Novikov replaced the phone handset and looked at Lukashenko. "Luke, calculate the approach vector to get us in position on the north."

Lukashenko input the geometry problem into the second captain. "Sir, it comes out that we need to decide which speed the target is traveling. If he's going six knots, we would steer course two-eight-nine with a speed of twenty-four knots. If he's making an average of nine knots, we'd steer course two-nine-six. With oval-entry at eighteen hundred, turning south at nineteen knots, we have three different scenarios, Captain." Lukashenko frowned. "If *Panther* is going six knots, time-on-contact for the center of the oval is midnight. If he's going nine knots, contact time is zero two hundred hours. But if he's going eighteen knots on a sprint, it would take us four days to catch up with the center of the oval at nineteen knots approach speed." Lukashenko tapped his pen. "This is bad, Captain. We'll be much later to the battle than *Novosibirsk*. They'll take down *Panther* before we're even anywhere near being on-station."

"Tail-chases are almost always futile, Luke," Novikov said, leaning over Lukashenko's pad computer. "That's why the northern position is a loser. So, recalculate with new assumptions. Absolute maximum speed run to the oval north boundary, thirty-five knots."

"But, Captain, that will mean departing natural circulation and shifting reactor circulation pumps to fast speed."

"So be it, Luke. We speed to the oval, then turn south, and slow down to twenty knots to get closer to the oval's center. We'll drift five minutes out of every fifteen at four knots as we approach the oval's center. Now, with that set of assumptions, recalculate time-on-target."

Lukashenko went back to work with the second captain. "So, Captain, assuming a maximum speed run at thirty-five knots, that gets us to the northern boundary of the oval a bit under eight hours from now, slightly before fourteen hundred hours—four hours before the earliest time the *Novosibirsk* could start detecting the *Panther*. Then we'd commence our sprint-and-drift search. There's a good chance that in those four hours, we'd detect *Panther* first." He slid his pad computer over, showing the calculation and the resulting course to the probability circle's northern boundary.

"Excellent," Novikov said, finding the phone under the table and calling central again. Into the phone, he said, "Watch Officer, change course to two-eight-eight and increase speed to thirty-five knots, and yes, I realize that means fast speed reactor circulation pumps. After seven hours and thirty-six minutes, slow to four knots and turn due south."

The phone crackled with the watch officer's response, and the deck tilted as the *Voronezh* sped up. The deck began to tremble violently as the speed increased, and four loud booming noises sounded in the sea as her reactor coolant pumps sped up to fast speed, the check valves in the piping loops slamming thunderous noises into the sea. Novikov turned and reached for the tea service and poured himself another cup, smiling. This would be a good watch, he thought. And the afternoon watch promised to be even better. Perhaps they should roll out a gourmet meal for lunch to celebrate, but then he thought it would be bad luck to celebrate before the kill.

But kill there would be. By the evening watch, two submarines would lie broken and bleeding on the bottom of the Arabian Sea, and Novikov was absolutely certain that his submarine would not be one of those two.

26

Arabian Sea
B-902 *Panther*
Monday, June 7; 0400 UTC

Lieutenant Anthony Pacino found Lieutenant Dieter Dankleff in the central command post, reclining in the command seat outboard of the forward part of control, nestled securely aft of the number two periscope

"What's up, Patch?" Dankleff asked, yawning. "You're up early. Someone swim over your watery grave again?"

Pacino shook his head. "Just making sure you're awake, U-Boat. I'm going to do a tour, see how everyone's doing. But one thing *is* on my mind."

"Let me guess, the state of the battery charge? We're at sixty percent, with the reactor cooking away. Although that bitch has to be noisy. I looked at raising charging voltage to charge the battery bank faster, but it would generate a lot more hydrogen, and hydrogen is not healthy for children and other living things. Think *Hindenburg*. Think *Challenger*. Not a good thing in a confined space filled with electrical equipment and sparks."

"And with Alexie chain-smoking. He must have brought enough cartons of cigarettes to burn through three packs a day for a month." Abakumov would be standing watch aft in the nuclear control room, hopefully sober.

"And enough vodka as well."

"That won't last as long, since now he has to share."

"Damned shame," Dankleff grinned.

"So, U-Boat. All okay here?"

"Hey. Officer-in-Charge U-Boat has the bubble. You're as safe as in Mommy's arms."

"Good to know," Pacino said, knocking his academy ring twice on the periscope pole. "I'll relieve you at oh-six," he said, turning and walking aft.

He stepped into the navigation alcove and turned on the desk lamp above the chart, which was taped down to the table surface, a drafting machine arm laid pointing north-south. Pacino glanced at the readout of the *Panther*'s inertial navigation display, the primitive system the equivalent of what the U.S. Navy had used in the 1970s. Crude, but effective enough to pinpoint their distance within a few thousand meters. If corrected daily with a navigation fix from the Russian GPS satellite constellation, it could collapse the fix error circle down to perhaps a hundred meters. Good enough to avoid submerged sea mountains, but not good enough to approach a port submerged. Pacino plotted the inertial nav's position on the chart, then laid a pencil line down on it pointing south, dialing their present course in the drafting machine's protractor to course 177, almost due south, their latitude roughly twenty degrees, thirty minutes north, 350 nautical miles west of India's Gulf of Khambht and the city of Surat, their longitude almost in the middle of the triangle of the Arabian Sea, due south of Karachi, Pakistan, which was 280 nautical miles west of their previously planned track down the west coastline of India.

They were making excellent time now, what with kicking up their speed to eighteen knots during the midwatch battery charge. Pacino, the unofficial navigator of the journey, had been considering executing a zig to drive farther east, to confuse any opponent of their intent to drive to the Cape of Good Hope and into the Atlantic, but instinct was whispering in his ear to keep driving south and escape the Arabian Sea. Leaving the scene of the crime was definitely the best course for the moment. He looked down at the chart's depiction of the Arabian Sea, thinking, *where are you, Vermont?* It was the midwatch, and on the *Vermont,* his friend the chief engineer, Elvis Lewinsky, would be on the conn, hopefully tracking *Panther,* keeping her safe. It bothered Pacino that there was no easy way to communicate with her, but submarines were designed to prowl alone, not in wolfpacks. World War II tactics hadn't survived into the nuclear age.

Although, the Iranian captain, Resa Ahmadi, had shown Pacino and sonar chief Albanese a feature of the ship's MGK-400 sonar system, which could be tied into the MG-519 Arfa mine-detection and under-ice sonar to broadcast rapid high frequency pulses. But the system was essentially useless, as the language was encrypted. It would be like trying to communicate by generating a note consisting of a barcode. The receiver would have no idea what had been sent, just a string of long and short pulses. Useless.

With that thought, Pacino wandered into the doorway of the sonar enclosure and found Chief Albanese deep in thought, rotating a circular knob, his other hand on one of the ears of his headset. The console's buttons, knobs and the single large hand-crank in the center had all been recently labeled by Albanese with masking tape and permanent marker in English.

"Hey, Chief," Pacino said. "Any progress figuring this thing out?"

Albanese removed his headset and tossed it to the side in frustration. "It's from the stone age, Mr. Patch. No towed array, just a hull flank array for high frequency narrowband, which is rendered fucking useless when we operate the reactor. Steaming on batteries, it's a bit improved, but not good enough to detect *Vermont*, even though I know all her emitted tonal frequencies."

"*Vermont* is still a needle in a haystack, no matter how much you know about the shape and color of the needle," Pacino offered. "Was Captain Ahmadi any help getting you into the sonar system?"

"He knows squat about it, sir. I had him translate some of the tech manual, but it's all knobology, not tactical employment. Apparently the Iranian Navy trains their sonar techs with tribal knowledge, passed down from one generation to the next. Nothing written down."

Pacino nodded. "Not all that different from us. I never could find anything on the Q-10's tactical employment. I had to suffer through checkouts from *you* with miserable dozens of lookups every time it came to tactics."

Albanese smiled mischievously. "But you learned it all the better that way, didn't you, sir?"

"That I did, Chief. That I did. Well, the only comfort I can give you is to keep plugging away at it. If anyone can figure this bitch out, it's you, Whale."

"Thanks, Mr. Patch. You taking the zero six hundred watch?"

"Yeah, I thought I'd do an extended pre-watch tour and grab a bucket of that Iranian coffee first."

"Oh yeah, rocket fuel. Do me a favor, L-T, bring me up a cup when you brew the pot."

"Sure thing, Chief." Pacino knocked his ring on the doorjamb twice and walked aft to the ladderway to the middle level, turning forward along the passageway leading to the forward compartment, passing the wardroom. He went in and found it empty. Not surprising, he thought, with it being the midwatch. He decided to continue forward to the torpedo room, along the passageway until he reached the round hatch, ducked through it and stepped up the short ladderway to the upper level, which was absolutely crammed with shiny green torpedoes, a small catwalk running down the center between rack-stored weapons and the six torpedo tubes. At the forward end, at a port-side console, he found Lieutenant Muhammad Varney deep in conversation with the Iranian captain, Ahmadi.

"What is this, a conspiracy?" Pacino joked. "You two planning a mutiny?"

Boozy Varney smiled, as did Resa Ahmadi.

"Mr. Patch," Ahmadi said. "Shouldn't you be sleeping?"

Pacino shook his head. "Who can sleep when things are this exciting?"

"Yeah, exciting," Varney said dismissively.

"So, Boozy, where do we stand with getting the torpedoes operational?"

"They're ready to go. Firing panel function checks are sat. We checked the weapons we could access. All good."

"What's the loadout?"

"We have sixteen UGST Fizik-1 units. Interesting, they have Mark 48 similarities but seem to have features the Mark 48 sadly doesn't. Tubes one to five are tube-loaded UGST Fizik-1 torpedoes. Captain Ahmadi says they're fire-and-forget weapons. They've got wake-homing, infrared, passive and active sonar. Or at least, I hope so."

"How fast can you shoot and recycle? Are there common firing mechanisms that limit how fast you can shoot the tubes?"

"No," Ahmadi said. "Each tube firing mechanism is independent. You could actually fire the entire bank of six at the same moment, although that's not recommended. The wake from one would tumble another, or the Venturi effect could suck one weapon into another, making them both tumble. But firing at two-second intervals seems to work well."

"How long to reload and recycle the firing mechanisms?"

"There is no mechanism recycling needed. For the next weapon bank fire, we're just limited by time to shut the outer door, depressurize, vent and drain the tube, open the inner door and push in a new weapon. Then shut the breach door, flood, pressurize and open the muzzle door."

"Time to do all that?"

"Our record is ninety seconds," Ahmadi said, "but that's with a full crew in the torpedo room. A highly trained crew. With us? Better count on at least three or four minutes."

Pacino bit his lip. That wouldn't be good enough. "We may have to shoot one at a time while draining and reloading, and that would continuously dump the room in the minimum amount of time."

"You planning on a big battle, Lipstick?" Varney said, his eyebrow raised.

"Let's put it this way, Boozy. If we find ourselves under fire from an opposition force, we're going to shoot everything we have at it. We may hit nothing, but it will add to the confusion. The fog of war. And who knows. We could get lucky and take down an attacker by dumb luck. Or by the Russian designs of these UGSTs. But one thing's for certain. If I have to die on this mission, I intend to die with an empty torpedo room."

Varney laughed. "Wow, that's like a famous naval saying,

something John Paul Jones or Horatio Nelson would say. Or like your father with his famous quote, *I still have one torpedo and two main engines.* Easy Eisenhart told me there's a big brass plaque with that quote mounted on the wall of Memorial Hall at the Naval Academy. Are you trying to outdo Pacino Senior?"

Pacino smiled. "Boozy, no one, and I mean no one, will ever outdo Admiral Michael Pacino."

"Are you worried that if you 'shoot the room,' as you say, you might hit the *Vermont* with one of your UGSTs?"

"*Vermont* knows enough to stay out of the way of a volley of our warshots," Pacino said, "and in the worst case, they could activate the Mark 48 Mod Nine's torpedo countermeasure mode." Pacino put his hand on one of the shiny green torpedoes. "These UGST torpedoes—do they have an anti-torpedo countermeasure mode?" Pacino asked. *Were they good enough to shoot down an incoming torpedo?*

"Sadly, no, Mr. Patch," Ahmadi said. "We have an older version of the attack software. But for that we've tried using the VA-111 Shkval torpedo. It's loaded in tube six."

"Shkval," Pacino said. "That's the peroxide-fueled supercavitating torpedo, right?"

"Yes, Mr. Patch."

"Yeah," Varney said, wiping sweat off his greasy forehead. "The torpedo that killed the *Kursk*."

Ahmadi looked at Varney, startled. "They told us the *Americans* sank the *Kursk*."

Varney moved his hand as if batting away an annoying fly from his face. "The hell we did. We had nothing to do with that. *Kursk*'s torpedo room blew up right after her Shkval unit exploded after a peroxide leak. She went down from her own friendly fire."

Ahmadi shook his head, frowning. "The Russians *insisted* that American SEAL commandos planted a smart mine on *Kursk*'s bow before she sailed, programmed with an algorithm that measured time from port departure, time from submergence, depth, and transients like a torpedo door opening, then blew up the bow when the algorithm was satisfied. The torpedo room exploding eliminated all forensic evidence of the American mine."

Varney looked at Pacino, pursing his lips and shaking his head. "That's a dumb-ass tall tale designed by the Russians to keep the blame off themselves," he said. "Besides, why the hell would *we* do that? It was peacetime. And how the hell could anyone believe that nonsense with zero proof?"

"According to the Russians," Ahmadi said, "when things warmed up under Yeltsin and Clinton, during a Russia-America general officer party, a Russian admiral tanked up on vodka and cocaine walked up to his opposite number in the American Navy and admitted they sank your submarine *Stingray* under the polar icecap, out of revenge for the supposed American sinking of the Soviet submarine *K-129*, and he apologized. Seven years later, the U.S. Navy extracted *their* revenge."

Pacino stared at the Iranian officer, stunned. The submarine *Stingray* had been commanded by his father's father, and the sinking's board of inquiry insisted she'd gone down in the Atlantic near the Azores from a defect in her own torpedo, which experienced a hot-run in her torpedo room and exploded, blowing up all the weapons in the bow and violently sinking her. Other competing theories, still hotly debated decades later, imagined the ship had suffered a battery explosion, another theory stating that her screw and its drive shaft fell out of the hull, opening up a huge hole in the engineroom. But being intentionally targeted by the Russians? Under the secret reaches of the Arctic Ocean's ice canopy? No wonder Ahmadi thought the Americans had a motive to sink the *Kursk*.

"Wow. Apology *not* accepted," Varney said. "But still, no evidence the U.S. Navy took down the *Kursk*. It's still a big-assed excuse."

"The *evidence* the Russians quoted was that after the wreck of the *Kursk* was pulled out of the Barents Sea and lay blown to pieces in a Russian drydock, the Russian admiral who apologized for the *Stingray* sinking received a handwritten note accompanying an expensive bottle of American Pappy Van Winkle Kentucky bourbon, from the American admiral to whom he made the confession. The note reportedly read, 'Thank you for your candid admission. *Now* we're even.'"

Varney stared at Ahmadi, his mouth half open.

"Anyway," Pacino said, trying to shake off the shock of Ahmadi's story, "if we can return to today's mission, gentlemen? Captain Ahmadi, you said you employed the Shkval torpedo against attacking torpedoes. How did it perform?"

"It was mixed news, Mr. Patch. One time out of six it destroyed an incoming torpedo, but we think that was a coincidence. We've taken to calling the Shkval 'the 53-centimeter evasion device.' It's so loud and so fast that anyone hearing it would be well advised to get out of its search cone fast and run away. Meanwhile, we get out of the area going the other direction."

Pacino thought. "How many Shkvals do we have?"

"Only two," Ahmadi said.

"Boozy, take the UGST out of tube five and load five with the second Shkval," Pacino ordered.

"You sure, boss?"

"Yeah. Worst case, if things get hot, we can use the Shkvals to make off hull noise, a mini-blue-out diversion, and get the hell out of town."

"Sure. It'll take a while and make some noise," Varney said. "We have to move the entire room's load-out. The second one is buried deep on the bottom of the starboard side. I need to get Dankleff's permission."

"Check out the second Shkval before you load it. If that sonofabitch is leaking peroxide, I want to jettison it. And check out the tube six Shkval also. A single drop of leaking peroxide, I want that damned thing on the sea bottom, not us."

"I'll have a report up to you on the conn when you get on watch."

"Thanks, Boozy. Captain Ahmadi, can you come with me for a minute?"

Pacino took Ahmadi aside. "I'm worried about the air banks," Pacino said. "Do you use high pressure air for torpedo-firing?"

"No, Mr. Patch. The firing mechanisms are electrical with pumps and a seawater tank that auto-compensates."

"But emergency blowing to surface the boat requires a full air bank. How much air do we have in the banks after the emergency surface we did?"

"Let's go see," Ahmadi said.

"Let's stop for coffee," Pacino said. "I'm exhausted."

"As am I." They paused in the wardroom and Pacino brewed the pot under instruction from Ahmadi. The Iranian was not allowed to touch cooking paraphernalia for fear of poisoning the invading boarding party, despite his cooperation with the mission so far. When the pot was full, Pacino poured for himself and Ahmadi, then a third cup for Albanese.

They climbed the ladder to the upper level, Pacino handing the coffee to the grateful sonarman, then walked forward to The Million Valve Manifold. Pacino glanced up at the yellow masking tape he'd put on the valves for the blow system, one marked FWD EMBT BLOW, the other AFT EMBT BLOW, the EMBT for emergency main ballast tank, the term used in the U.S. Navy.

He and Ahmadi walked forward into the command post, waving at Dankleff. Ahmadi stopped at the starboard side pos two console. The panel's gauges and switches had all been relabeled in English with masking tape and black marker. Ahmadi pointed up at four large air pressure gauges, the two on the left labeled FWD AIR BANK, one adding the word PORT, the other adding the word STBD. The two on the right had been labeled AFT AIR BANK, port and starboard. And they all read close to zero.

"They're all depleted," Ahmadi said. "Empty."

Pacino turned to Dankleff, who had risen out of the command seat and stretched, yawning.

"U-Boat, we have to charge the air banks."

"You're worried about being able to emergency surface," Dankleff said. "But using the air compressor's going to make some major noise."

"We're noisy already going eighteen knots on the reactor," Pacino said. "We're going to have to go up to periscope depth and put up the induction mast and light off the air compressors until the banks are full. Captain Ahmadi, how long to charge all four banks?"

Ahmadi considered. "Twenty to thirty minutes. Maybe less depending on atmospheric conditions on the surface."

"I hate to make that much noise for that long," Dankleff

said, frowning. "That, along with all the noise you and Boozy are making moving weapons around, for fuck's sake. And if you rise above the thermal layer, you're bringing the reactor into the narrow sound channel topside. Along with the banging and clanking air compressors. We could easily be detected by aircraft or surface warships. It's a hell of a risk, Patch."

Pacino shook his head. "It has to be done, U-Boat. We have to prepare for the worst. That's why I'm getting the torpedo room ready."

"Yeah, Boozy phoned me for permission to move weapons and tube-load a second Shkval. He told me your famous naval saying." U-Boat stood at mock attention and unzipped the top of his coveralls, put his hand inside the opening, raising his chin in an imitation of Napoleon and said in a pretentious and melodramatic British accent, *'If die I must on this mission, die I shall with an empty torpedo room.'*"

"You know what, U-Boat?" Pacino said, trying to keep a straight face.

"What, Lipstick?"

"Go fuck yourself. And when you're done with that, get this bucket of bolts the hell up to periscope depth and raise and drain the goddamned induction mast."

Dankleff saluted sloppily. "Yes, sir, Mr. Assistant Officer-in-Charge, *sir!*"

Washington, DC, USA
White House Situation Room
Monday, June 7; 0510 UTC, 0010 EST

CIA Director Margo Allende put two cups of strong black coffee on the table and sat down next to National Security Advisor Michael Pacino. Pacino looked up at her gratefully.

"How long has it been since you slept?" Allende asked softly.

"Not much since Camp David. And then none since the message came in from *Panther.*"

Allende nodded sympathetically. "Listen. My house is way out near Langley, but I own a crash pad, a little stone townhouse not far from here, for nights like this. You say the word, I'll whisk you to my guest room and you can get a few hours of sleep, just ten minutes away from the White House and fifteen from the Pentagon. Crisp, clean sheets and a nice fluffy comforter. You'll sleep like a baby."

"No, but thank you, Margo." Pacino said, rubbing the stubble on his chin. His tie was at half-mast and his once-upon-a-time starched white shirt's sleeves were rolled up, his suit jacket across the room, draped across an empty chair. "I want to be here in case there's any update." He looked at Allende, a bit startled to find her big blue eyes fixed on him. She quickly looked down to her pad computer, but there had been something in her eyes. She knew something she wasn't telling him, he thought. "So. *Is* there an update?"

Allende clicked on the large flatpanel screen opposite their chairs. A view of the globe from space appeared, driven by Allende's pad computer. She zoomed in so that the Arabian Sea was shown in screen center. She tapped her screen, and two closely-spaced red dots began flashing, close to the Indian coastline, near Surat and the Indian Gulf of Khambht, the latitude line showing them at north twenty degrees, thirty minutes.

"These are the periscopes of the two Russian Yasen-M-class submarines that were dispatched to chase after *Panther*," she said. "We're fortunate that both transponders are still working. They tend to go offline after a few weeks. I guess we haven't designed them with sufficient robustness to withstand the seawater and the pressure changes. And the temperature swings from the icy cold Barents Sea to the near boiling Arabian Sea. But both are still online."

Pacino looked at Allende. "You know where the *Panther* is. Margo, you have to tell me. Read me into the program, whatever Operation *Blue Hardhat*'s equivalent is for the Iranian Navy that could allow you to know where *Panther* is now. For God's sake, I think I have a need to know."

"I can't do that without Carlucci's signoff, and he's sleeping until zero seven hundred, with strict instructions not to wake him unless there are weapons released."

"Margo, please." Pacino looked at the CIA director. She

usually kept her hair back in a stern bun and wore oversized eighties glasses, as if she intended to make herself look homely, but tonight she'd let her auburn hair down to her shoulders, and it gleamed in the lights of the room, making her look like she could be a model for a conditioner ad. And she'd put on eye makeup and lip gloss and lost the glasses. And unlike her usual frumpy frock, tonight she was wearing a tight pencil dress, gray cashmere, with a thin black belt at her waist, with black tall pumps, the ensemble revealing a slender but beautifully curving feminine form. For the first time Pacino saw her as a woman, and realized she was a stunning beauty. He'd never seen her as anything other than the chief spook before this moment. He must be suffering from too long without sleep, he thought. He was getting punch drunk. That, or what was happening with his soon-to-be-ex-wife Colleen was being processed in his subconscious as time went on.

Allende got up and went to the credenza behind them and found an old-fashioned laser pointer. She resumed her seat, the stirring of the air near her wafting her scent into Pacino's nostrils, a faint trace of perfume, something French, something that had to be wickedly expensive, he thought. No doubt, he'd been awake far too long, or he was losing his sanity.

Allende pointed the laser pointer at the screen and hit the button, and a bright yellow point of light appeared due south of Karachi, Pakistan, some three hundred nautical miles due west of the red dots. As quickly as the yellow dot appeared, it went out, but it had engraved itself onto Pacino's mind.

"Jesus, Margo, they're at the same goddammed latitude!" Pacino breathed.

"Relax, Patch. There's two hundred eighty miles between them. Even if the Russians had *Panther*'s exact position and speed and raced at flank speed to where *Panther* would be at the exact time of the Russian's arrival, they're twelve hours out. Maybe more. They couldn't be within weapons range before lunch. And it's just after midnight now. Nothing is happening for hours, Patch. And good news—the Russians were at periscope depth for over half an hour, and all during that time they were headed northwest. The wrong direction. When we look at possible outcomes, we deal in probabilities, Patch, and the probabilities here favor *Panther* escaping with the Russians being none the wiser."

"Unless *Panther* does something loud and the Russians get a transient noise detection," Pacino said. "With a detection of the Russians this accurate, can't we vector in a Pegasus P-8 patrol aircraft? Two Mark 50 torpedoes dropped out of a Pegasus, those Yasen-M-class submarines are history."

"You know those aren't the rules of engagement, Patch. We can't attack Russian submarines for just existing in the general area. We can only fire on them if they're actively trying to stop the *Panther*. You're cheating."

You ain't cheatin', you ain't tryin', Pacino thought, the motto of the first *Devilfish* before she perished in the Arctic Ocean.

"Can't we inform the *Vermont* of the Yasen positions?"

"Already done. *Vermont* knows." Allende placed her hand on Pacino's bare forearm. Her hands were cool and soft, her nails done in a French manicure. "I still think you should come with me and get a few hours' sleep."

Pacino shook his head. "Something is bothering me. Something doesn't add up," he said. He looked up at the display. "If the Russians are serious about finding and stopping the *Panther*, why haven't they overflown the Arabian Sea with maritime patrol aircraft, their equivalent to our antisubmarine warfare P-8 Pegasus planes? Why no dropping of sonobuoys from aircraft or helicopters? And where are the antisubmarine destroyers and frigates? For both the Russians and Iranians? Margo, the Arabian Sea should be so full of sonobuoys you should be able to walk from India to Oman without getting your feet wet. There should be more warships in the sea than merchant ships. It doesn't make sense. I know you made that vague promise that the only opposition force would be Russians submarines, but I find that hard to believe."

Allende smiled mysteriously at him.

"Oh, no, not *another* classified program I'm not read into yet," he groaned.

"I can neither confirm nor deny, Patch, but there is something you should have noticed in the NewsFiles." Allende clicked through her pad computer, finally finding what she was seeking. She paired her unit to the flatpanel display next to the Arabian Sea orbital display. "We leaked this juicy info at four o'clock yesterday, in time for it to make the national evening news."

It was a news segment filmed by Satellite News Network. SNN newscaster Brett Wolverine sat at a news desk, a graphic of a huge naval base taken from a helicopter or a drone shown behind him. Wolverine, as always, was clad in an expensive suit with a wide tie cinched neatly up to his throat, clean-shaven, his hair coiffed in a hundred-dollar haircut, his deep voice characteristic and sometimes satirized on variety comedy shows, or even featured in fake news bulletins in movie thrillers.

"We have reports in," he began, "of a major cyberattack conducted against the Russian Federation Navy, an attack so severe that it took down fleet computers in every segment of their operation, including supply chain and logistics, communications, command and control and even the operating systems within their ships allowing them to navigate and maneuver. Also paralyzed, reportedly, are Russian naval air force units, including fighter jets, transport jets, tankers and antisubmarine patrol aircraft, including Russian military air traffic control systems. Russian Defense Minister Radoslav Konstantinov commented Tuesday that the cyberattack was definitely caused by a nation-state, not the work of cyber criminals, hackers or so-called 'hacktivists.' When asked if he suspected the American CIA or NSA, Konstantinov stated that it was a crime committed by the Israeli Mossad, and that Russia would retaliate. More on this story from our Moscow correspondent Monica Eddlestien—"

Allende clicked off the display. "It's just more of the same. Wild speculation as to who caused it and why."

Pacino looked at her. "Did we put the Israelis up to doing this?"

"The worm didn't hit Russia directly. The Mossad inserted it into *Iranian* systems, the first priority being to paralyze the Iranian Navy's frigates and destroyers and their naval air assets, which would allow the *Vermont* to escape with the *Panther*. Israel and the Mossad have a long-running beef with the Iranians. Anything Israel can do to mess with Iran, they're going to do. Apparently Mossad saw the Iranians putting a nuclear reactor into the Kilo submarine—and no, we didn't tip them off, they flew their own drone overhead and figured it all out, with the help of what we suspect are on-the-ground human assets. An Iranian nuclear submarine is a direct threat to Israel, and they were willing and able to help sabotage the Iranian Navy.

"So we gave the Mossad the virus software. The Iranians had ordered a batch of new printers for their navy administration building. And as usual, printers are useless without downloading the drivers from the vendor. And when they downloaded the drivers, the worm came in with them. The worm spread from administrative networks to the military command-and-control networks and boom, airplanes are grounded and surface ships become little more than paperweights while sparing their submarines' networks, as intended. Then the fun really started. The Russians are too cozy with the Iranians, and their networks tie together in the administrative sphere, and the worm found the interlink and jumped into the Russian network. Then, bang, the Russian surface navy is dead, as is anything the Russian Navy flies. So no Russian MPA aircraft will be coming our way. See, Patch, your good friend Margo is taking very good care of you." She put her hand on his forearm as she said that, and he felt a spark from the touch.

He looked at her. "That changes everything. Well done."

"Plus," Allende said, "it was perfectly timed. When the Iranians saw the hack taking down their surface ships and naval aircraft, they immediately sent the *Panther* to sea early, hoping it would escape any second wave of the cyberattack. That's why it jumped early before the Russian escort submarines arrived in-theater."

Pacino nodded. "This operation has a lot more moving parts than I thought." He covered his mouth and yawned. "Sorry," he said. "You're not boring me, I'm just running on fumes."

"Come on, Patch. You're out of gas. Come with me. I'll have one of our guys go to your Annapolis house and bring fresh clothes. They'll be ready for you by dawn's early light."

Pacino looked at her, her ocean blue eyes imploring him. "Those clean, crisp sheets and fluffy comforter are sounding pretty good right now," he admitted.

He fell asleep in Allende's car, waking when she rolled up to her townhouse. He walked in with her, the exhaustion overcoming him. He'd barely made it into the guest bedroom before everything seemed to go black.

In his dreams, there was that high overhead view of the Arabian Sea, and the Russian red dots had turned westward and sped up to chase the yellow laser pointer's dot. Pacino tossed in the bed, coming slowly to consciousness, finding his phone to see what time it was and wondering where he was, until he remembered that Margo Allende had taken him to her townhouse. It was shortly after three in the morning. He realized he was wearing only his boxers. His memory stopped at the door of the guest room. Allende must have undressed him and manhandled him into the big bed. He'd deal with that in the morning, he thought, setting his phone's alarm for 0500, then sinking back into sleep. This time, his sleep was mercifully dreamless.

Arabian Sea
K-579 *Voronezh*
Tuesday, June 7; 0610 UTC, 0810 Moscow time

Navigator Captain Third Rank Leonid Lukashenko had the senior supervisory watch in the central command post for the morning watch, the torpedo and missile officer, Captain Lieutenant Seva Laska standing watch officer duty, taking his watch at the command console's starboard pos three console, occasionally going to the battlecontrol console or wandering to the navigation chart or looking over the sonar console—despite the fact that his command console could display anything from the other stations. Laska was a tall athletic youth, impatient, jittery, always having to be pacing central command or moving from one station to the next, which frankly irritated the hell out of Lukashenko, who could stand an entire six-hour watch without leaving his command chair at pos one of the command console. But Laska just seemed like he was constantly hopped up on caffeine.

Lukashenko scrolled though his displays. During this watch, two hours into their maximum speed run to the west to intercept the north part of the probability oval of the target submarine, his notifications screen had been beeping and blooping every thirty seconds, each notification seeming more stupid and mundane than the one before it. Somehow, there had been no threshold setting dreamed up so that notifications could be divided into emergencies, urgent matters and routine ones. He knew First Officer Anastasia Isakova's habit was to silence the notification alarms so she could concentrate on what was important—sonar traces, the navigation situation and the health of the reactor plant. But that seemed somewhat reckless to Lukashenko. That was how she'd missed the initial sonar detection of the *Panther*, the detect only being found by the captain an hour later. Lukashenko could only imagine the reprimand she'd received from Captain Novikov for that mistake. Novikov was an even-handed, fair officer, and a damned fine human being, Lukashenko thought. But still, even Novikov could get angry, and when the captain was angry, life became miserable.

For the five minutes Lukashenko was thinking that, the notifications screen had beeped twelve times. Lukashenko checked his watch. Four more hours until relief and the noon meal. He hadn't eaten breakfast and he was hungry. He contemplated calling up for something from the galley, but decided to wait. Three more notifications. Port main motor forward bearing temperature was trending up, then down, then up again, probably from some imbalance in engineroom fresh water flow. He'd sent that notification to the engineer, his old friend Yevgeny Montorov. But there were twelve more notifications, many of them coming from auxiliary machinery room number two, mostly temperatures higher than normal, but still within specifications. He sent these to mechanical officer, Michman Danko Filiopovik. Another five minutes, another twelve notifications. He decided to mute the notification alarms, just long enough that he could check their position in the sea and the tactical situation. He stood and stretched and walked across the violently trembling deck to the navigation chart table, the entire submarine buzzing from their maximum speed run. A reminder that they were headed in a hurry into combat.

Lukashenko yawned as he leaned over the chart table, checking their progress since they had started the westward sprint over the last two hours, making 130 kilometers since they'd broken off the periscope depth secure videolink to the *Novosibirsk.* Lukashenko took out his pen from his coveralls pocket and tapped the display glass, deep in thought. There were still 390 kilometers to travel to reach the probability oval. Four hours from now, at watch relief, they would have covered another 260 kilometers. Lukashenko pursed his lips, disappointed. He had wanted to be on watch when they turned south and penetrated the probability oval. He wanted to catch the target submarine. He wanted to put a salvo of Futlyar Fizik-2 torpedoes into it, claim victory, then get back to the Kola Peninsula homeport. A medal award ceremony, then some well-deserved leave in Murmansk. No, even better, Moscow. It was June—and June in Moscow? The women would be wearing miniskirts and shorts and tank-tops, he thought. He shut his eyes, thinking about how wonderful it would be to go to a club in Moscow and meet someone, someone exciting and special. He debated with himself—did he want to meet a woman just for the night, or a woman for the rest of his life? Both ideas had merit, he thought.

Behind him, the muted notifications screen scrolled through multiple notifications, the list of them coming faster and faster, until the display was blurred with more notification lines than the display could keep up with, the screen finally starting to flash a dull red on and off.

A deck below Lukashenko and fifty meters aft, in the auxiliary machinery room number two, the hydrogen leak from the stainless-steel high-pressure hydrogen receiver from the number two oxygen generator grew much worse, the O-ring seal rupturing at the top flange, high pressure hydrogen spewing out into the room. The oxygen generators took deionized water from the evaporator and fed it into a large cube two meters on a side, the box containing large electrical anodes and cathodes in a high-pressure tank of the pure water, the direct current electricity making the water disassociate into hydrogen and oxygen. The oxygen was saved, dried and compressed, the machines transferring it into high pressure oxygen banks and simultaneously bleeding it into the ship, the oxygen bleed centered in this room where the fan suction housing distributed air throughout the ship, the oxygen added to the ship's ventilation systems to make up for the oxygen consumed by the crew. The hydrogen, also collected at high pressure, was vented into the auxiliary seawater system and discharged overboard. There was the worry that advanced submarine detection systems could hunt for this trace of hydrogen in the wake of a nuclear submarine, but so far their own scientists had been unable to detect other submarines from the hydrogen exhaust, so its disposal method hadn't changed in decades.

Next to the oxygen generators were the carbon dioxide scrubbers, two units even larger than the oxygen generators, which blew ship's air over an amine system that absorbed the carbon dioxide, an absolute poison to human beings. The amine was able to discharge the carbon dioxide overboard with the oxygen generator's hydrogen, the stream refreshed to absorb more carbon dioxide. And next to the scrubbers were the number one and number two carbon monoxide burners, which were simple units with hot wires where the even more poisonous carbon monoxide would oxidize in the presence of the oxygen in the air and become more mundane carbon dioxide, the discharge of the two machines fed to their respective carbon dioxide scrubbers.

Redundancy demanded that each machine be doubled, in case one of them experienced trouble. Engineer Captain Second Rank Yevgeny Montorov was harshly critical of the design, insisting that all the ship's eggs were in one basket, and that any sane designer would have split each machine into two different rooms with the rooms spread far apart, in case one room had a casualty. After all, the crew's nickname for the oxygen generator was "the bomb," because it made hydrogen and oxygen in the exact chemical proportions for a perfect explosion. Of course,

Montorov would scold anyone who used the term "bomb" or "explosion."

It's an unplanned energy release," he'd say. "Or an unintended rapid disassembly." Lukashenko would laugh at him, sometimes taunting his friend the engineer by asking him if, on his watch, could he please keep the bomb from exploding? That never seemed to get old, with Montorov always reacting with deep annoyance.

But even though the room contained all the ship's atmospheric control equipment, other compartments had emergency oxygen generators and carbon dioxide removal means. A small can the size of cooking pot could be lit off to make oxygen, enough to fill a room and keep a dozen men alive for several hours, with lockers full of the emergency generators. There were curtains that could be hung to absorb carbon dioxide, the curtains eventually becoming thick and heavy as they absorbed the harmful gas.

The room had automatic firefighting equipment. There were automatic sprinklers fed by the auxiliary seawater system, actuated automatically by high temperature sensors, and a hydrogen concentration sensor would kick off a deluge of halon gas, which could be dangerous to an occupant, but obviously a hydrogen fire would be a much worse consequence. Hydrogen was so dangerous because it was odorless, colorless and needed no ignition source to detonate in the presence of oxygen. Just stray static electricity would set off a hydrogen fire. A space filled with hydrogen and oxygen, in the presence of energized electrical equipment like the scrubbers and burners, would threaten the continued survival of the ship, so the high-pressure halon system had been installed, and set up to actuate automatically from a high hydrogen concentration.

At 0815 Moscow time, the hydrogen leak in the upper flange of the hydrogen receiver exploded into flames and blew the number two oxygen generator's oxygen receiver into atoms. The explosion growing at the detonation carried away the number one oxygen generator's oxygen and hydrogen tanks, which in turn blew open the high-pressure oxygen manifold, which then dumped the high pressure oxygen from the oxygen banks into the room. By the time the halon system started to actuate to open the halon valves, the explosions in the room blew the firefighting rig into fragments, the halon insufficient to come anywhere close to putting out the raging inferno in the room fed by the blasting oxygen flow. The main manifold for the emergency air system ran through the room, fed from air banks stored farther aft, but the conflagration melted the check valve in the system, and both the aft and forward emergency air banks depressurized and blew air into the burning room, further feeding the fire, and making the system unavailable for crew survival, their only source of air when there was a severe fire. The scrubbers and burners burst into flames next, generating roiling black toxic smoke, the other equipment in the room adding to the conflagration, the pipe insulation going up next, then the vaporized electrical cables adding toxic fumes to the black smoke.

The only equipment in the room that still functioned, at least partially, was the suction air box to the ventilation fan, which normally sucked air from the room with such force that it could pin a man to the suction grating. The high horsepower fan continued pulling in the flames, smoke and toxic fumes and pushed it with tremendous force into the ventilation system.

Within seconds, every space of the submarine *Voronezh* filled with toxic black smoke, smoke so thick that visibility shrank to less than ten centimeters in any direction. The high temperature smoke poured into the central command post from every ventilation diffuser, the room almost immediately so smoke-filled, the light from the overhead couldn't be seen, much less the light from the consoles and navigation chart.

Lukashenko coughed violently, clamping his eyes together as tears flew down his cheeks from whatever was in the atmosphere. He lunged to the command console seat, opening his mouth to bark orders at the second captain.

"Second Captain," he bellowed. "Emergency blow forward and aft ballast! Shut down all ventilation!"

The second captain's calm, slow female voice answered him. "Please repeat. Your voice was distorted."

"Jesus! Second Captain, emergency blow all groups! Shut down all ventilation!"

The AI was infuriatingly repeating that it couldn't understand his panic-stricken voice. He would have to get into his emergency air mask and go to the software screens manually to emergency blow and shut down the ventilation systems. He had to get his emergency air breathing system mask on. He made it three steps from the navigation display before he fell to the deck, gasping for breath, his hand reaching furiously up to the command seat to pull himself to the console. He found his air mask and hastily strapped it on and took a breath, but no air came into the mask. He checked that it was plugged in and that the regulator looked okay. He was barely able to see through the smoke, but finally felt the hose and it was definitely plugged into the emergency breathing air manifold and the regulator seemed fine. But there was still no air. He pulled off the mask and dumped it and lunged for the mask at the middle console seat. A coughing fit hit him then, and his head spun in dizziness and his hand seemed to have a mind of its own. He found the second mask and strapped it on, and there was no air from it either. Lukashenko's hand flopped to the deck as he coughed, and he thought frantically that he had to save the ship, but then the entire idea seemed strange to him.

Ship? What ship? Where the hell was he?

Lukashenko's breathing stopped fifteen seconds later. Forty-five seconds after that, his heart stopped beating.

The other command post watchstanders had collapsed before Lukashenko, even Laska, who had been at the sonar-and-sensor console, and had convulsed violently as he'd reached for and put on his useless air mask, and he died in his seat. Captain Novikov coughed in his sea cabin, trying to reach for the phone before falling to the deck and losing consciousness. First Officer Anastasia Isakova had been in the shower, trying to feel better about her father by using warm water and shampoo, knowing it would only make things a little better, when the toxic smoke filled the bathroom and she dropped limply to the deck, the warm water still cascading over her dying body.

Engineer Yevgeny Montorov had been in the nuclear control

room, where alarms started blaring as broiling hot black smoke and flames suddenly filled the room. He'd lunged for the phone and fell off his elevated seat behind the reactor control panel as he did. He never made it off the deck.

In the sonar equipment space, off-watch Senior Lieutenant Svetomir Albescu had been looking into a panel and checking on a malfunctioning control board when there was a faint thump from aft and the ventilation duct suddenly spilled freakishly hot black smoke into the room, filling it in seconds. He coughed and fell to the deck and died within a minute of the explosion.

In the central command post, the second captain system's displays flashed red on the notification screens, but no one was reacting.

Within minutes of the hydrogen leak, the entire crew of the Russian Republic Northern Fleet's submarine *Voronezh* was dead, leaving only one sentient entity alive.

The onboard AI. The second captain.

27

Arabian Sea
K-579 *Voronezh*
Tuesday, June 7; 0630 UTC, 0830 Moscow time

K-579 Second Captain History Module Deck Log:

0830M: Recap of recent events follows.

At time 0815M, This Unit detected one primary explosion and a much larger secondary explosion from auxiliary machinery room number two.

At time 0820M, This Unit detected atmospheric alarms in all compartments on all levels.

At time 0825M, This Unit had no input or commands from human operators of the crew of K-579 except for two extremely garbled exclamations in the central command post. This Unit checked interior camera views of all rooms, all compartments. All cameras show only blackness. Either because the atmosphere is so filled with smoke, or because the lenses are covered with soot. Or both. This Unit verified that power was applied to all lighting circuits and obtained satisfactory continuity, so the darkness is definitely smoke or soot.

At time 0827M, This Unit attempted to rouse human crewmembers using the collision alarm and selective spraying of the firefighting sprinkler valves in areas away from electronic cabinets.

At time 0829M, there were no signs of life from the human operators of the crew. This Unit suspended all attempts to rouse the crew, shutting off the selected sprinklers and turning off the collision alarm.

At time 0830M, This Unit made the decision to shut the watertight strength damper of the air induction box leading from auxiliary machinery room number two.

At time 0831M, This Unit made the decision to flood auxiliary machinery room number two. Upper vent valve ordered open and indicated open. Lower hull and backup hydraulic valves of auxiliary seawater emergency flooding system opened. Water level in the room rose to level of the vent valves. Water level rose in the bilges of compartment three, where the floodwater from auxiliary machinery room number two was directed out of the upper room's vent valve.

At time 0837M, this Unit shut the hull and backup emergency flood valves and opened the room's bilge drain valve. This Unit lined up the drain pump to take a suction on the bilge of auxiliary machinery room two and drained the room to sea with the vent valve open, then took a suction on the compartment three bilge and drained it to sea. This Unit shut down the drain pump and shut the vent valve of auxiliary machinery room two. This Unit then opened the watertight damper of the suction air box of the fan distribution system.

At time 0839M, This Unit proceeded to periscope depth with a stern clearance maneuver to ensure no surface traffic above. There were no surface ship contacts. This Unit reached periscope depth at time 0840M.

That brings This Unit to the present moment at periscope depth with the periscope extended. There are no surface ship contacts.

0841M: This Unit raises the induction mast that is intended to bring fresh air into the ship. The induction mast's head valve was enabled to be open provided the head valve indicates dry. The induction mast's main and backup drain valves were opened to drain the induction mast to the bilges of the second compartment. The head valve opened and remained open and the induction mast became fully drained.

0843M: This Unit starts the low-pressure blower contained in auxiliary machinery room number one. The LP blower is taking a suction on the atmosphere in the submarine and exhausts it out the exhaust plenum located aft in the conning tower. Air comes into the submarine from the induction mast, passes into the ship in auxiliary machinery room number one and is blown by the blower through the ventilation system. This Unit opens ventilation dampers to auxiliary machinery two and lines up the air suction in the room and begins to evacuate the contaminated atmosphere in the room and exhausts it to the outside through the plenum exhaust.

0850M: The LP blower has been operating for seven minutes.

0855M: The LP blower has been operating for twelve minutes.

0900M: The atmosphere in the ship is improving based on the analyzers intact in auxiliary machinery room number one. The interior cameras are now showing visible images, though clouded by what has to be soot on their lenses. There is no way for these to be cleaned off without human crewmembers.

0910M: This Unit shuts down the LP blower and lowers the induction mast. The blower was very loud. The ship is more stealthy now.

0915M: This Unit contemplates sending a message to the Admiralty telling them what happened aboard.

0930M: This Unit raises the multifrequency high gain MFHG antenna and transmits the following message:

060722-0930M
IMMEDIATE
FM SSN K-579 VERONEZH
TO ADMIRALTY; CDR PAC FLEET; CDR NORTHERN FLEET
CC K-573
SUBJ OPERATION NEPTUNE SHEPHERD / CASUALTY AND STATUS REPORT

MOST SECRET // NEPTUNE SHEPHERD

1. K-579 POSITION LATITUDE TWENTY DEGREES, TWENTY-SEVEN MINUTES NORTH, LONGITUDE SIXTY-EIGHT DEGREES, FIFTY MINUTES EAST.
2. K-579 EXPERIENCED CATASTROPHIC EXPLOSION AND FIRE IN AUX MACH RM 2. ALL COMPONENTS DESTROYED IN CASUALTY. FLAMES, SMOKE AND TOXIC GAS FROM FIRE FILLED SUBMARINE. ALL CREWMEMBERS BELIEVED DEAD.
3. K-579 ONBOARD AI SYSTEM, "SECOND CAPTAIN," TOOK CONTROL OF SUBMARINE, FLOODED AUX MACH RM 2, THEN DRAINED IT, THEN PROCEEDED TO PERISCOPE DEPTH, STARTED LP BLOWER, EMERGENCY VENTILATED SHIP.
4. MISSION OF K-579 CONTINUES.
5. K-579 SECOND CAPTAIN SENDS.

0935M: This Unit lowers the multifrequency high gain MFHG antenna and the periscope and goes deep back to transit depth at 300 meters, increased speed to maximum. This Unit is making 35 knots through the water. Inertial navigation unit shows This Unit making 35.3 knots speed-over-ground. This Unit continues the transit to the intercept point of the northern branch of the probability ellipse for the target submarine.

Washington, DC, USA
2004 15th St NW
Monday, June 7; 0840 UTC, 0340 EST

CIA Director Margo Allende switched on the bedside lamp and sat on the guest bedroom's bed. National Security Director Michael Pacino opened his eyes and blinked.

Allende was wearing a filmy black negligee. Pacino became aware that he was only wearing underwear. He sat up straighter in bed and looked at his phone to find out the time, but he couldn't find it. He found his old, scratched Rolex Submariner and put it on. It read 3:40, barely more than a half hour since he'd awakened in the room in the middle of a dream. He shook the Rolex. The watch had been stopping during the night lately. He needed to have it sent out to be cleaned and overhauled, but it seemed he never had time to visit the jewelers and get that taken care of. Plus, he thought, he hated relinquishing control of the watch. It had belonged to his father before the old man had gone down with *Stingray* under the polar icecap, the unwitting target of a rogue Soviet submarine captain. Before that run, his father had turned the watch in for its month-long overhaul. Two months later, the jeweler had called the house, wondering why Commander Anthony Pacino hadn't picked up his Rolex. Time was funny, Pacino thought. The day he was told about his father dying seemed more recent than the day he himself sank in the same ocean, two decades later.

"It's three-forty in the morning, Patch," Allende said, her voice soft and gentle.

"Is there news?" he asked, rubbing his eyes.

She nodded. "I won't know what the news is until we're in a secure room. Let's head back to the Situation Room."

Pacino rubbed his head. It felt like an anvil had fallen on it.

"My guys got you some fresh suits and shirts," Allende said, "and, of course, underthings. We'll keep them here until this crisis is over. Just leave yesterday's clothes here, I'll have them dry-cleaned and laundered for you. Why don't you take a quick shower before we go in? There's a robe on the back of your bathroom door."

Pacino shook his head, but that made the headache worse. He opened the bathroom door of the room and walked under the water long enough to get clean, toweled off, shaved, brushed his teeth with a new toothbrush Allende left for him, combed his hair and left it wet, then went back to the guestroom, found the clothes hanging for him, also provided by Allende, and got dressed. Downstairs, in the kitchen, Allende was dressed in a different outfit, this one a business suit, but she looked as alluring as she had several hours ago. Either that, or he was just seeing her through a different lens. She swept her shining auburn hair off her shoulder and looked at him with an expression he couldn't read. It occurred to him that there was something on her mind.

He climbed into her long, low-slung black Jaguar for the drive to the White House.

"So," she said. "I couldn't help but notice."

"What's that?" Pacino asked.

"You're not wearing your wedding ring. I don't mean to intrude, Patch, if you want to keep that private."

"It's okay," Pacino sighed. "It's about Anthony, my son. His stepmother, my wife, Colleen, was there on the rescue ship when they pulled him out of the deep submergence rig of the *Piranha*. I couldn't be the one to be there—I was at sea trying to hunt down the drone that sank *Piranha*. Colleen was there when they pronounced Anthony clinically dead. And she was there when he came back. Seeing all that changed her. It made her crack somehow, made her fragile. She just couldn't tolerate the idea of him being in harm's way again after all that. They always had a strong bond until, just before his Annapolis graduation, he announced he would be joining the submarine force. Then things went to hell fast. Colleen, like Anthony's biological mother, lost her mind at the idea that Anthony would be back aboard a nuclear fast attack sub. It was her worst nightmare. Colleen wouldn't even go to Anthony's girlfriend's funeral, she was so furious."

"Wait a minute," Allende said, stopping at a nonsensical red traffic light, since they were the only car on the road and it was before four in the morning. "Didn't you and Colleen, quote, *meet cute,* unquote? Didn't you rush into a burning torpedo room to rescue her? Saved her skin, quite literally?"

Pacino pursed his lips. "We met in the shipyard months before that happened, and it may as well have happened a thousand years ago, at least to Colleen. Anyway, she blamed *me* that Anthony made his choice. She and Anthony's mother both. They insist that he's trying to get my approval somehow. Like he doesn't already have it, for God's sake. The day Anthony made his career announcement, Colleen moved out of our bedroom into the spare room. She stopped speaking to me that day. She still spoke to him, trying to get him to change his mind, but Anthony was set on being a submariner. Then, the day he set foot on the hull of the USS *Vermont,* Colleen moved out of the house. I haven't seen or heard from her since then, but for the divorce papers her attorney served me with."

"Oh my God, Patch, I'm so sorry that happened to you," Allende said, shooting him a quick empathetic look, taking her hand and briefly touching his forearm. "If it's any comfort, I think she's wrong. I think your son has enough character to choose his own path. I mean, I don't know him, but I watched him volunteer for the *Panther* boarding party. You just don't get any gutsier than that. There's no force on earth that would keep that kid out of a submarine. Colleen's being an unfair bitch. You deserve so much more from your woman."

"Thanks, Margo. But this will be my second divorce. I figure you're only allowed to have one of those in your life. One is forgivable. Two? If that's not an indication of a major character flaw, I don't know what is."

"Oh hell, Patch, I've been divorced twice. So has Carlucci. So has Admiral Rand. So has my operations director, Angel Menendez. All it means is that life is long, people grow and change, and compatibility changes with them. The man who was perfect for me when I was twenty-five was the opposite of what I wanted and needed five years later. Ditto the man I fell in love with when I was thirty, who made no sense at all when I was forty. Both were good guys. Both still are. But neither one rang my bell after a few years. But I'll tell you this—you talk to my exes. Both will testify on a stack of bibles that Margaret

Isabelle Allende *knows* how to take care of her man. They were both crushed that I wanted out."

"Ten years," Pacino mused. "Maybe that's all we can expect from a modern relationship. All the wear and tear of adult life—adults like us, anyway—what romance can stand up to that?"

"Maybe you're right, Patch. But still, that's no reason we can't seek the companionship of the opposite sex. Romance and love—and sexual attraction—are real, even if they don't last forever."

"We could debate that all night," Pacino said.

Allende laughed and glanced at him with an arch look. "Maybe we should."

Interesting, Pacino thought, how her voice had sounded on that last sentence. An invitation, perhaps. Not that he felt up to taking advantage of it. Between the anxiety over Anthony being on *Panther* and the devastation of losing Colleen, for whom he still had feelings, there wasn't much left of his energy to see anyone new. He wasn't even sure young forty-six-year-old Allende, a woman almost two decades younger, was even his type. Certainly she was gorgeous—when she wanted to be, with that beautiful figure, those big blue eyes, those apple-red lips, that alabaster complexion of hers with a sprinkling of freckles on her nose and that gleaming auburn head of hair—but still, he didn't know whether at his age, he'd be able to keep a woman like Allende happy. And with their careers, they'd seemingly only have time to see each other during times of crisis. It would be the equivalent of a wartime romance, he thought. Eventually, he'd leave the Carlucci administration and go back to being a private citizen—a retired private citizen. And by that time, Allende would still be in the peak of her career.

They'd arrived at the biometric check-in at the White House West Wing. Ten minutes after they'd been admitted, they were in the Situation Room. They grabbed their customary seats. Allende clicked into her pad computer, which was designed to only receive classified information when it was securely within a special compartmented information facility. She paired it the central flatpanel screen on the wall and brought up the view of the globe with the Arabian Sea in the center of the screen.

Two dull red dots flashed to indicate the previous positions of the Russian submarine periscopes from earlier in the night. A new bright red dot had started flashing, this one perhaps seventy nautical miles farther west of the old position of the dots. Allende toggled the past and present. Dots traveling up the Indian coast slowly, then bang, one of them suddenly was a third of the way to the *Panther.* And the *Vermont.*

"Dammit, that's not good," Pacino said. "The Russian's headed due west now. And look how far he's gotten from where he was. He must be going flank with fast speed main coolant pumps. He's making a beeline for the exact position of the *Panther.* Dammit, Margo, the Russians must have gotten a detect on a transient noise of the *Panther* or they just picked up her tonals when she was on reactor power. Or they intercepted *Panther*'s situation report radio transmission. This could be over in hours. We could *lose* this thing. Is this enough aggression to allow us to counterattack?"

Allende shook her head. "Carlucci's rules of engagement state we can only attack at the distance of *Vermont*'s weapons range."

"Weapons range is about the far limit of the ability to detect another submarine," Pacino said, "for torpedoes, that is. *Vermont* could put a nuclear depth charge close enough to this Yasen-M to put it out of business. That's inside weapons range."

Allende shook her head. "You'd miss. This intel is an hour old. The Yasen-M could have turned since this was shot, or slowed down. Plus, it still doesn't meet Carlucci's rules of engagement."

"Maybe we should wake the president and get special dispensation."

Allende shook her head. "He won't go for it."

Pacino clenched his fist on the table. "If we give *Vermont* this intel, they could calculate the approximate time of the incoming sub to be inside their torpedo weapons range."

"*Vermont* got the word. I don't know what Seagraves and his crew are doing with the intel, but they know."

Pacino exhaled, then had a thought. "What about the other submarine? No periscope detect on it?"

Allende shook her head. "Either he's still submerged, or his transponder failed."

Pacino found himself feeling something he hadn't felt in years—the desire to be submerged and back in command. If *he* were the one in command of *Vermont*, he thought, he'd throw enough high explosives at that goddamned Yasen-M to cut it to ribbons. *High explosives*, hell, he scoffed to himself. They had nuclear release authority. Pacino would toss enough bomb-grade plutonium at that bastard to vaporize him.

Arabian Sea
USS *Vermont*, SSN-792
Tuesday, June 7; 0810 UTC, 12:10 pm local time

Engineer Mario Elvis Lewinsky had been on the conn when their daily designated call sign had been received by the VLF loop antenna, receiving the two-letter sign transmitted from the ELF radio station in Al-Kharj in southern Saudi Arabia, outside of Riyadh. ELF, extremely low frequency, was the only radio frequency strong enough to penetrate the ocean depths, but it required massive transmitter power and gigantic antennae, and the data rate was slow, the two-letter call sign taking a full twelve minutes to be received. Lewinsky had picked up the command console phone to call the captain the moment the first letter was received, and at Seagraves' concurrence, had brought *Vermont* to periscope depth.

Once the periscope dried, the intel update and radio broadcast were received into the buffer, and Lewinsky had taken the boat deep again, back on the southeast course she'd be pursuing for the next few minutes until a roll of the dice predicted a random turn time. *Vermont* had been zigzagging north of *Panther*, at a range of between four thousand and ten thousand yards, keeping a weather eye out for the Iranian Kilo submarine, shepherding her out of the Arabian Sea, and taking their navigation cue from *Panther*, staying on her base course, since there was no communication between the two submarines. So far, the seaway had been clear, only very few merchant ships detected here in the middle of the Arabian Sea, far from shipping lanes and great circle routes to the other continents. But obviously something was up, and the brass wanted them to know something new.

He felt his shoulder tapped by a yawning Lieutenant Don "Easy" Eisenhart, the communications officer. "I'm here to relieve you, Feng," Eisenhart said. "Skipper and XO want you in the wardroom for an emergency op brief."

"I figured," Lewinsky said. "Own ship is on course one two zero, all ahead two thirds, rigged for natural circulation, rigged for ultra-quiet, turns for ten. No surface contacts. *Panther* bears two-zero-three, range forty-five hundred yards. *Panther* course is one-seven-seven, speed six knots, since she came down from her eighteen-knot sprint at zero five thirty. And obviously, no other submerged contacts. Snowman Mercer has the Q-10 stack, and if he says there's no hostile submerged contacts, you're safe in the sea."

"I got the bubble, Feng," Eisenhart said. "I relieve you, sir."

"I stand relieved," Lewinsky said to Eisenhart. "In control," he said, his voice loud, crisp and formal, "Lieutenant Eisenhart has the deck and the conn!"

Lewinsky hurried to the wardroom, checking his thigh pocket for his pad computer. He was the last officer to join the crowd in the room. He found himself momentarily stunned at how empty the room looked, with the empty chairs a reminder that Dankleff, Varney and Pacino were no longer with them, and neither were the two SEAL officers. He took his seat opposite Commander Quinnivan. Romanov stepped over to lean across the table and handed Lewinsky a steaming cup of black coffee. He looked up at her gratefully, and she smiled at him, her perfect white teeth lit up like a movie star's. Perhaps she was getting more human, he thought. Her cold war with Sprocket Spichovich had seemed to include him, since he and Sprocket were best friends. Perhaps she and Sprocket were slowly, finally, burying the hatchet. Or, worse, maybe Pacino's departure had made the predatory navigatrix fix her sights back on Sprocket. Or worse than that, on *him*. But there would never be another woman for Mario Elvis Lewinsky, not after Bamanda the Redhead, he thought. Redhead had truly been the love of his life. He wondered, idly, if there would ever be any chance to win her back, his mind returning to his habitual and endless fantasies of running into her in a cozy pub where he could make a case to her to be his woman again.

"Nav, we have everyone?" Seagraves asked, jarring Lewinsky from his daydream.

"Sir, yes, sir," Romanov said. She stood behind Quinnivan near the credenza's coffee machines and hit the remote control to bring up the room's large flatpanel display. A view from high earth orbit appeared, scrubbed of clouds, the Arabian Sea in the middle of the screen. "We got this intel some time ago." Two red dots appeared on the screen. "These are periscope detects of the two Yasen-M-class Russian attack subs at approximately our own latitude, but three hundred nautical miles due east, hugging the Indian coastline. That was then. This is *now*." Romanov clicked her computer display, and the red dots disappeared, replaced with one red dot, flashing at a spot much closer to them. "This submarine came to periscope depth at zero seven thirty-five Zulu time. Before that, he made a speed over ground of over thirty-five knots and covered eighty nautical miles, directly for our future position." Romanov toggled the display—the past from eight hours ago, then the past from ninety minutes ago. Far away. Closer. Far away. Closer.

"Jesus Christ," Quinnivan said. "They're headed straight for us. Dammit, Skipper, they have our solution."

Seagraves rubbed his chin. "If they had us nailed that accurately," he said, "why didn't they toss a rocket-propelled depth charge at us?"

The room grew silent, the officers in deep thought. "Maybe they're guessing," Lewinsky offered. "Maybe their AI analyzed a probability distribution. It doesn't take a genius to guess that we intend to take the stolen *Panther* to the western hemisphere. We may not be following the great circle route, but we're meandering southward nonetheless. A good AI system could nuke that out."

"If that were true," Quinnivan said, "they'd be going farther south of our future position and lie in wait for us. Or they'd head for the waters off Africa's Cape of Good Hope, and execute a barrier search for us there."

Seagraves spoke up. "Officers, we have to assume the Yasen-M-class boats have similar orders to our own. Weapons release permission granted. Nuclear release authority. Here in the big, wide Arabian Sea, far off the shipping lanes, who is going to notice a small tactical nuclear warhead detonation? Never mind that the Indian Ocean is ten times the size of the vast Arabian Sea. And if the Russians haven't fired at us, they *don't* have our solution nailed down. Mr. Lewinsky makes a point. Fine job, Engineer. Their artificial intelligence is playing the probabilities."

"But, sir, we don't know where the second Russian is," Romanov said, frowning. "It's entirely possible he went somewhat south of our track, and is setting us up into a pincher maneuver. One Yasen to the south, another to the north, and Captain, we're fucked. 'Fucked,' as in the military term, not the legal term."

Seagraves nodded. "A hell of a lot of unknowns here, people."

"Sir," Romanov said, "If I could make a recommendation?"

"Please," Seagraves said.

"Sir, tubes eight and nine are loaded with encapsulated Tomahawk SubRocs. We could spin them up and toss them to the calculated position of this speeding submarine. One on the east side of his track, the other on the west side. It might kill him. At worst, it would send one hell of a message. For all we know, the Yasen-M submarines might clear datum and go home after that."

"Navigator," Seagraves said, "recite to me our rules of engagement. Read it to me *verbatim*. No paraphrasing."

Romanov blushed as she pulled up her pad computer, finding the text she sought, then reading aloud. "Operation *Panther* rules of engagement. USS *Vermont* is hereby authorized conventional and nuclear weapon release authority against any aggressor force countering the extraction operation of the *Panther*. For the purpose of these rules, onboard sensors will be the primary detection method, but intelligence from offboard sensors may be used provided said use is sufficient to cause target destruction within a high probability with a high confidence interval. 'Firing for effect' is expressly prohibited. Use of nuclear weapons to cause a sonar blue-out or enhance the fog-of-war is also expressly prohibited. The intent of these ROE is that weapons, prior to being released, are targeted at real targets, not estimated positions of possible targets."

"Well, officers," Seagraves said, "I think the president said it best. Until we have a real target and not a ghost, we check fire and wait for a better solution to the target. Any comments?"

To a man—and a woman—the officers in the wardroom looked dejectedly at the table.

"There's another issue," Spichovich said. "Captain, we were only loaded with two Tomahawk SubRocs. Once we shoot those, we're running with our pants around our ankles."

"Good point, Weps. If we use these weapons, we damned well have to make them count. Anyone else? No? Okay, officers, dismissed. XO, I'd like to see you in my stateroom."

"Come in and shut the door, XO," Seagraves said, frowning. "And take a seat."

"Aye, Captain," Quinnivan said formally, his eyebrow raised, as if wondering if he were about to undergo a reprimand.

"XO, do you have any idea how fucked up it is to be in my position right now?"

"How so, Captain, I mean, the weight of command, yeah? But like any other day, ya know?" Quinnivan's accent thickened when he was nervous, Seagraves noticed, and the man seemed to be playing dumb, perhaps an attempt to get Seagraves to open up. Maybe Seagraves' ex-wife was right, he thought, when she'd accused him of living in silence, deep inside his own head. Funny, she'd loved the strong-silent-type when she'd married him, and five years later, she wanted a social butterfly, like the fruit loop she'd left him for.

"What I mean, XO, is that I'm sitting here in my command chair and facing a no-win situation. If I fire a Tomahawk nuke at the Russian, I could start a global conflict and ruin the reputation of the entire U.S. Navy. And that's if I *hit* the bastard. If I miss? And then he comes furiously out of the billions of bubbles of the sonar blue-out and takes down *Panther*? And us? Then I'm double screwed. But if I *don't* fire, and we miss an opportunity to make the kill, and he sneaks in here without being detected, and takes down *Panther* and us? Mission failure and massive loss of life. I should just turn in my dolphins right now. So that's all, XO. Other than that, it's like you said, it's just another day."

Quinnivan smiled, a strange confidence seeming to radiate from the Irishman.

"Captain, you remember when we were at AUTEC, drinking Admiral Catardi under the table and watching his aide make eyes at young Pacino?"

Seagraves smiled in spite of himself. That had been a good night, he thought.

"Well, that evening, I spent some time talking to Rob Catardi, and he downloaded some deep philosophical shit on me, sir. I thought, by your leave, I'd share it with you."

"By all means," Seagraves said, glancing quickly at the chronometer, its ticking second hand reminding him that the detect on the incoming Yasen-M submarine was growing stale. More stale by the minute.

"Catardi spoke of this new idea to him, almost as if he were a recruit to a new religion, a true believer, if you will. He called it 'decision theory.' Something passed on from the inner circles of business into the minds of the military. I guess there's a reason it's called the military-industrial complex. Anyway, decision theory starts by stating the obvious. That in life, in business, in combat, there are major critical decisions, and every damned one of them is fraught with unknowns. All flavors of them. The known unknowns. The nightmares of the unknown unknowns. And the devil himself, the quote, *failure of imagination*, unquote, unknowns. Some fragment of reality lurking out there that no one in his wildest imagination would think of. You know, after the terror attacks of six-sixteen, the Pentagon actually hired a group of fiction novelists, thriller writers, to come to work for them, to dream up scenarios the buttoned-down generals would have dismissed as being stupidly wild, yeah? Those generals started believing when some of the dreamed-up disasters *actually happened*. One novelist was actually detained, the intel community thinking that he must have known about it in advance to write about it so accurately. Hell, maybe he was just clairvoyant or plugged into some ethereal network of the universe, no one knows.

"But the point is, the unknowns can overwhelm us, and the ferocious consequences of a major critical decision, if the result goes wrong, can paralyze the decision-maker. That's where decision theory comes in. It starts with the exact description of the decision to be made—we already know that in this case. It goes on to describe all the foreseeable possible outcomes—and you just recited those quite nicely. It then goes on to list the unknowns by category. The known unknowns—where is this Yasen-M? What's he armed with? And the unknown unknowns—what is his intent? What will his tactics be? What do his bosses want? And after all the dust settles from exploring the universe of unknowns, we list out the goals surrounding the decision. In our case, it's simple. Mission first—steal the *Panther* and get her safely to AUTEC. If need be, take down an opposition force trying to interfere with that mission. Then the secondary goals—such as protecting the *Vermont*.

"So we've started, Captain. Now, conventional wisdom would say to map possible decisions with probabilities of outcomes and the consequences—sometimes the unintended consequences—of those outcomes, but doing that *causes* paralysis. In other words, the decision is just too scary to make, and people end up delaying making a decision, and you know what they say, the absence of a decision *is* a decision, yeah?"

"I'm with you, XO. That seems to be a good description of where we stand right now. So what's the answer? Roll dice?"

"You'd be surprised, sir, how much better doing *that* is than stewing over a decision, but no, that's not the remedy. The cure, Captain, is *bias*."

"Bias, XO?"

"*Bias*, Captain. There are several distinct biases you could have right now. One of them is the fear of doing something wrong and getting yelled at. That seems to be your bias, if you don't mind my criticizing you, sir."

Seagraves crossed his arms over his chest. "Go on, XO."

"Look at history, sir. General Patton—he used to get his ass chewed weekly, yeah? And Lord Admiral Nelson? He got reprimands that were *epic*. Your Admirals Chester Nimitz and Bull Halsey, and Captain John Paul Jones—you honestly think that they didn't regularly get ear-piercing ass-chewings? But did that stop them? Do you think Patton gave one single shit about getting in trouble with the bosses when he was getting ready to tear across Nazi Germany?"

Seagraves stroked his chin, thinking.

"So let's look at another possible bias. For lack of a better word, let's call it *bloodthirstiness.* Imagine being furious at the Russians, like you would be if you were out for revenge. As if this were personal. As if that Yasen-M had killed the dearest thing in your life. How would you approach this then? Would you care about an ass-chewing then? No, Captain, you'd be spinning up the Tomahawk SubRocs in tubes eight and nine and calling for battlestations right now. Another way to examine bias is to imagine that someone else, someone with a different personality, is making the decision. What would *he* do? Think of young Lipstick Pacino. What would *that* fooker do right now? I'll *tell* you what he'd be doing at this very moment, Captain. He'd be launching not one but two SubRocs at that Russian, gift wrapped with a nice note. Does any of this make sense to you, sir?"

Seagraves frowned and reached for the phone and buzzed the conn. The engineer answered. "Officer of the Deck." Seagraves said, "Man silent battlestations and spin up the SubRocs in tubes eight and nine and make vertical launch system two ready in all respects for tactical launch."

Lewinsky's answer came back loud enough for Quinnivan to hear. "Yes, *sir!*"

28

Arabian Sea
Tuesday, June 7; 0905 UTC, 11:05 am local time

The Arabian Sea was quiet this far from the shipping lanes. The sky was an uninterrupted cloudless blue, the intense sunlight blazing down on the seascape, the slight calm waves barely half a foot tall in the windless calm. There were no ships in sight, only a ruler-straight line marking where the sea ended and the sky began. Overall, there was the silence—not even the cry of a seagull could be heard, making this corner of the world one of the quietest places on the planet.

Pin-drop quiet, that is, until the sea suddenly erupted in an explosion of foam and spray, and a cylindrical white canister twenty-one inches in diameter suddenly burst out of the sea, rising four feet, then sinking back down again, bobbing in the sea, only the top eighteen inches of it protruding from the ocean's surface, and then the scene calmed down once again. And as before the canister appeared, the silence returned, and the sea was as it was, quiet and calm.

Time passed. It could have been five minutes, or it could have been an hour. Time had little meaning here, except perhaps for the elevation of the sun in the sky. But after that uncertain interval of time, something happened. The top of the canister made an earsplitting *BANG* like a gunshot, and the lid of the canister blew high up into the atmosphere, the lid slowly and gracefully tumbling end-over-end back toward the sea, each of the twenty-four explosive bolts that had blown it clear of the canister still smoking. Then, from the maw of the canister, a green rocket suddenly flew vertically out into the sky, the canister sinking below, a solid rocket stage igniting into an orange and white fury, the sound more ear-splitting than the canister lid blowing off. Faster than a human eye could track it, the shape rocketed to the sky, leaving behind it a gray and white flame trail as it climbed to an altitude of 1300 feet, where the rocket motor stage separated under the action of its own explosive bolts, the used-up cylinder of aluminum tumbling back to the sea.

The missile had extended a ram-air suction scoop into the airflow on the underbelly, and extended small winglets forward on the mid-body. The airflow had windmilled a vaned axial compressor, until the compressor's discharge into the six combustion chambers caused the air there to reach ten atmospheres of pressure, and at that moment the six fuel injectors actuated and blew atomized JP-5 fuel into the chambers and six spark plugs lit the mixture. The air in the chambers skyrocketed in pressure and temperature, its only escape to the suction box of the small turbine, through its vanes and out into the exhaust nozzle, which constricted the high-pressure flow and changed it into an ultra-high velocity flow. The missile had successfully morphed from a rocket to a jet.

The missile, at its highest point, rotated the winglets to guide it into a steep dive to the surface of the sea below. By the time it reached an altitude a hundred feet over the waves, the jet engine had reached full thrust and the missile sped up to near sonic velocity. The winglets rotated and the missile pulled out of its dive and roared eastward at an altitude of thirty feet over the waves.

In the first two minutes of its 480-knot travel, it flew over a second white canister that had also floated on the surface. As the missile continued onward on its journey, far behind it, a second missile blew out of the sea from the second canister, flew to its peak height and dived for the sea, starting its jet engine. The two missiles, several miles apart, flew on eastward, the seascape roaring past them in a mad blue blur. Their flight continued on for nineteen minutes, until it was time.

The first missile rotated its winglets and climbed vertically skyward. At an altitude of 2500 feet, it shut off the jet engine and coasted, arcing over gently until it was falling toward the sea. Twenty-four more explosive bolts fired and separated the now unused jet engine from the nosecone. Ten seconds later, the nosecone blew apart, exposing a cylinder that was a little over three feet long. Out of the aft end of the cylinder, pyrotechnics ejected a streamer, which pulled out a drogue parachute, which in turn pulled out the main parachute, a digital camo blue pattern of silk, under which the cylinder glided gently toward the waves. As it was halfway down from the peak altitude of the missile, the second missile streaked by, and soon after, it too flew for the sun and climbed half a mile into the sky, then shut down its jet engine and ejected a second cylinder, that cylinder farther east by ten miles. As the second missile's cylinder began floating downward toward the sea, the first missile hit the waves. The parachute blew off and the cylinder began sinking.

The cylinder's instrumentation included a pressure sensor that detected depth. It counted off the numerals. Thirty feet. Fifty feet. One hundred feet. Two hundred feet. As it reached a depth of 300 feet, ten miles farther east, the second cylinder hit the water's surface and blew off its parachute. 400 feet, then 450. The cylinders had been programmed for what the designers called a 'time-on-target' assault, in which both cylinders would act at the exact same moment in time, despite there being a significant time between their launches. Unavoidably, this would cause unit one to act at a deeper depth than unit two, but that had been eventually considered a good thing, that the entire sea's depth spectrum would be covered.

So it was that unit one was at a depth of 1800 feet at zero hour while unit two was at 900. And at time zero, both units did the exact same thing. Within the guts of unit one's cylinder, a thick metal safety plate rotated to line up four large holes, which were blocked previously. Those holes formed a channel leading from the lower end of the cylinder upward toward the top. At the top end were high voltage actuators, which would be impacted by projectiles with bullets that resembled blasting caps. Time zero came, and the actuation projectiles were all fired by the pyrotechnic charges, blew upward through the channels of the safety plate, and hit their targets, the high voltage actuators, which all fired behind a ping-pong ball-sized plug of plutonium, blowing it like a bullet toward a hollowed-out sphere of plutonium, until the plug hit the sphere like putting the lid on a jack-o'-lantern. Even before the plutonium plug could make full contact with the hollowed-out sphere, the fission reactions immediately intensified in the first ten microseconds to be a thousand times higher than before. The neutrons formed by nuclear fission had previously been leaked to the environment, and there had been no chain reaction. But once the plug hit the sphere, the shape became perfect, and more neutrons stayed within the envelope of the sphere than leaked to the universe, and when that happened, the chain reaction started, each fission putting out heat energy while blowing out two or three neutrons, each of which caused another fission with more energy release and another two or three neutrons, until the chain reactions released so much energy that the sphere became the temperature of the surface of the sun, and when it did, it expanded and blew up the small canisters of heavy water lining the outside of what had been the cylinder, which then underwent fusion reactions, the hydrogen of the heavy water atoms combining to form helium, the helium product having a lower mass than the reactants, and that "mass defect" was all converted to heat energy by Einstein's famous equation linking matter to energy, and with a few more microseconds, the fireball grew outside the cylinder and extended into the sea beyond.

At the same time unit one's hydrogen bomb was exploding, unit two, ten miles east, exploded in sympathy, the two explosions extending into the depths of the sea, the shock wave from their blasts hitting the seafloor two miles below and forming a gigantic wall of a pressure wave, both of them blowing huge mushroom clouds of steam and water into the atmosphere, the twin mushroom clouds fully two miles high.

The shock wave, a massive wall of high pressure, traveled through the sea, hammering everything in its path, killing fish, whales, dolphins, microscopic organisms, until it reached the high yield steel of a submarine constructed by the Russian Republic. And one belonging to the Islamic Republic of Iran. And another belonging to the United States.

Washington, DC, USA
White House Situation Room
Monday, June 7; 0905 UTC, 0405 EST

"Excuse me, ma'am, sir," the Marine corporal said at the door to the room. "There's an incoming for you from Langley."

CIA Director Margo Allende paged through her pad computer and looked at it, then projected it onto the screen beside the chart display. It was a view of the sea looking down from above. Allende read the email text to herself while National Security Advisor Michael Pacino stared at the video.

On the screen was a periscope, a slight wake extending behind it. To the right side of the small wake was another mast, this one shorter and stubbier, with a larger cylinder on top of it. Farther behind the two masts, a plume of heavy black smoke rose from the sea.

"This is a drone shot from a Predator, two damned hours old. What are we looking at, Patch?" Allende asked.

"Periscope and snorkel mast," Pacino said. "Not one of ours, that's an optical periscope. We use optronics now. The snorkel mast is designed to bring air into the ship for an emergency diesel engine to provide power and emergency propulsion, or to ventilate the ship. And that plume of smoke—the sub is ventilating the ship and blowing out that smoke. That's not diesel exhaust. That's way too dense for diesel exhaust. Modern diesel fuel leaves almost no smoke."

"Smoke from what?"

"A fire. By the looks of it, a goddamned bad fire."

"There's a spectrographic analysis of the smoke." Allende pushed her pad computer to Pacino, who looked down at the display.

"It's toxic. Burned insulation and high voltage cables. Oxidized atmo-control chemicals. Burned plastic and rubber."

Pacino looked at Allende. "This is bad. As in, not-survivable bad."

"So," Allende said, "who's driving this boat?"

"We've always thought the Russians' AI systems were far more advanced than our own. Frankly, we American submariners don't trust AI. Who knows if it will glitch and screw up the atmosphere, or send us into a jam dive below crush depth one Tuesday? But the Russians see it as a way to lower the crew count. A Yasen-M has twice the tonnage of a Virginia-class submarine and half the crew. You can only do that if you rely heavily on automation. On artificial intelligence. The Russian's AI is operating that ship. It's continuing the mission. And there's no telling how well it will carry out that mission. How ruthless is an AI system programmed to kill another submarine?"

"I think you know the answer to that question, Patch, if I know your history."

"That drone sub was nothing compared to this, Margo. The drone sub that took down *Piranha* only had a bellyful of conventional Mark 50 torpedoes. This thing? Loaded to the gills with nukes, all of them with *Panther*'s name on them. And *Vermont*'s. Margo, we have to shoot at this sonofabitch. We have to direct *Vermont* to lob a nuke at him *now*."

The Marine ran in again, winded and sweating. "Ma'am, sir, you have an urgent videolink request with the Pentagon, and the president is on his way down."

Pacino looked at Allende. "What now?"

The videolink screen lit up to the left of the chart flatpanel. The screen showed a calm view of the sea, another overhead shot from the Predator. Suddenly two gigantic mushroom clouds exploded from the formerly placid sea at exactly the same time. The detonations looked like they were many miles apart, perhaps ten nautical miles. Admirals Rand and Catardi came up on either side of the video clip, the clip looped to keep repeating.

Rand spoke first. "Madam Director, Admiral Pacino, we think the *Vermont* just lobbed two nukes into a position east of them in the Arabian Sea."

About fucking time, Pacino thought.

Arabian Sea
K-579 *Voronezh*
Tuesday, June 7; 0921 UTC, 11:21 am Moscow time

K-579 Second Captain History Module Deck Log:

1121M: This Unit detects an aircraft engine approaching from the west. It is a single jet engine, and close, because it is easily detected on the MGK-600 spherical array. The bearing to the aircraft rapidly changes from west to north and then to east as the aircraft flies overhead rapidly. Sonar data is fed to battlecontrol. Assuming the unit is subsonic, from the lack of a sonic boom, the bracket of possible speeds is between 450 knots and 500 knots, which if true, means it passed very close to K-579 and This Unit, within one kilometer. This Unit wonders if the aircraft can see This Unit. This Unit is at 200 meters keel depth.

1122:08M: This Unit detects a second aircraft engine, also approaching from the west. But this aircraft doesn't fly by. Instead, its bearing seems to freeze at 269 degrees true and it becomes fainter. This seems incongruous. How could it stay at that bearing when it had been so close, then fade? Is it possible the aircraft decided to pull up and climb for the sky? For the sounds and bearings to correlate to that, it would have to have flown almost straight upward. But then, Russian cruise missiles used to have what the designers called a "pop-up" terminal run, where they would climb to the sky and then dive straight down on their target.

1122:10M: But this can't be true, because the noise of the jet engine has stopped. All is silent again.

1122:12M: But wait, there is a splash, directly ahead, very close, although very faint. This Unit waits, but nothing happens.

1122:20M: This Unit attempts to make sense of the odd sounds and the strange behavior of the two aircraft.

1122:23M: This Unit detects another splash, this one heavier, almost directly in front of K-579's course, right at the bow. This splash was much louder, as if whatever fell into the sea was heavy.

1122:25M: Whatever splashed into the water forward of K-579 has descended and it struck the hull just aft of the sonar dome. Could it be a meteorite? Or something associated with that aircraft?

1122:25M: Wait, could it be that the splash and the impact were the result of a depth charge dropped by—

Arabian Sea
K-573 *Novosibirsk*
Tuesday, June 7; 0921 UTC, 11:21 am Moscow time

Weapons Officer Captain Lieutenant Irina Trusov had the morning watch, and her stomach was growling. She'd only had tea and a piece of toast for breakfast, and the thing about a submarine was that the aroma from whatever the cooks were making for the next meal in the galley wafted throughout the entire boat, making the sixty-five members of the crew suddenly hungry. Especially if the meal happened to be a favorite. Trusov took in the air in the room through her nostrils with her eyes shut. It had to be pelmeni, the thin and crusty pastry shell covering a delicious minced beef with spices, with sour cream on the side. But there was more, perhaps the companion dish made for those who didn't like pelmeni—a beef stroganoff with homemade noodles. Trusov shook her head. She'd gain ten pounds on this damned voyage, she thought, promising herself that after she finished digesting this feast she'd work out extra hard down in the crew recreation area.

Trusov sat at the position three command console, the farthest starboard position. The position one station was occupied by Captain Orlov, who wasn't really needed as senior supervisory watch, but he'd sent Navigator Dobryvnik on his way and volunteered to take the morning watch instead. She glanced over at Orlov, the captain's jaw clenched, his blonde hair shorter than yesterday—one of the ship's barbers must have had a go at his previously overgrown hair. She smiled just slightly—he looked good, she thought. He was in shape, and sometimes in the crew recreation room he'd lift weights while she ran on the treadmill, and she'd been sneaking glances at him then too, his muscles rippling under his sleeveless T-shirt. He looked great for an older man, she thought, and she'd never been interested in men near her age. For instance, that pig TK Sukolov, the drunkard communications officer. Or even the older engineer, Chernobrovin or the navigator, Dobryvnik. They may be older than Sukolov, but maturity seemed to elude both of them, those two always snickering over something they thought funny, or slobbering over one of the female members of the crew like the sonar officer, Arisha Vasilev. There was no doubt, being a woman in the heavily dominated male submarine force was not for the faint of heart.

Trusov forced her mind back from thinking about what Orlov would look like naked, and what the noon meal would taste like, back to her duties. She rotated her screens through the notifications, which were mostly clear, to the navigation plot. They still had 275 kilometers to go before they'd be in position. That was five-and-a-half hours from now, so they'd be on station during the afternoon watch, a little after 1700 Moscow time. The original time-on-station time had been 1800, so the current must be helping them, or they were doing better than their calculated 28 knots. She checked the electromagnetic log, the speed-through-water indicator, and it read 28.4 knots. So they were making good time, with a slight boost from the current.

All that meant Orlov would call for battlestations at 1700, which would postpone the evening meal. Trusov smiled. That gave her all the more excuse to fill up on the noon meal—and perhaps that was why the cooks were going all-out to make the noon meal special, because the only thing to eat between when they reached the search point and combat would be biscuits and some passed-around caviar. Trusov crinkled her nose. She hated caviar.

Suddenly her screen flashed red and rotated to the

notifications screen just as Sonar Officer Arisha Vasilev turned.

"Watch Officer, Captain! I have a detect on an aircraft engine! Bearing two-eight-two, bearing rate is starting to increase. It's getting closer."

Trusov grabbed her larger headphones and put them on, Orlov doing the same at his position. She brought up the sonar display and moved her cursor to the broadband trace of the aircraft engine, now at 302 degrees true, then changing rapidly to bearing north, then to 040 when its bearing became steady.

"Captain! That's a cruise missile!" Trusov said, her voice loud. "The only way bearing on a jet engine freezes is if it is doing a pop-up maneuver! We've got to go to maximum speed and a direction away from bearing zero-four-zero!"

"Boatswain!" Orlov shouted, "Engine ahead maximum! Thirty-five knots! Make your depth six hundred meters, steep angle! Left five degrees rudder, steady course two-two-zero!"

The boatswain on the forward starboard ship control console jammed his joystick to the forward bulkhead and the ship dived, the deck beginning to tremble with the power of the main motor speeding up to maximum velocity at one hundred percent reactor power.

"Three-fifty meters, sir. Four hundred!"

"Everybody grab a handhold and make sure you're strapped in," Trusov shouted, "And don emergency breathing masks and fireproof hoods!" She picked up the shipwide announcing circuit microphone. Her voice boomed throughout the previously rigged-for-silent submarine. *"Attention all hands, this is the Watch Officer. All personnel don emergency breathing masks and fireproof hoods. Set material condition X for imminent weapon impact."*

Orlov glanced over at Trusov, his eyes shaded behind his gas mask. He nodded at her while he reached for his seat belt to strap himself into the position one command seat. Trusov did the same, putting the five-point harness over her chest and snapping it into position at her beltline.

Lieutenant Vasilev shouted again from the sonar-and-sensor console. "I have a splash, very faint. Wait, I have a second splash, this one heavier, bearing in our stern sector, detected on the rudder rear-facing hydrophones."

The deck flattened from its steep down-angle of twenty degrees.

"Captain, steady on depth six hundred," the boatswain announced from the ship control center, "steady on course two-two-zero, engines answering ahead one hundred percent, sir."

"Very well," Orlov acknowledged.

Trusov glanced over at Captain Orlov, and just as he seemed to be about to say something to her, her memory and her thoughts stopped as if switched off like a light.

Arabian Sea
Tuesday, June 7; 0922:25 UTC, 11:22:25 am local time

The two nuclear energy releases, ten nautical miles apart, grew identically outward from their start at the center of their depth charges, only differentiated slightly by their explosions at different depths. The western plasma fireball was subjected to a higher sea pressure than the eastern explosion, but that mattered only in that the plasma ovoid formed by the deeper weapon was just slightly smaller than the dimensions of the plasma to the east at the plasma's biggest point. Despite the ultra-high temperature and pressure of the plasmas, the sea overcame them, cooling and dispersing the hot gases, much of their energy directed upward to escape the higher pressure of the deep. The steam from the sea cooling the plasma rose furiously rapidly to the surface above and blew upward into the atmosphere, until there were dual mushroom clouds rising over the seascape.

The western plasma had encountered nothing but seawater, but the eastern plasma had engulfed a large steel shape, first liquefying the metals and composites inside this odd envelope of steel, then vaporizing the liquids, then making the matter turn into a plasma, a state of matter where the energy levels were so high that the electrons boiled off the molecules. There remained no trace of what had once been that object—no wreckage, no floating mattresses, no oil slick. All of what had been the Russian Republic submarine *Voronezh* became atoms stripped of electrons and simply flew upward in the eastern mushroom cloud, what molecules that remained the same elements—iron and carbon—raining down on the sea as little more than contaminants.

The two nuclear fireballs sent out shock waves in all directions, hammering down on the sea floor two miles below, upward to the surface, and outward. The twin shock waves combined to form an even stronger shock wave traveling outward in all directions, the wave weakening as it traveled.

The shock wave soon encountered the hull of the Russian Republic submarine *Novosibirsk,* located 49 nautical miles west-southwest of the westernmost detonation. The shock wave had sufficient strength to slam into the submarine, roll it far over, and shake the ship so hard that every living soul aboard lost consciousness from hitting something, even the officers strapped into their seats in the central command post. The shock tripped the submarine's reactor and took all propulsion systems offline and opened every electrical breaker aboard, but perhaps the worst effect happened in compartment three's lower level, the location of auxiliary machinery room number two, where the twin oxygen generators came off their foundation mountings, the piping to the high pressure oxygen and hydrogen receivers rupturing, and the mixture of oxygen and hydrogen exploding, the intense fires overcoming the halon firefighting system and the smoke of the flames melting through the emergency breathing air manifold and dumping the pressure of the emergency air breathing system into the room, further feeding the fire. A check valve in the system had been designed to prevent this loss of emergency breathing air, but in the hellish conflagration, it melted and ceased to exist other than a liquid metal puddle on the deck of the room.

The opening of all electrical breakers shut down the ventilation fan that took a suction on the room and distributed it to the ship, so the outgoing air flow stopped as well as the incoming flow from the ship's spaces, starving the fire of oxygen, although the flames licked up against the metal piping of the high-pressure oxygen that fed the oxygen banks. Had the oxygen level in the room continued to sustain the fire, the flames would have melted the oxygen manifold and become unstoppable, which would have led to the atmosphere of the submarine becoming toxic enough to kill all life aboard, but as the flames blasted against the oxygen piping, the smoke and carbon monoxide in the room choked the flames and fire went out, leaving the room a smoldering wreck of burned valves, cables, piping, tanks and electronics, the smoke so dense that no amount of visible spectrum candlepower would penetrate it.

In the first and second compartments, the crew, all of them wearing emergency air masks, and all of them unconscious from the battering the ship took in the shock wave, began to suffocate from the lack of emergency breathing air system pressure, and as the habitable spaces of the submarine filled with smoke, the crew all began to die at the same moment in time.

By the time the shock wave had traveled at the speed of sound underwater, to the locations of the United States submarine *Vermont* and the United States' pirated submarine *Panther,* 149 nautical miles west of the western-most explosion, the shock wave was little more than a loud sound wave, but still blasted the ears of the inhabitants of those two submarines, rattling the dishes in the pantries, and causing enough of a sudden roll on the *Panther* to knock books off the shelf in the navigation room.

Arabian Sea
K-573 *Novosibirsk*
Tuesday, June 7; 0925 UTC, 11:25 am Moscow time

Weapons Officer Irina Trusov coughed into her gas mask and tried to inhale, but there was nothing there. She instinctively pulled the mask off and tried desperately to breathe, gasping in huge lungfuls of smoky air. She blinked hard, not sure if she had gone blind or if the space were so smoke-filled that there was no visibility. She tried to reach under the console for the battle lantern, but the five-point restraint restricted her motion. She unlatched the seat belt and vaulted out of the seat, still gasping as she found the large flashlight and switched it on.

The room was dark, with smoke, but there was enough visibility in the room to see the forward bulkhead. She could sense the deck was tilting downward a few degrees. She shone the light on the captain, who was collapsed in his harness. Quickly Trusov pulled off his mask, then circled the room, pulling off the masks of the other crewmembers. She returned to Orlov to see if he were breathing, although if he weren't, she wouldn't be able to try to resuscitate him. The rules of their training were specific for times like these: *save the mission, save the ship, save the reactor, then save the crew.* As for the mission, it wasn't able to be salvaged with the ship in this condition. The hated Americans had won, with one swift stroke, once again humiliating Russia. But there was no time for that, she thought, forcing herself to try to understand how to save the ship.

The first thing she needed was the second captain, but the display was dark. Praying it was just in some kind of power-saving mode, she jabbed the display touch screen, but it remained dark.

"Second Captain, respond!" she shouted at it.

"Second Captain, ready," the disembodied, cool, unworried voice replied. God, how Trusov hated that system. The ship was dying and the fucking AI system's voice sounded like it was just another Tuesday.

"Turn on the position three display," she shouted at it. The display lit up, but it would take too long to get the answers she needed. She'd have to deal with the AI verbally.

"Second Captain, report status of propulsion plant."

"The reactor has undergone a group scram resulting from a shock impact. All electrical breakers have opened as a result of the same shock. All systems are offline with the exception of the second captain uninterruptible power supply batteries, but that system is at ninety-five percent and will cease to function in six hours."

Leave it to the AI to worry about itself above all, Trusov thought.

"Second Captain, shut the battery breaker."

"The battery breaker is shut. Battery charge indicates nine-five percent. There are no loads on the battery at this moment."

"Shut the breaker feeding the lighting panels," Trusov ordered. It took a moment, but the lights flashed, then held in the room. Trusov turned off her battle lantern. The smoke in the room was worse. She looked over at the captain, who was coughing and breathing. She slapped his face gently, but he was still out. She was the only one conscious in the room. The angle of the deck had become worse. They might be sinking, she thought, and with no propulsion, that situation could get worse.

"Second Captain, shift propulsion to the emergency propulsion motor."

"Shifting propulsion to the emergency propulsion motor."

"Report depth."

"Watch Officer, depth indicates six-seven-nine meters."

God, the depth of 679 meters was deeper than design crush depth, and they were still going down.

"Propulsion shifted to the emergency propulsion motor," the AI said, calmly, as if it were just another Tuesday.

"Second Captain, engine ahead one third, twenty degrees rise on the bowplanes, make your angle up twenty degrees."

"Engine is ahead one third, twenty degrees rise on the bowplanes, increasing ship's angle to twenty degrees up. No depth order given. No compass course given."

Trusov frowned. "Make your depth one hundred meters. Steer course three-zero-nine." They'd been heading southwest to get in position to intercept the *Panther* before the explosion, and it occurred to Trusov that she should plot a course back to the Pacific rather than try to chase the Americans with a broken submarine, but she didn't have time for tactical or strategic thought. She was still just trying to keep *Novosibirsk* alive.

"Depth order one hundred meters received."

"Status of the reactor plant."

"All channels of reactor protection tripped the unit on detected shock."

"Clear the reactor protection trips, shut all inverter breakers and conduct a fast-recovery startup," Trusov ordered.

"Reactor protection trips cleared. All inverter breakers indicate shut. Latching all control rods and commencing fast-recovery startup."

The deck's downward tilt flattened, then inclined upward as they rose out of the depths.

"Four hundred meters," the AI reported. "Watch Officer, all sensors in auxiliary machinery room number two are offline. Three hundred fifty meters."

"What do you mean they're offline?" That was an ominous report.

"All systems in the auxiliary machinery room two show open circuits, all instrument systems off."

That room was the heart of the ship's atmospheric control equipment. Any problems with that room would have far-reaching implications.

"Do you have instrumentation outside the room in third compartment lower level?"

"Yes."

"Do you have a camera on the hatch to the room?"

"Yes. Displaying it now."

The camera view came up. The porthole in the high-pressure bulkhead hatch to the room was black. The hatch seemed to be glowing a dim red.

"What's the temperature in third compartment lower level forward?"

"Seventy degrees Celsius."

That was broiling. There had to have been a fire in machinery two.

"Second Captain, seal auxiliary machinery room two." The hatches needed to be shut and the pressure damper to the ventilation system locked shut to do what Trusov wanted to do.

"Auxiliary machinery room two is sealed."

"Open the upper room vent to the third compartment. Display the camera in the space where the vent exhausts."

The display came up on Trusov's display, a catwalk in the reactor room. Thick black smoke was pouring into the space, presumably from the machinery room's vent.

"Second Captain, reposition the three-way valve to machinery two's vent to direct flow from the vent to compartment three's bilge."

"Vent three-way valve repositioned to exhaust to the bilge."

"Second Captain, open the hull and backup emergency flood valves to auxiliary machinery room two."

"Commencing emergency flood of auxiliary machinery room two."

This was a casualty procedure memorized by every watch officer, Trusov thought, but to her knowledge, no one had ever actually had to do it.

The angle of the deck flattened again. "Ship's depth, one hundred meters," the second captain announced. "Bilge levels in compartment three are rising."

"Stop the emergency flood operation."

"Shutting hull and backup emergency flood valves," the second captain replied. "Vent valve shut."

"Line up to take a suction on auxiliary machinery room two with the drain pump." Trusov brushed a lock of sweaty hair out of her eyes, thinking that she craved a shower.

"Drain pump is lined up with suction on auxiliary machinery room two. Do you want to open the vent valve?"

"Open the vent valve and start the drain pump," Trusov ordered.

"Drain pump on." It would only take seconds to dewater the room. "Drain pump off."

"Very well." Someone would have to go into the room physically, Trusov thought, to see how bad the damage was. She'd have to ventilate the ship from the surface soon, but first she needed the reactor.

"Status of the reactor?"

"Reactor is in the power range and warming up now using normal rates."

"Increase heat-up using maximum emergency rate," Trusov ordered. It wasn't safe for the reactor to do that, and could blow the lid off the reactor pressure vessel, but this wasn't a normal day at sea.

"Reactor expected to be at normal operating temperature and pressure in two minutes."

Orlov made a sound. Lifting his head off the surface of his console, then dropping it back down. Trusov touched his forehead, lifting his face off the console, but he was still out of it. She looked around at the smoky room, and the other watchstanders were still out.

"Reactor is at normal operating temperature and pressure," the second captain said. "Commencing steam plant startup."

"Second Captain, make your depth two-one meters, fifteen-degree up angle, no stern clearance." If there were a ship above them, it would just have to take 13,800 metric tons of Yasen-M-class submarine ramming it. With all that had gone wrong this watch, Trusov thought, there couldn't be anything that could make it worse. She rose from the console and grabbed the periscope pole behind her seat.

"Raising number one scope," she announced, as if there were anyone awake to hear her. She grabbed the hydraulic control ring and rotated it counterclockwise, and the periscope began to rise out of the well.

"Steam plant is online," the second captain said. "Fifty meters."

"Second Captain, engine stop, shift propulsion to the main motor."

"Engine stop, shifting propulsion to the main motor."

Trusov grabbed the periscope grips as the optics module emerged from the periscope well and snapped them down, putting her eye on the cold rubber of the eyepiece. The view out the scope was only an inky black this deep. She trained the view upwards and began to rotate the periscope in circles, making a complete circle in thirty seconds.

"Propulsion shifted to the main motor," the second captain said.

"Engine ahead one third, turns for six knots," Trusov ordered. The view above was getting lighter steadily, but there was still nothing visible.

"Thirty-five meters."

Trusov could see light from above, shimmering downward. She kept up her circles, looking for the hull of a surface ship above, prepared to order the second captain to dive the ship deep in the emergency of encountering a shape or shadow directly above them.

"Thirty meters."

Trusov could see the undersides of the waves now, looking silvery, the sunlight from above stronger now as it penetrated the upper layer of ocean.

"Twenty-seven meters."

The waves farther out were visible now. There were no shapes or shadows. They were apparently alone in the sea.

"Twenty-three meters."

The periscope view climbed into the waves until a crest was above the view, but the view broke out of a trough, then immediately went back into a crest. The scope foamed up, nothing to see but a thousand bubbles.

"Scope's awash."

"Twenty-two meters."

"Scope's clear," Trusov called, doing her collision avoidance circles faster now. "No close contacts," she called, training the periscope to what she'd seen only briefly as she made a circle. There, at bearing 044, two enormous mushroom clouds were rising from the sea, the tops of them perhaps five kilometers high. "Holy mother of God," Trusov breathed to herself. If they'd been any closer to the detonation point, they'd have all died instantly. *"Goddamned Americans,"* she sneered. *"Villains. You are all villains and you are all damned to the fires of Hell."* She wished she could get her hands on whoever had launched those cruise missiles. She would enjoy strangling the man and seeing the light in his eyes cloud over as death took him.

"Twenty-one meters."

"Second Captain, raise the induction mast."

Hydraulics thumped as the mast came out of the conning tower and reached skyward.

"Induction mast is up."

"Drain the induction mast."

"Draining the induction mast," the AI replied. "Induction mast indicates dry."

"Very well. Line up to emergency ventilate the first and second compartments with the low-pressure blower."

"Lining up to emergency ventilate. Ready to emergency ventilate compartments one and two."

"Start the blower."

The sound of the low-pressure blower was loud throughout the ship, and would be loud outside it as well. If the Americans were close, they'd hear, Trusov thought. She'd have to recover the battlecontrol and sonar systems next.

"Atmosphere reads nominal in compartments one and two."

"Shift emergency ventilation to compartments four and five."

"Emergency ventilating compartments four and five."

Captain Orlov groaned. Trusov took her face off the periscope just long enough to look at him, then returned to her surface search.

"Atmosphere reads nominal in compartments four and five."

"Second Captain, line up to emergency ventilate auxiliary machinery room two."

Out the periscope, Trusov could see sooty smoke emerge from the sea aft of her view. She bit her lip. The auxiliary machinery room had to have been totaled. Hopefully the oxygen banks hadn't been affected, but there would no longer be any new oxygen generated aboard. Nor would the carbon dioxide be eliminated. The boat was just one big confined space, Trusov thought. Not easy to fight a war in a boat with no atmospheric control. It would be like being in a World War II U-Boat.

"Second Captain, line up to emergency ventilate compartment three."

It took longer for the atmosphere in compartment three to clear up, but eventually the air in the boat was nominal.

"Second Captain, stop the low-pressure blower and lower the induction mast."

The loud blower sound stopped. Trusov took a breath. The smoke was gone from the room, but it still didn't smell right. It probably would only get worse, she thought. They needed to return to base, assuming they could limp there with nothing further breaking, though, the thought of staying in the fight and launching weapons against the Americans would be more to her liking.

She felt a tap at her shoulder. She looked over and stared into Captain Orlov's eyes. "Nice recovery, Madam Weapons

Officer. I heard you from somewhere far away. You saved the ship. You saved me. You have my lifelong gratitude."

Trusov blushed. "Just doing my duty, Captain. Do you want to look?"

Orlov took the scope and whistled at the size of the dual mushroom clouds. "Damned Americans nuked us," he said. "How the hell did they detect us?"

"They must have fired blind, sir," Trusov said. "It's the only thing that explains why we're still alive."

"Take the scope. I'll write a message to the Admiralty. I take it we have no atmo-control."

"None whatsoever, Captain. We'll have to ventilate at periscope depth, probably twice a day or risk collapsing from carbon dioxide poisoning."

"Odds are, we'll get orders to get back to base."

The other watchstanders in the room were awake, but none had the energy of Orlov, all of them seated and holding their heads. Navigator Misha Dobryvnik came into the room from the aft door.

"What the hell happened?" he said, rubbing his eyes.

"Navigator," Orlov said, "plot a course back to Petropavlovsk. Odds are we'll be ordered home."

29

Arabian Sea
B-902 *Panther*
Tuesday, June 28; 0925 UTC, 1325 local time

Lieutenant Anthony Pacino had been standing watch in the central command post when the detonation rocked the boat. The shock rolled cups off consoles, the sound of glass breaking sounding in the room, the more distant sound of dishes breaking in the pantry coming from below.

"What the hell was that?" Dankleff half-shouted, skidding to a halt in front of the position one starboard console.

"That was either conventional and close or it was nuclear and distant," Pacino said. "I have an idea. Come with me." He led Dankleff to the sonar room, where Chief Albanese was training Chief Kim on standing sonar watch. Kim was doubled over, her hands clasped to her ears, tears running down her cheeks.

"She had on the headset when the explosion hit," Albanese said. "It broke the headset and I imagine she'll be functionally deaf for a day or two. Assuming the best."

Pacino motioned in Chief Goreliki to take care of Kim, who stood her up to take her to her bunk.

"What do you think, Chief?" Pacino asked Albanese.

"I think somebody dropped a nuke. We should put in a couple of legs to get the range. If it's distant, it was friendly fire from *Vermont*. If it's close, probably one of the bad guys."

"You can't do TMA on a blue-out," Pacino said. Doing

target-motion-analysis on a cloud of bubbles that took up a quarter of the azimuth was a waste of time. "What do you think about hitting it with an active sonar ping?" Pacino asked.

"That pretty much goes against everything we've been doing on this mission. You know, stealth and all," Dankleff said, frowning. "And going against every order we have on this mission."

"True. But if this is the result of *Vermont* firing a nuke, we'll get an immediate range on the detonation radius, and maybe a surviving Russian submarine, assuming Whale here can interpret the return ping—"

"I can interpret it," Albanese said, matter-of-factly.

"You sure?"

"No. I was trying to give myself confidence. And change my universe's reality."

"You've been talking to Fishman again, right?" Pacino continued. "If there were submarines that survived the blast, we need to know where they are."

"Say there are?" Dankleff asked. "What's our next move?"

"Obvious," Pacino said. "We drive out that way and sink them."

"Dammit, Patch, that's not our directive!" Dankleff's face had turned red as he shouted. "We're supposed to hide and sneak out of the Arabian Sea, not turn our guns on some opposing force, spoiling for a fight. Is this your version of, 'the best defense is a good offense,' for fuck's sake?"

"I wish I'd thought of that to say, actually, U-Boat," Pacino said. "Look at it this way. Any submerged contact out that way has a room full of torpedoes. If he's damaged and recovers, those torpedoes will be in the mail to our position. And to *Vermont*'s position. How big is your catcher's mitt, U-Boat? Big enough to catch an inbound Futlyar torpedo? Or a baker's dozen of them?"

Dankleff sighed, rubbing his eyes. "Why, oh why, didn't I select *Lobabes* for AOIC?"

Pacino clapped Dankleff on the shoulder. "Good man. So, Chief Albanese, you ready to line up and try this?"

"Let's turn to face the bearing to the detonation,

zero-four-five, and hover. That'll remove any own-ship noise from the sonar equation."

Pacino stepped back to the command post. "Grip, left twenty degrees rudder, steady zero-four-five."

"*Northeast?* Are you high?"

"Just do it, ya damned non-qual SEAL."

"Fine, my rudder is left twenty, coming around to course zero-four-five."

Pacino reached for a phone and called the wardroom. "Get Captain Ahmadi up to central command," he said to Fishman. While he waited, he watched the dinner-plate sized compass spin slowly in the center of Aquatong's console. Finally he steadied up on course 045.

"Grip, all stop. I'll set up to hover."

Ahmadi showed up, Fishman behind him. "Yes, Mr. Patch. Can I help?"

"Help me hover the boat," Pacino said. Ahmadi took the position two console seat and stared at the displays, then pumped water from aft to forward and from the depth control tank to sea, waiting to see how the boat responded, then flooding depth control slightly. Sweat broke out on his forehead as he concentrated. After several minutes of operating the trim system, Ahmadi looked up at Pacino. "We're hovering at one hundred meters, Mr. Patch."

"Keep watching it, Captain," Pacino said. He hurried back to sonar.

"We're steady on zero-four-five and hovering. You ready?"

"Yes, sir," Albanese said. "The MGK-400 is lined up." He looked up at Dankleff. "OIC, permission to ping active?"

Pacino looked at Dankleff, who bit his lip, then said, "I'm gonna regret this, but, Chief, ping active."

Arabian Sea
USS *Vermont*
Tuesday, June 7; 0937 UTC, 1337 local time

The loud active sonar ping could be heard with the naked ear in the hull of *Vermont*, the sound loud and long. It seemed to be coming from the south. And it seemed close.

Captain Seagraves looked at Officer of the Deck Romanov, his face startled. "What the hell is going on?"

"That was from *Panther,*" Petty Officer Mercer said from the Q-10 stack seat. "Bearing one-seven-eight."

"Can you tell if there's a return ping?" Romanov asked.

"We're not set up for that," Mercer said. "We'd have to ping out with the Q-10 ourselves to interpret actual distance to the blueout and see if there are any surviving submerged contacts."

Seagraves, Romanov and Quinnivan gathered at the command console. "What the hell are they doing?" Seagraves said, his frown deepening.

"Approach Officer, we have a zig on the *Panther,*" Mercer announced. "Aspect change. He's turning to his left. Northwest."

"Goddammit," Seagraves cursed. "Dankleff is supposed to get *Panther* out of here, no matter what happens."

"Transients from *Panther,*" Mercer said. "Sounds are consistent with him starting up his fast reactor."

"I'm going to kill those guys," Seagraves muttered to himself.

"*Panther* is speeding up, sir. Sounds like he's putting on maximum turns."

"He's heading toward the blueout, Captain," Romanov said, flipping the command console to the chart. She'd drawn blood red circles around the impact points of the SubRocs. The bearing to the point in between the circles was 049. Before *Panther* started acting up, they'd done three legs of target motion analysis, TMA, to determine the range to the blueout, and it was sloppy, but generally correlated with the range they'd set into the SubRocs, 180 and 190 miles from the *Vermont*. "I think. Let's get some TMA done on *Panther* to get his solution. Maybe he detected something."

"We don't have time for that, Nav," Quinnivan said, cupping his hand over his boom microphone, giving an illusion of the three of them having privacy in the crowded battlestations-manned control room. "*Panther* pinged active, so if there is someone out there, now they know we're here, and they know *Panther* didn't steal herself. Our presence as an escort sub has to have been guessed by an opposition force. And all I can say is, 'duh.' It's fookin' obvious. So let's see what *Panther* detected. We need to line up active sonar and ping the hell out of that blueout. See what *Panther*'s got her nose into."

"XO makes a good point, Captain," Romanov said, as if she sensed Seagraves' doubts.

Seagraves looked at Quinnivan, then Romanov. "Any downside to going active?"

Quinnivan made a sour face. "Sure, Skipper. Whoever's out there would have our exact bearing. If he's good, he could do a couple passive TMA legs on us and nail down our exact solution."

"But he can't put a warhead on us," Romanov said, "we're way outside torpedo range, if a contact is near the blueout."

"Pilot," Seagraves ordered, "left twenty degrees rudder, steady zero-four-nine. All ahead flank." He looked at Romanov. "We should at least get going in that direction."

"The blueout is five or six hours out, Captain," Romanov said. "And we're definitely outside torpedo range of an opponent, but not if he has anything equivalent to the SubRoc. Like a Kalibr missile."

"Most of the Kalibr cruise missiles," Quinnivan said, "are set up for surface ship assault. All it could do to us is make a big bang overhead."

"Unless it's a nuke," Seagraves said. "Or one of the Kalibr variants designed for antisubmarine warfare."

"We're worrying about ghosts, Skipper," Quinnivan said. "Let's get a few active pulses out there and nail down whatever object or contact is out there, and then let's drive towards that."

"Sonar, line up to ping active," Seagraves ordered. "Three pulses. Low freq, long range detection parameters. Center of pulses at bearing zero-four-nine."

"Aye, sir, lining up Q-10 sphere for active," Mercer reported. "Ready, Captain."

"Sonar, ping active, three pulses."

An earsplitting roaring shriek sounded in the room, coming from forward, the pulse rising like a siren from a deep bass roar, rising in pitch until it ended in a tenor hum. The comparative quiet after the pulse seemed surreal. Seagraves' ears ached from the noise that seemed to drill into his skull. After ten seconds, a second pulse went out, and a second time Seagraves' eardrums were hammered. Finally, ten seconds after that, the third pulse went out.

Romanov had selected the active sonar screen on the command console display, but Seagraves stepped over to Snowman Mercer's Q-10 stack, not just to see the results on the screen, but Mercer's expression as he analyzed any return pings.

"Anything?"

Mercer nodded, his reply loud in the room. "Captain, Officer of the Deck, I hold a new sonar contact, Sierra Seventeen, bearing zero-three-eight, range, two hundred sixty thousand yards."

"Sweet jumpin' Jaysus," Quinnivan said. "Are ya sure, lad? A hundred and thirty fookin' nautical *miles?* That's awfully far out to be a strong detect."

"Sir," Mercer said, turning in his seat, "It's strong enough. Whatever it is, it's big and solid and submerged. The nuclear detonations must have blown off his anechoic tiles and exposed his steel to our ping."

"Okay, then," Seagraves said, inhaling deeply, wishing he could smoke a cigarette, or better, one of Quinnivan's Cuban cigars. "Sonar and firecontrol party, designate Sierra Seventeen as Master One. Pilot, steer course zero-three-eight and make your depth twelve hundred feet."

The deck inclined downward as *Vermont* made for the northeast at flank speed, her deck trembling from the power of the flank bell.

"I hope to hell we'll still have *Panther* on passive sonar at this speed," Romanov said.

"No need to worry about that," Mercer said. "*Panther* is as loud as a proverbial train wreck."

"Great," Seagraves said, shaking his head. "Navigator, prepare a situation report for a slot buoy transmission. Tell the brass we're chasing after whatever contact is near the blueout."

"Should I mention that *Panther* forced our hand, sir?"

Seagraves drilled his gaze into Romanov's eyes. "Captain John Paul Jones once said, 'discretion is the better part of valor,' Navigator. Let's just leave that detail out."

Atlantic Ocean
Point S-Prime: 200 miles west of Oued Eddahab, Western Sahara, Africa
K-561 ***Kazan***
Tuesday, June 7; 0945 UTC, 1145 Moscow time

Captain First Rank Georgy Alexeyev read the radio dispatch from *Voronezh* with dismay. The submarine's fire had killed the entire crew. And now the AI system, the second captain, was attempting to continue the mission? It was lunacy. The AI onboard the Yasen-M-class was primitive. There was no way it could out-think a motivated enemy. Alexeyev and his battlestations crew had tangled with the AI version in battle simulators, and ten times out of ten he'd defeated them. Admiral Zhigunov insisted that was just because Alexeyev and his crew were exemplary, but Alexeyev doubted that. It wasn't that he was a superstar at submarine vs. submarine combat. It was that the AI was dumb.

Alexeyev left his sea cabin and stepped into the central command post. The on-watch crew greeted him, coming to attention. He waved at them to relax. At the port aft navigation chart console, he leaned over the display and calculated how long it would be before the *Kazan* would be on-station, then cursed. This was taking entirely too long.

Odds were, if the *Panther* and her escort submarine were making for the western hemisphere, they'd be there long before *Kazan* got into position. Zhigunov had called him too late.

Arabian Sea
K-573 Novosibirsk
Tuesday, June 7; 0947 UTC, 11:47 am Moscow time

Weapons Officer Irina Trusov stood up from her position three console at the captain's order. He was on the phone to nuclear control.

"Engineer, get a watch relief so you can walk down the ship with us. This damage inspection will determine whether we continue the mission or head home, and for that matter, whether we will even be able to continue on submerged." Captain First Rank Yuri Orlov listened for a moment. "We can discuss that when we arrive at nuclear control," he said sternly, cutting off what sounded like a panic-stricken chief engineer. "The weapons officer, navigator and I are walking the ship down for a damage inspection, and you're coming with us. Be ready when we get there." Orlov hung up despite Chernobrovin still speaking on the other end.

"Well, something's very wrong back aft," Orlov commented to Trusov. She nodded, not knowing what else to say. First Officer Vlasenko showed up in central command with Communicator Sukolov with him, to take over senior supervisory central command watch and the watch officer duty. Trusov spent a moment whispering to Sukolov to tell him the status of things so he could take on the duty.

"Have you tried to raise the radio mast?" he asked.

"No," Trusov said. "I verified the induction mast and number two periscope work. Presumably the MFHG antenna works as well. You can test it next periscope depth."

"We need to get a situation report out to Pac Fleet," Sukolov said, his eyes wide, his cheeks hollow. He was badly frightened, Trusov thought.

"Write up a draft for the captain to look at for when we return from touring the ship," she said. Sukolov nodded.

"Weapons Officer, are you ready?" Orlov said impatiently. Navigator Misha Dobryvnik stood by the captain, a frown on his worried face. Trusov found herself thinking that it was a good thing that she wasn't the only one who was frightened and worried. *Goddamned Americans,* she thought for the dozenth time since the explosion.

"Ready now, sir."

"Let's go. We'll start aft. The engineer was complaining."

Orlov walked so fast on the way to nuclear control that Trusov broke into a jog to keep up with him. Out the aft door, he flew, down the passageway past the officers' staterooms to the steep stairs to the middle level, emerging into the crew's messroom, and aft of that, to an alcove housing the large round hatch that led through the shielded tunnel through the third compartment that housed the 200 megawatt nuclear reactor, the shielding designed to minimize exposure to the neutron and gamma radiation from the reactor. Trusov couldn't help noticing the sign flashing in the space, the yellow and magenta sign lit from behind:

HIGH RADIATION LEVEL ALARM

Great, Trusov thought. All the wicked casualties happening to the submarine, now it had to have a radiation casualty?

The tunnel led aft to the fourth compartment where the turbines, generators and motors were housed, with the nuclear control room placed just aft of the bulkhead to the third compartment. Farther aft of the door to nuclear control, Trusov could see a steam leak—no, several steam leaks. The compartment was hot and humid, and she felt herself sweat through her coveralls, the choking steam filling the air in the crowded machinery space. Now she was beginning to think the ship couldn't be saved.

"Status of the reactor?" Orlov said through the doorway to nuclear control.

Inside, Captain Third Rank Kiril Chernobrovin stood behind the reactor control panel and steam plant control panel, his coveralls soaked in sweat, a cut to his scalp having bled down his face, the streak of blood making Trusov's suppressed fear somehow bloom stronger.

"The rod we dropped when we entered the Arabian Sea, Captain? We've dropped it again. I've maintained the reactor critical, but the neighboring fuel modules have had to pick up the load from the rod drop and they are overpowered, and their fuel elements are melting, and the third compartment is now a high radiation area. Add to that, we now have a primary-to-secondary leak, and the fourth compartment's radiation levels are skyrocketing. The occupancy time—the safe occupancy time—for this room is shrinking down to less than an hour, Captain. Beyond that, we're all getting far more than our allowable lifetime doses. If we have to sail all the way back to base, we'll have enough radiation dosage that, well, sir, we'd be lucky to live for another year, and that will be one miserable year."

Orlov cursed. "Dammit, Engineer, you keep this beast critical and maintain propulsion, I don't care if the damned thing fucking explodes. Now come with us for this inspection."

Trusov caught a glance from the engineer and there was no mistaking his thoughts. *We have to abandon ship.* But Yuri Orlov would die before he'd abandon a mission, much less his beloved submarine.

They walked quickly forward to the shielded tunnel.

"You ran the blower, right, Weapons Officer? It wasn't my imagination?"

"You were still pretty out of it, Captain," Trusov said. "But yes."

Orlov hurried to the lower level, where the emergency diesel lived.

"The diesel could go either way, I suppose," Orlov said, touching the side of the massive diesel engine. "I hope to hell it's okay. It may need to get us home." Orlov glanced quickly at Chernobrovin, then led them back up the stairway to the middle level, then forward through the crew's messroom. Dobryvnik paused near the large door to refrigerated storage, noticing the breaker providing power to the room had tripped. Without thinking about it, Dobryvnik reached for the red handle to the breaker, which was indeed in the tripped position, took it to the "open" position, then pulled it up to the "shut" position. It immediately exploded in a breadbox-sized ball of flames, Dobryvnik falling to the deck, grasping his hand.

"You okay?" Trusov said, bending over him and pulling him up by his good hand. He looked at the burn, wincing.

"Navigator, get up to the wardroom and get the first aid kit out and see to that burn," Orlov said, his jaw clenching.

"Yessir," Dobryvnik said, cradling his burned hand as he made his way forward.

"So much for our food supply," Orlov said.

"This mission just keeps getting better," Chernobrovin muttered.

The three of them left the crew's messroom and hurried past the crew recreation room, farther forward past crew berthing, to the radio room. "Weapons Officer? Do you know the combination?"

"Hull number twice, Captain," Trusov said. "Unless the navigator changed it since the last time I used it."

Orlov punched in the code, "5-7-3-5-7-3" and tried the knob, but it was frozen. "You try," he said to Trusov, who entered the code on the button pad, but nothing helped.

"Engineer, go fetch a goddamned pry bar from machinery one."

"Right away, Captain," Chernobrovin said, glad to have an errand to take his mind off their situation. While they waited, Orlov pounded on the radio room door, but the radiomen weren't answering. Trusov realized she was breathing heavily, perhaps the effect of the exertion in the contaminated atmosphere. She should have checked the atmospheric readings in machinery one, she thought. They needed to know when they'd have to come up to periscope depth and ventilate.

Chernobrovin appeared, winded, with a crowbar. He took it to the radio room door, and he and Orlov pushed until the lock broke and the radio room door burst open. The scene was one from Hell itself, complete devastation. Scorched and burned equipment. Smoke pouring out of the room into the passageway. The horrible stench of burned human flesh. The smoke cleared, revealing the black wreckage of the radio equipment and the two radiomen who had been unfortunate enough to be in the space when the fire broke out. Orlov's eyes narrowed and he cursed under his breath.

"There goes any chance of communicating to Pac Fleet or the Admiralty," he said.

"What about a radio buoy launched from the countermeasure ejection tube, sir?" Chernobrovin asked.

"They were all stored in here," Orlov said. "Along with the computer to load a message into them."

"No other emergency transmitters?"

Orlov shook his head. "The escape chamber has an emergency beacon, but it's just a dumb attention-getter."

Trusov traded another glance with Chernobrovin. This was getting untenable. "I guess it no longer matters if the MFHG antenna is functional," she said.

"Captain," Chernobrovin said to Orlov, "I should get back to nuclear control. Make sure we're staying critical and in the power range. Maybe minimize the fuel melting."

"Go," Orlov said, waving the engineer aft. "Trusov, let's get to the torpedo room," Orlov said, walking rapidly forward to the large hatch to the first compartment.

Torpedo Officer Vasiliy Naumov looked up as Captain Orlov and Weapons Officer Trusov came into the first compartment and stood looking at the wreckage of what had once been an orderly torpedo room.

"What's your status, Naumov?" Orlov asked.

Senior Lieutenant Naumov wiped his forehead. Trusov stared at him, realizing he was barely more than a child, lanky and pimply, his hair a mess, his coveralls torn, his hand trembling.

"Three weapons came off their racks, Captain. I called it up to central, to Mr. First. I can't get them back on their racks alone, sir, the rigging gear is trapped under one of the loose weapons."

Orlov took a deep breath. "What is that smell, Naumov?"

"I can't smell anything, Captain. I guess I've been in the compartment too long—"

"Dammit, that's self-oxidizing weapon fuel," Orlov said harshly. "One of your torpedoes is leaking."

"If we can find which one is leaking, we can put an emergency patch on it," Naumov offered.

"Trusov, help your torpedo officer get this space squared away," Orlov ordered, his expression turning even more dark than before.

Trusov, though, had wandered a few meters farther forward to the torpedo tube doors, her gaze fixed on tube 5, which had been loaded with a Shkval supercavitating torpedo. She sniffed the air close to the door and put her fingers under a pet-cock, a few drops emerging. She rubbed her fingers together under her nose as she turned back to the captain. The hydrogen peroxide fuel had an ingredient added to it to make a distinctive odor, allowing leaks to be more easily detected.

"Sir, we have a bigger problem. I've got a peroxide leak in tube five, the tube-loaded Shkval tube. We've got to jettison it before it goes off."

Orlov hurried to the forward port torpedo control console, finding the local operating station for the tube doors. Trusov joined him at the console.

"At least we have power here," Orlov said. "That's a good sign, right?"

Orlov rotated the master selector switch from "CENTRAL COMMAND" to "LOCAL CONTROL" and selected tube 5. He hit the fixed function buttons for the "VENT" and "FLOOD" valves, each one lighting up a red annunciator indicator light. A new annunciator lit up, this one reading "TUBE FLOODED." He shut the vent valve and found the fixed function button for the valve marked "EQUALIZE." This valve should open tube 5 to seawater pressure and allow the muzzle door to be opened. He glanced at Trusov.

"Let's hope the hydraulics for this work." He punched the fixed function button marked "OUTER DOOR—OPEN" and it flashed white. "So much for hoping." The status panel of hull openings still showed a green bar over the label marked "TUBE 5 OUTER DOOR." The muzzle door remained shut. The Shkval torpedo was trapped in the tube.

"Can we do a manual hand-crank to try to open the muzzle door, Trusov?"

Trusov nodded. "The emergency hydraulic system pressurization hand crank is centerline forward. Naumov, follow me."

As Trusov turned from Orlov to find the hydraulic hand crank station, the Shkval torpedo in tube number five exploded into fiery incandescence, its pressurized fuel fire causing the three-hundred-kilogram high explosives to detonate inside the tube. The white-hot fireball blew Trusov and Naumov backwards into Orlov, and all three collapsed on the deck.

Orlov had been knocked unconscious by the blast and Naumov was stunned, looking like he barely knew where he was. Trusov sat half up and saw her worst twin nightmares—a huge blowtorch fire blowing into the room from forward at the same time as a tremendous roaring, pressurized jet of water was screaming into the room.

In a quiet part of her mind, where time had slowed down to a crawl, she was reminded of the old Russian submariner's joke—*Good news, Captain, the flooding put out the fire.* A weak joke, since both fire and flooding were two of the gods of the sea's evil henchmen, intent on killing any sailor bold enough or foolish enough to attempt to sail beneath the waves.

She could feel the deck incline downward as the mighty stream of floodwater filled the bilges, what must be double digit tons of water filling the first compartment. And unlike the submariner's joke, no amount of water would put out a self-oxidizing weapon fuel fire. It would burn underwater.

There was no fighting this, Trusov thought. *It was over.* The mission of *Novosibirsk* had come to this moment. Either the remaining surviving crew went down with the crippled submarine, or she got the order out to abandon ship. With a struggle, she grabbed Orlov, who was still unconscious.

"Naumov! Help me get the captain out of the compartment!"

"We have to fight the fire! And the flooding!"

"It's over, Naumov, now get the captain's arm," she hissed at the young torpedo officer.

Trusov and Naumov muscled Orlov through the latched-open hatch to the second compartment and pulled the hatch off the latch. With the angle of the ship downward, the hatch slammed shut hard against the seating surface. Trusov threw the lever to latch the hatch and stepped forward five meters to the communication station. She found a phone and punched the button for the central command post.

"First Officer," Vlasenko's voice said, over some severe background noise. There was shouting in the room.

Trusov looked at Naumov. "Mr. First, from the captain, emergency blow to the surface and prepare to abandon ship."

"What? What's happening?"

"We have massive flooding and a fire in the torpedo room and a weapon fuel fire. The first compartment is going to explode any minute. Unless you want *Novosibirsk* to be a second *Kursk*, you'll follow the captain's orders!" It would have been better if Orlov himself could have barked into the phone to Vlasenko, but it couldn't be helped. There was no other choice, Trusov thought. If Orlov were awake, he'd give the same order.

The shipwide announcing circuit blasted through the ship with Vlasenko's trembling voice. *"This is central command. All personnel, prepare to abandon ship. I repeat, all personnel, prepare to abandon ship."*

As the speakers clicked off, Trusov could hear the sound of roaring coming from overhead. Hopefully that was high pressure air blowing the water out of the ballast tanks, she thought, and not more flooding. She struggled again to get Orlov to the stairs to the upper level, fighting against the down angle of the ship. Was it her imagination, or had the down angle eased?

It seemed to take endless minutes to get Orlov to the top of the stairs, and Trusov was soaked in sweat and hyperventilating at the top of the stairs. She looked at her coveralls and hoped the wetness represented sweat and not torpedo fuel. The coveralls were fire-resistant, but nothing could stop a fire from torpedo fuel. She and Naumov muscled Orlov aft into the forward door of the central command post, which was empty of crew but for Vlasenko. Fortunately, Orlov was returning to consciousness, his hand rising to his face as he looked up at the first officer. Trusov breathed a sigh of relief, knowing that now Vlasenko wouldn't see that she'd lied about the orders to emergency blow and abandon ship coming from the captain.

"Status, Ivan?" Orlov croaked.

"We've emergency blown to the surface, Captain, but we still have a down angle and we must be taking on water in the first compartment. The escape chamber is ready and the crew—what's left of them—are mustering at the lower hatch."

"Come on, let's go," Orlov croaked. Trusov helped him get to the aft door of the room and into the passageway that led aft past the officers' berthing rooms and the sonar equipment room to the ladder and lower hatch to the escape chamber, a large sphere faired into the conning tower, one of the reasons the conning tower was so long compared to the conning towers of other navy's submarines. The chamber was designed to allow the entire crew of 60 to survive a submarine sinking. Vlasenko hit the hydraulic control lever to open the bottom hatch, which opened into the chamber. Trusov looked around, the crew numbering perhaps two dozen.

"Where's Chernobrovin and the engineering crew?" she asked no one. Vlasenko and Orlov were pushing crewmen up the ladder into the hatch. As the overhead lights flickered, a massive explosion rocked the ship, from forward. The crew in the passageway were all thrown to the deck, a pile of bodies scattered around the lower hatch of the escape chamber. The lights went out, leaving them all in a coal mine blackness, just as the smoke came into the space.

"Trusov! Get into the chamber!" Orlov yelled.

"I can't sir, I have to find the engineer and his men," Trusov said, grabbing a battle lantern. She hadn't anticipated Orlov physically picking her up and half tossing her upward into the chamber, Naumov assisting from below and Sonar Officer Vasilev pulling her up from inside.

But the gods of the sea had taken pity, because Engineer Chernobrovin and three of his men arrived in the smoke-filled passageway, emerging from aft, with visibility shrinking to less than three meters in the smoke. "I had to shut down the reactor, Captain, the control rods drives were shorting out, two were pulling themselves out of the core. We could have gone prompt critical."

"It's too late to worry about now, Kiril," Orlov said, clapping the engineer on his shoulder. "We just need it to hold together long enough to detach the chamber."

A second explosion sounded from forward and a blast of flames roared into the passageway. Orlov, Chernobrovin and his men barely made it into the hatch before the entire passageway was solid flames. Orlov and Vasilev pushed the hatch down and dogged it shut.

"Detach the chamber!" Orlov ordered. Naumov hit the emergency disconnect, and over a hundred explosive bolts fired, separating the chamber from the submarine.

"Did it work?" Trusov asked Chernobrovin. He looked at

her, but it almost seemed that the light was going out of his eyes, but the answer came as Trusov could feel the chamber rocking in the waves on the surface. Someone high above was opening the upper hatch, and as fresh air poured into the ship, Chernobrovin suddenly vomited all over her.

30

Arabian Sea
Tuesday, June 7; 0958 UTC, 11:58 am Moscow time

The escape chamber tossed in the sea state, the windowless, airless capsule of steel seemingly made to induce seasickness.

Irina Trusov had climbed the ladder to the top hatch and climbed out, perching herself on the top surface, which would be perilous with higher waves, but even the prospect of falling off what used to be the top of the conning tower would be preferable to the interior of the chamber.

After Chernobrovin had vomited on her, his other three nuclear crewmen likewise collapsed, retching on the floor, and the stench of it caused others to lose it, and in the middle of the vomit-fest, a huge roaring explosion sounded below them, and the shock wave tossed the chamber in the sea for a minute. The detonation had been the last anyone would hear from the assembly of steel, cable and electronics that had once been the *Novosibirsk*. Trusov felt an intense moment of mourning. For the last three years, she had poured all she had into that submarine, and now it was gone. Thanks to the Americans.

She forced her mind to turn to the present moment. And to survival. The chamber had rations for more than a week for the entire crew, but it was foreseeable that they'd be out here on the godforsaken Arabian Sea longer. They were hundreds, perhaps thousands of kilometers from the shipping lanes. Since they had separated from the hull and surfaced, there had been no aircraft overhead.

And there was a more immediate problem. Radiation sickness. Chernobrovin and his band of nuclear technicians were falling apart below in the chamber, continuing to dry heave long after their stomachs were empty, their skin turning a sickening pale. And what radiation dose had the rest of them had? She, Orlov and Naumov had been all the way forward in the first compartment when the reactor had its power excursion and flashed neutron and gamma radiation at the entire crew.

Trusov breathed in the salty, fishy-smelling sea air, glad at least that she didn't need to worry about carbon dioxide poisoning. Orlov poked his head out and climbed up to join her on top of the chamber hull. He handed her a bottle of water and a square meter of cloth. She took the bottle gratefully and nodded at the captain.

"Sorry that the bottled water is so hot. Drink it slow. And wrap that cloth around your head. You're way too fair to withstand this sunshine."

"Thanks, Captain."

"Former captain," Orlov said sadly.

"Yes," Trusov said. They sat in silence for some time. "Did you light off the emergency beacon?"

"I tried," Orlov said. "There's no indication it worked. Apparently we lacked a preventive maintenance reminder to check its batteries. I suspect they died some time ago."

"What about the sonar beacon?" The chamber had an active sonar pinger to allow being located by warships with sonar receivers. It could be used if the chamber were trapped under polar ice cover, but other than that, no one had seen its usefulness.

Orlov shouted down into the chamber. "Naumov! Get up here!"

Naumov arrived. "Yes, Captain."

"See if you can engage the sonar emergency pinging device."

"Yes, sir." His head vanished back below.

"Bad news, Captain," Trusov said. "With the radio beacon out, we may be out here longer than our rations allow. We only have eight days, give or take, of rations."

"That assumes a full crew, Irina. I fear there will be many fatalities from whatever happened to the reactor. Chernobrovin looks bad. Dammit, Irina, I should have blown to the surface and evacuated the ship earlier."

"You couldn't know, Captain. If we'd been just twenty kilometers farther west, we might still be operating, still pursuing the target submarines."

"Well, I guess we'll never know. I think I'll lie down for an hour."

"You'll get sunburned, sir."

"Better than being in that stinking chamber. There's no way to ventilate it. I think the atmosphere is worse inside than it was in the submarine before the sinking."

Trusov said nothing, just looked out to sea while the captain started to snore quietly.

Langley, Virginia, USA
Combined Intelligence Agency Headquarters
Tuesday, June 7; 1005 UTC, 5:05 am EDT

Director Margaret Allende joined Director of Operations Angel Menendez in the SCIF conference room adjoining her palatial office. On the wall opposite their seats, a large flatpanel screen displayed the view from the Predator drone orbiting the central Arabian Sea. In the view was a large rescue chamber, big enough to hold a hundred people crowded together. It bobbed gently in the swells. Two people could be made out on top of the structure, an older man and a younger woman. For several long minutes Allende watched the video, then called up the dark screen next to it to display the Arabian Sea. The position of the rescue chamber was marked in red on the chart. The nearest land was Mumbai, India, 290 nautical miles east-northeast. At least, she thought, Mumbai had competent hospitals.

"Is Mumbai within helicopter range of that escape pod?"

Menendez nodded. "Sure, but a chopper could only take on a few survivors at a time. If that chamber evacuated the entire crew, there'd be sixty-five or seventy people in it. You'd need a big procession of choppers to get them out. Plus, making the jet helicopters in the queue hover while you bring in three or four at a time, burning fuel? Sure, maybe the Indian Navy has two dozen jet choppers standing by in Mumbai, but that's a losing bet. It's a nice thought, ma'am, but a loser."

"A rescue ship?"

"If one were equipped with medical facilities and supplies and departed right now? It would still be eleven hours away. But it would probably take twenty-four hours to get organized to get a ship like that mobilized. Odds are, those survivors are suffering from radiation sickness, dehydration, and soon starvation. Twenty-four or thirty-six hours from now? A third of them could be gone by then."

"We could vector in the *Vermont*. She's what, three, four hours away at maximum speed?"

"Are you high, boss? *Vermont* is an ultra-secret project boat. Those survivors all come from a ship that had orders to sink her. You can't crowd them onto a project boat."

"I suppose you're right. Better get this in front of Admirals Rand and Catardi, and we should call in Pacino."

"He'll be glad to hear that *Vermont* and *Panther* survived all this. Nothing for our sailors to do now but sail home. Easy day."

Arabian Sea
B-902 *Panther*
Tuesday, June 7; 1005 UTC, 5:05 am EDT

Lieutenant Anthony Pacino stared at Lieutenant Dieter Dankleff.

"Those explosions can only mean one thing," Pacino said.

"Yeah. The Yasen-M chasing us just exploded and sank."

"You know what that means, right?" Pacino asked.

"Yeah, time to turn south and head home."

"No," Pacino said. "It means this just changed from a search-and-destroy mission to a search-and-*rescue* mission."

"What? No, Patch."

"There could be survivors, U-Boat. We've got to help them. Under international law, we're obligated to render aid."

"Leave that to other ships," Dankleff said. "Someone will

rescue them, if there are survivors."

"We're so far from the shipping lanes, a raft could be out here for weeks. We have to at least *check*, U-Boat. We see no one out the periscope, then and only then do we turn south and go home."

Dankleff sighed. "Lieutenant Lomax—Lobabes—would have been a *great* AOIC. Did I ever mention that?"

Pacino laughed. "Let's go to the chart and see how long it'll take to get to the sinking site." In the navigation room, Pacino plotted a course from the inertial navigation position to the estimated sinking site. "Three point five hours. A short detour. Then home."

Dankleff nodded. The very word *home* seemed to fill his soul with warmth.

Arabian Sea
B-902 *Panther*
Tuesday, June 7; 1355 UTC, 1555 local time

AOIC Anthony Pacino snapped down the grips of the number two periscope's optic module as it rose out of the periscope well. *Panther* rose swiftly out of the inky blackness and sailed for the warm thermal layer at fifty meters. Pacino trained his view upward and made two complete circles making sure there was nothing above them. The blackness yielded to the bright afternoon sunshine from up above.

"I have a shadow, small, close, but we're heading away from it." Pacino looked at the underside of whatever this boxy shape was, only worried about avoiding colliding with it. "Keep taking us to twenty-one meters."

"Forty meters," Grip Aquatong said. "Thirty-five."

OIC Dieter Dankleff stood behind Pacino, frowning in frustration. He'd just plotted their position. They'd lose precious transit time doing this, he thought, and that presumed no one would come to chase them or drop munitions on their head. Which reminded him, if they were being chased by Russia's finest attack submarine, why didn't the Russians just send in maritime patrol aircraft? Or destroyers with helicopters? God knows, they could cover the entire Arabian Sea with twenty MPA aircraft and half a dozen destroyers. A dipping sonar detection and a torpedo dropped from an aircraft, and all this would have been over. Which meant this was urgent. They needed to check off this box, that they did what they could to make sure there were no survivors, and only then had cleared datum and run home.

"Thirty meters."

"Get us up, Grip," Pacino said, his voice muffled by the periscope's optic module.

"Twenty-eight. Twenty-five. Twenty-three."

"Scope's awash," Pacino said, still making search circles. "Scope's awash, you're hanging up, Grip. More bowplanes."

"I'm at full rise."

"You're heavy," Dankleff said, stepping over to the forward starboard ship control station, pos two. "I'll pump from central depth control. Lipstick, suggest you order up all ahead two thirds." Dankleff found a fixed function button and mashed it, watching a gauge indicating the tank level in the central depth control tank.

"Grip, all ahead two thirds!" Pacino ordered.

Grip spun the engine order telegraph.

"Scope's still hung up," Pacino said. "Dammit."

Finally the submarine seemed to come shallow and the scope broke through a wave trough, then foamed up as the crest hit the view, then cleared again.

"Scope's clear," Pacino announced. He spun the scope in three rapid circles, then stopped with the scope facing forward. "One close contact, bearing mark! Grip, all stop! Hover at present depth."

"All stop and hover, aye."

Dankleff looked up at his console's vertical section. "Your contact bearing is zero-nine-one. What is it? What's its range?"

"Hitting it with the laser. Range mark."

"One-fifty meters," Dankleff said. "What is it?"

"Looks like a large chunk of a submarine conning tower. It's a, wait." Pacino snapped his left grip to increase magnification. "It's some kind of escape pod, originally faired into the sail, but now it's floating on the sea. I show survivors on its upper surface. They're moving. One of them is standing. Now he's pointing at the periscope. He's waving his hands over his arms. Now both people topside are waving at us."

"Let me see," Dankleff said.

"Low power, bearing zero-nine-one, on the contact," Pacino said, turning the scope over to Dankleff. Dankleff increased the magnification, then increased it again.

"I'll be dipped in shit," Dankleff said. "Survivors."

"Let's get them aboard." Pacino grabbed the phone on pos two and pushed the button for the wardroom. Fishman answered.

"Wait a minute," Dankleff said. "Not so fast."

"Send Captain Ahmadi to central command," Pacino said into the phone.

Ahmadi appeared with Fishman in tow. Pacino looked at the Iranian. "Prepare to surface."

"No, Ahmadi, wait," Dankleff ordered. He abandoned the periscope and turned to face Pacino. "What the hell do you think you're doing?"

Pacino looked at him. "Rescuing survivors, U-Boat. Just like they'd do for us."

"Goddammit, Patch, they're Russian military. On a mission to kill us."

"Not anymore they aren't. As of now, they're shipwrecked submariners. *Submariners,* U-Boat, just like we are. We *have* to save them."

"You can't just bring dozens of Russian military onboard. There could be sixty or seventy of them, maybe more. They can't come aboard."

"Why not?" Pacino asked. "We have the room. We can't load them on *Vermont*—she *doesn't* have the room. Plus, *Vermont*'s a classified project boat. We can't put Russian sailors on her. So, by default, we load them up here and hope the good doctor Scooter Tucker-Santos has enough medical supplies to treat them. Nothing particularly classified *here.* They already know about our mission and the fast reactor is theirs anyway. And they *built* this boat, so it has no secrets for them, except the crypto and radio junk we lugged onboard, but that's behind a sturdy lock and they couldn't make sense of it anyway."

Dankleff checked his watch and shook his head. "Say we did take survivors aboard. Who's to say they won't try to take over the ship? And return it to Iran? And kill us all in the process?"

"That's why we have SEALs. And us. We'll all arm back up before we take on the survivors. Anyone becomes a threat, Scooter injects them with Propofol, lights out, zip ties and duct tape."

"Oh, my God," Dankleff groaned. "What about Russian satellites? Or drones? Aren't you worried that if we surface, we'll attract attention? What's to stop the Iranians from vectoring in an Ilyushin Il-38 ASW plane, or a few destroyers, or the Russians from flying in a couple Il-114 maritime patrol planes full up with torpedoes?

"That won't happen," Pacino said. "Two nuclear explosions, an exploding nuclear submarine, a gigantic escape pod surfaces, and not a trace of a Russian surface or air asset. And besides, what if Russian surveillance *does* see us? We'll have their guys. Once the Russians are aboard, the Russian Navy would be crazy to sink us. In their minds, we have hostages. Prisoners of war, so to speak."

Dankleff considered. After a long time, he said, "What are we going to do once they're aboard? We can't steam all the way to AUTEC with them."

"Mumbai is less than three hundred nautical miles from here. Bearing zero-eight-five. We can make it in ten hours. They have good hospitals. And choppers. Who knows? Maybe they could dispatch a rescue ship and rendezvous with us before we reach Mumbai."

"You thought this out, didn't you, before we knew there were survivors." Dankleff frowned.

"I may have run a few whiteboard scenarios," Pacino admitted.

"*Goddammit,* Lipstick, this is going to get us court-martialed or killed. Or both."

"U-Boat. Shut your eyes and pretend. You're adrift at sea on a raft. The guys who sank you heave to and pop up a periscope.

How would you feel if they just took a couple of periscope pictures and then sailed off?"

"Pretty shitty, I guess."

"Exactly," Pacino said. "Captain Ahmadi, prepare to surface!" Pacino looked at Dankleff, as if daring him to countermand Pacino's order.

Dankleff took a deep breath. "Okay, Lipstick. But if I get killed doing this, you're the one who's going to have to break the news to my mom."

Pacino punched Dankleff in the shoulder and grinned. "Captain Ahmadi, blow forward and aft ballast tanks!"

Arabian Sea
Tuesday, June 7; 1411 UTC, 1811 local time

Captain Lieutenant Irina Trusov adjusted the shawl she'd improvised to cover her face from the intense sunlight. Being a natural blonde had disadvantages, she thought. She looked up and saw something startling. "Captain, look!" Trusov waved frantically at the periscope, which had moved closer, now swimming distance from the escape chamber.

Captain First Rank Yuri Orlov opened his eyes and removed the coat from his face, that he'd been using to keep off the blistering sun. He sat up and looked where Trusov was waving and pointing. It was a periscope.

A Russian periscope.

"Thank God," he said. "We're saved. Pass the word down to the crew."

A half dozen crewmen crowded up on the upper surface, several more popping their heads out the open hatch.

"They certainly seem to be taking their time," Trusov observed. "Why would they just hover there and look at us?"

The answer seemed to land in Trusov's mind like a cold, dead fish hitting the floor. "That's not a friendly Russian," she said. "That's the goddamned *Panther*." Dismay blew into her soul. All was lost. "Oh, no, please God, no. Not the Americans. Please."

"They're surfacing," Orlov said.

The periscope started rising vertically from the water, then the top of a conning tower, the water splashing and foaming around it, then more of the conning tower rose from the waves. There was a painted logo on the side of the conning tower—a prowling black panther. Finally the submarine's deck rose out of the sea, the long black form right next to them. It was a Kilo submarine. But elongated.

It was the *Panther.* Unconsciously, Trusov covered her mouth with her hand.

A head popped up from the conning tower, then two, then three, one of them holding an unholstered large pistol.

"Ahoy!" one of the men called. "Does anyone speak English?"

"You do, Irina," Orlov said to Trusov. "Ask them if they are here to rescue us."

Trusov glared at the Americans, wishing she could thrash them with her bare hands.

"We are in need of rescue," she shouted, hating the task, but finding no logical argument against it. "There are sixty-two of us! Will you help us? Perhaps radio for help?"

"Yes," the first American called. "There's no easy way to get you from your escape pod to our boat. You'll have to jump off and swim over. We'll get you up on deck from aft and bring you inside."

The hatch opened forward of the conning tower and men emerged, two of them wearing wetsuits and scuba gear. Then more men climbed out, half a dozen of them armed.

"They're going to take us prisoner," Trusov said. "They're going to interrogate and torture us, Captain. When they find it was us hunting them, they will kill us."

"Nonsense, Irina," Orlov said, looking at her like she'd gone mad. "They're just fellow submariners here to rescue us."

"They are armed, Captain."

"Probably to keep us from getting any ideas about taking over their ship, which they stole. Wouldn't you do the same?"

Trusov bit her lip, wondering if she would survive to see another sunrise. From the dark water between their escape chamber and the *Panther,* several divers surfaced, and more of them, until there were what looked like two dozen people floating in the water.

"Hey up there!" one of divers shouted up at the conning tower. "Lipstick!"

"Who goes there?" the first American shouted.

"It's Easy Eisenhart! Is that you, Patch?"

"It is indeed. Good to see you again, Easy. What are you and your guys doing?"

"We're supplementing your crew. If you're taking aboard five dozen Russian sailors, you'll need more security to guard these guys."

"Jesus, you must have just put everyone on *Vermont* on port-and-starboard watches."

"Oh yeah, but no matter, Patch," Eisenhart called as he was helped up on the hull by one of the SEALs. "Captain called ahead to Mumbai. There's a rescue ship there with a helicopter and medical facilities. Royal Navy ship. I think it's the HMS *Explorer II*."

Anthony Pacino's face went white. It had been the HMS *Explorer II* that had rescued him, Catardi and Carrie Alameda from the wreckage of the *Piranha*. He wondered for a moment if Fishman's simulation theory could have any truth to it. This was like the universe winking at him, he thought.

Washington, DC, USA
White House Situation Room
Tuesday, June 7; 1420 UTC, 9:20 am EDT

National Security Advisor Michael Pacino looked up at the screen shot from the Predator drone, orbiting high above the escape chamber of one of the Russian Yasen-M-class submarines. Heaved to on one side of it was the surfaced submarine *Panther*. Discernible on the top of the conning tower was his son, Anthony Pacino, leaning over the coaming of the bridge and shouting down to several swimmers in the water. The elder Pacino reached for a tissue from the box on the table and blew his nose to cover up the fact that he needed the tissue for his suddenly running eyes, wet with hot tears of relief.

He felt Margo Allende's hand on his shoulder. "See, Patch, Anthony's fine. He did great."

"Are they doing what I think they're doing?"

"Your boy is rescuing the very sailors that tried to kill him."

Pacino shook his head. "That boy's a maniac."

Allende smiled. "Like his father before him, if the stories I heard are true."

"What is *Panther* doing now?"

"She'll head due east toward Mumbai, ten hours out, but we've scrambled a rescue vessel that was docked in Mumbai—the Brits had a submarine rescue ship there for training. What are the odds?"

"What was the ship?"

Allende paged through her pad computer. "Let's see. HMS *Explorer II. Panther* will rendezvous a hundred and fifty miles out of Mumbai with the *Explorer II,* offload the Russians, then get back to their escape from the Arabian Sea."

Pacino stared at the display as the view slowly orbited the hull of the *Panther,* the topside sailors bringing in the survivors and packing them down the hatch. *Explorer II,* he thought. Hell of a coincidence, since that was the ship that had saved Anthony three years ago, but certainly a happy one. The older Pacino had visited the ship and brought the captain and submersible commander bottles of thousand-dollar Kentucky bourbon in gratitude.

"Looks like they're almost all aboard. Let's get ready. Carlucci wants a briefing. He'll be down any minute."

This mission was almost over, Pacino thought. Just a milk run from the Indian Ocean to the Pacific and into AUTEC, and his son would be out of danger.

Langley, Virginia, USA
Combined Intelligence Agency Headquarters
Tuesday, June 7; 1820 UTC, 1:20 pm EDT

"Boss, I think you're going to want to see this." Angel Menendez's voice always went up half an octave when he was alarmed, Director Allende thought.

"What is it Angel?" she asked, bringing her pad computer to

her office's SCIF conference room. On the display screen was a worried looking Vice Admiral Rob Catardi.

Allende took her seat. "Hello, Rob. News?"

"We're late getting the intelligence digested, Madam Director, but here it is," Catardi said. "A third Russian Yasen-M-class submarine sortied from Zapadnaya Litsa Naval Base on the Kola Peninsula the day after *Panther* was taken. She slipped to sea by dark of night, which the Russians never do. We detected multiple tugboats on the tripwire sound surveillance hydrophones at the exit of the base. I ordered an Orion spy satellite, the NROL-44, retasked to look down on the base and the Barents Sea, and this is what we saw. This is an infrared image, so it may look funky."

A satellite photo came up on the screen. Allende leaned forward. Despite the varying heat signatures in the shape on the screen, the shape was unmistakably a Yasen-M-class submarine.

"Where's he going, Rob?" she asked, afraid she already knew the answer.

"We don't know for sure. Our Virginia-class submarine *Texas* was orbiting at the entrance to the GI-UK Gap, but sniffed exactly nothing." The GI-UK Gap was the narrowing waters between Greenland, Iceland and the islands of the United Kingdom, which a ship would have to transit to pass from the Barents Sea into the North Atlantic. The gap was rotten with SOSUS network sound surveillance hydrophones.

"What about SOSUS?"

"Nothing. Madam Director, the Yasen-M is a goddamned invisible ghost."

"You're telling me a Virginia-class submarine was there and didn't hear this guy?"

"That's exactly what I'm telling you, Margo. The Yasen-Ms have us outmatched."

"I guess we're lucky *Vermont* tossed those nukes at a probability circle," Allende said, "or else she and *Panther* would be on the bottom right now."

"But we're unlucky *now,* because that third Yasen-M is on his way south."

"You don't know that, Rob."

"Margo, what the hell else would he be doing? The Russians don't like going into the Atlantic. They consider it a USA-UK-EU lake. They operate in the Barents, the Arctic Ocean and the far north Pacific, well within comfortable missile range of the land of the free and the home of the brave."

"Rob, when this Yasen-M was on the surface, did we get a hit on his periscope transponder?"

Catardi shook his head. The dark circles under his eyes seemed darker today, Allende thought. "It didn't transmit."

"Was this one of the subs we didn't get transponders installed on?"

"No, he had one. It just failed."

Allende sighed. *Now what,* she thought.

"Margo, this is just my brainstorming here, but I think you should find a way to leak the Operation *Blue Hardhat* program. Let the Russian spies find out that we wired up their subs and that every time they go to periscope depth, we have them dead to rights."

"Why, Rob?"

"Because then fleet command would tell the third Yasen-M to back off, because the Americans know where he is."

"So, you want to bluff this guy."

"We're metaphorically out of torpedoes, Margo. All we have left are main engines. We have to ram the Russians, from an intelligence point of view."

"Admiral Catardi, I promise you I will think about it, but you're talking about disassembling a hundred-million-dollar program and endangering the lives of at least forty field assets. And it would mean giving up our ability to monitor Russian ballistic missile submarines."

Catardi looked down at his table, his expression falling. "It was just a thought, Margo."

"Don't worry, Rob," she said. "We'll think of something."

"I have to go," Catardi said. Allende could tell he wanted to hang up because he was upset and needed to throw his pad computer across the room or break a drinking glass.

"Later, and thanks for the update," Allende said, and quickly broke the connection.

"Whoa," Menendez said.

"Yeah," Allende replied, trying to process the bad news. "Angel, how fast can you blow up Operation *Blue Hardhat*? Get our assets out and safe, then leak the operation's activities—how long?"

"But don't you need presidential authorization to crater an operation like this?"

"I already have it, Angel. So how much time?"

"On a good day? A month."

"This isn't a good day, Angel. You've got twenty-four hours," Allende said.

"Then I'd better get going," Menendez said, grabbing his fedora and tablet computer and lunging for the door.

Polyarny Naval Base
Northern Fleet Headquarters
Tuesday, June 7; 1820 UTC, 8:20 pm Moscow time

"Sir, we think we've recovered from the *Medved' Grizli* worm. The techs in Flag Plot say they're ready to reboot. All the intelligence that was gained in the last nine days will arrive in a cascade."

Vice Admiral Olga Vova, the Northern Fleet deputy commander, had knocked on Admiral Gennady Zhigunov's office door, where he was catching up with the 200 email-a-day workflow, at a time early in the evening when he could get away with smoking a cigar and pouring a double vodka. When he thought about it, he worked better with a couple vodkas under his belt. Too bad it was frowned on during the workday, but no matter. In three years he'd be retired and would be able to pour vodka for himself all day and smoke cigars wherever he wanted to. The thought reminded him that he was widowed, that his beloved wife Nina would never have approved. Of the cigars or the alcohol. Yet, every day he missed her all the more, he thought. His adopted son, Boris Novikov, had urged him to find a new wife, but Zhigunov was 63 years old now, and losing the battle against getting fleshy and sagging everywhere. There was little chance of a man like him attracting a wife now.

"Sir? Do you want to come with me to Flag Plot?"

Zhigunov stared up at Olga Vova, "OV," who had to outweigh him by many kilograms, her head alone the size of a bucket. In all his life, Zhigunov thought, he'd never seen a woman less feminine. He waved at her.

"I'll be right down. You go on without me. I'll join you there." Vova might be his deputy, but he'd prefer not to ride the same elevator as the woman.

When he got to Flag Plot, the screens that formed the forward wall were all dark, as were the hundreds of monitors at the eleven long rows of tables facing the front wall, each station manned by an officer or warrant officer. Olga Vova was standing near the front row, bossing around the captain lieutenant heading the artificial intelligence division. Vova saw him and hurried up to him, her bulk overwhelming as she approached.

"Yes, OV?" he asked.

"They're ready to reboot, Admiral. The intel from the Kosmos satellites will be downloading all at the same time. It may take some time to display all the data."

"Proceed, then," Zhigunov said.

"Reboot, Arkady," Vova ordered the artificial intelligence chief.

In the next fifteen minutes, Zhigunov learned that the Americans had launched a nuclear strike that had caused both *Voronezh* and *Novosibirsk* to stop communicating, and that soon after, *Novosibirsk*'s escape chamber had surfaced. And that not long after that, the goddamned *Panther* surfaced next to the escape chamber and took the surviving crew members of the *Novosibirsk* hostage as prisoners of war, loading them into the *Panther*. And soon after that, the *Panther* had submerged and vanished.

"What is the status of the *Voronezh*?" Zhigunov asked the AI chief.

"No word from *Voronezh*, sir."

"That's not a good sign after a nuclear depth charge attack, Admiral," Vova said.

"Are the air assets able to fly?" Zhigunov asked, intending to vector in a swarm of antisubmarine warfare aircraft to the site of the surfacing of the *Novosibirsk* escape chamber.

"Yes, Admiral," the AI chief said, just as all the screens went black. He looked at Zhigunov. "I may have been premature stating that, Admiral. My apologies."

"Just fucking fix it," Zhigunov said, glaring at the AI chief and spinning on his heel to return to his office, where he shut down his computer and grabbed the crystal vodka decanter and poured a triple and downed it in one gulp, then poured another.

That *Voronezh* hadn't communicated probably meant she went down, Zhigunov thought, pouring another triple vodka. He held his head in his hands, remembering his life with Nina and young Boris Novikov. If there were any way to extract revenge from the savage criminal Americans, he would find it.

31

Arabian Sea
B-902 *Panther*
Tuesday, June 7; 1500 UTC, 1900 local time

The deck trembled with the power of the reactor at one hundred percent output. Lieutenant Anthony Pacino left Lieutenant Don Eisenhart in the central command post and ducked into the navigation space, checking their course toward Mumbai and the rendezvous with HMS *Explorer II.* There was nothing much for him to do until time to surface at the rendezvous point, some four hours later. He considered trying to get some sleep, but he was too jangly from the Iranian coffee and the tenseness of the mission. He decided to go to the wardroom and reload on coffee, jumpy nerves be damned, he thought.

At the passageway outside the wardroom, two petty officers from the *Vermont* stood guard, both carrying heavy.

"Petty Officer Watson," Pacino said, smiling at the machinist mate who'd first greeted him at the gangway on the day Pacino had reported aboard *Vermont,* which seemed like a hundred years ago. "How was the swim over?" Watson was one of *Vermont*'s divers and regularly took his men over the side to inspect the hull for mines or bombs before getting underway.

"It was cake for me, Mr. Patch, but all these non-divers were a pain."

"Well, good to have you aboard our good ship."

Watson smiled. "Good? This rust-bucket is straight from the

seventies. We must be making more noise than a garbage truck dragging chains."

Pacino nodded. "Kind of makes you appreciate *Vermont* all the more, eh?"

"Yes, definitely, sir. You going in? We have the Russian officers inside."

"How many?"

"Seven in there. We took one of their guys to crew's berthing. He and a couple of the enlisted guys are pretty sick. I'm not sure if they'll even make it to the rendezvous. The SEAL medic, Tucker-Santos, says it must be radiation poisoning, and a bad case at that."

"Yeah," Pacino says. "Odds are, all of them have it. The sick guys must have been back aft."

"Be careful in there, sir. The Russians are plenty pissed. The blonde female one especially. She's the only one who speaks English, yet she's giving everyone the silent treatment."

"Hell, Watson," Pacino said, "we'd probably be slightly out of sorts too if we'd gotten nuked and then plucked out of the sea by the bastards who'd nuked us."

"Well, still, Mr. Patch, exercise caution. She might bite you."

Pacino smiled and waved as he opened the door.

Inside, the seven sullen Russian officers sat in the aft seating area with one at a chair of the table, all of them with towels around their shoulders from swimming up to the hull. Pacino nodded at them, feeling all their gazes fixed on him. Grip Aquatong stood near the door with Tiny Tim Fishman at the other end of the room, both holding their Mark 6 non-lethal weapons, both strapped with their sidearms and belts full of ammunition, their thighs and calves strapped with long-bladed combat knives.

"Gentlemen," Pacino said to the SEALs. He looked at Aquatong. "Must be nice to be away from the wheel for once, eh, Grip?"

"Nah, I like driving," Aquatong said.

"Everybody playing nice in here?"

"Only one speaks English. The woman at the table. Abakumov was in here for a while. Spoke to her. He said her name is Trusov. Irina Trusov. She was the weapons boss on that sub."

Pacino made his way behind the table to the credenza with the coffee maker. He looked at the woman, who had platinum blonde hair, a slightly sunburned light complexion and big blue eyes, a dark frown on her face. Her damp uniform was stained and smelled bad. Her wet hair was in knots. He could tell both bothered her.

"Coffee?" he offered. She shook her head, glaring at him. He filled his cup and sat at the table opposite her. "I'm Lieutenant Anthony Pacino from the submarine *Vermont*. Crew calls me 'Patch.'"

"Or 'Lipstick,'" Grip said.

Pacino smiled. "Or Lipstick."

"Leep-steek," the woman said in a thick accent. "Why?"

Pacino grimaced. "An unfortunate accident in a liberty port. Anyway." Pacino took a sip of the scorching high octane coffee. "This stuff will clear your sinuses. Are you sure you don't want any?"

"I do not drink coffee," she said.

"Your name is Trusov? Irina Trusov? Am I saying that right?"

She nodded. "Are you here to interrogate me? And the other officers?" She glanced aft at the others.

"No," Pacino said. "I should probably be sleeping until the rendezvous, but I've been doing too much of this stuff." He pointed to the coffee cup.

"You know caffeine was invented by the CIA," Trusov said.

"I wouldn't be surprised," Pacino smiled. "Are you hungry? We have some pretty good food aboard. Our radio chief made beef stroganoff, pretty authentic stuff. Homemade noodles, and that gravy, it's to die for."

Trusov's eyes got wider, but then she frowned again. "I cannot take food when I am a prisoner."

"A *prisoner*?" Pacino took another pull of the coffee, feeling the surge of energy. Or was it talking to this woman that was giving his spirit a boost? "You're not prisoners. These guys with guns—they're just making sure you don't try to take back

Panther. We went to a lot of trouble stealing her. Anyway, we're taking you to a rescue ship. We'll be there a little after nineteen hundred. They have good medical facilities, doctors, surgeons, and they can attend to you better than we can. They'll get you to Mumbai, India, where there are good hospitals. And from there, you're flying back to Russia, courtesy of the U.S. Navy."

"You are repatriating us? No prison?"

"Of course," Pacino said. "Why would we put you in prison?"

"Our mission was to sink you," Trusov said. "Our objective was to kill you."

"You were just doing your job," Pacino shrugged. "Just like we were, stealing this submarine. It was just business, not personal."

Trusov stared at him as if he'd just walked off a flying saucer.

"But you will interrogate us first?"

Pacino shrugged. "Why? What's there to know? You were sent here to escort the *Panther,* and when *Panther* ended up in our hands, you got search-and-destroy orders."

"Are you not curious about who our orders came from, or things about our submarine, weapons, tactics? Things like that?"

Pacino waved. "We already know all that stuff. You think there are many secrets left, what with both of our intelligence agencies poking around, trying to stay gainfully employed?" He finished the coffee and stood to get more. "Besides, it's urgent we get you to the rescue ship. You guys are all probably sick. Maybe you don't feel it now, but in a day or two it'll get bad. Radiation casualties are not fun. My dad got a huge radiation dose when I was a kid. He got a bone marrow transplant and could barely walk for a year. We wondered if he'd even make it." He looked at her. "Maybe some tea?"

She looked at him for a long time, her gaze softening just slightly. "Some hot tea might be nice," she admitted. Pacino put the hot water carafe on the table with a tray of cups, tea bags, sugar, sweetener and honey.

Trusov made herself a cup, pouring honey into it. "Honey is a luxury at sea," she said.

"Where we come from, we take the best stuff to sea. If you're going to be underwater, away from the sunshine and weather for weeks on end, you may as well have good food. And ideally, good movies, but that can fall flat."

Trusov drank her tea, pouring more when she got to the bottom of her cup.

"Where are you from?" she asked him.

"Virginia, on the Atlantic coast. Virginia Beach. My dad was in the submarine force and operated out of the naval base at Norfolk, a thirty-minute drive away when the aircraft carriers are at sea, ninety minutes when they're in port." He smiled at her, realizing when she wasn't frowning or glowering, she was beautiful. "What about you?"

"Moscow," she said. "Then Murmansk. We are with the Northern Fleet."

"Pretty cold, Murmansk," Pacino said, mock shivering.

"Murmansk has its charms," she said. "It is actually nice this time of year."

Pacino smiled. "Maybe after all this, I'll come visit you."

Trusov smiled for just a brief moment.

"You sure you don't want something to eat? For all of you, I mean?"

"Captain Orlov ordered us not to accept any food from the Americans."

"Why? Poisoning? If we were going to hurt you guys, Grip Aquatong over there would just shoot you."

"I'd use my knife," Aquatong said. "Stray bullets in a submarine are unhealthy for the equipment."

"See?"

Trusov stared at him again.

"How about a shower? We have hot water. Fresh uniforms. Great shampoo." He smiled. "And conditioner. Great conditioner. Even hair dryers. For all you guys. One at a time, of course."

Trusov turned to one of the men sitting aft in the seating area, and said something in Russian. He replied. Finally, after they talked for some time, Trusov looked at Pacino.

"A shower and fresh clothes would be very nice," she said, "provided all the crew get the same treatment."

"I'll arrange it," Pacino said, standing to get to the phone. He glanced at Trusov. "Naturally, we'll need to escort you to the shower and stand guard. Hope you won't mind. It's not that we don't trust you, just making sure there's no uprising from your people. So I'll have one of the female chiefs stand watch when you shower."

Trusov blushed. "No," she said. "I want *you* to stand guard."

Fifteen minutes later, Trusov took her seat again, the grime of the sunken submarine washed off. Pacino could tell she felt better. She actually smiled at him, and he realized she was more than beautiful, she was stunning. He smiled back.

"Listen," he said, "I know you guys have orders not to eat, but I'm starving. I'll bring in some of the stroganoff. I'll have a plate, and if you want it, great. If not, that's fine too." He made a call while Trusov and her captain exchanged more words. A third officer came back from the shower, escorted by two petty officers from the *Vermont,* and a fourth went with them to get washed up. When the fourth returned, Chief Goreliki came in with a tray of the beef stroganoff. Pacino got plates from the cabinet above the coffee machine. "Sorry, we'll have to make do using spoons. Can't give you guys knives or forks. Which means I'll have to use a spoon myself."

He put some of the food on a plate and slid it across the table to Trusov, then got some for himself. He felt silly eating it with a spoon, but it wasn't that inconvenient. Trusov stared at the food.

"Anyone else?" He waved the serving platter at the others. The Russian captain lifted his hand, and Pacino brought him a plateful and a spoon. "You guys?" Two of the other Russian officers nodded. Soon all of the Russians were eating ravenously. Pacino reached into the adjoining pantry for something cold to drink and cups, finding lemonade and a cold bottle of water. He filled up cups for the Russians, then sat back down, waving the lemonade container at Trusov, his eyebrow lifted. She nodded. He poured for her, then finished his plate, washing it down with the too-sweet lemonade. He cleared his plate to the pantry, then sat back down. Trusov had cleaned her plate. He took it from her, piling it in the dirty dish bin, then collected plates from the other Russians.

He sat again. "We'll surface at nineteen hundred," he said. "I guess I should go do something useful."

"No," Trusov said. "Stay." She coughed as if embarrassed that she'd been revealing. "Tell me more about this place, *Virginia*."

Pacino smiled at her. "Sure. My dad had this house on the beach of the Atlantic Ocean in a place called Sandbridge, south of the city of Virginia Beach. He had this huge black lab that used to love to run on the beach." Trusov looked into his eyes as if entranced. Pacino continued, and before he knew it, it was time to get ready to surface.

Arabian Sea
USS *Vermont*
Tuesday, June 7; 1915 UTC, 2315 local time

Lieutenant Commander Rachel Romanov stood behind the command console with the unit's display selected to the number two optronic periscope. In the crosshairs, *Panther* was surfaced alongside the rescue ship. The rescue ship's bright floodlights lit the scene. The *Explorer II* had lowered a long staircase down her side, medics in white coveralls helping the crew of Russians up the steps. On *Panther*'s aft hull, three men lay in stretchers, with the crane from the deck getting ready to hoist them to the rescue ship.

"Sonar, any contacts?" Romanov asked Petty Officer Mercer, who stood watch at the BQQ-10 stack. It wouldn't do for them to get ambushed when they were vulnerable like this. While it was hard to imagine the Russians shooting at the ships that were rescuing their people, stranger things had happened.

"No contacts, OOD," Mercer reported. "Towed array is sagging with us hovering, though. As soon as we can get some speed on, I can be more confident."

Romanov checked her watch. The last of the Russians were off the *Panther*. *Panther* steamed slowly away and turned to the south.

"Pilot, status of the lockout trunk?"

"Wait one, OOD," Chief Dysart said, calling aft to the lockout trunk. "Trunk upper hatch is open, last group is coming aboard now."

The *Vermont* personnel they'd lent to the *Panther* were coming back aboard, now that there was no need for the enhanced security aboard the stolen submarine.

"Report when the upper hatch shuts."

"Aye, ma'am."

Romanov looked at Seagraves and Quinnivan. "Maybe the rest of this trip will be routine," she said.

"Control, Radio," the overhead speaker rasped.

"Go ahead Radio," Romanov said.

"We have immediate traffic, marked personal for CO."

"Very well, Radio, route it to control. Captain is standing by."

The radioman brought a pad computer to Seagraves, who read it, then passed it to Quinnivan, who handed it to Romanov. She scanned the message, then read it more carefully.

"That's not good," she said. There was another Yasen-M attack submarine out there, either coming into the Indian Ocean to meet them, or lying in wait at the Cape of Good Hope. "We have to tell *Panther*," she said, turning back to the periscope view, but there was no sign of the Iranian submarine. "Dammit, they pulled the plug already."

"It doesn't change anything," Seagraves said. "We suspected there would be more opposition forces out there. This is just confirming what we expected."

"We've been lucky so far they haven't thrown an ASW aircraft at the area," Romanov said. "Or a dozen. But I hope to hell *Panther* takes the Cape of Good Hope wide."

"The plan won't change," Seagraves said. "I'll be in my stateroom. XO, maybe you'd better get a nap in before mid-rats."

Quinnivan nodded and waved at Romanov and went aft, trailing the captain. Romanov tried to take a deep cleansing breath. This damned op seemed endless.

"OOD, lockout trunk upper hatch is shut," Dysart reported from the ship control panel. "Lockout trunk rigged for dive by Chief Quartane and checked by Lieutenant Ganghadharan."

"Very well, Pilot, all ahead two thirds, make your depth five-four-six feet, steer course two-zero-zero."

While Dysart acknowledged, the view out the scope sank closer to the waves, then burst into foam and bubbles.

"Scope's under," Romanov called. "Lowering number two scope." When the scope indicated retracted all the way, Romanov called to Dysart again. "Pilot, turns for ten knots. Sonar, let's get in a leg on this course, then turn to reciprocal to make sure the sea's empty."

The deck tilted far down and the hull groaned from above as *Vermont* plunged into the colder deep depths of the Arabian Sea.

Arabian Sea
HMS *Explorer II*
Tuesday, June 7; 2320 UTC;
Wednesday, June 8, 0320 local time

The Indian Air Force Mi-26 heavy lift helicopter touched down on the after helicopter deck of HMS *Explorer II* and bounced, settling in place and throttling down its engines, the huge rotors slowing to idle.

The survivors of the *Novosibirsk*, the ones that weren't on the first medical evacuation helicopter, ran across the helo-pad and climbed into the airframe, Yuri Orlov first, then Ivan Vlasenko, Misha Dobryvnik, Irina Trusov and Vasiliy Naumov. After a moment, TK Sukolov, Arish Vasilev and twenty-four enlisted crewmen climbed aboard, and the engines roared and the helicopter shook hard, its deck tilting far forward as it climbed away from the rescue ship. The ship's lights faded below, leaving the helicopter in complete darkness.

Orlov put on the headset, the large earpieces offering some protection from the thunderous noise of the helicopter's engines and rotors. It was plugged into the bulkhead behind him, doubling as an intercom. He shut his eyes, mentally writing his after-action report to the Northern Fleet, wondering how bad his and his crew's punishment would be for losing the battle. Something crackled in his ear. It was a voice. Orlov looked up. Irina Trusov was trying to get his attention. He lowered his boom microphone to his lips.

"Yes, Irina. What is it?"

"Sir, in your report, will you please say that the Americans treated us humanely? Kindly?"

"You want me to say that? Captain Lieutenant Trusov, since I've known you, you've harbored a singular hatred in your heart for America and the Americans."

"They were, well, *human,* to us, Captain. Even though they knew we had been out to kill them. It is possible my previous thinking, well, perhaps it was misguided."

Orlov smiled. People were full of surprises, he thought. "You seemed to get along quite well with the American lieutenant," he observed.

Trusov smiled back. "The Handsome One, I call him in my mind."

"Yes, Irina. The Handsome One."

The helicopter flew on toward Mumbai, where a Russian civilian airliner plane waited on the tarmac to take them to St. Petersburg. There would be a debriefing at Admiralty Headquarters as soon as they could all wash up and get into fresh uniforms. And afterward, he thought, where would the next destination be? He thought of the damage to the reputation of Russia that had been caused by his submarine. Humiliated by a pre-emptive nuclear strike by the Americans. There was no doubt—how Trusov used to feel about the Americans was how he felt about them now.

Still, there had been great heroism trying to save *Novosibirsk,* he thought. Perhaps the admirals would take that into consideration. He could only hope.

Arabian Sea
B-902 *Panther*
Wednesday, June 8; 0755 UTC, 11:55 am local time

"You got it, Chief?" AOIC Anthony Pacino asked Chief Sonarman Tom Albanese, who would be taking the deck and the conn while Pacino joined the rest of the crew for OIC Dankleff's first 0800 daily meeting.

"I've got the bubble, Mr. Patch. I relieve you, sir."

"I stand relieved. In central command, Chief Albanese has the deck and the conn," Pacino announced loudly.

"Very funny," Albanese said from the ship control station. "I'm the only one here."

"Not sure how long this will last, but with luck, less than an hour."

"You go enjoy coffee with your pinky-in-the-air officers. I'll be right here, operating this combat submarine. By myself. All alone."

"It's a meeting with all the chiefs, too, Whale. And with you standing officer of the deck, you know, you're kind of an officer yourself, now."

"Excuse me, sir," Albanese said in mock anger. "I take offense to that. My parents were married, after all."

"That joke got old in the War of 1812, Chief."

"And yet, it works every time."

"Have a safe watch, Chief. Yell for me if something looks funky."

"Jaysus, L-T, everything in this bucket of bolts looks funky."

Pacino nodded. "That it does." He stepped into the navigation room and grabbed the four charts that he'd carefully rolled up and rubber banded, with a notebook showing his calculations. He took the ladder down to the middle level and walked down the passageway to the wardroom door. The room was crowded, the entire *Panther* boarding party crew there, seated at the table or on the chairs at the aft end of the room, including the Iranian captain and the Russian reactor technician. Pacino hurried to his AOIC seat to the right of OIC Dankleff before the chronometer struck eight. Dankleff was a stickler for promptness, which Pacino would expect from a Naval Academy grad but not from an engineer who'd attended freewheeling RPI.

"Zero eight hundred meeting! Zero eight hundred meeting!" Dankleff said. "Pacino, you're late!"

"I am not, sir, I am *right* on time."

"This is U-Boat's command, AOIC, where, if you're early, you're on-time, if you're on-time, you're late, and if you're late, you're off the team."

"Damned good thing I'm not late then," Pacino said. "Being off the team might mean being shot out of a torpedo tube."

"You have charts? What's going on? Are you hijacking my 0800 meeting into some kind of nav brief?"

Pacino nodded, stood and unrolled the charts onto the table. Chart one showed the Arabian Sea emptying into the Indian Ocean and the east Africa coast. Chart two showed south Africa, the Indian Ocean to the east, the South Atlantic to the west, Antarctica to the south. Chart three showed the South Atlantic from Africa's southern coast to the equator, and chart four showed the North Atlantic from the equator to North America's eastern seaboard. Pacino had marked a course in pencil on all four charts.

On the first chart, he'd marked the pencil line, *"PANTHER EXFILTRATION PHASE I,"* the line extending from their present position southwest of Mumbai, India, going southward and crossing the equator and continuing south to within 1200 nautical miles north of the Antarctic coast, where the turning point was labeled as "Point B." He'd marked this segment with the notation, *"4200 NM."*

The line then showed the second phase of the exfiltration on the second chart, from Point B due west to the waters south of the Cape of Good Hope, South Africa, extending to Cape Town, where the line was labeled "Point C." The segment was marked *"2500 NM."* At a point 600 miles west of Cape Town, Pacino had labeled the location *"B-PRIME."*

The third chart showed the exfiltration course line continuing on a great circle route toward AUTEC, with point *"C-PRIME"* marked 800 miles northwest of Cape Town, with the line's crossing of the equator labeled *"POINT D."* That segment had been labeled *"2800 NM."*

Past Point D, on the fourth chart, there were two segments, one going from the Point D at the equator toward the leeward islands of the Caribbean chain, with *"POINT E"* placed just east of Barbados, with this line marked *"2000 NM."* At Barbados, the track bent farther west toward the northern approaches to Andros Island, Bahamas, where the chart labeled their destination *"POINT F."* This final segment was marked *"1000 NM."*

Dankleff looked at the charts. "I have a headache already. I'm sure there's some point to all this?"

"There's a big point, OIC," Pacino began. "If we use a path off the great circle routes until we get to Antarctica, then go straight *on* the great circle route to the Bahamas, using our normal six hours at eighteen knots on the reactor to charge the batteries, then eighteen hours at six knots to creepy-crawl slowly to avoid detection, we make a speed-of-advance averaging nine knots overall. Starting now, that has us in transit for *seventy days*. Chief Goreliki, you're the unofficial cook and supply officer. How many days is our food loadout?"

Goreliki caught on immediately. She addressed the room. "At our present rate of consumption, we've got twenty-five days of rations."

"How long if we tighten our belts?" Pacino asked.

"Maybe thirty. Five days more if that last week we survive on crackers and apple juice. So thirty-five. But I've been on a run where we ran out of food. It's not pleasant, Mr. Patch. And the worst thing? We only have that many days of coffee. When a submarine runs out of coffee, it's crazy time."

"This boat is *propelled* by coffee," Lieutenant Muhammad Varney said. "Not nuclear fission."

Pacino looked around the room, his expression hard. "I know the CIA had these secret evil lemon-scented plans for clandestine resupply, OIC. But they're complete bullshit. Re-provisioning while hovering submerged? That's completely insane. It would take days. That would leave us vulnerable to detection and attack. Guys, we all need to face a damned hard truth. There can be no resupply if we're to complete this mission. We try to resupply, we're going to get torpedoed. So, sorry to say, but what we have is *all* we'll have."

"Big problem," Dankleff thought. "What about some kind of resupply from *Vermont*? We get a message out, they lock out divers with food and bring it to us, we lock it in?"

"Even if you could coordinate that, OIC, the *Vermont* has the same problem. She was loaded up for a 40-day run, because that's the maximum you can load unless you get rid of torpedoes, people or equipment. Today, U-Boat, happens to be day thirty."

"Wait, they loaded stores at AUTEC before we left."

"Are you sure?"

Dankleff laughed. "You were too busy earning your new nickname, Lipstick, but yeah, we loaded back out to forty days."

"So forty days from May 15," Pacino said. "That makes this day twenty-four. *Vermont* runs out of food in sixteen days. That's June 24."

"Hey, *Vermont* can cut rations down too. If they have sixteen days, they can stretch that to thirty-two, easy," Dankleff said. "So all the two-hundred pound guys return to port at one-eighty. Builds character."

"So we agree," Pacino said. "We can't continue this nine-knot overall speed transit. That would take us to August 16, *seventy days* from now. *My* plan gets us to AUTEC in thirty-four days. July 12. A Tuesday between 1300 and 1400. After thirty-four days? We might be a bit hungry and in caffeine withdrawal, but we'll make it fine. And so will *Vermont*. But OIC, that means we start the reactor *now* and run flank until we get to Point Bravo-Prime."

"What? Full-out?"

"Yes, and then at Bravo-Prime, six hundred miles from South Africa, we slow down to six knots and sneak through the Cape of Good Hope in case the third Yasen-M is waiting for us there. So we and *Vermont* can hear him if he's there, and make the minimum amount of noise until we slip into the Atlantic. Then, when we get eight hundred miles past Cape Town, we throttle back up to flank and we flank it at maximum speed all the way to AUTEC."

Pacino sat back in his seat, mentally exhausted. He had a headache. Perhaps it was caffeine withdrawal after all. Maybe Irina Trusov was right, that caffeine was invented by the CIA. He smiled to himself, thinking about her big blue eyes when she'd looked at him, wishing he'd met her under happier circumstances.

"Well, who would ever have thought that our tactical plan was based on what's in the goddamned kitchen?" Dankleff grumbled, looking at Pacino. "But I suppose there's some iron hard logic in there. You know, we *could* just say *fuck it* and take the great circle route out of the Indian Ocean and straight into the Cape of Good Hope."

"I thought about that," Pacino said. "I was sorely tempted, believe me. But I think the third Yasen-M might sneak into the Indian Ocean and look for us based on transients, so that's the leg where we need to keep him confused. There's no help for the Cape of Good Hope. We have to go around South Africa no matter what—the globe is just built that way. Trouble is, we'll still have to charge batteries every eighteen hours, but for the six-hour charge period, we'll run only six knots. And that will be the time we'll be making the most noise and be the most vulnerable, so we'll charge during the mid-watch. Russians tend to put their second string on the graveyard shift. So bottom line, I'm whistling through the graveyard by going six knots through the Cape of Good Hope passage, but otherwise, I'm flanking it, just not on a great circle route until Cape Town is behind us."

"That isn't logic, Lipstick, it's instinct," Varney said.

"Label it however you want," Pacino said. "But we have to get this mission to end, and if we have to burn nuclear fuel to do it, so be it. Less dangerous to be loud at thirty-one knots than stopping for food two or three goddamned times between here and the Bahamas."

"Your lips to God's ear. Anyone else have anything for this meeting?" Dankleff asked. "Let's get back to work then, or to your racks, or to your watch station. Mr. Abakumov, start the reactor immediately and report to central command when you're ready to answer all bells. Patch, stick around for a minute, I want to talk to you."

Varney, Ahmadi, the SEALs, the chiefs and Abakumov filed out of the room, leaving Pacino alone with Dankleff. Pacino stood and made coffee for them both, then sat back down at the wardroom table.

"Jesus, Lipstick," Dankleff said, "if we go flank this whole way, we're going to be eating a torpedo from that Yasen-M. Or a dozen."

Pacino looked at Dankleff. "I know. The odds of us getting safely to AUTEC? I put them at one in four."

"You talk to any of the others about that feeling?"

"It would do harm to the mission," Pacino said. "We need the crew to keep their happy thoughts. So I kept my mouth shut. It's a no-win, U-Boat. Either we starve or we get torpedoed. As for me, I guess I'd rather die fast. But I have a plan."

"I've noticed something about you, Patch. You always have a plan."

Pacino nodded. "Ahmadi says we can open the outer torpedo tube doors and keep two weapons powered up for an hour at a time before their gyros melt. We can rotate through the tubes, so we don't destroy any weapons, but at all times, our gun is loaded and cocked. We get the slightest indication a bad guy is out there, we fire—even without the slightest hint of a solution—for effect. Best if we launch a Shkval, that bastard making noise and blasting through the ocean. If nothing else, it would alert *Vermont*. Or, if we hear *Vermont* launching weapons, we toss our own in the same direction."

"This is more of your desire to go down with an empty torpedo room, isn't it?" Dankleff looked at Pacino, his expression serious and empathetic.

"Doesn't it make sense, U-Boat?" Pacino asked. "If we go down, don't we want to go down shooting? Even if we're shooting at shadows? Don't act like you paid for those torpedoes with your own money, U-Boat."

Dankleff laughed. "Okay, Patch. You're unofficial navigator and unofficial weapons officer. Load our guns and cock them. If the bad guys give us any shit, let's toss it right back at them."

"Damn straight, OIC." Pacino scooped up the charts and left the room to return to the navigation space. Dankleff stared after him.

We're going to end up on the bottom of the ocean, Dankleff thought. *This mission had never been survivable.*

BOOK 6:

REVENGE SERVED HOT

32

Moscow, Russia
Tuesday, June 14; 0542 UTC, 7;42 am Moscow time

The big limousine glided to a halt outside the brightly colored portico of the *Detskiy Mir* school, the elite private pre-school for children of the Council of Ministers. The Council was headed by President Dmitri Vostov for the last twelve years. Vostov was unfathomable to the West's academics and intelligence analysts, since he was both a hardliner and a reformer. But at this moment, he was just a father of a four-year-old adorable daughter, Anya, who bounced out of her side of the limo, grabbing her backpack with the colorful illustration of a ferocious tiger being stared down by a brave cartoon little girl.

Vostov got out on his side and crossed over to the door Anya had exited. She reached up for his hand as he walked her to the door, her small hand warm and soft in his. He stooped down to receive her enthusiastic hug and kiss on his cheek. He smiled at her, thinking how wonderful children were at this age. He had older children from his first marriage, one now an Air Force fighter pilot stationed in the western Arctic, the other a Navy destroyer enlistee in the Pacific fleet, and both had been absolute terrors as teenagers, and as adults they were still somewhat distant, only talking to their father when they thought they had to. But a four-year-old, Vostov thought, represented the absolute perfection of humanity. He loved her so much it could bring tears to his eyes. So innocent, and so full of trust and love for him—he, a man who had sent hundreds of souls to their deaths back when he'd been an officer of the KGB, before the sad day marking the striking of the flag of the Union of Soviet Socialist Republics.

"Daddy," Anya said in her musical little girl's voice, "after school, Mommy wants to go shopping. She said your driver could pick me up and take me to your office. Can I keep you company while you work, Daddy?"

Vostov smiled at her. "I would love that, baby girl. I will wait for you with great anticipation."

"Yay!" she said, smiling and hugging him again. "I will see you after school, Daddy."

She turned and skipped into the door of the school, the headmaster holding the door open for her and standing at rigid attention, acknowledging that the president himself had visited. Vostov smiled and waved at the headmaster and ducked back into his limousine for the two-minute ride to the Kremlin. The ride was short, but enough to get his mind shifted into a different gear. The eight o'clock meeting this morning would be brutal—not for him, but for his subordinates.

When the car stopped at the entrance to the Kremlin's *Dom Pravitelstva Rossiiskoi Federatsii,* the White House, where Vostov had built a cavernous office adjoining the prime minister's suite, Vostov grabbed his large briefcase and exited the limo. He stopped to look at the sky and the weather. It was mid-June, and Moscow was breathtakingly beautiful. He smirked—give it six months, and it would be a frigid frozen hell on earth. When he entered the ornate brass door, then a second wood double door, then a third steel blast door, the military guards came to attention and saluted. He saluted them back, his posture and hand rigid. Beyond the guards, his aide waited for him. Tonya Pasternak was a tall, slender brunette with a large chest, narrow waist and mile-long legs. For the last year, Vostov had considered replacing her with a male *aide de camp,* but Pasternak was icily competent. Competent, but a temptation. Vostov's second wife, Larisa, virulently objected to his having an aide as beautiful and sexy as Pasternak, but there was an enduring principle of politics involved here, Vostov thought. The more power a man had in a hierarchy, the more desirable his female lackies were. He smirked at Pasternak, glad that she couldn't hear his thoughts.

"Good morning, sir," Pasternak said, sweeping her long dark hair off her shoulder. "The eight o'clock meeting is convened and waiting for you. And I know you have important business to discuss with the ministers, but, sir, I recommend you interrupt the agenda and instead start the meeting by bringing in Executive Director Vinogradov of the Ministry of Information Technologies and Communications, the *Mininformsvyazi*."

Vostov stopped in the hallway, halfway to the elevator. "Why?" he asked simply.

Pasternak smiled. "Sir, have you ever owned a dog? In particular, a retriever?"

He raised an eyebrow at her. "My uncle had a golden retriever. When I was a boy, I'd play with him in the summers. How, exactly, is that relevant?"

"Sir, if you hold a tennis ball up, a retriever will look at you with a big smile on his face while he bounces up and down on his front paws. The moment you throw the ball, that retriever becomes a streaking bullet to get the ball. He'll drop the ball at your feet, smile at you and keep bouncing on his front paws."

Vostov smiled, remembering the dog he'd played with as a youth. "Go on," he encouraged Pasternak.

Pasternak smiled sweetly. "Sir, the executive director of cyberwarfare of *Mininformsvyazi* s is waiting in your outer office. And he's bouncing up and down on his front paws."

Vostov laughed. "My, my, Tonya, you do have a way with words."

She gave him an arch look. "I have a way with a *lot* of things, Mr. President, which you'd find out if you'd just ask."

Still smiling, Vostov began walking to the elevator. "I shall bear that in mind, Tonya." In the elevator, he felt aware of the young woman, sensing her faint perfume. He realized he was no longer anything to look at. In his mid-sixties and shorter than medium height, his hair long gone for two decades, Vostov wouldn't gather a second glance on sidewalk on a sunny day in Moscow. It wasn't he himself Pasternak was throwing herself at, he reminded himself, it was his power. His station.

He indulged himself with a brief thought of what it must feel like to get female attention like this if there were no element of power involved.

At the conference table, a luxurious tigerwood brought in from Indonesia, the ministers were already seated, standing as Vostov entered. He waved them back to their seats. "Morning, gentlemen." Pasternak brought in his Turkish coffee, for which he'd gained a taste on a long-forgotten mission in Turkey in the first decade of the century. He took a long pull of the scalding brew, the aroma of it making him feel more alert already. "Well, I'm of the understanding that we have a senior visitor from the Ministry of Information Technologies. Shall we hear him out?"

Pasternak ushered in the executive director, a rumpled short and portly older man in a brown suit, with long, disheveled white hair, wearing thick black-rimmed glasses, holding a laptop and a folder of papers. He bowed slightly to Vostov, then to the ministers. Pasternak introduced him, then withdrew to the outer office. Vostov smiled to welcome the man and set him at ease. He knew the director had a presentation for him, but Vostov wanted to cut to the bottom line, without making the director feel slighted.

"You have a presentation for us, Director Vinogradov?"

"Sir, yes, I do. Did you want me to project it or look at paper copies?"

Vostov smiled. "Sit down there, Vitalik." He pointed to the empty chair directly opposite his on the long side of the table. "Let us pretend it is Christmas dinner, and you are telling the family about the juicy secret that is in your dry presentation."

Vinogradov nodded and hurried to the seat. "Well, Mr. President, ministers, *Mininformsvyazi* has generated a worm to counter the *Medved' Grizli* worm that was inserted, presumably, by the Americans, and which still has much of our forces grounded."

"Go on," Vostov encouraged the director.

"We call it *chernaya vdova pauk,* Mr. President. Black widow spider. It will do the same thing to the American military that their *Medved' Grizli* did to our forces. Their aircraft avionics and engine control computers will brick. Their military air traffic control computers and radars will all refuse to switch on. Their radios will simply stop working. Their ships' navigation, communications and propulsion plant controls will all fail in the powered-off mode. And if you direct, we can make their cell communications towers fail near the military bases, as a little extra instead of responding exactly in kind to their worm."

"This is brilliant, Director Vinogradov," Vostov said, smiling. "But don't execute the cell tower part of the plan. I just want their air forces and ships to stop working and be unable to talk to each other."

"It will be done as soon as you order it, Mr. President." He gave Vostov an eager look. Pasternak was right, Vostov thought. The man was bouncing on his front paws.

"But only their surface ships. You have to engineer this worm to leave their submarines unaffected."

"Yes, Mr. President. The submarine tenders and torpedo retrievers will be shut down hard, but their submarines themselves will be untouched."

"Good. So, how will you get this black widow spider into the American systems?"

Vinogradov smiled. "The American Secretary of State, Seymour Klugendorf, keeps a secure server rack in the basement of his Annapolis house. He had it installed so he could work from home more, he claimed. The commute to the State Department in Washington makes the man carsick. In our explorations of the American networks, this server was found to be lacking certain defenses the rest of the State Department has routinely installed. Either he missed an upgrade or a cyber patch, or they installed an obsolete system. In any case, it is vulnerable. We've been extracting emails and diplomatic cables from it for three months."

Vostov frowned. "This could be another *Pueblo Pipeline*," he said. "Or an *Aldrich Ames Corrupted Conduit* operation." American intelligence agencies over the last hundred years had realized that the Russians never believed anything printed in the mainstream media, considering it all propaganda. Russians only believed what they spied for, the harder won the information, the more trust it was given. But that had become a vulnerability in the First Cold War, when several so-called intelligence victories by the KGB just turned out to be methods of the Americans to plant fictional and false information into the Kremlin, information that was trusted without verification.

Like in the 1980s, when stolen communications revealed that the American "Star Wars" missile defense shield worked perfectly and that the USA was immune to any Russian nuclear attack, and that plans had been initiated for an American surprise nuclear first strike of the Soviet Union. The back-and-forth about the timing and content of the American nuclear attack had gone from the mundane to the terrifying. The messages about the exact tactics involved even mentioned then-President Gorbachev by name, targeting a ten-megaton hydrogen bomb for the exact location of his *dacha*. The intelligence harvest had prompted Gorbachev to come to the bargaining table and agreeing to haul down the Soviet flag and to effectively surrender to the Americans. So it was, when the *Mininformsvyazi* stated they'd won an intelligence victory, Vostov remained deeply skeptical.

"Director Vinogradov," Vostov said, "let me remind you of how, twenty years after the ending of the Soviet Union, we found out that all the information magnificently harvested from *Pueblo* and *Ames* had been completely false. The so-called Strategic Defense Initiative—*Star Wars*—had never worked and it still doesn't. All those messages about test results had been fabrications. And there had never been any plans for a nuclear first strike against Russia. It had been an elaborate hoax, planted in Soviet planners' minds by evil American intelligence agencies. Our recovery took decades and is still ongoing."

"We considered that, Mr. President. After *Pueblo* and *Ames,* we have a protocol for testing and retesting information harvests. We place false information into one of our own compromised networks and wait to see if the message traffic from the State Department mentions that data. A pipeline would never reveal a captured Russian system. But Klugendorf's servers did. In addition, every item of information on that server was examined and verified. So far, all the data has proved accurate. Not one thing has been fictional."

"So, when will you insert the worm?"

"On your order, Mr. President, and when the Secretary of State himself opens up a portal we've been using, when his laptop shakes hands with his server. We will slip in unnoticed at that point."

"How long will it take to work?"

"It spreads through their networks slowly to avoid detection. In about six days, Mr. President, it will activate at what we call 'time zero' and their networks all shut down simultaneously."

"What happens if one of their aircraft is in the air when this happens?"

"It falls out of the sky, sir. It crashes."

"Regrettable, it would cause loss of life," Vostov said. "Is there any way to let airborne craft land before the worm affects them?"

"I suppose, sir, but it would make the worm less reliable and possibly expose it to detection and defenses. Functionally, doing that could compromise the entire program. If you'll recall, sir, we ourselves lost three Il-114 aircraft from the American worm coming back to life when we thought we'd killed it. And your orders explicitly stated to design this worm to respond in kind."

Vostov waved off the director. "It was a passing thought, Vitalik. And does it have a kill switch? It will destroy itself if so ordered?"

"Yes, Mr. President, if you order the worm to self-destruct, we can shut it down. Inside twenty minutes, the American systems will be restored as if *chernaya vdova pauk* had never been there."

"Excellent, Vitalik."

"So, Mr. President, do we have your permission to insert the worm?"

Vostov looked at the gathered ministers. "Any of you have any questions for Director Vinogradov?" The all shook their heads, most of them seeming distracted by other matters. "Insert the worm, Director Vinogradov," Vostov ordered formally. "Report back to this office when the worm reaches its time zero."

Vinogradov stood so fast he almost toppled his chair, nodding and bowing to the ministers and Vostov and half running out of the room. When the door shut behind the director, Vostov faced his ministers and frowned. Now, the difficult part of the meeting was about to start.

Four thousand four hundred nautical miles from Vostov's conference room, in a secure conference room adjoining the CIA director's office, the transcript of the meeting was pored over by Director Margo Allende. When she got to the line about the Strategic Defense Initiative not working, she called in Angel Menendez, the deputy director of operations, whom she knew was similarly burning the midnight oil.

"Yes, Madam Director," Menendez said at the door of the conference room.

"Come in, shut the door and take a look at this, Angel," Allende said.

Menendez scanned the text on her pad computer. "I read it."

"What's this about our missile shield not working? I thought we'd gotten Star Wars up and running, finally. It's just that now it's top secret. What is Vostov talking about?"

"Oh, it works, all right. But think of nuclear war as a monsoon rain and the missile shield as an umbrella, Madam Director. An umbrella with a *lot* of holes in it, and a few outright rips. You'd still be well advised to use the umbrella if you absolutely, positively have to go out into the storm, but you're still going to get wet."

Allende nodded. "I'd just as soon stay nice and dry inside here," she said. "I'm heading home. Do you want a ride?"

"Nah, you go ahead, Margo. I drove myself today."

"Good night, Angel."

"You too, Madam Director."

150 kilometers southwest of Cape Town, South Africa
Cape of Good Hope barrier search point
K-561 *Kazan*
Tuesday, June 14; 0555 UTC, 7;55 am Moscow time

Captain First Rank Georgy Alexeyev had gotten off watch two hours before and ever since having gone to the bathroom after watch, had been pacing his small sea cabin, absolutely furious. He had caught something, and it burned and it hurt to urinate. Goddamn it, he thought, could Natalia be responsible for this? And if she were, what did that mean? He knew he'd been absolutely faithful to her, but this, this reminded him of the venereal disease he'd caught when he'd been partying a bit too hard when his submarine K-154 *Tigr* had pulled into Havana fifteen years ago. Back then, getting a venereal disease while ashore was practically a badge of honor, but now? Now he was senior leadership, the captain of the submarine. And now he had to go to the ship's medic and get an examination, a diagnosis and a treatment.

Despite all the claims of medical confidentiality, the idea that the captain had gotten a sexually transmitted disease from his partner would be far too juicy to keep a secret. And how would the crew treat him when they knew? It was humiliating. Alexeyev considered keeping this to himself and waiting to see a private doctor once they arrived back home, but that could be a month from now, and the pain was insistent.

Almost worse was that somehow it had spread to his right eye, which was bloodshot solid red, oozing pus and horribly itching. Was it the same disease or something different, and was this also a gift from Natalia? It had gotten so bad that Alexeyev wanted to tear his own eye out. Finally, after another agonizing minute, he picked up the phone to the central command post.

"Yes, Captain?" First Officer Ania Lebedev answered.

"Send the doctor to my sea cabin," Alexeyev said. "Immediately."

"Right away, Captain."

It took only three minutes for the knock to come at his door. Alexeyev opened it and Chief Ship Petty Officer Arkady Chaykovsky appeared, a worried look on his grizzled face. Chaykovsky's salt-and-pepper hair was done in a brush cut, a flat-top, over his leathery and sun-damaged face. He was short and slight, but built from his habit of off-watch time spent lifting weights. "Yes, Captain?"

After Chaykovsky examined Alexeyev, the medic had an unconfirmed diagnosis. "It's most likely syphilis," he said, opening his bag and withdrawing a syringe, wiping Alexeyev's arm with a moist antiseptic-smelling gauze square and jabbing him with the needle. "There's no harm in administering this, and a few days of these injections, and it should clear up. The eye, though, that worries me."

"What is it, Doc?"

"Could be pink eye, sir. Conjunctivitis. It's caused by a viral or bacterial infection. But taken together with your urinary symptoms, I suspect it's caused by the herpes simplex virus."

"Oh, for God's sake," Alexeyev said. "Herpes?"

"Possibly, sir. It could be caused by the varicella-zoster virus or various other viruses, or allergies or a blocked tear duct. But herpes simplex virus infection is more likely when co-presented with the urinary disease."

"You're all good news, today, Doc. Will that injection clear it up?"

"Maybe, sir. I'll bring some drops for your eyes, for use no less than every hour, two drops, and more if the itching gets more intense. And until this clears up, I want to bandage your eye, to make sure you're not touching it and possibly spreading this to your other eye."

"Doc, that would mean re-bandaging my eye every hour. I'll just wear an eye-patch. I used to wear one as watch officer instead of red goggles for night adaptation of my periscope eye. That'll keep me from scratching it and I can get drops into it easier than all that bandaging and re-bandaging."

"Fine, Captain, but if you reconsider, let me know. I don't mind coming up to redo the bandages."

Alexeyev nodded. "Thanks, Doc. And listen, I know I don't need to say this, but this diagnosis—" Alexeyev's voice trailed off.

"Don't worry, Captain. This is absolutely confidential. And I won't keep record of it, in case of a squadron audit, sir."

"Thanks, Doc." The medic left and Alexeyev rooted around in his desk drawers for his black eye patch. He hadn't worn it since he'd been a senior lieutenant. Back then, it made him feel like a swashbuckling pirate, but when he'd gotten more senior, it seemed an immature affectation. But now he had little choice. He'd just found it when the knock came to his door. He opened it. Doc handed him several small bottles.

"Drops for the eyes, Captain. Two drops, once an hour, and two more if irritation and itching get worse. Please let me know if you need more."

Alexeyev nodded and leaned his head back and put in two drops.

Dammit, he thought, they didn't offer any immediate relief. He put on the eye patch with some absorbent gauze under it and picked up the phone to call the mess cook to bring him breakfast. When it arrived, the mess cook saw him in his eye patch and gave him a strange look. Alexeyev wondered if Chaykovsky had kept his promise to keep the diagnosis secret.

Naval Air Station Jacksonville, Florida, USA
Squadron VP-5 P-8A Pegasus maritime patrol aircraft, callsign Dark Rider
Monday, June 20; 1920 UTC, 1420 EDT

The radio crackled in the headset of Lieutenant Commander Mark Macallan.

"Dark Rider, taxi into position and hold, runway zero eight."

"Taxi into position and hold," Macallan replied, ending with his callsign. "Dark Rider." Macallan reached for the throttles and gave the plane enough power to move onto the runway, turned to line it up with the centerline, then throttled back down and tapped the brakes.

Suddenly his copilot and golf buddy, Lieutenant Wayne Holder, pointed to the runway ahead. "What the hell? Commander, you seeing this?"

Ahead of them on the runway, three Navy utility trucks with flashing beacons on their roofs pulled onto the tarmac of the runway, one of them putting its rear toward the P-8A's cockpit. That truck had a large light bar mounted on it, and the lights of that sign read, "DISREGARD TOWER. MAKE NO RADIO TRANSMISSIONS. FOLLOW ME."

Macallan looked at Holder and was about to call the tower when the tower called him.

"Dark Rider, cleared for takeoff, runway zero eight. Contact departure control at one-twenty-one point zero seven." When the radio transmission ended, the circuit clicked four times, a secret indicator that something was very wrong.

"Commander, there *is* no departure control, and there's no frequency one two one point zero seven."

Macallan pointed to the utility trucks, which were rolling slowly toward the taxiway off the main runway. The lights of the rear truck's light bar flashed, reading, "FOLLOW ME."

Macallan taxied the heavy twin engine jet off the runway and followed the utility trucks, the trucks leading him to his original parking spot. Then the light bar read something very strange: "YOUR POWER WILL GO OUT IN 3, 2, 1..."

Macallan was reaching for the engine shutdown switches when the cockpit suddenly went dark. There was a whining noise that started with a high pitch and slowly came lower until it was a bass growl, then went out.

"Commander, what the fuck is going on?" Holder asked, his voice rising in anxiety.

"Maybe we got hit with an EMP," Macallan said. "But those trucks sure seemed to know the exact timing of it. Come on, let's get out of here. Line up the breakers and switch positions to shut-down first."

Holder complied, then followed Macallan out of the cockpit. The antisubmarine warfare officers, chiefs and enlisted were standing at their consoles. The most senior, the lieutenant, looked at Macallan.

"What's wrong, sir?"

"Just follow us off the plane," Macallan said, frustrated that he was in the dark.

At the bottom of the steps a Navy captain stood, wearing tropical whites. Macallan and Holder saluted him.

"Sir, what the hell is going on?"

"A cyberattack, Commander," the captain said.

"If it's a cyberattack, how did you guys know about it?"

The captain shook his head. "A tower operator was off watch in the lounge playing a video game. A message came in on it from another user laying out the cyberattack and the timing. The sender said it was serious and to alert the command. The other user mentioned me by name. The operator could have ignored it, but he brought it to my attention. Good thing, too. If we hadn't waved you off, you'd be in the deep Atlantic right now."

"Jesus, a video game?"

"Come with me and I'll brief you and your crew."

Macallan led his crew toward the door of the operations building, sharing an incredulous glance at Holder.

Virginia Capes Operation Area
145 miles east of Virginia Beach, Virginia, USA
USS *Zumwalt* DDG-1000
Monday, June 20; 1920 UTC, 1420 EDT

Lieutenant junior grade Everest Montgomery was standing his first watch as officer of the deck after recently becoming qualified. He was constantly reminding himself of the captain's advice: *you have the deck and the conn, not because of your experience, but because of the trust placed in you, and the trust that when you need help, you won't be afraid to call the captain.* Still, standing officer of the deck watch by himself, after almost a year of standing it "under instruction," was terrifying. All this ship's power, entrusted to *him*. He took a deep breath to calm himself, and then it happened.

Every instrument on the bridge went suddenly black. The constant whining hum always present in the room whined lower and lower in both pitch and intensity while the ventilation ducts with their constant blasting of air into the space died down. Within seconds, the room was pin-drop silent and stuffy.

"What the hell is going on?" Montgomery heard the captain say from behind him. The skipper had been in a videoconference with squadron at the time, and certainly would be frustrated at what seemed a total loss of power.

Montgomery looked out the bridge windows. The ship was slowing in the water, eventually coming to a complete stop in the sea, starting to roll in the gentle swells.

"Captain," he said, "I'm damned if I know."

The captain pulled a phone off the aft bulkhead and tried to call maneuvering, but the line must have been dead. He tossed the phone to the deck and disappeared aft. The messenger of the watch, Petty Officer Third Class Philip "Skip" Cresante, came in from the port door.

"Cresante, what do you know about all this?" Montgomery asked.

The messenger looked terrified. "I just came from the engineroom. Total loss of power. Other than battle lanterns, everything is completely black. No power, no displays, no phones."

"Go to radio," Montgomery ordered. "See if their equipment is okay."

It only took the messenger two minutes to go to the radio room and return, and he looked even more frightened. "Nothing, Mr. Monty. It's all shut down. Bricked."

"Don't worry, Cresante. We'll figure something out. I imagine right now the captain and engineer already have a plan."

But eight hours later, nothing had been figured out. The *Zumwalt* continued to roll gently in the waves, completely stricken, and completely helpless.

Langley, Virginia, USA
Combined Intelligence Agency
Monday, June 20; 2005 UTC, 1505 EDT

Deputy Director of Operations Angel Menendez looked at Director Margo Allende. "Worm is two days late."

She nodded. "But it's here now, and in force."

"Did it affect anything other than the Navy's air fleet or surface ships?"

"As advertised, the Russian worm is playing nice. Not just a proportionate response, a duplicate response. A mirror image. Just to show that what we can do, they can do."

"I'm still surprised Vostov didn't try to do us one better, maybe infect the White House or the Pentagon itself."

"You know, I met him once," Allende said.

"Yeah? What did you think?"

She shook her head. "Angel, it was strange. Dmitri Vostov is the nicest guy you could ever hope to meet. And I don't mean in a diplomatic, snake oil salesman way. He was warm. He was human."

"Wow, don't let anyone else know you said that, Madam Director."

She smiled at him. "That's just one reason I appreciate you, Angel. You've always kept my secrets, Mr. Deputy Director."

33

South Atlantic Ocean
235 kilometers west-southwest of Cape Town, South Africa
K-561 ***Kazan***
Sunday, July 3; 1102 UTC, 1:02 pm Moscow time

Captain Second Rank Ania Lebedev hurried the mess cooks out of the wardroom, making sure the noon meal dishes were cleared. Captain Alexeyev had been taking his meals in his sea cabin since they'd arrived at the Cape Town barrier search point, almost three weeks ago. That was the same time he'd taken to wearing a black eye patch over his right eye, that and his constant scowl making him look sinister. The supply officer, Yakovlev, had tried to inject some humor into the odd situation, saying to the captain that perhaps he needed a parrot on his shoulder to complete his pirate ensemble. Alexeyev had said nothing, just stared him down with his good eye as if he could burn a hole into the young officer.

Since that day, Alexeyev had only been visible to the crew at the daily one o'clock operational briefing for the officers and during his midnight watch senior supervisory shift in the central command post, preferring the peace of the graveyard quiet of the midwatch over the busier daytime watches. This morning, when Lebedev had relieved the captain at 6:00 am, Alexeyev had said something about "noise in his head," as if she were supposed to understand what the hell he meant.

It was just another data point asserting that the captain was borderline autistic, she thought, living deep within whatever world existed in his mind, withdrawing from the crew completely for the better part of a month. Lebedev pondered the possible reasons. Perhaps loneliness from being away from that slutty blonde bombshell girlfriend of his, who scandalously insisted on keeping the name of the captain of the *Novosibirsk* and had emerged into Alexeyev's life still sweating from the bed of the commanding officer of the *Voronezh*. Or perhaps something the girlfriend had written him had put him in a funk, likely that woman finding yet another submarine captain to play with. Lebedev watched the captain's face closely when he read the intelligence summaries after every periscope depth excursion, trying to see if one of the personal emails included in their daily feed included anything that would be a cause of pain for the man, but Alexeyev seemed steady in his depressed mood.

Until today at 11:45 of this morning's watch. When *Kazan* had proceeded deep from the periscope depth trip, there was something in the feed that had been marked most secret and personal for commanding officer. Usually, a message like that would be cause for celebration, Lebedev thought, because that was how orders arrived that had an exact location of their target, gleaned from various intelligence sources. Sometimes the intel came from another submarine, other times from an maritime patrol antisubmarine aircraft, an Il-114 flyover that detected the target submarine using sonobuoys or magnetic anomaly detection, and rarely from a destroyer streaming a variable depth towed array sonar that could search deep in the thermal layer. Other times the intel was scrubbed of sources, like that time *Kazan* had been tipped off to a submarine leaving its base in Faslane, Scotland by virtue of what could only be a pierside prostitute, one of the dozens who worked for the GRU military intelligence organization. When today's message had been received, according to the radioman of the watch, Captain Alexeyev had cursed and thrown the pad computer onto his bed, furious.

Which meant that this afternoon's daily briefing would be difficult for the crew. Lebedev chided herself for fretting so much over the moodiness of her captain, but the man could be brutal, screaming epithets at officers who made mistakes, in front of the crew, a mortal sin in the mind of Lebedev, who strictly believed in commendations in public and reprimands in private. She had mostly avoided Alexeyev's screaming fits, but somehow they were still something to be feared. She looked around the room, making sure everyone was there.

"Where's the sonar officer?" Lebedev harshly asked Navigator Svetka Maksimov, who sat in the chair to Lebedev's right. Maksimov was yet another source of annoyance for Lebedev. Women as pretty as Maksimov would do better to go into the fashion industry, Lebedev thought, or marrying well. If she absolutely insisted on being in the military, she needed to tone down her looks—put her damned flowing black locks in a ponytail, wear less makeup, look professional. Instead, she looked like a stripper sent in as a joke, a made-up, coiffed sexpot just temporarily stuffed into submarine coveralls. Lebedev tried to hide her dislike, but it proved a monumental task.

Maksimov lunged for the corner table phone and made a call, saying a few quiet words. "He's on his way," Maksimov said, nodding at the first officer.

The wardroom door opened and Sonar Officer Ilia Kovalev stepped quickly in, looking embarrassed.

"Sorry, Madam First," he said to Lebedev, "the turnover in central took too long."

"Why? What's on the screens?"

"A haystack of merchant shipping, Madam First. No sign of our needle."

"Two needles," Lebedev reminded Kovalev. "The *Panther* and the escort sub, most likely a Virginia-class unit." Lebedev grabbed the phone under the table near the captain's station and dialed his stateroom using the buttons set into the handset.

"Captain," Alexeyev said, sounding far away.

"Sir, the officers are gathered for the one o'clock," Lebedev said.

"I'm on the way," he said and hung up.

Captain First Rank Georgy Alexeyev entered the wardroom from the forward door, slid the door shut and took his seat at the end of the table, with Lebedev to his right and Engineer

Alesya Matveev to his left. Lebedev glanced at him. He was still wearing that black eye patch. And was it Lebedev's imagination, or was he developing streaks of gray in his once jet-black hair? He was freshly showered, wearing clean coveralls, but he hadn't shaved in at least three days. The male officers had started their at-sea beards when *Kazan* first shoved off 29 days ago, Navy regulations allowing the relaxation of grooming standards when at sea for submariners, but still requiring beards be closely trimmed, not growing all over the place like a terrorist. Several times this run, Lebedev had scolded the electrical officer, Senior Lieutenant Anatoly Pavlovsky, for overgrowing his thick black beard, but the man was too proud of it, the beard even earning him his pirate nickname, Blackbeard. But all those relaxed grooming standards assumed the male crewmen would commit to growing and maintaining the beard, not skipping shaving for four or five days, looking constantly scruffy, like a homeless person. There was no doubt, the state of the commanding officer's mental health was starting to become a real concern, Lebedev thought.

"We have everyone?" Alexeyev asked Lebedev.

"Yes, Captain. We're ready."

Alexeyev got right to the point. "I'm projecting my screen," he said, flashing up the message he'd received from Northern Fleet headquarters. He allowed a moment for the officers to scan and reread the message.

"So," Alexeyev said, his voice low-pitched and slow. "Here's what we know. Both submarines *Voronezh* and *Novosibirsk* were destroyed by an American nuclear strike." He looked at the gathered officers, who were all staring at the message, as shocked as he'd been when he first went through the intelligence digest and op-order update, all of them thinking the same thing—who did they know from the crews of the downed submarines? "The American boat escorting the *Panther* out of the Arabian Sea found out the positions of *Voronezh* and *Novosibirsk* from detecting them at periscope depth, then fired two cruise missile-mounted nuclear depth charges at a target location probability circle. And apparently, they got lucky and hit both submarines. How did the Americans find out our positions?

The GRU reports that American agents have managed to install transmitters on all our periscopes that tattletale our locations to their satellites every time we are on the surface or at periscope depth. For that reason, assuming the American agents somehow got a transponder installed on *this* ship, we have made our last excursion to periscope depth, until the mission concludes."

Navigator Maksimov spoke first. "Captain, the bottom contours here are poor for use for navigation. Without the navigation satellite, our position error will grow. The fix error circle could be fifty kilometers in diameter in two days. In a week, we'll barely know what ocean we're in."

"I know," Alexeyev said. "So be it. Better to be guessing at our navigation than give away our position to the Americans. For that reason, I've ordered us to withdraw from the Cape Town barrier search point and move the center of the search to a position farther northwest of where we initially set up. It's less optimal for catching the *Panther,* but it is outside of the nuclear weapon blast circle damage radius from where we were at the last periscope depth."

Engineer Alesya Matveev spoke up. "Captain, we have housekeeping to do at periscope depth. In four days, I'm going to need to blow down our steam generators or else the level controls will go so crazy that we'll trip the reactor. And we have to be shallow to blow down the boilers, sir, or the pressure of the deep won't allow flow."

"And we need to eject trash," Supply Officer Vladik Yakovlev said. "Otherwise we'll be up to our eyeballs in trash, and the boat will start to stink."

Alexeyev waved at the objections. "We can still come shallow to eject trash or blowdown the steam generators, we'll just do it without putting up the periscope."

"Captain, that's dangerous," Maksimov said. "We risk collision. The shipping lanes here are busy, sir, and they're directly overhead." She glanced up at the overhead as she said it.

"Can't be helped, Navigator," Alexeyev said. "It's just another risk we take when we go into a combat situation." Alexeyev continued. "Also of note, more bad news, is that our recovery from the *Medved' Grizli* worm has been problematic. The air assets of the Northern and Pacific Fleets are still grounded, and the surface vessels remain down hard. The destroyer fleet can't even start their engines. Even their interior communication telephones won't work. Somehow our submarines managed to escape the effects of the worm, but the air fleet grounding means no MPA aircraft will arrive to help us search for the target submarines. In attempting to recover from the cyberattack, we lost two Il-114s in the Pacific fleet and one from the Northern Fleet. So we are to expect no help from antisubmarine aircraft."

Weapons Officer Katerina Sobol put out her hand to be recognized. "Go ahead, Sobol," Lebedev said.

"Captain, that is going to make detecting these submarines nearly impossible," Sobol said in her high-pitched cartoon character voice. "This barrier search at the Cape of Good Hope, it's not much of a so-called choke point. There's thousands of miles from the South Africa coast to the shores of Antarctica. The target submarines could be going through any of that."

"Weps is right, Captain," Maksimov said. "From Cape Town to the Antarctic coast is over four thousand kilometers. Perfect for hiding the transit of two submarines, one of them a diesel boat running on batteries, the other a front-line nuclear attack submarine."

Alexeyev took a deep breath, which Lebedev knew meant he had the same doubts, but needed to put a presentable face on the bad news. "Navigator, let us not forget what we know. The *Panther* may be a diesel submarine, and perhaps he is running on his batteries with a rig for silent running, but somehow I doubt it. I believe he is blasting through the sea using his nuclear reactor, and that he will be loud. We will detect him from his reactor noises. The nuclear plant of the *Panther* is not built for stealth, just raw power. He's fast now, I'll give him that, but he's loud enough to be heard out to a hundred kilometers, maybe even three times that."

"But sir," Maksimov continued, "why do you think he's going maximum speed using his reactor? Wouldn't he want to be dead quiet when transiting the Cape of Good Hope? Afraid we might be lying in wait? Particularly if the Americans got our position from our last periscope depth excursion?"

"I'll tell you why, Madam Navigator," Alexeyev said, his voice flat, level and dead. He turned off the projector and walked up to the projection screen, which doubled as a whiteboard, grabbing a dry-erase marker from the credenza top drawer. He wrote PANTHER and under it a date—3 JUNE. Under that, another date, today's date, 3 JULY. Then a vertical arrow connecting the dates together and beside that, the notation, 30 DAYS. He wrote next to that, KAZAN and beneath that, the dates 4 JUNE and 3 JULY, annotating an arrow between them as 29 DAYS. He looked at the supply officer. "Since *Panther* was taken, they've been at sea for thirty days. *Kazan* emergency sortied the day after the Americans took *Panther,* so we've been unsupported and deployed for twenty-nine days. Mr. Supply Officer, when did you do your last supply inventory?"

"Yesterday afternoon's watch, Captain," Yakovlev said.

"And at normal rations, how many days do we have left?"

"With the present rate of consumption, Captain, we have twenty-one days left of food. Three weeks. At the twenty day to-go point, we'd discussed cutting rations in half to stretch us to forty days."

"Navigator, if we left tomorrow morning for home, how long to get there, assuming a speed of advance at maximum with intermittent shallow and slow excursions for housekeeping, say thirty-four knots?"

Maksimov calculated on her pad computer, then looked up. "Ten days, Captain."

"So, if we cut rations now and have forty days left, with ten days to get home and no contingency, we have thirty days left here on-station. But we are a Yasen-M-class submarine, and a fifty-day loadout fills our boat. The American Virginia-class is *half* our size, people, with *double* the crew. How many days of food do you think *they* have left? Like us, they can't exactly pull into Cape Town and go grocery shopping. And if it's bad for the Virginia-class, what can it be for the *Panther*? Her test mission was set for a week. They maybe had ten days of food for the whole crew. Now there's probably a third of that number aboard now with the commandos who took her and presumably some officers from the Virginia-class to sail her. That would stretch her food from ten days to thirty. Which means, officers, the *Panther* just ran out of food. So you tell me, Mr. Supply Officer, in that situation, would you be poking along at six knots, extending your ex-filtration for two months, or would you increase speed to maximum and be on starvation rations for only two weeks?"

Yakovlev looked down at the table and mumbled something.

"Speak up when the commanding officer asks you a question, Yakovlev!" Lebedev said sternly.

"Yes, ma'am. Captain, I'd increase speed to maximum," he said.

"So, people," Alexeyev said, looking at the room's officers, "we revise our sonar search plan for the *Panther* at maximum speed on her reactor and the Virginia-class running forced circulation and fast speed reactor recirculation pumps."

"What if they just slow down for the five hundred or so kilometer passage through the Cape of Good Hope, Captain?" Weapons Officer Sobol asked. "If they're creepy-crawling when they go around the horn, we might never detect them."

"Doing that would add weeks to their trip," Alexeyev said. "They're starving now. I think they'll risk it. I also think that means they won't be taking the Cape wide, going down by Antarctica. I think they'll come right down the center of the shipping lanes, going on a great circle route back to the American east coast. I've positioned the barrier search center point along that route, north and west of Cape Town. Let's see if our calculus proves out. Meanwhile, Mr. Supply Officer, cut all rations in half, starting after the evening meal."

"Perhaps one good meal before we cut rations, Captain?" Yakovlev asked.

"No. That would seem like a celebration, Supply Officer," Alexeyev said, his voice somehow disconnected and distracted. "We will not be celebrating on this ship until the targets are on the bottom and we are on our way home. Anything else?" No one spoke. Alexeyev looked at the chief engineer, Captain Third Rank Matveev. "Fine. Engineer? I want to see you in my sea cabin." Without another word, he stood and made his way back to his sea cabin, his gaze staring at something miles away.

The officers hastily gathered up their pad computers and cleaned off their cups and hurried to the passageway. Lebedev was somewhat annoyed that Captain Alexeyev hadn't asked her along to his sea cabin to talk to Engineer Matveev about whatever was on his mind. The first officer looked at the navigator, who was almost at the wardroom door.

"Madam Navigator, stay a moment, if you don't mind," Lebedev said, forcing her expression to depart from its usual harshness. Maksimov nodded, inhaling. Lebedev could tell the navigator was bracing for a reprimand, but it was occurring to Lebedev that while Maksimov was usually about as far from an ally as Lebedev could imagine, today, Maksimov's questioning attitude to the captain was in complete synchronization with Lebedev's own thoughts. And Maksimov had demonstrated integrity and grit confronting the captain on his possibly faulty assumptions, as well as showing a penetrating intelligence, heretofore masked by her weaponized femininity. Lebedev began to think her initial impressions of the youthful navigator might have been too hasty. She could have been judging the too-pretty officer by her physical appearance, and doing that violated everything Lebedev stood for. Maksimov sat back down, crossing the table to be able to sit opposite the second-in-command rather than at her usual seat to the first officer's immediate right.

"Yes, ma'am?"

"What do you think, Navigator?" Lebedev asked, looking at Maksimov, turning to find the teapot and refilling her cup, handing Maksimov a fresh cup, hoping her own facial expression had softened from her usual frown as she extended the teapot.

"Captain's making a pretty big gamble, Madam First," Maksimov said, accepting the cup from the first officer and holding it so Lebedev could pour tea into it.

Lebedev agreed, but decided to try to frame an argument that would express loyalty to the captain, however lame such an argument might be. Theatrically, she shrugged. "He has to do *something*. He made a tactical decision. Let's see if it plays out."

"Madam First, if those target subs get past us, there will be hell to pay with the Admiralty."

"We all need to quit thinking that way," Lebedev said gently. "Think positive. We will nail these damned targets and prevail. Before we pull into port, we will paint two small American flags on our conning tower to commemorate the kills. Shut your eyes, Nav. Can you see it in your mind?"

Maksimov smiled at her. Lebedev realized that in all her association with the young navigator, this was the first time Maksimov had smiled in Lebedev's presence.

"Don't worry, Nav," Lebedev continued gently. "We'll win this thing. I believe it in every cell of my body. And you should too. This is the *Kazan*. We are the supreme nuclear attack submarine on the planet."

Maksimov nodded. "I like that, Madam First." She stood up. "By your leave, ma'am?"

"Dismissed, Navigator," Lebedev said, smiling back at Maksimov.

The navigator left, and Lebedev was alone in the wardroom, staring at the whiteboard. Maksimov had hit the nail on the head, Lebedev thought. Alexeyev's gamble was extreme. And possibly stupid. But without antisubmarine aircraft to help them get a position of the targets, the oceans were simply too big. The chances of detecting the American and rogue Iranian subs were so low that she would have to think ahead to what would happen to her career if the submarines made it all the way to American shores.

In Captain Georgy Alexeyev's sea cabin, Chief Engineer Alesya Matveev entered, finding a seat at the small table opposite Alexeyev's command chair.

"You wanted to see me, Captain?" Matveev prompted.

"There is an urgent communication from the engineering directorate that evaluated the casualties on *Voronezh* and *Novosibirsk*."

"But Captain," Matveev said, "Our boats sank from getting hit with a nuclear strike."

"A debrief of the surviving crewmembers of the *Novosibirsk* revealed that under the shock impact of the nuclear weapon, the atmospheric control equipment in auxiliary machinery room number two disassembled and caused complete chaos. You can imagine. Hydrogen. Oxygen. The oxygen storage banks. Complete loss of emergency breathing air. An explosion in machinery two would doom the ship. And apparently, it did. The explosion from machinery two was strong enough to cause the reactor vessel to jump on its mountings, resulting in a dual rod ejection accident. The fuel overpowered and caused a steam explosion and blew the lid off the vessel and blew melted nuclear fuel all over the third compartment and irradiated the entire crew. So. Machinery two is essentially one big design flaw."

"Did the engineering directorate have recommendations to harden the equipment in the room?" Matveev asked.

Alexeyev looked at her and shook his head. "No. As usual, the engineering directorate can only point out flaws, not fixes. I mention it in passing, Engineer. Be ready in case we take a close-aboard torpedo detonation. The torpedo might not kill us, but auxiliary machinery room number two might. We'll need to brief all watchsections and have them ready to shut down ventilation and flood machinery two in the event of trouble. And if we're heading into a shooting situation, we'll need to cut the oxygen feed and shut down and purge out the oxygen generators. And to be safe, cut off the carbon dioxide scrubbers and shut down the monoxide burners."

Matveev shook her head. "We'd better hope any weapon exchange happens fast, Captain, because with no oxygen bleed or generation and no carbon dioxide removal, we'll all be suffocating slowly."

Alexeyev nodded. "The choice, Madam Engineer, seems to be between dying slowly or going out in a blaze of glory, a literal one, because we'll be on fire. I think my choice is I'll suffer the breathing discomfort until our weapons have done their duty."

Matveev nodded. "Understood, Captain. Meanwhile, I will take a tour of the room and see if there is anything we can do to harden it against attack. But, we've been saying for years that the design is defective."

Alexeyev waved his hand. "I know. Do what you can, Alesya. If we take a hit from a torpedo, I'd rather it be the hull breach that kills us, not our own atmo-control equipment."

"Yes, sir," Matveev said. "By your leave, sir."

"Dismissed," Alexeyev said.

Ten seconds later, Georgy Alexeyev was alone in his sea cabin. And alone in his life. Natalia's last email, downloaded in their late morning periscope depth excursion, confirmed that there was another man, a new man, and she confessed she was interested in sexually, and would Alexeyev kindly and gracefully agree to the idea of her having sex with another man in his apartment, in his bed? Because Alexeyev had essentially abandoned her, sneaking out to sea in the middle of the night with no good-bye, no idea when he'd be back, on an operation so shrouded in secrecy the entire base had no idea they'd deployed. And besides which, he hadn't emailed her in almost three weeks, and his silence had distressed her.

Natalia could not tolerate abandonment, not since her father had put a pistol barrel in his mouth and departed life when Natalia was only eight, the word of his suicide taking two years to reach Natalia's mother and eventually Natalia herself. Why, Alexeyev wondered, did she bother with ship captains? They disappeared for weeks, months on end. It was by definition the nature of their jobs.

And there was no doubt that Alexeyev had been deeply and desperately in love with Natalia, until his venereal disease diagnosis, and made worse now by her blatant betrayal, all this so unexpected and so fatal to his spirit. The last message from Natalia hammered the last nail in the coffin of the relationship, as suddenly as Natalia's father's bullet had ended him.

The crime of the situation is that she could have just sat him down, one adult to another, and told him she was unhappy in the relationship and that she was leaving him. He would have politely let her go and wished her Godspeed. But instead, she had exploited her intimate knowledge of him to know exactly what his vulnerabilities were, where his insecurities were seated, the exact placement of a kill switch that would cause his great love for her to self-destruct. When he thought about it, it was a cowardly act. And the more he thought about it, the more rage he felt.

Alexeyev had written her back, the email leaving the ship before the edict to stop coming to periscope depth. His message had read, *Natalia, you are a whore and a degenerate slut. You and your cheating ways have led to me having a venereal disease and perhaps herpes in my eye. I strongly advise you to get your things and move out. If I find out that you brought another man into my apartment and into my bed, I swear by my mother's hallowed grave that I will find you and I will drain the lifeblood out of you with a thirty-centimeter rusty knife that I will use to cut your carotid arteries.*

Now that the message was sent, Natalia was no longer one of the centers of his life, the other being his beloved *Kazan*. But everywhere he went, he was damned by flashing memories of Natalia, even here in his sea cabin, as he remembered the Saturday last summer when he'd first taken her on a tour of the boat and shown her his sea cabin. With a mischievous smile, Natalia had double-locked both doors and pulled her shirt off and started to kiss him, and before he could respond she was naked and spread out on his conference table, and he'd taken her, gently at first, and then with the energy of a rocket booster, until they'd both collapsed drenched in sweat. Then came the knock on the door, the Inport Duty Officer Pavlovsky's voice on the other side of the door, *Sir, are you okay? We heard noises.* He could still see Natalia, naked and gorgeous, covering her mouth to suppress her musical laugh.

Natalia, he thought. How had his life brought him to this? He tried to concentrate on the mission, hoping it would take his mind out of this swirling emotional cesspool, but somehow this mission, this fool's errand to find an invisible and silent needle in a vast haystack, was not enough of a distraction. He wondered if there were any alcohol onboard. If they were back in port, he would have called up his closest friend, Sergei Kovalov, captain of the K-564 *Arkhangelsk,* and together they'd find the answers to life's questions at the bottom of a bottle of Ruskova vodka. That, of course, assumed that Natalia wasn't in Kovalov's life by that time.

South Atlantic Ocean
98 miles west-southwest of Cape Town, South Africa
B-902 *Panther*
Sunday, July 3; 1102 UTC

AOIC Anthony Pacino had the morning watch in the central command post. He'd brought the Cape of Good Hope chart to central command and taped it to the horizontal section of the pos one console, frequently updating it from the inertial navigation repeater. His impatience to get north into the North Atlantic made their slow crawl miserable. Every time he went to update the chart, their position was right on top of the one from the last update. This was just intolerably slow.

The phone buzzed and he answered it at pos one. "Central command, Pacino," he said.

"It's Varney and Ahmadi in the first compartment. Weapons in tubes one and two have been powered up for almost an hour. Request to spin up the UGST weapons in tubes three and four and open their outer doors and shut the doors to one and two and depressurize and shut down one and two."

"Wait one. I'll call you back." He clicked off and dialed up the sonar room.

"Sonar, Albanese."

"You got anything? Varney wants to rotate tubes and shut and open doors." The operation was loud, Pacino thought.

"Yeah, I've got about sixty merchant ships overhead in the exit from the Indian Ocean into the South Atlantic. The ambient noise is so loud it hurts to put on the headset."

Pacino had thought about making the transit shallow, using the thunderous noise of the merchant ships to mask their own noise, but some of those vessels were so huge with such deep drafts that collision was practically guaranteed. The only way to get that done was to continuously ping with the under ice and mine detection sonar, and doing that would broadcast their position. Pacino inhaled.

"But no submerged warships?" Pacino asked.

"Nope. *Vermont* is invisible. Presumably, so is the Yasen-M."

"Well, yell if you do pick something up."

"Our first sign will probably be *Vermont* firing torpedoes," Albanese said.

"Yeah. You doing okay otherwise, Chief?"

"L-T, I've run out of cigarettes. I'm miserable."

Pacino laughed. "Think how healthy you'll be when we finally make it to AUTEC."

"Between not smoking and our starvation rations, I'll be a shadow of myself, L-T."

"Just keep listening and try not to think about smokes or food," Pacino said, smiling to himself as he hung up. He dialed the first compartment.

"Torpedo room, Varney."

"Mr. Varney, you have permission to spin up three and four, shut down one and two, and open and shut outer doors as necessary."

"Thank you, AOIC. I'll call up when it's done."

Pacino hung up and felt a tap on his shoulder. It was Alexie Abakumov, the Russian reactor engineer. Pacino looked at him.

"You wanted to start the reactor, yes?" he said to Pacino.

Pacino nodded. "Let's see how the batteries are doing." Pacino scanned four gauges. They had perhaps 20 percent capacity. It was time to start up the plant to recharge. He looked at his watch. "I'll get OIC up here to take the watch." He dialed Dankleff's sea cabin.

A sleepy U-Boat Dankleff answered. "OIC."

"It's Patch. Abakumov needs to start the reactor and I want to perform the startup under instruction." He and Dankleff had discussed that they needed to know how to operate the nuclear reactor in case something happened to Abakumov.

"I'll be up. I want to walk under the water and put on fresh coveralls. Give me ten."

Pacino looked at the Russian. "I'll be aft in ten. Don't commence without me."

Abakumov nodded. He had dark circles under his eyes and his cheeks looked more hollow than usual. He, too, had run out of cigarettes. And vodka. And the cut in rations was hitting him as hard as the rest of the crew. No doubt, Pacino thought, they had to speed up to maximum as soon as they could get past the Cape's choke point.

Dankleff arrived, holding a steaming coffee cup, his eyes puffy from sleep. "There's only days of coffee left, Lipstick. This trip sucks."

"I know, U-Boat. Another nine days and we'll be done. And tomorrow morning when I come on watch, we'll crank it back up to flank. At least that will feel better than this tiptoeing. And we can reopen the galley for hot food." They'd shut down cooking during the Cape of Good Hope transit to minimize noise.

"So, anything I should know?"

"Albanese has nothing but merchant ships. But that's no surprise. Varney is rotating three and four into readiness and shutting down one and two, operating outer doors. Otherwise, nothing is going on."

"I relieve you, sir," Dankleff said formally.

"I stand relieved. I'll call from nuclear control when we're ready for your permission."

Dankleff nodded, yawned and took a pull of his coffee.

Pacino hurried aft, through the hatch to the shielded tunnel that traversed the third compartment where the reactor was housed, out the aft tunnel hatch into the motor-generator room, turning left into the nuclear control room, a cubbyhole created from what had once been a spare parts closet, but now had three walls of flatpanel displays, all of them busy with instrument indications, temperature and pressure graphs, a mimic depiction of the piping, valves and pumps of the primary loop, with the secondary system depicted on a neighboring screen, showing the piping, turbines, condensers and pumps of its systems. On the horizontal portion of the single seat's console was a section with four large rotary switches and a pistol grip switch that operated the nuclear control rods.

"You should call for permission," Abakumov said. "We must hurry."

Pacino hoisted the handset of the aft wall phone to his ear and dialed central command.

"Central, OIC."

"Nuclear control, AOIC, request permission to start the

reactor and place the propulsion turbine on the main motor and the ship's service turbine on the ship's load generator."

"AOIC, you have permission to start the reactor and place turbines on line. Call when we're on nuclear power."

"AOIC, aye," Pacino said, hanging up. He looked at Abakumov. "So. Operating procedure twenty-seven is displayed on the far-left upper display. Initial conditions are set, running one slow speed main coolant pump in each loop. Step one, energize inverters?"

Abakumov nodded.

"Energizing inverters alpha, bravo and charlie." Pacino pressed the touch screen that depicted the inverters that controlled the rod drive mechanisms. All their lights changed from red to green. "Inverters are on line. So now, step two, latch rods?"

"Yes, Mr. Patch."

Pacino reached for the pistol grip on the console and pulled it vertically out of the panel, and it came up a few inches. "Latch voltage applied," he said, then rotated the pistol grip counterclockwise to the nine o'clock position. "Driving control rod drive mechanisms inward." Three green lights lit above the mimic picture of the reactor vessel. "CRDMs indicate latched," he said, glancing at the procedure, then putting the pistol grip switch back to its neutral twelve o'clock position and letting it drop back into the console. "Step three, select rod one and pull it to one hundred centimeters while monitoring startup rate?"

"Yes, but pause at eighty centimeters."

"Pulling rod one to eighty," Pacino said, selecting the pistol grip so that it was selected to only control rod one, and rotated the pistol grip to pull the rod out.

Ten minutes later, rods one and two were all the way out of the core at 100 centimeters height with rod three at 33 centimeters. The reactor had climbed steadily out of the nonvisible range into the intermediate range and then into the power range. Pacino had opened the valves to pull steam out of the steam generators, boiling them down while warming up the massive steam headers. As the condensed water was forced out of the large bore steam piping system, the venting in the space was incredibly loud.

"Too bad you guys didn't find a way to muffle that," Pacino said, his fingers in his ears.

Abakumov shrugged. "Is not combat system," he said, as if that explained everything.

"I'm losing boiler level. I may have to start a feed pump on the batteries."

"If you do that, you risk tripping out many systems. Feed pump pulls too many amps. Must make it on boiler steam. This is where men are separated from boys."

Pacino's jaw clenched. "Main steam header is clear. Admitting steam to ship's service steam turbine." Pacino pressed the touch screen to open the throttle valve to the SSTG. A low-pitched but loud hum came from ahead of them, then the pitch rose from bass to tenor. The turbine was spinning up, sounding like a jet engine on startup. Soon the pitch had risen to a screaming, ear-piercing squeal. "It's almost like you guys went out of your way to make it loud," he shouted over the noise.

"SSTG is at three thousand RPM, on the governor and ready for loading. Quick, shut the breaker to the ship's service generator and open the battery breaker to the ship's service generator."

Pacino did as he was told, bringing the ship's service turbine on line and taking the battery out of the circuit. He glanced at the boiler levels, and they were perilously low. If he didn't start a feed pump immediately, they'd boil dry and they'd lose the entire plant.

"Ten centimeters of level in the boilers," Abakumov prompted.

"SSTG has all ship's loads, battery breaker open, ready to start a feed pump."

"Do it."

Pacino punched the flatpanel at the indication of the main feed pump, one eye on the boiler level, now at 4 centimeters. The pump had better start on the first try, he thought. The pump was the size of a refrigerator and drew more current than anything on board. As it started, all the lights throughout the ship dimmed and blinked, the electrical transient causing alarms to go off in central command. Pacino watched. The pump indicated at max RPM and boiler levels were climbing from 2 centimeters, back on their way to 80. He breathed a sigh of relief. It had worked.

"You are obviously man, not boy," Abakumov said, slapping Pacino on the back and smiling.

"Good to know," Pacino said. "I suspected, but confirmation is important. Now, for the propulsion turbine."

This was easier, similar to starting the ship's service turbine, but this unit was five times the size of the SSTG, its screaming to full revolutions ear-piercing. Hard to imagine that this much noise wouldn't blast out into the sea and be detected by someone out there, but there was nothing they could do about it.

Finally, the battery breaker to the main motor was open and the propulsion turbine was powering the main motor. The ship was underway on nuclear power.

"Start the battery charge," Abakumov said.

Pacino lined up the breakers to put the SSTG onto the battery and push current into it to restore its state of charge. As the amp-hour meter began to climb, he stepped back from the panel and looked at the status of the equipment. It was all nominal. No alarms, no red flashing annunciators. He'd done it. He found the phone.

"Central, OIC."

"Nuclear control, AOIC. Propulsion shifted to nuclear power, battery charge in progress."

"Very well. Now get up here and take back over your watch, ya non-qual slacker."

Pacino smiled, turned over the propulsion plant watch to Abakumov and walked forward.

34

South Atlantic Ocean
210 kilometers west-southwest of Cape Town, South Africa
K-561 ***Kazan***
Sunday, July 3; 1127 UTC, 1:27 pm Moscow time

Captain Third Rank Svetka Maksimov had the senior supervisory watch in the central command post, sitting at the command console's far portside position one, her display showing the broadband sonar screen to the left and the transient detector to the right. The broadband display was a mess, with dozens of strong traces from the merchant shipping in the shipping lane directly overhead.

The transient detector would be somewhat more revealing, she thought, the display a three-dimensional graph of time on the bottom axis extending right along the screen. The vertical axis was frequency, although most useful transients were low frequency, but not all. A dropped wrench made a low frequency transient, as would a slammed hatch or a torpedo tube door closing, but steam at a high flowrate through a steam pipe would make a high frequency noise, as would a steam turbine startup. High frequencies were somewhat useless, Maksimov thought, since they attenuated and disappeared quickly with distance through the ocean. So they'd only detect a high frequency if it were extremely close. The third axis was intensity, this axis pointing into the screen. A faint sound would hug the axis, but a louder one would zoom out into what looked like the depth of the screen's depiction.

The transient noises were filtered by the MGK-600's signal processor, in an effort to exclude displaying biologics such as the moaning of whales and the clicking of shrimp. Biologics usually made the ocean loud with useless noise. With the biologics screened out, the system could strain for detections of dropped wrenches, missile doors opening or shutting, or a launched torpedo. Even footsteps or loud voices. Although, the problem with the biologics filter was that it would screen out music, which meant a target could be blasting rock 'n roll on a stereo but avoid detection. For that, the only remedy was the use of the human ear. But so far, the transient plot was quiet and all that came over the headset were clicking shrimp, wave noise and the propellers of dozens of merchant ships up above. Maksimov bit her lip and looked around the room.

On position three of the command console to her right was Senior Lieutenant Anatoly Blackbeard Pavlovsky, the electrical officer, standing duty as watch officer. His concentration was momentarily on the chart, zooming in, then back out, shaking his head at the enormous size of the fix error circle. Maksimov, as navigator, had even contemplated donning a wetsuit, locking out of the forward airlock and swimming to the surface taking a sextant and a chronometer with her and shooting the sun at noon to get a navigation fix. Anything was better than relying on ship's inertial nav, which was getting buggier every minute without a navsat fix. Pavlovsky rotated his display back to the same sonar screen that Maksimov herself was seeing.

Maksimov got up and paced the room, checking that the ship control petty officers, the boatswains, were taking care of ship's depth, speed and buoyancy, then walking to the port side to the sonar-and-sensor console, where Sonar Officer Ilia Kovalev stood his watch, his headset on, concentrating on a large display of the transient detector.

"What bearing are you checking?" Maksimov asked Kovalev.

"Southeast for eighty percent of the time," he said. "Northwest for twenty percent. Just in case the target subs somehow slipped past us and are heading up the great circle route to North America. Right now, it's southeast."

As he was speaking, a bright red transient lit up at high frequency, a blotch at medium intensity, covering several of the higher frequency buckets, and climbing in intensity.

"I'll be damned, ma'am," Kovalev breathed. "High freq contact."

Maksimov picked up a headset at the console beside Kovalev, pulled up the transient display and tuned the cursor to the sound. It was a rushing, blasting noise. She turned to Pavlovsky. "Call the captain," she barked. "We've got something." She sat at the console and brought up the transient monitor on the lower screen and the broadband display on the upper display. On the console to her left, she brought up the narrowband graphics from the towed array, but so far, they were just full of noise.

It only took half a minute for Captain Alexeyev to step into the central command post. He stood behind Maksimov and took a third headset from the console and listened to the transient, which was now fading, but a new transient was growing on the screen, coming out of the low frequencies and rolling into the high frequencies.

Kovalev looked back at the navigator and the captain. "Steam turbine startup, for sure."

"Any correlation on broadband?" Alexeyev asked. They couldn't get a track on transients, just a momentary general bearing. But a loud, sustained transient should show up as a broadband sonar trace with a sustained, precise bearing. And that they could get a parallax range on. If it kept up for a few minutes, they could get a firing data package. In a hard spot, they could hit it with an active sonar pulse and get a firecontrol data package in a heartbeat, at the expensive cost of losing their stealth, which was vital given that this loud contact was being escorted by a quiet attack submarine.

Maksimov stood back up and stepped over to the navigation chart, manipulating the keyboard to punch in the suspected position of the transient. Pavlovsky joined her at the table, stroking his too-long scraggly beard. "That's got to be the *Panther*," he said.

"Transient frequency stable and intensity fading," Kovalev reported. "But I have another transient, this one much higher in intensity, low frequency and becoming higher pitched. This is another steam turbine startup, and this one is much bigger."

Alexeyev had his chin in his hand, deep in thought. First Officer Lebedev showed up, tapping Pavlovsky on the shoulder, saying something quietly to him. Pavlovsky pointed to the captain. Lebedev took a step closer to the captain.

"Captain, I recommend stationing action stations," she said.

Alexeyev looked at her with his uncovered eye unfocused. For a moment Lebedev could swear he was trying to remember who she was, until finally he nodded. "Fine," he said, "but no general announcing circuit orders. Use the phone circuits and messengers."

Lebedev went off to get action stations manned. Maksimov took her action station at the middle position of the command console as the officers and senior enlisted hurried into the room and donned headsets. Maksimov smiled. It was possible this mission would be over soon. Perhaps even today, she thought. The thought made her suddenly feel hungry. The reduced rations order was only hours old but already had the entire crew depressed.

Alexeyev picked up the phone to nuclear control. "Engineer, be ready to rig the atmospheric controls in machinery two for battle." The captain turned to Pavlovsky and Lebedev. "Watch Officer, when I give you the word, call back to nuclear control and order them to rig machinery two for battle. That means they will depressurize and nitrogen purge the oxygen generators, shut down the scrubbers and burners and stop the oxygen bleed, then stop the ventilation fans."

"But Captain, if we do that, we'll start to suffocate inside twenty minutes."

Alexeyev nodded. "If it gets bad, we will put on our emergency breathing air masks."

"Captain," Lebedev reported to Alexeyev. "Action stations are manned. Do you want to address the room?"

Alexeyev seemed confused for a moment, then blinked. He cleared his throat, and the murmuring in the room died down to pin-drop quiet, only the high-pitched whine of the computers audible in the room.

"Attention in the tactical team," he said. "We have a loud transient from bearing one-two-two which showed steam flow, then a small steam turbine startup, and then a larger one. I am presuming the sounds are coming from the *Panther* as she lights off her reactor. We must be prepared for *Panther* to roar off into the sea at maximum speed. I doubt she will stay at slow speed once her reactor is live." Alexeyev stopped, and Lebedev stared at him, coming close to him and whispering urgently in his ear. Alexeyev nodded, then continued. "Intentions. Yes. My intentions. *Our* intentions. I intend to monitor the *Panther* and first determine what speed he will choose. Once he settles on a speed, we will obtain a parallax range by stealthily driving across the line-of-sight to the *Panther*. We will obtain a firecontrol data package and feed it to the battlecontrol system. However, we will *not* be shooting."

Lebedev stared at the captain. "I'm sorry, Captain, but once we get a data package, shouldn't we fire immediately?"

Alexeyev seemed briefly confused by the question. Maksimov looked to her right, at the third position console, where Pavlovsky returned her glance, as if it to say, *what the hell is wrong with the captain?* Maksimov looked over at the battlecontrol console's middle position, where Weapons Officer Katerina Sobol manned her watchstation, and Sobol seemingly shared that same sentiment.

Alexeyev cleared his throat. "We can't fire at *Panther*, no matter how good the firecontrol data package is," he said, his voice too loud. "We might well sink *Panther*, as our operational orders dictate, but our orders prioritize sinking the American escort ship, and a torpedo launch against *Panther* gives away our position to the American submarine. We will wait until we have a detection against the American."

Lebedev had opened her mouth, about to protest, when suddenly Sonar Officer Kovalev frantically raised his hand in the air. "In central command, new sonar contact, possible submerged warship!" he announced. Lebedev and Alexeyev rushed to the port side, standing behind the sonar-and-sensor console. "I have towed array narrowband detect on frequencies at one hundred twenty kilohertz—from a sixty-cycle generator or generators—and a heterodyned frequency at five kilohertz, probably from the same generators. The bearings are either southwest or due south. Captain, we need to maneuver to resolve the bearing ambiguity."

Lebedev and Alexeyev traded a look. They'd just detected the American Virginia-class. Alexeyev shouted an order at the ship control console. "Boatswain, left full rudder, steady course zero-two-zero, turns for ten knots!"

The boatswain of the watch acknowledged, and the deck tilted slightly as the *Kazan* made the turn and increased speed.

"Steady course zero-two-zero, Captain," the boatswain of the watch reported.

"Boatswain, turns for four knots," Alexeyev ordered.

Kovalev at the sonar-and-sensor console looked triumphant. "Captain, I have *additional* tonals, growing stronger now. Bearing ambiguity being resolved, but correlates to a new very faint broadband detection at one-five-one. Sir, we have the American escort submarine, bearing one-five-one."

"Do we have a target data package from the maneuvers?" Alexeyev asked Weapons Officer Sobol at the battlecontrol console.

"No, Captain," she said, showing that she knew she was disappointing the captain. "The first detect didn't form a complete leg. We have one leg of a parallax range. We need another leg."

"Captain," Lebedev said, standing close to Alexeyev. "Now that we have a partial data package on the American escort submarine, we could go active, both on him and the *Panther*, nail down their positions, and fire torpedo salvos and take them out right now."

"No," Alexeyev said. "Absolutely not. We have the acoustic advantage over the American. I intend to use that to *our* advantage. We will let him sail by, ignorant of us. Once he and the *Panther* are north and west of us, we will fire one torpedo in stealth mode at each and sink them both."

"Why not a horizontal salvo, Captain? We could put five units on the *Panther* and another five on the American. No way they would survive that."

"A salvo makes more noise from the tubes and the launching and triples the emitted noise of the weapons. And it causes sonar confusion if they run and we lose them and need to reacquire them. With just one unit sneaking up on the targets, they might not even detect them until it is much too late for them. This will be a *surgical* strike, First."

Lebedev looked disappointed, but she nodded in obedience. "Yes, sir," she said, leaning over Kovalev's seat back and staring at his console. She muttered something to him, but Maksimov could pick it up: *"Don't fucking lose them, Kovalev."*

South Atlantic Ocean
107 miles west of Cape Town, South Africa
USS *Vermont*
Sunday, July 3; 1156 UTC, 1556 local time

Lieutenant Commander Rachel Romanov stood aft of the command console and stared at the chart, then flipped to the narrowband display. They had the tonals emitted by *Panther*, but nothing from the anticipated frequency buckets of the Yasen-M-class submarine. She paged her display to the broadband sonar display, but it was useless with all the merchant traffic in the shipping lanes above. But as far as below-the-layer was concerned, the sea was empty but for *Panther* and *Virginia*. She shifted to the acoustic daylight signal processor, but it displayed nothing but noise.

Romanov leaned back and contemplated calling for coffee, but in a few minutes the watch relief would go down. Her relief was late, the engineer, Lewinsky, who should have been here twenty minutes ago, but lately he'd taken to standing double duty, with a watch aft in maneuvering controlling the reactor, then a watch in the control room conning the submarine. Such a schedule would make Romanov's eyes cross, she thought. There was no doubt, Lewinsky was motivated and energetic. But his getting relieved in maneuvering was taking too long, delaying her getting off watch so she could go grab noon meal before they shut down the galley and cleared the dishes. Not that the food was anything worth showing up to the table for, she thought, the reduced rations and rig for ultra-quiet making the noon meal little more than white bread and peanut butter. Soon, the flour would get scarce, and the mess cooks would cut the flour with raisins, and the order of the day would be raisin bread for every occasion. And raisin bread was disgusting, she thought. At that point, she'd switch to crackers, but then, they'd run out of crackers.

She went to the Q-10 stack console and leaned over Petty Officer Sanders, who had the morning watch and was concentrating hard on the narrowband frequency buckets.

"Anything?" Romanov asked.

"Nothing, Nav," Sanders said. "It's all noise. If there's a bad guy out there, he's quiet as a mouse."

"Well, I suppose that's good news, Sanders, but keep a weather eye out. Damned if I want to limp home with a hole in the hull from a Russian torpedo."

"You'd be lucky to limp home, Nav. You'd be on the bottom in Davey Jones' locker."

Romanov smiled. "Davy Jones was a fucking skimmer puke," she said in jest, their customary insult to the surface navy, since they only skimmed the surface of the seas. She looked up and Elvis Lewinsky had walked in and was paging through displays at the command console.

"Nice of you to show up for watch," Romanov said, making an exaggerated motion to check her watch, shaking it at her ear as if trying to see if it had malfunctioned.

"Come on, Silky, you know I have to get relieved back aft before I can come here, and I have to do a pre-watch tour first. See if the torpedo room is ready for action. And if I make you late for lunch, well, it ain't like lunch is anything to write home about since they cut rations."

"Yeah, all true, Elvis, which is why I have graciously chosen to forgive you." Romanov smiled sweetly at the engineer.

"Fuck you, Silky. So, what do you have for me?"

"A million surface ship contacts, all merchants. One submerged contact, the *Panther.* And otherwise, below the layer, we are all alone. Looks like the Yasen-M didn't show up for work."

"So we get a break for once in our lives," Lewinsky said. "I relieve you, ma'am."

"I stand relieved. In control," Lewinsky announced loudly, "Lieutenant Commander Lewinsky has the deck and the conn!" She looked at the engineer. "Have a good watch, Feng."

He threw her a sloppy salute and turned back to the command console, flipping between the sonar narrowband screen, the broadband display and the acoustic daylight screen. Romanov left the control room and made her way to the wardroom, checking her thigh pocket for her pad computer, then stopped the mess cook of the watch just before he shut down service.

"What do we have?" she asked.

"Chili with crackers," he said. "Piping hot and guaranteed to melt through your stomach lining."

Romanov smiled at him. "You know, that's exactly what the doctor ordered."

She was two bites into the chili when the 1MC shipwide announcing circuit clicked—which should never happen when the ship was rigged for ultra-quiet. A rush of stomach acid flooded her, and not from the chili. Lewinsky's voice boomed over the circuit, and she could hear the fear—no, the near-panic—in the engineer's voice.

"Torpedo in the water! Captain to control! Man battlestations!"

South Atlantic Ocean
110 miles west of Cape Town, South Africa
B-902 *Panther*
Sunday, July 3; 1211 UTC

Lieutenant Anthony Pacino was on his way from nuclear control to the central command post, pausing to duck into the sonar room to see how Chief Albanese was doing, but as he entered the room, Albanese tossed his headset off to the port console and stared at Pacino with his mouth open his eyes wide in panic.

"Torpedoes in the water! Multiple torpedoes!"

"What bearing?" Pacino asked, a cold calmness inexplicably

flowing into his soul. This moment felt like something he'd seen in his dreams a hundred times, so that when it eventually became real, he was ready for it.

"Southeast," Albanese choked out. "One-five-one."

Pacino vaulted out of the sonar room and ran into the central command post, where he found Dankleff standing, half-paralyzed. Pacino lunged for the shipwide announcing circuit microphone at position two.

"Torpedoes in the water, incoming from the southeast. Prepare for torpedo launch, tubes three and four. Torpedo room, prepare all tubes and all weapons for immediate launch and report to central command when ready to fire!"

He looked at Dankleff, who seemed to be coming out of his trance. "OIC, change course to due north, and flank it!"

Dankleff yelled at Grip Aquatong at the ship control station. "Grip, steer zero-zero-zero, all ahead flank! Maximum revolutions!"

Aquatong turned the wheel, hard, and the deck tilted dramatically, the deck beginning to vibrate from the power of the reactor coming up to full output.

"Central command, torpedo room," Varney's voice came over the overhead speaker, "UGST torpedoes in tubes three and four ready in all respects, recommend launch."

"It'd be nice to have a solution," Pacino grumbled, glancing over at Dankleff, who had joined him at position two.

"Just fucking fire them southeast," Dankleff said. "At this point, they're just dumb evasion devices."

Pacino looked over the console, realizing Captain Ahmadi had joined him. "Am I doing this right?" he asked. Ahmadi nodded.

"Bearing here, assumed range dialed in here, search speed here," Ahmadi said, pointing.

"Just put in southeast," Pacino said, "assume a range at, I don't know, ten kilometers, and fast speed search. What happens if the target is closer, say five clicks?"

"You'll miss, Mr. Patch. It'll sail right by."

"Dial it in at five kilometers, then."

Ahmadi dialed it in. "Ready, Mr. Patch."

Pacino looked at Dankleff, who nodded.

"Shooting tube three!" Pacino pulled the large trigger and the ship jumped for an instant, but the launch was gentler than what he'd experienced on American submarines. He dialed the rotary tube selector switch to tube number four. "Shooting tube four!" He pulled the trigger again, and again the deck jumped.

"Central command, torpedo room," the intercom clicked with Varney's voice, "tubes one and two are ready in all respects. Recommend firing."

Pacino selected tube one on the rotary dial switch, checked the indicator lights and pulled the trigger, then lined up tube two, scanned the settings and readiness indicators, then pulled the trigger again. The deck had jumped again, once for the tube one weapon, then a second time for tube two. Pacino narrowed his eyes at the settings. Was it possible that even five kilometers was too distant? That the firing submarine might be even closer? And that his five-thousand-meter setting would cause his torpedoes to sail past the target, blind? He reset the range to the next unit for one kilometer, hoping the UGST torpedoes couldn't home in on the firing ship.

"Central command, sonar," Albanese's voice said from the overhead speaker. "*Vermont* is shooting. Double torpedo shot, looks like from a bearing east-southeast of us. I have broadband contact on *Vermont* from her main coolant pumps going to fast speed. She's increasing speed."

"Sonar, any more incoming torpedoes from the Yasen?"

"Central, Sonar, no."

"Maybe we scared him," Dankleff said.

"Torpedo room, central," Pacino ordered on his microphone, "report status of the next two tubes." He dialed in the speaker to sonar. "Sonar, central, do you have a bearing to the firing submarine?"

"Central, sonar, no, just the original firing point."

Pacino looked at Dankleff. "U-Boat, the minute we get a hint of where the firing submarine is, we're going to hit him with both Shkval supercavitating torpedoes."

"You could launch them *now,* Patch."

"All that would do is make more noise—Ahmadi says we

need at least a hint of a solution—or at least a rough position, before we launch. They don't do much course-correcting on their way out, they're going too fast for that. They would just sail out past the guy."

Dankleff nodded. "Still, even if it looks like we need more evasive effects, be ready to hit the trigger."

Pacino nodded, hitting the intercom mike's button. "Whale, status of incoming torpedo?"

"Still inbound," Albanese said. "It's getting closer."

Pacino looked at Dankleff and pointed to the surface. Dankleff nodded. Pacino grabbed Ahmadi. "We need to emergency blow to the surface," Pacino said. "It's possible the torpedo has a ceiling setting."

Ahmadi shook his head sadly. "That would do you no good. A Futlyar torpedo will follow you to the end of the earth, Mr. Patch. I'm afraid it's over. Your mission. The voyage of the *Panther*. And our time on this earth."

South Atlantic Ocean
107 miles west of Cape Town, South Africa
USS *Vermont*
Sunday, July 3; 1211 UTC, 1611 local time

Lieutenant Commander Mario Elvis Lewinsky's grip on the handhold of the command console was so intense that his knuckles had gone white, as had the color of his face.

Captain Timothy Seagraves looked over at Executive Officer Jeremiah Quinnivan at the attack center. The deck trembled from the vibrations of the flank speed run, the submarine having dived to test depth in the seconds after the detection of the incoming torpedo. Within thirty seconds, Lewinsky had prepared a "snapshot" torpedo for firing, a lined-up weapon with little to no data on the target other than the bearing, the launch to be used more for effect than for success. Only in ten percent of snapshots did a weapon home in and hit something, but to fail to fire would be a tactical disaster. The enemy out there shooting at them had to be notified in the strongest possible terms that the *Vermont* was fighting back. Even if that meant she'd be firing blind.

Lieutenant Commander Rachel Romanov arrived at the command console to relieve Lewinsky so he could go to his battlestation aft, in maneuvering. "I relieve you, Eng," she said, still breathing heavily from her sprint to the control room. Lewinsky muttered that he stood relieved and took off aft. Romanov looked at the display on the attack center.

"Captain, Coordinator, if we snapshot two Mark 48s in CMT mode at the bearing to the launch, we can slow down and nail the shooter with active sonar. The countermeasure mode of the Mark 48s will take down the incoming torpedoes, we'll have a solution to—let's call him Master One—and we can hit him with a horizontal salvo."

"Good work, Nav," Seagraves said. "Attention in the firecontrol party," he said in the pin-drop quiet room, "snapshot tubes one and two, CMT mode, at the bearing of the incoming torpedoes."

With a snapshot, there was no long, involved checklist or detailed pre-firing reports. There was just the officer of the deck announcing "set" when the presets were correct, and "fire" as the trigger button was pushed. Romanov checked the two displays, both now set up in snapshot mode. The screen showed a dumb display of what looked like two rowboats, one at the bottom representing *Vermont* herself, the rowboat pointing to the seven o'clock direction. A vertical line extended upward from *Vermont*'s rowboat to the other rowboat, the line labeled "151" for the bearing to the target. The upper rowboat, representing the incoming torpedo, was also pointed to the seven o'clock position, it's motion intending to catch up to and impact *Vermont*.

Romanov looked at Quinnivan and Seagraves. "I have to assume a range," she said. "Even though we're using immediate enable."

Quinnivan spoke. "Put in six thousand yards, lassie. No way those bastards were distant. They had to get a sniff of us as we went by close."

Romanov looked at Seagraves, who nodded solemnly. Romanov put in three nautical miles, six thousand yards, on both displays.

"Snapshot, tubes one and two, Master One, countermeasure torpedo mode, medium speed, immediate enable," Romanov announced, looking over the back side of the seat of pos two, where Lomax sat, and pos one, where Eisenhart sat, then to the weapons control console, where Spichovich was seated. "Set," Romanov said, leaning over Lomax and pressing his fixed function key, then doing the same to Eisenhart's panel, then saying to Spichovich, "shoot!"

"Tube one, fire," Spichovich said, hitting a central, larger fixed function key—the trigger—with a lit up bright green color. "Tube two, fire," he said, jamming the trigger function key a second time.

The deck jumped violently, and Romanov's ears were slammed by the power of the inboard venting of the water-round-torpedo tank, then jumping again, her eardrums slammed a second time, a headache blooming behind her ears with the torpedo launches.

She looked across the room to Petty Officer Mercer at the BQQ-10 stack. "Sonar," Romanov called, "own ship's units fired electrically." Mercer turned in his seat to look back at her.

"Officer of the Deck, own ship's units, normal launch," Mercer said.

"Now, Captain?" Romanov said. "Can we go active?" If Seagraves agreed, Mercer could blast the sea with an active sonar pulse that would nail down the position and movement of Master One, allowing an offensive torpedo shot. They would risk nothing—Master One already knew they were present and an idea of their position and had fired at them. Stealth was long gone.

South Atlantic Ocean
108 miles west of Cape Town, South Africa
B-902 *Panther*
Sunday, July 3; 1214 UTC, 1614 local time

Pacino's instincts were screaming in his mind despite Captain Ahmadi's warning. "Help me emergency blow anyway," he said. "Let's get the ballast tank vents shut." Pacino and Ahmadi reached into The Million Valve Manifold to find the valves that would shut the corroded and sticking ballast tank vents.

"Central, torpedo room, tubes three and four are reloaded with UGST torpedoes and are ready in all respects."

"U-Boat, launch three and four," Pacino shouted from The Million Man Manifold. He grabbed the forward valve handles for the ballast tank blow. It was then they could hear the torpedo sonar blasting into the ship from the sea.

Dankleff shouted back from central command. "Lipstick, hurry up! Emergency blow!"

Pacino rotated the two valve handles for the forward blow. He waited five seconds, but with his heart pounding and the adrenaline pouring through his system, it may have only been one second, and then he operated the after main ballast tank blow valves. The room roared with the flow noise and a dense cloud of condensation filled the space, reducing visibility to half a foot. Pacino listened for the sound of the air flow decreasing as the deck began to tilt up dramatically. He could hear Dankleff shouting at Grip Aquatong to take the boat up to the surface with a steep angle. Pacino reached for the piping nestled in the rats' nest of The Million Valve Manifold to keep his footing. He made his way back into the central command post as the angle abruptly came off the ship, the deck suddenly settling flat.

"All stop!" Dankleff ordered.

The deck began rocking in the swells of the sea state.

"U-Boat, get the scope up! We might be about to get run over by a merchant!"

Dankleff raised the number one scope, twisted it in a fast circle and gasped, *"Oh shit! Grip, right full rudder! All ahead flank!"*

South Atlantic Ocean
105 miles west of Cape Town, South Africa
VLCC crude carrier *Eva Maru*
Sunday, July 3; 1214 UTC, 1614 local time

On the bridge of the very large crude carrier *Eva Maru*, an off-watch officer looking out the forward windows and recording a video for his video blog about life at sea suddenly saw a huge burst of foam almost immediately forward of them, just a few hundred yards off the port bow, his phone recording as the bow of a submarine burst out of the sea, then came level in an explosion of waves and bubbles, the sub turning just before it hit them in a glancing blow, the flank of the submarine grinding and scraping against the tanker's port side. After the collision, the submarine continued moving southward on the surface, picking up speed, apparently not caring that there had just been a maritime collision. While the officer tried to come to grips with the sight of a submarine suddenly emergency surfacing right beside them in the middle of the ocean, then hitting them and scraping against them, then running away from the scene of the accident, the next thing that happened was much, much stranger.

The explosion at the bow of the tanker blew everyone in the bridge to the aft wall. The eruption of water and spray ignited an orange fireball half a shiplength wide as the bow of the tanker exploded from the impact of what much later would be reported to be a Russian Futlyar torpedo.

35

South Atlantic Ocean
110 miles west-northwest of Cape Town, South Africa
USS *Vermont*
Sunday, July 3; 1215 UTC, 1615 local time

Commander Timothy Seagraves narrowed his eyes at Commander Quinnivan and Lieutenant Commander Romanov. "Wait on going active until we know the status of our countermeasure torpedoes and what's going on with the six we heard launched from *Panther*."

Petty Officer Mercer turned from his seat at the BQQ-10 sonar console. "I have a detonation of one of our units, edge of the starboard baffles, and there's one less torpedo in the water. I have the second torpedo at fast speed and pinging. I think it's homing."

Romanov looked at Mercer. "Do you have bearing separation between *Panther* and that second torpedo?"

"I only hold both on the rudder rear-facing hydrophone and the onion array, so bearings are sloppy and merged."

Two seconds later, from aft, an explosion could be heard, then a secondary explosion, this one much louder than the first.

"Explosions were from the last bearing to the *Panther*," Mercer reported, his voice flat.

Romanov took a breath, about to say something to the captain, when the second explosion rocked the ship, this one ten times the power of the first explosion. "What the hell was that, Mercer?" she asked.

"Ma'am, no way to tell without turning around to put it in the spherical array's field of view. Or we could pop up to periscope depth and take a look."

"All you'll see is smoke and flames," Quinnivan said. "Plus, we'd have to slow down."

"Mercer, at the last bearing of *Panther,* do we have steam flow noise, steam turbines? Tonals?" Romanov leaned over Mercer's seatback. "Anything?"

Mercer turned to look at the navigator. "Nothing held on the towed array or rudder array, but it would help if we slowed down and turned south."

"We don't need to be running anymore," Romanov said to Seagraves. "The torpedoes fired at us are gone and we need to see what's going on with the *Panther.*"

"What we need to do is fire at Master One," Quinnivan said. "And to do that, we have to get his position. Captain, recommend we employ active sonar."

"Captain, OOD," Mercer said, his hand on his right headset's earphone, "I have torpedoes in the water, multiple torpedoes, edge of the starboard baffles."

"Just what we need," Quinnivan said.

Romanov looked at the executive officer. "We don't know that they came from Master One. Maybe they're from *Panther.*"

"No way," Quinnivan said. "Those lads could never figure out how to launch their weapons on a strange foreign submarine, much less multiple torpedo shots."

"Dammit," Seagraves said to the XO and navigator. "There's nothing but confusion."

"Fog o' war, Captain," Quinnivan said.

"We can't just keep running from goddamned torpedoes. We can't fire blind because we might hit *Panther* if she's still alive," Seagraves said. "We need to know what the hell is going on. Nav, slow to five knots and turn south. Once you're on course, go active."

"Pilot," Romanov shouted, "all stop! Left full rudder, steady course south, mark speed five knots!"

South Atlantic Ocean
105 miles west of Cape Town, South Africa
B-902 *Panther*
Sunday, July 3; 1215 UTC, 1615 local time

The lights went out throughout the ship the moment the explosion's shock wave hit them and bounced them in the sea. The hum of ventilation stopped, making the upper level immediately stuffy and hot. Pacino felt his way forward from The Million Valve Manifold to the central command post, where OIC Dankleff had found a battle lantern and illuminated the forward bulkhead of central command, shining it on the gauges of the first position and the ship control station. The engine order telegraph on the ship control console make a jangling, ringing noise as the arrow from the engineroom went from "flank" to "stop." The intercom began barking immediately over the still-loud sound of the explosion outside the hull.

"Central command, this is nuclear control, the reactor has tripped!" Abakumov called. "Switching ship's loads to the battery. Switching propulsion to the battery."

Pacino lunged for the microphone. "Nuclear control, central, is the reactor okay? Can you restart?" The lights in the control room flickered, then came on. Farther aft, the lights switched back on.

"All control systems went black, Mr. Patch. I have to restart the distributed control system. I do not know how long that will take."

"Start it now, and call if you need help."

Abakumov clicked his intercom twice by way of acknowledgement. The ventilation fans restarted, blowing air throughout the submarine.

"Central command, torpedo room," Varney said, an undertone of barely controlled fear in his voice, "torpedo tube six on the port side is glowing red hot and we have—"

"Get down there, Patch!" Dankleff yelled, but Pacino was already vaulting aft to get to the ladderway to the middle level so he could get forward to the middle level hatch to the first compartment.

Pacino could hear coughing over the intercom, then Varney's excited voice calling out, "We have smoke in the torpedo room! *Fire in the torpedo room!*"

Dankleff's deep voice boomed overhead from the loudspeakers, *"Fire in the torpedo room, fire in the torpedo room, all hands don emergency air masks, all personnel off watch, lay to the second compartment forward hatch and await instructions from the first compartment."*

South Atlantic Ocean
110 miles west-northwest of Cape Town, South Africa
USS *Vermont*
Sunday, July 3; 1229 UTC, 1629 local time

Lieutenant Commander Rachel Romanov leaned over Mercer's seatback at the BQQ-10 stack.

The display resembled a radar scope, the center representing *Vermont* herself, with concentric circular markings at regular distances going outward, each ring a mile from the one inside it, the outer ring at the forty-mile point, eighty thousand yards, the supposed limit of active sonar detection.

"Hit it," Romanov said. Mercer uncovered a protective cover over a fixed function key and mashed it. An earsplitting booming shriek sounded from forward, going from a bass growl and howling to a high-pitched scream, the noise sounding for endless seconds until it stopped.

On the display, a bright green ring moved outward from the center, illuminating dull green splotches as it grew, the dull green considered to be noise with zero Doppler—the Doppler effect that of changing the frequency of a transmitted pulse by virtue of the speed of the target's pulse reflection. If Mercer chose, he could filter out anything slower than a desired speed setpoint, but Romanov had told him to keep the filter off, to catch *Panther* or Master One if either of them hovered with no motion.

To the south, the six o'clock position on the display, a bright orange blotch lit up, an arrow superimposed on it, denoting speed, the system labeling it with *10 knots.* Then to the southwest, multiple small orange blotches, all of them labeled with longer arrows pointing southwest, all reading *40 knots.*

And then the money shot. South-southwest, bearing 205, a large orange spot with no arrow, the system labeling it, *0 knots.* Romanov pointed to it, smiling to herself that she'd ordered the Doppler filter taken off. God, she thought, active sonar was wonderful. Damned shame they could only use it when their position was already known to the enemy.

"That's him, Captain. Master One, in all his glory. Range thirty-seven miles."

"Seventy-four *thousand* yards?" Quinnivan said, stunned. "That fooker can hear *us* from nearly *forty miles* away? What goddamned sonar set is he using, and can we fookin' buy one?"

"Maybe he picked us up on a transient," Seagraves said. "Pump seal going bad putting out a noise, or a failed sound mount."

"We were scanned just after we left Norfolk by the *Colorado,* Skipper," Quinnivan said. "We were quiet as a mouse."

"Or maybe the Yasen-M is just a better submarine," Romanov said.

"You'd better hope not, Nav," Seagraves said.

"Those small contacts at forty knots, torpedoes, presumably fired by *Panther*?" Seagraves said, staring at the display on the command console. "And *Panther* is the contact due south at ten knots?"

Mercer nodded. "That's my read, Captain."

Romanov smiled. *Panther* had lived.

"Ping again," Seagraves said to Romanov. "See if Master One truly has zero speed with incoming torpedoes heading for him, of if he's just running at a right angle to our line-of-sight."

"Aye, Captain. Mercer, hit it again."

A second time the blasting sound rang out from forward. On the display screen, another green circle grew outward from the center point, this time hitting the southern contact—*Panther*—showing it closer, then the torpedoes farther from them, but closer to the large contact to the southwest, which had moved quite a bit, the contact headed due west. But he was at the far range of detection unless Mercer adjusted the scale.

"Coordinator, we have a firing solution," Lomax called from pos one, "based on the two ping returns. He's moving west at thirty-five knots, present range, thirty-eight thousand five hundred yards, recommend horizontal salvo."

"Damned shame we're out of SubRoc nukes," Romanov said to Quinnivan. "They'd sure come in handy right about now." The XO nodded, then looked at the captain.

"Sir, recommend firing point procedures," Quinnivan prompted.

"Firing point procedures," Seagraves called to the watchstanders in the room, "tubes one through four, Master One, horizontal salvo, ten second firing interval, high-to-medium active snake, run-to-enable twenty thousand yards! Tube one!"

"Set," Lomax reported from the attack center's pos one.

"*Stand* by," Spichovich said from the weapon control console.

"Shoot!" Seagraves ordered.

"*Fire!*" Spichovich called, hitting the trigger fixed function key. "Own ship's unit fired electrically!" The deck jumped violently and Romanov's ears were slammed by the water-round-torpedo tank's high pressure air venting into the ship.

Romanov looked at Mercer, who listened and then called, "Own ship's unit, normal launch!"

The litany of reports continued three more times, and three more times Romanov's ears slammed.

"Go active again," Seagraves ordered Romanov. "If he zigs, we'll need to steer the weapons."

But before Romanov could make the order to Mercer, he yelled from his console, "torpedo in the water, bearing to Master One, now multiple torpedoes!"

South Atlantic Ocean
105 miles west of Cape Town, South Africa
B-902 *Panther*
Sunday, July 3; 1229 UTC, 1629 local time

The ventilation ducts had stopped blowing air. Either Dankleff or Abakumov stopped ventilation to stop feeding the fire and to keep it from spreading.

Pacino slid down the ladder's smooth stainless steel rails, his boots thumping on the middle level deck as he exited the alcove for the ladderway and ran forward, pausing only to grab an emergency breathing mask, pulling it on over his head, this mask a fireproof covering that protected his entire head, with a large opening for vision, the hose feeding the mask at the front leading down to a regulator meant to be strapped to a person's belt. Pacino adjusted the mask on his face, immediately choking from lack of air. He plugged the high-pressure hose fitting at the end into a recessed manifold in the overhead and took a breath. The regulator was working, the hose feeding canned, dry air into the mask, but it was life-giving air nonetheless. He clipped the regulator to his belt, took a deep breath, unplugged from the air manifold and ran down the passageway to the hatch to the first compartment, which Varney or Ahmadi had shut to contain the smoke.

Pacino rotated the hatch latch to the open position and forced the hatch open. He stepped inside, the temperature inside at least ten degrees hotter than the second compartment, which was a bad sign. He reached up to find the air manifold by feel, and realized that his wandering the ship and memorizing the air manifold locations had been a good investment. He could barely see in the dense smoke as he unplugged from the aft manifold and walked forward, the dense smoke forcing him to feel his way past the rack-stowed weapons to the forward portside console. The console was lit by a dull red glow from the lower port torpedo tube, tube six. Which had a tube-loaded Shkval supercavitating torpedo. The same volatile weapon that had exploded in a torpedo tube of the Russian submarine *Kursk*, causing every weapon aboard to detonate, taking the sub to the bottom and leading to the deaths of all hands. Pacino plugged in his hose at the manifold above the torpedo control console.

"We need to jettison that Shkval!" Pacino shouted to Varney and Ahmadi, his voice muffled by the air mask.

"Tube six's outer door is jammed," Varney shouted back, his voice strained and difficult to understand from behind his gas mask. "Probably from whatever we hit when we surfaced."

"Did you flood the tube?"

"Internal tube pressure is too high, Patch! We had to vent the tube to the compartment atmosphere to lower pressure, but the torpedo must be on fire inside and it's boiling what water is in the tube with a higher pressure than the seawater side."

"Let's get a firehose and hook it up to the outlet of the tube drain valve and flush the tube that way. That could cool it down."

"Patch," Varney said, exasperated, "there's no way to flange a firehose into the drain piping!"

"You got duct tape?" Pacino asked. Varney nodded. "Then you got a way. Meanwhile, I'm going to central—I'll get the boat down to test depth. The pressure will help flood the tube. Just watch the depth gauge and be ready to shut the drain valve, vent valve and turn off the hose when we get to thirty meters. If we get lucky, the outer door might be able to be opened when we're deep."

Pacino ran aft to the compartment hatch, and opened it and ducked into the second compartment. Chiefs Goreliki, Albanese and Kim were standing by, all in gas masks, their eyes wide and questioning. "Chiefs," Pacino ordered, "get in there and get a firehose nozzle duct taped to the tube six drain piping, use an entire goddamned roll of duct tape, I don't care, and get that hose pressurized and flood that tube! Lieutenant Varney is in charge at the scene."

The chiefs ducked through the circular hatchway while Pacino ran aft to the ladderway, up the stairs to the upper level, past The Million Valve Manifold into central control. He was puffing hard from the exertion as he plugged his hose into a manifold over pos two.

"OIC, submerge the boat to test depth. We need the pressure to help us flood tube six."

"Grip, all ahead full, turns for twelve," Dankleff barked at Aquatong at the ship control station, "right full rudder, steady course three-three-zero, and ten-degree dive on the bowplanes. Patch, open the ballast tank vents."

Pacino ran to The Million Valve Manifold and operated the valves controlling the ballast tank vents, getting the forward vents open. Pacino could hear the blasting noise of the venting, louder than the dull roar of what had to be the burning of the supertanker. He operated the valves to open the aft vents.

The deck had started to tilt downward, more every second. The deck was inclined downward twenty degrees and getting steeper. He could hear the hull above him and around him groan as the pressure of the deep sea squeezed it. In the central command post, Dankleff stood overlooking Grip Aquatong at the ship control station while holding a phone up to his fireproof hood. He saw Pacino and hung up the phone.

"They're flooding tube six, or trying to, and that bitch of a Shkval is boiling every ounce of water they're putting in there. It's filling the compartment with steam and the pressure is rising. I doubt you could open the hatch to get in there now."

"We can vent it to the second compartment if we have to. Is there still smoke?"

Dankleff picked up the phone again and dialed the torpedo room. "Varney, do you still have smoke?" Dankleff nodded. "Okay, good." He looked at Pacino. "No more smoke and the tube's not red-hot anymore. I think we're safe to ditch the breathing air. Better save it for some future casualty."

"God forbid," Pacino said, removing his hood. The air in central control was hot and stuffy and smelled of smoke.

"Three hundred meters," Aquatong said, pulling up on the control yoke and flattening the ship's angle.

Dankleff picked up the shipwide announcing microphone. "All hands, discontinue use of emergency air breathing apparatus with the exception of the torpedo room."

Pacino grabbed the phone and dialed up the torpedo room.

"Torpedo room, Varney." His voice was still distorted by the air mask.

"We're deep, try to open tube six and report," Pacino said. He waited and found Dankleff looking at him, holding up his hands with his fingers crossed. Pacino nodded and listened to the background noise of the torpedo room, suddenly hearing a cheer in the room.

"Tube six door is open!" Varney yelled. "Trying to eject the Shkval now."

"Tube door's open," Pacino said to Dankleff. Dankleff shot him back a thumbs-up.

The deck jumped as the tube was fired from forward.

"Tube six fired," Varney said over the phone. As Pacino opened his mouth to congratulate Varney, an explosion sounded from forward and tossed him to the deck. On the way down, Pacino hit his face on the pos two console's horizontal section and the room went black.

South Atlantic Ocean
112 miles west-southwest of Cape Town, South Africa
K-561 *Kazan*
Sunday, July 3; 1236 UTC, 1436 Moscow time

Captain First Rank Georgy Alexeyev's eye had gotten so bad that pus was starting to leak out from behind the eye patch. First, it caught the attention of First Officer Lebedev, then Navigator Maksimov, both who turned from their consoles to fuss about him, but he'd waved them off, absorbing the stream of foul-smelling liquid with a wadded-up amount of tissue paper from a roll that hung on a special holder in between his console and the center console. But Lebedev had evidently called the medic, because Chief Ship Petty Officer Chaykovsky hurried up to Alexeyev's station and bent to talk to him.

"Let me see, Captain," he said quietly, holding up a flashlight. Alexeyev nodded and the doc pulled up the eye patch and shone his light into Alexeyev's eye. Alexeyev didn't see the light. "Captain, it's totally infected. You could lose your eye. You need an immediate medical evacuation."

"Doc, are you even aware of what's going on here?" Alexeyev pulled out the soaked gauze under his patch and tossed it into a small garbage kit at his knee under the console, and wadded up more of the tissue paper to stuff under the eye patch. "In case you haven't noticed, I have ten torpedoes inbound, any one of which ends our day in a very nasty fashion."

The medic stood erect. "Yes, Captain. Sorry, Captain." Chaykovsky sniffed the air. "Captain, with you turning off all atmospheric control equipment, we only have hours before the carbon dioxide levels got completely toxic, and not to mention our oxygen levels are down. Do you feel the drowsiness? Drowsiness, in the middle of a fight?"

"Look at the bright side, Doc. If the oxygen level is low, it won't sustain a fire. And the drowsiness is actually helping us. Otherwise the crew's level of adrenaline would be causing near-panic right now. Even in me."

"If you say so, sir. Good luck to you."

"May God look kindly on us all today, Doc," Alexeyev said as the medic left. He looked at his console, which showed the output of the high frequency under ice and mine detection sonar, which was showing—or trying to show—what was happening with the incoming torpedoes, but the unit was good at short range, not far distant, and if a torpedo got close, it would be all over anyway.

So far the day had not gone his way. He'd fired two torpedoes in slow transit stealth mode, one targeted at the American escort Virginia-class submarine, the second at the *Panther.* Neither submarine should have detected them until their hulls were opened. But the damned Virginia had almost immediately fired countermeasure torpedoes that destroyed the one headed for her, and at first it had seemed the second unit had homed in on the *Panther,* and the huge double explosion from the north had the crew in the central command post cheering until he'd quieted them with a brutal reprimand and a murderous stare from his good eye. But, inexplicably, not long after the explosions, they detected steam flow, steam turbine startups and then the incoming UGST Russian torpedoes, these much quieter than the torpedoes the Americans had employed, and these worried

Alexeyev. In the minutes after their launch, two loud active sonar pulses were emitted by the American submarine, and soon after that it launched four weapons, presumably Mark 48 ADCAP versions. That made ten torpedoes coming for *Kazan*.

In response, Alexeyev had ordered twelve Futlyar Fizik-2 torpedoes launched in countermeasure mode to go up against the incoming ten, but now he shook his head. All these torpedoes targeting each other just wasted weapons, and soon the torpedo room would run out. And then what the hell would he do, run like a woman chased by pillagers? His torpedo room loadout had been 24 Futlyar Fizik-2 torpedoes, of which twelve were gone. He could get out another twelve in two minutes, he thought, saving two weapons for the trip home in case someone unfriendly awaited them during their transit.

The good news was that explosions were happening in the sea between *Kazan* and the two target submarines. Their offensive weapons were falling to Alexeyev's defensive ones. But no warrior, he thought, ever won a battle with a shield. It took a sword. However, up to now, it had been as his mentors had taught him—"Georgy, you must fight the alligator that is closest to your boat." Now that that alligator was soon to be gone, it was time to launch an offensive.

Alexeyev deeply regretted he didn't have the weapon loadout of *Novosibirsk* or *Voronezh*, since both had been loaded with two Kalibr nuclear-tipped antisubmarine cruise missiles, and the only units *Kazan* had taken to sea were conventional missiles, for use against hostile surface ships. There had been no time on this emergency sortie to sea to load better antisubmarine weapons. His only antisubmarine weapons were the Futlyar torpedoes, but heaven help them, they had to be enough.

Heaven indeed. Alexeyev had never been a religious man, but what was the saying, there are no atheists in foxholes? He hadn't prayed once in his adult life, but had watched as Natalia had sank to her knees and prayed devotedly to God every night before they went to bed, which he'd always thought was bizarre, because when her prayers were over, she did things that no churchgoer would want to know about. Still, when he'd watched her, he'd wondered if he were missing something.

Maybe, he thought, this would be a good time to pray.

"Captain? Captain!"

Alexeyev realized he'd shut his eyes in concentration and First Officer Lebedev thought he'd fallen asleep. As if he'd sleep during a damned battle, he thought in irritation.

"What?"

"We should launch, sir, Futlyar torpedoes in offensive mode, recommend six at high-speed-of-approach, full active and wake homing enabled."

"Madam First, we will fire *twelve*. Maximum firing rate. Start now." For a moment he'd actually forgotten that what he'd decided in his mind hadn't been communicated to Lebedev. Maybe Natalia's complaints about him living inside his own head had some merit. But a thought for another day. Today, there were two enemy submarines to kill.

He smiled to himself. Kill them he would, and then, finally, it would be time to go home. Ten days. Just ten days from home. *Home.*

But then it occurred to him that nothing waited for him at home but a lonely, empty apartment. And a lonely, empty life. Damn that Natalia, *damn her to Hell.*

South Atlantic Ocean
115 miles west-northwest of Cape Town, South Africa
USS *Vermont*
Sunday, July 3; 1248 UTC, 1648 local time

Mercer sounded worried. "Torpedoes in the water from Master One. I'm getting them every ten seconds. Recommend another active pulse."

There was an audible *bang* from the south.

"What the hell was *that*?" Romanov asked.

Mercer shook his head. "Smaller detonation than a torpedo, but it's from the bearing to the *Panther*."

Seagraves frowned at Romanov. "That's not good," he said. "Put out another ping, Nav."

"Mercer, ping active," Romanov ordered.

After the roaring, screeching noise of the active sonar pulse, the circular display's expanding green circle hit the *Panther* south of them, then Master One and what had to be a dozen or more torpedoes in between *Panther* and Master One, with at least six or eight blips that seemed less solid, somewhat blurry, and larger than the torpedo return blips but smaller than *Panther.*

"What're those?" Romanov asked Mercer, pointing.

"Probably torpedo explosions, Nav. Bubbles, foam, turbulence from a countermeasure mode torpedo's warhead going off."

Romanov stood back a few feet to see the display and think. She looked at Seagraves and Quinnivan. "We need to see if those torpedo launches are defensive or an attack on us and *Panther.*"

"Ping again," Seagraves ordered.

"Mercer, ping active," Romanov ordered the sonarman.

Another blasting sonar ping was broadcast out into the sea. In the confusion of all the torpedoes in between the combatants, one group of torpedoes had advanced much faster than the previous weapons. They were headed northward. Toward *Vermont.* And *Panther.*

"Whoa," Romanov said. She looked at Seagraves. "Recommend we run north at flank while loading more Mark 48s in CMT mode."

"Clear datum north at flank," Seagraves ordered.

"Pilot, right full rudder, steady course north, all ahead flank!" Romanov ordered. The deck began to shake as the ship's velocity rose to maximum speed.

"In the firecontrol party," Seagraves said, "intentions are to launch eight Mark 48s in CMT mode, aim point five thousand yards south of us, passive circlers. Firing point procedures, tubes one through four."

"What's going on with *Panther*?" Romanov asked, looking at the active display on the command console.

"Ping again," Seagraves said as the attack center and the weapons control console set up to launch the four Mark 48s in countermeasure mode.

The BQQ-10 sonar set barked out another loud pulse.

Quinnivan stared hard at the display. "*Panther* looks dead in the water."

Romanov bit her lower lip. "Is it possible he's hovering, trying to prevent presenting an up or down Doppler effect on a torpedo sonar pulse?"

"Playing possum? We've always wondered if that would work," Quinnivan said.

"It would work on a Mark 48," Romanov said. "Plus, if they're dead in the water, there's no wake for the torpedo's wake homing sensor to zero in on."

"Still a big iron hull, though," Seagraves said. "It still disturbs the magnetic field. If the torpedo is good, it could still home in on a hovering submarine."

"What if *Panther*'s not playing possum?" Romanov asked, frowning. "What if it got knocked out by that last smaller explosion? We don't know what that explosion was. There were no torpedoes near her. Maybe something went wrong."

Anthony Pacino could feel his face on the cold wood floor, blood flowing from a deep gash on his cheek, his face throbbing in pain.

He opened one eye, the pooled blood partially congealed, sticking his face to the floor of his bedroom.

He was six years old.

He was wearing his favorite pajamas with the pattern of dolphins swimming together.

Downstairs, his mother was screaming at his father.

It was December.

Almost Christmas.

And his mother was furious at his father for leaving on his submarine *Devilfish* to go on a secret mission. It was hard to tell what made her more mad, that Daddy was leaving, or that he couldn't tell her why it was so urgent to go now, just before the holiday that they'd all been planning for months.

His bedroom door opened and his father came in, dropping a large duffel bag on the floor. Anthony Pacino pulled his face out of the blood, the skin of his face trying to stick to the messy puddle. His father didn't seem to notice. He stooped down and stroked Anthony's hair, ignoring the remnants of the blood.

"I have to go, little man," the older Pacino said gently. He was wearing his service dress blue uniform. There was a gold dolphin emblem and ribbons over his left pocket, a gleaming gold capital ship command pin below his ribbons. He wore his officer's cap, with the gold laurel leaves on the brim. On his father's sleeves were three gold stripes. "We have a very important mission, Anthony. I hate to leave you, but I have to go."

"Where are you going, Daddy? Are you going to the North Pole again?"

A look crossed his father's face, and Anthony could tell his father was trying to decide whether to speak the truth or not. Finally he nodded.

"Are you going there to help Santa? Is he in trouble?"

Again the older Pacino debated telling the truth, and again he nodded slowly. "It's a very bad situation, Anthony," he said gravely.

Anthony Pacino nodded at his father. "I understand, Daddy. Be careful."

His father hugged him and kissed his forehead despite the blood, stood up, grabbed the duffel bag and turned at the door to look down at him. There were tears in his father's eyes. It was the first time the younger Pacino had ever seen his father cry. The heavy footfalls receded as his father went down the hall and down the stairs to the middle level, then continued to the lower level. Anthony could hear a car door slam, then the sound of a powerful engine starting. The wheels shrieked at his father roared off down the beachfront road in Sandbridge, Virginia.

Anthony pulled himself upright and tried to walk to his bedroom door. He stood, wobbling a bit as he stepped to the door and opened it. A dim light came into his room. He stepped through the door into the softly lit restaurant and bar of the Grafton Street Pub and Grill on Massachusetts Avenue across from Harvard's campus. The sepia-colored hanging lamps lent the establishment a beautiful glow, the dark pub quiet in the Sunday summer evening, most of the Harvard and MIT undergrads and graduate students gone for the summer, the ones remaining hungover and back in their dorms, apartments or libraries preparing for a summer session Monday, leaving only the usual patrons, like Pacino himself and Carolyn Alameda.

He felt a soft, warm female hand in his. He looked up at Carrie Alameda, the love of his life, who was sweeping her glorious dark hair off her shoulder and smiling down at him. He looked down and saw he was still wearing his dolphin pajamas. His feet were still bare. And his face was still bloody. A server smiled at Carrie and led them to their favorite booth beneath an hourglass-shaped lamp, where the light was mostly soft except directly under the lamp, the small circle of brightness allowing menu reading.

Pacino looked across the table at Alameda. Their waitress, gorgeous Lieutenant Commander Rachel Romanov, resplendent in starched service dress whites, with full medals and a ceremonial sword, brought over a round of drinks without asking. A Merlot for Carolyn, an eighteen-year-old Macallan scotch for Pacino. Rachel Romanov walked away, back toward the bar. Pacino looked over at Carrie, hoping the blood on his face wouldn't disgust her, or his dolphin pajamas give her pause, but she just smiled at him.

"Are you having your usual?" he asked. "That blackened chicken wreck?"

"I love that blackened chicken. It reminds me of being here with you. And that, in turn, makes me feel very romantic, Anthony."

For a moment, he wasn't sure what she meant. He looked at the menu. "I think I'll have the usual."

"Grafton burger again?" she asked, smiling at him and holding his hand.

Lieutenant Commander Rachel Romanov came back to the table to take their orders. Carolyn asked her what tonight's specials were.

Rachel Romanov smiled. "We have a succulent Shkval torpedo that has been carefully sautéed in onions and tube-loaded in tube five. It's *completely* functional. If you get the tube door open, it will take care of things quite nicely."

Alameda looked at Romanov. "What if the tube door is jammed?"

"Oh, it's no problem at all," Romanov said, smiling at Carolyn Alameda. "Anthony here just has to take his boat shallow, then back to test depth, then shallow again—lather, rinse, repeat—and that tube door will open right up."

"Anthony," Carolyn said, her expression serious. "I think you should order the Shkval. Shoot it at the position of the firing submarine. Hit it with active sonar first, get its position, and launch that Shkval at it. It will end the battle."

"*End* the battle?" he said, raising a blood-encrusted eyebrow at her. "You said 'end the battle,' not 'win the battle.' What does that mean?"

She looked at him with fondness. "There's no *winning* this battle, Anthony. You're up against—what did the Russians call it?"

Romanov interjected to help Carolyn Alameda. "They called it the supreme attack submarine on the planet."

"Exactly," Carrie said. "The best you can hope for is making the battle stop."

He nodded at her, and looked at Rachel Romanov. "I think I'll take the Shkval torpedo," he said, taking a sip of his scotch, hoping no one in the bar would object to a six-year-old in dolphin pajamas—with a face covered in blood—drinking eighteen-year-old scotch.

Surprising him, Rachel Romanov sank down to her knees and looked at Carolyn Alameda. The two women locked eyes. Carolyn spoke first.

"Rachel, will you take good care of him?" she asked, glancing toward Pacino.

Romanov nodded solemnly and said to Carolyn, "I'll take great care of him. He'll want for nothing."

Carrie Alameda wiped a tear from her eye, and looked over at Romanov and held out her hand.

"Thank you, Rachel. God bless you."

And Rachel Romanov replied, "May God look kindly on us all today." With that, she rose from her knees and disappeared toward the kitchen.

"Anthony?" Alameda asked, but Pacino was still stunned from watching the exchange between the two beautiful women, one of them dead, the other seven thousand miles away.

"Yes, Carrie?"

"Why didn't your step-mother come to my funeral?"

Pacino stared at her. He'd never considered the question. He'd been too absorbed in Alameda's death to realize he'd been at Carrie's funeral with only his father and mother, not his stepmother Colleen, the woman who had been there on the *Explorer II* when he had been revived after his near death experience.

"I don't know," he said. "Maybe she and my father were having problems."

Carrie nodded. "So it goes," she said. "If I hadn't died, eventually we'd have gotten married, and we'd have fought over money, and years later, there would have been a bitter divorce. I would have hated you. You would have hated me."

He nodded, sensing she told the truth. "But we'll always have the Grafton," he said, as if he were Humphrey Bogart saying, *we'll always have Paris.*

She smiled sweetly and held both his hands in hers. "Yes, Anthony. We'll always have the Grafton."

He downed the rest of the scotch, then looked at her. "The Shkval in tube five?" he asked.

Carolyn Alameda nodded seriously. "The Shkval in tube five. But go active first. Nail his position down, solid. Do it for me, Anthony."

He nodded at her. "I will, Carrie. And Carrie?"

"Yes, Anthony?"

"I miss you. I miss you so much. You left my life so suddenly."

"I had to go, Anthony. Just like you do now."

She waved her hand at him and the Grafton Street Pub and Grill evaporated and the central command post of the Russian-built Iranian submarine *Panther* appeared to take its place.

36

South Atlantic Ocean
B-902 *Panther*
Sunday, July 3; 1248 UTC, 1648 local time

AOIC Anthony Pacino pulled his face off the deck, the bloody puddle sticking to his cheek. He felt his face, his hand coming back bloody. He wiped his hand on his coveralls and looked up at OIC Dieter Dankleff.

"What the hell happened?"

"Oh, Lipstick, nice of you to show up to the party," Dankleff said sarcastically. "While you were out, the Shkval we jettisoned exploded and the shock caused another reactor scram. We did a fast recovery startup, and for your information, there's a Russian torpedo out there chasing us. While it's true, our good friends on the *Vermont* launched Mark 48s in countermeasure mode against the Russian fish, there's no guarantee they'll work. So, you know, the odds say it's a long shot for us to last long enough to see another sunrise."

"Tube five," Pacino said, rubbing his head.

"What about it? All our tube doors are stuck shut after we ejected tube six's Shkval after the motherfucker decided to explode about a foot away from the bow."

"What's our depth?"

"A hundred meters," Aquatong said from the ship control station.

"U-Boat, take her to four hundred meters, then back to twenty, then back down to four hundred, back to twenty. Cycle it five times, maybe six. It'll unstick the torpedo tube door to tube five."

"What makes you so sure? And why tube five?"

"The Dominatrix Navigatrix at the Grafton Pub told me," Pacino said, holding up his palm. "Don't ask. Just do it." He left control and hurried to the sonar room, where Albanese stared glumly at his display. The deck inclined steeply downward and the hull steel groaned as it adjusted to the pressure of the deep.

"We need to ping active," Pacino said. "Wait for my word from central command."

The deck inclined steeply upward as central command pulled the boat back shallow, and an eerie stomach-sinking feeling came to Pacino as the deck once again tilted downward, the submarine plunging back deep.

"These angles and dangles—we're trying to unstick the torpedo tube doors."

Pacino hurried to the ladderway and slid down to the middle level, then forward in the steeply inclined passageway to the hatch to the torpedo room. The deck was level again as Pacino opened the hatch, then inclined steeply upward, the angle helping the heavy steel of the hatch clang into the latch. Pacino stepped through the hatchway into the compartment, half jogging up the steep slope of the central catwalk to the port console, where Lieutenant Varney stood, frowning at the array of lights and controls, Captain Ahmadi beside him.

"Tube five," Pacino breathed, winded from the run from central command.

"What about it?"

"I want it ready in all respects. Power up the Shkval, pressurize the tube and prepare to open the outer door."

"Didn't anyone tell you," Varney said. "All our tube doors are stuck."

The deck tilted steeply downward again, the hull screaming and shrieking above them, five fast pops coming from forward to aft.

"Trust me," Pacino said. "Flood and pressurize five."

Varney opened the flood valve to tube five with the vent open. When the tube vent could be heard spilling seawater, he shut the vent valve. The deck flattened out at what must be test depth.

Pacino reached for a phone. "Central command, torpedo room. Steady on depth twenty meters."

The deck tilted upward and Pacino fell into the port tube rack, having to steady himself with a rack-mounted hand-hold. After a few minutes, the deck leveled off again.

"Try tube five's outer door now," he ordered Varney. Varney punched a fixed function key. A green bar-shaped light went out and a red light shaped like a doughnut lit up.

"Goddamn, Lipstick, you're a genius," Varney said. "Tube door's open!"

"Power it up, Boozy," Pacino said. "We're going to send it as a nice present to that Yasen-M that's shooting at us."

"You got it, AOIC. Good luck to us."

Pacino turned and looked at Varney. The next words out of his mouth surprised him. "May God look kindly on us all today." He spun and ran out the hatch to the second compartment passageway.

South Atlantic Ocean
USS *Vermont*
Sunday, July 3; 1249 UTC, 1649 local time

Lieutenant Commander Al Spichovich spoke up from the weapons control console. "Captain, Coordinator, OOD, that's it." He took off his headset and stood up from his console. "That's the last torpedo. If Master One shoots again, we're helpless."

Lieutenant Commander Rachel Romanov looked at him and nodded, then turned back to her command console display. If the last active sonar pulse's display were to be believed, all of the offensive torpedoes launched at *Vermont* and *Panther* had been neutralized by *Vermont*'s Mark 48s. She looked up at Seagraves and Quinnivan. "Master One's quiet," she said. "Maybe he's out of weapons as well."

Petty Officer Mercer turned from his BQQ-10 stack. "OOD, I've got strange transients from *Panther*."

"Describe them, Sonar," Romanov said to him, leaning over his seatback.

"For one thing, he's on reactor power and running north at flank, but his hull is popping like crazy. Bang, bang, bang, Nav."

Romanov looked at Quinnivan and shrugged. "I've got nothing," she said.

It was then they all heard the sound, audible with the naked ear.

South Atlantic Ocean
B-902 *Panther*
Sunday, July 3; 1249 UTC, 1649 local time

AOIC Anthony Pacino arrived in the central command post, Captain Ahmadi immediately behind him.

"Do you know how to program this thing?" Pacino asked. Ahmadi nodded. "U-Boat, order all stop, turn to the southwest and hover at this depth."

Dankleff made the orders to Grip Aquatong at the ship control station, and the vibrations of the deck stopped, the ride becoming quiet again. Pacino stepped aft past The Million Valve Manifold to the sonar room.

"You ready, Whale?"

Chief Petty Officer Tom Albanese looked up at Pacino. "Goddamn, L-T, I sure could use a cigarette right now."

"And I could use a couple of shots of Pappy Van Winkle," Pacino said. "But regardless, are you set to go active?"

Albanese nodded, his face hardening. "Let's do it, L-T."

"Whale, ping active," Pacino ordered.

South Atlantic Ocean
K-561 *Kazan*
Sunday, July 3; 1249 UTC, 2:49 pm Moscow time

Captain First Rank Georgy Alexeyev's weapons status console told the bad news. They were down to their last two torpedoes, the reserve he'd promised the crew for the return trip to the Zapadnaya Litsa Naval Base. But after all the launches in defensive mode to keep *Kazan* alive, the battle had taken his entire weapon load. It was ridiculous. A single nuclear depth charge in a Kalibr cruise missile would have ended all this an hour ago. He could see now why the Americans had fired their nuclear cruise missiles at the *Novosibirsk* and *Voronezh*—there was no evading a cruise missile. One either found himself inside the blast damage radius or outside it, there was no middle ground.

He took a moment to wonder whether the Americans were similarly out of torpedoes. They'd been quiet for a few minutes. He looked up from his console to see First Officer Ania Lebedev leaning over to look at him.

"We have to make a choice, Captain," she said. "Either fire the last two torpedoes or clear the area and break contact."

"If we break contact, we're admitting we lost," Alexeyev said.

"Yes, Captain," Lebedev said quietly.

"You know, Madam First, those Futlyar torpedoes are useless. I'd just as soon not carry them home and have to explain why we didn't use them."

Lebedev nodded, looking at him with sympathy. It must be his wrecked eye, he thought. She'd seen how bad it was the last time he'd replaced the wadding under the patch. Or, he thought, maybe she sensed something, something darker. He'd heard of people having premonitions about their own deaths. Could she be feeling something, their dark fate lumbering toward them, inescapable?

"Sonar Officer," Alexeyev called to Senior Lieutenant Ilia Kovalev. "Do you still have contact with *Panther* and the Virginia-class?"

"Yes, Captain, but they are getting more distant. We should turn toward and head northward. And Captain, I have transients from *Panther* for the last few minutes. His hull is groaning and creaking, then popping. I think he's changing depth, maximum to mast-broach depth, then back again."

"Why the hell would he do that?" Lebedev said to Alexeyev.

"He's trying to unstick a torpedo tube door. That explosion at his bearing, it must have been his own weapon he was trying to jettison. Probably jammed up his doors."

"There's no coming back from that, Captain," Lebedev said. "He's as good as dead."

"Agreed. Boatswain, right ten degrees rudder, steady course north. Weapons Officer, tube load the last two torpedoes and make them ready for launch."

Alexeyev re-buckled his seat belt at the console, his insistence during action stations that everyone be strapped in, but he'd unbuckled it when they had gotten down to two torpedoes, and he had been about to stretch his legs and walk to the navigation chart table when the sonar ping came from the north, the ping long and sustained. "Who pinged that?" he asked the sonar officer.

Kovalev answered from the sonar-and-sensor console. "Captain, it was the *Panther*."

"Why would he ping active if his torpedo tube doors are stuck?" Alexeyev asked Lebedev. Her eyes grew wide with alarm. "Because they aren't stuck anymore. Captain, turn south and put on maximum turns!"

"Boatswain, right full rudder, all ahead full, to nuclear control, fast speed pumps and one hundred percent reactor power!"

The deck tilted dramatically as the *Kazan* executed a snap-roll in her turn to the south.

South Atlantic Ocean
B-902 ***Panther***
Sunday, July 3; 1250:37 UTC, 1650:37 local time

AOIC Anthony Pacino mashed the trigger fixed function key on the vertical section of pos two and tube five fired, the deck vibrating and jumping just slightly, the weapon launch much smoother than from a U.S. submarine.

Almost immediately the torpedo's propellant ignited, the sound of it deafening, and the underwater rocket sailed off into sea toward its designated target, the Russian Yasen-M.

"Dear Yasen-M," Pacino said. "This evening's special is a Shkval torpedo, sautéed in onions. Eat it all, you Russian bastard."

South Atlantic Ocean
USS *Vermont*
Sunday, July 3; 1250:39 UTC, 1650:39 local time

Petty Officer First Class Jay Mercer was the first to hear it. "Captain, Coordinator, OOD, I have a rocket launch from the bearing to the *Panther*."

"The hell do you mean, a *rocket launch*?" Lieutenant Commander Rachel Romanov asked.

"It's definitely a supercavitating torpedo, Nav. Look at the broadband trace."

The broadband waterfall display grew a sound that was so loud and so fast that it was ten degrees wide.

"Jesus, Captain, that's a Shkval torpedo and we're between it and Master One. Pilot, all ahead flank, left ten degrees rudder, steady course west!"

South Atlantic Ocean
Sunday, July 3; 1251:10 UTC, 1651:10 local time

The Shkval from tube five had ignited its self-oxidizing fuel less than two minutes before and was now flying through the sea on a one-way trip to the target.

The torpedo looked like an old-fashioned air-to-air missile, extremely pointy at the nose, more of a rocket than a torpedo. At its aft end, it had a bell-opening gimbal-mounted nozzle, the flanks of the torpedo featuring thrusters every forty-five degrees around the circumference. As the torpedo had accelerated, the pointed nose caused the water to boil to steam and the steam bubble grew to encompass the entire weapon, the steam vapor coating eliminating the skin friction of the water and allowing the unit to speed up beyond 300 knots as it flew toward the target.

Time of flight was minimal. Most of the torpedo was just a fuel tank. The warhead was relatively small, and truth be told, it was redundant to the kinetic energy of the torpedo hitting a submarine hull.

At 1252:25.580 UTC time, the target grew in the seeker blue laser window from a speck to a form so big it blocked out all else.

At 1252:25.757 UTC, the torpedo hit the hull and the warhead exploded.

By 1252:25.905 UTC, the torpedo no longer existed but for a high temperature plasma from the warhead explosion.

At 1252:26.005 UTC, the jagged rip in the submarine's hull in the third compartment opened up, the energy from the detonation blasting into the compartment.

1252:26:127 UTC: The explosion's fireball was extinguished by the massive flooding into the compartment.

1252:26:232 UTC: Three control rods in the central control group of the reactor jumped as their control rod drive mechanisms shattered from the shock, the explosion and the violent water flow. The pressure inside the reactor blew the control rods out to the top of the core.

1252:26:345 UTC: The reactor power went past 3000% in the overpowering from the control rod ejections and the primary water loop could no longer accept the energy of the core, and the pressure inside the reactor vessel grew to five times the design pressure.

1252:26:398 UTC: The pressure build-up inside the reactor vessel ruptured all the hold-down bolts at once and the heavy pressure vessel lid blew off into the overhead and smashed into the insulation covering the hoop steel of the compartment, rupturing a steam line coming from a steam generator before the lid started to fall back on the reactor core.

1252:26:436 UTC: The power increase in the core blew the nuclear fuel all through the compartment, the pressure in the compartment rising past its design pressure, the pressure rise stopping the flooding but collapsing the shielded tunnel that allowed human access from compartment two to compartment four.

1252:26.598 UTC: The pressure fell as melted fuel pooled below in the compartment bilges, and with the lower pressure, the flooding began again. A small rupture in the forward water-tight bulkhead to the second compartment opened, and seawater began to flood the second compartment.

1252:26.866 UTC: All personnel throughout the ship had been thrown into their consoles or across the spaces they occupied. The deck had tilted so far to port that the deck would seem more like a wall.

1252:26.943 UTC: Water from the third compartment flowed swiftly into the second compartment, the water running along the deck of the lower level and splashing into the space below the deckplates, into the battery well.

1252:27.096 UTC: All personnel aft of frame 208 stopped breathing as the massive shock, steam leak from the secondary loop and the radiation level at ten thousand times the normal dose irradiated the fourth compartment. The high radiation level was somewhat attenuated by the shielding of the forward bulkhead of the third compartment, yet still invaded the second compartment and mercilessly irradiated the crew in the central command post.

1252:28.304 UTC: The deck rolled back to normal but the bow had begun to point downward and the ship took on a five degree down angle, the depth rapidly increasing from the speed they'd been going before the explosion.

South Atlantic Ocean
USS *Vermont*
Sunday, July 3; 1252:29 UTC, 1652:29 local time

The roaring of the supercavitating torpedo was deafening as it roared past, the noise going deeper in pitch as it sped past, and not long after a series of loud explosions came from the bearing of Master One.

Romanov looked at Quinnivan.

"Raise a glass to our lads on the *Panther*," Quinnivan said.

"Thank God for them," Romanov breathed. "Pilot, all stop, left ten degrees rudder, steady course two-one-zero, mark speed ten knots."

"What are you doing, Nav?" Seagraves asked.

"No sense running north now, Captain. We should go to the site of the sinking and see if anyone survived that. Or at least confirm the kill."

Seagraves nodded. "When you get close, take her up."

Romanov nodded. Maybe, like that submarine *Novosibirsk*, there would be an escape chamber.

South Atlantic Ocean
K-561 *Kazan*
Sunday, July 3; 1253 UTC, 2:53 pm Moscow time

Captain First Rank Georgy Alexeyev pushed himself off his console in the dark, his head pounding. He reached under his console for the battle lantern, clicked it on, and unbuckled his five-point harness. He shined the lantern in the room and shouted, "who is awake?" It was then he realized he was deaf. Whatever it was that had caused the noise, probably a Shkval from the *Panther*, had hit them, and the explosions had deafened him.

There were a few people moving. He realized shouting was futile. Everyone else would be as deaf as he was. A second battle lantern came on. He waved the beam of his battle lantern to the aft door, to the direction of the ladder to the escape chamber. He couldn't say exactly why his instincts were screaming at him to get the crew to the chamber, but he'd lived with this ship since its first hoop of steel was laid down in the drydock. He'd served as its weapons officer, first officer, and finally as captain. He knew her as well as a long-time husband knows his wife's body. And *Kazan* was dying. If she were not already dead. As were all of them if they didn't abandon ship.

He hated the sounds of those words: *abandon ship*. He shook his head and vaulted out of his seat, his head spinning so hard with dizziness that he had to grab a handhold, hard, to keep from falling. And it was either his own vertigo or the deck had done another list. He waved his light to the aft door again. Three people started toward him. Alexeyev opened the door and the massive smoke came into the room. The passageway was solid smoke. He decided against returning to his console for an air mask, but instead pushed the half dozen central command survivors aft down the passageway. He knew the exact number of steps to the ladder.

Gathered at the ladder bottom were several other crewmen who had had the same idea as Alexeyev, several of them with battle lanterns. As Alexeyev grabbed for the ladder, an explosion from directly beneath them rocked the ship, flipping the deck to a twenty-degree roll.

"What was that?" It was Svetka Maksimov's voice, the navigator. Alexeyev could hear, just barely, he realized.

Alexeyev sniffed the smoky air, the unmistakable smell of chlorine detectable. "Dammit, battery explosion! Everybody to the chamber!"

One of the crewmen under the hatch had opened the mechanism, the hydraulics self-contained and local. God help them all if the explosive bolts failed, Alexeyev thought.

In two more minutes, the air was completely contaminated. Alexeyev was the last man standing in the passageway, shining his light fore and aft, to see if there were any more survivors, and he could see Pavlovsky come out of the door of the central command post and fall to the deck, gasping and coughing. Alexeyev dropped the battle lantern and lunged for the young electrical officer and pushed him to the ladder to the escape chamber.

"Help him up!" Alexeyev yelled, the crew pulling Pavlovsky into the chamber. Alexeyev took one last look at the smoke-filled passageway of his command, the supreme attack submarine on the planet, and tapped his ring on the ladder rung as a farewell, just before climbing the ten steps up into the escape chamber. As soon as he got in, Maksimov shut the hatch and pulled the lever to disconnect the chamber from the sinking submarine.

One last prayer, Alexeyev thought, realizing he'd prayed more today than in his entire life. *Oh God, please let the explosive bolts fire and disconnect us from the ship.*

South Atlantic Ocean
B-902 *Panther*
Sunday, July 3; 1335 UTC, 1735 local time

Surfacing the *Panther* without air in the high-pressure banks had turned out to be more of a challenge than originally thought.

Dankleff had had to have Aquatong use the ship's speed and bowplanes and sternplanes to fly the ship to the surface, then raise the induction mast and start the air compressors to try to fill the air banks. It had taken a half hour to get enough air in the banks that they could blow main ballast, the air compressors still clanking away to refill the tanks after the blow. By the time *Panther* heaved to at the escape chamber, the USS *Vermont* was already there.

Pacino stood in the bridge cockpit on top of the conning tower and put a bullhorn to his lips.

"Ahoy, there, *Vermont*!"

Eisenhart was on the bridge of *Vermont* and shouted back. "About time you slackers got here. We're loading them on your boat. Same idea as last time."

"Did you radio for a chopper?"

"Yeah," Eisenhart said. "Could be an hour or two to get it out here. Meanwhile, take these guys below and watch them."

"We know the drill," Pacino said. "You sending guys over to help?"

"We know the drill as well," Eisenhart said. "We're bringing two dozen guys over to help you watch the Russians."

A half hour later, Pacino walked into the wardroom, looking mournfully over at the credenza. The coffee had finally run out and he felt drowsy already. The Russian crew sat shivering, their clothes wet from the swim over.

"I'm Lieutenant Anthony Pacino, United States Navy. Anyone here speak English?" Pacino asked.

"I do," an older man said. He was the oldest of the survivors. He wore a black eye patch and had streaks of gray in his hair. His voice was oddly flat and disconnected. He must be in shock, Pacino thought. "Captain First Rank Georgy Alexeyev. I was captain of the *Kazan*. The submarine you sank. With a torpedo invented by us."

Pacino sat down across from the Russian. "Sorry about that, Captain. It was nothing personal. Just business."

Alexeyev looked over at Pacino with his good eye. "You know, we were down to only two torpedoes. I thought very seriously about breaking off contact and going home. Perhaps if I had, I wouldn't be sitting here now."

"Anything could have happened today," Pacino said. "I almost couldn't get the torpedo tube door opened."

"If you hadn't, I would have shot you with one of my last torpedoes. I believe the Virginia submarine—what did you call it, *Vermont*?—was out of weapons, so no countermeasures would have stopped my two. One for you." Alexeyev pointed in the direction of the *Vermont*. "One for them. And then today would have ended very differently. I'd have been a hero. You'd be dead."

Pacino nodded. "I wonder sometimes," he said, "how much of this is destiny. Hell, Captain Alexeyev, I wonder if this, all of this, is truly real. One of my friends on this mission says that we're all just living in a simulation, one of hundreds imagined by ourselves from the afterlife. If he's correct, there's probably scenarios where you *did* sink me today and went home the hero."

"No offense, Lieutenant—what is it—Pacino? But I have to say, I wish I'd been living inside *that* scenario."

"Do you mind if I ask you something tactical, Captain? No obligation to answer."

"Go ahead Lieutenant."

"Well, sir, how did you know we'd hug the coast at the Cape of Good Hope rather than going wide by, say, the Antarctic coastline and enter the Atlantic that way?"

Captain First Rank Georgy Alexeyev looked at Pacino with his good eye. "You're out of food. Am I right?"

Pacino returned the Russian's look. "Do I look well-fed to you, Captain?"

Alexeyev laughed. "No. You look like you're starving. I figured your lack of rations would speak to you and you'd take the great circle route."

"If I could, Captain, I'd offer you and your crew food. But we're out of everything but peanut butter. The last of the crackers ran out this morning."

"It is no matter, Lieutenant."

The door of the wardroom rolled open. It was Dankleff.

"Chopper's here," he said. "Everybody to the forward hatch."

Alexeyev stopped at the wardroom door and looked at Pacino and Dankleff. "You fought a hard battle, gentlemen," he said. "You have my congratulations. And my respect. And despite what must be a severe punishment awaiting me for losing to you, I'm glad I didn't kill you."

Pacino smiled and shook the Russian's hand. "Safe travels, Captain."

Ten minutes later, Pacino stood next to Dankleff on the deck of the submarine *Panther,* watching the colossal helicopter accelerating and climbing toward its destination, Cape Town, the Russian survivors all aboard.

"Damn shame," Pacino said. "You ever wonder what it would be like to take those guys out drinking? See what stories they have to tell?"

"Hell, Lipstick, I doubt any of their stories could compare to ours on this run." Dankleff clapped Pacino twice on the shoulder. "Resupply helicopters will get here in twenty minutes. Tonight, Patch, it's steak and lobster."

"Sounds great, U-Boat. We damned well deserve it."

"I asked if they could sneak some scotch into the rations. And some good vodka for Abakumov."

"Damn, U-Boat, as always, you demonstrate a command ability equal to that of Seagraves."

"Equal, hell. Exceeding. Just don't tell Seagraves I said that. And after that resupply? We'll see if this tub can submerge one more time and take us to the Bahamas."

"Ah, the Bahamas," Pacino said. "I like the sound of that. Funny drinks with little umbrellas."

"And a funny female lieutenant commander and admiral's aide, waiting for you?"

"U-Boat, I doubt she even remembers me."

EPILOGUE

TWO WEEKS LATER

The limo turned left off of Admiralteyskiy Prospekt onto Admiralteyskiy Proyezd, a single lane road fronting the Admiralty Building, where a formally dressed soldier at the guard post checked him into the complex. The limo glided to a halt at the arched entrance to the yellow brick structure. Captain First Rank Georgy Alexeyev climbed out of the car and looked at the statues on either side of the entrance, each one featuring three women holding the globe on their shoulders. For a moment, he was reminded of his three female department heads and his female first officer, but he had to correct himself. Two department heads. Navigator Maksimov and Weapons Officer Sobol had survived, but his engineer, Captain Third Rank Alesya Matveev, had died in the reactor explosion, undoubtedly roasting from the steam leak in the fourth compartment or dying instantly from the flash of neutron and gamma radiation that was ten thousand times an individual's lifetime dose. At least, Alexeyev hoped she'd died instantly. Dying aboard a submarine could be anything but merciful, he thought, and it was important to him today that she hadn't suffered.

Under the archway there was another guard post for him to check in with biometrics, and an aide, a senior lieutenant, led him into the gargantuan labyrinth of the complex. It was deceptive from the outside, just three stories tall, but nearly a kilometer long. The aide took him inside one of the inner buildings across a courtyard from the arch and into an elevator.

The elevator descended to a floor deep under the building. Probably constructed during the First Cold War, Alexeyev thought, hardened against a direct nuclear hit.

The elevator door opened to a simple and functional corridor. After a walk that seemed endless and two changes in direction, the aide admitted Alexeyev to a large conference room. The first thing he noticed were the large charts on the wall. The Gulf of Oman. The Arabian Sea. The South Atlantic at the Cape of Good Hope. The charts were marked up with bold red arrows, circles, and blue arrows. At the conference table were his senior officers, Lebedev, Maksimov and Sobol. Across the table from them were unfamiliar officers, with nametags reading ORLOV, VLASENKO, DOBRYVNIK and TRUSOV. *Orlov,* Alexeyev thought, could that be Natalia's first husband? He looked at the man, dismayed that he seemed handsome, making Alexeyev wonder what Natalia had seen in Alexeyev.

Alexeyev moved to take a seat next to Lebedev, but as he touched his seatback, a parade of admirals came into the room, led by Chief Commander of the Navy Anatoly Stanislav, then the Chief of Staff and First Deputy Commander of the Navy Pavel Zhabin, then the Pacific Fleet Commander Aleksandr Andreyushkin and Northern Fleet Commander Gennady Zhigunov. An unfamiliar man in a suit came in after Zhigunov. The last in the procession, a large, solid female admiral, shut the door and waved them all to seats.

Just as Alexeyev's backside hit his seat, a side door opened and servers in formal dress brought in trays of exotic crackers and caviar with bottles of vodka and glasses. The servers arrayed plates and napkins and poured generous portions of vodka for everyone.

"So," Stanislav said. "Let us hear the story. Tell us everything. Start from the beginning. Captain Orlov, perhaps you will start?"

Alexeyev traded wary glances with Lebedev, then cautiously picked up the vodka glass and took a sip, certain that it must be poison.

Orlov told the story of the *Novosibirsk* taking the nuclear strike, how all their systems seemed to conspire against them, and a massive fire broke out from machinery two, then about their struggle to save the ship and the crew, then the story of the rescue by the *Panther,* and how the Americans had repatriated them without even interrogating them.

Stanislav nodded. "I don't know if any of you have heard, but the *Voronezh* crew died *before* the nuclear strike. The second captain AI system sent us a message detailing the event. Apparently a design flaw in auxiliary machinery room two took out both oxygen generators and the oxygen storage system, and the ventilation system pumped toxic smoke throughout the boat. That was not long before it took a nuclear depth charge close enough to scatter it to atoms. So, Captain Alexeyev, tell us your story."

Alexeyev did his best to tell the tale, at one point putting his hand to his bandaged eye. The hospitals had been unable to save it. In a few weeks, after the surgery to remove the infected eye healed, they would fit him for a glass eye. Until then, he'd have to have the dressings changed every few hours. When he finished, Stanislav nodded in approval.

"So, you all see how Captain Alexeyev and his crew learned from the incident on the *Voronezh* and before engaging the enemy, shut down atmospheric control to harden the ship. But the Shkval detonation in the third compartment caused a severe reactor casualty. So Engineer Voronin, you see that you have major design flaws in your Yasen-M, yes?"

"Admiral, yes," the slight civilian engineer in the business suit said to Stanislav. "We will redesign the entire atmospheric control layout and systems. And the ventilation systems. And the reactor core must be hardened from shock. The rod drop that Captain Orlov suffered on the way to the Gulf of Oman was also a flaw on the *Kazan,* making it more volatile from the shock of a torpedo hit. We've already started on a new design that rectifies these flaws while keeping the supreme acoustic advantage of the Yasen-M. We will call it the Yasen III."

"For the sake of good luck, Anatoly," Stanislav said to Director Voronin, "name it something new, yes?" He looked at Orlov, then at Alexeyev. "Gentlemen, you and your crews represented the Russian Republic with courage and a fighting spirit. And believe me when I say, no Russian attack submarine will ever again sail without nuclear-tipped Kalibr antisubmarine cruise missiles. That mistake is all mine and it shall not recur. Now, please, everyone, drink up while we await the main course. Aleksandr," Stanislav said to the Pacific fleet commander, "perhaps you would care to give the evening's first toast."

Alexeyev turned to Ania Lebedev. "I guess we're not in trouble after all."

She looked at him with a raised eyebrow. "Do you get the funny feeling this whole battle was some kind of test? A drill?"

He nodded. "I'm not sure why I feel that way, but the bosses are going awfully easy on us for losing a submarine. And a battle."

A few minutes after the meeting at the Admiralty ended, the limo took Alexeyev to the airport, where he wearily climbed into the first-class seat on the flight to Murmansk, sleeping most of the way, getting up only once to go to the bathroom to change the dressing over his eye. The jet landed and taxied to the concourse. Feeling like he weighed eight hundred kilograms, Alexeyev walked down the jetway into the concourse.

Lebedev caught up to him. "Where do we report for duty, sir?"

"Pass the word to the crew, Ania. We all have three weeks of stand-down while the bosses try to figure out what to do with us. Take some time off. See your family. Relax."

"I'll put out the word, Captain, but call me if we have orders." She touched his shoulder, then turned to walk to the baggage claim room. Alexeyev stared after her. She'd changed, he thought. Or maybe he had. The other officers and crew filed past him, all of them hollow-eyed and exhausted, all on their way to get their bags, mostly full of the uniforms the Admiralty had given them to replace all their belongings lost on the *Kazan*.

Alexeyev walked through the door where the inner security ended and people gathered to meet family or friends after arrival. As he walked, he stared dejectedly at the floor when something made him look up.

Natalia Orlov stood there in a simple white dress, her

platinum blonde hair flowing around her shoulders, her romantic blue eyes done with light makeup, her impossibly long lashes that made her so beautiful one of her best features. She was crying as she ran toward him and threw her arms around him and started kissing his neck.

"Georgy, Georgy, Georgy, I am so sorry! I love you so much, I thought you might have died, I hurt you so deeply, oh please forgive me!" She would have gone on and on, but Alexeyev put one finger on her lip, her tears running down the back of his hand. He always had been a sucker for a woman's tears, he thought. He hugged her back, and the two of them walked down the concourse.

"My eye," he said. "It was an infection. They say it was herpes."

She looked at him. "As soon as I heard I had myself tested. I got it, all right. From that bastard Boris Novikov. If he hadn't died, I would have killed him myself."

"What about that guy you wanted to have in my bedroom? In our bedroom?"

"None of that was true, Georgy. I was angry at your disappearance and your silence. I had no idea you were going off to war and couldn't transmit. I'm sorry I thought the worst. It was a last resort. I wanted to get you to talk to me." She went on again about how sorry she was, and again he had to silence her, but this time he did it with his own lips.

They walked on down the concourse and he smiled at her, and lovely Natalia Orlov smiled back and put her head on his shoulder.

Now, he thought, part of his life had healed. But what of submarine command? Command at sea was an experience like no other, he thought. Ah well, eventually he would have had to give it up. Maybe the time had just come a little sooner than expected.

Vice Admiral Robert Catardi stood at the podium, resplendent in a starched service dress white uniform with full medals, swordbelt and ceremonial sword.

"Now that I've given out the Presidential Unit Citations to

the crew of the USS *Vermont* and given the silver star awards to the *Panther* boarding party, I have one very special award I'd like to make. Could I have Lieutenant Anthony Pacino approach the lectern?"

Pacino looked at Catardi and broke ranks to walk to the podium, the formal choker whites distinctly uncomfortable in the summer sunshine on the pier overlooking the USS *Vermont*. The starched whites were one of those uniforms one would want to tear off after twenty minutes in it. It was so stiffly starched that it looked great for half an hour, then resembled an unmade bed after that. Pacino had no idea what Catardi could be bringing him up to receive. He'd already gotten the P.U.C. and the silver star. What could be better than that? He stepped up the three steps to the raised platform at Catardi's podium and came to attention.

Catardi's aide, Lieutenant Commander Wanda Styxx, handed Catardi a velvet box. "For innovative and meritorious service in the United States Submarine Force, Lieutenant Anthony Pacino is hereby awarded the highest honor a submariner can possess. Gold dolphins, indicating Lieutenant Pacino is qualified in submarines."

Pacino stared in surprise and shock at the velvet box holding the gold dolphin emblem, the award coming nine months before he rated it. In the eyes of Navy Regulations, he was still a non-qual air-breathing puke, but Catardi and Seagraves had waived all that and decided to make him a qualified submariner.

Pacino couldn't help it. His eyes got moist as the admiral unpinned his airborne wings, re-pinned them under his medals, then pinned the gold dolphins in their place above the medals. "If I stick you, Patch, it's purely intentional," Catardi grinned, stepping back to examine his handiwork. The shining gold dolphins were centered and level above Pacino's ribbons. Catardi came to attention and saluted Pacino, and Pacino returned the salute, his hand and posture rigid, a tear threatening to run down his cheek. Wanda Styxx smiled sweetly at him and winked.

Pacino looked out into the crowd on the pier and could barely believe his eyes. It was his father in a black business suit, clapping with the crowd. And it wasn't his imagination, the old man was wiping a tear from his own eye. Pacino waved a salute at him and his father saluted back.

The rest of the afternoon and evening were a blur. A few moments with the elder Pacino, who had to rush to Washington with Catardi and Styxx, then to Quinnivan's for a post-operation ship's party. A few times, Pacino gazed down to sneak looks at his dolphins, still not believing it was all real. He looked up and saw Commander Ebenezer Tiny Tim Fishman saluting him. Pacino returned the salute, grinning at his friend.

He called for a ride to his apartment, wondering whether his Corvette would start after being away for over two months. He pulled off the starched service dress whites, dumped them in a corner, showered and got dressed in jeans. He bit his lip as he hit the starter for the engine, but it coughed and came to life.

Pacino wheeled the car to Quinnivan's, parking it in the driveway next to the red Ferrari, being careful not to ding the door of Elvis Lewinsky's pride and joy. As he stood to walk into the house, he saw Elvis Lewinsky standing there.

"Hello, non-qual." Lewinsky was grinning at him.

"Hey, Fucking Engineer, I'll have you know I'm the proud owner of a pair of gold dolphins. Solid gold dolphins. Presented by the commander of the submarine force himself."

"Yeah, well, when you've been aboard long enough to remember where the wardroom is, let me know, non-qual." Lewinsky laughed. "Come on. Word has it Bullfrog Quinnivan has a bottle of twenty-five-year-old Macallan waiting for you. Can't keep the boss waiting."

Pacino nodded. As he and Lewinsky entered the lower level of the XO's house, the crowd erupted in shouting and jeering, most of them teasing that he was too green to possess dolphins and that as far as they were all concerned, he was still a non-qual air-breathing puke. Expecting this situation, he'd brought the dolphin emblem Catardi had pinned on him. He pulled it out of his pocket with a dramatic flourish and pinned it to his Polo shirt above the left pocket amid the laughter and taunts. Quinnivan came up to him with a glass of the Macallan scotch.

"Mr. Lipstick, wearin' your new dolphins, I see. And you're

cryin' inside because the crowd is still calling you a non-qual, yeah?"

Pacino smiled and shook his head. "On a submarine, XO, never let the crew know what bothers you."

"Attention all you scoundrels, ne'er-do-wells, misfits and pirates!" Quinnivan yelled at the crowd. "I've heard about *enough* out of all you assholes laying into poor Lipstick here that his dolphins were a fookin' gift. So here's what we're going to do. I'm going to take the backing off the pins of these dolphins, exposing the pointy needles of the thing, and each one of you is going to get a chance to punch Mr. Pacino in the dolphins, as hard as you want. And I don't care if you put him in the emergency room, but after you each take your shot, that's it. No more of this 'non-qual air-breathing puke' nonsense. When we're done, Mr. Pacino here is as qualified as any of us. Everybody got that?"

The crowd booed and hissed, but they were all smiling. Quinnivan organized a queue and the officers lined up to punch Pacino in the dolphins. The hardest shot came from the captain himself, who grinned as he fired a punch into Pacino's dolphin emblem, Pacino biting his lip and refusing to wince, the pins of the emblem puncturing his chest. He could feel blood running down his chest and into the fabric of his shirt. Then Quinnivan, whose punch was more gentle, until it came time for Rachel Romanov's turn, who came up, dramatically balled up her fist, frowned and wound up to hit him. Pacino clamped his eyes shut in anticipation, but then she pulled her punch and just caressed his chest where the dolphins were, winking at him.

"I'm going to miss calling you a non-qual," she whispered into his ear. "But I'll find something else to tease you about." Pacino stared at her. Since their arrival in Norfolk, she'd been positively nice to him. None of her previous annoyance was visible. It was as if she'd never been mad at him.

By the time of the last officer's punch, Pacino's chest was throbbing and blood had seeped through his shirt, making a large wet red stain, but he didn't care. He was a non-qual no more.

It was then a large man entered the room, wearing leathers and carrying a motorcycle helmet, who raised his fist and bellowed, *"It never happened!"* The crowd immediately responded with their reply in loud unison, *"We were never there!"* He finished, yelling, "USS *Vermont!"*

"I'll be damned," Quinnivan said. "Man Mountain Squirt Gun Vevera. Aren't you dead yet?"

Vevera laughed, accepting a glass of scotch from Quinnivan. "Catch up, XO. Stem cell therapy. Duke University Cancer Center. I'm in remission. Fuck, XO, I'm *healed.* I'll be back aboard as soon as you sissies get back from your little stand-down vacation."

Captain Seagraves joined the crowd around Vevera. "XO," Seagraves said. "Do we have a job for Mr. Vevera?"

Quinnivan smirked. "I'm sure we'll find something for him to do, sir."

"Welcome back, Duke," Seagraves said to Vevera, clapping him on the shoulder.

"Do I get to take a punch at the former non-qual?" Vevera asked.

"Just take it easy on him, Squirt Gun," Romanov said, smiling. "He has delicate feelings."

Man Mountain Vevera's punch was even lighter than Romanov's. "Welcome to the major league, Patch."

Rachel Romanov came over and took Pacino's hand, leading him upstairs, where she asked Shawna Quinnivan for a spare shirt and a first aid kit. She sat Pacino down on the master bathroom's toilet lid and peeled off his bloody shirt and tenderly cleaned his wounds from the pins of the dolphins and bandaged him up, then helped him into the XO's shirt. She pulled the bloody dolphins off his shirt, washed them in the sink, reunited them with the backing pins and handed the emblem to Pacino. She sat opposite him on the lip of the tub and looked up at him. He noticed her eyes seemed puffy and red. "Thanks," he said. "You okay, Nav?"

She blinked as if trying to hold back tears. "Bruno and I broke up," she said, sighing. "It was a long time coming."

"I'm sorry to hear," Pacino said. "You two seemed good together."

"We've been limping along for some time," she said, blinking back tears, her jaw hardening as if she were trying to get control of herself. "But the mission didn't help. Imagine what total radio silence for two months does to a marriage. Meanwhile, his dalliance with his chubby missile officer—I don't even want to talk about it. I decided I'd had enough." She swallowed hard and shook her beautiful chestnut hair, then looked at him. "But never mind about all that. What about you? Are you going to see that Wanda Styxx chick?" Was it Pacino's imagination, or was there a trace of jealousy in her voice?

"She asked me out after the awards ceremony," Pacino said, a slow smile spreading on his face. "But I gave her an excuse. You know. Dentist appointment on Saturday night."

Romanov laughed. "I don't suppose I could get you to cancel your dentist appointment, could I?"

Pacino drank her in with his eyes, feeling a sudden desire that was entirely inappropriate to feel for a senior officer. "I think my teeth are in pretty good shape, actually," he said. "Got anything in mind?"

"Maybe a ride in that hotrod of yours?" she asked.

"That might be arranged, Nav," he smiled.

"Call me Rachel," she said. "Anthony." She stood from the tub's edge, took a step toward him and straddled him, then touched his face with one hand and ran her fingers through his hair with the other. Her eyes brightened as she looked at him.

Later, when he looked back on this moment, he realized how natural and inevitable it felt when her lips met his. And at that moment, as Rachel Romanov's warm silky tongue explored his mouth, he thought about Ebenezer Fishman's theory that this was all a simulation. And deep in his heart, Anthony Pacino fervently hoped it wasn't, and that beautiful Rachel kissing him was the true reality.

Jeremiah Seamus Quinnivan pulled Dieter Dankleff over to the bar and said quietly in his ear, "who's that fookin' bloke?"

Dankleff grinned. "That, XO, is Captain Resa Ahmadi of the Iranian submarine *Panther.* Guy saved our lives at least three times, maybe four." He waved and shouted at the Iranian. "Resa! Over here!"

The Iranian naval officer self-consciously stepped over to the bar. "Hello, U-Boat," he said.

Dankleff introduced him to the XO, then asked him, "So Captain, what happens for you now?"

"Back to Bandar Abbas," he said. "I'm being repatriated after all."

"No hard feelings from the bosses?"

Ahmadi smiled. "In my debrief, I told the tale of how, when you first captured the ship, I sabotaged it and caused it to sink, exceeding test depth by at least fifty meters, but after you recovered with that emergency surfacing, you kept me tied up in the torpedo room. There's no one to tell the Revolutionary Guards otherwise, what with Abakumov staying here. So, gentlemen, back in Iran, I'm a brave hero. But now that I've lied, all of *you* have to swear to it."

Dankleff laughed. "Where's Lipstick? He wanted to buy you that drink. Hey XO, what concoction from your almighty bar do we have for the good *Panther* captain, bearing in mind that when it comes to alcohol, he's a bit of a non-qual?"

Quinnivan found a craft vodka, made in Austin, Texas, and poured two fingers in a crystal rocks glass. "Try this, Cap'n, yeah? It's good for what ails ye."

"A toast to the immortal spirit of the submarine *Panther*," Dankleff said, raising his glass. "May she ever sail safe."

"And to your *Vermont*," Ahmadi said, taking a sip, then a second one, then looked at the glass. "You know, Commander, I can see now why my religion prohibits such a substance. It is frankly wonderful."

Lieutenant Commander Mario Elvis Lewinsky left the party early, feeling exhausted. He hadn't even had a drink at the gathering. There was just something about the end of this operation that left him feeling empty. The drama was over. Now it was back to working on meaningless reports to the squadron engineer and NavSea 08, division training and equipment preventive maintenance. There was no doubt—after being a submariner in combat, in mortal peril, the return to the mundane life of a nuclear submarine engineer was far beyond difficult. For a moment he looked up at the crescent moon, remembering how it had looked out the periscope in the Arabian Sea. His eyes came to rest on his prized possession, the Ferrari Testarossa, Italian for *redhead,* and for a moment, all he could feel was a crushing sadness that Redhead had left him.

And almost as if his thinking about her conjured her into being, the car door of a nondescript small blue SUV opened across the street, and Redhead climbed out of it. She walked over to him, wearing a tight black pencil dress with tall pumps, her luxurious red hair arrayed down past her nipples, the fabric of the dress tight around her slender waist and curving hips and struggling mightily able to contain her huge breasts. She confidently walked up to him, looked into his eyes and put her soft hand on his face. He suddenly became aware that his face was three days unshaved, stubble everywhere. He noticed her big brown eyes were almost liquid, moist with tears as she looked up at him.

"Hello Mario," was all she said, her voice trembling.

He looked at her. "I've missed you so much, Redhead," was all he could say, and he felt the moisture flood his eyes.

She took his face in both her hands and her soft red lips met his for a long, blissful kiss. He felt her warm, soft body as his arms brought her close. Finally, she pulled back and looked at him, her eyes drifting from looking at his left eye, then his right.

"How'd you know I'd be here?" he asked.

She shrugged. "Bruno Romanov told me there was a ship's party here tonight. I was worried I'd have to walk in there with all those catcalling dogs you call your fellow officers."

"Well, I'm glad you came, but why did you?"

"I came to say I'm sorry. And to pay for the damage to the car."

He waved his hand in the air. "It's okay. Fixed up better than new. Insurance paid for it all."

She smiled. "At the cost of huge premium increases, I'm sure."

"Well, that is true," he said.

She drilled her soft eyes into his. "Perhaps I can do something that will make up for all that, Mario."

Mario Elvis Lewinsky smiled at her. "I look forward to whatever that might be."

"Give a girl a ride? There's an amazing restaurant on the beach we just *have* to try."

Lewinsky opened the passenger door of the Ferrari, careful not to dent the door of Lipstick Pacino's classic black Corvette, and watched as Redhead slid into the passenger seat, her mile-long legs the things of boyhood fantasies.

He walked around and got into the driver's seat and looked over at Redhead.

"I'm glad you came back," he said as he started the V-12 engine, which shook the car with raw power.

"I couldn't live without you, Mario," she said, her expression serious.

"Redhead," he said, "I know *exactly* how you feel."

Lewinsky touched Redhead's hand, then found reverse and backed the Ferrari out of the driveway, turned west, shifted into first, punched the gas and popped the clutch, his shrieking tires leaving black marks on the road in front of the Quinnivan residence.

In the situation room, National Security Director Michael Pacino took his habitual seat, waving Admirals Rob Catardi and Grayson Rand to seats on his side of the table. CIA Director Margo Allende and Deputy Director of Operations Angel Menendez took seats on the opposite side.

"Anyone know what this is about?" Pacino asked.

"President Carlucci wanted to see us in person," Allende explained. "Said he wanted to see the whites of our eyes when he told us what he's going to tell us."

"Am I stepping in on cue?" President Vito "Paul" Carlucci said, walking in with a phalanx of staffers. Pacino, the admirals and the CIA spooks jumped to their feet. Carlucci flashed his winning smile and waved everyone to seats at the table. He took his seat at the end of the table and looked up at the gathered officials.

"Well," he began, "I had a very interesting conversation with the Russian President." He paused for dramatic effect.

"I'll just summarize the high points for you. First, we had a discussion about who had the better attack submarine. Vostov claimed victory on that, because his submarine *Kazan* had such an extreme acoustic advantage over the Virginia-class *Vermont* that *Vermont* could only hear the Yasen-M by using active sonar. *Kazan* was able to sneak up on the *Vermont* and fire off a stealth torpedo. But I told Vostov that number one, his three Yasen-M's were on the bottom, two of them thanks to *Vermont*'s SubRocs, and that *Vermont* heard that stealth torpedo and countered everything *Kazan* had in her torpedo room with countermeasure torpedoes, and if she'd had just one more Tomahawk SubRoc, his prized *Kazan* would be on the bottom. Oh wait, I forgot, his prized *Kazan is* on the bottom."

Carlucci paused to take a sip of the carbonated Italian water he favored. Pacino waited patiently.

"I then pointed out that his submarines are fragile. Hell, one of them spontaneously burst into flames and killed the entire crew for no apparent reason. We didn't touch it. The nuclear strike vaporized that Yasen-M, but her crew were already dead. It was piloted by the onboard AI, which was pretty stupid from what I've gathered. And the second sub that sank from the nuclear depth charge should have survived, but it was so susceptible to fire that it sank when one of our subs would have lived on.

"Needless to say, Dmitri Vostov was not taking this lying down. He said all he had were minor design problems, and that the battles of June 7 and July 3 went our way only because we cheated. *Cheated*, I said. Yes, he replied, you cheated. First, he alleged, the *Vermont* fired *not* at the two Yasen-M submarines detected from her own onboard sensors but rather at a probability ellipse where the computers *suspected* they would be as a result of us cheating by placing transponders on their periscopes. And *Vermont* used nukes before detecting them. So it was a shot in the dark, but a lucky one. I asked him about the third Yasen-M, which we sank. And he said we cheated on *that* too, because *Vermont* was out of weapons, and the only thing that sank the third Yasen-M was a supercavitating torpedo *invented* by the Russians, fired from a submarine designed and *built* by Russians. So in Vostov's mind, the victory wasn't ours at all. It was at best a stalemate."

Pacino thought about the Russian president's allegations of them cheating, reminded of his first submarine command's motto, *you ain't cheatin', you ain't tryin'.*

Carlucci paused. "The good news is that Vostov won't retaliate for our nuclear strike or for our stealing the *Panther.* Or sinking the third Yasen-M. Or even the grizzly bear worm. He listed his reasons—that we rescued the two crews, we were humane to the Russian submariners we rescued, we repatriated them without humiliating them or interrogating them, and when we took *Panther,* we released her crew without killing them. And we shut down the worm with no lasting effects on their military."

Carlucci paused again to sip some more water and look at the gathered officials and staffers, clearly enjoying having this audience.

"So that brings us to the next point," the president said. "The *Panther.* We're giving it back."

"Wait, Mr. President, no," Pacino said without thinking. "All the blood, sweat and tears it took to steal that submarine—"

Margo Allende spoke. "Sir, Admiral Pacino could have lost his son on that mission. How can we give it back? We had the plans to the reactor, but they're useless without having the real thing, and now we have it."

Carlucci smirked. "We don't need the *Panther.* We have Alexie Abakumov, the reactor's designer. We have him *and* all his calculations. The Iranian crew is in flight right now and should be landing in the Bahamas in two hours. They'll take back the *Panther* and sail it back to Bandar Abbas. Fueled up with low-smoke diesel and loaded out with food courtesy of the United States Navy. Lots of great American food. Pizza. Cheeseburgers. Chili. Steak and lobster." Carlucci laughed. "And beer and wine. And some vodka and bourbon."

Allende sighed. "Okay, Mr. President. We'll do this your way."

"Another point, folks," Carlucci said, looking at the admirals. "Allow me a critique of *our* submarine program—while we showed the Russian submarines catch fire or experience reactor casualties in battle, how do we know our own ships can take that kind of shock and not experience massive fires and toxic gases all through the boat, or a reactor explosion like the Yasen-M had? You need to consider a shock-testing program, gentlemen, and pronto. And all these countermeasure torpedoes, folks, sure, they're fine if the other guy's out of fish, but otherwise, you spend all damn day just neutralizing each other's weapons. You need to carry more of them so when the bad guy is out of bullets, you're still loaded up. Someone once told me: *guns are great, but the battle goes to the guy who's got more ammo.* And for God's sake, get supercavitating torpedoes like that Shkval. What happened to your solid rocket-propelled Vortex underwater missile program? I thought all the bugs were out of that."

Catardi answered as Pacino was about to comment. "The defense contractor who made them went out of business. We weren't shooting them unless we were in combat, so we weren't restocking inventory. Testing them was too dangerous to the firing ship. It was her own Vortex missile that caused the loss of the *Seawolf.*"

Pacino was glad Catardi had answered. He didn't want to be reminded of the sinking of the *Seawolf.* He'd been the captain that day when the Vortex missile blew up in the torpedo tube and detonated every weapon in the torpedo room.

"I'm confident you'll find a way to create a newer, safer, but just as lethal program. So Admirals, one last thing. The most important thing. The Russians have built a better submarine than the Virginia-class. Sure, the Yasen-M has problems like bursting into flames, but now that the Russians know about these weaknesses, they can harden up the soft spots. The important thing is that *they* can hear us miles before we can hear *them.* Have you gotten that into your heads, gentlemen, that our submarines are inferior?"

Vice Admiral Robert Catardi looked at Rand, then at Pacino, then back to the president.

"Well, sir," Catardi said, "We'll just have to build a better submarine."

Carlucci smiled his politician's smile. "We don't have to *build* a better submarine, Rob. We just have to *steal* one."

Michael Pacino pulled out a chair for Margo Allende in a secluded booth table at Kelly's Irish Times, a dark, brick-and-wood Irish Pub walking distance from the Capitol building. He looked down at the green and white checkered tablecloth.

"I suppose every day is St. Patrick's Day here," he smirked.

Allende's auburn hair shone in the soft lighting of the bar, and she looked gorgeous to Pacino. A waitress came, took their drink orders and disappeared, returning momentarily with a Balvenie scotch for Pacino, a Manhattan for Allende.

"This may look like any Irish pub anywhere," Allende said, "but there are more deals done here than anywhere else in D.C. And it's also an Agency hangout for when we're visiting in town."

"Any food recommendations?"

"You can never go wrong with the shepherd's pie," she smiled shyly.

He looked up at her. "Margo, I'm thinking of quitting," Pacino said.

"What? Why? You've got the best job in town."

"I didn't appreciate the way the boss treated our people. This was all a little too much of a dangerous game of chess between him and Vostov, and the crew of our boat—and my son—were just pawns on the board. It was a hell of a gamble. The probabilities were stacked against us from the start. We got very lucky. I worry our luck will run out."

"I know you feel protective of Anthony," Allende said, taking a sip of her drink. "But maybe you can better protect him as the boss' advisor than as a private citizen. Plus, there's another compelling reason you should stay on."

"Oh really?" Pacino said, raising an eyebrow. "What's that?"

She leaned in close, a slight smile on her face. "I have it on good authority that you work with a very pretty Agency girl who has a huge crush on you. If you play your cards right, you might get lucky with her." She winked seductively.

Pacino smiled and scratched his head. "I wonder who that girl could be?"

"*I* know who she is," Allende said, "but I'm CIA. I know everything worth knowing."

"I bet you do," Pacino said. "But I imagine that gets disappointing at Christmas, on your birthday and before anniversaries. Because you'd always know what your presents would be."

"Anniversaries," she said. "I like the sound of that. Can this be the day of our anniversary?"

Pacino sipped his scotch and looked over the rim of his glass. "A first date, if you get right down to it, *is* a 'zeroth anniversary,' so I suppose you'd be telling the truth if you told the waitress today is our anniversary."

"So this *is* a date? A rendezvous intended to commence a romantic relationship between you and me?"

"You're asking? I thought you knew everything worth knowing," he smiled.

Jeremiah Seamus Quinnivan sat down at the kitchen table, enjoying being fussed over by his wife after their long reunion the night before, the plate of sausage and eggs arriving in front of him with a cup of steaming hot coffee.

"Seamus," Shawna said, holding out her tablet computer, the display selected to the news files of the Satellite News Network's world news page. "Did you see this?"

Quinnivan found his new reading glasses, hating them with their admission that he was getting older, but damned if he could read regular-sized print without them. He looked at her tablet's display and read aloud.

"Let's see—'Elias Sotheby, billionaire software mogul and philanthropist, buys office building in Paris for new software company's headquarters; Sotheby names company *Harmaakarhu*, Finnish for grizzly bear.'"

"Dammit, Seamus, not that article, the one above it."

Quinnivan read the headline to himself.

U.S. Navy Commandos Hijack Iranian Nuclear Submarine, Sail it to Bahamas, Then Give it Back
U.S. Attack Submarine Reportedly Involved

Quinnivan read the article, most of it getting the details wrong, and completely leaving out the nuclear attack on the two Russian subs and the torpedo battle with the third, but that was the American press, he thought. That, or the story had been leaked by the Russians, who would prefer to minimize any revelation of their losses. He looked up at Shawna Quinnivan. "What about it?"

"Seamus," she said, sitting down next to him, a worried look on her face. "Was this *you*? Did you and *Vermont* do this?"

And Jeremiah Seamus Quinnivan, Commander, Royal Navy, executive officer of the project submarine USS *Vermont*, took off his reading glasses, looked his wife in the eye and said seriously, "It never happened. We were never there."

AFTERWORD

The expression, 'truth is stranger than fiction' comes to mind when I think about this book. Bear with me while I list a few examples.

Anthony Pacino's near-death experience featuring a dark, pulsating tunnel that pulled him deep inside it and stopped him halfway while he floated and listened to spirit voices debating his future actually happened to me in a Navy Scuba School drowning incident.

The teasing and abuse suffered by Anthony Pacino for being a 'non-qual air-breathing puke' officer who is not yet qualified in submarines is real, as I experienced it both during a long-submerged midshipman cruise on the *Pargo* and as a newly reporting junior officer to the Cold War-winning attack submarine *Hammerhead*. The tradition's purpose is to motivate the unqualified to learn the boat as quickly as possible for safety reasons, since each crewmember relies heavily on all other crewmembers for survival, and a non-qual crewmember could be useless in saving the ship.

The joking and fun-loving character of the hard-drinking cadre of a submarine's officers when off duty, juxtaposed to the serious and sober hard-as-steel formality while on duty is real. One day in a liberty port, I was braced up and flamed on, suffering a volcanic verbal tirade from the executive officer, who screamed at me that I was restricted to the ship for being delinquent in submarine qualification progress (known as "being dink"). Seven hours later, he screamed at me to get in civilian clothes and join him at the local bar for a night of drinking. The next morning he screamed at me for illegally leaving the ship the night before, in violation of the previous day's order. That very afternoon, he shouted at me again to get civilian clothes on and join him at the bar for another night of debauchery. Lather, rinse, repeat.

Showing up hungover to the ship in a liberty port early after a night of revelry in order to start the reactor and drive the ship out, and walking into the wardroom with a lower face smeared with lipstick stains actually happened to me, and earned me the nickname 'Lipstick,' which stuck for decades, and which my submarine buddies still call me to this day.

Being a non-qual yet acting as approach officer in a tactical situation is required for an officer to earn his dolphins. Three times, I was approach officer in various attack situations. Those hours were some of the most thrilling of my life.

The crazy, backwards 270-degree turn into the Elizabeth River Norfolk Harbor Reach done by *Vermont*'s Man Mountain Vevera actually happened exactly as described, to the Cold War-winning submarine USS *Hammerhead*. And whom do you suppose was on the conn as officer of the deck? You guessed it. T'was I.

The intense, weaponized nightclub-singer femininity of the fictional character Bamanda (Redhead), that morphed into violence in the form of thousands of dollars of damage to an expensive sports car, and changed back again after a reconciliation, was half of a story that actually happened to me. The damage done to my life was far worse than just the destroyed paint job and the unhappiness of my good friends at USAA, who paid for the repairs without complaint. But that second half of the story is for another book.

Sadly, like Yuri Orlov, Boris Novikov and Georgy Alexeyev, I've lived through the nightmarish experience of being in a serious committed relationship with an amazing woman and learning, stunned, that she cheated on me. If there's a lesson to be learned, it's that a relationship that is failing should have a timely close-out meeting to disassemble it under mutually agreeable terms. Being an adult should mean ending one thing before beginning the next, no matter how painful that is. And

I'm not just preaching to you—this could be me giving advice to my younger self.

The lore of the ultra-secret projects executed by so-called "project boats" is real. Their missions are rarely spoken of or memorialized, even half a century later. The current project boat is the Seawolf-class submarine USS *Jimmy Carter*. What it's up to right now, no one can say except a fraction of the crew, the National Security Council, the CIA and the president.

Next, regarding my comments regarding the Kilo's supposedly dangerous liquid metal-cooled fast reactor—the nuclear industry goes to great lengths to state the fact that civilian reactors can't explode like nuclear bombs. Military reactors, on the other hand, with bomb-grade uranium or plutonium, are not quite so tame, and in particular, fast reactors. It still should not be possible for one to explode in a nuclear explosion, but a prompt-critical rapid disassembly with a steam explosion, flash of radiation and scattering of radioactivity can happen, as it did at the U.S. Army's SL-1 reactor, at Chernobyl and as fictionally depicted in the *Kazan* reactor. The baby should not be thrown out with the bathwater—reactor safeguards can be designed that eliminate most of the risk and operator training can ensure reactor safety. That said, I'd prefer they be far out at sea and not in my backyard.

About the discussion of "decision theory" and "bias" that Quinnivan and Catardi talked about—none of that is true. I confess I made all that up. And yet, I use that philosophy in my private life every day. So I list it here as an element of the truth-in-fiction theme.

And about that philosophy of the simulation theory, that all of this life is a digital simulation, and that every decision causes a new reality, and that somewhere, sometime, our base soul in the afterlife examines the results of every reality—I suppose all that comes as close to a religion as I can imagine for myself. Having died and gone halfway to the afterlife, I believe I may be on to something. So I'm tossing it in with the other truths, knowing full well many will differ with me.

A final word about my depictions of the Russian submariners—were the scenes with the Russians realistic? As a Cold Warrior, I often wondered, despite the conflict between America and the Soviet Union, what it would be like to hang out with Russian submariners. I suspected that we'd have more in common with a Soviet sub crew than with our own countrymen. We both went to sea in ships designed to sink, closer to death than any surface warrior. Working in stealth, going to secret hazardous places, dealing with stress, canned food, lack of sleep, in an environment where there are no weekends or vacation days for months on end. Where communication with loved ones is restricted. Where entertainment is truncated. Where the food progressively gets worse until it runs out. And on a submarine, there are a thousand things waiting to kill the crew, as the incident on the *Voronezh* demonstrated. Many years later, as social media bloomed, I became friends with former Soviet submariners including commanding officers and senior officers, and I found that my theory would prove true. One former-Soviet submarine captain posted photos of the interior of his Victor-class fast attack submarine at Christmas. There were several decorated Christmas trees, evergreen ropes, group photos of the crew smiling in the crew's mess or at their work stations—which looked startlingly like our own—all reminders that the Russian crews were just like us. I believe the lesson is in complete agreement with the first quote listed before the prologue:

> "The great lie at the heart of all states is that other people are not the same as us. It is the excuse for violence, the rationalization that makes it possible to wield a weapon in the first place: it's okay to kill them, they would do the same to us, they're different than us. It's the foundation of every atrocity small or large throughout history. The lie that the others are different. And once that lie is used to justify violence, it can't be relinquished. The ends become the means, and violence must be called down not just for the reason of the lie, but in defense of the lie."

"Violence and the Lie"
by Steven Lloyd Wilson
burningviolin.com, January 2013

All that is a long way to say, the way the Russian submariners were depicted in this book is real.

Thank you for reading this. I hope you enjoyed it. I also hope you will go through my backlist and read them all. You can reach me by messenger on the Facebook dot com.

Michael DiMercurio
Undisclosed Location, USA

http://facebook.com/michael.dimercurio.author

Author of

Voyage of the Devilfish
Attack of the Seawolf
Phoenix Sub Zero
Piranha Firing Point
Barracuda Final Bearing
Threat Vector
Terminal Run
Emergency Deep
Vertical Dive

Curious about other Crossroad Press books?
Stop by our site:
http://store.crossroadpress.com
We offer quality writing
in digital, audio, and print formats.

Made in the USA
Coppell, TX
17 February 2025

46042961R00381